CW01561970

To

Brenda,

with love and best wishes.

William [illegible].

COVER DESIGN WILLIAM HURST.

COVER PHOTOGRAPY. JAMIE THOMSON.
WWW. FACEBOOK. COM/JAMIETHOMSONPHOTOGRAPHY

`THERE IS A CRACK, A CRACK IN EVERYTHING,
THAT'S HOW THE LIGHT GETS IN...`

LEONARD COHEN.

Names, characters, businesses, places, events and incidents are either the products of the author's imagination or used in a fictitious manner. Any resemblance to actual persons, living or dead, or actual events is purely coincidental.

THIS BOOK IS DEDICATED TO;
LORRAINE WALLS and KIMBERLEY JOHNSTON.

TWO VERY SPECIAL FRIENDS.

CHAPTER ONE.

HARRINGTON SQUARE. SHEFFILD.

Tracy Hillman hung the last garment on the line and looked up at the October skies, wondering if the rain would hold off long enough to dry her day's washing. Her husband, Doctor John Hillman was off to the surgery, which was in the city centre, three miles east of here, where they lived in their detached house in Harrington Square, Sheffield. Tracy didn't mind living here, although, it was rather too quiet at times, for her liking, but, there were far worse places they could be living, she surmised, plus, it was only a couple of hundred yards or so from the primary school where her two daughters attended.

All said and done though, the street was rather uneventful, and some would say, boring, but then again, anything in comparison with her previous life-style, would, she supposed, seem boring. 'How time flies' she thought to herself, looking at her daughter's clothes on the wash line. Angela was seven now, and Amy, five. There were no other children in this street for her daughters to mix with, which was another down side to dwelling here, but the girls hadn't ever mentioned this fact to her, and so she didn't ever bring the subject up. Most of the residents in the Square were retired couples, and although they were alright in their own way, she always felt just a little alienated to them. They were all stuck in their ways, and sometimes, she felt, stuck in a time zone. The conversations which did take place between her and them, were usually quite short, and mostly about the weather.

She picked up her wash basket and peg box, and made her way back inside, once more glancing at the untrustworthy skies. Once inside, she put on the kettle for the first of many coffees that she would consume during the course of the day. The routine, for this day, was the same for every other day. Get the kids up for school, make their packed lunches, and then their breakfast's, then her husbands' breakfast, then her own, walk the kids round to school, and return, just in time to kiss her husband goodbye as he headed off to the surgery, and then, and then the silence, the emptiness, the solitude. As she made her cup of instant coffee, she heard the letter-box rattling in the hall, just another boring little statistic of her day, to retrieve the day's mail. She walked slowly down the hall, sighing as she picked up the bundle of letters lying on the floor. Most of them junk mail, and none of them, she observed, addressed to her, not one.

Sometimes it seemed to her, that she had suddenly ceased to exist outside of this house. The four letters in her hands, which merited any importance, were all addressed to John. One from the health board, one, from the youth club he helped to run in the city centre, and two from the Church, where he took the Sunday school lesson each week. He insisted on all the family attending church, which meant, that even on a Sunday morning, she would not be rewarded the luxury of a lay in. The routine was just the same, only for different destinations. "What difference does it make if I attend church or not. If people, are unwell, they'll still have to come to see you, whether or not I go to church". She remembered the look on her husband's face. It cut through her, like a shard of glass.

"We go to church Tracy, because we believe in God, we are a Christian family, of which I am the head, you would do well to remember that".

She remembered it alright, she would never forget it. She was now beginning to see the disadvantages of having such a short courtship. They had only courted for a few months before marriage was first suggested, and that suggestion, made by John Hillman, of course. Tracy herself hadn't even given thought to such a binding commitment, but, eager to leave her past as far behind her as she could; she accepted his proposal of marriage.

Almost ten years now. "God, where has the time gone". She put the mail in its appointed place, where John had told her to put it, indeed insisted she put it. Strange, how you never see the signs of any bad habits in people when you're in love with them, or even if you only think you're in love with them, which, it seemed to Tracy with each passing day, was the case in this instance. When she thought about it now, it was easy to see how she never noticed anything out of the ordinary with him. They had met in London where Tracy was living, and where he was studying so hard to finalize his qualifications to the medical board, and to prove to them that he would be a successful practitioner. During the course of this time, she hardly saw him, and so there was little chance of her picking up on any of his faults. Having been living on her own his absences had been practically unnoticed. She sat down by the kitchen table to drink her coffee, knowing now, that if she had spent any length of time living with him, then, most definitely, this marriage would not have taken place. She loved her kids, and couldn't imagine the world without them, but, it was fact, she had jumped in to this relationship blindfolded, and now, ten years down the line, she was regretting it.

They had moved up here soon after the medical board had decided John had qualified as a general practitioner, and had given him this post, at the Sheffield medical centre. He was on a two year probationary programme, and, of course, he had passed with flying colours. That was ten years ago. At first, when they came up here, they stayed with his parents, until this house came on to the market. There didn't seem to be anything out of the ordinary regarding them, they went to church every Sunday, nothing unusual there, but, in hind sight, there was something strange about the way John's mother spoke to him, and he to her. It was almost childlike, the way she addressed him, as if she were speaking to a juvenile, or even, a child.

She sighed, as she drained her coffee cup. Maybe it was just her; Tracy thought to herself, after all, what did she know about family life, she had been kicked out of her home by her father after she had got herself pregnant at an early age. She begged her father's forgiveness, but to no avail. From that day on, she had never made any contact whatsoever, either with her mother, who, in fairness had tried to defend her, or her father. That was the last experience she had ever had, of family life. She found a doctor in the city who performed an abortion, and then proceeded to fund herself into college, and then on to university, where she studied English and Law.

It had all gone wrong for her there, as well, she lost her place due to a fight she had with a fellow student, breaking the young man's arm in several places, after he had secretly filmed them making love, and had put it on the internet. His actions had gone practically unpunished, but she was expelled immediately. That was that, and that was the end of any dream she had of making a success of herself. From that day forward Tracy had no choice but to live by her wits, which she did, with a group of people she had met, and who had given her some kind of semblance of a family life. Now this, this was her life, running a home for her disciplinarian husband, who had very different ideas about bringing up children, than she had, and for her girls, whom she loved dearly. As she washed her cup she began to think of the time she had spent with John's parents, and was kicking herself for not reading the signs of his abnormalities back then. She remembered one occasion when John's parents had left the house to visit someone, and knew for certain that they would be away for some length of time. She had undressed to her underwear and then shouted on him to come and see something. When he opened the bedroom door, she opened her legs, and with her pointing finger, summoned him to the bed.

His reaction put her into a state of complete shock and embarrassment. "Tracy"! There'll be time enough for that when we're married, you should be ashamed of yourself, if you think for one minute that I would tarnish my parent's house with that kind of behaviour in their absence, my God woman, control yourself"! It was as if they had never made love when they had been in London, as if they had never spent a single night together. She remembered how humiliated she felt that day, and also how guilty, and for what reason? Why did she indeed feel ashamed, when there was no reason for it, she was only behaving like any other woman would do in the same circumstances.

His reaction cut through to her very soul, and she swore to herself, that from that day forward she would never again make herself available to him in any such manner, no matter how he may change when they got their own place. It was at that point, she realized now, that she should have made her exit. It was all too easy to see it now, but, perhaps she was in love with him then, maybe love had

made her blind, maybe. She flicked the switch on the kettle for the second of her coffees. What made matters worse, was the fact that she had given up smoking almost a week ago, after becoming so tired of his lectures about polluting the house and the kids, and him, with her filthy habits.
She placed another nicotine tablet under her tongue and tried to convince herself of all the advantages of not smoking, but today, for some reason, she couldn't stop herself thinking about all the negatives, living with mister so bloody perfect Doctor John bloody Hillman. "Huh, I didn't even smoke in the house when I was smoking; I always went outside to smoke, just like I was made to, like a good wife, doing exactly what I was told".

Her mind went back on to the subject of sex again. She laughed at the thought of what she was referring to, as 'sex'. The 'love making' was regimental, and consisted of little or no foreplay. He was a well-endowed man, but just did not have a clue. Even in London, when he had obviously pretended to be a regular guy, she had to take matters into her own hands, which had turned her on at the time, thinking that it was part of some erotic sex game he was playing with her. Now, whenever she suggested something a little different, she was frowned upon, and condemned.

"I know you weren't a virgin when I met you Tracy, and that part of your life does not concern me, but don't try and educate me with all of your carnal knowledge, and your filthy games which you have picked up over the years, because I am just not interested, ok"?

Again the words cut her deep, making her feel that she was some kind of uncontrollable nymphomaniac, who could not help herself. "What an existence", she thought to herself, to be living like this in the twenty-first century. Again, the biting negativities about living with John Hillman hit the forefront of her mind. As if going to church on a Sunday morning wasn't bad enough, he made the girls go to the Sunday school class in the afternoons. John took the Sunday school lessons as well. It had to be said, that both of the girls enjoyed it, but Tracy put that down to their ages, once they were a little older, they would soon lose interest.

As Tracy stirred her coffee, she knew she was going to have a bad day. She wasn't sure if it was because she had stopped smoking that she felt constantly irritable, or if it was just the plain and simple truth, that she had grown tired of living with this man who would have been better suited in the nineteenth century in some little Victorian village. She could do with a cigarette now.
"Deep breaths Tracy, deep breaths" he had told her, the cravings would soon pass. Today though, the cravings were not passing, in fact they were getting worse, stronger even. She took another sip of her coffee, and then picked up her purse from the table, "to Hell with this". The shop was only a few yards around the corner. "I'll just buy ten" she thought to herself, but then, as she was walking, she thought, why? Why will you only buy ten, do you want to smoke Tracy"? "Yes, yes I do want to smoke, well then, why are you only buying ten cigarettes".

As she entered the shop, the bell above the door clanged horribly as usual, and then again as she closed it. Mister Timothy Black, a resident of Harrington Square was in conversation with Mrs Miller, the shop owner, about some sort of flower seeds, and the best time of year to sow them. "Good morning Mrs Hillman", he managed to say in between his conversation with the shop keeper.

"Tracy", Tracy said.

"Good morning Mrs Hillman", said Mrs Miller.

"Tracy", she repeated, "it's ok to call me Tracy".

Timothy Black said, "Well, I must be off, can't stand here chattering all day, there's lots to do, good day now". The old man opened the door, CLANG! Then, as he closed it again, CLANG!

Tracy's nerves were grating. "Now then young lady".

CLANG! "Forgot my brolly" said Mister Black, "I'd forget my head if it wasn't screwed on, CLANG!

"Yes now Mrs Hillman, what can I get you"?

Tracy took a deep breath, but it was no good, her temper had snapped. "Fuck, do you know this Mrs Miller, I've clean forgot what I came in for, oh yes, cigarettes, and a bottle of vodka, that was what it was, oh, and a bottle of coke, the proper stuff, not that diluted rubbish, because I'm not fat, anyway, the diet coke doesn't compliment the vodka the same, don't you think, Nancy"?
"I, em, I don't know Mrs Hillman, I don't drink".

"I haven't had a drink for a while Nancy, but I'm going to have one today, I think I've earned it, and a few cigarettes as well".

"I shouldn't think that Doctor Hillman will be too pleased with that Mrs Hillman, if you don't mind me saying, what with the girls to pick up from school and everything".
"Well Mrs Miller, I do mind, and on top of that, it has nothing whatsoever to do with you, what I do, but to put your mind at ease, John's mother will collect my children today, so you have no need to worry any further on that subject, ok"?

"I'm sorry if I offended you Mrs Hillman" said Nancy Miller, putting Tracy's money into her till.

"Why" said Tracy. "Why"?

Why what"? said Nancy Miller.

"Why won't you call me by my name, I've lived here for the best part of ten years, and yet no-one around here calls me by my name. When you get married around these parts, is there some unwritten law which says that you lose your Christian name, everyone around here calls each other Mister or Mrs".

"Perhaps our ways around here are rather different to what you were used to when you lived down in London, Mrs Hillman".

"Oh I see Mrs Miller, I see it now, because I'm not born and bred here, I have to prove myself worthy of living among you, is that it? Well, as far as my days down in London, as you put it, are concerned, I used to really enjoy myself down there, I always seemed to have a smile on my face in those days, and plenty of sex,

Mrs Miller, plenty of good sex, and good times, something you wouldn't know about Nancy".

"I know, young lady, I have spent my life dedicated to one man, and I'm proud of it".

"Yes, I'll bet you are Mrs Miller, and rather lucky you were, to find a man old-fashioned enough to put up with your irritating ways, because I sure as Hell couldn't put up with the way you all go about your days up here, and so, I don't suppose that I'll ever fit in with the community, certainly not in your eyes anyway. Where I lived in Knightsbridge Nancy, they didn't pass their time discussing flower seeds, I can tell you that for nothing, I miss my nights out down there Nancy, I miss the good old fashioned sex sessions I had down there, you know, with real men, men who knew how to treat a lady".

"A lady, huh", said Nancy Miller, handing Tracy her change. Tracy was going to say something else, but Nancy interrupted her: "Good day Mrs Hillman".

Tracy looked straight into the woman's face, "And good day to you as well, hypocrite". CLANG.

"Why are you calling me a hypocrite"?

"Because, Nancy, you look down your snobby nose at people who purchase cigarettes and alcohol but you don't mind making a profit from them, do you"?

"I would appreciate it if you no longer came into my shop, is that clear"?

"Very" said Tracy, "took my money first before you said that though, you old crow, didn't you". CLANG

There would be trouble about this, Tracy thought to herself. Well, so be it. It wasn't just about today, that little bust-up. It had been building up for some time. She began to realize that she had been kidding herself on about being happy, rather than face the truth, and admit to herself that she had made a major mistake, and that she wasn't happy at all. Hell, she was thirty-four, not sixty-four. "I am the head of this Christian family" indeed. In all honesty, she had been with young men in their teens who had given her better sexual attention than her husband, and that, even with the gift he had been given, was the truth. Whether women would face up to it or not, the fact remained that any successful relationship had to have a healthy sexual bond between the two of them, and an appreciation of each other, never taking the other for granted, and always considering the other's needs. There wasn't much chance of that happening here, not with holy Willie at the helm.

As she turned the corner an old man called Stan Morrison was busy plucking weeds from underneath one of his prize Cherry Blossom trees. "Hello there young lass, do you think the rain will stay away"?
"Hello Stan, how are you today"?

"Oh busy lass, very busy, this is me tidying up the garden before I set off for America, I'm going to visit my daughter and son-in-law, and my three lovely grandchildren and they live in California lass, so they do".
Tracy smiled at the pleasant old man. "Very nice Stan, you'll be looking forward to that then, are you not"?

The old man got up from his knees with a grunt, and came over to the garden wall. "To tell you the truth Mrs Hillman"

"Tracy, please Stan, call me Tracy".

"Well Tracy, to tell you the truth, I've been like a child a week before Christmas, not been able to sleep lass, or anything, bloody up drinking tea and peeing all bloody night lass, you know, with all the excitement.

Tracy noticed a tear in old Stan's face as he said, "This will be the first time in three years that I've seen them all, aye, I'm looking forward to it lass, I mean Tracy, Mrs Hillman".

"Well I'm glad for you Stan you enjoy yourself when you're over there".

“ Oh I always do lass, this will be my third time, they take me out for drinks and everything when I’m over there lass, the last time I was there, the buggers got me drunk, so they did lass Tracy Mrs Hillman”.

“Did they indeed” said Tracy, “Do you like a drink then Stan”?

“Oh lass, when Gladys was still alive, she and I used to go to the club on a Sunday afternoon. We’d have a few games of bingo and a few drinks, and listen to the singers in the singing competition, oh aye, watch all the young ones performing their favourite songs, and some of them are really good lass, Hell lass, some of those young girls hardly wear anything these days, Hell, I never saw Gladys wearing anything like that, unless it was time for bed and even then, Christ”.

“How long has Gladys been gone Stan”?

“Three years Lass, aye, three years Mrs Tracy. She used to say to me, if I go first Stan, you make sure you get yourself out of the house, don’t be sitting around vegetating, get yourself down to the club, and mix with people, because Stanley Morrison, if you go first, I’m telling you now, I’ll be out there, and doing my best to enjoy myself, you remember that”.

It sounded to Tracy, that Stan had recited Gladys’s words, to the letter. “Well there you are then Stan, when you come back from the States, you get yourself down to the club on a Sunday afternoon, and enjoy yourself, and remember, Gladys wanted you to do that”.

“Aye but lass, Tracy, people talk around these parts, it wouldn’t look very respectful, you know, for Gladys”.
“Will you answer me honestly Stan, if I ask you a question”?

“Of course lass”.

“Ok, what do you think Gladys would say to those people, Stan.”

Stan laughed, “Oh I know what she’d say alright”.

"Well, there you are then Stan you get out and enjoy yourself, and fuck them".
"Oh hell lass Tracy hell Mrs Tracy".

"Take care Stan, and enjoy your holiday".
"Oh I will, thank you, Mrs Hillman Tracy". Stan Morrison went back to his weeding, smiling to himself.

Slowly, but surely Tracy's day was improving. As she got to her gate the old lady from across the street, Mrs Semple, came out of her house, a nice but rather nosey old biddy.

"Mrs Hillman Mrs Hillman", she shouted, as though someone's house was on fire. "Mrs Hillman, there was a few spots of rain in the air, so I took your washing in".

"That was very nice of you Mrs Semple, but the rain's gone off, so you can hang it back out again thank you" said Tracy, kicking the gate closed behind her.

Mrs Semple stood at Tracy's gate, bemused.

"Nosey old bat" thought Tracy to herself. She placed the bag on the table with her vodka and her cola. Then she pulled out a packet of cigarettes and opened them. She lit one up and inhaled deeply, sheer bliss. Outside in the garden, she could see Mrs Semple hanging out her washing again. "That'll learn you" she said out loud, as she tapped out the number for John's mother. She too, was a nosey old twat, always wanting to know about their affairs, and, of course, her golden boy would always fill her in with every detail, her only boy, an only child.
"Hello? Anne, it's Tracy, Tracy, do you think you could pick up the girls from school? No there's nothing wrong, it's just that I think that John has been working so hard these days; I thought I would treat him to a nice surprise dinner. What? No I'm not cooking it, I meant take him out for a meal. Well, if you could have the girls overnight, that would be really nice of you, thank you Anne, you're an absolute angel, you really are, bye. Huh, it's a wonder you didn't smell the smoke over the phone". Just as Tracy was opening her vodka, the

phone rang. “Yes Anne, there’s two bags of clothes for the girls in your spare room, Papa John took them over last week, remember? Ok Anne, thank you again. “Papa John, for God’s sake”, said Tracy, as she poured her first drink, “It’s not as if there are two papas for the girls to get confused”.

That had been her husband’s idea, “papa John, dear fuck!” Tracy took a drink of her vodka and coke. She stubbed out the cigarette in the ash tray that she had to hunt out from under the sink where she kept all her floor cleaners and dusters. The front door bell rang. “Thank you Mrs Semple! They’re like bloody children, they really are, wanting you to praise them and thank them, trying to win your favour”. The door-bell rang again. “Thank you Mrs Semple”!! As Tracy lit up another cigarette, she looked into her back garden. Mrs Semple was still busy.

She went to her front door and opened it. Sharon Hartley was making her way down Tracy’s garden path to the gate. She had left two bags on Tracy’s steps. “Hello” said Tracy. Sharon stopped, and turned to make her way back up the path.

Keeping her voice down, Sharon said “Mrs Hillman”

“Please, call me Tracy”.

“Well, Tracy , I hope you don’t mind, I was hunting through my attic, and I came across some children’s books and games, I thought maybe your girls could have some use for them, I don’t mean to offend, but, I’m moving away soon, and I hate throwing things away”.

I’m not offended, Sharon isn’t it”?

“Yes that’s right”.

“Come on in Sharon, I was just having a coffee”.

“If you’re sure”?

“Of course I’m sure”, said Tracy.

John had warned Tracy about this woman. Under no circumstances was she to have anything to do with this woman. “She is no better than a whore, different men at her house every week. She is the biggest disgrace of this whole area, she has broken up more marriages than I could possibly count, a slut if there ever was one, now I’m warning you Tracy, stay well clear of her”.

Sharon Hartley was a thirty-two year old widow, very attractive, and always immaculately dressed. Yes, she liked her men, but in this day and age what single woman didn’t? She had no children, so what was a woman her age supposed to do? All the residents around here would have preferred if she’d taken up gardening or joined the bowling club, like all the other widows or widowers around here. Tracy had always secretly admired this woman, for more reasons than just being independent. “Come on in Sharon, it’s about time we got acquainted. Actually, I lied about the coffee Sharon I’m having a drink, would you care to join me”?

“Oh, it’s only”

“Listen Sharon, who cares what time it is, now, will you join me”?

“Well, maybe just a quick one then” said Sharon, smiling.

“You’re moving soon you say”?

“Yes, I’m going back down to London, I don’t really fit in up here, it’s not the people’s fault, it’s me. I think they are stuck in their ways up here, you can’t blame them for not accepting people like me”.

“People like you? Huh, join the club Sharon, and I’m married to a doctor, a bloody religious doctor at that. Do you know what that’s like Sharon? I’m expected to be a pillar of the community around here. Dress like a frump, which I do, always watch my P’s and Q’s which I do, well, until today anyway, go to his stupid bloody church meetings, cook dinner, wash clothes, keep the house clean. Oh, he does the garden, says it’s a man’s job. I once mowed the lawn Sharon. He told me that I hadn’t done it correctly, and that, though I meant well, I was to leave the men’s jobs to the men. It’s a bloody pity he doesn't remember the men's jobs when he's in the bedroom. Oh, I'm so sorry Sharon, I got carried away there, sorry, it's just that you are the first person in an age that I've had to talk to, a bit too much information there, sorry".

"That's alright Tracy, I can see already that your life certainly isn't a bed of roses, it's strange though isn't it, I mean he comes over as such a nice man, very popular with the rest of the residents in the square".

"Oh, he's popular with them, of course he is, because he's one of them, he's right up their street, if you pardon the pun, but believe me Sharon, you don't know the half of it. His bloody parents as well, who the hell talks to their son like that, at his age, and him a bloody doctor as well, even the girls look sometimes when his mother is talking to him, I can see them laughing, they think she's playing some kind of game on their behalf, but she's not". Tracy sighed and said, "Sharon, I apologise for this, for goodness sakes, you come over here just to give me some books for the kids, and you get this, I'll shut up about him, God knows, I shouldn't burden anyone else with his personality, if you can call it that".

"Tracy, honestly, I don't mind, and you obviously need to get this off your chest, it's ok, really".

"Would you like another drink Sharon? I'm having another".

"Well, if you insist, Mrs Hillman".

Tracy laughed. "That's another thing Sharon, about living around here, have you noticed too, they never refer to each other by their Christian names, it's always Mister and Misses, it drives me mad, I mean some of these people have known each other for years and years, and yet it's still Mister so and so, or Misses so and so, it's like watching an episode of some Victorian drama. I don't think I've ever heard a single swear word coming out of their mouths in all the time I've lived here".

Tracy poured two more generous amounts of vodka and coke and returned to her seat. She lit up another cigarette, and inhaled deeply.

Sharon said, “Does he know how you feel Tracy, have you tried talking to him”?
“Huh, Sharon, talk? You’re joking, with Doctor John Hillman, you don’t talk, you listen, and he does the talking”.
“I see” said Sharon, “well it seems that you have a problem Tracy, I mean, if it’s as bad as you say it is, and I’m not doubting you for one second, then, you’ll have to do something about it Tracy, you can’t keep on living like this girl, it’ll kill you”.

“I know Sharon, I would have left him years ago if it wasn’t for the girls, they love their daddy, that’s the thing, and their grandparents. If I take them away from them, they would never forgive me. On top of that Sharon, they would have to change schools and everything, it’s too much for them, I couldn’t expect them to go through all that, just because I’m not happy. There are four of us in this family, and three of us are as happy as could be, so, I’ll just have to grin and bear it Sharon. Imagine the villain I would be round here, if I left Doctor John Hillman, and took his children away from him, God, it’s bad enough now, their opinion of me, imagine if I did that”.

“Well, you’re going to have to do something Tracy, you know that, or you’ll wind up in some bloody loony bin somewhere”.

“I’m already living in a prison Sharon, or at least that’s how it feels, I have no friends around here, come to think of it, I have no friends whatsoever. If I go into the city to buy anything, I have to take the girls with me, he insists, and God forbid if I buy myself anything fashionable.

“No, take that back Tracy, you’re revealing too much cleavage, you look too cheap in that, for goodness sakes woman, you are the wife of a Doctor, at least try and act accordingly, even if it goes against your nature, your days for that lifestyle are gone, you don’t walk the streets now, I have improved your way of life, at least honour me with your attire when you leave the house to go anywhere, try and raise your standards a little”.

“He said that Tracy”?

"Yes, or words to that effect".

"I can tell you now Tracy, if my husband had spoken to me like that, then I can honestly say; right here and now, that I would be doing time, because I swear I would have cut his throat as he slept, and I kid you not Tracy. You can't keep living like this, you don't even have a life, goodness sakes, nobody should be expected to exist in this manner in this day and age, you'll have to put your foot down and make a stand for yourself. Threaten him with leaving Tracy, tell him you are no longer prepared to live like this, and if he doesn't change his ways, you'll find somewhere else to live, you and the girls, give him that in his pipe to smoke and see what his reaction will be, it might make him sit up and take notice Tracy, that this is the twenty-first century and that the days for bullying your wife are over". "Well, whatever you thought of me Sharon, this is what it's like for me, this is what it's like to be married to John Hillman. Today though Sharon, I'm having a drink, and some cigarettes, fuck him. Anyway, to talk to him in that way would be to no avail, he would end up lecturing me, it always ends up like that. He cannot be wrong Sharon, and remember, he has God on his side.

"It just goes to show" said Sharon, "from where I was standing, you look like the perfect happy little family you hide your unhappiness well Tracy".

"I have to, for the kids, the last thing I want them to think is that their mother dreads the arrival of each and every new day, so I have to pretend that I'm happy, or at least content. Like I say Sharon, you are the first person I have confided in. I can't even talk to any of my neighbours about what it's like living like this, because they are exactly the same as him, they would go back and tell him everything I said, so, I'm trapped in this, this living bloody nightmare, and looking to everybody else in the world, that I'm a happy little housewife".

"Yeah, they're a queer lot around here Tracy, in this square I mean. They're like a frozen little segment of Victorian times that has escaped evolution somehow. Progress does not apply to this little hidden corner of England, and its residents do not wish to know about life in the twenty-first century. When I lost Peter, they were all sympathetic and kind-hearted, offering their condolences and prayers for me. Two years later though, when I tried to move on with my life, and brought a man home with me, well, that was the end of any sympathetic gestures from them. From that day forth Tracy, I was known to them as a harlot, a whore, and a nymphomaniac. I was given the cold shoulder by most of the people around here, your husband included, although, I must say Tracy, you've always spoken to me whenever we've passed each other".

Tracy smiled. "What, what's so funny"?
"He forbids me to talk to you Sharon, he has informed me to steer clear of you, in fact I think his exact words were. Under no circumstances was I to have anything to do with you. You have broken up more marriages than he could possibly count".

"And yet you've invited me into his house, to drink vodka with you at half past ten in the morning, my God Tracy, what would he say if he were to come home now, unexpectedly".

"Wrong Sharon, I have invited you into *my* house, this house was purchased by me. Contrary to what Mister John Hillman would have everyone believe, it was me who purchased this Sharon. Oh, I let his mother and father believe they were helping us, when I allowed them to give us four thousand pounds as a wedding gift, let them believe they were helping us get a deposit together to buy our first home. I thought it would help the relationship between us, especially when they knew that I had no parents. They were quite happy about that, because it meant that they'd have no rivals whatsoever when it came to grandchildren. Everything they do is for John and the kids though Sharon, nothing is for me, in fact, they look down on me as much as their son does, I am second grade in their eyes, and that's because I had a life before I met him. It's like this marriage is a punishment to me because I hadn't met him when I was a virgin, that's how it feels. I'll let you into a secret Sharon, as to how I was able to buy this house. It was because of what I done in my past that I was able to afford this house, and it's something that I'm not particularly proud of either".

Sharon shifted uneasily on her seat. Tracy picked up on it. "What's wrong Sharon?"
"Can I have another cigarette please Tracy"?
Tracy handed Sharon the packet, and then gave her new friend a light.
"What is it Sharon"?

"I know Tracy, I know how you got the money, I've always known".

Tracy lit herself up a cigarette. "There's no way you could know that Sharon, no way whatsoever".

"It's a small world Tracy, and you never know who you're speaking to. You see Tracy, you used to do some favours for certain people down in London, didn't you".

"Yes I did, for lots of people, so what has that got to do with anything".

"You were closer to those friends than you were to any other weren't you, Paul Trent, Tracy, Paul Trent is my brother, my name before I married Peter was Sharon Trent, that's how I know Tracy".

I haven't had any contact with Paul for years, and I know they say he's dead, but he was too smart Tracy, he's not dead, he's just gone into hiding. He's probably got himself a new identity if I know him".

Tracy felt shell-shocked. Eventually, she composed herself, and said. "Well, if you haven't spoken to your brother in years, how come you know how I obtained the money"?

"Your cousin told me, Angela".

"What? You've spoken to Angela? Where is she, is she alright, I mean, what, how did you"?

"Relax Tracy, she's fine, Angela's just fine. She told me what you did, and why you did it, and to be quite honest Tracy, if I had been in your shoes, I'd have done the very same".

“When did you last speak to her Sharon”?

“A couple of days ago, on the phone, that’s who I’m moving in with when I go back down to London”.
“Oh my God” said Tracy, scarcely able to believe what she’d just heard. Her hands were shaking as she poured another vodka, the neck of the bottle tinkering on her glass.

“Tracy, relax, she’s fine, she got to see you last year and her nieces that she hasn’t been able to approach”.
“What do you mean, she got to see me”?

“She was here last summer Tracy. Her and I sat on the step and watched you playing in the garden with your girls one evening, that’s what I say Tracy, you look like a happy little family”.

“Why didn’t she come over to see me Sharon”?

“And say what Tracy? She had no idea how you would react, and what if you kicked up a fuss, and got the police involved, remember, she’s still missing, presumed dead, but if they were to find out she was still alive, they’d have her locked up for the rest of her life. She wanted to come over, believe me, she was crying, but she was crying because she thought that you were happy, achieving what she could never achieve now, and that was to have a family, she was crying because she was happy for you”.

It had been almost eleven years since Angela had tapped Tracy on the head reassuringly, way up there in the Lake District, and told her to enjoy her life. Her cousin Angela Phorbes, the woman who had turned her back on everything she had going for her in her life, to run with the most ruthless gang that had ever existed in the history of Britain. Turned her back on the promising career she had with the police force, and the marriage she had been planning with her fiancé. Tracy had betrayed them all, Paul Trent, Amy Smith, Linda Evans, Rodney Miller, better known as ‘Tools’, and her cousin, Angela Phorbes. Tracy had picked up more than half a million pounds in reward money, for the betrayal of her dear friends. She had even named her children after two of them. All these years of guilt and regret and unhappiness had finally caught up with Tracy Phorbes. She sat now, sobbing bitterly into her hands at her kitchen table, feeling more alone now, than she had ever felt in her entire life.

Sharon stood up and put her hand on Tracy's shoulder. "It's alright Tracy, really, it's alright, Angela bear's no grudges to you, and she still loves you".

It took Sharon a full five minutes to help Tracy regain her composure. "Come on, no more vodka for you, a cup of coffee is the order of the day". Sharon screwed the bottle-top back on and sat the bottle down on the table then she picked up the glasses and poured down the sink the remainder of the alcohol. She washed out the glasses and placed them on the table as well.

Sharon had made two mugs of coffee, by which time Tracy had full control of her emotions once again. Sharon sat opposite her friend, smiling. "I've put a note inside one of the bags Tracy. It has my forwarding address on a piece of paper, along with my mobile phone number. I wanted to stay in touch with you, and to let you know that I am unlike the rest of the residents around here, and that you could trust me with anything you wished to tell me. If I'm totally honest with you, the books and games in the bags are brand new as I'm sure you'd have noticed once you'd looked at them. They were Angela's ideas, and she sent me the money up to buy them, she insisted. So, Tracy, you're not as lonely as you thought you were, at least not any more, can I tell Angela that she can come up and visit you some time"?
"Of course Sharon, and you, please don't forget me when you're away, I'll keep in touch with you constantly with texts and 'face-book', don't leave me here, forgotten, please".
"Now that I know you Tracy, I would never do that, now, I will finish this coffee and I will make myself scarce before your husband gets back and accuses me of leading you astray, can't have him thinking his wife is a whore as well, now can we"?
"Sharon he"-.

"It's alright Tracy, I know what he thinks of me, I don't care, and you shouldn't care too much about him either. From what Angela told me about you, I'm quite surprised that he's still alive. She said

you have a vicious temper, and that even 'Tools' was it? Was very wary of what he said to you, and he was a big muscular hunk of a man, John's a bit on the thin side, if you don't mind me saying".
" He's a fucking hypocrite as well Sharon, with that opinion he has of you, huh, I watched him last summer, as he was out cutting the grass, properly of course, when you walked past with a pair of shorts on. His eyes never left your arse until you were round the corner. I had to turn my head. He came racing in here and up the stairs, where he gave himself a cold shower. He came back down stairs, and I burst out laughing. When he asked me what I was laughing at, I had to tell him it was something the girls had been saying to each other."
Sharon smiled. "It must be hard for you Tracy, living with a man like him".
"I love him Sharon, or at least I did, but he won't love me back. Most of the time, it's like I'm not here, he plays with the girls, not that I'm complaining about that, but if he's not here, he's at the youth club, or a church meeting, or he's in the bloody surgery. The only time I see him is when it's time for bed, and then he's reading some bloody medical document or something, anything but spend time with me, as a wife, if you get my meaning, bed time is just that, bed time, time for sleep, and then Sharon, the whole bloody procedure kicks off again, as soon as the alarm clock goes off, welcome to my nightmare".

Tracy's doorbell rang. She stood up, and walked to the door, wiping tears from her face before she reached it. Tracy opened the door. "Misses Hillman, it's starting to rain again, I was wondering if you wanted to get your washing back in, I'd give you a hand to"-.

"Misses Semple, Tracy sighed, do you know what a lesbian is, do you? Sharon, could you come here please for a minute. Sharon, this is Misses Semple, Misses Semple, this is Sharon, you don't know Sharon, although you've gossiped about her from time to time, I think John said that you're name for her was a Jezebel. She lives down there in the end house, Misses Semple. Tracy pointed down to Sharon's house. Now, Misses Semple, my husband, Doctor John Hillman, will not be home until at least six-thirty, my children are being looked after today by their grandparents, and so, Sharon and I are off to bed until nearer that time. If you want to take my washing

in then please feel free, in the meantime though, Sharon and I are off to bed to eat each other".
"That means lick each other's vagina's Misses Semple" interrupted Sharon, "until our hearts are content, good day Misses Semple".
The old lady put a hand up to her mouth as if she were going to be sick. As the nosey old biddy trundled down the path, Tracy shouted after her.
"Misses Semple"! The pensioner turned round. Tracy placed her hand on the outside of Sharon's breasts, gently squeezing, and then the two young women kissed each other full on the mouth.
Misses Semple shook her head and mumbled something about poor John and London prostitutes.
"There, I shan't be bothered by her again, nosey old twat that she is".
"Oh, you've done it now Tracy", laughed Sharon, we'll be the talk of the square now for the next few days".

"We always are Sharon, whether or not we do anything wrong".

CHAPTER TWO.

"What's Angela been up to Sharon, all this time?"

"Well Tracy, she's only just got back onto her feet recently. She had a raging heroin addiction she lived with for years. She funded her addiction through prostitution and shop-lifting whilst living down in London. She had met up with a bunch of young fellow addicts, and together, they used their wits to survive".

"How on earth did you meet her"?

"It was by sheer chance Tracy. I had been down visiting some friends, and was waiting in a pub to kill time before the train arrived. She happened to be sitting at the next table to me, and we just started talking. We were just talking casually, until I mentioned that my brother lived there. I happened to mention his name, and suddenly, I had her full attention. She began to ask me questions about him, I think it was to see if I was telling the truth or not, you know, in case I was some C.I.D agent still looking for her. Eventually, she believed me and became more friendly towards me. I don't know what it was about her, I just felt so sorry for her, I mean I've seen a thousand addicts, but, she was a mess, I mean a real mess, and yet I could tell that there was this class person underneath all this misery in her face. I wrote her out a cheque for two hundred pounds and handed it to her. I told her, it was entirely up to her what she done with the money, but if she spent it on heroin, we would never meet again, however, if she decided to do something about her habit, I would help her get over her addiction, and we would become friends for life. I gave her a card with the name of someone who helped me when I was an addict, and told her to tell them who had sent her. She went to see them Tracy, and after a long hard battle spanning almost three years, she conquered the habit. That was seven years ago, and, as you know now, we're still friends, and very close ones, as you can see by the information she gave me about you and the rest of that gang you hung around with".

Tracy sat, completely mesmerised by Sharon's story. She lit up another cigarette and handed one to Sharon.

“Can I use your toilet please Tracy” said Sharon rising to her feet. “It’s with all this bloody vodka and coffee”.

Tracy showed her where the bathroom was. She returned to the kitchen, taking a handful of kitchen roll and blowing her nose. At that precise moment the back door opened and in walked Doctor John Hillman.

“What! What in the name, Tracy! What is going on here, my God! And you’re smoking in the house? Tracy? Drinking? dear sweet Lord. What the Hell Tracy! He could hardly speak with the shock of what he was witnessing. Worse was to follow. Sharon had not heard the back door open, and so, in an attempt at cheering Tracy up, she had removed her top. She was going to make a joke about lesbianism, and so wandered through to the kitchen exposing her breasts through her see-through lace bra, and teasingly calling, “Misses Semple, Misses Semple, come and lick me baby, come and suck honey”.

The joke would have been bad enough, even as things were, but the fact that Misses Irene Semple and Doctor John Hillman were the best of friends, only made the joke even more sick than it was.

“I’m so sorry” said Sharon, “I didn’t realize you were here Doctor Hillman, I’ll get my top and leave”.

“I bloody well think you’d better” said Hillman. Suddenly, Tracy felt a wave of anger wash through her very soul. She became a completely different person. She was no longer, the Harrington Square Tracy, but the other Tracy, whom Angela had told Sharon about, the one who would take “no shit” from anyone.

Tracy stood up now, looking directly into the eyes of John Hillman, and exhaling smoke directly into his face. “You’re not going anywhere Sharon, sit down”.

John Hillman’s face was white, with shock, and with rage. He lunged at Tracy, in an attempt to pull the cigarette out of her hand. She swung with her right foot, with lightning speed, and caught him square between the legs, sending him buckling over in agony, and clutching his testicles. "Come on John, deep breaths man, deep breaths, the pain will soon pass, come on, you're the doctor, deep breaths".

The pain, as yet, was not subsiding for the doctor. He cursed as he lay on the floor, and pointed with his right pointing finger at Tracy, "You, you fucking bugger bitch bastard that you are, you're nothing but a bloody fucking whore! That's all you are, that's all you'll ever be, and you, you fucking bitch fuck that you are, you filthy fucking whore in my house you bastard, you fucking Misses Semple you bastard whore"!
Sharon stood up to leave. "Sit down Sharon, I've already told you, you're not going anywhere, it's this piece of shit who is leaving, and he's not even leaving in my car either Sharon, he can get a fucking taxi over to his mama's, or his father can come for him. Mummy will kiss them better for you as well. Tell her I'll be over for my children in the morning. We are going through to my living room Sharon". Tracy suddenly pulled Sharon's bra, exposing her breasts. "There, you perverted bastard, take a good look, you've been trying to for as long as I can remember, you sick fuck that you are". Tracy looked down upon her husband and said "I'm going out there to retrieve my car keys, if you as much as say one word to this woman while I'm outside, then I promise you here and now, you will regret it".

As soon as Tracy was outside, Hillman hissed through his teeth and through his pain, "You fucking black fucking whore bitch that you are, you pox infested bastard, how dare you come into my house you scab that you are". Tracy returned moments later. "Did he say anything Sharon, I thought I heard something".

"No. No he didn't Tracy".

On her way back into the house, Tracy had picked up Amy's skipping rope, which had been lying in the garden. Sharon had seen the rope in Tracy's hand, and therefore said that Hillman had said nothing.

"I did say something to your whore friend, I told her she is a scab, just like you, you are both whores and buggering bitches, the two of you, nothing but scum . Huh, try and improve you into a descent honest woman, and to try and educate you into something resembling a descent citizen, and this is the thanks I get, you fucking whore you!"

Tracy quickly wrapped the skipping rope around Hillman's neck, and coiled it round three times. She then began to batter his mouth as hard as she could with the wooden handles of the rope. After almost half a minute, she stopped. All of Hillman's front teeth were now broken, as well as his tongue being badly cut. Tracy's husband lay on the kitchen floor, barely conscious. She was not even out of breath, as she unwound the rope from his neck, and then proceeded to call an ambulance for him.

"Emergency! How do I know, I'm not a doctor, it's for Doctor Hillman, he's got a very sore mouth, some broken teeth, and I think one or two of his fingers could be broken as well, what? This is Misses Hillman, Doctor Hillman's wife, try and hurry please, he's crying with the pain".

Tracy had just replaced the phone, when it began to ring. "Hello? Oh it's you Anne. John? Yes John's here, he can't speak just now, he's got a very sore mouth, what?" Tracy turned to her husband and said. "Your mum says have you tried T.C.P. pastels John, she says they worked wonders with her ulcers.

There was silence on the other end of the line. It was Anne Hillman taking in the information that her brain was giving her. Eventually, she said, "Have you been drinking Tracy, are you in a restaurant somewhere"?

"No we're not in a restaurant, we're in my kitchen, that's where we are, I wouldn't be seen dead with that fucking mental holy Willie creep, in any restaurant for fuck sakes, talk sense woman, for once".

"Put my son on the phone at once, you are drunk Tracy, I can tell by the way you're talking, we'll talk about this tomorrow young lady".

"Go and fuck yourself you old hag that you are, and don't ever come round to my house ever again, or I'll knock your fucking teeth out as well, do I make myself clear, now go and sort out the spare room for your darling little mixed up fucking useless boy, goodbye". Tracy put down the phone.

"I think I should leave Tracy, I think I've caused enough trouble for one day, you've hurt him badly Tracy".

"Please Sharon, stay for half an hour after this piece of shit's been taken away, and just for the record, none of this was your fault, this has been building up for years, I should have left him years ago".

Fifteen minutes later the ambulance pulled up outside the front of the house. Two paramedics came to the door. "Come on you" she said to her now, ex-husband, "get your arse up and away to fuck out of my sight, away you go and live with your mummy and daddy, tell your mother I'll be round in the morning to pick up my children". One of the paramedics looked at Tracy with a cold stare, sensing that she had caused the damage to the doctor's mouth.

"What the fuck are you looking at" she said, "I can't help it if he fell, for goodness sake, just get him away to fuck out of my face, and off my property".

Tracy followed the two paramedics down her garden path, as they helped Doctor Hillman into the ambulance. Just before he boarded it, she said, "Keys please".

Hillman fumbled in his trouser pockets for a moment or two, and then threw the set of keys onto the ground. Tracy picked them up and said "Thank you, now fuck off out of my life, you mental bastard". She had only just got back in the house when the telephone rang again. She sighed heavily as she once more picked up the hand set. "Hello Anne, your son? No, he's not here, he's off to hospital, with broken teeth, I broke them, he's also got bruised testicles, I kicked them, he's got two, maybe three broken fingers, I broke them. Anne, no, just shut up and listen, make the spare bed up for your darling boy, he'll be coming home soon licking his wounds, I'll be round in the morning to collect my children, tell them I love them, goodbye Annie". Tracy knew Anne Hillman despised being called that name, Annie.

Tracy sat down again at the kitchen table. "Are you alright"? said Sharon, rather taken aback at Tracy's outburst, but remembering what Angela had told her about her fiery cousin.

"I'm fine" said Tracy, "It's just that. I've had it Sharon, living in a world of pretence with that, that twat of a man. I've tried Sharon, I really have, I've bent over backwards to make this marriage work. It's all him though, everything and everyone has to revolve around him, well no more. All this lot around here as well Sharon, Misses Hillman this, and Misses Hillman that, not once in all of these years have any of them called me by my first name, they make me sick, they do". Tracy poured herself another vodka. "I'm sorry about all this today Sharon, I really am. If I hadn't done anything though, he would have made you leave, and then my life would have been sheer Hell for God knows how long, he wouldn't have ever let it drop. No I've, I'm glad Sharon, I'm glad I've finally had the guts to make the break; he was bloody killing me mentally. Please, have a drink with me Sharon. Help me to celebrate my new beginning. I'll make a fresh start with the girls, I'll put this on the market, it will sell, and then I want to get as far away from all of these fucking mental people as possible. It's not Sheffield either Sharon, hell the people around here are brilliant, and very easy to get on with, it's just this bloody square, the square that time forgot".

Sharon laughed as she poured herself another drink. "I know Tracy, you're right there as well, it's as soon as you leave this square, everyone becomes normal again and you kind of forget how odd the residents of this bloody Harrington Square really are".

"They're not long in reminding you though, are they, once you return to it. I got banned out of a sweet shop today Sharon, did you know that"? Sharon burst out laughing. "Yeah, I'll have to drive into town now for everything. Well, at least I'll keep my sanity; it'll be worth it just for the peace of mind that I won't have to endure their senseless banter from now on".

Sharon ended up staying at Tracy's house for her tea, and then the two women went out for a few drinks later on. Tracy felt that she had to get to feel what it would be like living without him breathing down her neck. When they returned, Tracy attempted to call Anne

Hillman's house, but as soon as Anne heard Tracy's voice, she hung up the phone. "Ah well" said Tracy, "It's only to be expected, after all, I'll be the first woman, apart from herself, of course, to give him a hiding he won't forget".

The two women sat talking into the early hours of the morning, when, eventually, Sharon said she would have to leave, that was at two fifteen a.m. Tracy Hillman undressed for bed, and wondered what she would do now, and how her life would be, bringing up her two daughters on her own. It shouldn't be that hard, she thought to herself, I've done tougher things in my life than that, and more frightening things. She would be fine, all three of them would, she would make sure of that, and of course, they would have their Auntie Angela coming to visit them from time to time.

CHAPTER THREE.

John Hillman senior stood at the front door of the City General hospital, tapping his left palm with the leather strap of his car keys. He had been here now for almost fifteen minutes, after receiving a call from one of the hospital staff, requesting transport home for Doctor John Hillman junior. Senior had been told at reception that his son was on his way down with a nurse. He was still rather confused as to what the hell was going on. His wife hadn't really made much sense when he returned home with his grandchildren. Anne had told the girls to go and play, and then she spurted out some story about Tracy being too drunk to speak, and that she attacked "Our John".

Young John had said that when he had arrived home, that woman from across the road was in the house, parading about half naked. She and Tracy were smoking. He said that the whole house stank to the high heavens of cigarette smoke and vodka. "Goodness knows what's been going on in that house when our son has been busy down at his practice, God knows".

Then the phone had rang and a member of staff at the General had asked him to come and pick up his son. As Hillman senior had made his way to the car, his wife, still frantic, was saying to him, "You should have heard the language coming from that girl's mouth John, I've never heard the likes in my life, like a demon she was". He had climbed into his car and closed the door, grateful more than ever, that B.M.W. made soundproof vehicles.

The sixty-three year old retired judge stood on the step, still tapping the strap of his car keys, awaiting his son, and to hear the actual true account of events which had taken place earlier that day, minus the dramatisation that his wife had no doubt added to the story, in order to help turn him against Tracy. She had never been Anne's favourite person in the world; of course, no-one would be good enough for her precious son. John Senior entered the hospital again to see what the holdup was. As he approached the elevator, the doors slid opened and accompanied by two nurses and an elderly lady, John Hillman junior stepped out into reception, where his father stood waiting.

Doctor Hillman's lips were blue and very badly swollen. Stitches had been put in his mouth. The hospital dentist had worked on John's mouth extensively for almost two hours, capping, and saving what teeth he could, and extracting the ones which could not be saved. His father took one look at him and immediately realized the seriousness of his son's injuries. So Anne hadn't been blowing everything out of proportion after all. As father and son walked outside to the car, Hillman senior said, "I don't know what to say son, I mean, whatever I thought of her, I certainly didn't expect this".

John Hillman junior shook his head and pointed to his mouth. Senior understood, it was either too sore for him to talk, or he just couldn't.

By the time father and son arrived home, Anne had the girls bathed and into bed. As Hillman opened the door he was bombarded with a hail of questions about his son, as if he were four years old, and as if he were not even present. "What did they say? Is he alright? Is there much damage to his mouth"? Suddenly, she looked at her son's mouth, and putting up her hands to her mouth, she said, "Oh my sweet mother of Jesus, would you look at this, heavens preserve us". She looked at her husband again. "What did they say? Is he going to be alright"?

"He'll be fine Anne, it'll just take a bit of time for his wounds to heal, he's had extensive dental surgery, he'll only be taking liquids for a while, but he'll be fine, he's made of good stuff", said Hillman in an attempt to brighten up his wife, and to stop her from stressing so much.

"You must be starving" she said to her husband. To John Hillman junior, she said "I'll warm you up some tomato soup, will that be ok"?

Doctor Hillman shook his head and pointed to the ceiling, meaning that he wished to go to bed.

"Oh, right you are John; I'll look in on you throughout the night".

Doctor John Hillman lay in the bed his mother had made up for him, wondering what he had done to offend his God, to make his wife turn on him like that. He had no idea that he had in fact, for the last few months been suffering from Schizophrenia. To his way of thinking, God had allowed Satan to enter his wife's body and turn her into a demonic bitch. "What did I do Lord" he thought to himself. "I can't think why you would do this to me".

Down stairs in the living room, John Hillman senior sat with his wife talking about the course of events of this very strange day. "I can't believe Tracy would do something like this, it's just so out of character for her, I think it's the drink that has made her act this way, she's never touched the stuff before. She probably has had something bothering her that she didn't want to bother John with, and so she's had a drink, thinking that that would help her. Obviously, drink doesn't agree with her, she'll probably wake up in the morning Anne, and I'll bet you she won't be able to remember a thing".

"Rubbish John, that's wishful thinking and fine well you know it. If you had heard the way she spoke to me, anyway, how would you explain that whore woman, strutting around the house half naked, how would you explain that? I'll tell you this John Hillman; there is no way our grandchildren are going back to that house that much is for certain. I mean, what's going on in that house John, when our son is at his surgery. How many other times has that, that ,whore been in that house, strutting about half naked in our grandchildren's home? Oh no, they're not going back to that. Now, you're a retired judge John, you get in touch with the police, and you tell them what has happened there today. Get some court order put on her, that she can't come here until she's had some help with her drinking problems".

"Do we have to do this Anne? Look, it might be that they can sort this out, they might get back together again, but if we do this, it will only make matters worse, for everyone, for John, for the kids, for us, and for Tracy. Anne, she won't remember a thing, I'm certain of it".

Anne Hillman sighed. "For someone who has sat in a seat of authority for thirty-two years John Hillman, you are a remarkably gullible man, do you know that? Of course she's going to say that! She's going to say sorry, and that the whole incident is just a blur to her. "Oh I can't remember a thing". How long have we known her John, huh? Nine or ten years? What do we know about her before that? Huh? Nothing! We know that she lived in London, that's all, that's all we know.

She met our John when he was at Oxford and going into London at weekends. She told us that both of her parents were dead, she didn't tell us how they died, or if she was close to them, or anything. When we first met her we asked her what she was doing for a living. She told us she was a hairdresser. Can I ask you a question John, how many thirty-odd year old hairdressers do you know, can buy a Two Hundred and Fifty thousand pound houses, cash"!

Hillman looked at his wife. "Yes John, it's true".

"I thought they had a mortgage Anne"?

"A mortgage! Said Anne, "Oh no John, John told me, she paid it cash. When we gave them that money, I thought like you that we were helping them get a deposit together, that's what young John had us believe. A year or so later, I got the truth out of him. Now you tell me where a girl that age can get that kind of money John, now if you cherish your grandchildren, then you get on that phone and you speak to whoever you need to speak with, and you tell them everything, because I'll tell you something for nothing, if you allow her to come and pick up those children tomorrow, you can kiss them goodbye, for good, because we'll never see them again. Make your mind up, and just think of those two little girls up there, and that half naked whore while you're at it".

Half an hour later, Anne Hillman came into her living room with a plate of French toast and bacon and eggs for her husband. John Hillman senior was on the phone talking to someone. She placed the tray on the table and returned to the kitchen to retrieve the two mugs of tea, muttering to herself something about naked whores, and children having to live in the filth and mire of their parent's sexual fantasies. "Bloody crying shame, it really is" she said, putting down the two mugs of tea.

"Well it's done", said John Hillman, "I just hope we're doing the right thing here".

" Of course we are John, for goodness sakes, you're not telling me that you would even consider those children returning back there after what she has done to their daddy, would you"?

"All I'm saying Anne, is sometimes couples can resolve situations like this, and sometimes they get back together, that's all I'm saying".

"You would allow your son to go back with that"?

"Allow, for goodness sakes Anne, he's in his bloody thirties, he's not nineteen any more, he's a bloody man, and a doctor at that, who deals with all sorts of people and their problems, allow for God's sake".

"John Hillman! Mind your mouth man, taking God's name in vain indeed", she said, in her strong Irish accent.
"Ok Anne, just calm down, I'm sorry, let's have our supper in peace, huh? Let's not fall out with each other, we'll see what happens from here, anyway, John can't talk just now, so how come you know all the details about this woman and everything"?

"Because, Mister Hillman. Misses Irene Semple, a good friend of our John's had the decency to go to the hospital and stay with him. John wrote all the details down about what had happened, and anyway, Tracy had been rather nasty to poor Misses Semple earlier on in the day, that's how I know, not that it's of any importance how I found out. The fact is, I know everything that happened in there, that's what's important".

CHAPTER FOUR.

Nancy Miller was placing an assortment of fruit in display trays outside her shop when the police car went cruising past, and turned into Harrington Square. It was seven thirty a.m. "I wonder what's been going on round there last night" she said to her husband Joe, who was sorting out newspapers for the, already half an hour late paper boy.

"Mmm?" said Joe, with a ballpoint in his mouth.

"The police Joe, they've just gone in to Harrington Square, it's only half past seven in the morning".

"I know, I'll kick his bloody arse when he gets here, that's twice in two weeks".

"What"? said Nancy, carrying another box of fruit outside.

"What"? said Joe.

"Listen to me Joe, I'm not talking about the bloody paper boy, Honestly Joe, I wish you'd get a hearing aid or something, you're getting worse, I SAID, the police have just gone into Harrington Square, I was just saying, I wonder what's been going on there last night".

Joe sighed heavily, as he got to his feet. "Nancy, you've always got to think the worst, haven't you, hell. So the police have gone into Harrington Square, does that have to mean that someone's in trouble, hell, you're worse than the buggers who print these bloody newspapers".
"There's something up Joe, you mark my words, they wouldn't come around here at this time of the morning, I'm telling you".

"Maybe they're taking a message round to Doctor Hillman or something, there might be an emergency at the hospital or something, it doesn't always have to be something nasty Nancy hell". Joe Miller loved his wife with all of his heart. His wife Nancy loved him equally. She had loved this man from the first day she set eyes on him at school. They had been engaged for eight years before Joe had finally popped the question. All through their courtship they had planned out things they would do together throughout their lives, which included having two children. When Nancy had been informed, three years into their marriage, that she could not have children, it broke her heart. She thought she would lose her husband, for she knew he had his heart set on having a family. But Joe had stayed by her side and supported her through a very bad spell of depression, and loved her just the same as he always had. They had discussed adoption, but had rejected the idea. The end result of all this, was this banter between them, a kind of friendly rivalry between themselves, each trying to prove the other one wrong. They themselves, becoming the bickering children they couldn't have.

Joe was still sorting out his newspapers when Misses Irene Semple walked into the shop. "Good morning Mister Miller" she said, as she picked up a newspaper from the shelf.

"Morning Misses Semple, how are you on this fine morning".

"Well. I'm afraid I don't know where to start".
Joe's back was turned to the old lady. "The baker van hasn't been yet" he said.

"I beg your pardon" said Misses Semple, "the what"?

"The baker hasn't been yet Misses Semple, there's no tarts".

"What's he saying Misses Semple, good morning to you" said Nancy Miller, heading to the back of the shop with two empty cardboard boxes.

"Good morning Misses Miller" said Irene Semple, "he misheard me I'm afraid, I said I don't know where to start, and he thought I said I wanted tarts".

"Oh I know, I've been telling him to get himself a hearing"-.

"Where the bloody hell do you think you've been mister, it's nearly bloody dinner time hell!!"

The young paper-boy looked past Mister Miller, and spoke softly to Nancy Miller, for he knew which one of the two was his real boss.

"I'm sorry Misses Miller, I'm sorry I'm late, but my rabbit died, and my mum insisted that I buried it before I done anything else, that's why I'm late, I'm sorry".

"On you go Colin" said Nancy Miller, you're not too late, we won't dock your wages will we Joe no we won't, and when you're finished you can get yourself a nice apple and orange from the tray outside to take to school with you, ok"?
"Thank you Misses Miller, and thank you Mister Miller".

"Don't thank me boy, it's her you need to thank hell".

Colin Rees's waterproof jacket already contained three oranges and three apples, but he felt better now that he'd had actual permission to take some fruit. After Collin had left the shop, Mister Miller said, "It's all very well being soft with them, but you give them a bloody inch, and they'll walk all over you, little buggers that they are".

"Listen to him Misses Semple, the softest touch this side of Sheffield".

Eventually, the subject got back on to the police car. "I'm telling you Misses Miller, that Doctor Hillman's wife, yesterday, I got the shock of my life with that one, I really did. First of all she was filthy mouthed with me, told me she was a lebsian, and kissed her, you know, that bloody tart from the corner". Joe looked up. Then the next thing I knew, the ambulance comes to the house, to take Doctor Hillman away".

"Misses Semple" Joe smiled, "I think sometimes you get a little like my wife from time to time. He's a doctor ladies, sometimes he has to go with the ambulance, it's part of his job, dear dear ladies hell".

“Mister Miller” said Irene Semple, “Doctor Hillman had to be helped to the ambulance by two of those medical people, his mouth was bleeding badly. I saw him throw his keys onto the ground as well. Misses Hillman was drunk, and that woman was in her house. Misses Hillman was laughing at her husband. After the ambulance pulled away she informed me that she had to get back into bed with her lebsian lover, she said she was missing her”.

Nancy folded her arms and looked over to her husband, smiling at how Misses Semple had pronounced lesbian. “Well? What are you going to say about that Joseph”?

Joe looked at the two women. “Hell”.

Tracy got up out of bed with a thumping headache. Sharon had gone over to her house and brought back more vodka and gin. The two women had sat talking until after two in the morning, at which point Sharon had returned home, very drunk. As Tracy entered the kitchen she looked at the clock on the wall. It was seven forty-five. She opened the cupboard and took out a small tub of paracetamol tablets.

Although her head thumped, she remembered every single detail from the previous day. Amy's skipping rope lay on the floor, with blood stains on it. She would buy her a new one. She had made herself a cup of coffee and was now standing by the kitchen window drinking it. No regrets whatsoever, she thought to herself. It had been coming on for a long time. She wondered how much longer it would have gone on if she hadn't started drinking yesterday. "Not long" she said out loud, as she picked up the skipping rope. Her life had taken yet another twist. Here we go again, she said to herself, only this time you've got two little girls to think of, not just yourself.

As she enjoyed her last cigarette in the quietness of the early morning, she remembered her days with her friends in the years gone by, Paul Trent and Tools, Amy, Angela and Linda. The beating she received from Linda in the back of the car, she would never forget, but then, it was fully deserved, there was no question about that. The house in which she now lived was bought with the price of that beating. If her cousin Angela had not stepped in, she would have died, that was for certain. At the end of the day though Tracy, you betrayed them for money. John McRae, and Sandra Bellingham, the detectives, had made her out to be some kind of hero, for putting her life at risk to track down the villains, who had been killing at will. She remembered reading a couple of years later that John had died, trying to overcome bank robbers. He had been shot, and died instantly. What made his death even more tragic was the fact that the robbers, moments later, gave themselves up," A bloody shame, rest in peace John McRae."

She washed her coffee mug and picked up the wall phone. "Here goes. Hello Anne? It's me, just letting you know I'll be round for the girls in ten minutes".
"Will you indeed" came the reply.

"Yes I will, can I speak to them please"?

"No, they're getting ready for school you can speak to them when you get round here, not before".

The phone went dead. It was understandable, thought Tracy, after all, she'd given her golden boy a sore mouth. "I'll bet its bloody sore now" she said out loud, as she stubbed out her cigarette. "That'll learn you to try and stamp your authority onto the weaker sex". Fifteen minutes later, she had had a quick shower, and was now reversing the Volvo V 70 out of the drive, and on to the main street. She had only driven about twenty yards when the police car drew along- side of her and signalled for her to pull in.

"Shit!" She hadn't quite fastened her seat belt and she knew the police officers had noticed this. One of the officers came round to the driver's side. "Good morning" she said, trying at least to look like she was unfastening her seat belt.

"Switch off the engine please madam".

"Tell me" said the officer. "Do you think that you are somehow exempt from the law for some reason"?

"No. I-"

"Why did you not have your seat belt on then"?

"I was putting it on when you pulled me up, I'm on my way to pick up my children".

"Not yet you're not madam, can I smell alcohol"?

"Not now, I mean, I had a couple of drinks last night, but I don't drink much, it was only"

"Step out of the car please madam".
"Why? I mean why do I have-"
"Just step out of the car please madam. I won't ask you again. At eight twenty-five on this Wednesday morning, the two police officers made Tracy do a series of balancing exorcises right in the middle of her street, in front of all her neighbours, right in front of her own house. Three times as many tests as was legally required. Tracy could feel her face glowing with the humiliation of the situation she was now in. Then the dreaded statement.

"Are you prepared to take a breath test and a blood test madam? Do you agree to that"?

"Agree? How can I not agree"?

"That's entirely up to you madam, but I would strongly advise you to comply".
"What about my car"?
"Arrangements will be made for your car to be taken to the police car park. If you pass the tests, then you'll be allowed to drive it away, if not, your car will be put in the car pound until further notice, now then madam, give me your full name and address".
"Why can't we do this at the station along with the tests"?
"Madam"
Tracy was now past the embarrassed stage and could feel the adrenalin rising up. She began to think of a set up. That's what this was. She would have to go along with it in the meantime. She sighed, "My name is Tracy Hillman, I live at twenty-six Harrington Square, Harrington, Sheffield. She went on to give the names and ages of her two children and her husband's name and age. The two policemen kept taking it in turn to ask her needless questions, even asking her, her in-laws names and addresses. At that point Tracy cracked. "You have no need to ask me their bloody names because we both know, that it's been those two who have put you up to this, haven't they"?

One of the two officers walked over to the police car and sat in at the passenger side, leaving one foot on the road; he picked up the receiver and spoke into it. Tracy was raging. "They have, haven't they, they've set me up here, I knew it!"

"Madam, I must warn you"
"Warn me? Go and fuck yourself you useless brainless bastard that you are. See? Your friend can't hear me from back there, because that's what I think of you, the two of you. A pair of fucking lap dogs, that's what you are, arresting me at eight o clock in the fucking morning, you're never usually going around until ten thirty, it's a fucking set up and you know it, and if you don't know it, then you're even more fucking stupid than I took you for".

The policeman sighed, "Misses Hillman"

"Don't Misses Hillman me, I no longer wish to be associated with that family, thank you".

The policeman spoke to her again. "Would you like to get anything from your car Misses Hillman, before we go down to the station"?

Now it was Tracy's turn to sigh, "Yes I would thank you" she said softly, "I would like to get my bag and my jacket".

"On you go then, Misses Hillman".
"Fuck" Tracy thought to herself, even the police, Misses Hillman. Tracy walked over to her car and took out her bag and her jacket. She thought about the friends she had so badly let down all those years ago, and what they would have done in a situation like this. "It's no good thinking about them now, anyway I was never as brave as they were, I wouldn't get very far".

Tracy had calmed herself down. If there was any chance whatsoever of her being let off with a warning, then she had better cooperate in a less aggressive manner, goodness knows her chances were slim enough without jeopardising them any further. She handed her car keys to one of the officers, and then climbed into the back of the police car. One of the policemen got in to the back of the car and sat beside her. She thought this a bit strange, seeing as how she wasn't hand cuffed, but she said nothing, she had already said enough. As the police car pulled slowly away, a young lady in the corner of

Harrington Square was talking on the phone to her friend in London, telling her that she might wish to come up here for a few days, because a relative of hers had got herself into a situation. She would even go as far as to say she was in a bit of trouble.
As the police car crawled past the corner shop, Nancy Miller and Irene Semple stood where they had been now for over twenty minutes, waiting for the police car to come out of the square. Nancy Miller stood with her hands on her hips, as Tracy stuck up the middle finger of her right hand in her direction, licking it in the process. The young policeman sitting beside her only smiled, but said nothing.

"I knew it" said Nancy Miller to her friend, "God knows what she's been up to. Mark my words Irene, once they've lived in that bloody city down there, they can't change. It's her poor husband I feel it for, and those two little angels, that's who I feel it for".

All the way to the police station, there wasn't a word spoken, either from her, or from any of the officers. She had got over the embarrassment of what had just happened to her in her own street. No doubt they would all take Doctor Hillman's side and condemn her as some kind of evil alcoholic demonic bitch. If she felt alienated before, well, now she would really find out what getting the cold shoulder meant. She didn't care too much though about that. As soon as possible she would put her house up for sale, and begin again with the girls somewhere, although she knew that they both loved their daddy, and their grandparents, that part of it would be the tricky bit, try and explain to them why she was leaving their daddy, when, in their eyes he was all but a perfect father, who had done nothing wrong.

As the police car pulled up in front of the station, she couldn't help feeling that something was wrong, other than the trouble she was in. The whole unfamiliarity of the arrest, something or other wasn't right, didn't feel right. She remembered what Anne Hillman had said to her, "You can speak with the girls when you get round here, not before". Well, whatever was going to happen, she would find out in due course. She would find out alright. The verbal hurricane which was about to batter into her would sweep her away into a world that even she could not imagine.

The first policeman spoke; "Misses Hillman, I must advise you that you are now under arrest on the suspicion of driving a vehicle whilst under the influence of alcohol, and for also, in that same vehicle, being in possession of a large amount of cocaine, with intent to supply". He produced the bag of cocaine from his jacket pocket, and handed it to his partner. He then fastened a hand cuff to Tracy's left wrist, and his right wrist. He tugged three times with his arm, and then took the hand cuffs off again. "Also for resisting arrest and for blaspheming at an officer bearing the Queens uniform, and for using that same foul language on the Queens highway at the top of your voice. Anything you say may be-"

"Oh fuck off! What is this? Is this some kind of joke? Have the Hillmans put you up to this. Bloody hell, cocaine! Get to fuck"!

She was soon to realize that this was no joke. The seriousness of the crimes she was being framed with was starting to sink in. She knew only too well the consequences of carrying large amounts of cocaine, and there was absolutely nothing she could do to prove that she had been set up. She was up against it here. Twenty minutes ago, she was frustrated at the thought of being late to pick up her girls, now, she was wondering if she would see them again, at least not in the foreseeable future. Panic was beginning to set in. She would say nothing from this point on, she would not speak another word, not until she had a lawyer with her. The bitterness she had felt towards her husband, was fast turning into hatred, and not just to her husband, but with his parents as well, supposedly honest church going God fearing people. "If I get out of this" she thought to herself, "I'm going to make them suffer, they'll pay for this. As the two policemen walked her up the steps to the front door of the police station, they both began to push and pull her, making it look like she was struggling against them. She said nothing to them as they played their game. She could only see the face of her husband, and the faces of the hypocrites who had brought him into this world. "Come on you little whore" said officer John Flemming, "spoiled little fucking bitch that you are, let's see you get your candy ass out of this mess, whore"!

Tracy was taken into the police station handcuffed to Officer John Flemming. In front of them, Officer Anthony Park held the door open for his colleague and their prisoner. Nothing at all of what Tracy thought would happen, did happen. The place was virtually empty, save one young lady behind a desk, tapping away on the keyboard of a computer, and a sergeant standing over the young lady's shoulder. The sergeant looked to be around fifty, with thin grey hair, and almost bald up the middle.

"This is her sir" said Officer Tony Park, as they approached the desk. Park placed the cocaine on the desk along with the list of charges. The sergeant sighed. "Right boys, take her through". Tracy was led through a set of double doors, the hinges badly needed oiled, and down a long corridor to a room at the bottom. Flemming stood with his prisoner, as Park stood and fumbled with an enormous set of keys. Eventually, after about a minute, he found the correct key for the door.

"Put a label on it" said Tracy, sarcastically to the officer, "and then you won't have as much trouble next time".

Not one word was spoken by the two policemen; instead, Flemming dragged her in by the handcuffed arm, and roughly pushed her down onto the one and only seat in the room. Once seated, Flemming then reached inside his jacket pocket with his left hand and pulled out a key. Moments later, Tracy's hand was released.

"Stand!" said Flemming.

"What"? Tracy said.

"Do you want me to-"? Officer Flemming unleashed a very hard blow with his right hand onto Tracy's left cheek. The blow had been dealt with sufficient force, to knock her off the chair, and onto the cold tiled floor. "Stand"! Officer Flemming repeated.

Still in a sitting position, Tracy said, holding her cheek, "Did that make you feel tough sonny? Huh"?

With the back of his right hand, he unleashed an even harder blow to Tracy's right cheek. "Stand" he said.

Tracy got up to her feet, slightly dizzy from the blow. This time she decided that silence was once more the best policy. Tears were rolling down her face from the pain of the blows. She stood with her hands by her sides, looking down onto the polished tiled floor. Park closed the door and stood by the side of the chair with his arms folded.

"Strip" said officer Flemming, "start with your shoes".

Tracy sat down on the chair to take off her trainers. This time the back of his' hand caught her square on the nose. "Stand"! He said again, this time shouting.
Once more Tracy picked herself up, and the chair which had been knocked over with her.

"Strip"! Said Flemming. "Start with your shoes".

Tracy bent down, as if touching her toes, and began to untie her trainers. When she had taken them off she was unsure of what to do. Blood was now trickling down from her nose and onto the floor. She decided to leave her trainers on the floor. She then stood straight up and began to unbutton her blouse. Park stood grinning and nodding, rolling on the balls of his feet. Tracy took off her blouse.

"Belt". She unfastened the belt from her jeans, and rolled it up into a neat circle and tucked it into the right foot of her training shoe and laying her folded blouse neatly on top of them. As she took off her jeans, Officer Park, arms still folded, walked around to the back of the chair, and bent down, just as Tracy was bending down.

"Nice" said Park, arms still folded, "Nice". He took up his position once again as Tracy took off her jeans and folded them on top of the other articles of clothing.

"Bra"!

The blood was now flowing freely down Tracy's face under her chin and down onto her breasts. Again, arms still folded, Park moved from his position, this time right in front of Tracy, beside his colleague. As Tracy pulled off her bra, Park cocked his head to one side and closed one of his eyes, as if he were taking aim down the barrel of a rifle. "Sit"!
Tracy sat down on the chair, tears and blood flowing down her face. Park walked over to a small sink in the corner of the room and returned with a dry cloth and a handful of paper towels. He threw them onto the floor. Flemming barked, "Clean the floor, and then clean yourself".

With that, he picked up Tracy's belongings and placed them inside a black polythene bag, turned with Park, and left the room. As they slammed the door, two or three of the paper towels flittered along the floor. She heard the key jangling as the door was locked. Tracy picked up the bone dry cloth and walked over to the sink. She soaked the cloth with the water from the one and only tap, cold. She could feel her eyes puffing up. The cheek bone on the left side of her face was tender to the touch. She looked into the small plastic mirror on the wall. Her eyes were beginning to turn black. Her nose felt blocked and stuffy, as if she had a cold. Surely they couldn't get away with treating people like this. One thing she was learning quickly though, speak only when spoken to.

Half an hour or so later, she had cleaned the floor and herself. Her nose had stopped bleeding and she felt marginally better. There was no heating in the room, only an old fashioned oil heater. She would not dare turn it on. There was a small single bed in the corner of the room, with one thin grey blanket. She wrapped the sheet around her shoulders and was sitting once more on the chair. After a while she had to lift her bare feet off the floor, it was too cold. She sat cross legged and looked around the room. Three of the walls had been painted a horrible bottle green, painted over plaster. The fourth wall, the one with the heavy door glossed black, were just bricks painted white. There were posters pinned on the wall in various places, all warning that, whoever was looking at them, would not escape justice. One of the posters read, in large print; IN YOUR LIFE THERE ARE TWO PATHS YOU CAN TAKE. THE RIGHT ONE, OR THE WRONG ONE. MAKE SURE THAT WHEN YOU

LEAVE THIS ROOM, YOU CHOOSE THE CORRECT DIRECTION. CRIME DOES NOT PAY.

Were they not going to give her, her phone call? How long would she be kept here, and most importantly, how long did they intend to send her to jail for. She knew she was going to jail, it was only a question of how long for. Why had they planted the cocaine on her like that? She was in big trouble without actually doing much wrong. Was all this retaliation for what she'd done to John Hillman. She sat shivering under the thin sheet, knowing that this was turning out to be the nightmare of all nightmares. Tracy had never been in prison in her life, but she knew only too well the implications of being caught in possession of cocaine, especially the amount they had planted on her. She was in big trouble, and there was no fancy pants lawyer could get her off with this, even though she was innocent.

A few minutes later, she heard the keys fumbling in the lock again. This time there was nothing remotely funny about it. In walked officer Park followed by the sergeant who had been in the reception area when she came in, lastly, her father-in-law, John Hillman. "Stand" said Officer Park.

Tracy stood up and folded the sheet she had wrapped around herself, and placed it neatly on the chair behind her. John Hillman made a gesture to the officer, who immediately left the room, returning moments later with a small coffee table. Park then left the room again, this time returning with a padded easy chair. "That will be all officer" said Hillman. Park left the room for the third time, this time closing the door behind him.

The sergeant handed Hillman a small brief case. "Would you be wanting any refreshments sir" said the sergeant.

"Hillman, not looking up at the sergeant, but instead, taking papers from the case said "Just a coffee sergeant thank you".

Tracy watched with fear burning inside her, as her father-in-law laid out documents onto the small table. The sergeant left the room, closing the door behind him. "John I'm sorry about-".

"Don't" Hillman snapped, as he wrote on a piece of paper! "Officer!" The door opened and in walked P.C Park. "She's speaking out of turn again".

In four quick strides officer Park was at Tracy's side. He grabbed the petrified woman by the hair, and pulled her along the floor over to the sink. He turned the tap full on and thrust Tracy's head underneath the freezing cold water. After a minute or so, he pulled her from under the tap and began to slap her head and face, and then her ears, throwing her onto the wet floor. She sobbed on her hands and knees. Park then kicked her on her backside. Tracy fell flat forward on her face. "Sit" Park barked at her again.

Tracy, still sobbing, struggled to her knees, and then up on to her feet, face ablaze again with fresh pain, and now completely deaf in one ear. She made her way back to the chair. John Hillman, still writing, did not look up from the table. "Thank you officer, that will be all for now". Park left the room, and closed the door.

Tracy sat sobbing on the chair with her head in her hands. Blood was coming from her nose again. Her mouth was also bleeding. In her left ear, she could only hear a ringing, humming pitch. She felt dazed and very confused. She needed to wipe the blood clean from her nose, but was too frightened to leave the chair and retrieve the kitchen roll, in case there would be more punishment dealt to her for not asking, but she was sobbing so badly, that she couldn't have spoken if she tried.

"Officer" cried Hillman. The door opened and Park entered the room. "Tell the sergeant I want a large pot of coffee, and two mugs, Tracy and I are going to have a little chat" now hurry up man; I have a busy day in front of me".

"Yes sir". Park left the room.

Once again, there was only Tracy, and her father-in-law in the room. After almost a minute of complete silence, Hillman said, "Do you know what's funny Tracy? I'll tell you, my wife thinks that I'm on your side, can you believe that? You and I know different though, don't we Tracy. I must be a bloody good actor, that's all I can say".

Tracy had a good idea of what was coming next. This was about the children, it had to be, and he would offer her some kind of deal. The first thing she had to do, was get herself out of here, she could be of no use to her children for as long as she was in here. It was clear to her as well, that she would not be allowed to talk to a lawyer, not yet anyway. She would have to go along with whatever this bastard put forward to her, that was her only option. Officer Park returned with a large tray and two pots of coffee with two mugs.

"That will be all, you can return to your duties now". Park, once again left the room.

Hillman rose to his feet, and poured two mugs of coffee. "You take sugar don't you Tracy. He came over to the chair where Tracy sat. "Here you are, drink this, you'll feel much better". He handed her the mug. "It's a shame you had that fight with the girl in the next room isn't it Tracy"?

Tracy did not reply. "It's a shame you were caught in possession with all that cocaine as well isn't it, drink your coffee dear. You see, every way you look at this Tracy, you lose. What I propose to you is, oh I nearly forgot. Hillman reached inside his jacket pocket and pulled out a packet of cigarettes and a lighter. He handed them to Tracy.

"Thank you" Tracy spoke, but sounded like a whisper.

"You're quite welcome my dear, now, what I propose is, that you sign full custody of the children over to young John, I've got all the papers here ready, and guess what Tracy, the bloody cocaine disappears, gone, just like that, also all the other charges, gone, as well, now, I know how much you love your children, so, you can see them once a week, every second week you can have them stay over at your place, now how does that sound, you must sign over full custody though, you understand".

As Tracy took a drag on her cigarette, she said, "and if I don't sign"? Hillman sipped his coffee and said "Tracy, you know, you know what happens if you don't sign. It's quite possible those two girls of yours could be well into their teens before you got out. I would be doing my best to keep you in there, and I know quite a few people in the prison service who owe me lots of favours, now please, let's not talk about walking down that road Tracy, don't make me do that to you dear. I am giving you this option Tracy, because I'm fond of you, I am offering you, your life back. We both know if these charges go ahead that John will automatically get full custody of the children. So you see, it is no big deal to me whether you sign or not, only, if you don't sign, you will be taken directly to the courts in the morning, and then, as I say, you know the rest. The pain you have experienced today, well, let's just say that that would become part of your everyday life in prison, again, I would personally see to that, of that, let there be no doubt". Hillman took another sip of his coffee and said, "I would much rather sort this out amicably, wouldn't you my dear"?

Tracy sighed, and said "May I put my cigarette out at the sink please"?

"Of course my dear, here, I'll do it for you. I have an odd one or two you know Tracy, Anne doesn't know though, she would make my life hell" he said, as he walked over to the sink. He ran the water over the cigarette butt and then threw the stump onto the floor "More coffee my dear"?

"Yes please" whispered Tracy again. Hillman walked back over to the coffee table and brought over the pot. After he poured himself another cup, he sat back down on the padded chair again. "May I have one of those please Tracy" he said, pointing to the cigarette packet. Tracy stood up and walked over to her father-in-law and handed him the packet. He took one out and lit it, and then handed the packet back to her. "Here Tracy, you sit on this chair, it's much more comfortable than that one, put your feet up on the cushions, warm them up".

As Tracy traded seats with her captor, she said, "May I have another cigarette please"?

"Of course my dear, they're yours, only, it's up to you how long this packet has to last you". Hillman pulled the plastic chair over beside the coffee table. He lifted a pen from the table, and offered it to Tracy. "It's up to you my dear, but this has to be sorted out today, one way or another".

Tracy flicked ash onto the floor. "I'll sign it" she said at last, "as long as I can see my girls every week Mister Hillman".

"You have my word Tracy, read it if you wish, I promise you, you will see your girls every week".

Tracy glanced at the form Hillman had handed to her. She knew only too well, that this man could definitely not be trusted. She also knew that he would have her in court the next day with God knows what other charges pinned to her name, there was no choice. She signed the papers.

"This one as well please Tracy, it's for John's solicitor, a copy". Tracy signed the duplicates as well.

Now she would find out if he was going to keep his word.

"Thank you my dear, the children will be well looked after, I promise you". He folded the two pieces of paper and put them into his briefcase. He stood up and walked over to the door and shouted for the sergeant.

"Oh God no" Tracy cried, almost bursting into tears.
"Relax Tracy, you have nothing to worry about now, I promised you".
Less than thirty seconds later, the sergeant knocked on the door and came in. "Go and fetch officers Park and Flemming would you sergeant," said Hillman.
"Right away sir, is everything alright sir"?
"That's none of your business, now go and do as I've told you".
"Yes sir".
"Yes sir" repeated Hillman. He took a draw of the cigarette and exhaled smoke up into the air, as he slowly paced around the room.
"Just flick your ash on the floor Tracy, it doesn't matter my dear, we won't be cleaning it up".
Officers Flemming and Park entered the room. "Sir" they both said in unison.
"Manners gentlemen, manners, you see that Tracy, their sergeant, their superior, knocks on the door before he enters, but these two, these two feel free to just to walk in unannounced on two people's conversation, no respect whatsoever Tracy".
"Sir we thought-"
"See? Tracy? There they go again, butting in when they've not been invited to. You" Hillman pointed to Park, "Go and get this young lady's clothes, and be quick about it". Park hurried off, closing the door behind him. Flemming stood to attention, directly beside the chair that Tracy was sitting on. Hillman rubbed his chin as if he needed to shave. "There's something I need to know officer Flemming, something which is rather confusing me at the moment". There was a knock on the door. "Come in Park, you're a bit late in trying to prove you've got manners now don't you think". Park came in carrying Tracy's clothes. "Alright you two, turn your twisted heads away while the young lady gets dressed, you've had your share of perversity for today".

The two police officers looked at each other, wondering where Hillman was going with his dark sarcasm. As Tracy began to dress, Hillman said to the officers, "What did I ask you to do, concerning this young lady here, when I spoke to you on the phone this morning, what did I specifically ask you to do, can you remember"? Park spoke first. "Sir, you said to rough her up a bit".

"That's correct officer Park that is exactly what I said to you, I said rough her up a bit, and give her a fright. When she's finished dressing, I want you to take a look at her face, or what's left of it, and explain to me, just what exactly you two think you were doing, to put the girl in this condition, I mean look at her, this is what you call roughing up huh? Well, I'm glad I didn't tell you to beat her up, you should be ashamed of yourselves, but I'll bet you're not, I'll bet you had a good laugh while you beat on her, and as for that treatment that you gave her at the sink there, well, I think I'll give you a taste of your own medicine gentlemen, what do you say to that, and I think it's only fair that young Tracy here gets to see you getting a hammering, do you think that's fair, you pair of lick arse sons of whores that you are. You' better strip to your underwear gentlemen; it'll be easier for the hospital staff to set about your injuries when you arrive at the A and E.". Hillman poured more coffee for himself and Tracy, and then pulled out his mobile phone. "Hello? Yes just come in Carla, the desk sergeant will show you where we are. Sit down Tracy, and enjoy this my dear. Watch now, as these two heavy handed bullies take a bit of their own medicine".

The two policemen had ignored Hillman's request of stripping down to their underwear. Park took off his jacket. "Whatever you've got lined up Mister Hillman, then get one thing straight here, we are going to defend ourselves, don't think we're just going to stand here while you attempt to humiliate us, and remember, this was your idea, if someone gets hurt, then it's your blame, we were only defending ourselves".

"Indeed gentlemen, I would hope you would attempt at least to defend yourselves, to the best of your ability, at least, shall we say". There were two soft taps on the door. "Come in Carla, my dear, come in and say hello".

A young woman of about twenty-five, walked into the room. She looked to Tracy that she would weigh, perhaps eight stones, and that if she were soaking wet.

"Carla? This is Tracy. Tracy? This is my personal assistant Carla Paganni. Now, just take a look at the mess these two have made on Tracy's face here. What I want *you* to do Carla, is to hurt these men in such a way that they may think twice about throwing their weight about on young girls".

Carla whispered something into Hillman's ear. Hillman smiled at Carla, and said, "You feel free my dear, you break as many bones as you wish, Tracy?

This is for you my dear".

Carla looked at Tracy, and repeated, "This is for you Tracy, I'm going to hurt them really badly, the way they've hurt you".

"Come on then dick heads", said Carla," ready when you are".

Hillman sat back on the chair sipping his coffee and enjoying another cigarette. There was never a shadow of doubt what the outcome of this confrontation would be. It was a foregone conclusion.

"Take your time with them Carla, inflict as much pain on them as you possibly can my dear, let them feel what it's like to be humiliated, and make sure you break a few bones my dear, I like to hear the bones crack Carla".

CHAPTER FIVE.

Sharon Hartley gazed out of her window holding a mug of coffee in her left hand. A cigarette burned in her right hand. She flicked ash from the cigarette into an ashtray she had placed on her window sill. It was almost midday. Two hours earlier she had watched a small mobile crane pull up across the road and tow Tracy's car away. Before the truck had arrived, several of the neighbours had made a point of stopping on their way past to look into the car, to see if there was anything interesting inside for them to gossip about. What made people behave in this manner, thought Sharon to herself. Of all the troubles there were in the world, people still got some kind of thrill about gazing upon other people's downfalls or mishaps. Around these parts, the people had set themselves a standard, a beaten track, and God help you if you step off that beaten track, they will make you feel like a leper. Of course, if she had known what the people around here were really like, she would never have purchased the house. Her husband Peter had loved the house though, and, the fact that he had only a couple of miles or so to drive to get to his work, added to its appeal. "A home is what you make it Sharon he had said", and of course this was true.

She shouldn't let people get to her, and ordinarily she didn't, but as Tracy Hillman was now well aware, the people around here had a way of getting under your skin, they weren't long in letting you know if they weren't happy about something you'd said or done.
Sharon snapped herself out of her daydream, and began wondering again what had happened to Tracy. She's been away for nearly four hours. No way would she pass any blood test this morning, that's for sure, she would still be way over the limit to drive. Even so, even if they'd charged her with drink driving, she should surely have

been home by now. Maybe she's gone to her mother-in-law's to sort things out with the children, who knows?

As Sharon took another sip of her coffee, a black Mercedes SL 500 pulled up outside of her house. It was Angela Clark, formally known to her friends as Angela Phorbes. She was looking well, with her blonde shoulder length hair, black leather jacket, and jeans which looked like they had been sprayed on. "Ooh, fancy boots as well" said Sharon out loud. Her figure looked immaculate. Angela took one case out of the trunk of her car, and made her way to the front door. The doorbell rang, and then Angela was in the house.

"Hello? Sharon"?

"In here" Sharon said.

"Hello darling" said Angela.

"Hello babes" said Sharon.

The two friends hugged, and kissed each other on the cheek.

"Would you like a coffee Angela" said Sharon, removing the ash tray from the window sill.
"Oh I'd love one; I only stopped once on the way up here. So what's been happening to Tracy then" Angela said, as she followed Sharon through to the kitchen.
"I've told you everything all wrong Angela, you see, I thought she was happy with her life, I thought she was quite content, but, looks can be deceiving". Sharon explained everything to Angela what had happened the day before, and all the things Tracy had told her.

After half an hour Angela said, "I see, and she's not back yet"?

"Nope, and they've taken her car away as well. God knows what's going on".

Angela smiled, "She really leathered her husband did she"?

"Put it this way Angela, I'm glad it wasn't me she was upset with, I can tell you that. You'll get the full story when she gets back".

"Are you sure she'll be ok with me" said Angela.

"Are you kidding, that girl broke her heart yesterday, over you, it seems like you are her hero. She wanted to give you money, kept asking if you were alright. Then I told her about you being here last summer, and that was it, she sat breaking her heart, as if she'd missed the last chance of ever seeing you again. She's going to need your friendship Angela, there's going to be trouble about what she's done to her husband, you know, involving the kids. I don't think it's going to be as easy as she thinks. I've watched that guy, and he really loves his kids, I mean really loves them, and I don't think he's going to let things go just quite as easy as Tracy thinks".
"Well, first things first" said Angela, "we'll see what she says when she gets back".
"Whenever that will be" said Sharon, looking up at the clock, which now read Twelve- forty five. The two women returned to the living room with their coffees.

"Do you have a cigarette Sharon, I've ran out, I'll have to get some". Sharon handed the packet over to Angela. As she lit the cigarette, Angela looked out of the living room window again. "Is that Tracy's car, there's a blue Volvo parked in the drive".

Sharon stood and looked out. "Yes it is, she's back. Angela, make yourself at home sweetheart, I'm going over there to see if she's alright. I'll bring her over Angela, I won't tell her you're here, what a surprise she'll get". Sharon took one more mouthful of her coffee and then left the house.

As she made her way across to Tracy's house, she thought to herself, that's strange, they picked up her car by pick-up truck this morning, and yet, by the looks of it, they've let her drive it home, surely they wouldn't let her drive it back here, if she were over the limit, and she knew for certain that Tracy would be, without a shadow of a doubt. Anyway, she thought to herself, there's something not right here. As Sharon rang Tracy's doorbell, she was still worried about what had happened this morning, nearly five hours ago. She saw the silhouette of Tracy through the frosted glass door.

"Hello? Who is it"?

"It's me Tracy it's Sharon, are you alright"?

"You'd best go Sharon I'll give you a call some time".
"Is everything ok Tracy, are you sure you're alright"?
"I'm fine, now please Sharon".
Sharon knew that something was wrong, something was very wrong. There was silence but Tracy was still at the door. "Tracy? Tracy, I've got someone in my house who's longing to see you".

There was no verbal reply, just the sound of Tracy unlocking her door then Sharon could see her moving away from it. She opened the door and stepped inside. Tracy sat in the living room on her sofa with her back to Sharon, she was lighting up a cigarette. "Tracy? What's wrong" said Sharon, "What's happened this morning, something's wrong". Tracy looked round at Sharon and said, "Oh yes, something's wrong alright, I've signed my children away Sharon, I've just signed my girls out of my life".

"Oh my God Tracy who done this to you"? Tracy's left eye was almost closed. There was bruising to her left cheek, and her bottom lip was badly swollen. There was a deep split in her top lip. Her whole face was puffed up. "Who the hell done this"?

Tracy burst into tears. Sharon sat down beside her new friend and put her arm around her shoulder, and with her other hand, she tapped Tracy on the head, ever so gently. "It's ok angel, we'll sort this out, don't you worry about anything, we'll sort this out, whatever has happened".

"He, he, made me, sign Sharon, he made, he made me sign. I had to. He made me sign my babies. They were going to put me. He's not what I thought. They were going to put me in prison. She beat up two policemen, I had to sign Sharon, he was ruthless. They had cocaine, I was going to jail for a long time".

Sharon hugged Tracy and told her to take it easy, that they would sort everything out together. Sharon Hartley got up and walked over to Tracy's telephone. A few seconds later she said, "Could you come over here please Angela". Then she whispered, "It's even worse than I thought".

Less than three minutes later, Angela stood in the doorway of Tracy's living room. It took Angela and Sharon a full half hour to get Tracy calm enough to tell them everything that had happened. After Tracy had finished explaining everything, Angela said, "Well now Tracy Phorbes, your father-in-law thinks he's a bit of a wide boy does he, we'll see how much power he has just shortly; make no mistake about that babes. I'll find out where he's coming from, and when I do, then we'll play with him, we'll play with his emotions".

"That girl" said Tracy, "that chauffeur of his, she kicked those two policemen to unconsciousness, she never even used her hands once, I've never seen anything like it".

"Well, I've got a little friend I carry around with me at all times, he'd put an end to all her fancy footwork pretty smartly, I've never met anyone who could out step him, he hurts them. You'll have your girls back Tracy, don't you worry about that, it may take a little time, but you'll have them back, I promise you. Auntie Angela will have them back with their mum, you can rest assured on that. Meanwhile, you just play their little game; you just go along with it Tracy let them think that they've beaten you, no pun intended".

MORNINGSIDE.

Carla Paganni stopped the B.M.W. outside of John Hillman senior's new home. The half mile drive up to the house was beautifully landscaped with Pine trees and shrubs. Oaks and Douglas firs were also in abundance throughout the seven acres of land, which surrounded Hillman's property. There had been a house situated where his house now stood. Hillman had wanted to renovate the property, but as soon as Anne Hillman had discovered that the house was not a listed building, she insisted that it be taken down, and a new one built in its place.

The whole project had cost Hillman, one point seven million pounds from start to finish, and had taken almost a full year to complete. Builders had used the original sand stone from the old house, but extra stone had to be bought to finish the house to Hillman's specifications. Because the house had been built with the original stone, it gave the place all the character that the previous house had. Even though the house was brand new, it looked a hundred years old. It had elegance and grace, style, and above all, it kept Anne Hillman happy, which, at the end of the day, was the only thing that mattered in Hillman's mind, anything for a peaceful life.

The house consisted of six full size bedrooms, three lounges, three bathroom and shower rooms, a games room, a library, a massive kitchen, and one large dining room. A builder's pick-up, sat outside the house, in the spacious parking area. A cherry red Porsche 911 3.3 also sat outside of the property, which belonged to Carla Paganni.

“Now then my dear” said Hillman, “would you like to see inside my new house”?

“If you wish Mister Hillman” said the young lady, as she unfastened her seatbelt.

“They tell me it’s almost ready my dear, Misses Hillman has given me no peace since the first block was laid, every blooming day she has gone on about it. She thinks that you can build a house like this in a couple of weeks Carla; she knows nothing of the skills and patience required, or indeed the expense of such a project. She is one of those people who flicks a switch and expects a light to come on, having no idea or interest why the light comes on. Everything has to be done yesterday for Anne, I’m afraid”.

“It’s certainly big enough, Mister Hillman, it’s very impressive”.

“Oh, but wait until you see inside my dear”. Hillman dug into his inside jacket pocket, and pulled out a brown leather wallet. He pealed out five fifty-pound notes and handed them to the young lady.

“Sir, I can’t take all that for-”.

“Oh yes you can my dear, you did me a huge favour today. Those scoundrels deserved what they got. You see Carla, I did not want the girl harmed, only frightened, maybe a little ruffled, nothing more, the rest, I would have done, but those two, well, they had themselves a good time inflicting pain like that onto the girl, no, you take the money Carla, you earned it my dear, now, come and have a look, you’ll love it I’m sure”.
“I’m sure I will” said Carla, as she put the money into her handbag.

As they entered the house, a drill could be heard in some distant part of the house. “Hello” shouted Hillman, when the noise from the drill stopped.

“Hello” came the reply.

“It’s me Billy, Mister Hillman”.

A moment later, footsteps could be heard from upstairs, and then descending the three tear staircase. A man of about sixty years of age came down to greet Hillman. "Ah Carla, this is Mister Billy Waite, Billy, this is Miss Carla Paganni".

"How do you do miss" said the builder.

Hillman smiled at both of them and then said, "This man, Carla, along with one or two trusted friends of his, built this house from its foundations to its present form. This gentleman is not just your average builder Carla, but is, a stone mason, a dying breed, a real builder Carla".

"I'm very pleased to meet you sir" said Carla".

"The pleasure is all mine, young lady" said Mister Waite. "Mister Hillman, I'm pleased to inform you that the electricians have finished this morning and that all of your appliances are now installed and fully functional".

"Splendid" said Hillman.
"Your snooker table was installed yesterday, and is ready and waiting your pleasure sir. The games room has been carpeted, and your bar installed and fully stocked, as requested. The carpet fitters will be here tomorrow to lay the rest of your flooring. They've been waiting for the painter and decorators to finish off. All being well sir, you and Misses Hillman will be able to move in any time after the weekend".

"Thank you Billy" said Hillman, "for everything, not just for building the place, but for keeping all the other contractors on their toes, and for keeping them to that high standard of craftsmanship that you yourself work to".

"It's my pleasure Mister Hillman".

Hillman looked all around the hall and up and down the whole house from where he stood, impressed with what he was looking at. "I think he deserves a little bonus, don't you Carla"?

"It's a beautiful house Mister Hillman".

"Indeed it is Carla, now then Billy, I am going to have a few friends round fairly soon, I would like to invite yourself and your lovely lady wife along with another friend of yours and his wife, I'll let you know when it will be".

"Thank you very much sir, oh, your telephones will be installed tomorrow morning".

"Thank you Billy" said Hillman, dipping in to his jacket pocket once more, this time producing a cheque-book. He scribbled something in the book, and then tore out a leaf, and handed it to Billy Waite.

"Mister Hillman, you have already paid me for my work, I don't think you need pay me any more sir I am already happy with our agreement, and more than happy if truth be known".

"On the contrary Mister Waite, people like you are very hard to come by, now please, take this, and buy Misses Waite something nice, do you hear me, I insist".

"Well, if you insist Mister Hillman".

"Indeed I do, now, I am going to show Carla around the house Billy, you just ignore us as we wander around".

"Yes sir, Mister Hillman, and thank you again".

"You're welcome Billy" said Hillman, as he began the tour of the house with Carla.

Builders being builders, no matter of what quality, have an age-old habit of having to look at cheques when they're handed to them. Billy Waite would put it down to being ripped off too many times. As soon as Hillman was out of sight, he looked at the cheque. He smiled. "Pay Mister William Waite the sum of five thousand pounds only". "He's not a bad old twat really. Buy Misses Waite something nice Mister Hillman, Yeah right".

CROMWELL ROAD. (SHEFFIELD)

"Listen John" Anne Hillman said to her son as she handed him his cup of tea. "You know our new house is nearly finished, well, your dad and I have been thinking, we want you to have this house as a gift".

"Mother, I don't need you and dad to come to my rescue every time something goes wrong in my life, I can stand on my own two feet you know, I'm not exactly destitute".

It was as if John hadn't said a word. "Now we'll be moving in to our new house within the next few weeks, your father has seen to the deeds for this house and such. He has also seen to it, that the children get new swings and climbing bars installed into the far end of the garden. He's doing the same over at the new house, oh, they'll love it over there, they really will".

"Mother, they were asking for their mum this morning, Amy is upset, they both are, they love their mum".

"Well, be that as it may, they'll see their mum soon enough, unfortunately. If it were up to me, she wouldn't be seeing them again, bloody tramp that she is, her and that bloody strumpet from across the street, two of a kind, those two".

"I don't know how dad got her to sign full custody to me; I know how much she loves her girls".

"Do you John, do you really know? She phoned me up and asked me to take the girls. She lied to me, saying that she was going to take you out for a surprise dinner, when all the time, she was planning a drinking session with that whore, in her little girl's house, in their home, love John? I know how much she loves them alright. Imagine, if I had to go over there for something, God forbid, but imagine if I had. Amy and Angela opening the door, only to be confronted with a house full of cigarette smoke and a drunk mother, and a half naked whore running around the house on top of all that, huh! Love! She gave you full custody of the children John, because she knows fine well that you are a better parent than she could ever hope to be, that's why, it's no mystery John, it's common sense, I mean, it's not as if your father has gone round there and beat her up now, is it, he's not exactly forced her to sign those papers".

John smiled, even though it hurt his mouth when he did. "I doubt if he could mother, even if he wanted to".

"Well, there you are then, stop feeling guilty about winning the rights to your own children. She signed those papers knowing full well that she didn't stand a chance in court, that's all. She may be callous John, but she's not stupid".

"No she's not." Hillman mumbled to himself.

HARRINGTON SQUARE.

Sharon Hartley was in Tracy's kitchen. "Looks like you're out of tea bags Tracy", she shouted through.

"Oh I'll nip round to get some" Tracy shouted back through, and then remembered Misses Miller had barred her from using the shop.

"I can't go after all" said Tracy, "that lovely Misses Miller has barred me, I forgot".

Angela couldn't help bursting out laughing. "I'm sorry Tracy, but I've heard it all now, a thirty four year old mother of two, banned from the local sweet shop".

"Very funny" said Tracy, with a smile, it's no laughing matter Angela, they're fucking mad around here they really are".

"I'll nip over to my house and get some "said Sharon.

"No, I'll tell you what" said Angela, "I'll go to the shop, from what you two have told me, they'll have been gossiping good style about you Tracy, and your car being towed away, well, I'll give them something to gossip about, now, where's this shop"?

Tracy gave Angela money to get her more cigarettes when she was there. "What are you going to say Angela" said Sharon.

“Oh, I’m just going to knock Doctor Hillman off his pedestal, that’s all, a bit of old fashioned gossip, that’s what they like around here isn’t it”?

The three young women laughed. “Angela, be careful what you say” said Sharon.

“Why? They don’t know me from Adam, I can say whatever I like”

Joe Miller was sorting out his tinned fruit, placing them neatly onto the shelves, as Angela entered the shop. A young boy was making his way out of the shop. “Now don’t you be late in the morning Colin, do you hear me” said Nancy Miller, putting the thirty pence Colin had spent on gum, into the till.

“I won’t” he said, as he nudged past Angela.

As quick as lightning, Angela dipped her hand inside the lad’s coat pocket and pulled out a half pound bar of chocolate. She lifted it high above him and said. “Hey, have you paid for this, has he, excuse me, has he paid for this”?

Colin Rees’s face went bright red.

“No, no he hasn’t” said Nancy Miller, but he’s going to, that’s coming out of your wages young man, and this really is your last warning, if I ever catch you stealing from me again, then that’ll be you, no job”.

“Stealing from you? Hell” said Joe, “stealing from you? I’ll kick your ruddy arse boy, that’s what I’ll do, and don’t think I won’t boy, hell, because I bloody well will Christ, stealing with that chocolate”.

“That’ll do Joe, he gets the message, goodness me man, you’ll have him hanged before long” said Nancy Miller”.

He bloody well should be banned” said Joe, “he bloody should be” Joe said, looking at Angela for some kind of support.

The boy stood with his head bowed, and eventually said, "May I go now"?

"Yes you can go now" said Nancy, "but just remember Colin, this is your last chance do you hear me"?

"Yes Misses Miller".

Angela could not resist the temptation. "Hey lad, you look like a well-mannered boy, do you not think you should apologise to these nice people, you're a lucky boy, the fact that this nice lady and gentleman have not given you the sack, do you know that"?
He nodded his head slowly and said "Sorry Misses Miller, Mister Miller".

"Now" said Angela, don't you think it would be the right thing to do, if you put the chocolate back as well, that would prove to these nice people just how genuine you are, that would be the manly thing to do".

Again Colin nodded. He walked forward and replaced the bar of chocolate where it had been.
"There now", said Nancy Miller, as if she were soothing her own child. Joe Miller's bifocals hung on a chain around his neck. He lifted them up onto his nose, but still looked over, rather than through them at the boy, still not totally convinced of Colin's honesty.

"There" said Angela, "does that not make you feel better? Now that you've admitted to doing wrong, you can start from afresh again, I'll tell you what I'm so impressed with you, that I'm going to buy you that bar of chocolate".

"It doesn't matter" The young boy muttered.

"Oh but it does matter young man, honesty is always the best policy, you'll learn that as you go through life" said Angela, patting the lad on the head.

Joe Miller lifted the last tin of fruit from the box on the floor, and placed it neatly upon the shelf. "Yes you will boy hell, you will learn that, bloody chocolate hell".

Nancy looked at Joe shaking her head, "Give it a rest Joe will you".

Angela picked up the bar of chocolate and said, "Here you are young man". As Colin raised his hand to receive the chocolate, Angela, knowing full well what the boy had hidden under his coat, pulled quickly on the Velcro strip at the front of Colin's jacket. "Oh my father in heaven" said Angela, with one hand held up to her mouth. From under Colin's jacket, out fell, two more half pound bars of chocolate, two mars bars, and a bag of
peppermint creams. "Saints preserve us" said Angela, pretending she was about to faint. "Lord help us".

Joseph Miller had spent the last three years of his teens, and the first four years of his twenties, in the army. He had been taught combat, in all kinds of conditions, extreme heat, extreme cold, how to fight in jungle warfare. He had been taught how to drive various vehicles, and above all, he had been taught, self-control. At five fifteen on this Wednesday, the tenth of October, he still had all of these attributes to his name, except for the last one.

"You little buggering Nazi that you are", he roared, as he lifted up the tin he had placed so neatly on the shelf, and threw it in the direction of Colin Rees, who was now making his way out of the shop as fast as he could. The tin, for a good job, thought Angela, sailed over the boy's head, and went straight through his own shop window, causing it first to creak, and then, after a few seconds, to completely shatter and disintegrate over all of the beautifully assorted fresh fruit display. Angela squealed as high pitched as she could, trying her best not to laugh. To make matters worse, Joe had attempted to get up too quickly to chase the boy, and had lost his balance completely. He hurtled into a display pyramid of baked beans.

Angela actually fell to her knees with laughter. She had to place both of her hands over her face to prevent the Millers from realizing the hysterics she was in. Her shoulders were shaking. Nancy Miller,

thinking that Angela was crying, came round from behind the counter, herself suffering from shock, with the noise and her husband's violence. With Angela on her knees, Nancy Miller put a hand upon her head. "There there now, madam, Joe will be alright, he's just lost his temper a bit, now don't you be frightened now madam. He's ruined all that fruit though, look he's under those tins".
Angela was certain she was going to wet herself.
"He did say you know, so he did, he did say that boy was no good, he's always said that, for six months he's said so".

Joseph Miller emerged from under the baked beans. His brow was cut, just above the eye. His knee was on one of the bars of chocolate, which was now smashed to pieces within its wrapper. "Hell, I'm sorry Nancy, I'm sorry madam, but I'm bloody sick of that boy, to the back teeth".

Angela had calmed herself down now, but found it hard to say anything. Only one leg remained on Joe's glasses, and the chain was burst. The single leg swung to and fro` as Joe got to his feet with a grunt. "Christ fuck it just shows you doesn't it madam, eh"?
Nancy Miller at last regained some composure. "Can I get you anything madam, before we close the shop, I'm afraid I can't sell you any fruit".
"Hurt your fucking foot? My brow needs stitches woman hell!" Cried mister Miller.
This was not the time for bringing up any gossip about Doctor Hillman, thought Angela to herself, that would have to wait until another day.
Three hundred and ninety-two metres away, Colin Rees made his way home on his bicycle, with only one tin of sliced peaches for all of his troubles.

MORNINGSIDE.

John Hillman senior walked along the loose gravel car park with Carla Paganni. "You have a very beautiful house Mister Hillman" she said, as she climbed into her car.

"I do indeed Carla, I hope Misses Hillman appreciates it as much as I do".

"I'm sure she will, it's so spacious, oh, I almost forgot" said Carla. She handed John Hillman a letter she had put in her glove compartment. " It's from Heather" said Carla, " She said I had to wait until you read it, to see if there were any messages you wanted to pass on to her".

John Hillman took out a pair of reading glasses and put them on. After a minute or so he looked up from the letter and said, "Yes, yes I do have a message for her, tell her". He trailed off, looking up at the laden skies, as if seeking divine advice. "Tell her to leave this one alone, tell her, under no circumstances has she to bother with this one, it's not safe, tell her. Make sure Carla, whatever you do, make sure she gets that message".

"I will sir, you can count on it".

"Good, now, I must be off Carla, I have lots to do today and a nagging wife who is so hyper-active, you wouldn't believe it". As he walked away from Carla, he said, "I'll be in touch my dear". Hillman stood on the steps of his new house, which he and his wife had named Morningside, and watched the cherry red Porsche disappear around the bend of his drive. He was just about to go inside when Carla's car came reversing back onto the car park, followed by the carpet fitter's van, and the police car. Carla had switched her engine off, and was now waiting for a signal from Hillman, a special little code they had. The van pulled up alongside the steps of Hillman's house. Hillman looked at his watch. The driver got out and walked around to the steps. "You're late" said Hillman.

"No sir, we're early, we're not supposed to be here until tomorrow morning, but Mister Waite phoned us and told us we had access to another four rooms if we wanted to make a start today. It leaves us less to do tomorrow sir, we know how eager you are to move into your new home".

"Oh, ah well then" said Hillman, "you carry on then".

"Right you are sir" said the driver.

The police car had parked about twenty metres from Hillman's steps. Hillman walked slowly down the steps and along the loose chippings until he was at the driver's door. It was chief inspector Robert Denby. There was no-one else in the car. The door opened, and Denby climbed out. "Just what the hell do you think you're playing at John" said the chief inspector, almost whispering.

"I beg your pardon" said Hillman.

"I've got two good officers lying in hospital with broken arms and ribs, one with a broken leg. One of them is seriously concussed John, what the hell do you think you're playing at"?
"Playing? Robert. Playing? Is that what you call it, I'm not playing anything. I have an ex daughter-in-law who has been set about by your two good officers, they got off lightly, I can assure you. That young woman's face is going to take weeks to heal, her eyes are

closed, and her face is badly swollen, if anyone was playing, then it was your officers, they got what they deserved".

Denby cleared his throat, trying to keep his cool, and not shout out loud. "The girl was beat up under your orders, and fine well you know it".

"That is where you are wrong Robert" said Hillman. "My orders were too rough her up a little bit, give her a fright, not knock the life out of her, no those two got what was coming to them".

As Denby started to get back into the car, Hillman leaned over the door and said, "You haven't got a complaint to make, have you Robert"?
"No. It's just. I've got to cover for those two officers, there's a gap to fill".
"Well, cover for them then, you haven't got time to sit here all day have you, goodbye Mister Denby, mind how you go now".

Robert Denby started up the car and reversed back, a little more quickly than he should have, causing the back wheels to spin as he did so. He drove off at a more sensible speed, disappearing round the bend at the corner of the drive. Hillman gave the thumbs up sign to Carla. She drove off down the hill. "Be very careful Mister Denby", Hillman whispered.

HARRINGTON SQUARE.

Tracy, Sharon, and Angela all sat laughing at the story Angela had just told them. "I'm beginning to see what you mean Tracy, about the residents in this square. If those shop owners are anything to go by, honestly, I thought my sides would split, you've never seen anything like it, that old boy, he's lovely".

"Yeah, he is nice" said Sharon, "he doesn't seem to be the same as the rest around here. He seems to take a dim view on gossip, although, with that hearing problem, he is a laugh, everything always seems to backfire on him. It's a bloody shame, him being married to that".

"Now" said Angela, "nobody twisted his arm, now did they"?

"I wouldn't bet on that Angela" said Tracy.

After a few minutes, Tracy said she was going up stairs to phone her girls. "I don't want them seeing me like this, but I have to speak with them".

"Well", said Angela, I'm going to get some take away food, what would you like Tracy"?

"Oh, I don't want anything, I'm not hungry".

"Now you listen here madam" said Angela, "I know you've had a rough time lately, but you have to be strong, now you eat, because, if you don't put the fuel in". She pointed to her stomach. "Then the engine won't run". She pointed to her head. "Now what kind of take away do you like"?

"Oh, Indian, if you insist, but just a small curry".

"I'll come with you" said Sharon, "I'll show you where they are".

As Angela stood up, she walked over to Tracy, and bent down on her hunkers in front of her. "Listen to me Tracy, I made a promise to you about your children, and I'll keep my promise, but you've got to promise me something, you promise me you'll be strong through all of this. You have to pretend you have accepted the situation. Now, if he lets you have the children every two weeks, then that's how we'll get them back, except, it won't be you taking them away, it'll be me. After a few weeks, the girls will be used to seeing me coming about the house. You can tell them that you and I are old friends or we went to school together or something, but we mustn't let them know that we're related, in case they tell the Hillmans, but, one day, you'll phone the school, and tell their teacher that their aunt is picking them up early.

The girls will be quite happy to come with me, especially when I tell them that they are going to see mummy every day from then on. Meanwhile, those Hillmans will come roaring and shouting round here about it not being your day to pick them up. Of course, you won't have made the phone call, it will be me. You will then fly into action, and panic, start cursing them, demand the police get involved. "If anything has happened to my girls" and remember, "My girls, I'll kill you all, you bastards that you are, you corrupted bastards". Call them what you want
Tracy, they'll be too shocked to realize, they will be frantic". Tracy smiled. "Now you be nice and cheerful to those little girls of yours, after all Tracy, it could have been so much worse, they could have had you banged up for carrying cocaine. You've done the hard bit babes, you got yourself out, and well done, but now it's your turn to

play, you're cooking the dinner now, and you know what they say, revenge is a dish best served cold". Angela gently tapped Tracy twice on the head, and kissed her on the cheek. "I won't be long".

"Angela" said Tracy, as she got to the door.

Angela turned, "Yeah"?

"Thank you" said Tracy.

"There's no need to thank me, we're more than just relations, we're a special kind of family Tracy, and I will defend you to the death, my angel, you'll have your kids back, don't worry".

HEATHER'S HAIR SALON AND BEAUTY PARLOUR. (SHEFFIELD)

Heather Bradley sat in the small room at the back of her salon, carefully scanning a list of girl's names on her computer, when Carla Paganni knocked and entered the room. Heather, a twenty-eight year old ex- prostitute, had been set up in business by an ex punter, a certain Mister John Hillman senior. She had two girls working in the salon with her, and made enough money to pay the girls a decent wage, and take care of the general running of the shop. Her real profits came from the girls who worked on the streets for her. John Hillman took only twenty per cent of Heather's profit, but in return, Heather had to provide runners for him, whenever there were parcels to pick up at certain harbours. The girls Heather chose were informed of what they were going to collect, and therefore knew the implications should they ever be caught. For taking these risks, Heather would pay them quite substantial amounts of money. Heather let the girls keep fifty per cent of their earnings, which left her a healthy thirty per cent. Hillman said she was crazy, and far too soft with them, but then had held his hands up. "It's up to you, my dear, they're your girls, it's not for me to interfere". All of her girls had places of their own. Some had flats near the city centre, some had apartments on the outskirts, but all, had places to go. The term, *Working the streets,* was only a figure of speech, although sometimes some of the girls still ventured out.

Nothing at all had to be connected to the salon, in any way. Carla Paganni was the collector, and so no-one ever undercut Heather, ever. Heather, a beautiful blonde haired young woman, had put herself through college with her hustle money, and had gained all of her qualifications to obtain her license as a beautician. Her dream was to own her own boutique, but that was a long way off yet. "Hello Carla" said Heather make yourself a coffee honey if you want".

Carla put the kettle on. "How are you Heather, are you ok"?

"Fine" said Heather, "I'm just, there's three girls not working tonight, and I'm going to need one of the girls who is working to drive over to Manchester for John, that's only going to leave five working girls, bloody hell, only half a work force".

"No" said Carla.

"What"?

"No, I gave John your letter, and he told me to tell you, under no circumstances were you to touch this. That was his message".

"Oh fucking hell Carla, I've gone and made arrangements, when did you give him the letter"?

"This afternoon Heather, I'm sorry, I put it in my glove compartment yesterday, and I forgot about it, I'm sorry".

Heather sighed. "It doesn't matter, I'll sort it out, and anyway, it'll give me an extra girl making money".

She picked up a small mobile phone from her desk and pressed a few digits. "Hello? Dave? It's off, what? I can't help it; I've just received word that I've not to touch it, ok? That's all I know. Dave? A word of warning, get that gear out of there fast. The man said under no circumstances, now when he says that, then it usually means a bust, just letting you know, I'll be in touch, bye".

"Sorry Heather" repeated Carla, "I should have got word to you sooner".
"Forget it; did you not make me a cup of coffee Carla"?
"I thought you had one".

"It's cold, fuck Carla, I hope those boys in Manchester don't get caught with that cocaine".

"So do I" said Carla, "I'll feel responsible if they do".

"Well, it can't be helped, that's life" said Heather.

"Yeah, it just about will be life if they get caught with that much cocaine, poor bastards".

HARRINGTON MEDICAL CENTRE.

Doctor John Hillman felt very strange as he got out of his father's car, less than twenty metres from the staff doors at Harrington Medical Centre, very strange indeed. He had been absent from work now for nearly a month. Although his mother and father had more or less sorted everything out for him, including the children, and a house for the three of them to live in, something still wasn't right. He knew how much the kids missed their mother, and he felt for them, but no matter how much they missed her, or him for that matter, because he admitted to himself that he did miss her, there was no way he would ever go back with her, even if she begged him, he couldn't, not after that. "Oh God" he sighed, as he made his way to the surgery doors. "Why Lord? Why are you putting me through all this misery? Have I not been a good Christian, is that it? Huh? Surely there's worse than me going about". He kept asking in his head. " Surely there's worse than me, I mean, I don't sell drugs on to kids, I don't run brothels, I live clean and simple, I look after my children Lord, I look after the patients who come in here, I mean, fuck sakes Lord, why the fuck pick on me? Huh? What a fucking fucked up God you are, you really are, what a fucking twat!"

"Good morning doctor Hillman". A young secretary called out to him, as he came in the door.

What sort of a stupid name is that, he thought to himself. "Good morning Maureen".

"It's good to have you back with us doctor, hope you're feeling better".

With us? Thought Hillman, with us? Are you a doctor you little trollop, are you? Are you part of this medical team here, you little fucking slut, are you? I doubt whether you could spell tonsillitis, you jumped up little tramp that you are.

"Yes I am Maureen, thank you. Do you think you could bring me a cup of coffee to my office, when you get a moment".

"Certainly doctor Hillman, I'll bring you one straight away".

That's more like it, you little cunt, you fetch me coffee when I click my fingers, you lick my arse madam, because I sure as fuck will lick yours at the first opportunity, right Lord? Huh? Think you could set that up for me Twat? Lord, I mean? "Thank you Maureen".

"It's my pleasure doctor".

Doctor Hillman, carrying a brand new black leather brief case, made his way down the corridor to his practice. I bet I know what your pleasure is, you little fucking scrubber, I bet you like it hard up the arse lady. Hillman continued his way down the corridor whistling the twenty-third psalm, and continuing to feel strange.

MORNINGSIDE.

At long last, the Hillmans had moved into their new home. After weeks and weeks of packing things away and bringing boxes and bags to the house, they had finally moved in. Hillman could start to unwind now. His wife would have enough things to do to keep her going for two lifetimes, and when she was like this he hardly heard a word from her. She was happy, and he could tell. This was the house she had dreamed of, where they could spend the last of their years together, and quietly live out the rest of their retirement. She stood now with her husband looking out to the far end of the garden where the swings and round-about had just been erected. "Do you think they would like a paddling pool or a sand pit John"?

"Mmm"?

"I said, do you think sand pit or pool, which do you think the girls will prefer"?

"Anne" said John Hillman, "I'm sure you'll know much better than I what little girls like to play with. I'm sure that whatever you decide, they'll love it, I'll leave it to you my darling". Hillman knew only too well, that if he'd picked either one, his wife would have inevitably chosen the other. He played safe.

Anne Hillman walked over to the breakfast bar and handed her husband a mug of tea. "I wonder how our John is doing on his first day back at work it can't be easy for him John".
Hillman sighed and closed his newspaper; there was no way he was going to get peace to read it. "Oh he'll be fine Anne" he consoled his wife. "He's made of good stuff". He decided he would patronise her. "It'll take more than that to keep our John down you should know that by now my dear, he's a fighter".

"Yes I know John, but he needs company, he needs female company, you know? He needs to get out and mix, socialise with people. He was off work there John for a month, he never once went out. He hasn't even went to church since that carry on, have you noticed. He hasn't been down to see anyone down at the youth club either".

"Anne, for goodness sakes woman, would you stop giving yourself things to worry about. We've just got moved in here and all the stress from that is over, so you've got to give yourself something else to worry about haven't you. He's not been anywhere because his mouth has been so bloody sore it's only just healed recently. Where do you think he'd go with all his mouth stitched up, Christ, give the man a bloody chance".

"John Hillman!! I swear it, if you ever use that language in here again I'll wash your mouth out with soap and water, what kind of talk is that, at your age John".

"Sorry, Anne, I'm sorry, I'm only trying to put a point over". Again he patronised her. "I'm only sticking up for my boy Anne".

Anne Hillman said, " I know you are John". She tapped her husband lightly on the shoulder three times. "God bless you John Hillman, the world could do with a few more like you, that's for sure. You read your paper I'm going to do some ironing. You're a good man" she said, as she left the kitchen.

As he reopened his newspaper to where he had been reading, the front doorbell rang. "I don't believe it" he muttered, as he closed the paper once again.

"I'll get it" his wife shouted from somewhere in the house. He heard his wife's voice and another woman talking. Anne walked into the kitchen followed by one of the most beautiful young women he had ever seen in his life. The young lady was dressed in a pale blue jacket with skirt to match. The skirt, about knee length, hugged her shapely hips. She wore black tights, or stockings, he would have loved to find out which, a deep blue low cut top, but not too low. Around her neck she wore a very expensive gold chain with a disc in the centre.

"This is Miss Julia Peters" said Anne, "she is from the art school she's trying to sell some of her paintings, to raise herself some money to further her education".
"Is she now" said John Hillman. The young lady offered her hand to Misses Hillman and then to Mister Hillman. "It's a pleasure to meet

you my dear" he said, as he rose up from his chair at the breakfast bar. "Always nice to meet young women who are trying to better themselves. Well now, do you have any paintings with you my dear"?
"Yes sir, they're outside in the car, may I show some"?
"You certainly may" said Hillman.
"Thank you". She left the kitchen, and went out to her car to get her paintings. As she left, Anne Hillman said, "You see John? That's the kind of girl I would like our John to take up with. You can tell by the way they dress you know. She's beautiful, she doesn't have to flash her backside or her boobs to get noticed, no, she's pure class John, it stands out a mile".
"Well, if her paintings are any good, I might buy a couple to help her out you know? Maybe young John might want to buy a couple when he gets home Anne, huh"? He gave his wife a wink.
"Oh now John, that's terrible, Anne blushed, you shouldn't do that".
"You said it yourself Anne, he could do a lot worse you know".
"Oh now John" she giggled.
"Hello".
"In here my dear" said Hillman, "we're just going to have some coffee, would you like some"?
"Oh yes please" said the young lady.
"Now then, let's have a look at these paintings of yours, let me clear this breakfast bar for you" he said, removing a cup and his newspaper.
"This is most kind of you both" said Angela Phorbes, as she lifted the first of her paintings up onto the table.

HARRINGTON MEDICAL CENTRE.

"I wonder what's wrong with him" Maureen whispered to her colleague, at reception. "It's twenty past eleven, and he's only seen two patients all morning, since nine o clock, and even they were only in for a couple of minutes each. "I've asked him if he feels alright" said Maureen", and he assures me he's fine, but every time I press the buzzer to his office, and ask him if he's ready for his next patient, he just says, not yet Maureen, not yet. I think I'll tell Doctor Phitspatrick, he'll look in on him".

"You'll be lucky" said Sandra Smith, Maureen's colleague, "there's only two Doctors on today, Doctor Phitspatrick is run off his feet".

At eleven twenty-four a.m. John Hillman was on the internet, scanning the pages for massage parlours. "You would think they would just come out and say it, wouldn't you" he said out loud, "whores. I only want to fuck somebody". Then it was back to his singing, "*My soul he doth restore again*".

Doctor Gerald Phitspatrick knocked on the door of John Hillman's office. "Ok in there John" he shouted in his bold Irish accent.

"Yes fine Gerald".

"Well, I could use some help here Doctor, we're kind of snowed under John, do you mind taking some patients in here, to clear up the backlog, there's people in there been waiting for over an hour man".

"No problem Gerald, send them in, tell her to send them in, tell Maureen. *Yea though I walk through death's dark...* Send them in Ger".

MORNINGSIDE.

"Julia Peters" was showing John Hillman a beautiful water coloured landscape when Anne Hillman came back into the kitchen, after she had been putting rubbish in the bin outside. "My goodness me Miss Peters" she said, in her strong Irish accent, as she walked over to the sink, that's a rather expensive car you have out there, for being an art student, if you don't mind me saying".

As quick as lightning, Angela Phorbes said "Oh it's not mine Misses Hillman, it belongs to my brother, he lets me borrow it when he comes up from London, not that that's very often".

"I see" said Anne Hillman, what is it that your brother does dear"?

"Oh, he's an estate agent, free-lance, he says it's better not to work for anyone else if you can help it, otherwise you tend to get the tarry end of the stick. It was he, who paid for my first two years at college".
"Well, he must think a lot of you Miss Peters, that's all I can say".

"Julia, please, call me Julia, yes he does Misses Hillman, he's taken care of me since I was ten, that's when we lost our parents".

"Oh my poor girl, what happened if you don't mind me asking"?
"Not at all, they were on holiday in Italy, when the car they were travelling in, collided with a coach, they were both killed instantly. Our only aunt was in the car with them, she died too".
"I am so sorry my darling" said Anne, "you poor child, you didn't get much of a start in life did you"?

"Oh, Terry's looked after me, that's my brother, he's been kind".

John Hillman cleared his throat. "Well now my dear, these paintings are very good, very good indeed, look at this one Anne" he said, getting up from his seat to take a bottle of wine from the rack he had installed at the far side of the kitchen, "Isn't it beautiful"?
"It certainly is" replied his wife. "You know John, this would look lovely at the top of the staircase, don't you think"?

"Yes it would" he said, as he popped the cork of the bottle of wine he had chosen. "Now then, my dear, how much do you charge for a painting like this, it is unique, isn't it"?
"I'm afraid not, I've had ten copies made from that one, but this one is the original though".
"Ah well then" said Hillman, then it is unique in its own way isn't it"?
"I suppose so" replied 'Julia Peters'.
"How much my dear"?
"Well, I was kind of hoping I would get fifty pounds for it".
"Fifty pounds"? Mocked Hillman "My dear, the very first thing you have to learn, the very first rule in setting yourself up in business, is, never ever sell yourself cheap, if you do that, then you'll end up doing it all your life, big mistake. Any fool can see that this painting is worth at least two hundred pounds, what do you think Anne"?
"Surely" replied Anne Hillman, although she knew her husband was being kind to the girl.
"There now, I'm offering two hundred for this one". He picked up the landscape. "Do we have a deal Miss Peters"?
"Mister Hillman, it's too much, it's not worth that much".
"Ah ah, there you go again now, don't do it my dear, don't sell yourself cheap. Now, let's have a glass of wine to celebrate your sale, shall we"?
"Well, if you're sure Mister Hillman".
"Of course I'm sure" he said, as he handed the young woman and his wife a glass of wine each. "Here's to a long and distinguished career in the world of fine art, may you flourish from this day forth in everything you do, bottoms up".
"Cheers, thank you Mister Hillman, thank you both".
"You are quite welcome young lady, quite welcome".

HARRINGTON MEDICAL CENTRE. 3.50.pm.

Gerald Phitspatrick tapped twice on the door of Doctor John Hillman's office. Having received no reply, he opened the door and walked in. John Hillman sat on his chair with his head resting on his two folded arms on his desk, fast asleep. "John! John"!!

Hillman sat up quickly, "Huh"?

"John" said Phitspatrick, "I think you need some more time pal, you are obviously nowhere near ready to come back to work, hell John, you've only seen four patients all day, you need some more time. I'm not being funny, but you are no good to anyone in this state, you'll only make yourself ill. Now, you get back off home, and I'll see about getting a replacement for you, until you have recovered sufficiently".

"Well, I suppose I could take another two weeks, I am feeling a bit tired, but how will you cope Gerry"?

"I'll cope fine with a replacement, you don't worry about that, you just get yourself better".

Hillman stood up. "I, eh, I think you're right Gerald".

"Of course I'm right, now you go and freshen up, have Maureen get you a coffee before you drive, do you hear"?

"Yes I will Gerry, I will".
"Good man, now off you go, and take it easy ok? You take as long as you need".

"Thanks Gerry, you're a mate".

"On you go John, now take care, and remember the coffee".

"I will". Hillman picked up his bag. He took his bible from his desk, and carefully placed it inside the briefcase. "See you Gerry".

“Yeah see you John, watch how you go”.
Hillman left the office, closing the door behind him

Gerald Phitspatrick was pressing the digits on the telephone, when something caught his eye. As he looked at the computer screen, he saw a naked red haired woman sitting on a sofa with her legs wide open, her hands wrapped around a pair of voluptuous breasts. The logo above her head, read, COME AND SEE ME ANY TIME, I’M VERY CHEAP, AND I ALWAYS PLEASE. CALL ANGEL ON…

HARRINGTON SQUARE.

Tracy and Sharon were having a coffee out in the garden when Angela returned. "Hi girls" she said, as she brought a cup of coffee out to join them. "What have you two been up to when I was away, you've not been annoying your neighbours again with your lusty lesbian sessions again have you? You've not been teasing that old Misses Semple again".

Tracy and Sharon laughed. "No, nothing like that Angela, what have you been up to"?

"Well now, where do I start? I went into town this morning, and I came across a market. I browsed around for a while, and I came across these paintings, all done by the same artist, six of them in all. I paid only eighty pounds for the six. I then had a brainwave or something, an idea, we'll say, and I went up to the Hillman's house, and posed as a student. He only paid me two hundred pounds for one of the paintings".

"Angela, be careful" said Tracy, "They may seem to be a nice placid old couple, but believe me".

"Oh I know Tracy, I know, but I was careful, I was cunning, I had them eating out of my hands in the end".

"Did they see your car Angela" said Sharon.

"I told them it belonged to my brother, they took it all in, don't worry, I wouldn't put you in any danger Tracy. I was just trying to see what kind of people they are, that's all, I won't even see them again".

Tracy took a sip of her coffee and then said, "I hope not Angela, I thought I knew that old bastard, thought I had him sussed, and then look what happened".

"I know Tracy, but you had no reason to doubt who he was, or should I say, what he was. I, on the other hand, know how much of a ruthless bastard he is. He's one of these wide boys, who fancies himself as some type of gangster, getting other people to do his dirty work for him, he'll get what's coming to him, believe me, just leave him to me babe, I'll repay him for you".

Just at that point Tracy's doorbell rang. Angela and Sharon left by the back of the house. Tracy looked through the slats of her gate and saw her ex-husband's car parked at her house. As she opened her front door, she sighed with relief to see that Angela had parked her car over at Sharon's house.

Doctor John Hillman didn't even look Tracy in the face, instead, he looked at his feet and said, "I was wondering if you wanted to spend some more time with the girls this week, I have some tests to undergo at the hospital and I won't have much time with them, but if you have things planned for this week, then it doesn't matter, my mother will have them".

"No I don't have anything planned, what could I, thank you John, thank you so much, I really appreciate this".

Hillman turned away, and began to walk back down the path. "I'll pick them up on Friday afternoon, about three".
He got into his car and drove away. He was obviously going to his mother's now to get the girls, but he'd said nothing more. He'll just drop the children off when he returns. He was so distant now, she couldn't help noticing, not just to her, that was understandable, but deep, not the same person at all, weird. Sure enough, fifteen minutes later, he pulled up outside the house. Hillman got out of the car to let young Amy and Angela run up to the house and to their mother's arms. He took two hold all bags from the boot of the car, and laid them gently on the pavement. "Friday" he said, as he got back into his car and drove away, not even waving to his kids.

John Hillman had business to see to, there were whores out here who needed seeing to, hundreds of them, who needed to be fucked hard and to be taught a lesson, not to be flashing off their bodies on the bloody streets and making themselves an abomination in the eyes of God. There was work to be done. "I don't know why Lord, you just couldn't come straight out with it, and just tell me what you wanted

me to do, didn't have to put me through all that" he said out loud, as he drove through the city.
"But I'll do it for you Lord, I'll learn these whores a lesson, I'll dispose of the lusty bastards for you, if that's what you want Lord".
Hillman had no idea how ill he was. Schizophrenia has many forms and makes the sufferer react in many different ways. As far as he was concerned he was in full control of his actions, and his actions were perfectly normal, never thinking that the voice of god in his head was, to say the least, abnormal.

OAKWOOD ESTATE. (EAST SHEFFIELD.)

Steven Todd lived on the top floor of the high-rise flats in the centre of Oakwood Estate. He had been a drug addict since the age of thirteen. He was now twenty-nine. He was no longer a drug addict, nor an alcoholic. Never again would he rely on cocaine or heroin or vodka, or anything else for that matter, because his body lay, one hundred and sixty-two feet below his balcony, burst and broken, over what was left of the roof of a Ford Orion.

Cocaine had been delivered to his door, three days previously to this one. He had become greedy and had come up with some cock and bull story about his flat being burgled. His flat was being robbed now, as Carla Paganni retrieved what was left of the cocaine, and the money that Todd thought was safely stashed in the corner of his bedroom ceiling. Carla smiled and thought to herself, as she pulled out the canvas bag, "Always the ceiling, what makes them think that the ceiling is the best place to hide anything". She had arrived at Todd's flat fifteen minutes earlier, for the money off the cocaine he was supposed to have sold on. It was then that he'd come up with the story about being burgled. " Tell him I can't help it, he knows the risks around here, it's just tough that's all, there's fuck all I can do about it, that's it, fuck him".

"Is that what I tell Mister Hillman, Steven, fuck him"?
"Yeah, fuck him, and fuck you too, for that matter, and if you don't get your sweet little arse out of here, I might just fuck you, got it"?
"Carla sighed, "Yes I've got it, I'll tell him, not like that, but I'll tell him Steve. Listen" she said, "business aside, do you fancy going out for a drink some time, I quite like you, I'd like to get to know you a bit better, you know"?
"Sure, hey, look, I'm sorry I snapped at you just there, I mean, I'm just as annoyed as anyone about being robbed you know".
"I know" said Carla, "He'll understand Steve, when I tell him. Hey, is there any chance of a coffee Steven before I go"?
"No. it'll have to be tea, tea or water, that's it, that's all I've got".

"Tea will be just fine, sugar and no milk thank you Steven".
"Good, that's handy, because I've got no milk either.

Carla opened the door which led out to the balcony. "Wow, what a view" she said, as she looked over the edge down to the ground below.
"What"?
"I said what a great view from up here".
"Oh yeah" he said, returning with two mugs, one in each hand.
"Can I drink mine out here please Steven"?

"Sure, if you want, you get good fresh air up here, that's one good thing about living up here; it's good for getting rid of hangovers too".

"I'll bet" she said. As he handed her a mug, she took a sip of the near boiling liquid, and then threw the tea straight into his eyes. He had only just begun to scream, when she grabbed one of his arms, and with one lightning quick move, she spun him over the top of the safety rails. She stood and listened for the three point seven seconds it took for Todd's body to splatter over the roof of a car. "Ooh, I'll bet that didn't hurt Steve, I'll pass your message on though, fuck him that was it Steven wasn't it? Fuck him"?

By the time Carla left the back of the flats, a large crowd had gathered around the front, and around what was left of Steven Todd's body. "It's one of those fucking junkies who live up there" one old man said to an elderly lady, who replied, " It's a bloody shame though isn't it, a waste of a young life, tragic".

"Tragic fuck all" replied the old man, he would have killed you or me for the price of a fix, and never think twice about it, that's just the way it is, fuck him".

Carla couldn't help but laugh as she drove through the town with the radio on. She was singing along to an old Van Halen song. "*Jump, might as well jump, go ahead and jump. JUMP*! Oh" she laughed, "Stop it Steven, you're killing me", she laughed some more. "Ha, fuck him"?

“What do you think dear”? Said Hillman, standing on the wooden step ladder holding, the painting against the wall.

“I think it looks, well, it kind of clashes with the wallpaper, don’t you think John”?

“I think it looks fine” he said, knowing that because of what he had just said, he had doomed the painting to another part of the house. “Wait for it” he said to himself, five, four, three, two”

“Don’t you think it would look nice hanging in the games room dear, there’s nothing at all hanging in that room”.

“Yes it would dear, you’re absolutely bang on again, it will look perfect in there, I’ll hang it up after dinner tonight. I’m going to my study; I have a couple of important calls to make”. Hillman walked from the hallway and into the kitchen, where he picked up his glass of wine from the breakfast bar, then made his way to his study.

“It’s a shame young John missed that young lady today, you know, the artist”?

“Oh yes” said Hillman, “Never mind, I gave her a card with John’s address on it, she said she might call in on him some time”.
“Well there’s a good chance she’ll catch him in, because he told me he’s taking some more time off, he says he needs some more rest”.

Hillman stopped in his tracks. “He said that? Are you sure Anne”?
“Of course I’m sure, he was here today. He brought the girls home, then he went off on his own. Then he came back and told them they were going to stay with their mummy for a few days”.
“And you didn’t object to this”? Said Hillman, taking a sip of his wine.
“John, no matter what I may think of the woman, she is still their mother, and those little girls love her to pieces, there’s nothing you nor I can do about that John”.
“Well, you’ve changed your tune have you not Anne”?

“It’s not a question of changing my tune, we have to do what’s best for those two little angels, that’s what’s important here Mister Hillman, changing my tune indeed” said Anne, as she made her way to the kitchen.

“Have you ever heard the likes of it, deary, deary me”. Hillman sighed and went in to his study. “Huh, my son’s a lady boy by the looks of it. More time off for receiving a smack on the mouth by a lady at that, bloody pink team”.

Five minutes later he was talking to one of his associates. “Any luck on the Merc Charlie”. Hillman had made sure he walked `Julia Peters` out to her car, personally, so as he could get the registration of her car.

“Yes” said the man on the phone. “I don’t know what’s going on John, but according to the D.V.L.A. the owner of that car is not Julia Peters, her name is Angela Clark, C.L.A.R.K. That’s it John there’s nothing else, she has no criminal record. She lives at Twenty-four Henry Street, and that’s Isle of Dogs, London, that’s it buddy, that’s all we can get”.

“Thanks Charlie, you’re a pal”.

“No problem, any time John, bye”.

Hillman replaced the telephone back on to its cradle, and sat tapping his teeth with his pen. After a few seconds, he began tapping the digits for Carla Pagannis’ mobile phone. “Hello? Carla? Yes how are you my dear”?

“I’m fine Mister Hillman”.

“Carla, I want you to do me a favour my dear, would you”?

“Anything sir”.

“Yes, I want you to look out for a black Mercedes SL five hundred”. He told her the registration. “Now the driver of this vehicle should be a blonde young lady, roughly about the age of twenty-eight to

thirty-four, somewhere around that age, as I say, roughly. Now I don't want you to approach her in any way, just make a note of addresses she visits, or bars, hotels, you know, after a few days come and tell me what you've got ok"?
"Sure Mister Hillman".

"Oh, how did you get on with Mister Todd Carla"?

"Ah, bad news there sir, he said he lost it all, he said he was robbed and there was nothing he could do about it, oh yes and he said fuck you, he told me to say that to you, fuck you Mister Hillman". There was silence on the phone for a few seconds, then Carla said, "I got most of the dust back for you Mister Hillman and four thousand pounds he'd been hiding from you".

"Good girl Carla, I sincerely hope that you hurt him bad my dear, to teach him a lesson".

"Afraid not sir, he didn't feel anything, other than some hot water on his face".

"Explain"?

"I threw him over the balcony sir".

"And what? He landed in water what"?

"No sir, he lives in the high rise flats over in the East of Sheffield, he lived on the top story sir".

"Oh I see Carla, he's dead"?

"Yes sir".

"Ah, very good my dear, very good indeed, was his body all twisted and mangled Carla"?
"Don't know sir, I never looked, there was no need to, we were nearly a hundred and seventy feet up in the air".
"I see my dear, I would imagine there would be one almighty splat though, wouldn't you say, Carla"?

"Definitely sir".
"Very good, now you know which bank account to put that money into".
"Yes sir, Mister Hillman".
"Yes, I tell you what Carla, just put three in Carla, you keep a thousand for yourself".
"Oh Mister Hillman, there's no need for all that".
"Yes there is, now you keep in touch with me concerning the Mercedes honey, ok"?
"Thank you Mister Hillman".
"No, thank you Carla, fuck him indeed".
"I'll be more ruthless next time Mister Hillman".
"Good girl, talk to you soon, bye Carla".

FINCHLEY STREET. (NEAR CITY CENTRE.) 2AM.

Susie Monk walked along to the edge of the street. She never went any further than this, normally. She had a rule that she kept, to stay in the busy area, because it wasn't safe any further than here. Not because of rival prostitutes, although sometimes battles had occurred between them, but because of the creeps who roamed the streets at nights in this area. In the busy areas, the police had long since given up on picking up working girls, since a simple phone call to Heather, and in turn, another to Mister John Hillman sorted everything out. If they were picked up, they were usually back out working the streets within the hour. Tonight, however, Susie had been very quiet, and had gone to her friend Jenny's house for a couple of drinks. The taxi she had ordered for one o clock had not arrived, and so she decided to walk back to her place, armed only with a pepper spray and her pride. As she walked, she became more and more nervous. She kept looking behind her, to convince herself that she wasn't being followed. She kept walking briskly. "Haven't made much money tonight" she thought to herself, but then, there were always spells like this. You could make an absolute fortune in one night, and then nothing for the next three nights. Tonight was just one of those nights where she had made next to nothing, tomorrow was another day.

Five minutes later she started to feel safer as she entered the busier areas, near the City centre. All the other girls who worked for Heather had sent her text messages, saying that they had had quiet nights as well. Some had gone to a night club, and some had just gone home. She felt confident enough now to stop and light up a cigarette. She inhaled the smoke and then exhaled it up into the frosty air. Still the streets were eerily quiet, especially for this time of night. As she walked back towards the city centre, headlights began to shimmer some light from behind. As it approached, the vehicle pulled over to the wrong side of the road, so that the driver was level with Susie as she walked. The driver's window of a Ford Transit rolled down. A young handsome man about the age of eighteen smiled at her.

"There you are, I've been looking for you since midnight".

"Well, you haven't been looking hard enough then, have you, because I've been working since nine o clock last night, I'm finished for the night".

The Transit rolled along at the same speed that Susie was walking. "Carla told me I would find you up here".

"Did she now"?

"Yes, and she said that if I asked you nicely and gave you a generous tip, that you would oblige, she said you wouldn't be able to resist the money".

"I see, and how do you know Carla"?

"Carla and I are friends, she saved my life once when I was getting beat up badly by a couple of jerks, huh, they ended up in hospital, and I think they were there for about three weeks. I met her a couple of times after that, and we ended up kind of mates, you know, my name is Terry, Terry Gibb, come on Susie what do you say
"Who's in the back of your van"?

"No-one, honestly".

"Yeah sure, like I'm going to believe that".

The young man stopped the van and switched off the ignition. "Here". He handed the keys to Susie, and stepped out, walking away from her until he was about thirty yards off her. He sat down on the pavement. "There, I'll sit here until you check the back of the van, the door's open, take a look, why would I lie to you about that? If I as much as move from here you can throw those keys down that drain there and scream your head off.

"Susie thought to herself, "this guy is crazy or he's desperate to have sex with me". She walked to the back of the van, and looked at Terry. He hadn't moved. She quickly opened the back door of the van and stood back.

"Alright"? Terry shouted up at her.

"Yes, alright" she replied, "come on back here to your van before a policeman comes and lifts you".

Terry walked back up to her, smiling. "You are crazy, do you know that"?

"Yip, come on Susie, what do you say, can I come back to your place, please"?

"Alright then" she said, "But don't leave it so late next time".
"I won't" he said, "But I'll pay extra though".
"No, that won't be necessary, not this time, don't make a habit out of this though" she said with a smile.

"I won't, I promise". He opened the passenger door for her, and then got in the driver's side. "Do you mind if I stop for chips Susie, I'm starving".

"Go on then" she smiled. Now she really did trust him, as they drove off.

As Terry Gibb drove, Susie said, "What kind of car does Carla drive".

"Susie, for God's sake darling".

"Well, you said that you two were friends, what kind of car does she drive"?

Terry smiled and said, "She drives a Porsche Nine eleven, three point three, cherry red, now, can we please drop this nonsense"?

Susie leaned over and kissed him on the cheek.

"Yes we can" she said, in a soft sexy voice. "We're going to have a good time, you and me".

Terry smiled. "Thank you Susie".
"I'll tell you what" she said, "seeing as how you've been such a good boy, I'll let you stay all night how does that sound"?

"That sounds like sweet music to my ears babe".
"Good" she said.

"Sizzling Susie, that's what your girl friends call you isn't it"?

"Now how might you know that young Terry"?

"Carla told me".

"Did she now, just wait until I see her".

By the time Terry pulled up alongside Susie's flats, he had already finished his chips. "I've never seen anyone eating as fast as that in all my life" she said, as she fumbled in her bag for her keys, "you must have been starving Terry".

"Oh I was, I haven't eaten anything since lunch time".

"Well, I hope you're going to give me something nice for my supper".

"Oh you bet I am, I've been trying to find you for days Susie".

"Do you live round here Terry"?

"No, I live over at Oakwood, it's not too far from the city centre, it suits me fine".

"It's kind of rough out there is it not, you know drug dealers and gangs and shit, I heard about that guy yesterday, jumped from the top storey, poor bastard, did you know him Terry"?

"Yeah well, I knew of him, can't really say I knew him".
Susie lived on the second floor of the block. They climbed the concrete steps up to her apartment, number 6b. Across the hall, in number 6a, Susie's pal Rose was entertaining one of her clients, a new client in fact. Rose had never come across one like this before. Her gentleman friend insisted in reading a passage from the bible before starting proceedings. "Oh well" thought Rose, "It takes all kinds". Now he was kneeling by Rose's bed, saying a prayer. She

watched in fascination as the man knelt naked by her bed. The longer his whispered prayer went on, the harder his penis got. "Suits me" said Rose, quietly, as she started to undress

Susie and Terry entered the flat. There was a coat rail in a very small hallway inside the apartment. "Hang your jacket up there Terry, I'll get you a beer, beer or lager Terry"? Susie shouted through from the kitchen.

"Oh, lager please". Terry walked through to the living room. Susie had thrown her hand bag down on to the sofa. "Do you like living here Susie" he shouted through, as he fumbled inside her bag, "got it".

"Well, it's not exactly the Ritz now is it, but it does me, it's comfortable. As she came through with his lager and a vodka and coke for herself, she said, "I've been here for nearly five years now. The flat is owned by my boss Heather".

"Yeah, I know". "Don't tell me, Carla told you".
Terry just smiled, and sipped his lager. "Is there anything you don't know about me Terry"?

Suddenly, Terry's expression changed. "Yeah, I don't know why you choose to be a fucking whore, I don't know that, why you choose to fuck men off, you little tramp bastard that you are, instead of working like the rest of us, you little dog bastard that you are".

Susie was stunned, and frightened at the same time. "Terry? What on earth"?

Terry produced the pepper spray he'd stolen from her bag, and sprayed it straight into Susie's face. She fell off the sofa onto the floor. He grabbed a handful of her hair, and pulled her head back again, giving her another full blast in her eyes. He let go, as she choked and coughed, struggling to get her breath.

"Right boys, she's all yours" he said as he sat back on the sofa to drink his glass of lager. Susie's bedroom door opened and out came eight men, all wearing white face masks. Their expressionless masks stopped just under their noses, so that their mouths were fully exposed.

Without speaking a word, four of the men picked her up off the floor, and carried her through to her bedroom. Two others went in to Susie's kitchen and carried a dining table through to the bedroom. Susie was bent over the table with her hands straight out, palms down. One man opened a tool bag they had brought in with them, and produced an electric drill. A massive ball of cotton wool was stuffed into her mouth and then taped with masking tape. Still without a word spoken, the man fired up the drill, revving it in his hand four times. All the men held her hands down as they drilled four inch screws into the back of her hands, right through into the table. Two screws in each hand.
The pain was unbearable for the girl. Almost unable to breathe, she could feel her stomach tighten. She was going to be sick. She knew that if she was sick, she would choke to death. She fought hard to keep down the bile. The eight men left the room and closed the door behind them.

One of the men took out his wallet, and peeled off two hundred pounds in twenty pound notes and gave them to Terry. "Now, fuck off kid". Terry Gibb left Susie's flat and trundled down the steps, as if he had just delivered a parcel, whistling a tune as he made his way outside to his van. Now, where would he find his pusher at this time of the morning? Already, the chances would have been fifty- fifty if he could have remembered the whore's name. He started up his van, reversed back, and then drove off into the night. "Kinky bitch" he said.

Inside the flat, the men had returned to the bedroom. They had left Susie in there for almost twenty minutes. One man went back into the tool kit, this time producing a Stanley knife. Susie felt the cotton wool being ripped out of her mouth.

"Please, she whimpered, please I".

She felt a hard hand being clamped across her mouth, then two words only. "Be quiet!"

The man with the Stanley knife began cutting her clothes off, piece by piece, until she was finally naked. One by one, all the men took it in turns to rape Susie Monk.

"Please" again she whimpered. This time, the man who told her to be quiet, went into the tool bag and brought out a length of heavy-duty electrical cable, like a length of flex. Another gag was stuffed into her mouth. Then the man began lashing her back with the cable. After five lashes, the men began to rape her again, this time penetrating her anus. After a couple of minutes, another man took over. "Enough" the man with the flex said.

The skin on Susie's back was burst open in several places. "Salt" One of the men left the room and returned with a tub of salt and a bottle of vinegar. The flex man nodded his head. His friend poured vinegar over Susie's wounds, and then poured salt over them. He rubbed them in. "Enough!" Flex man began beating Susie again on the back, this time using all of his power.

After a few moments Susie's back was just raw flesh, there was no skin left. Small pieces of her skin hung like scrap paper. Flakes of it lay on the floor all around the table. She had lost consciousness and was only being held up by the screws in her hands. Then the screws were taken back out of her hands. That woke her up again, because the pain was worse than when they were put in. Her body slumped to the floor, but was quickly picked up again. Some of the men held her, while the others took turns at raping her again. While all this had been going on, a camcorder had been recording all the events of their sick show.

All the men taking turns aiming the camera at the unfortunate girl. They threw Susie's body onto the sofa. Flex man began lashing her body again, this time on the front. Lash after lash he swung the cable, each stroke making a new red line on the defenceless girl's body. He pointed to the man who was holding the camera. The man pointed the camera to his face. At the same time, he pressed some digits on his mobile phone. A few seconds, and then, "Paganni, I should get here as soon as you can, if I were you, to Susie's place, you may, you may not, be able to save her life. She isn't pretty any more, but she is alive, just, that's more than I can say for my friend Steven Todd.

Now I've filmed all this for you to watch, and to warn you, you little Italian cunt, that you are not getting away with this anymore". He pointed to the unconscious girl on the sofa. "We'll spare her, maybe, but we will not spare you. You are next little madam, enjoy the film". The camera went on to Susie again.. Flex man lifted up her leg, and fired a shot from his gun straight through her ankle. He then repeated the same act on the other leg. "Right, let's go".

As the unconscious girl lay bleeding from her wounds, flex man pulled out a ten pound note from his pocket and stuffed it up Susie's vagina. "Thank you Susan", he said as he smiled at the camera. Suddenly, all the men were gone from Susie's house. Once or twice the girl came round to something resembling consciousness. Through the blur that was her vision, she could make out her cat Tigger, warming himself by the gas fire. She thought she could hear him purring, but the sound was getting fainter and fainter, until she couldn't hear anything at all.

By the time Carla Paganni got to Susie's flat, the girl lay dead, or rather, sat dead. Carla had to run through to the bathroom where she was violently sick. She herself, had inflicted some nasty wounds to people in her time, but this, this was something she had never seen before. The extent of Susie's wounds would be enough to make anyone sick. Susie was unrecognisable, just a bloody pulp of raw flesh. Her breasts had been lashed so severely, that the nipple of her left one, hung only by a piece of skin. Her face had been unbelievably whipped into mush. Carla had to fight to stay in control. She could feel herself beginning to shake, all over her body. She had to try and think straight. She would have to inform John Hillman about this, it didn't matter that it was three o'clock in the morning, she would have to tell him everything. "I'll tell him before I call the police".

She drove through the city centre, and then the two miles or so out to Morningside. She tapped his number on her phone, as she sat outside his house in the car park. There were no lights on in his house anywhere. Finally he answered the phone.

"Hello, who is this"? He said, in an angry voice.

"It's Carla Mister Hillman, come to your front door, its important".

"Carla? What's wrong"?

"Come to your front door Mister Hillman".

"Coming, I'll be there in a minute!"

"Who is it dear" said Anne Hillman.

"It's nobody, I mean, it's Carla, she needs to talk to me about something, go back to sleep dear".
Hillman was at the door in less than two minutes, standing with his blue tartan dressing gown and pyjamas to match. "What's wrong Carla" he whispered. "Can't this wait until the morning"?
"No it can't wait. This can't wait, I. I have to tell you now, she. They've beaten her to death. They've beat, she's dead. Susie's dead, they, I can't wait, I'll phone".
Hillman could plainly see the stress the girl was under. He took her by the arm into the house. Twenty minutes later, she had completed the story, from the phone call she got, to the point where she sat now in his study.
"Did this man mention my name Carla, I mean, does he know you work for me"?
"No, I don't think so; he didn't mention your name".

"Ok Carla, go back over there and phone for the police from Susie's house. Don't touch her Carla you didn't touch her did you"?
"No, I couldn't if I tried. Mister Hillman, they've lashed her to death sir, they've, they've skinned her alive. She's been shot in both ankles, even if she had survived, she was never going to walk again, they say I'm next. They've left a camera recording on the table, aimed at poor Susie. I turned it off when I got there".
"Right, now you have to be strong Carla, don't worry, they won't be back at that place tonight, you get that camera and you bring it here tomorrow. Now, I'll call Heather. Once you've called the police, you go to Heather's house ok"?
"Yes".

"Good girl, here have a brandy before you go. He poured Carla and himself a large brandy. "We'll get to the bottom of this Carla, don't worry, we will find out who has done this, and when we do, we will deal with it our way".
As Carla pulled in to the street where Susie lived, she groaned with misery. "Oh no" she said as she pulled up outside her friend's flat. The police were already here. As she climbed wearily up the concrete steps she thought to herself, "Now I have to pretend that I'm arriving for the first time. When she got to the second level, there were two policemen standing outside the door, but not Susie's door.

They were standing outside Rose's door, Susie's friend. "Do you live here madam" one of the policemen asked her.

"No, I'm here to visit a friend in this flat officer". She pointed to Susie's door.

"I'm afraid there's no-one in there madam, we've knocked three or four times, there's no reply".

"It's ok officer, I have a key, we're friends you see and I-".

"I see, well, just wait there a minute Miss, there's been, something's happened. I'm afraid the lady who lives in this flat is dead Miss, do you know her, I mean, did you know her"?

Carla looked at the two policemen in total disbelief. "Yes. I. we're friends, its Rosie, we are friends, she eh. Carla's mind was racing. This was now worse than she could ever have imagined, and it was getting worse by the minute. "They've done Rose as well" she thought to herself. Oh shit, no, please God. She thought that they would have said something about that though, they hadn't even mentioned Rose.

Inside Rose's flat D.I. John Crosby stood with his legs astride and his hands on his hips, staring at the wall in front of him. Beside him stood D.I. Deborah Knowles. Although only thirty six, she had seen some horrendous sights in her ten years at this post, but the sight before her and her colleague rated right up there with the worst of them. "What do you make of this Deborah? I've never seen one killed like this before. A religious freak it would seem". Written on the wall, in the victim's blood there was a verse from the book of psalms; YEAH THOUGH I WALK THROUGH THE VALLEY OF THE SHADOW OF DEATH, I WILL FEAR NO EVIL, FOR THOU ART WITH ME, THY ROD AND THY STAFF, THEY COMFORT ME; SURELY GOODNESS AND MERCY SHALL FOLLOW ME ALL THE DAYS OF MY LIFE, AND I SHALL DWELL IN THE HOUSE OF THE LORD FOREVER.

The woman's body had been laid across a table directly in front of the scripture. Her throat had been cut, and her wrists, and there was a gaping hole in her stomach. A chair had been placed in front of the young woman, so that whoever had done this had sat and watched the young lady die. They had stuck drawing pins in her chest to form the shape of a cross, from just under her throat, to the base of her belly. The drawing pins had been pressed in three wide, up and down, so that, from a distance it looked like she had a giant gold cross pinned to her body. "Weird" said Crosby.

"Aren't they all" said Knowles.
"Yes mam, they certainly are".
The girl's legs were tight together, with her arms straight by her side.
"Ah well, there's nothing we can do until forensics get here" said Knowles.
"They're never in any hurry are they" said Crosby.

"No, and who can blame them John".

The living room door opened and one of the police officers came in. "Miss Knowles, there's a young lady here, says she's a friend of the dead girl, and a friend of the girl next door. She says she has a key for that flat".

"Ok, let her go in, don't let her come in here whatever you do. Tell her to stay in there and we will come and talk with her directly".

Carla knew she had to be quick. She stepped inside the flat and put the camera into her hand bag. Carla knew as well, that the two police officers outside the door would not have been trained for the sight that was about to be bestowed upon them. She had to act like she would have done, if she were seeing the sight for the first time, although, there wasn't much acting involved. Clutching her bag, Carla came out of the flat, walking slowly, at about six inches to a step. With her left hand, she pointed to the door she had just come out of.

The two young policemen looked at Carla, and the open door. "Go back inside Miss, there'll be someone out to speak with you shortly".

Carla kept coming, six inches at a time.

"Go back in Miss, you can't-".

"She's dead". Still pointing back at the door, "Susie's dead".
"Who's dead? Joe, keep her here until I have a look. It's probably delayed shock, about her friend in there".

PC Johnstone went in to Susie's flat. His friend and work colleague Joe Harvey waited outside in the hallway with Carla Paganni. They did not wait for long. Johnstone came rushing out, vomit spewing from his mouth, like it was being shot out of a cannon.

"What the fuck? Said Harvey, "what's going on man, what is it"?

"Susie's dead". Said Carla, out loud. "Susie and Rose are dead." She began sobbing bitterly. Carla Paganni, at this point, was not acting.

When John Crosby and Deborah Knowles walked into Susie's living room, they could not believe their eyes. "For fuck sakes" Said Crosby,

"Oh my Christ, what the fuck have they done to her". Deborah Knowles looked at Crosby in disbelief.

"Oh my God Deborah" he said, they've even shot right through her hands, her hands and feet, poor woman". He looked again. "Is it a woman"? For the first time in his career, Crosby looked away with his face in his hands.

Carla sat on her knees out in the hallway, also with her face in her hands, sobbing uncontrollably. Now she could let out her true emotions. Deborah Knowles shouted out to the two
policemen, "Hey, one of you two, Hey, would one of you two please get this girl out of here, take her outside for God's sake".

Crosby could no longer keep the contents of his stomach in. He tried his best to find the toilet in time, but he did not make it. He whooshed out a flood of vomit so severe, that it splattered up the wall opposite from where he stood. Deborah Knowles felt her guts tighten up but managed to keep control of herself, at least until two minutes later. She had been walking around the sofa looking for weapons or anything that might point the way to find the animals or animal who had committed this horrendous crime, when she came upon a pint glass tumbler. Putting on a pair of polythene gloves, she held it up to her nose and sniffed.

It took about two seconds for her brain to register what had been in the glass. Maybe if that had been all she'd found in this house, her stomach would have held out, maybe, but when confronted with this poor retch on the sofa, and the realization of what acts had befallen this girl, on top of all the other tortuous events she'd had to suffer, it was just too much. Every human being has a limit to what they can endure visually. Mister Crosby and Miss Knowles had reached theirs within three minutes of each other.

HARRINGTON POLICE STATION. SHEFFIELD.
5. AM.

"Why can't you let me go, I've told you everything I know", Carla Paganni pleaded.

"You can go soon Miss Paganni, I promise you, it's just that you are the only one, it seems who knew these girls well. Can you think of anyone they have fallen out with recently that would make them do this? Did they say anything about any nasty tricks lately, any awkward ones perhaps, ones who wouldn't pay up, anything"?

"I've already told you, no, now why can't I go home"? She began sobbing again. At that point, the interview room door burst open, and in walked John Hillman senior, and a Mister Robert Mclelland Q.C. Carla sprung up from her chair and threw her arms around her friend, knocking over the chair she'd been sitting on, as she did so. "They won't let me go Mister Hillman" she sobbed, "I've told them all I know, and they still won't let me leave".

"There now, my dear" whispered Hillman, "It's going to be alright, don't you worry now, you're coming home with me in a minute". Hillman looked at John Crosby, Deborah Knowles, and Sergeant Richard Price. "How long have you had her in here"?

"Mister Hillman, with all due respect sir" said John Crosby, "we-". "How long"?

"About two hours John" said Deborah Knowles.

"Two hours? After what she's been through tonight, what kind of people are you in here, my God, can't you see she's still suffering from shock"?

Robert Mclelland wrote something down in a small note book he had taken from his pocket.

John Crosby sighed, exasperated. "She can go now John".

“You bet your fucking life she can go now, and don’t you ever call me by my Christian name again, you idiot that you are, do you hear me, because if you do, you won’t have a job by the following morning”.

“John, he’s only, we’re only trying to piece some clues together to find out who committed these murders”.

“Murders”? Said Hillman, “Murder you mean”?

“No sir, murders, there were two girls killed in those flats last night”.

“Jesus Christ” whispered Hillman, still embracing Carla.

“What? And Carla discovered them both”?

“No sir” said Crosby, “We got an anonymous phone call from a man, saying there was one less hooker to worry about on the streets of Britain, he said she is to be found in number 6.a. Fedgley Green. We went down and discovered a young woman’s body. Whilst we were there, your Carla appeared and went in to the neighbouring flat, only to discover the second victim. We were asking her these questions, Mister Hillman in order to find out who these girl’s enemies are, or if she knew of any. Carla says she knows both girls, they are all friends. Now I know this is not very pleasant Mister Hillman, but I’m afraid it is necessary, now, take her home by all means, but we will have to speak with her again, whether you threaten me with my job or not. I am trying to do my job Mister Hillman, so I warn you sir, don’t you ever interfere with police work again, or call me anything other than D.I. Crosby, or I’ll knock your nose right through your face, do you understand me? John? Now, take the young lady home, or wherever you’re taking her, and we’ll be in touch with you, when we need to talk to her again, and that will be tomorrow”. Crosby walked over to the Q.C. and snatched the note book from his hands. He tore out the only page which had writing on, and handed it back to him. “And you can fuck off too” said Crosby, “bursting in here unannounced”.

CROMWELL ROAD.

Doctor John Hillman lay on his bed, naked, on his back, with his hands behind his head. A glass of beer sat on his bedside table, half finished. He went over and over the course of events of the previous evening, and how that evening had ended, in the early hours of this morning. "Well Lord, at least she got a good seeing to before meeting her maker, I don't think I ever hammered my own wife as hard as that, it was most enjoyable, thank you Lord. Are there any more you wish me to deal with, because if there is, just you let me know? I hope you didn't mind me draining her like that, I love to see the blood flow Lord". He took a sip of beer. "The shock on that whore's face, when I made the first cut on her wrist, she was so far gone, enjoying me Lord, that I don't even think she noticed at first. It wasn't until she saw the blood spurting up about a foot high from her arm that she realized what I had done, and, of course the second wrist was done while she was still in shock, I mean that was two main arteries severed, there's no coming back from that Lord, is there? You remember how hard my cock was Lord? Of course you do, you were there, you were guiding my hands. My favourite was her face, when I rammed the broken bottle right into her soft belly, how she sat up bolt upright as I twisted it round and round, deep into her stomach. I swear Lord, I could hear her fleshy intestines bursting and twisting, ripping and giving way to the force of the rugged glass, but you know me Lord, it can't be about my fun all the time, I had to speed up the process a little. As I slashed her throat Lord, I could have sworn I heard her say, "Why". It might just be me Lord, but I swear I heard her say that, she certainly tried to say something before the red line began to flow".

Doctor Hillman sat up slowly on his bed, lifted the glass, and drank the remainder of his beer," Ah, lovely". He then picked up a cigarette packet from his dresser, and took one out. He lit it up inhaling deeply, then exhaling the smoke up towards the ceiling. "Now then Lord, the next time you want me to rid you of another sinful woman like Rose, you just let me know, and I'll go back to my father's house, and sneak out that book he keeps hidden from my mother with all those girl's names on it, and how much they charge for those very vile things they do with all of their disgusting habits, just speak to me a name Lord, the next time I'm reading it. They have to be taught a lesson, beguiling people the way they do for money...you just point them out Lord".

MORNINGSIDE.

Anne Hillman was cooking her husband's breakfast when he entered the kitchen. He walked over to his wife and put a hand on each of her shoulders, standing behind her, and kissed her on the cheek. "Good morning darling" he said.

"Good morning sweet" she replied, "How is she"?

"Oh, she's still sleeping Anne, poor thing, what a bloody shock to her system though, coming across that poor girl's body like that".

"John". Anne sighed, turning over pieces of bacon on the grill pan, "We are living in a very sick world, my love, I thank goodness we have the grace and mercy of our living God. Oh, how he's blessed us John, and protects us from all that goes on around us. We are so lucky to have the things in life that we have, so lucky".

"Yes we are my love, but God helps those who help themselves".

Anne Hillman smiled as she put bacon and fried eggs onto a plate for the one and only man in her life. Hillman sat down at the breakfast bar. "Have the police phoned yet Anne"?

"No, I expect they'll be giving her time to get over her ordeal". Hillman snorted with bacon in his mouth, "I wouldn't count on it dear, Carla is the only one they have to talk to who knew those girls, they won't be giving her too much time, you can rest assured on that".

"John, I've been meaning to say, and I know it's none of my business, but how does Carla know these girls"? She began to almost whisper, as if God would be offended if He heard her even talking about this. "I mean, Carla works at the hair salon, and she runs a few errands for you, but, girls like that? Carla"?

"Anne, before you get yourself all worked up, just forget about it. In all my years of judging, I have seen some pitiful sights my dear, let me tell you, and contrary to what most people think of prostitutes, or working girls, as I would prefer to call them, they are human beings with feelings, just like you and I, so don't look down on them like they were mud, because they are more honest than some of the people running this country, and anyway, working girls have their hair done too Anne, that's most likely how our Carla met those girls. I'm going outside for a cigarette Anne, if Carla comes down make her something to eat".

"And when did you start smoking again Mister John Hillman"?
"Anne, just, just don't ok? Not today Anne. He went outside with his mug of tea and sat on the summer seat he had erected, facing the city.

"Look at him" thought Anne Hillman to herself, "a more caring man, you just could not meet". She smiled. "He even finds good things to say about prostitutes, the very scourge of our towns and cities, he even finds good things to say about them,
what a man you are John Hillman, you are a diamond in the dust, that's what you are".
As it turned out, Hillman was right. Carla had come down the stairs half an hour after her host. She had been struggling to force down the bacon rolls Anne had insisted she ate before she did anything else, when the phone rang. The police wished to speak with her again this afternoon. She was now outside on the summer seat with John Hillman. "Carla, when we get back from the police station today, we're going to have to watch that film you know, as unpleasant as that may be. We have to find out who these sick people are".

"You're coming with me"?

"Of course I'm coming with you, and so is Mister Mclelland. This time Carla, you'll find that it's a lot easier, now that you've had time to adjust to the situation. They won't be keeping you there for long today, don't you worry about that my dear. Now I'll get that camera off you and put it in my study, we'll watch it when we get back. I've told Heather that you'll be staying here for a few days, until things calm down a bit".

"They said, Mister Hillman, they said I was next, and they meant it sir, they are going to get me for sure, it's not a question of if, only when, Mister Hillman".

"Now don't you be worrying about that, my dear, we'll watch the film and then we may know just who it is we're dealing with, and we'll get to the bottom of all this, make no mistake about that my dear, now come on, get yourself ready and let's get this over and done with Carla".

"I can't for the life of me understand though sir, why they would go to all those lengths to show everything on the camera
concerning Susie, and yet not mention one word about Rose, that's got me baffled , Mister Hillman".

"I know Carla, that one's puzzling me as well."

"I warn you Mister Hillman, when we watch what's on this film, be prepared for the most horrendous violence you have ever seen, I saw the condition of her body when they were finished with her, and I must admit, I'm not looking forward to seeing how they put her in that state sir".

Hillman smiled at Carla, "My dear child, I have seen things that you couldn't dream in your worst nightmares, believe me".

"Well, all I can say Mister Hillman is, whatever you have seen, this will undoubtedly be up there with the worst of them, make no mistake about that".

Angela and Sharon were out in the garden at the back of Tracy's house, playing a ball game with Angela and Amy. Tracy was putting the last of the girl's clean clothes into their bags. It was 1.40.pm. She was just about to shout outside to see if Angela and Sharon wanted a coffee, when the front doorbell rang. She put down the bag and went to answer the door. Tracy nearly dropped with fright. Doctor John Hillman stood on her front step. "Hi, I know I'm early Tracy, but I'll have to pick up the girls now, I'm going away with them and my mother for the weekend, I hope it's not too inconvenient, is it"?

"Em, no, John, em, they're out playing in the back garden with, em, with Sharon and her friend".

"That's alright Tracy, I'll wait for them, I want a word with Sharon and you anyway, if you don't mind".

"Now John, look" said Tracy, "we made an agreement".

"Tracy it's alright, it's not bad, it's nothing bad, I just need to speak with you two alone for a couple of minutes, do you think Sharon's friend could keep the girls outside while we talk"?

John Hillman stood before his estranged wife, dressed in a pale blue trendy t-shirt, dark blue levies, and a pair of trainers. Tracy had never seen him in trainers in all of their time together, or jeans for that matter.

"Yeah, I'll just go and tell Sharon, do you want a coffee John"?

"Please Tracy, thank you".

A few moments later, Sharon walked in to the living room, wearing a peach coloured top, with white shorts and sneakers, not really knowing where to put herself. Hillman stood up when she entered the room. A minute later, all three of them sat, each with a cup of coffee.

"This won't take long ladies" said Hillman. "The first thing I must do Tracy, is apologise for the kind of life I have given you for the past ten years or so".

"John please"

"Tracy, please, let me finish, this is not a... I know there is no chance of us getting back together, I'm just simply saying sorry for the way I have been with you. You are a very beautiful woman, and I was very lucky indeed to have you in my life, and to have two beautiful little girls to you. I blew it Tracy it was nobody's fault but mine. Sharon, you are also a beautiful woman, and I most humbly apologise to you for the way I spoke to you that day in here, I had no right whatsoever to call you those names. Tracy was right Sharon, I did used to look and lust after you, but look at you, look at the both of you, what man in his right mind wouldn't lust after you, I don't apologise for that, but I do for being such an idiot. I only hope", he looked at Tracy, "that you can find it in your hearts to forgive me, I can understand if you can't".
Tracy and Sharon sat speechless for a few seconds. "I hope you can forgive me John" said Tracy, "for being such an animal that day, but I felt trapped, and I felt downtrodden".

"You were Tracy, that's how I made you live, that's what I'm sorry about, I was lucky you didn't bloody shoot me. Sharon? Can you forgive me, for my slanderous outburst"?

"Of course John, there's nothing to forgive really, you were in the middle of a row with your wife, and I was out of order making jokes about Misses Semple".

"Thank you, thank you both for being so understanding, I was a fucking clown".

Tracy spun round and looked at John. The first swear word she had ever heard him utter, apart from *that* day. Now, on top of the swearing, he was getting cigarettes out of his pocket. "Do you mind if I em"?

"No" said Tracy, "you eh, you carry on".

“I don’t go to church as often now”. He held up the cigarette packet, “as you’ll have gathered, it was taking over my life, so it was, and I ended up losing you over it. Well, the next girl I get, I won’t be losing over going to church too much, I promised myself that. I feel more confident with myself these days, how about you Tracy”?

“Yes, I’m happy John, I only hope you’re happy”.
“I’m just fine Tracy, I just, oh, look at the time, I’ll have to get the girls”. Hillman stood up. “Well, I’ll see you again Sharon and thank you again sweetheart for forgiving this stupid man”. He took her hand and kissed it. Then he walked over to Tracy “May I”? He leaned over and kissed Tracy on the cheek. “I’ll see you, take care”. With that, he picked up the girl’s holdalls and walked out the back door. Tracy followed him outside.

“This is Angela John, Angela this is John”.

“I’m very pleased to meet you Angela, I’m sorry I can’t stay, I have to be off now, we’re all going away for the weekend with nana, aren’t we girls”?

“Yes” said Amy, “we’re going off to see the Loch Ness Scotland monster, aren’t we daddy”.

“Yes we are angel, so come on, let’s be moving, it’s been nice meeting you Angela, perhaps I’ll see you again sometime”.

As Tracy walked to the car with John Hillman, he turned and said, “I’ll let them come a bit more often Tracy, and I meant what I said in there, I do regret blowing my time with you. I wish you luck Tracy, with whoever you decide to spend your life with, just don’t be getting tied up with any holy Willie, come on girls, give mummy a kiss, come on, big kisses”.

As Hillman got into the car, Tracy said, “John?”
“Yeah?”
“Thank you”.
“For what”?
“Just for what you’ve done today, for saying those things. That took guts”.

"Thank you Tracy, for waking me up to reality, and oh, Tracy"? He stuck his head out of the car window. Tracy bent down to hear him whisper. "Tell Sharon I still lust after those legs". Tracy laughed, as she waved to her children and her ex-husband. For the first time in ten years or so, John Hillman had made her laugh. She went back inside and broke down on the sofa, where she sobbed for a full twenty minutes.

In the car, John Hillman sang a song along with his children. "Right, all together now you guys, Onward Christian soldiers, marching as to war, WITH THE CROSS OF JESUS GOING ON BEFORE!". In his mind, he spoke to his God; "There now Lord, do you see what I can do with your help? Right into the fucking whore's den I was, right in, sitting talking and lusting after the whores, what a beautiful world it is Lord, what a beautiful fucking body that Sharon has, you know who I mean? Whore Sharon Lord? The one outside was the best though, and I know, I know, I'll have to wait until you tell me, I'll wait, and then I'll make them pay for being such teasing whores, they will repent my Lord, one way or another, they'll repent. Fucking beating *me* with a skipping rope...whore"!!

John Hillman waved goodbye to his wife and son, and his grandchildren on the steps of his house. He watched as the car disappeared round the bend of his drive, then went back inside to pour himself a drink. Carla was in the shower. "Thank goodness for that" he mumbled, as he lifted his scotch from the drinks cabinet. "Maybe get some peace round here and sort out this bloody mess". He lifted up the day's newspaper. The story about Susie Monk was on page four, a whole page of it. There were no photographs. At least they had the decency to keep those venomous bastards out of the flats. If the public were to see the mess of those poor girls, it would undoubtedly cause a national panic. Carla Paganni came down the stairs wearing a light grey pair of jogging bottoms and a lemon top. She was brushing her wet hair, and humming a tune. "You sound a lot better" said Hillman.

"I am Mister Hillman, I've got my head round everything that's been going on, and I've accepted it. Now I have to find out who's behind all this. I have to warn you one more time Mister Hillman, that what we are about to see will not be pretty, I saw the end result of what they'd done to Susie, I have no idea what they did to put her into that state, but I saw the end result".

"Yes I know Carla, you've told me, now; I want you to look out for any familiar faces you might see here. Even if you just know one face Carla, just one, that's all we'll need. I promise you we'll get all the names we need if we can just get one, one single name Carla. Hell Carla, I don't particularly want to see what they did to that poor girl, I just want to see who these animals are".

"Mister Hillman I-".

"Call me John when she's not around Carla, you know that".

"John, I know I'm ruthless when I dish out punishment, but I never inflict pain on to anyone who doesn't deserve it, but these, these, animals have picked on a young twenty year old girl, and Rose, Rose was only twenty six, and they've taken their lives away from them, it's not fair sir, I mean, John, they were in the prime of their lives".

"I'm going to get the camera Carla, you fix yourself a drink my dear, the sooner we get this over and done with the better".

As they sat down to watch the gruesome film, Carla could feel her stomach start to tighten. Hillman put a hand around her shoulder. "Be brave now child, it's alright, we'll be alright. Whatever threats they make to you here on this film, remember, I won't let anything happen to you, I promise my dear". After they had rewound the tape, Hillman pressed play.

Straight away they were both disheartened. All the men wore masks, every one of them. "Bastards!" roared Hillman. They watched as Susie Monk was brought before the camera. She was snorting and coughing, struggling to breathe. "Bastards have drugged her".

"No sir" said Carla, "If they only had, that's pepper spray, all the girls carry one, in case of a nasty punter, it demobilises them for a few minutes" said Carla, as they both watched Susie being dragged into the bedroom. At first she was just being held there, then two of the men came in carrying a kitchen table. Susie was made to stay on her feet, but was bent, thrown over the table. Her hands were placed in front of her. Then, whoever held the camera pointed it to a tool bag on the floor.

"Oh sweet Christ no" said Hillman, as he watched the drill being brought out of the bag. By the time the camera had been put back on to Susie, her mouth had been gagged and taped. " Oh Lord no, oh shit". Hillman forced himself to watch, as they proceeded to drill Susie's hands onto the table. The camera went back on to the tool bag. Another man's hand was filmed as he pulled out a Stanley knife. The camera went shaky for a few moments, and then steadied, as Susie's clothes were cut piece by piece from her slender body. Finally she was naked. "Carla, pour us another drink please, big ones" said Hillman, almost crying, "two big ones my dear".

Carla, standing by the cabinet, forced herself to watch, in between pouring the drinks. The camera zoomed in on Susie's backside, and stayed there for a short while, then it was back in the living room. Whoever had held the camera last, had forgotten to switch it off. It was still filming and aiming directly at Michael Gibb, quite clearly being handed a bundle of notes by one of the masked men. Seconds later, he was off the screen again. Carla, filled with rage, and revenge now, quite calmly walked over to the sofa and gave Hillman his drink. " Rewind it John" she said. Hillman had missed it, it was so fast. "Rewind it, I'll tell you when to stop, there! Pause it there John".
"Oh dear Carla".
"Ah ha" said Carla.
"Please tell me you know him my dear, please".

"I'll tell you better than that John, not only do I know him, I also know where he lives. We have no need to watch any more of this sick show, God bless Susie. Would you like to get naked with me John, and finish our drinks in the hot tub"?

"I thought you'd never ask my dear, I'll fetch a bottle up each, it's going to be a long night I think".

"Yes it is" said Carla.

"And it's going to be the last normal one for a certain Mister Gibb. From this piece of junky shit, I swear I'll get all the names we need".

"And remember dear" said Hillman, "you promised me you were going to be more ruthless".

"After what they have done to my friends John, I'll never be anything else, ever again".

"That's the spirit my dear, that's what I like to hear, that's the Carla I know".

"No, the Carla you know frolics playfully with you, when Misses Hillman's away".

SHEFFIELD MORTUARY.

Detective John Crosby stood beside D.C.I. Deborah Knowles, while Ashley Barnes, the police pathologist made her way around what was left of Susie Monk's body. She was dictating to another young lady whilst she made her examination of the dead girl. All four of them wore face masks. When Ashley had finished, she summoned Crosby and Knowles over to her. "I'm finished here just now, I'll wash up and we can talk in my office, I'll be able to tell you what you need to know from my notes. Would one of you put the kettle on when you're up there, I'm dying on a cup of tea".

Knowles and Crosby didn't know if the last remark was a joke or not, neither one said anything. They walked up a steep narrow staircase of eight steps, and opened the only door at the top. The pale green door had a homemade sign stuck crudely onto it, it read; *Ashley Barnes Criminal pathologist.*

Deborah opened the door and was quite surprised to see a well-furnished little office, which had all mod cons, and where you could quite easily wile away the hours if you were not too busy. She picked up the kettle and handed it to John Crosby. "Would you like to do the honours John". Crosby was about to leave the room and go back down stairs to fill the kettle. Knowles said, "John, behind you".

Behind John there was a door, and a sign saying; wash room and toilet. Crosby had just filled the kettle and walked back into the room when a young blonde haired girl stepped into the office.
She wore a tight red sweater with a low cut plunge line, a black mini skirt with high heeled ankle boots, with fancy chains round the sides. The girl looked like she was heading to the disco.

"Yes, can we help you"? Said Crosby.

"Oh you found the kettle then" said the young lady. Crosby's face went red, as he realized who the young lady was. Knowles smiled at her colleague, "that's two in a minute John, good start to the day".

“What” said Ashley, “Did you think Mister Crosby, that all pathologists were frumpy old men and women with old fashioned spectacles that cover half of their faces? Oh I know I dress a bit racy” she continued, “but that’s just me, if you’ve got it, flaunt it, that’s what I say”.

“Indeed” said Knowles, smiling, “I’m quite sure you won’t hear any objections from Mister Crosby here”.

“Well, allow me to introduce myself, I am Ashley Barnes, criminal pathologist”.

“How do you do” said Knowles, “I am D.C,I. Deborah Knowles, and this is detective John Crosby, and as you know, we are here to find out what we can about the murders of those two poor girls lying down stairs”.

They all shook hands. “How long have you been in this job Miss Barnes” said Knowles.
“Five years, well, five years fully qualified, I spent three years down at Thames Valley, training, and studying”.
“You don’t look old enough to have spent eight years in this game” said Crosby.

Ashley crossed her long legs, “Oh I’m old enough Mister Crosby, believe me”. She then stood up and walked over to the kettle, which was now boiling, “tea ok for everybody?”

“Tea’s fine” said Knowles, smiling again, this time at the girl’s attitude and her fine figure, and she could see that her colleague was already besotted with the girl.

Crosby wiped sweat from his brow. “Hell, it’s hot in here” he said.

“It’s not really, it’s just that it’s so cool down there, that when you come in here to a normal temperature, and then a beautiful half naked woman like me comes in, it does tend to make the hetro men get a bit sticky under the collar. Deborah Knowles burst out laughing along with Ashley

Five minutes later, the conversation was anything but light hearted. Ashley Barnes was now referring to her notes. "We've found traces of copper in the young lady named Susan Monk"

"Copper"? Said Knowles.

"Copper" repeated Ashley, "The poor girl has been literally flayed alive".

"But how the hell, Copper"?
"Quite simple, she wasn't beaten with a whip, she was beaten with an electrical cable, which had been skinned down, probably to the last few inches. Each blow would have inflicted unbelievable pain to our young friend, hence the gag. She has been severely buggered, raped, what you thought were gun wounds, were in fact, drill holes. They drilled right through the poor girl's hands. According to her wounds, they've used quite considerable sized bits as well, probably four inch screws or there about. They screwed her hands to the table; the poor wretch wasn't going anywhere. Even if she passed out with the pain, and I assure you, she did, she would not fall to the floor, the screws were keeping her upright. Judging by the samples of the D.N.A. there were six men involved in this particular attack, maybe more, we're still looking".

"Holy Christ" said Crosby, "This has to be revenge, surely, revenge for something".

"That's not my job Mister Crosby, that's yours. All I'm telling you, is what has been inflicted upon this girl, and for their finally, they ejaculated into"-.

"Yes, I know that" said Knowles.

"Of course, they made her swallow it though I think the poor girl would be almost dead by this point, that, I cannot tell, at the moment anyway".

Ashley Barnes continued, "Now then, the other girl. She looked at her notes again, and then crossed her luscious legs again. "Miss Rose Cranston, she died rather quickly as compared to her friend.

Rose would have drifted off into unconsciousness very quickly, there would have been very little struggle. The difference between the two girls is this. Ashley sipped her tea and lit up a cigarette. Rose only had sex with one man, she was not raped. Rose's… juices were flowing, if you catch my drift, she said to Deborah, the man wore a condom. Rose knew who was making love to her, or at least, she was comfortable with who was making love to her, she was enjoying it, was, I hasten to add" said Ashley.

While she was enjoying it, her gentleman friend has then taken a very sharp instrument and slashed her wrists, both of them. He has then proceeded to ram her belly with some sort of glass object, possibly a bottle. I'm guessing she would be dead in less than fifteen minutes with the severe blood loss. Oh, the drawing pins were added after her death, to form some sort of decorative religious symbol of some sort, goodness knows. Now, as I say to you both, it is not my job, and I certainly wouldn't dream of trying to tell you yours, but it seems to me, that the man who killed Rose is not one of the men from the neighbouring flat, but, that's not for me to say, he may have been along with them and decided to do Rose on his own". Ashley lifted her hands in the air, "Who knows".

"Mmm" said Knowles, "well, thank you for all of your help Ashley, you've been most helpful".

"Any time" she said. "I'm having another cup of tea, would you like another"?

"Yes please" Said John.
"No thank you". Said Knowles, "we'd better be getting back, hadn't we John"?
"Yes mam, we'd better".
Deborah smiled again at Ashley. As Knowles and Crosby reached the bottom of the stairs, Crosby said, "Oh, I've left the car keys in that office" Deborah smiled to herself, as she walked on, "I know you did John". Crosby tapped on the door.

"Come in".

"I'm sorry Miss Barnes, I've left the keys on the table".

"Oh" she said, putting a tea bag in her cup. "Would Friday be alright John"? She smiled.

"Friday"?

"Yes Friday, for to go out for a drink with you, that's why you left your keys wasn't it"?

"I em, I thought, maybe".

"Is Friday night alright John"? She turned and looked him in the eyes.
"Thank you, I mean yes, Friday's fine, yes please".
"I'm the one who is supposed to say yes please John, here's my address. She handed him a card. Pick me up at eight, and good luck".
"Good luck"? said a fumbling John Crosby.
"With the murders, silly".
"Oh yes, thank you, and thank you".
"See you Friday John" said Ashley, smiling.

Crosby was grinning from ear to ear when he got back to the car. Deborah took one look at him. "I take it she said yes then John".

"What are you on about Deborah"?

"Leaving your keys" she said, "I take it she said yes"?

"Deborah, I don't know where you get this stupid, yes, she said yes, fuck, was it that obvious"?

"Transparently so John I'm afraid".

"Oh well, it doesn't matter, she said yes". Deborah smiled and waved up at Ashley's window. Ashley waved back.

OAKWOOD. ESTATE.

Carla Paganni's Porsche sat in almost the same spot where the Ford Orion had sat, which had taken the full weight of Steven Dodd's body. Michael Gibb lived in the same block of flats as Dodd, but at the far end of the building. She had been here now for nearly an hour, waiting for him to make an appearance. She knew he was in because his van was parked across the road. It had been five days now since the murders of her friends. One of Carla's many qualities was patience. She would wait all day if she had to, because this was one fish that wasn't getting away. He lived near the top of the tower block, so there was not much chance of him spotting her car from up there. As Carla looked in her rear view mirror, a young girl came out at the entrance of the flats. She wore a short denim skirt with trainers. She wore a white top, which was no longer white. It looked like it had been thrown in the washing machine with a load of colours. "Now then, who are you waiting for missy"?

She looked like a junky. "Come on Michael, let it be you". A few moments later, Michael Gibb appeared. "Yes" said Carla, "Now let's go for a ride Michael".

Half an hour later, Michael Gibb sat with Rachel, his girlfriend, and Carla, in John Hillman's house. "He said he won't be long" said Carla. "You can relax Michael, he knows you had nothing to do with those murders, he just wants to ask you some questions about Oakwood, there's a couple of suspicious characters over there, he wants to know if you know them, that's all".

"And why am I here," said Rachel.

Carla smiled at the girl. "You are here, my sweet, because it's not very nice being left outside in the car while your boyfriend is in here drinking beer, that's why. You'll both be on your way in less than an hour, unless of course you have something to hide, do you Michael"?
"Of course not".
"Well then" said Carla, "you have nothing to worry about".

"If my van gets stolen Carla".
"Your van will be fine Michael, relax".

"Hello young lady" said Hillman, coming into the lounge, carrying a camcorder, and what might your name be"?

"Rachel"

"Rachel? That name goes all the way back to biblical times, did you know that? Way back to the Old Testament, my dear, what a lovely name it is too. What would you like to drink my dear, would you like, now let me guess, wicked"?

"Smirnoff Ice, if you have it".

"Smirnoff Ice for the young Rachel, Carla, and you sir, what would your pleasure be, don't tell me, lager"?

"Yes please".
"Yes please" repeated Hillman "and what's your name sir"?

"Michael".

"Lager for Michael Carla, and Smirnoff Ice for Rachel. I knew he would drink lager Rachel. I knew that because I watch films my dear".

Rachel looked at Michael and said, "He's weird".

Hillman was connecting the video camera to the T.V.

"We're going to watch a film today Rachel, when Carla brings the drinks back. Do you like horror films my dear"?

"They're alright" replied the teenager.

"They're alright, but not your favourites though, no, I didn't think you looked the type to go for that kind of thing. What about you, do you like horror films Michael"?

"Yeah, I don't mind them, they're alright".
Hillman smiled at the young lady. "They're alright, your boyfriend doesn't scare easily Rachel, he must be very brave".

"He's weird" Rachel whispered again.

"Ah, here's Carla with the drinks everybody, show time".

Carla handed the teenagers their drinks. Hillman said, "are you a local girl Rachel, do you live with your parents"?
"No, I come from Aberdeen".

"Aberdeen my dear the granite City".

"Yes" the girl said, almost impatiently.

"I see, are you down here on holiday"?

"No" she sighed, "I ran away from home two years ago, I've been living in a town in the South West of Scotland called Dumfries. I've only been in Sheffield for three weeks; I met Michael in the Sheppard's Arms".

"I see, so your poor parents don't know where you are"?

"They're not poor, they're bastards, utter bastards, no-one knows I'm here".

"Oh dear, it's a shame you feel that way about your parents".

"Huh, you haven't met them".

Hillman aimed the remote control in the general direction of the television set. In fact, he was aiming it at a control box high above the television. Rachel heard buzzing noises and locks clicking all around the house, doors and windows.

"What's that" said Rachel.

"Relax my dear, it's just the security locks, we don't wish to be disturbed during our film now do we"?
Michael shifted uneasily in his seat, for some reason he didn't feel very comfortable at all. Hillman stood up from the chair he was seated upon. "I want to use this girl Carla, she would make a good working girl".

Rachel looked at Hillman. "I'm not looking for work thank you".

Hillman ignored the girl's reply. "She's got a good body, lots of men would like to be with her, she'll make us a lot of money".

"Right, that's it, you sick old cunt I'm out of here!!"

Rachel put down her half-finished bottle, and got up to leave. Neither Carla nor Hillman made a move to stop her. There was no way out. Every door was locked and the whole place was soundproof. Hillman looked at Michael Gibb. "Now then young man, how much do you value your life"?

"Sir"?

"I'm not repeating the question".

"I, eh, I do. I do value my life sir, very much so".

"Do you really, well, I am going to ask you series of questions, of which I already know the answers, clear"?

"Yes sir".

Now Michael was beginning to break sweat.
"Ok" said Hillman. "Rachel, come and sit down here my dear, next to Carla, there's a good girl, finish your drink child, no one's going to hurt you".

Carla tapped the cushion next to her. "Come on Rachel, it's alright sweetheart, come sit next to me here".

Eventually, Rachel sat down next to Carla.

"Now then young sir, how's your memory"?
"It's fine, as far as I can tell sir".

"Well" said Hillman. "Let's see how far that is. Where were you last Thursday night, let's start with that shall we"?

"Last Thursday night, I don't think I was out".

"Remember Michael, I already know the answers".

"Yes sir, you said, no, I don't think I was out, oh, I think I went for some chips, but that was all, I went back home and I think I watched a late film".

The smile that had been on Hillman's face suddenly faded. "I see" said Hillman, "and that's your final answer is it"?

"Yes sir".

"Yes sir" said Hillman, to Carla Paganni. "Another lager Michael"?
"Yes please, if that's alright". Michael was trying his best to act cool.

"And you my dear, another Smirnoff Ice"?

Carla smiled at Rachel, "it's alright Rachel".

Rachel nodded. "Carla, would you do the honours my dear".

Carla got up and asked Rachel to give her a hand to carry the drinks over. Rachel carried her own drink and Mister Hillman's, Carla carried her drink and a can of lager. She sat her drink down on the coffee table, and then, just as Michael was draining his glass, she brought the can hard up under his chin, so that the glass burst in his mouth. Rachel screamed. Carla sat back down on the sofa. "It's alright sweetheart, when you've seen what's on this film, you'll want to kill him, I promise you. Mister Hillman gave him a chance there to save his own life, we were only going to put him in a wheelchair, but now, because he's a lying little bastard, he's going to die".

Hillman said, "Carla, could you go and get a basin or something, I don't want rat's blood on my new carpet, misses Hillman would go frantic".

Gibb was crying, as he carefully pulled out pieces of glass from his tongue and held them in his hand. "As far as you can tell Michael huh"? Said Hillman.

Carla came back with a basin. "Here you are liar" she said, "Think yourself lucky I didn't make you eat it".

"Right" said Hillman, "Lets watch the film, there's no point in asking him any more questions". Rachel sat sobbing on the sofa, absolutely terrified.

"Rachel, we're the good guys, honestly darling" said Carla. Watch the film and see what he had planned for you".

"Indeed", said Hillman, "but don't you worry my dear, Uncle John and Carla are going to look after you now".

They made Rachel watch the full horror unfold on the screen. She had heard on the news about the two prostitutes being murdered; now she was watching the whole grisly episode unfold before her very eyes. She watched in horror, as Susie Monk was buggered and then beaten with a raw electrical cable. The girl on the screen couldn't scream because her mouth was stuffed with a gag. Gibb looked at the floor as blood streamed from his mouth into the basin. Susie's back was being ripped open with every stroke of the whip. The copper tongues, like red hot needles greedily ripped out pieces of flesh each time the flex made contact. "Rewind it John, to the place, you know where".

"Why are you doing this" said Rachel, "What have I done to you, why are you making me watch this"?

Hillman paused the film, and pointed to the screen. "That's why my dear, that's why I'm making you watch it". He pointed to Michael

Gibb on the screen, receiving a bundle of notes. The only unmasked man in the picture. Hillman pointed to the real Michael Gibb, "He did that Rachel, he did that, all those nasty things to Susie, and then he left without a care in the world while that poor girl got flayed alive. Now, Carla and I have not even seen the end of it yet, but we will now, and the worse it gets for Susie, the worse it gets for him, this is what he had lined up for you Rachel, you were next on his list".

HARRINGTON SQUARE.

Angela sat with Tracy and Sharon in Tracy's living room, each of the girls drinking a glass of vodka and coke. "I know Tracy, how easy it is to be taken in with an act like that". She was referring to Doctor Hillman's new lease of life, and sudden change in his behaviour. "Believe me Tracy, no matter what he says, it's only a matter of time before he asks you out, don't fall for it".

"If you don't mind me saying Tracy, Angela's right, I mean, I saw his face that day, I saw his eyes, the rage, the fury, it just seems to me to be a bit too good to be true".

"I know" said Tracy, "I know, it's just, well, what I would have given for him to be like that in our marriage, hell, he made me laugh, his new clothes, bloody smoking, hell, he even swore, in fact, for the first time in all our time together, he was just like a regular guy, you know? Talking, admitting he'd been lusting after Sharon all this time, he just seemed so honest".

"Oh he's good" said Angela, "I'll give him that, but mark my words Tracy, wait until he's asked you out a couple of times, and you've refused, see if he stays the same after that. He's softening you up by bringing your little girls round more often, and letting them stay a bit longer, don't fall for it. At the end of the day though, it's your decision, and whatever you decide, we're still your friends, we'll always be here for you, don't think I'm trying to dictate your life to you, because I'm not, I only want what's best for you that's all, and if you think that means getting back with John Hillman, then so be it".

Tracy took a sip of her vodka. "No Angela, no chance, you're both right, he is playing a game of some kind. I know he's changed, I even said as much the other day, but it's not for the better, whatever is going on in his head, that's for sure, and besides, look what his father done to me in order to obtain his grandchildren, no, you're right Angela".

“Tracy, you should see this new house of his, this father-in-law of yours, this guy has got money, and plenty of it, and I intend to find out where he’s getting it from”.

“Yes” said Tracy, but you can’t go back to that house now Angela, not now that John has met you, and just hope that he doesn’t describe you to his parents, or you’ll have senior on your ass”.

“Tracy, I understand your concern for me, but I don’t have the same fears that you have, they have no hold on me, I would kill them without a second thought babe, I may even have to before we’re finished”.

“Hillman has a weapon too Angela, he has that Carla girl, and I’ll tell you something now, you would have to shoot her, and that, only if you were quick enough to get your gun out, because there’s no way anyone’s getting anywhere near her, I saw what she done to two six foot plus policemen who tried, so, whatever you plan to do Angela, plan it carefully, because the Hillmans are a very dangerous family to fuck about with these days”.

Rachel White was carried out of Hillman's house, sedated. Hillman put the girl down gently on the back seat of his B.M.W. and closed the door. Michael Gibb was not so lucky, his hands had been tied behind his back and his feet tied together. He was being dragged by the feet by Carla, his face scraping on the granite chippings of Hillmans parking area.

"I'll give you a hand to put that in the boot my dear".

"It's ok John, I'll manage it".

A couple of minutes later, the four were off to a certain location that Carla had chosen. "Don't worry Mister Hillman, I'll get all the names we need from that piece of shit in the boot, I'll get to the bottom of this. Young Rachel there, she'll be out for a couple of hours or so, I'll have all the information we need by the time she wakes up".

Hillman said, "The child was sick with fear as she watched those animals taking Susie's life like that, most dreadful Carla, those people, they need to receive similar treatment my dear, you need to really go to town on these scoundrels Carla, hurt them seriously".

"Oh don't you worry about that John, I'll hurt them for Susie and Rose. They took the lives of two very close friends, who had nothing to do with anything I might have done to offend them, they should have just came for me, instead of torturing and killing two innocent girls. It would have been better for them if they had come for me first, because then they might have stood a chance. Once I get the names off that shit in the boot, then none of them stand a chance of survival, and I couldn't care if there are two hundred in their gang, they are all dead, every single one, Even if there was anyone there who only made the tea John, they are all dead, I'll learn them to make threats to me, huh, I hope for their sakes they're prepared to try and carry their threats out, either way, they are in for a shock, they'll pay John, believe me they'll pay for their sick show".

When they reached their destination it was pitch black. "Carla, I hope you're sure about this" Hillman whispered in the car.

"I'm sure, don't worry John".

"Where are we"? Rachel was awake.

"It's ok my dear, don't you worry now, we're heading back soon".

Carla said nothing at all, as she got out of the car, and opened the boot. Hillman said to Rachel, "she's just going a walk with that dog my dear to find out the names of those bad people who did those horrible things to that girl you saw on the film, she won't be long, I know Carla, and she won't be long my dear".

Two minutes later, Carla Paganni, with a small torch in her teeth laid Michael Gibb on a banking. All Gibb could see was the blinding light of the torch, and the dark outline of Carla's body. "Now then Michael, you know you're going to die, right"? He nodded. "Well then, seeing as how you didn't actually rape Susie along with your animal friends, I'm going to give you the choice of how you die, now I think that that is really good of me considering the circumstances, don't you"? Gibb did not even attempt to answer. Carla smashed a blow onto his swollen mouth with the heel of her hand. "I said, that is good of me to give you that choice, isn't it"?

He managed to nod. A small piece of glass had been wedged between his teeth, and had gone up into the roof of his mouth splitting the skin. He screamed with the pain. "Hush now! Or I'll whack you again. Now, here's a pad and a pen, because I know it's hard for you to talk. Write down all the names of those animals you met up with in Susie's flat, don't worry, there'll be no come back, you have nothing to fear, because you're already dead, now start writing. The more names you give me, the quicker you'll die, be awkward, then I will be too".

For Michael Gibb, there was no escape; this was it, the end. This girl meant business. He could not begin to tell Carla that the whole thing was a stitch up. One of the men had approached Michael, telling him about a party, and that a certain girl had a fantasy about being gang banged. They told Michael where to find the girl, and said they would pay him two hundred quid if he could bring her back to her flat, and then turn nasty on her. They would then come out and fulfil her fantasy. The girl was a prostitute, and a friend of the man who spoke to him. Michael's job was to make it as real as possible. The man told Michael that all the men were friends of the girls' but that they weren't going to reveal their identity until the end. He told him the girl's name and some other information about friends of the girl, just to make it as believable as possible.

Michael couldn't see any harm in what the guy wanted, and so he agreed, and now here he was, only moments from death, because he'd been tricked by a gangster. He would have one last chance, if Carla permitted him this one thing, he had nothing to lose. She had given him a piece of paper and told him to write down all the names of those who had taken part in the murder. He wrote down; PLEASE LET ME WRITE SOMETHING DOWN, THEN I'LL GIVE YOU THE NAMES OF ALL THOSE I KNOW. Carla looked at the paper. "You've got five minutes, for everything, now move".

Michael wrote down everything that had happened to him concerning the gangster and Susie. After he'd written it down, Carla took the piece of paper from his shaking hands, and read it. "You poor bastard" she sighed. "They stitched you up, oh kid you're a silly boy, what the fuck are we going to do with you, eh? You're as innocent as that slip of a girl in the car aren't you"?

Michael Gibb began to cry. "I'll be back in a minute boy". Less than five minutes later, Carla returned. "Come on kid, let's get you to a hospital, after that, you work for Mister Hillman, agreed"?

Michael nodded, and tried to say yes. John Hillman drove as fast as the law would allow him, to get Michael to a hospital. "We weren't to know son, I mean that girl was our friend, it looked like, well you know? Is that all you know? Four names"?

"It doesn't matter John" said Carla, "one would have been enough". Outside of Sheffield general, Hillman sat with Carla and Rachel in the B.M.W. Carla had been in the hospital with Michael, who needed emergency treatment. Before they'd given him the anaesthetic, she told him she would wait for him outside. Hillman spoke to Carla. "Are you sure he's as innocent as he says he is Carla"?

"Of course he is John; you only have to look at the film to see that, I'm annoyed at myself for not spotting it in the first place".

"Explain"?

"Mister Hillman" said Carla, "he wasn't wearing a mask, now, even as green as he is, even he wouldn't be stupid enough not to wear a mask if he knew he was being set up. He knew nothing about it; he thought they were telling the truth about the gang bang being a fantasy thing. He wouldn't think, that's why the main man wanted him out of the way as soon as possible, he'd be happy with his cash".

"Keep an eye on him Carla, you never can tell".

"I know John; I'll take care of him. He can stay at Heather's until I find him somewhere, once he's recovered enough, he can do some running for you".

"Alright Carla, I'll leave that up to you to sort out".

Hillman then turned and spoke to Rachel in the back seat. "As for you my dear, you have struck gold. Carla here will take you to Heather's place where you will be looked after properly. You will be fed, and given a room, or maybe a place of your own, Heather will see to it. What is it you take my dear"?

"I'm sorry"? Said Rachel.

"What do you take my dear, come on, don't be silly, we know how you live, you have no fixed abode, what is it"?

"Cocaine if I can get it".

"Oh you'll get it, you'll get as much as you need".

"Take note of that Rachel, as much as you need, not as much as you want, there's a difference" Said Carla.
"Indeed" said Hillman. "And, of course, once you're getting as much as you need, there won't be any more need for you to go out shop lifting, understand"?

Rachel sighed, "Yes".

"Now then, tomorrow, or the day after, Carla will give you some money, and you and her will go shopping for clothes and shoes ok"?

"Why? Why are you doing this for me, I'm not going on the game for anyone, is that clear, you can stick your money, I won't do that, I've still got my pride".

"Have you indeed" said Hillman, "good for you, but let me ask you something, and all I ask for is an honest answer, that's all I ever ask for. Where did you meet Michael"?
"I told you, in a pub".

"In a pub" repeated Hillman.

"How much money did you have when you met him, forgive me for asking, it's just that you said you belonged to Aberdeen, and you ran away from home, and then lived in Dumfries, then you came here, so how much money did you have when you met Michael in the pub"?

"I had about fifty quid, something like that, why"?

Hillman ignored her reply. "How much do you have now, I mean to your name, your whole fortune, how much my dear"?

"About fifteen pounds".

"Fifteen pounds, and how long will that last you Rachel, it won't even buy a decent meal. Where were you planning on staying? Don't tell me, Michael said he would put you up for a couple of weeks until you got yourself up on your feet, am I right"?
"Yes, he said that".

“Fine, only you told me in my house that you weren’t looking for a job, isn’t that what you said”?

“Yes, well, not that kind of job anyway”.

“I see” said Hillman, “well, what kind of job then, what qualifications do you have, do you have any”?
Silence.
“I see, so unless you find a cleaning job, or stacking shelves or something, you’re kind of stuck, aren’t you, and what happens if Michael and you fall out, that’s the end of that isn’t it. Back out on the streets, looking for another Michael, someone else who’ll be kind to you. Let me make one thing clear to you Rachel, kind people are about one in five hundred, the other four hundred and ninety nine are like those men you saw in that film. Now, what do you say, you stay at Heather’s for a couple of weeks, you can cook or clean for your keep, I’ll still give you the money, there’s no catch, if you still feel the same way after that, you can walk away, how’s that? You won’t be getting a better offer than that my dear, this side of the next blue moon, I can tell you that for nothing” said Hillman.

Carla looked over the seat and took Rachel by the hand. “If I can say one thing Rachel, Mister Hillman here is a man of his word, I can vouch for that. I was just like you Rachel, I had nothing, I had no-one, I had nowhere. Now, I have a healthy bank account, I have a car, and I have lots of friends. I have loads of clothes, and we girls, we love our clothes now don’t we”? Rachel smiled. Carla squeezed her hand gently. “So, do we have a deal”?

“If I still feel the same way in a couple of weeks, I can walk away”?

“Of course” said Hillman, “and you can keep the clothes you buy, how does that sound”?

“Yes sir, I’ll do it, and, and thank you”.

“You are more than welcome my dear” said Hillman, “Now would you excuse me for one moment; I have something rather important to talk about with Carla”.

Rachel watched from inside the car as Carla and John Hillman stood talking about something or other. There wasn't really much of a risk involved in what she'd agreed to, after all, Hillman was right, she had absolutely nothing, therefore she had nothing to lose, and she needed clothes, badly.

"Alright my dear" said Hillman, as he and Carla climbed back into the car.

"Yes, fine Mister Hillman, thank you".

"Splendid my dear."

Just then, Carla's mobile phone rang. Hillman watched the colour drain from her face. Whoever was talking to her was giving her some grave news. Carla switched off the phone.

"Carla? Carla? What is it girl"? What's wrong, tell me".

"Excuse us a minute again Rachel, Mister Hillman and I need to speak".

The two of them once more got out of the car and walked a few steps away from it.

"What's wrong Carla" whispered Hillman.
"It was them again John, they've just told me, they've killed Michael Gibb".
"What? They must be bluffing Carla". He pointed over to the hospital.

"John, they even told me what ward he's in, they've done him John, and I'm next they said. They said they've been following my every move".

"Fuck" said Hillman, "The boy will still be under the anaesthetic, he might be in theatre now, surely they can't-".

"They have John, trust me they have".

“Right, let’s get the girl round to Heather’s, don’t let on about any of this to her whatever you do Carla. How on earth”?

“It doesn’t matter how John, the fact remains that they have, that’s what we’ve got. We have to act on that information. I’ll get a couple of hours at Heather’s place, and then I’m going to pay a visit to the first of those names I have. Now John, I have to start kicking ass here, I’ve got to start paying them back for Susie, for Susie and Rose. These bastards do not know the meaning of the word ruthless, but I swear to God, they will soon, I owe that much to Susie”.

Less than a hundred yards from where Carla spoke to John Hillman, nurse Sandra Stiller hadn’t noticed the little pieces of pillow material lying at her feet, as she rolled the trolley out of ward six and down to the theatre where surgeon Alex Worthington stood with his team, awaiting Michael Gibb and the delicate work ahead of them, to repair the young man’s inner mouth.

“He’s out” said nurse Stiller, bringing the trolley to a halt. “He hasn’t even mumbled a word all the way down here”.

“Have we lost him already nurse” said Worthington. He was referring to the sheet which had been placed over the patient’s face. “He looks like a corpse, can he breathe under there nurse”? As Worthington pulled back the sheet from the young man’s face, he froze. A single neat half inch hole was in the centre of Michael Gibb’s brow. “Call the police” he said calmly, at first, “call the police”.

He lifted the young man’s head gently, and as he did, the pillow lifted up with it. His brains were mixed and mashed with the contents of the pillow. He placed the head back down and sighed. No-one had heard his request it seemed. “WOULD SOMEONE CALL THE BLOODY POLICE PLEASE, NOW!!!”

MILLBURN AVENUE.

Carla Paganni sat in John Hillman's B.M.W. outside of number twenty-two Millburn Avenue. She had been here since five thirty am. It was now nine fifteen. The list of names given to her by Michael Gibb, sat on her lap. Number one on the list was a certain Mister James Fisher. Carla had known this man for some time now. He was a user, and had, in the past, been a customer of Mister Hillman's, until one day James had got a little heavy handed and stole cocaine from one of Hillman's runners.

He had been let off with a warning. Today, Mister Fisher would not be so lucky. Carla looked over the top of her magazine as a young blonde haired girl came out of Fisher's house. Carla knew this was not Fisher's wife. She got a good look at the girl as she walked past the car sending a text message to someone. This could be tricky thought Carla; she may be on to me, and giving information to someone of my whereabouts. "I'll soon find out" she thought, as she got out of the car. "Excuse me" Carla shouted. The girl stopped, and much to Carla's surprise, began walking over towards her. "I'm sorry to trouble you" she said to the blonde, "I'm looking for number Twenty-two, is it anywhere round here"?

The girl pointed down to the house she had just come from.

"It's down there" said the girl, "just down there on your right".

"Thank you" said Carla. "That would be a Mister James Fisher, am I right"?

"Yes, well, I only know him as James, I don't know his surname".

"I see" said Carla. I'm from the council you see, and it seems, according to my records, he's been paying too much rent. I have a cheque here for him; it's quite a substantial amount as well".

The young lady flushed. "Oh, well, I'm going back down to his house in an hour or so, I could give it to him" she lied.

“I’m sorry” said Carla, “I’m afraid I have to hand it to him in person, or his wife, of course, are they both in”?

“No, only James, his wife’s away for a few days with his kids, I actually think that she’s left him. He’s in bed, so you’ll have to knock loud. He’s tired; he’s had a busy night”.

“I see” said Carla, smiling. “Well thank you for your help” said Carla, “I would”--

“This cheque” said the blonde, “Is it more than two hundred pounds? He owes me that much you see”.

“Oh yes” said Carla, “It’s more than four thousand pounds”.

The girl went flush again.

Carla almost burst out laughing. “Well, I’ll have to go, goodbye”, said Carla.
“See ya” said the blonde.
“You greedy little tart” Carla said to herself, as she walked down towards the house. She walked round to the back of the house and tried the back door. It opened. Once inside, she closed it and locked the door, putting the key in her jeans pocket. She looked briefly into the living room, no-one, and no dogs. As she climbed the stairs, she began teasingly calling out, “James”? No answer, almost at the top of the stairs. “James, I’m coming for you James”.

“Go away Amanda, I’m fucking knackered you little whore, you’ve fucked me out bitch, fuck off like I told you, little annoying twat, I’m trying to fucking sleep here”.

Carla followed the voice and found the bedroom. She pulled out her pistol, complete with silencer attached. Down on her knees, she slowly made her way to the edge of Fisher’s bed. “JAMES!!!”

Fisher sprang up, sitting bolt upright. “Look you little fucking, oh fuck”.

"Exactly James" said Carla, "Oh fuck. Now then James, names James".

"I don't know anything, I swear".

"You're" Thud. "Deaf" Thud."

"AAARRRRGGGGHHH". The two shots destroyed the tops of both his arms. "Before you die James, I've got four names, yours was one of them, but you're just shit, I need bigger names"'

Blood was spurting from the damage caused by the 3.57 I.M.I. automatic pistol. One of the few semi-automatic pistols which fired Magnum 3.57 cartridges. His gaping wounds now soaking his bed sheets. Come on, you might as well tell me, you're dead in twenty minutes anyway, come on, don't make me hurt you any more, names please".

"I don't know, help me please, please don't let me die".

"I'll help you if you give me some names". Carla stood by the bed. "Come on James, neither of us have much time to fuck about here, who's your main man"?

"I...only… know one name, Carla I swear, it's, Steve Temple, that's all, that's all I know, that's all I know Carla, I swear".

"Hmm" said Carla, "Were you in the video James"?

"No, no it wasn't, I wasn't part of it".

"Well, why would young Gibb tell me you *were* part of it, huh? I don't believe you James, and we both know that you have a master's degree in lying. I can tell James when you tell a lie, you're lips move".

"Carla, I swear".

Carla pulled back the sheets from the bed. She pulled the quilt back then pulled down his shorts.

"Last chance James".

"I don't know Carla, just Temple".
She fired another shot, this time into his groin.
The burning pain that Felder suffered, was indescribable, as he choked out something incomprehensible, the incoherent words coming out as a whimper.
"Well James, you won't be in any more films will you. *Your* bleeding to death is dedicated to my friend Susie, think of what you did to her as your life drains away from you, and think yourself very lucky that I don't have time to make you suffer, you got off light you fucking vermin that you are, goodbye James".

By the time Amanda Pearce returned to number Twenty two Millburn Avenue, her friend James lay dead, staring straight in front of him. The girl was so gullible, that, after she had made a phone call to a certain Mister Steven Temple, she went back up stairs and searched frantically for a cheque from the council.

SHEFFIELD GENERAL.

Deborah Knowles and John Crosby stood in the corridor as the forensic team put the body of Michael Gibb into a body bag.

"Do you think this is connected to the murder of the prostitutes Deborah? Said Crosby, As he sipped the scorching black liquid that was supposed to be coffee.

"Yes I do" she replied. "There's something going on here John that is even bigger than we initially thought. This is the drugs world John, believe me, and I'll tell you something else", She whispered in Crosby's ear as a nurse walked past, "There's a lot more to come, I wouldn't mind betting. This looks like tit for tat. This will go on until one of the gangs feels justified, you mark my words".

"Yeah, but whoever did this Deborah, just walked in here and blew the guy away, it doesn't say much for the hospital security does it".

Deborah walked down the corridor a few paces and went into a room. Crosby was about to follow her. "Wait here a minute" she said. She walked out, a few moments later wearing a white jacket and trousers, and a green mouth mask over the top of her head. "How long would it take you John to put one of these on". She pointed to the mask on her head. "Look how busy the place is, look at the size of the place, there are people coming and going around here all the time, students, doctors nurses, janitors, nobody has got the time to stop every stranger they see and ask them who they are. That's it John, it's as easy as that. Come on let's get down to the morgue. By the way John, speaking of tit for tat, how did your date go with the lovely leggy Ashley"?

"It was all right" said Crosby. "I'll bet it was" said Deborah, smiling.

LONDON ROAD.

Carla knew she was going to have to bide her time to get near Steven Temple. At least now though, she knew who her enemy was. Now she could watch him, if only from a distance. Temple was well known in the drugs world, he carried a lot of punches. Few people ever crossed this man. Those who had, lay somewhere hidden in the ground, or, their ashes were scattered to the wind. None of them still had the privilege of breathing. She was going to have to be very careful. Temple's house sat back from the rest in London Road. His house was very similar to John Hillman's, other than the fact that this one didn't have nearly as much ground to it. The house had obviously been built long before any others around this area.

If Fisher had been telling the truth, then this man would indeed be the ring leader, although, she doubted if he would have been present at Susie's execution. He would leave that to his dogs. "He'll be pissed off now" she thought to herself, although that was what she wanted. Carla started the car, and drove down towards Temple's house. As she got to the end of the road, she turned right, as if she was going into Temple's drive. Instead, she stopped the car, picked up a small pair of binoculars and focussed them onto the three cars parked outside of his house. She quickly jotted down the three registrations, and then reversed back out onto the street and drove away.

Inside the house, Steve Temple sat tapping his fingers on the huge oak table in his study. Amanda Pearce did not know who Carla Paganni was, but had given a perfect description of her when she had phoned Steven Temple about Fisher's murder. She sat now, at the table with a very angry Temple. "You stupid little bimbo cunt, you might have known she wasn't from any fucking council, you might have warned James".

"Mister Temple, I"-

"Shut the fuck up, while I think, fucking bimbo, you are one dizzy fuck are you not? Fucking junky slut!"

“Papa, papa, shouted Amy and Angela as they came running into the kitchen, each with a present for their grandfather.

“Hello, my babies, hello, hello, hello, mmm”. He kissed each of his granddaughters on the cheek. “Oh I’ve missed you, little angels”.

Amy cried out, “Papa John, we’ve got you a present from the Loch Ness Scotland monster, papa”.

Hillman laughed as he accepted the parcels from his excited grandchildren. “My goodness me, presents for papa, I think I’m the lucky one today, two presents, oh, and look” said Hillman, here comes my favourite girl as well, as Anne Hillman entered the kitchen, and my favourite son as well, oh this is all too much for one day”.

“Your only son” said Hillman junior.

“Yes” said Anne Hillman, smiling, “but I’m not so sure about his only girlfriend”.

“You’re not papa John’s girlfriend Nana” said Amy, laughing.

“Of course she is” said Hillman. “She’s the best girlfriend papa John has ever had”.

“Hmm” mumbled Anne, putting the kettle on. A few minutes later, Hillman, and his wife and son sat at the breakfast bar in the kitchen, each with a cup of tea.

“It was lovely up there John, you should have come with us, the scenery alone, was worth the trip. It’s hard to imagine, you’re still in Britain when you’re up there. I’ve got some beautiful photos John; I hope they turn out alright. If we hadn’t built this place John, I’d be encouraging you to buy a house up there near Loch Lomond. Scotland is so beautiful John”.

Amy spoke up, still full of excitement. "Daddy, show Papa John on the telly, me and Angela and you on the boat. Daddy was rowing the boat Papa, on the Loch Ness Scotland".

"Was he indeed" replied Hillman. "I'll show Papa later girls, I have to unpack the camera and everything and connect it to the television. I'll just go and set it up dad in the study, if that's alright". Doctor Hillman stood up and unpacked one of the bags. "I'll just go and set this up now, or we'll never get any peace, I won't be a minute". As John Hillman junior left the room his mother said, "This break John, it's done him the power of good, he's a different man. We visited a few places up there, but oh John, Loch Lomond, goodness me the beauty".

In the study, Hillman junior was setting up the camcorder. After he had set it up, he turned to leave the room. A single piece of paper lay on his father's writing desk. On that piece of paper, were four men's names. It simply read; 1 James Fisher. 2. Henry Felder.3. Joseph Dougan.4. Paul Crane.

John Hillman took a pen and a piece of paper and copied the names down, putting the list into his pocket. As he was returning back to the kitchen, he tried to remember where he had heard that name. " James Fisher, James Fisher, was he a patient of his.
How do I know that name"? He was starting to feel strange again, almost dizzy, fuzzy headed. Suddenly, he remembered where he had heard the name. It had been in this morning's paper, lying on the floor of his house. James Fisher had been murdered.

"Alright son"? Said Hillman, as John entered the kitchen.

"Yeah, fine dad, and you? Have you been alright here yourself, you've not been getting up to any mischief now, have you, while me and mum's been away"?

Hillman never flinched. "Son, my days for any mischief are well and truly over, that's for sure, I did all that before I met your mother John".

"Did you now" laughed Anne Hillman.

Suddenly there was a raging battle taking place in John Hillman junior's head. "*Lord God would you please fucking shut up a minute while I deal with this, I know I get the picture, give it a fucking rest Lord please*". Young Hillman picked up the newspaper from the table and put it on the breakfast bar. He opened it up to page four. On the left hand page there was a small photograph of James Fisher. Beside that, there was a small headline which simply said; Mysteriously Murdered. Young Hillman pointed to it. "Did you see that dad, murder over at Millburn, James Fisher, did you know him"?

"I've never heard his name in my life son, it's a mystery to me, probably drug dealer's son, it usually is".

"*I'm listening Lord, I know he's a fucking bastard liar, I know, but leave it with me, I'll get to the bottom of it, just see if I don't*".

HEATHER'S BEAUTY SALON.

Carla Paganni entered the salon and asked one of the girls if Heather was in today.

"She's coming in this afternoon Carla, she says she has company at home and she wants to spend a little time with them. Carla went through to the back of the shop, into Heather's office, and switched on the computer. After scanning the screen for a few minutes, she switched it back off, and left the shop, saying goodbye to the girls as she did. Heather knew that Carla was always scanning her computer, but never once objected.

John Hillman had told her to do so from time to time, so there would be no point in objecting. Carla drove round to Heather's house, which was less than three hundred yards from her salon. She pressed the doorbell twice. A few moments later Heather opened the door.

"Hi Carla, come in, your friend is in the shower, she won't be long, coffee Carla"?

"Yes please babes, I could do with one. As soon as Rachel is ready, I'll take her over to John's, I have to take his car back and pick up mine, then I have to take her shopping".

"Hell Carla, you look exhausted, you need to sleep. Heather gave Carla her coffee and the two friends sat on the sofa.

"Who was the hit Carla, did I know him"?
"A certain Mister James Fisher, it was a couple of days ago, but I've been running round like nobody's business, I needed something to calm me down. He refused to grass on his scum friends and so I just let him bleed to death. He was one of the bastards who done Susie and Rose".

"This Fisher, is he the same creep who stole all that cocaine off our young friend that time"?

"The very same, but he won't be stealing anyone else's cocaine. This is getting bigger all the time Heather. There's someone who fancies a bit of John Hillman's pie, and they quite fancy their chances at taking over from him. These gangs, they're getting more and more brave, I mean, John only has me to protect his interests, if these lot were to force the issue, well, there wouldn't be much I could do, and he's in no hurry to hire any more heavies to help our cause. He doesn't realize Heather, just how lucky he's been having control of your girls and all the major drug deals around here, without challenge, but those days are coming to an end, this is going to get out of control, if he doesn't do something about it. I have a list of names Heather, which I am going to see to, but if these people I am going to kill, happen to be in the same gang, well, you can only imagine what will happen, there will be consequences. I know now, who my enemy is, at least I have that, but, I'll have to act very cautiously, to say the least. I'll have to change my car as well, they know my Porsche".

"Well, if you don't mind me saying Carla, it's quite hard not to notice your car, a bloody Porsche for goodness sakes, talk about show".

"I know Heather, I know, bloody exotic car, but that's me, if you've got it, flaunt it. At that moment Rachel White came into the living room, wearing only a pair of Heather's shorts and a cropped top, her ample breasts protruding through the flimsy material.

Heather smiled at Carla. "Well, I had to give her something to wear while I was washing her jeans and things. Rachel had no idea how provocative she looked.

"Jesus Christ Heather, don't let any of your girls see her like that. They'll either eat her alive, or they'll forbid her from working with them, hell, this thing will take all their business away from them, she's just a machine, she's built for it, she's a fucking money machine, I mean I'm sitting here, and I want to fuck her".

Heather smiled at Rachel, "all right babes"?

Rachel came and stood at the living room mirror. “What”? She said.
“I have to agree with you there Carla” said Heather, “she’s bringing out the rug muncher in me as well, Jesus!
I’m just saying to Carla sweetheart, I’ve got your clothes in the washing machine. Won’t be long, then you can go shopping with her”.

MORNINGSIDE.

Doctor John Hillman sat at the breakfast bar with his list of names he'd found in his father's study. He sat sipping his coffee and scanning the names before him. His father and mother were off to church with the girls, so he knew he had at least an hour of peace and quiet. He sat, tapping his fingers on the bar, half whispering, half talking to himself, or to his God.

"Felder, Felder, I know I've heard that name Lord, Felder". He got up from the stool and went upstairs, returning moments later with three or four sheets of paper in his hands. "Now then" he said, as he lay the sheets of paper out neatly in front of him. He had the lists of all his patients in the last two years. "Let's see now, Felder, I know that fucking name Lord". He ran his finger down the list slowly. There were four rows of names on each of the four sheets. Half way down the third row of the third sheet, he stopped. "Ah ha, Felder Nancy. Nancy Felder, she's an old biddy, I wonder if this is her son or a relation of hers on this sheet. He stared at her name for a few seconds in total silence, and then, "*Look, how the fuck am I supposed to concentrate if you keep interrupting my bastard thoughts, just tell me that*!!"

He then went quiet again for a few seconds, staring at the name on the list. Then, like an unruly child in the classroom, he began to snigger through his nose, before bursting into laughter. "I get it now Lord, you fucker, you want me to deal with this old girl, she's the whore, is that it? Fuck Lord, you had me there, you fucking twat that you are, you know how to wind people up don't you, you're fucking playing with me. Ok, I'll do it". Half an hour later, he had the names and addresses of the mothers of the other men on the list as well. "So that's it Lord, huh? You want me to do all these old whores. They must have thought that you would forget all of their sins from their younger days, but no, you don't forget anything at all Lord, do you, I mean, I didn't even do anything wrong did I, and look how you punished me, with Tracy and the other whore, you fucker that you are. I'll take the old whores off the breathing list though, you just leave your dirty work to me, I'll sort it for you. As for Tracy and the other tramps, I'll get them in my own time, and in my own way, if you don't mind. I don't want you on their side this time either, imagine, having to go to hospital, because your wife's just beat your mouth with your kid's skipping rope, you rotten bastard that you are. You're just lucky you've got me on your side". He took the lists back upstairs singing; "Jesus wants me for a sunbeam".

BRAITHWAITE ROAD. 2.35. am.

Carla had ran the number plates through John Hillman's associates, and had come up with this address where she now sat, in Heather's Mondeo, twenty yards or so from Mister Henry Felder's house. A tough character who was well known for his, behind the back type of attacks. "Dirty Harry" he was named, by some of those who had the misfortune of crossing his path. This man would shake your hand, and then, when your back was turned, he would stick a knife in. Night clubs were his favourite playgrounds, both for women, and for making underhanded drug deals behind his boss's back, with his boss's merchandise of course. He had back rooms in some of these places, where he would bring customers who wouldn't, or couldn't pay up the money. One way or another, they paid. Henry Felder was one of Steve Temple's top dogs, if not *the* top dog.

Carla looked at her dashboard. It was 2.35.am. Lighting up a cigarette, she looked up and down Braithwaite Road. It was eerily quiet, this being one of the roughest parts of Sheffield. Everything happened in this street. You could buy the company of a woman, a gun, drugs, clothes, higher a killer, you could buy a car, of any description, you just might have to wait a couple of hours, and if you were unfortunate enough to walk through this area, not knowing where you were, and you had enough money or jewellery on you, you could even buy your own life, although that would depend on the individuals who mugged you.

Carla looked in the mirror. A car was coming from behind her. It was a taxi. A dark haired girl in her twenty's staggered out from the cab. Seconds later, out came Mister Henry Felder, looking completely sober. His light grey suit matched his hair, although he was only forty three years old. He was always dressed immaculately. He guided his drunken lady friend gently by the arm in the direction of his house. Carla knew she would have to work fast. She got out of the car, but did not close her door. She was at his back in no time at all. She quickly placed a thumb behind each of Felder's ears, and pressed, a trick she had learned from one of her martial arts instructors. Felder dropped to his knees. Carla then smashed her elbow into his throat. He fell face forward on to the pavement. The drunk girl began to scream, but only for a second. Carla repeated the thumbs trick on her. As the girl dropped unconscious, Carla turned once more to Felder. He was struggling to breathe. She opened the boot of the Mondeo and lifted Felder, who was still choking, and threw him in. She then took out her trusty I.M.I. Desert Eagle, and fired a shot through his hand. Then she did the same with his other hand. "There now Henry, I'll see you soon sugar". She closed the boot and got into the car, and drove away, leaving the unconscious girl on the pavement. As she drove, she looked at the dash again, it was 2.37.am. "You're getting sluggish Carla" she said.

Henry Felder lay crumpled in the boot, still struggling to breathe. Both of his hands completely destroyed, shock setting in, and an overwhelming need to be sick. Panic was now setting in as well. He knew who it was, who had done this, he also knew she was far from finished with him. His mobile phone rang in his pocket. What Henry Felder would have given to have been able to answer it, if he could have answered it, he could have been helped, but he no longer had any hands, he no longer had any hope.

Carla pulled up at the old air field. The place had never been used since the Second World War. Some fathers or boyfriends would bring their sons and daughters or their girlfriends up here for their very first driving lesson, just to let them get used to the gears. Apart from that, only the odd teenage couple would enter one of the old munitions huts, where they could bonk away in peace until their hearts were content. Just a mile and a half strip of runway, which had once been smooth tarmac, but which was now rough chippings and pot holes, a skill in its own right to be able to manoeuvre them. Carla opened the boot, aiming the gun at Felder's face. "Come on, out you come scum, your time is up Harry for bullying and manipulating people, your ticket is up hard man. She pulled him roughly by the wrist, "come on hard man, out you get". He fell out of the car, groaning, as he fell hard on both of his knees. "What are you crying like that for hard man? Just because you fell on your knees?"

"Please Carla, I can explain, I can, it wasn't meant to happen like that Carla, I swear to you".
"Stand up!!" Said Carla, "Yes, it wasn't meant to happen like that eh? But it did happen didn't it, and you were there, you helped murder my two best friends didn't you, did you enjoy your gang bang, you and your dogs did you? Did you"?

"Carla, we, there was only one girl, I swear to you".

"Yes Susie in one flat and Rose in the other, you sick bastards".

"No Carla, there was only the one girl, I swear to you, it just got out of hand, I swear it was only one Carla, please, please". He began to cry. "There was only one girl Carla, I swear to you, I don't know anything about any other girl".

"Answer me this, and you'd better answer me honestly, were you one of the men with the masks"?

"Carla I, how could I-"

The force of the shot, shattered his whole knee cap, making it look like he had deliberately kicked out at Carla's car. "Felder screamed and fell to the ground. Carla bent down and emptied his pockets. She opened the back door of the car and brought out a rope. "You're going to be on another film today dirty Harry, I'm sending this one to your boss as a warning, and to prove that even hard men like you, drop their guard once in a while, and the trouble is Harry, people like me are watching and waiting for it to happen. Tough hard man. Huh! That poor girl, you fucking bastards. There wasn't a piece of skin left on her body, well guess what Harry" she said, as she tightened the rope from his good leg to the back bumper.

"Please Carla" whimpered Felder, "I beg you".

"Yes. Please, Harry, I heard my friend saying that on the film you made, and did any of you listen to her plea? No, did you fuck listen". Carla went back to the car, this time returning with a camera. "Remember this Harry? Now then, what do I do to, oh yes, that's it. "Smile Harry, smile for Mister Temple, show your boss how intimidating you are now. Are you listening Temple? This is what you'll get if I receive one more threat from your monkeys. Now, I'll make an example of this runt, and then we leave it. Now, you can see where we are, I'll leave what's left of him in that first hut over there". She pointed the camera to where she referred to. "So that you can give it some kind of burial. For your own good Mister Temple, you'd better call a halt to your silly games, because if you don't, I'll personally see to it that all your men are taken down, one by one, and then I will come for you. Now this, what you're about to see, is for Susie and Rose".

She turned the camera to Felder. "Any last words scum cunt"?

"Please Carla" Felder whispered.

"Yes, I do believe that that was Susie's last words, as you wish. I hope you're going to suffer some of the pain that my friends had to. Oh, I nearly forgot Harry, come here". She pulled out a knife from her jeans and cut the clothes from Henry Felder's body. "I'll have to be quick Harry to cause you as much pain as possible, or else you're going to die on me through blood loss, and that wouldn't be fair on Susie and Rose now would it Henry". She sat the camera down on a flat piece of stone, and looked through the view finder. "There, perfect". She leaned over and spat on Felder's face. "Before you pass out with the pain, just remember what you done to my friends".
With one of Felder's legs tied to the under-side of the car, she drove up the rough gravel road, dragging the naked man about twenty miles per hour. She felt it was the perfect speed to inflict as much pain as she could, to this vermin. Up and down the runway she drove at the same speed, and then, for the final time, she drove back down towards the huts doing almost seventy miles per hour at one point.
Justice was done for Susie and Rose, unless Temple ignored her warning.

POLICE MORTUARY. SHEFFIELD.

Ashley Barnes was once more dictating all the details of the deceased's injuries to a young girl, when Deborah Knowles and John Crosby entered the room. "Busy" said Knowles, in between Ashley's dictation.

"Yes I am Miss Knowles and getting busier all the time these days, hi John".

"Hi Ashley" replied Crosby.

Knowles turned and smiled at Crosby, and then looked back at Miss Barnes, who, Knowles could tell, was smiling under her mask. "Shall we wait up stairs, if that's convenient"?

"Of course" said Ashley, I'll be up in a minute or two, you know where I keep everything".

"Thank you" said Knowles. Into Crosby's ear, as they made their way up the steps, she said, "I don't know about me Ashley, but I'll bet Mister Crosby here knows exactly where you keep everything".

"Leave it out Deborah" said Crosby, laughing, as they entered the room.

"What" said Knowles, "I'm only telling the truth John".

"Deborah" sighed Crosby, "we are here on official police business, now, could we please keep it like that, as you know, I never mix business with pleasure".

"Is that a fact John, well, I seem to recall someone deliberately leaving their keys here on this very table in order to arrange a date with a certain Miss Barnes, am I right, I mean, was that in work time, or your own time, can you remember"?

"Who's on their own" said Ashley Barnes as she entered the room wearing a tight v necked sweater incrusted with mock diamonds around the v and around the short sleeved arms, tight pale blue jeans, and trainers. Her golden hair hung loose, and shone like a picture, thought Deborah Knowles. Her makeup looked like it had been applied by a professional. "Who's on their own" the young lady repeated.

"No-one" said Crosby, "we were just talking shop Ashley".

"Coffee Ok"? Said Barnes.

"Coffee's fine" replied Knowles.

In less than two minutes, Ashley was explaining in detail, all of Michael Gibb's injuries. John Crosby cleared his throat, and then said" I thought it was just one gun shot that killed Mister Gibb".

"So it was" said Ashley, "One shot killed him, but he had been brought in by a young lady, he needed emergency treatment to his mouth. By the looks of it he had been caught badly on the mouth with a tumbler, glass had cut through all of his gums, top and bottom, also, the roof of his mouth as well; in fact, there is still glass inside his mouth now. He was in a bad way, before he was shot. His nose had been broken as well; in fact, I think he's been put under, even before he's been shot. He wouldn't have felt anything, he was out. "Now" said Ashley, as she sipped her coffee, "That guy had a bad day, that's what I'd call a bad day".
"Did anyone get a description of the young lady who brought him in" said Knowles.
"You'll have to ask at the hospital" said Barnes, "they don't tell me anything down here, I must have done something wrong in a previous life or something, to be stuck with this job".
Deborah smiled at Ashley, "You love this job, I can tell".
"Yes, I must admit, I do get a certain pleasure from poking about the human anatomy".
Crosby blushed again. "What's he like" said Knowles, you've got him like a school boy Ashley, he's blushed more times than a chameleon".
"Please" said Crosby, could we please talk about what we're here for, instead of trying to take the piss out of me, can we"?
"We're finished with the business John" said Knowles, Ashley's told us all we need to know about poor Mister Gibb".
"That's right" said Ashley, "you've only got Mister Fisher to hear about now".
Knowles and Crosby spoke together. "Fisher"?
"Yes" said Ashley, he was brought in after Gibb, not long after Gibb anyway, what, you two didn't know"?
"No we didn't, we haven't been told".
"You see that John"? Said Ashley, "I get told absolutely nothing, and you get told absolutely nothing, haven't we all got great jobs you guys, huh"?

FINCHLEY COURT.

Doctor John Hillman waited in his car for the nurse to leave number twenty-seven. The rain battered hard down on the roof, almost drowning out the voice on his radio, prattling on about the weather. In his mind he was having a conversation with his God. "She's been in there now, for the best part of an hour, can't you make something happen so that the nurse can move her arse out of there? I mean, here I am, doing your dirty work and all you can do is make it fucking rain, I'll tell you what, if she's not out of there in five minutes, I'm out of here, I'm fucking warning you. You're just fucking me about, and I'm about at the end of my tether, you better fucking wise up here buddy, or you can get some other fucker to do your dirty work for you, "I HAVE GOT KIDS YOU KNOW", he shouted out loud. The rest of the statement had been in his head. It was as if the divine being had heard him. "About fucking time too, come on you lazy little fuck, how long does it take you to change a dressing on an old woman's leg? You see? That's why you'll never be anything other than a nurse young lady, spend half the day talking about the bastard weather, and the other half drinking fucking tea, you guzzling little tramp that you are, go on, get into your fucking Polo, and fuck off!!".

The small blue car disappeared down the street into the sheets of rain, which seemed to be coming down even harder now. Nancy Felder stood at her kitchen sink rinsing the two cups that she and Nurse Morrison had been drinking from only minutes before. Her doorbell rang. "Oh Tiddles, Miss Morrison must have forgotten something" she said to her two year old cat, as she dried her hands on the tea towel. "Coming," she sang, as she made her way down the hall, with her new bandage from her knee to her ankle. She slipped on the chain, and pulled the door open, as far as the safety chain would allow. "Oh, em, who are you? What can I do for you"?

"It's me Nancy, it's Doctor Hillman. The man pulled down the hood from his waterproof jacket.

"Oh, so it is Doctor, I'm sorry, the nurse has just been".

"I know Nancy, that's why I'm here, I have to check up on their standard of work, to make sure you're getting the best possible treatment, you see, I pass on my remarks to the medical centre, you see, and they assess her progress, now how about a nice cup of tea

Nancy, you and me, and maybe a nice scone or a biscuit or something".
Nancy Felder smiled. "Of course Doctor, I'll just put the kettle back on, it'll still be hot".
"Yes, I'll bet you were fucking hot in your day Nancy eh"? He shouted through, "Bet you took some cock in your time Nancy".
Nancy could not hear what Doctor Hillman was shouting because of the kettle coming to the boil. "I'll just be a minute Doctor; I can't make out what you're saying".
"Hah, make out, I'll bet you made out a few times Nancy eh? Tried to hide your sins all these years Nancy, isn't that so, whore!!"
Nancy came through carrying a tray. "There now Doctor, you help yourself now, do you hear"?
"Yes I hear Nancy, I hear a lot better than you, but listen, don't you think you're a little too old to be offering sex to people like me"?
"Doctor Hillman, I really don't, are you feeling alright Doctor, you don't look too clever to me".
Doctor Hillman opened his briefcase and pulled out a length of cheese wire. "I'm fucking fine Nancy, honest, never been better. Tiddles made the mistake of nudging the back of Hillman's leg "What's its name Nancy" he said, holding the cat up in the air.
"That's Tiddles" said Nancy, "and you're Nancy's little helper aren't you, you're Nancy's little protector, that's what you are".
Doctor Hillman looked into Nancy's eyes. "Are you fucking kidding me Nancy? This, this piece of fluff is your protector? You've got to be kidding me".
"Doctor Hillman, I was only-".
Hillman wrapped the cheese wire around the cat's neck, and pulled with the two wooden handles at each end. Nancy Felder screamed as the cat's head came clean off and rolled onto the coffee table.
"Look, look" said Hillman, "Look at him kicking now, front legs and back, "It's no good kicking now, you little bugger, you can't protect her now, you've lost your head". Nancy had fainted and fallen to the floor. Hillman sat her up and patted her brow with one of the table napkins. "Come on now Nancy, wake up, wake up and confess to the Lord just how much of a whore you've been, tell him how much money you made with your arse when you were younger, come on, he knows already, just confess to the Lord how much of a sinful whore you really were, and all will be well". The old woman was barely conscious as Hillman placed the wire around her neck. "No?

You're not going to tell him? Ah well, let's sing a song before you go. What's your favourite"?
He squeezed and squeezed with all his strength. The wire cut into her neck and throat like butter. Blood flowed down all around her shoulders. She made a final gurgling sound, then her head went limp. Only her spinal cord prevented it from falling to the floor. Three minutes later, Doctor John Hillman had his hood up again and was making his way back to his car, the rain pelting down as hard as ever, as he heartily sang; " *ASK THE SAVIOUR TO HELP YOU"*. He sang as he drove away and headed for Morningside. "Oh, I've got to get juice and sweets for Amy and Angela before I get back".

Twenty-one minutes and eighteen seconds after he'd taken the life of Nancy Felder, John Hillman sat on his mother's rug, colouring in pictures with his two little girls, his hands, not even as much as shaking, as he shared the crayons with his children. "*Listen, you ungrateful bastard, I'll get them for fuck sakes, can't you just let me have some time with my daughters first? Do you think I've got nothing better to do than to kill whores for you all day, is that it*"?

CHAPTER SIX.
LONDON ROAD. SHEFFIELD.

Paul Crane sat with Joe Dougan and Amanda Pearce around the table in Steve Temple's study. They had each been summoned personally by Temple. "Here we go again" said Crane, a twenty-eight year old ex-army man, "Earache because you didn't recognise Carla Paganni". He pointed to Amanda.

"Hey Paul" she retaliated, "can you recognise anyone when you haven't even met them before, because that's some trick if you can do that, smart ass".

"Yeah, come on Paul" said Dougan, an Irish mercenary with over a hundred dead men to his name. Dougan, now in his thirties, looked at Crane, "Anyway, we don't know what this is about". Amanda Pearce knew exactly what it was about, but chose not to tell the two men in front of her.

"Where's Henry anyway, why is he not here"? Said Dougan.

"You know why" replied Crane, "it's because Henry is so far up Temple's arse, only his feet stick out, the crawling bastard".

Steve Temple walked into his study. He had in his hand, a small jiffy bag, which he sat on the table. He looked at Amanda. "Go and fetch drinks you, and don't take all day about it".

Amanda knew what they all drank. She also knew which way they all liked their eggs in the morning. Soon they were all seated, and all with a drink. Temple pulled out a compact disc from the bag, and put it into the DVD recorder. "This is not nice, I warn you" said Temple. "If you are going to be sick bitch, then you make sure you make it to the bathroom, or else I'll rub your face in it".
"Where's Henry" said Crane, "Have you not sent for him"?

"Henry's in here". Temple pointed to the DVD. At first there was just haze and snow on the television screen, but then, the unmistakeable face of Henry Felder came into view. Henry's face was twisted and contorted with pain as Paganni's voice came over. As she spoke the camera went down to where Henry's hands should have been, then the camera focussed on his right knee, it was missing, only skin and bone protruding through his trouser leg.

"Ah fuck" said Dougan, "Who the fuck".

"Wait" said Temple. "The horror has not begun yet". They all watched the screen, as Carla drove past, dragging something resembling a bundle of red rags. Temple turned off the recorder. "That was him folks, that was our friend Henry Felder being dragged along the ground at seventy miles per hour. That is what we're up against here. She is no joke people. You underestimate her, and you're dead, you all make sure never to make that mistake. She said that's it. If we leave her alone, there will be no more killing. Now then, what do you think, bearing in mind, what you done to her friends".

"I say leave it be" said Dougan, "At least until all this lot calms down, until *her* guard has dropped".

"Huh, you'll wait a long time for her guard to drop, believe me".
"Well" said Steve Temple to Crane, "I know you and Henry didn't get on that well, but you were partners".
"Yes I know Steve, but all said and done, no-one deserves to die like that, poor bastard".
"What? And those girls deserved to die the way they did, is that what you're saying? Look, I need you to do something Paul".
"What's that"?
"Paganni left instructions where we could find Henry's corpse, would you go and get him for me"?
"Yeah, but there won't be much to get Steve".
"I know, but get him, leave him outside of the mortuary, they'll do the rest, maybe dental records or something".
"It's a fucking shame" said Dougan, "Hell, he's only got his poor mother, old Nancy, this could kill her Steve, he was just saying the other day how frail she was getting, poor old bugger".
"Well, he's gone now boys, there's nothing we can do now".

"She's fast Steve, this Paganni bastard" said Crane.

"Yeah, so it would seem, and getting a bit ruthless in her old age as well. We'll leave it boys just now, if she keeps her word, we'll leave it".
"So Henry dies for nothing then, is that what you're saying" said Crane.
"I said, we'll leave it for now Paul, right"?
Crane sighed, "Right".
"I also said, for now Paul, I didn't say Henry died for nothing, just get his body please, or what's left of it".

FINCHLEY COURT.

Two police cars and an ambulance sat outside Nancy Felder's house. The ambulance's blue light flashing furiously in the darkness. Deborah Knowles and John Crosby stood in the living room of Nancy's house. Crosby stood with his hands folded, shaking his head. "I don't believe it Deborah, I really don't, what on earth could this old woman do to upset anyone, I mean, what sick bastard could find it in themselves to slaughter a pensioner in this fashion"?

Knowles shook her head. "John, you've been in this game long enough to know that there are no limits to what a human being is capable of doing".

"Yeah but Deborah, look, look how she's been killed, her head's hanging off". He pointed to the table where Nancy was slumped, her blood covering most of the white table cloth. "They've even done the same to the poor fucking cat". As they watched the forensics doing their job, the telephone rang in the hallway. "I'll answer that" said Knowles. John Crosby stood shaking his head and cursing with disgust as the medical team put Nancy's body into the bag, and carried her out to the ambulance. He looked to the floor, where the cat's head lay, three feet from its body. "What kind of sick fuck can do something like this"? He asked one of the forensics.

"Beats me," the man answered, shrugging his shoulders.

"Beats you"? Said Crosby, "you couldn't give a fuck could you, you're not one bit interested, that poor old woman, and you shrug your shoulders, beats you? You need to change your job pal" said Crosby, "you'd be better emptying fucking bins, beats you. You bunch of ruthless bastards the lot of you."

The gentleman in question, pulled his mouth mask away from his face, and sighed. "Listen here, super cop, don't you dare criticise me, or any of my team on how we handle our jobs, don't you dare. If you had seen half of the things that we see and have to deal with, well then maybe you could talk, but you haven't. Do you know what it's like to enter a house where the young mother has died with

an overdose, and has lay for over a week before anyone discovered her body, and then to find, that her baby has died of starvation in that time, do you know how that feels? Or to discover a pensioner's body which has lay for even longer than that, and when you come to move the body, you discover that there are rats eating him from the inside. Let me tell you something smart boy, we have to go home to our wives, and try and live a normal life, we have to play games with our children and be happy for them, we have to shut out what we see in the course of a day's work, so don't fucking stand there all high and mighty looking down at the rest of the world. Yes, I'm sorry about that old girl, and yes, my heart bleeds for her, but it's happened, and it's not my job to wonder who or why, that's your fucking job, so instead of moaning at me, why don't you make my job easier by going out there and catching the culprit, and leave us to do our job in here, we'll let you know if we come across anything, that stupid bitch you have with you, did it ever occur to her, that the murderer might just have used that phone, huh? Now, her prints are all over it, makes our job harder see? Now fuck off the pair of you!!"
Crosby held up his hands. "I'm sorry, I'm sorry, it's just this, this sickness that people have, they're inhuman, please accept my apologies, I wasn't thinking".

"Well, you just think the next time, before you start shouting off your mouth, now, if you don't mind, we have work to do".

Deborah Knowles came back into the living room. "Let's go John; we're off to see your girlfriend down at the morgue that was Ashley on the phone. Someone dumped the body of Misses Felder's son on the steps of the morgue, or what was left of his body. Seemingly, he's been dragged naked from the back of a car at considerable speed. She just warned us, if we are squeamish, to be prepared for a horrendous sight. She said there is very little skin left on the body. The forensic man smiled and replaced his mask. This address and phone number were written on a piece of paper and stuck on the bin bags to which he had been placed inside".

"Do you think it's the same murderer Deborah"?

"Well, let's go and see what Ashley says".

LONDON ROAD.

The following morning Steve Temple sat at his breakfast table with his morning paper opened up in front of him. The headline on page two read; 'Mother and Son brutally murdered'. Temple exhaled cigar smoke onto the newspaper. "You little bastard Paganni, you fucking little bastard that you are, you killed his mother as well, little fucking Italian whore that you are, you are one dead bitch, I'll drag *your* fucking body up and down Division street, I swear. You are one dead bitch" he muttered, as he lifted his mobile phone.

MORNINGSIDE.

The sun shone brightly through the kitchen windows of John and Anne Hillman's beautiful mansion. Hillman stood at the large patio window which faced the children's play area. It also faced a thick wooded part of his property, where a sniper could easily lie in wait and pick him off at will. Joseph Dougan was doing just that at this very moment in time. Dougan had received a phone call telling him exactly what had to be done. "As quick as you like" said Temple, "Kill them both, kill their grandchildren as well" he had said. "And get Paganni, alive if you can, dead or alive, just get the bitch. We will wipe the whole lot out, do Hillman's son too, if he's there!!"

God indeed, must have been on Doctor John Hillman's side today, for he lay in his own bed, in his own house in Cromwell Road. His two children as well, lay in their own beds.
Dougan lay perfectly still in the midst of the woods that surrounded Morningside, peering through the telescopic sights of his Barrett M.82, which had earned him over one hundred and fifty thousand pounds to date, from mercenary killings. His, and many other mercenary's favourite sniper rifle.
Anne Hillman walked over to her husband who was standing by the window looking out onto his beautiful property. "It gives you a

sense of freedom, doesn't it Anne"? He said, as he took the mug of tea offered to him.
"It is lovely John, I have to say, we are lucky John, to have all this". Anne had retrieved her own cup, and was now sipping her tea. Hillman didn't even hear the glass of the window break. He only heard the mug in his wife's hand tinkle as it was held up to her mouth. Amy's certificate for being pupil of the year was pinned to the wall, twenty-five feet behind Anne's head. It was now sprayed with blood and flesh. Anne didn't seem to move for a couple of seconds, and then she fell silently to the floor in a crumpled heap.
Hillman saw the horror right before him; it took a few seconds for his brain to take in the information. It soon became clear, as his wife lay on the floor, only shuddering down one side of her body. Her left arm and her left leg shaking furiously, in a final death dance, her brains scattered from where she lay, right up to Amy's award.
"Oh no" John Hillman cried, with his hands right up to his face, "Oh no Anne, please, not you Anne, not you". He looked to the trees outside and spoke to them. "Not her" he said, standing up and pointing to the floor, "Not her, she doesn't know anything, not Anne, she's nice, she's my... she doesn't harm anyone".
The first bullet caught him in the Adam's apple. The second shot caught him on the philtrum, exploding out through the top of his head, both shots being fired in rapid succession.
"And it's goodnight from him", said Joseph Dougan, almost a hundred and fifty metres away, as he began to take his rifle apart.
In the kitchen, the pool of blood in which John and Anne Hillman lay, was growing forever larger, as the toast popped up, semi scorched, just the way the Hillman's liked it.

Tracy, Angela and Sharon had decided to go out for a couple of drinks. As it turned out, it was the best thing that could have happened. While they were out, they met Heather Bradley the hair dresser with a young friend of hers named Rachel White.

They found themselves sitting next to each other in the night club, and before long, they all began talking to each other. They were all getting on so well, until Tracy nearly dropped with fright, as Carla Paganni came in and sat down next to Heather and began talking with her.

"That's her Angela" said Tracy, through the volume of the music that was playing. "That's the girl who put those police officers down at the station".

"Calm down Tracy, I know who she is; she won't be starting anything in here, just stay calm". After a couple of minutes, Carla came over to Tracy, and sat down beside her. "How are you Tracy, I see all your wounds have healed up babe, you're looking well".

Tracy introduced Angela and Sharon to Carla, and from that point on, the rest of the night was a total success. Carla explained why she had set about the two officers and swore that her father-in-law had not ordered any beating to be administered. The longer the night went on, the more they enjoyed themselves, even to the point of being up dancing with each other. The only time in the evening when Tracy thought
there would be trouble, was when two young men approached Rachel, and it was no wonder they had approached her. Heather had dressed her in a pair of denim shorts, which were slightly too small for the girl, making the cheeks of her backside to be half exposed when she stood up to walk. Rachel also wore a top that tied just under the breasts, so her midriff was exposed. Heather had talked her into getting her belly button pierced, so there was a blue mock diamond shining there, adding to the girl's sex appeal.

The two young men had come and sat down while Carla and Heather had been up dancing. When Carla returned to her seat, it was occupied by one of the hopeful youths, who had just looked at Carla when she stood waiting for him to give her her seat back. "What"? Said the youth to Carla, which turned out to be the last word he spoke that evening. Eleven seconds later, he and his friend were carried out unconscious by two of the doormen. "See what you mean Tracy, she's good", said Angela. The two doormen then apologised to Carla for the inconvenience. The rest of the night was really enjoyable, and the first night that Tracy could remember actually laughing and joking, and not having to guard her every word.

After the night club, Sharon invited everyone back to her place, where they all were now, at eleven o clock in the morning, all eating bacon rolls and drinking tea. As Sharon got up to make more tea, she said, "Tracy, John is over at your house, he's got the girls in the car".

By the time Tracy had found her shoes and put them on, John was pulling away. "Shit!" said Tracy, "And my mobile is over the road in my house".
"Use my phone Tracy" said Sharon. "It's alright Sharon; I'll have to be getting back over now anyway, I'll phone him when I get in". She smiled and said "Maybe the girls are going to stay with me again, that would be brilliant, anyway, thank you all for a lovely evening last night, I really enjoyed myself, perhaps we could all do it again soon".

Everybody agreed that that would be a great idea. "I'll see you two later" she said to Angela and Sharon, as she made her way back to her own house, feeling guilty for not being there when the girls came to see her, although she had nothing to feel guilty about.

MORNINGSIDE.

As Doctor John Hillman drove up the gravel drive of his father's house, he felt a sense of uneasiness. "What's wrong daddy" said Amy, "Why aren't you singing songs today"?

"I don't know darlings" he said, "We'll sing soon".

"I'm going to sing for papa John and Nana" the little girl went on.

"What was it"? Hillman thought to himself, what was different today? Then, he knew. His God was not talking to him today, that was it, yes, but something more, something else didn't feel right. As he got out of the car, he said, "Wait in the car girls, just for a minute".

"Are you going to sneak up on Papa John daddy, is that why we've to wait in the car"?

"Yes that's it, that's it girls, now you stay in the car until one of us comes out, ok"?

Hillman found himself praying that the front door would open, and that his mother would come out to greet him, or his father. Neither appeared. He opened the door and nervously called out, "Mother, Dad, Is anyone home"? He waited for an answer. Nothing, only silence. He walked through the main lounge and down the hall towards the kitchen. Then the voice in his head, as he reached the door. "WAIT TILL YOU SEE THIS, LOOK AT THE MESS ON THIS FLOOR, SEE? LOOK AT ALL THIS BLOOD ON THE NICE CLEAN FLOOR, OH LOOK, THERE'S YOUR MAMA LYING WITH HER HEAD ALL MASHED UP, SEE? AND SEE HERE, HERE'S YOUR OLD DAD LYING SHOT UP TOO. LOOK AT THE BULLET HOLES, LOOK? ONE, COUNT THEM, ONE, TWO. THERE'S TWO HOLES IN YOUR FATHER, AND HOW MANY IN YOUR MUMMY'S HEAD?

John Hillman staggered out of the kitchen; he was finding it hard to take a breath. His legs felt weak, cold sweat ran down his back, his hands were shaking. Still the voice in his head ; " LETS GO BACK INTO THE KITCHEN JOHN, LETS TAKE ANOTHER LOOK SHALL WE. WE WON'T GET INTO TROUBLE JOHN, MUM WONT SAY ANYTHING TO US, HOW CAN SHE. TWICE, DADDY'S BEEN SHOT, LOOK, GO ON JOHN, LOOK AT ALL THE BLOOD AGAIN, MUMMY'S BLOOD AND DADDY'S BLOOD MIXED TOGETHER". "SHUT UP!!!SHUT UP"!!! "WAS THAT YOU JOHN? WAS THAT YOU WHO SPILLED ALL MUMMY AND DADDY'S BLOOD ON THE FLOOR, WAS IT"? SHUT UP!! "YOU DON'T KNOW DO YOU? JOHN". "SHUT UP BASTARD SHUT UP!!!

Hillman was frantic, as his mother's voice called to him, "JOHN HILLMAN!!! "YOU JUST GET YOURSELF THROUGH HERE YOUNG MAN, AND GET ALL OF THIS BLOOD CLEANED UP, OR YOU'RE GOING BACK INTO THE DARK CUPBOARD". His mother stood at the door, pieces of flesh and brain tissue clung from the side of her head, then his father's voice. "COME ON SON, HELP YOUR MOTHER, YOU HAVE TO LEARN HOW TO BE A GOOD SON, AND STOP FUCKING THINGS UP". He was hallucinating. " OH WELL, IF YOU'RE NOT GOING TO HELP US, WE'RE JUST GOING TO LIE DOWN AGAIN AND STAY DEAD, YOU'VE HAD ENOUGH CHANCES IN YOUR LIFE, YOU LITTLE SPOILT BASTARD THAT YOU ARE, FUCK YOU, WE'RE STAYING DEAD, WE'RE STAYING DEAD, AND WE'RE NOT GETTING BACK UP EITHER".

When John Hillman turned round again, both of his parents were lying where he found them. "I CANT HELP YOU" he cried, "I WANT TO HELP YOU, HONEST, BUT I CANT, THEY'VE KILLED YOU BOTH, CAN'T YOU GET THAT INTO YOUR HEADS"?

Angela and Amy stood at the entrance of the kitchen, watching their daddy on his knees, crying and praying, and looking at the large pool of blood in which Papa John and Nana lay, very still.

By sheer chance, Carla was coming up the drive in Heather's Mondeo, to see Mister Hillman about what she intended to do next, when the two little girls came out of the house, crying.

"Whatever is wrong girls" she said to the children. Angela sobbed, "Daddy's crying on the floor, and Papa John and Nana are lying in the big blood".

"Oh shit" thought Carla to herself. "Tell you what, I'll phone your mummy on my mobile, and you talk to her, while I go and speak to daddy, ok? Then I'll come back out and take you over to your own house with mummy, ok girls"?

Carla got Tracy on the phone. "Tracy? Problem, I don't know what's happened here" said Carla, "I've got your two little girls here, they're crying. They're saying that their Papa and Nana are lying in blood, and that their daddy is crying on the floor, keep them talking Tracy, until I go and see what the hell has happened. I'll tell John I'm bringing them over to your house, ok? I'll be as quick as I can".
"Carla"?
"Yes"?
"Be careful, I don't think John is quite himself these days".
"I will, see you later". "Right girls, here's mummy on the phone, talk to mummy, I won't be long, now, you don't leave the car angels, do you hear? Stay in the car until I come back out".
As Carla entered the house, she could hear John Hillman junior sobbing somewhere in the distance, he was also talking. "Why? Why have you done this? I was doing everything you asked me to, I always do, so why did you let this happen, especially to her, what has she done wrong? She's not a whore is she"?
"John" said Carla, softly, as she stood at the kitchen doorway.
"Carla" said John, pointing to his dead mother, "She's not a whore is she"?
"No John, not at all".
See? Even Carla says, so fucking why? Huh? What the fuck is it with you, why don't you ever give me a break? Just fucking lay off, will you"?

Carla walked over and looked at Mister and Misses Hillman. After looking at the bodies, she turned and looked at the kitchen windows, and knew exactly what had happened. So, mister Temple had no intentions of stopping the wars. Fair enough she thought, have it your own way Steven, but don't say you weren't warned".

HARRINGTON SQUARE. (TWO DAYS LATER.)

Angela Phorbes pulled up in her Mercedes outside of Sharon's house. She had been in and around the city listening for any stray talk concerning the Hillman murders. Gang warfare was so common now, that the police tended to turn a blind eye on these matters, knowing full well that the gangs would sort it out in their own way, and in their own time. To be caught up in anything like this these days, was just your tough luck, you got yourself into it, you get yourself out of it, it was as simple as that. "Have you seen Carla today Sharon"?

"She's over at Tracy's, she's helping with the kids, hell Angela, those poor children saw their grandparents lying dead in a pool of blood. They also saw their dad going barking mad, they've got him in the hospital just now. He's suffering badly from shock, poor sod, I mean, I know he was a bastard to Tracy, but no-one deserves to see that".

"The thing is Sharon, young John doesn't know that his father was a ruthless gangster, let's face it Sharon, that's exactly what he was. His own wife never knew either. As far as I can make out, John Hillman has been the main supplier of cocaine around here, and in Manchester, down Chesterfield, and all around these parts. Lately though, there have been gangs wanting in on the action, they want a slice of the cake, and who can blame them, but as soon as anyone tries to move in, he sends his faithful Carla in to deal with them, and she usually does, only the gangs are getting bigger and stronger now, it's only a matter of time".

"Now then, it's my guess, that whoever killed the Hillmans, are going to be coming after Carla as well. I don't want her over at Tracy's house, even though she means well. These people are ruthless; they don't give a fuck who else they take down. If they track Carla to Tracy's house, then Tracy and the kids get it too. If those children had been at their grandparent's house the other day, they would be dead. They are playing a psychological game with Carla, they want her to feel isolated, and that's why I think Carla is kind of clinging on to Tracy, I'll have to talk with her. I think, for

Carla's sake, it's time to move away from here. Believe me Sharon; you don't want to be going shopping around Carla these days. For all we know, there could be someone watching Tracy's house right now".

"Angela, you're scaring me".

"Good, because this is serious Sharon, this is no game here that they are playing, this is the real thing, the big picture, these guys want in on the action, they want control of the drugs Sharon, and now that Hillman is down, there is nothing to stop them, they'll just want Carla out of the way for peace of mind, nothing else, she no longer is a danger to them".

Angela picked up Sharon's phone and tapped out Tracy's number. After Tracy had handed the phone to Carla, she and Angela spoke for almost fifteen minutes. It was arranged that Carla would stay with Angela down in London, along with Tracy and the girls. They would move down with Sharon, this very night. Later, Carla would come down with Angela. Neither of the women were to tell anyone anything, not even Heather or young Rachel, no-one must know.
By nine thirty that evening, Tracy had packed, only what they needed. Sharon had done the same. Angela kissed Sharon on the cheek, as she handed her, her house keys. "I'll see you both in the morning, but I'll phone you when Carla and I are setting off. Tell Tracy to drive carefully and tell her not to worry, everything will be fine".

Tracy pulled up in her Volvo and peeped the horn. Sharon kissed Angela once more and then left the house. Angela stood at the window and watched the car disappear around the corner. "We'll be ok down there Tracy" she whispered, though it was more of a prayer than a statement.

Angela phoned Carla. "Get your things Carla, and don't be late".

"I won't" she replied, "I can't afford to be late, they've got a price on my head Angela".

Temple had put the word out among all the other gangs. "Twenty thousand to anyone who gets me".

"Who told you this Carla"?

"A friend, she told me to clear out as soon as possible".

"Carla, just come round now, don't pack anything, just come round right now, we have to move fast, I'm at Sharon's house, now please hurry".

"I'll be right there".

"Oh and Carla"?

"Yes"?

"I've got all the lights off in Sharon's house, so don't think that I'm not here, the door's unlocked, just hurry".

Five minutes after Angela had phoned Carla, a car pulled in to Harrington Square. It went down to the bottom of the street, reversed and turned, and was now parked outside of Tracy's house. Angela felt the reassuring presence of her magnum Colt Python in her hand bag. It was obvious someone had told Steve Temple that Carla had been here. As she looked through the tilted blinds at the stranger in the car, she knew that if Carla had come out of the house right now, she would have been shot. Angela also knew that she would have to work fast. The one big advantage she had going for her, was that none of Temple's men knew what she looked like.

She casually walked out of the house and made her way over towards the car outside of Tracy's house. The car was a black Jaguar of some sort, she wasn't sure of the exact type, and anyway, that was the least of her problems. A man of about twenty-five sat at the driver's wheel. There were no other passengers. As Angela approached, the driver's window rolled down. "Hello stranger" she smiled, "Haven't seen you round here before, are you going to be another customer of mine? I'll have to score you fast before the other girls see you, won't I, what do you say handsome"?

"Not tonight darling" said the young man, sharply, "Maybe some other time".

"Ok" said Angela, "Maybe some other time, oh, could I bother you for a light"?

The young man pushed the automatic cigarette lighter into the dash.

"Are you on business handsome? You're not a policeman are you"?

"Yes" he sighed, "I'm on business, and no, I'm not a policeman". The cigarette lighter clicked, and the young man pulled it out and held it up for her. Angela lit her cigarette. "Now please, could you move on, because I'm waiting for someone".

The security lights were on in Tracy's house. Angela smiled and pointed up. "Does your business live in there"?

"Yes, now please move away or I will call the cops".

Angela had already pulled the gun from her bag, while the lighter had been heating up "right, I'm off then, I don't want any trouble with the police", as she began to walk away, she turned and said, "Just one more question".

"What"?

"Is it Tracy or Carla you're after"?

Suddenly, she had the man's full attention. He put his hand into the inside of his jacket pocket. By the time it reached there, three of his fingers of his left hand had been blown off. "Now now" said Angela, as she walked over to the car again. "Carla or Tracy" she said, as she shot him in the opposite shoulder.
"AAArrgghhh".
"Ssshhh" she said, as the third shot was fired into his right thigh. "Carla or Tracy? The quicker you answer the quicker I'll stop".
The young man panicked, and foolishly attempted to turn the ignition key. "Oh I see" said Angela. "Carla". She put the gun against his head and pulled the trigger for the fourth time. The roof

of the car was pelted with the insides of the man's head, as were both passenger windows and the windscreen, where Winnie the Pooh, and Tigger both held their cheerful smiles as pieces of the man's brain slid down both of their faces perched on the shelf at the back of the car.

Carla came out of the house having watched proceedings from Tracy's bedroom window. "Right, let's go" said Angela, "before they send someone else round here".

"What are we going to do with him"? Said Carla.

"Nothing, it'll give the neighbours something to talk about when daylight comes".

"No" said Carla, "if we don't move that car then Tracy will get roped into it, the police will track her down, and they'll think she had something to do with her in-law's murders as well".

"Fuck!!" Ok Carla, you drive the Jaguar behind me, we'll drop this off before we get onto the M1, right, let's go".

Carla pushed the corpse over onto the floor. She quickly wiped the driver's seat with his jacket. "Fucking blood everywhere Angela, just one shot would have been enough girl, fucking fingers all over the place here" she muttered to herself.

Twenty-five minutes later, Carla was in Angela's Mercedes heading down the M1, and hopefully, to a new start. They would soon find out how much of a grudge Steve Temple held. He had it all to himself now, everything. There was no John Hillman to hamper his plans. No Carla Paganni to wipe out his numbers. The trouble was, was that enough? Could he live with the fact that she was still alive? "We'll just have to wait and see" said Angela, "that's all we can do".

How Steve Temple would react the next day, when he would be informed about his brother being discovered in his Jaguar, shot to ribbons, and abandoned in a ditch, a little outside of Stavely on the A61, would be anyone's guess.

SHEFFIELD GENERAL.

Deborah Knowles and John Crosby sat in a private room given to them by Ellen Shields, the hospital administrator. “Always try and do our best for the police whenever we can” said Ellen to Deborah.

“Thank you” said Crosby, “We’ll be as quick as we can”.

Still looking at Deborah, she said, “There’s no hurry, I’ll send down nurse Bell as soon as I can, she was the one who spoke to the young woman you wish to question”.

“Thank you again” said Crosby to Ellen’s back as she left the room. “I hope they don’t take as long to perform an operation as it did to set us up in here, or we’ll all be in trouble” said Crosby, impatiently.

“Now John, they’re doing their best for us, let’s not knock it ok”? On a small table in front of them was a small portable T.V and a video recorder. Beside these, and neatly placed in order were a stack of video tapes containing all the footage of the hospital’s security for the last three weeks.

“Well” said Crosby, “might as well start scanning these tapes, this could keep us here for the rest of the day”, he sighed.

Deborah shook her head and smiled, as she took out one of the tapes from its box. She pointed to the spine where, quite clearly, in black marker pen, were the details of dates and times. “You really will have to learn John about patience; it is a virtue you know. Now, what was the date that young mister Gibb was brought in”?

Crosby examined his mobile phone for a few seconds and then told Deborah the date. “Do you keep everything on that phone John? Don’t you take the time to write anything down these days”?
“There’s no need to, I can keep all I need on this, and it saves on paper, you know, the environment and everything”.
Still smiling, she said, “Come on, get the tape in, smart ass”.

They watched the tape for Michael Gibb being brought in through the main entrance, and then they watched it again, nothing. Crosby picked up the next tape and looked at the date on the box. "It'll be on this one Deborah, if he was brought in after midnight, it would register as the next day on the camera".

"You don't say" said Deborah. Crosby ignored the sarcasm. Sure enough, ten minutes into the film, the main entrance doors opened and a couple came in together. The young woman had her arm around the man's shoulder helping him up to reception. Just then, a nurse came on the scene and began talking to the couple. Even from this angle they could plainly see blood oozing from the man's mouth onto the polished floor. For just one brief second, the young lady glanced at the security camera. "Pause it there John. There, that's the woman we need to speak to, it's a pity the film is black and white" said Knowles. "Never mind though, maybe nurse Bell can tell us a bit more about her".

"I've seen her before though" said Crosby.

SHEFFIELD PSYCHIATRIC CLINIC.

"He's away, he is" said the tall male nurse as he left the room which was now home to Doctor John Hillman. The tall man continued to talk to his work mate, "It's all been too much for him, finding his parents murdered like that Tom, his mind has decided to fuck off somewhere, take a long vacation, maybe Malibu, maybe South of France, who knows? But it's left no forwarding address, and it sure as hell doesn't know when it's coming back. The shell in there", he pointed with his hooked thumb in the general direction of the room he had just left, "is basically shut down to the rest of the world, he's fucked at this moment in time. The shrink's gonna' take one look at that and tell us to get the funny coat, you wait and see if I'm wrong".

"You don't know that Billy, the guy is in deep shock, fuck, give him a break man".

"Tom, I'm telling you, he's in here until we get pensioned off, you mark my words, hell, five minutes ago, I thought he was talking to me, turns out, he was arguing with God up there, and muttering something about stretching the whore's necks in here, I mean, what the hell has that got to do with shock, was his mother a whore? No. he's fucked Tommy, swearing like that, and then the next thing he's singing "Shall We Gather at the River", so if that don't qualify him for the penthouse suite, then my daddy's a pigmy.

The two men walked down the corridor towards the canteen for their lunch break, each putting forward their point of view as to whether Doctor Hillman would make a full recovery or not. Both were in agreement about one thing, there would be no early release, he would be here for quite some time, and they could only hope that during that time, Doctor Hillman's mind would find it in itself, to drop them a line and let them know he was coming back home completely refreshed. They could still be heard talking as they turned at the bottom of the corridor, more than fifty yards from Hillman's room.

They had only just begun their lunch when the emergency buzzer reverberated around the corridors. The red light flashed furiously above the door of number 22, which happened to be the room where they were keeping John Hillman. Hillman had decided that it was about time that someone took these whores they were sending in to change bed sheets, into hand and show them the error of their ways. "They shouldn't expect to be allowed to come in here, laughing and giggling like the whores that they are, and not get a bloody good seeing to, for no charge, of course. When I get out of here" he said to the young nurse he had gripped by the hair, "and get all that blood cleaned up, you're all really going to get it". Hillman had the unfortunate girl pinned over the bed, his erect penis jammed up the nurse's anus. When Tom and Billy entered the room, Hillman was in full flight, the girl screaming with the horrendous pain, and he, shouting out loud, singing in rhythm to his strokes, "Mine eyes have seen the glory".

SHEFFIELD POLICE STATION.

Knowles and Crosby were looking at the statement nurse Emma Bell had given them at the hospital. Nurse Bell had given them an accurate description of the young woman who had brought in Michael Gibb. In front of them, on the table lay a piece of paper with three names on it. Carla Paganni's name was at the head of the list. "I think it's her Deborah" said Crosby, tapping the pointing finger of his right hand on the paper, "I'm sure of it".
"Well, we'll take them one at a time John, we'll just speak to them in the order they've been written down". Deborah looked at her colleague, "Well we know John, we've seen Carla Paganni driving Mister Hillman senior around on many occasions.
"So"?
"Well, Hillman and his wife were shot dead the other day, now, if that was Carla Paganni at the hospital.."
"What"? Said Crosby.
"Nothing, I eh, I think she's linked to those murders John, I do, it's only a gut feeling, but I think she's part of what 's been going on around here, I can sense it, let's go and speak to her".
"Well, we'd better not keep her too long in the station Deborah".
"Don't worry John; because if I'm right, then she'll be in jail before long, I really do think that she has something to do with this"

THE M. 1.

Carla Paganni and Angela Phorbes were approaching Rugby. "Do you fancy something to eat"? Angela said to her companion.
"Not really, I could use a cup of coffee though" replied Carla. The Mercedes turned off the motorway and headed into the roadside services. "It probably won't taste anything remotely like coffee Carla, but I think I'll join you. We'd better bring them out to the car though; we can't smoke in there". Ten minutes later, both women were carrying two cartons of coffee each and were heading back to the car.
"By the way Angela, thanks".
"For what"? Said Angela.
"For doing this for me, I mean, I know you're doing it for Tracy and the kids, I know that, but for letting me come down here with you, you know"?
"There's no need to thank me Carla. When we all met in that night club back there, well, it kind of felt like I'd known you and Heather all my life, I think it's because I've known girls like you all my life, something along those lines, why I took a shine to you. You have a bad reputation Carla, it wasn't so long ago, I had a bad reputation, along with two female friends of mine, and a male friend".
"Where are they now Angela"? Said Carla, opening the first of her cartons, "If you don't mind me asking, all settled down with families, I expect"?
Angela opened her coffee carton. "No, three of them are dead. My male friend was shot in the head; he got careless and forgot to check behind a door, that was that".
"Poor sod" said Carla, "You can never be too careful, what about your female friends, were they killed at the same time as your male friend"?
"No. I killed them later on that day".
"I see" said Carla, lighting up a cigarette.
"I had to Carla, they were going to kill Tracy".
"Why? What could Tracy have done for them to want to kill her"?
Angela sighed; "She shopped us all to the police".
"You're joking, what, Tracy"?
"Yes Tracy, it wasn't as simple as that though Carla, there was a lot of money at stake.

Whoever could give the police any details about our whereabouts, were offered a lot of money, a lot. We were wanted Carla. At one point, they were going to bring in the armed forces to help catch us; it was starting to get out of hand. That's when we were just going to crash a house and just lie low for a while. We spotted a house, and we went to take it. It all went wrong. Angela lit up her cigarette. "Boy, did it go wrong".
"How come you were never caught, I mean, if you killed two people"?
"Oh, I killed more than two people Carla, believe me".
"But you were never caught, how come"?
"Because, after I'd killed those girlfriends of mine, well, let me put it this way, I died. Tracy and I made a deal. She got the reward money, and I got my freedom. If I remember correctly I think my body is lying somewhere in one of the lakes up near Kendal, or somewhere up there in the Lake District. Angela Phorbes lies dead up there somewhere".
Angela Phorbes"! Said Carla, "You're Angela Phorbes? Fuck!"
"No Carla, I told you, Angela Phorbes lies dead up in the North of England, you have the pleasure of speaking to Angela Clark".
"God, I remember all the fuss they were making, trying to catch you all. They said you were all ruthless killers".
"I suppose we were Carla, but it was never as bad as they said it was, we never killed just for the sake of killing, it was either self-defence or revenge. That guy I killed there back in Sheffield is the first in ten years. I don't feel any worse or any better for doing it, it just had to be done. It was either him or you, either way, one of you were going to die, it might as well be him, anyway, I kind of like you Carla".
"I'm glad" said Carla, smiling, "thanks Angela".
"You're welcome".
"I would do the same for you Angela".
"Would you? Would you really"?
"Yes I would" said Carla.
"Good, because I don't think that Temple will rest until he hears you're dead".
"I know".
"When we get down to London Carla, you should stay out of sight for a while. Get your hair dyed, dyed and cut; you need to make yourself look totally different to how you look now. This Steve

Temple, he could make phone calls to other people to look out for you, it doesn't have to be one of his gang remember. Twenty grand is twenty grand, there'll be a lot of junkies going around who would kill for twenty quid never mind twenty grand. The advantage we have Carla, is that none of Temple's men know what I look like, in fact, they'll think you've taken off yourself, but you're not on your own Carla, you can rest assured on that".
"Thank you Angela".
"It's ok Carla, I've been where you're hanging, and it's not much fun, I know. You need a friend or two in this day and age to get by. The whole country is filled with gang warfare. The government paint the public a very different picture, they tell us that everything is under control. Bull shit, they haven't got a clue what's going on in the country, there are more illegal immigrants on this Island than they could ever hope to know about. People die here every day Carla and no-one ever gets to know about it, because they're turned into ashes, or they're buried away in some woods. It's all about survival kid, and you haven't got to have any remorse, or else you'll be the one who ends up dead, take it from me Carla, you have to be in this game to win, to survive, or don't bother taking part in the game at all. I don't know Carla, how much of a bodyguard or a hitter you've been for John Hillman, but you'll have to get even more ruthless if you are going to stay alive, believe me. The game is going to get tougher now, you'll see, especially if they've got a twenty grand price tag on your head".
"Where am I going to stay Angela, I've got my bank book here and my cards, but hotels these days."
"You won't be staying in any hotel Carla, we want to stay alive. Hotels are too dangerous anyway, lots of people go to sleep for the last time in hotels Carla, no, you'll stay with me, it'll be safer".
"Do you have a gun Carla"?
"Yeah, a magnum three fifty seven Anaconda".
"Wow, where did you get that"?
"I don't know, John Hillman got it for me. I notice that you have one as well Angela, what a mess you made of that guy back in Sheffield".
"Yes well people should be nicer to each other shouldn't they, because you never know when your time is up, so they say"?
"It must have been an experience, running around in a gang like you guys".

"It was Carla, both exciting, and frightening from time to time. You would wonder some days, was this it? Was this the day they would catch up with us, was this the day the police would kick in the door, and have you locked away for the rest of your life, and they could still do it Carla, if you went to them now with information about who I am, you see? Trust Carla".
"Yes, and you can trust me when I say that I feel safer with you, and that, if I can help it, you won't be far from my side, you can trust me when I say that Angela.
Angela threw her cigarette butt out of the window. " Right, homeward bound, we'll be down there in no time Carla, give your mind a rest for a couple of days, not having to look behind your shoulder, of course, you can only have that comfort staying indoors".
"I just wish I could have told Heather though" said Carla, "Let her know that I'm alright".
"I'm going back up there Carla, in a couple of days, I'll let her know, in the mean time you don't even call her on her mobile, clear?"
"Yes"
"Good, because you never know Carla, they could have some-one up there watching her every move, in fact, they probably will".
"I would like to have been at John Hillman's funeral as well Angela, I know I can't go, but the man was good to me you know"?
"Yes I do Carla, but you can't, or it'll be your funeral three days after his".
"That poor woman as well, his wife Anne, she was nice Angela".
"Yeah, but it's like I said Carla, in this day and age, its dog eat dog, ruthless".
"How did you all get together Angela, how did you pick your friends"?
"I didn't, they picked me. I was a police woman; we were answering a domestic disturbance. The two policemen who were with me were both shot dead. I was raped, gang banged in fact, Linda and Amy helped them".
"Oh fuck" said Carla, "And these people became your friends"?
"Strange world Carla, that's all I can say".
"I don't think I want to hear any more Angela".
"Good, because I'm tired of talking about me, tell me about you Carla, how did you get caught up in the drugs world".

“There’s not much to tell Angela, compared to you. I’ve lived a sheltered life, until I met John Hillman”.
“My life was the same Carla, until I met a man called Rodney Miller”.
“Fuck in Hell, I’ve heard that name as well”.
“Yes, you know that name, but very few knew the man, those of us who did, loved him, just ask Tracy. They were very wild days Carla, and half the time I was out of my face with just about any type of narcotic known to man. It’s a miracle I’m still here”.
“I’m glad you are Angela”.

LONDON ROAD SHEFFIELD. 7.15. A.M.

Steve Temple was taking his morning shower. A young blonde haired girl by the name of Amanda Pierce lay in his king sized luxury bed, fast asleep. She had spent the night with her boss; not wishing to lose out on an opportunity which had presented itself after Steve had drank the best part of two bottles of wine. She also knew, and accepted the fact that she meant absolutely nothing to him whatsoever, and that she was there to serve a purpose, and that, only if required. She would cook meals now and again, do a little cleaning in the house perhaps and of course, sexual favours, when required. That was it, that was all she was, and she didn't care, because in return, she got as much cocaine as she wanted, and she got a roof over her head, for no charge, and she didn't have any bills to worry about, so, all in all, she thought, she didn't have a bad deal. She had to bear the brunt of Temple's sharp temper now and again, but, there were more advantages than disadvantages to being his dog's body. She knew women who were married who had worse deals than this.

Temple was humming away to himself and thinking about the revenge he had taken on Carla Paganni. By killing her boss, she had no-one to rely upon, no-one to turn to. She would know to keep her nose out now. Paganni would be warned, "Stay out of trouble or the next time, you die, last warning".

Everything was his now, with Hillman out of the way, there was no-one left to challenge him. He would take over the prostitutes as well, plenty of money to be made there. He had just dried himself, coming out of the shower, when his doorbell rang. He glanced at his watch as he was putting it on. "Who the hell can that be at half past seven?" He was just at the foot of the stairs when it rang again. "I'm coming I'm coming, fuck sakes, where's the fire!!" He opened the door. Officers Feld and Johnstone stood on his top step.

"Mister Temple? Mister Steven Temple"?

"Yes, what's the problem officers"? He knew there had to be one; why else would they be here at this time of day.
"Can we come in sir; we need to have a word with you".
"Sure, come in, I was just about to make coffee, would you like one"?
"Eh, yes please, I'm afraid we have a bit of bad news for you sir".
"What? Is it my mother? Is she alright? What?"
"I think it would be best if you sat down sir".
"Right, that's enough, now I'm demanding to know, now what the fuck is it"?
Officer Feld took a deep breath. "Sir, you have a brother called William"?
"Yeah, Billy, what's he been up to, listen, if you've got him locked up, I'll pay the bail, or the damages, there's no problem, what's he done now"?
Temple got up to retrieve his cigars. He lit one up.
"We em, we found his car just outside of Stavely, a black Jaguar".
"Was he speeding? Is he dead"?
"We don't know if he'd been speeding sir, but, yes, he's dead. The thing is sir, he, em, he was already dead when his car was dumped".
"How do you know that"? Said Temple with a slight tremor in his voice.
"He'd been shot sir, quite a few times. We need you to come in and identify the body, I know it's hard sir, but there's only you or your mother, we thought that you'd be more capable of doing it. Temple sighed, as he went to the cabinet to get himself a whiskey. "I must warn you sir."
"Look, don't fucking warn me, I'm having a fucking drink, my brother's dead, and I'm having a drink, fuck off!"
"I didn't mean that sir, I meant, prepare yourself for a shock sir, your brother's face, you won't be able to, does he have any birth marks".
"Fuck! What's she fucking done!?"
"She sir?"
"I'm sorry officers, I'll tell my mother in my own way".
"Will you be alright sir?"
"Yes, I'll be fine. What time did you find him"?
"It was about two thirty this morning sir. A lorry driver was pulling into Stavely when he noticed the vehicle lying in the ditch, and he alerted us".

"Was there anyone else in the car with him"?
"No there wasn't sir, forensics are examining the car now. I know it's a bad time sir, but, do you know of any enemies he had, any grudges anyone has held on him, anything"?
Temple swallowed the remainder of the whiskey in his glass. "None that I know of, Billy kept his comings and goings to himself, he was a bit of a loner always has been".
"Do you know where he worked"?
Temple smiled. "Billy hasn't had a job in over eight years, he didn't sign on or anything, but he had the best of everything".
"That's what we were thinking sir, having a car like that, they don't grow on trees".
"I'd like to be left alone now" said Temple, placing his empty whiskey glass onto the coffee table.
"Well" said Feld, "I'm sorry to be the one to bring you this bad news sir, but, if you could come over sometime today and identify your brother, I know it's difficult. You can be assured sir, we will be doing everything in our power to bring to justice your brother's killer or killers, but if you can think of anything at all, please do not hesitate to contact us".
"If I think of anything, I will, now please, could you let me have some privacy".
"Good day to you sir" the two officers said as they stepped out of Temple's house, down the steps and into the car park. "Take it easy sir" one of the officers said, as Temple went back into his house. Amanda Pierce was now sitting at the coffee table with her arms folded onto it, and her head bowed.
"I'm sorry Mister Temple, about Billy".
"You heard"?
"Yes sir, I awoke when I heard the door being knocked. Was it that woman, do you think sir"?
Temple sighed as he poured himself another whiskey, and Amanda vodka and coke. "Yes Amanda, it was that woman alright. Do you know Amanda, I kind of admire her. No matter how much I hit her, she always comes back and hits me harder. I better think here, before I jump into any kind of retaliation. Either that, or find my mother somewhere else to live first".

SHEFFIELD PSYCHIATRIC HOSPITAL.

Doctor John Hillman had now been officially classified as insane. His belongings were packed in a suitcase. His wallet, along with his credit cards were all put into a plastic bag. They lay neatly on the table beside the case. John Hillman himself sat on his flat bed in the corner of his room with his head in his hands. In his pocket was the key for the cell door, the key he had secretly obtained whilst the two male nurses were battling with him, disturbing his fun with the "whore" nurse. It had only been by chance that it was the key for this door, but in Hillman's mind, it was God giving him a helping hand. He was now going to be moved to a more secure unit.

"I told you" said Billy, to his work colleague. "I told you he was away with it, I'll be glad Tom, when they get that fuck out of here, he gives me the willies, so he does. He's seen three shrinks now, and they've all certified him insane, now, they can't all be wrong, hell, he was raping poor Maria there, singing religious songs at the top of his voice".

"Yeah, I know Billy; I got that one wrong pal".

"Sure did" said Billy Swan, draining the last of his orange juice from the carton. "I tell you Tom that could have been me or you". Tom and Billy looked through the reinforced glass of the room of John Hillman's cell. Swan put the key into the door and turned the handle. "You gonna' be nice and quiet Mister Hillman"? Hillman nodded, but did not even look up from the position he was in. "That's good then" said Swan, "Because I don't want to be slapping the funny coat onto you again, d'you hear"? Again, Hillman nodded. "Good, now I've come to tell you something doctor. You know you're being moved, right"? Another nod. "Yeah well, there's been a mix up; they're not coming for you today. Instead, they're coming for you tomorrow morning, you got that"?
"Yes" said Hillman. In his mind, God had intervened and given him an opportunity to escape.

"Right, so you've got one more night in here, you make sure, it's a quiet one, ok? Don't you be causing any of the night staff any bother now? We'll be finished in a few minutes doctor, I'd like to wish you all the very best of luck ok? You'll be away by the time we get in tomorrow morning. We wish you a full recovery Doctor, now, you take care".
Hillman looked up and said "Yes gentlemen, take care, you do that will you"?
"Now then Doctor Hillman, there are two police officers wanting to have a word with you, Tom and I are going to be sitting right beside you, ok? So no funny business".
Hillman looked up at the giant nurse. "What do they want to talk to me about"?
"I don't know" said Swan, but you make sure you behave yourself, that's all, do you hear me"?
Another nod.
"Right, we'll be back in a few moments with the officers. The two male nurses made their way round the corridors to the visitor's waiting room, where Deborah Knowles and John Crosby sat patiently, awaiting permission to speak with Doctor Hillman.
Swan opened the door of the waiting room. "Right you are officers, oh shit!"
"What"? Said Crosby.
"She's a woman" said Swan.
"I sincerely hope so" said Deborah Knowles, "there's a problem with that"?
"You bet your life there's a problem, nobody told us there'd be a woman here".
Tom Mitchel spoke up and looked at Deborah. "You see mam he em, Doctor Hillman, he raped a nurse the other day, buggered her, to be precise, he's been officially declared insane".
"You bet" said Swan. "Now, we may have to put a security jacket on him, for your safety miss. We presumed it would be two male officers interviewing him, I mean, we'll be there, right beside him, but, for your own safety, we'll have to put on a funny coat".
"Safety" repeated Swan. "Well gentlemen, whatever you have to do, just do it, because we really need to speak with him, it's of the utmost importance".
"Right you are mam, we'll just go and get him fitted up".

"Do you usually let your patients roam around the wards, free to rape nurses? Mister Mitchel."
"He wasn't roaming around miss, the nurse was in his cell changing bed covers, and by the way, up until that point, there was no reason whatsoever to suspect that Hillman was dangerous, in fact, up until the incident with the nurse, he had only just sat around singing his religious songs and praying and shit".
Deborah Knowles spun round and looked at John Crosby. Both of them smiled at each other, remembering the young prostitute who was found dead with the religious verse written on the wall. "Thank you nurse" said Deborah Knowles, you have no idea how much you have helped us, you get his funny coat on boys, thank you".
The door of John Hillman's room rattled once again with the sound of a key in the lock. "Mister Hillman" said Swan, "I'm afraid we'll have to put on the jacket again, before you can speak to the police officers, can't be helped".
"Why? I'm not dangerous any more" protested Hillman.
"No. You're not dangerous any more, unless of course, that person happens to have a pair of tits and a pussy, that is, so come on, don't make us have to be all tough with you now, this being your last night here and all".
"Can I have it taken off again after the police have been"?
"If you behave yourself you can. You make sure you behave yourself, now, there's a nice lady coming to talk with you, if you conduct your behaviour like I know you can, then the coat will come off, deal"?
"Deal" said Hillman.
"Ok then, just don't you be calling her a whore or anything, 'cos she sure as hell 'ain't no whore, got it"?
"Got it Billy".
"Ok then" said Swan, tightening up the straps of the straight jacket. Let them in Tom, you come and sit over here doctor, in the middle of these three chairs here". Mitchel had sat three chairs down one side of the table, and two chairs on the other side. The suitcase containing Doctor Hillman's belongings now sat on the floor. The plastic pouch which contained Hillman's wallet and credit cards still sat neatly in the centre of the table.

John Crosby entered the room first, followed by Tom Mitchel, and finally Deborah Knowles. Hillman did not take his gaze off the

small spider which was making its way up the far wall of the cell. "Mister Hillman" said Billy Swan, "These two people are police officers, they would like to ask you a few questions, are you alright with that"?
"Certainly Mister Swan" replied Hillman, still staring at the spider.
Deborah Knowles looked first to Crosby, and then to Swan and Mitchel. "Do you think you could leave us alone with him, he's got his strait-jacket on, he can't do any damage, it's just to make him feel a bit more at ease".
"I don't know about that" said Swan "He's a bit risky".
"It'll be alright" said Mitchel, "and anyway, like she says, what harm can he do, plus, we'll be right outside the door".
"Well, I suppose, but only for a few minutes, alright? I don't want anything else going wrong".
"We promise" said Knowles, we'll just talk to him for five minutes, ok"?
Swan and Mitchel left the room. Still, Hillman's gaze was on the spider. "Mister Hillman" said Knowles. When you entered your father's house, is it true you found them lying in a pool of blood, your mother and father, is that true"?
"Yes" said Hillman, sighing, I must have said that now about fifty times, what's your point, because if you think for one minute that I killed my own parents then you have another thought coming".
"No, Doctor Hillman" said Crosby, "We definitely don't think that, that's not why she's asking you that question".

"Now, try and think Doctor Hillman" said Knowles, "Were there any tramps or whores in your father's house, when you discovered the bodies? We all know John, that they are disgusting people, these whores, and they must be punished, going around there, flashing their bits to everybody who'll look at them. God is watching them, ready to punish, now, Doctor Hillman, were there any tramp bitches in your father's house that day, tell us, and we'll hunt them down and punish them for you".

"You'll punish them for me? Miss Knowles, "not for God? I must say, I am a bit disappointed with the angle of your questioning. Your job is to find the killers of my parents. You obviously have no idea where to start looking, and so, well, let's blame their son, that'll do, as long as we get someone to pay the penalty, everybody will be

happy, am I right Miss Knowles, I'll bet I'm not a million miles from the truth, and anyway, why would there be whores in my father's house"?
"Why indeed" said Knowles. There was silence for a few moments, Hillman once more fixing his gaze on the spider. Suddenly Knowles said, "Do you know a Miss Carla Paganni, Mister Hillman"?
"Yes, she works for my father, well, she did".
"When was the last time you spoke to her, can you remember"? Hillman looked up at Knowles, who was now standing with her back to him.
"I, em, I, no, no, I can't remember, it may have been the day before my parents were killed, I can't be sure".
"Didn't she arrive the day your parents were murdered"?
Crosby looked at Knowles and winked, and then said to Hillman, "We just have one more question sir, before we leave you in peace. Do you remember a patient of yours, an elderly patient called Nancy Felder, do you remember her"?
Hillman thought for a moment. "I have so many elderly patients; it's hard to keep track of them all, why, has something happened to her"?
"No" replied Knowles, "She was asking for you, when we told her that you'd been struck off the list, and that they had declared you a threat to society, and that you are now, a nothing, a vegetable, going to be in some institute for the rest of your life, and that it's a good job your parents are already dead, you sick fuck, because you drove them into the deepest shame for bringing you into this world. She seemed to think very highly of you, God knows why".
"That's right" said Hillman, staring right into the eyes of Deborah Knowles, "God does know why, and I would advise you young lady, not to take the Lord's name in vain, it can be very unhealthy for you".

"Yes" said Knowles, especially if Doctor Hillman is prowling the streets it can, good day, ex doctor. Wherever they are taking you, we'll be back to talk to you, don't worry about that".

"Ok then, I won't, and oh, Miss Knowles"? Knowles turned and looked at Hillman, who was now smiling broadly, "Tell Nancy I was asking for her will you"?

Crosby tapped the door twice. Billy Swan opened the door and said, "Everything alright"?
"Yes, could we have a word with you Mister Swan"?
"Yeah, just let me take off his strait-jacket".
"Do you think that's a good idea Mister Swan"?
"He'll be alright, there'll be nobody else going in there tonight, he only seems to be dangerous around females. Three minutes later, both Swan and Mitchel stood in the waiting room looking down at the floor, both of them with their arms folded.
"I'm telling you both now for your own sakes" said Knowles, be very careful around that man, both of you. I don't know what those shrinks were thinking about, but I can tell you now, that that man in there is as sane as you and me, he is evil, I'll give them that, but he's sane, be very careful gentlemen".
As Deborah Knowles and John Crosby made their way across the car park, Crosby squinted at Knowles through the drizzle. "Do you think he killed Nancy Felder Deborah"?
"Without a shadow of a doubt he killed her, and Rose the prostitute, he didn't kill Henry Felder though, I think that that was just a coincidence. The sooner we speak to Carla Paganni the better".
The drizzle sheeted down even harder as the two officers got into their car. "Fucking weather" said Crosby, as he took off his coat inside the car. "There's something about Hillman, the father I mean" said Knowles. "That night Carla discovered Susie Monk's body, remember"?
"How could I forget" said Crosby, rubbing his fingers through his wet hair. "Well remember when we were questioning Carla about the girls"?
"Yes"?
"Hillman came storming in with that bloody Q.C., and started shouting the odds. Don't you think it's a bit strange that Carla, as far as I can recall, didn't make any calls, am I right"?

"I don't remember her making any calls, what's your point"?

"My point, Mister Crosby is this. If Carla didn't make any phone calls from the time she was at Susie's flat, until she got to the police station, then how did John Hillman know she was there, and not only know, but got himself a Q.C. at that time of the morning"?

"Deborah, I have to hand it to you, that's why, I suppose I'll always be a junior rank to you, I bloody missed that, fuck, I never gave it a thought".
"Tell you the truth John; it only just came to me the other night as I was lying in my bath tub. Another thing John, if he knew she was there then he probably knew why she was there. He also said that he understood there was only one girl murdered. He didn't know about the other until he got to the station. Remember what Ashley thought? She said it was a different killer who had done Rose than the ones who'd done Susie."
"Coincidence John, that young Hillman has killed a girl next door to where Susie was being murdered. I think Carla already knew what she'd found that night? Remember John, you and I were as sick as dogs that night. Carla never turned a hair, oh she cried a bit, but that was it, don't you find that a bit strange John"?
"Yes I do, and I can clearly see that I am going to be no good whatsoever to you in this case".
Knowles smiled. "Don't beat yourself up John, like I say, I only thought about this the other night, now, come on round to my place, I'll cook you a nice dinner, that's if Ashley and you have nothing planned for tonight do you"?
"No nothing planned, she says she's busy all week".
"I'll bet she is, and she's going to get a lot busier, make no mistake about that".
"What's that supposed to mean Deborah"?
"It's not supposed to mean anything, stop being so bloody defensive will you, goodness sakes man, calm yourself down will you".
"No, but when you say, I'll bet she is, you think she'll be seeing other men don't you"?
Deborah smiled, shaking her head. "Light me a cigarette up will you, you silly bugger".

HEATHER'S SALON.

Joe Dougan and Paul Crane entered the salon where Heather and her girls were all busy at work, cutting, perming and rinsing, even sweeping, as was the job given to young Rachel White. "Good morning ladies" said Crane, "We would like to speak to a certain Heather Bradley, which one of you lovely ladies goes by that name"?

At first, all three of Heather's hair stylists did not answer. Even young Rachel only looked up from her sweeping, but said nothing, simply because the two men didn't look very pleasant.

One of Heather's oldest and best customers quite innocently said, "Here you are young man, she's hardly ever in the shop these days, you've actually caught her working".

"Thank you madam" said Dougan, not even looking at the woman who had spoken to him. "Is there somewhere we can talk" said Crane.

"In here" said Heather, "Won't be long Misses Mcfall, I'll just be a few minutes". "Rachel, you make Misses Mcfall a cup of tea babes will you"?

The two men walked into the room at the back of the shop behind Heather. Dougan, being the last one in, closed the door behind him. Paul Crane spoke, even before Heather got a chance to.

"Where is she"?

"Where is who"? Said Heather, "Who are you talking about"?

Crane said, "If you answer me like that again, I'll kick you in the teeth, and then I'll drag that little sweeper in here, and rape her in front of you, now, where is she"?

Heather looked Crane in the eye. "I don't know, honestly, I don't know. She came in the day after John Hillman was killed, and I haven't seen her since, I swear, that's the truth. She said something about taking a holiday for a couple of weeks because she had no employer now, and that she was going to get her head together, try and work out what she was going to do next. She asked me to lend her some money until she was back on her feet".

“What did you say”? Said Crane, “Did you give her the money”?

“I said of course I would lend her some money, but she never came back to me, as I say, that was the day after John Hillman was killed”.
“You’re certain you haven’t seen her since then”?
“I swear to you, I haven’t, she hasn’t even phoned me or text me or anything”.
“Right” said Dougan, handing Heather a plain white card with three different mobile phone numbers on it. “If you hear from her, or if you hear of her whereabouts, you phone one of these numbers, and you let us know, alright”?
“Sure I will, yes”.
“Listen” said Crane, almost whispering, “If we find out that she’s been here and you haven’t got in touch with us, well, let me put it this way, those girls through there will be out of a job, do you catch my drift Heather? You, my dear lady will have nowhere to live either”. “Come to think of it miss” said Dougan, you might not need anywhere to live. Get one thing clear in your mind miss Bradley, we don’t make threats, only promises”.

John Hillman sat at his table staring up at the ceiling. "She knows Lord, that bastard police woman, she knows". He was talking in his head. "As sure as a cat's a hairy beast, she knows. Now, where's all this protection I was promised? Huh? Where"? The word "where" was spoken out loud. "You promised me full protection from all of those interfering bastards, now where is it. Do you know, I've a good mind to just walk right out of here, and shut you right out of my life, let you do your own dirty work, how would you like that, huh? Letting them come in here and talk to me like that, don't you think you've put me through enough? I've lost my wife , my kids, my mother and my lying bastard father over you, is there anything else left you can take from me? Oh yes, yes there is, isn't there, because as long as I am certified insane, then there is no way I can inherit any of the things which have been bequeathed to me in my mother and father's will is there?"

"It's a wonder you didn't spill the beans on me three years ago when I sorted out that little fifteen year old whore, remember? When she came to my surgery wanting to be put on the pill, saying she loved her boyfriend? Boyfriend my arse Lord, coming in there with her little skirt all the way up her arse. They never found her body did they? And they never will, provided you keep your fucking mouth shut Lord. Now you'd better start helping me out here, or you're on your own, this is your last warning Lord, "Cut me some fucking slack, will you"?

At 11.15. pm the guard who sat at the table, and who monitored the internal locking systems, and for the outside mechanisms, went for the first of his tea breaks on his night shift. Tonight was no exception. Hillman listened intently as the guard's squeaky boots could be heard heading down the corridor to the tea rooms more than sixty metres away. He slipped the key into the lock and turned it. The lock sprung open echoing and reverberating down the corridor. After he'd left the cell, he locked the door behind him. Under the covers of the bed he had placed pillows and cushions, rolling them up to make it look like there was a body in the bed. It would buy

him some valuable time when the guard came round at around 2 am to check the cells.
He walked quietly and confidently down the corridor towards the main exit. What was the bloody point Lord, of having all these security cameras around the place, when the two men supposed to be monitoring them spent most of their time playing cards and pool, or darts in another room, "I mean what's the bloody point"?
Hillman pressed the first security button on the panel on the wall, which opened the first door, the unbreakable glass door. It opened, buzzing quietly as the glass panel slid to one side. He then pressed another button on another panel. This one would allow the huge oak doors to open up and let Doctor John Hillman obtain his freedom, and allow him to carry on his good work. There was a loud buzz, and a couple of lights flashed red and green on the panel, and then the locks could be heard clicking. It sounded to Hillman like there were huge bolts being slid open, and then, at last the doors began to rumble as they slid slowly open. To Hillman, it felt like an eternity for the doors to open wide enough for him to step outside. Once outside, he pressed yet another button on yet another panel, and watched as the huge doors began to close behind him. He drew a deep breath of the cold fresh night air and said. "Now then Lord, where to"?

HENRY STREET. ISLE OF DOGS. (LONDON.)

Tracy, Sharon, Angela and Carla, all sat in Angela's living room.
"Being down here Carla will give you some breathing space" Angela said. She went through to her kitchen, and returned with four mugs of coffee. "Stay here as long as you like Carla; I know you have no employer now".
"I have no anything Angela, the clothes I sit in, maybe a couple of changes that's it".
"Don't worry about that Carla, we'll soon sort that out" said Angela. "I'm just glad we got you down here in one piece".
"I have to thank you, because if I'd stayed up there, I would have been dead within the week, I just hope they don't go after Heather".
"That's exactly why Carla, I got you down here without Heather knowing where you are. I know she's your friend, but believe me, it's better that she really doesn't know where you are. Do you have her number? I'll call her tomorrow to see if anyone has approached her".
"I'd better keep these kids indoors Angela" said Tracy, "Just in case the authorities have reported them missing".
"No, I'll tell you what Tracy, you phone the school, tell them you are taking them on a holiday, just as long as they know they're safe, that'll keep them from doing anything stupid like putting the girl's faces on TV. You can take the kids out down here Tracy, nobody will be looking for you down here, unless, of course your ex-husband comes down, and I don't think there's much chance of that happening any time soon. Plenty shops for you down here Tracy, I know how much you love to shop, this is London Trace, you're back in London, you'll be able to shop until you drop down here girl" Angela laughed.
All the women laughed, but it was mostly from relief, rather than humour.

HARRINGTON POLICE STATION. .SHEFFIELD. 8.40. AM.

Deborah Knowles and John Crosby were sifting through the results of some of the forensic evidence which had been brought in. "That's it confirmed then" said Crosby. "D.N.A. had been taken from Nancy Felder's house. It had also been taken from John Hillman's mansion. Young Hillman's D.N.A. had been taken from that house. "Yip, there's your match John, it's him. Well, at least we've got him safely tucked away from harm's way, he can't kill any more pensioners, and he's going nowhere real soon. Now, all we need to do is go and speak to Miss Carla Paganni and see what she's been up to in the last few weeks. I'll get a couple of cups of coffee John, you go and phone the funny farm and see where they intend to take Mister Hillman".
Deborah was writing down the number for Heather's hair salon when Crosby returned. "Where are they taking him John"?
"Nowhere"
"Nowhere? They're keeping him there"?
"Nope".
"Explain"?
"He's, wait for it, he's missing".
"What"?
"He's missing".
"You're joking, right? You're not joking, are you John".
"No mam, someone went to give him his breakfast this morning, he wasn't there. His cell door was locked, there was security on the main exit all night, and he's gone. Cameras and everything, he's gone".
"I don't believe this" said Knowles. This is just fucking marvellous isn't it, just when we think it's all piecing together nicely, I don't think I can stand any more of this. Come on John, let's go and see who was on duty last night, let's see how this bastard has done this".

Billy Swan and Tom Mitchel stood in the office of the psychiatric clinic, along with Deborah Knowles and John Crosby. Sarah Barkley who was the main administrator, sat on her chair by her desk. She had only two years to go until she retired from her thirty-two years here at the centre. In all of her time here, she had run the

place as smooth as velvet. Never once had there been as much as a blemish on her record. Today, she was a very angry woman. A very thin woman, with thinning grey hair, tied back in a bun. Bright red lipstick with a deathly pale complexion, Crosby thought she looked like a very poor drag queen.
"Sit down everyone" she sighed. "Now, where are the security staff who were on duty last night, or should I say, were supposed to be on duty".
"If I could just say something Miss Barkley" said John Crosby, "All my colleague and I want to do is look at the footage of the security cameras last night, just to see how Hillman got out, and when he got out, this man is very dangerous and he needs to be put back under lock and key as soon as possible, we owe that to the public. I appreciate that you may have disciplinary action you may wish to take, but this is of no importance to us, every second that this man is loose is crucial to the safety of the public".
Barkley looked over the top of her glasses and said, "Mister"?
"Crosby, Detective Inspector Crosby".
"Well Mister Crosby" said Barkley, "If you'd had the decency to let me finish, I was just going to ask one of these two gentlemen to go and fetch you the tapes".
Almost one hour later, Knowles and Crosby emerged from the psychiatric clinic; none the wiser as to how Hillman had made his escape. It turned out, that the night shift were prone to forgetting to switch on the night cameras, especially when they had a pool competition going on which could last most of their shift. "Hmph" said Crosby, as he and Deborah made their way back to the car park.
"They even have a league table between the eight of them, can you believe that? Meanwhile, Britain's worst serial killer since Harold Shipman, just up's and away at will, he gets in and out of there with more ease than us".
"This will go nationwide John" said Knowles, "His face will be on every T.V. screen up and down the country. When Hillman sees that, it may trigger him off into killing again, or, he could go into hiding, that, believe it or not, would be the worst scenario".
"Yeah, and those incompetent bastards in there had him under lock and key".
As they approached the car, Crosby said, "What now?
Where do we go from here"?

“From here John, we go and get some coffee, after that, we go and speak to Heather Bradley, see if she knows where Carla Paganni is, and then, we go over to John Hillman senior’s house and have ourselves a good look around, I mean a bloody good look around because I think that there’s a connection between all of these murders that have been taking place. There’s more than Doctor John Hillman at work here, and I want to find out what the hell the connection is...and we will”.

LONDON ROAD. SHEFFIELD.

Steve Temple sat on his reclining chair in his study, sipping at his whiskey. Across the room sat Joseph Dougan and Paul Crane. "Did you talk with Miss Bradley" said Temple, not looking up from his glass.
Crane spoke. "Yes we did Steve".
"And"?
"She doesn't know where Paganni has gone. She said that Paganni had asked her for a loan of some money so that she could take a break or something. Bradley had told her that she would lend her the money, but she hasn't returned. Miss Bradley went on to say that she hasn't even bothered to text her or anything, no phone calls, nothing. When she tries to phone Paganni, her phone is always switched off".

Temple looked at the two men. "Do you think that Miss Bradley is telling the truth"?

Both Dougan and Crane answered, almost in unison. "Yes she is. We told her what would happen if she was lying".

Temple got up from his chair, and walked, slightly sluggishly over to his drinks cabinet. "Do you know where I was today? I had to go and identify my young brother's body, that's where I was".
Dougan looked at Crane. Temple poured himself another generous glass of whiskey. "Could hardly do it boys" he sighed, and then repeated, "Could hardly do it. What a fucking mess boys, what a fucking, shot half of his face off, fingers, bits off his hands, half his fucking head off, shotgun I would say, or a cannon, something, what a fucking mess, that was my kid brother, fuck, never, never, I've never seen anything like that in my life, then I had to, guess, guess what I had to do next, I had to go and inform my old mother, I had to lie to her about, what a fucking mess". Temple slumped back down onto his chair. He picked up one of his cigars from the jar on the table. He meant to speak but it came out as a whisper. "Help yourselves boys". He lit up his cigar and looked down to the floor. "That was my kid brother. Mother, she was, oh fuck, Jesus Lord". Crane thought that his employer was going to break down.

To try and save him the indignity, Crane said, “If, or when we find her, I’ll kill her boss, I promise you”.
“Kill her? Kill her for what”?
“You know, for killing your kid brother Steve, that’s for what”.
“Really? Well, let’s just recap here for a minute, shall we? And you, Mister fucking Irish marksman fucking mercenary, what did you do to her friends, look at the mess you left her friends in, you and your fucking dead beat friends”!
“Now just a minute here Steve, you were the one who told us to kill that whore friend of hers, you said it was revenge for that young boy who was thrown off the ledge in those flats over at Oakwood”.
“Yes, kill her, shoot her in the fucking head, at least make it sudden, and just one, not two of them. One of those girls was raped repeatedly and buggered, you screwed her hands to the table, you sick fucks, and if that’s not bad enough, you whip every bit of skin off the poor girl’s fucking body, I mean, you’re hardly in any position to talk about revenge now are you, and I’ll tell you something else Mister Dougan, she won’t rest until she’s got you, until she’s got every single one of you who were there, and believe me, she will, huh, shoot her? I think you’d better Joseph, because if she sees you first, then you won’t get the chance. Fuck! Sticking drawing pins into that other girl’s body in the shape of a cross, what the fuck is wrong with you, what the fuck was that all about”?
Dougan raised his hand up in protest.” I’m telling you Mister Temple, for the last time, that was not us, now I’m not telling you again, who fucking knows who that was, but it was not us.
Now you fucking tell him Paul, and get it into his head once and for all”.
“He’s right Steve that was not us, we knew nothing about it”.
Joseph Dougan turned and walked to the door. When he got there, he said, “I’m sorry about your brother, you know where I’ll be if you need me”.
As Dougan opened the door to leave, Temple said, “Joseph”.
Dougan stopped and looked back.
“I’m sorry”.
“Sure” said Dougan, as he left and closed the door behind him. There was silence in the room for a few moments until Temple said to Crane, “Did you play any part in that”?
Crane nodded his head. “Well, I’m telling you Paul, for your own sakes, watch out, now that Hillman’s dead, she could become even

more dangerous, we've taken away the source of her income. Before, she had no choice, running around for him, doing her little errands. Now, she can stay in hiding for as long as she wants, pop up her pretty little head whenever she wants to pop one or more of us off, and then duck back into hiding. Do you know what I think Paul? I think she got a list of names off James Fisher before she shot him, that's what I think. She's got a list Paul, and all of our names are on it. If we don't kill her, well, it's only a matter of time, watch your back Paul, whatever you do, don't drop your guard, because if you do, you will never know that you did".

Knowles and Crosby had been in the mansion for almost an hour. Knowles was searching the study, Crosby, all the upstairs rooms in the house. The only place left to look now was the safety box in the corner of Hillman's study. She phoned the company whose name was on the safe and told them who she was, and that it was of the utmost importance that she gained access to it. To be fair to the company, they refused to tell her the combination until they had proof. She told them who to speak to and gave them the number, telling them to call her back on her mobile phone once they had confirmation as to who she was.
She was standing on the top step smoking a cigarette when Crosby came outside. "Nothing" he said, "Except this". He handed her a piece of paper with a list of names on it. "I haven't read them all" he said, I don't even know what the list is. It may well be a list of guests for a function, something like that, who knows".
Deborah glanced at it and was just about to hand it back to John when a name caught her eye. "Look at this" she said, "this looks interesting".
"What's that"?
"Look" she said, pointing half way down one of the columns. "Nancy Felder, and look, it's got a cross beside her name. There are no crosses beside any of the other names. Look beside her name as well, her son Henry Felder. There's no cross beside his name and yet he died the same day as his mother. Now then John, you and I both know that Doctor Hillman killed Nancy Felder, but who killed Henry, not Hillman, I'm guessing. Coincidence? Do you think, that they died on the same day? It's just the same as the prostitutes, both killed on the same night, but by two different killers. Why would Hillman have a list with both of those names on it, and how many more names on here were at risk"?
"Are", corrected Crosby.
"What"? Said Deborah.
"Are, how many more of those names *are* at risk, he's escaped remember".
"Keep a hold of this John, this could end up being crucial in our bid to finding Hillman again".
"Yes, or Paganni" said Crosby.

"You're getting better all the time John" smiled Knowles, "You really are".
"Better, but nowhere good enough mam. I honestly think that Hillman is far more dangerous than he's been credited, and I also think he's nowhere near finished his killing spree. You saw the writing on that bedroom wall mam, the twenty-third psalm and all that. You also heard his personal threat to you when he told you to be careful not to take the Lord's name in vain…I think he thinks he's killing for God".
"In which case John, his work is never-ending. I think we'd better warn all prostitutes to be on their guard, and not just round this area".

HENRY STREET. ISLE OF DOGS. LONDON.

Angela had punched in Heather's number. Carla sat beside Angela at her kitchen table. Heather told Angela everything that Dougan and Crane had said to her. "They're blaming Carla for the death of Temple's brother. I'm sorry to say this Angela, but tell Carla, never to return to Sheffield whatever she does. If she does come back up here, she's dead, there is no question about that. Temple's numbers are increasing too, as he takes over from Hillman. He's got pushers up here by the score, it's just not safe for her to be here tell her. If they even think I've spoken to Carla, they'll burn my shop down, with me in it most likely. Maybe some time in the future I'll come down there and visit her, but not just now, definitely not just now. I've got those two thug's numbers Angela, if that's any use to you".

"Could be Heather. I might just give them a call, and have a chat with them, give them something to think about. Oh, how is young Rachel doing, is she alright"?
"Yes, fine, good little worker she is".
"Ok Heather, take care" said Angela, "get in touch with me if you need any help, don't hesitate".
"I won't" Said Heather, as she switched off her phone and turned to speak to Paul Crane who had threatened to cut her throat if she let them know what was going on. "They're in London, now, can I please get on with my job"?
"What's the address"?
"I don't know the number, but its Henry Street, Isle of Dogs".
"Who's she staying with"?
"I don't know, I really don't know, she just said she was alright".
"If you hear anything else from her, then you let her know I'm on to her, you tell her that if she calls back".
Crane took note of Angela's number, punching it into his own phone.
Angela told Carla everything Heather had said. Carla sighed. "It's a shame I got caught up with all this. You know Angela, all I ever wanted was an average life, a good little job, a car, some money in the bank, you know? But now look what's happened, I'm down here sheltering with a friend, from people who are trying to kill me, this is

Britain Angela, this is not America, I didn't think these things happened here in England".
"I've got news for you Carla" said Angela. "Britain changed a long time ago, and it didn't change overnight. There's all kinds of things happened to this country over the years, but the poison that runs through its veins now, has set right in, and there's no antidote, there's no cure. Drugs, violence, prostitution, computer fraud, pornography, these are the things that feed this country now; this is the sludge that flows through the veins of Britain now. It's no good feeling sorry for yourself Carla, or anybody else for that matter, we are here to live out our lives,
live your life out as best you can, have as much happiness in your life as possible, because one day, somebody calls time, and that's it, no more, gone, and by the way Carla, you didn't think these kind of things happened in Britain? You threw a man from the top floor of a block of flats, you little bitch, don't give me that shit".

Angela got up and poured water into the kettle. She sat down again, this time right beside Carla. She took hold of Carla's left hand and said, "I've not known you for long Carla, but in the time I have known you, I've grown to like you. For as long as you are here, I want you to know, that you are more than welcome here. Stop thinking about John Hillman now, he's dead, he's out of your life, but because of the life you had up there, working for him, these people are trying to kill you. No matter how much you liked it up there, you can't go back. Down here though, you're safe from them, they can't get to you down here, and anyway, you're not on your own any more, they'll have two of us to face if they did come looking. You'll be fine here Carla. Now then, Tracy and Sharon are off to the city with the kids. They'll be away for at least three hours; would you like to take our coffees through to the bedroom"? Carla nodded. Just as Angela was stirring the coffee cups, her phone rang. She picked it up. "Hello"?
"Hello? Could I speak to Carla please? Tell her it's Steve".
"I'm afraid you have the wrong number, there's no-one here with that name".

"I don't have the wrong number and I'm certainly not afraid, but if you don't put Carla on, or if you switch off your phone, then you should be afraid. I know that you live in Henry Street Isle Of Dogs,

now don't you make me come down there and get her. Put her on, I won't ask you again".
"Ok, I'll put her on, but let me make this clear to you, any threats you make to her, you make to me, you're messing with the big boys down here Mister Temple, and don't you ever threaten me again, because we know where your mother lives, and you, for that matter. This is London, Mister Temple, the games they play down here have very different rules to the games you play, now here's Carla, be nice".

The call came back for Deborah Knowles. The company had given her the security combination for the safe. As she turned the dial round to the last digit, she heard it click, and the small metal door opened up. “Now then John, let’s see what Mister Hillman senior has been keeping secret from everyone.”

Inside the safe, were sheets of paper. A bundle of about fifty sheets Deborah guessed. There were also four neat bundles of fifty pound notes, each bundle about an inch thick, and a cassette tape for a camcorder. She held it up to John. “Would you like to do the honours it may be porn you know, could be home-made porn, we may find people on there who we already know of”.

“Yeah, and it could be boring holiday footage, which, knowing my luck, it will be”. Crosby disappeared into the lounge to look for a camcorder. Deborah Knowles began to look through the sheets of paper. Most of them were from the bank, some from insurance companies. Mister and Misses Hillman’s birth certificates, also wedding bands, and then. “What’s this Mister Hillman”? In her hand she held a piece of paper with four names written upon it. 1. James Fisher. 2. Henry Felder. 3 Joseph Dougan. 4.Paul Crane. “John! John could you come in here for a minute please”.

John Crosby would have dearly loved to have been able to go back through and speak with Deborah, instead, he lay now on the floor of the lounge with his throat cut from ear to ear. Lying face down, his clothes had been split from the nape of his neck, down to his rectum. The Stanley knife had then been drawn right down the length of his body, right through the flesh and the muscle, right down to the spine. The man had practically been filletcd.

“John, you’re not watching that porn in secret are you, I’m going to tell Ashley what you’ve been up to”. She walked through to the study, looking at her list of names. She was now less than four feet from her colleague’s body. “John, do you know what I think”? She was standing in something wet. And then she saw what lay at her feet. After two seconds, her breathing became tight and short, It was only because of the clothes she knew it was John Crosby. The blood spill was so immense that he was otherwise unrecognisable. "Oh shit. Oh no. God John, how could, oh fuck. Jesus Lord no, oh fuck John, look at the, oh Christ no please John"! With shaking hands, she pulled out her gun, and made her way down the passage towards the kitchen. On the floor of the kitchen were two chalk shaped drawings where Mister and Misses Hillman had lay. On the kitchen table was a note.

The note read; to Deborah Knowles,

WE'RE GOING TO THE MANSION ON THE HAPPY DAY EXPRESS,

THE LETTERS ON THE ENGINE ARE J.E.S.U.S. THE GUARD SHOUTS OUT FOR HEAVEN, WE GLADLY ANSWER, YES!!!!!!! WE'RE GOING TO THE MANSION ON THE HAPPY DAY EXPRESS.

Deborah struggled to make it outside in time before emptying her stomach onto the steps of John Hillman's house. She called in for immediate assistance, and armed police officers. It was safer for her to stay outside just now, much safer. She found herself shaking uncontrollably, she felt numb, cold and numb. John Crosby, her favourite by far, of all her colleagues had been taken from right underneath her nose.

HENRY STREET. ISLE OF DOGS. LONDON.

"Pack some things Carla, we have to move fast" Angela said, as she opened a holdall bag.
"Why"? Said Carla, "Everything's alright, he just said so".
Angela stopped in her tracks. "Do you really think so Carla? Why do you think he said that? I'll tell you. He said that Carla, to make you feel exactly like you do right now, so that he hasn't panicked you, don't you get it? So that you'll stay right here Carla, and so that you're easy to find, Easy to kill Carla!! Now get some clothes and hurry, I'll leave a note for Tracy and Sharon, tell them to stay at Sharon's sister's house, until we get back. Bring your gun Carla, and any other weapons you may have".
"Where are we going"?
"We're going back up to Sheffield to put an end to all of this. He's not going to forgive you for killing his brother, and even if I told him it was me who killed him, he wouldn't believe me. He's gunning for you Carla, and that's the end of it". Angela scribbled a note for Tracy and Sharon and placed it upon the coffee table. "Now then Carla, let's be going doll. Once we're out of London I'll feel a bit better. He may have people watching this house already, I don't think so, but you never know we'll just have to take that chance".
"What are we going to tell him" said Carla, pulling up the zipper of her black leather bomber jacket.
"Tell him"? Said Angela, "We're not going to tell him anything, we're going to kill him. First we take his tough guys out, that should be easy enough, they don't know what I look like. Then we take him".
"It's a good job we hadn't taken any cocaine before he phoned us" said Carla.
"I know, we probably would have invited them all down for the weekend".
The two young women laughed as they left the house, albeit, a rather nervous laugh. "Are we not taking your car Angela"?
"Nope, we're taking a taxi to the station and then we're taking the train. If they are watching us Carla, we can dodge about from train to bus to taxi to train. There's less chance of them trailing us this way, and anyway, if I want to take a car up there, we'll just steal one".

“Have you done that before”?
“Don’t be fucking stupid Carla, does a dog lick its balls”?
“Everything seems easy to you Angela”.
“Listen Carla, can you kill someone without thinking about it”?
“Yes”.
“Good” said Angela, “because that’s going to come in quite handy”.
“I know *you* can Angela, I saw you”.
“You bet” said Angela. “He’s wanting you dead Carla, not just for revenge either. Now that Hillman has been eliminated, he wants everything and everyone connected to him out of the way. He’s preparing to take over, before one of the other gangs beats him to it. Your boss was making a hell of a lot more money than you thought Carla. No wonder he was able to buy you things like that fancy car you ran around in. Did you fuck with him”?
The abruptness of the question seemed to take Carla by surprise.
“Well, did you”?
“Sometimes”.
“Nothing to be ashamed of Carla, self-preservation is a necessity in life”.

Deborah Knowles waited outside while the police gunmen made their search of the house. The chief of police sat in her car beside her. "Can you remember Deborah, what happened? Was there a noise, a struggle, was-".

"Do you honestly think if I heard a suspicious noise or a struggle that I wouldn't have had my gun out, do you?

"No, I'll tell you what happened alright. They had that sick fuck Hillman in a mental institute under lock and key where he could harm no-one, but those incompetent fucking bastards in there just let him march right out of there again, while the security cameras were switched off, and while the security staff played fucking pool, and now my good friend and colleague lies in there practically halved in two, that's what happened. I mean what the hell are they doing in that institute, are they merely cagophilists"?

Chief of police, sixty-one year old Terrance Davis, blew out of his mouth, as if he were exhaling smoke. "I know it must be hard Deborah, I know, but you have to -".

"Hard"? said Knowles, "hard? You bet your life its hard Terry when that sick fuck was already locked up. We were more than half way to solving all these murders round here, now? Now we're going to have to watch as other people die. This, this lunatic, is now going to have himself a field day, he could have killed me as well in there, he could have killed me, and I wouldn't have heard him coming. He's playing a game now, he spared me just so I could see how good he is, and you've got fifteen men in there with guns, all chasing their fucking shadows because he's not there, he's long gone. He's probably out there among those trees and bushes, out there pissing himself laughing at us all making perfect fools of ourselves, hard? No offence Terry but you haven't got a clue, none of you, just what you're dealing with here, and he is only one. There are dozens of killers all around here involved in gang warfare. Gangs, drugs and prostitution. Oh it's hard alright Terry".

Deborah got out of her car and stood on the loose gravel car park. A cold wind blew from the North West onto her, but for now, it felt soothing on her burning face. She felt a lump in her throat as an ambulance went past her, and up towards the huge house, to collect one of the nicest people she had ever met in her life. She thought she'd done well hiding her jealousy from him when he had made the date with Ashley. It didn't matter now; no-one was getting him.

One by one, the police marksmen came down the steps in their navy blue bullet proof uniforms, complete with helmets and visors. A few came out from the bushes of the grounds surrounding the house. None of them had fired a single shot. "Of course not", she thought to herself," he's long gone, hell, he's had enough time now, he could be anywhere, bloody miles from here, probably is".

Davis got out of the car. "Deborah"? She turned to look at him. "I've been thinking".

"Don't tell me, you think I've been working too hard lately so why don't I take a couple of weeks off, is that it? Is that what you've been thinking"?
"No, I think you should take a couple of months off, that's what I've been thinking, maybe even longer, because if you don't, I think you're going to have a nervous breakdown, and then we'll lose you permanently, and I don't want that to happen". As Davis went on about all the reasons why she should take a break, the two ambulance paramedics came out of the house carrying the body bag which contained the remains of her trusted colleague and friend John Crosby.

"I'm sorry John" she whispered, "I'm so sorry".

Davis's voice cut through her thoughts. "I want you to go home Deborah, and think hard about what I've said, you're going to end up killing yourself young lady, and then you won't be able to solve anything, take a break, recharge you batteries".

"Sir" she said, in a soft whisper. Now the wind was cutting into her. "If I take a break now, I know I'll never recover, never. Everyone knows their own limitations, now if I keep busy, and stay on the job, this job, then I know that gradually but surely, I will recharge my batteries, give me someone else to work with, and I'll be fine, I promise, but, if you force me to take time off, I'll sink, I just know I will, I'll sink into a deep depression that I'm not sure I could resurface from. I'm asking you as a friend Terry, please, let me be, let me carry on with this case".

The ambulance drove slowly past Deborah Knowles and chief of police Terrance Davis. She looked first at the ambulance, and then to her superior. "I owe it to him" she said. Terrance sighed, and looked down to his feet. "So be it Deborah, as you wish".

Three hours later, after all the forensics had finished and all the necessary photographs had been taken and questions had been asked, there remained in the car park, only Deborah's car. In the back seat, was John's overcoat, still damp from the soaking they got the other night? She looked from her car to the house, thirty yards away. Such a beautiful house that was, up until two weeks ago, just that, somebody's dream. Now, on the floor of that beautiful house, there were chalked out silhouettes of three bodies. For such a young house there was already a sinister feel to it, almost like it was haunted. She had to admit, she did not expect young Hillman to come back here of course, but John Hillman would know we were thinking that, the element of surprise. "He got us there Mister Crosby, he certainly did".

The last two policemen came out of the house and made their way over to Deborah's car. "Excuse us `mam, but we've been instructed to stay here over night and guard the place. We were just going down to pick up our car at the bottom of the drive, and then we're going to get ourselves something to eat, we were just wondering if you wanted anything"?

No thank you lads, but I'll stay here until you get back, I may go back in to take another look around".

"Well, be careful mam you-".

"Why? There's no-one in there. I think fifteen armed policemen would have found him if he was still there".

"Yes mam, but would you like one of us to stay with you, keep you company".
"No, no you carry on with what you're doing, I'll be fine".
"Mam, with all due respect, I'm afraid I'm going to insist that one of us stays with you, it'll make us feel better".
"Ok then officer" said Knowles, smiling, "If you feel so strongly about it, then by all means".
P.C . Johnston said he would stay with Knowles. His colleague P.C. Feld, began the long walk down the twisting drive to get to the patrol car and then on to get the fish and chips for his friend and himself.
Back in Deborah's car, she said, "Do you smoke P.C. Johnston"?
"When I'm not on duty mam".
"Here" she said, "don't be silly, have one now, I think you deserve it".
"I'm sorry to hear about your partner Miss" he said, as he lit up the cigarette.
"Yes, I'm going to miss him a lot".
"Was he married mam"?
"No, no he wasn't. This, what happened today, was the very reason he told me, why he would never get married. He said he wouldn't want any wife or children to live with the heartache of something like this. That was typical of the man officer, always thinking about other people's feelings. How long have you been in the force officer Johnston"?
"Five years this Christmas mam".
"Five years? I bet it feels like fifty"?
"Not really, but then, I haven't had any real bad things to deal with yet miss, well, until I saw Mister Crosby today".
"You'll see a lot more of that before you're off this earth I can tell you. You wouldn't believe some of the sights I have seen. It makes you wonder sometimes how people can do these things to each other, it beggars belief".
"It's beyond me mam".
"Yes, and it's beyond me as well constable".
Deborah decided she would not go back in the house today, after all. She would go home and put her feet up, catch up with some sleep, if at all that was possible. "Tell you what" she said to Officer Johnston," how's about I drive you to the bottom of the drive, see where your pal has got to with your chips".

“Thank you mam I don’t know where he’s got to. he’s been gone now for over half an hour, the chip shop’s only a few hundred yards away, he’ll be chatting to Veronica who works in there, he’s fancied her for six months now, but he’s frightened to ask her out”.
Johnston began to laugh, thinking about his colleague’s shyness.
“What’s so funny Johnston? Lots of men are shy to talk to women at first, you shouldn’t laugh”.
“Mam, she’s, she’s a scrubber. Emily, who works there as well, said that everybody but the tide has taken her out”. Johnston could not control his laughter and blasted out a hearty burst, much to the amusement of Deborah.
“I see” she said, as she continued driving, smiling at the thought of these two colleagues having a joke at each other’s expense.
“I know a girl like that as well” said Deborah, “These scrubbers, they don’t just work in chip shops Johnston, take it from me”.
When they reached the bottom of the drive, they could see the patrol car was still there. They could also see that officer Feld had fallen asleep. Johnston immediately defended his colleague. “Mam, I hope you don’t think that we spend our shifts sleeping, it’s just that we were due to finish at two o clock this afternoon, but with all that’s been going on today, we were asked to stay on. He told me the other day mam that he hasn’t been sleeping well lately”.
“Well, you go and wake him up”. Deborah was smiling. “We’ll say no more to anyone else about this; I know what it’s like to be over worked”.
Johnston got out of the car and walked up to the patrol car. He opened the door and shook Feld by the shoulder. “Come on Joe, don’t do this in front of royalty, fuck sakes man”. It wasn’t until he shook him again, that he noticed something on the floor, a pool of blood. He lifted up Joe’s head, and saw the knife sticking out of his throat. “Oh no” said Johnston, as he made his way back over to Deborah, who was scrutinising a piece of paper again on her lap.
“Mam”?
“Yes”?
“He’s dead”.
“What”?
“He’s dead mam, he’s got a knife sticking out of his throat”.
“Oh fuck” said Knowles. “Call up for assistance Johnston. I don’t believe this day, I really don’t. This bastard is just killing for fun, he’s taking the piss”.

Officer Johnston had called for assistance. Deborah was looking at officer Feld. "It's not a knife Johnston, not an ordinary knife anyway; it's a scalpel, a surgeon's knife. The bastard was still here. How could he have stayed around here and not be seen? Hell, there were five or six armed officers in these woods, how the hell did he manage to evade them". Officer Johnston was shaking slightly, and looking nervously around the wooded area. Darkness was falling, fast.

"Don't worry Johnston, he's gone this time".

Fifteen minutes later, yet again, the grounds and the house of John Hillman were being searched thoroughly. Officer Johnston had been sent home, and told to remain there until further notice. The man was heartbroken that his friend and colleague had been taken so brutally. Deborah Knowles, knew how he felt and was feeling sorry for him. Once again she stood talking with the chief of police.

"He may be declared criminally insane, but he's one clever bastard. The newspapers are going to have a field day with this. He must have been around when the marksmen were looking for him, he must have been".

"Of course he was" said Knowles, lighting up yet another cigarette.

"Where though" said Davis. "There were policemen everywhere".

"Think about it Terry, there's only one place he could have hidden, one place where they would never dream of looking".

Terrance Davis looked at Deborah, and then slowly followed her head as she turned to look at the corpse.

"Of course" he smiled. "The bloody police car, the bloody car, the cheeky bastard".

"Yip, he just got himself all curled up on the floor in the back of the car, and waited. Van loads of marksmen went past him, no more than four feet from him. It was just a bonus for Hillman that officer Feld came to the car by himself. It might have been a different outcome had Johnston came down here with him".

"Yes" said Davis, "It could, we could have been looking at two corpses in there right now".

"He'll lie low now" said Knowles, "He's made his point".

"Which is"?

"He can kill, when and where he pleases".

LONDON ROAD. SHEFFIELD.

Steve Temple stood at his living room window, wearing his black suit and white shirt and black tie. One hand was in his trouser pocket, the other held a glass of whiskey. It was the day of his brother's funeral. His mother, Sarah sat on the sofa with two of her sisters, talking about how good Billy had been, and how he would have done anything for anybody, a good boy through and through. Temple stood looking out at nothing in particular; he was trying to make a decision in his mind. Should he let Paganni live, and therefore take over the whole city without any interference from anyone, or should he have her killed and be done with it. He looked round slowly at his mother and his aunts. If he put the word out to kill her, and then somehow, something went wrong, then he knew he would be burying his mother soon as well. "That's the way the little Italian bastard worked". He rubbed his chin as though he needed to shave, then he looked over to Joseph Dougan, nodding his head for to follow him into the kitchen.

"Go down Joe, after the funeral go down. Stay down there until you get her. You might have to survey the place out for a couple of days, until you find out who that is, that she's living with.

You want her out then"?

"No, I want to put a do on for her and make her my wife, of course I want her out!! You see that old woman in there Joe? She's all I've got left in the world. You fuck this up, and that little bastard will find her, and she'll drag her body along that fucking airfield just the same as she did to Harry Felder, now, I couldn't live with myself Joe, if that were to happen. So you get down there, and you do her, nice and clean, no fancy stuff. A couple of bullets in the head, or slit her throat, deep, whatever, just make sure she hasn't got a pulse when you leave, got it"?

"No problem".

"Hey! don't say no problem, don't ever say that! That is one clever little fucking I-tie, just fucking do it Joseph".

"Boss, have I ever let you down before, ever"?

"No you haven't pal, no you...but there's so much at stake this time Joe".

"Boss, don't worry".

Angela Phorbes sat in the taxi with Carla Paganni, fifty yards down the road from Steve Temple's house. "You go to the hotel Carla, I'll take a good look at this Steve Temple and his hit men" she whispered to her friend. Just before she got out of the taxi, she gave Carla some money. "Now then Carla who's his main men".
"A certain Mister Joseph Dougan, an Irish mercenary, about thirty-eight thirty-nine, and a guy called Paul Crane, a well-built bouncer come body builder type of guy, almost skin head, good looking, but a bit of a bastard. It's him I think who gave all the orders, you know, that night with poor Susie. I'm certain it was him who used the electrical cable to whip off Susie's skin".
"Will they both be here at this funeral"?
"I would say, Temple probably has them taking a cord. If they're there, they'll probably be in the second or third car".
"Right, I'll see you in an hour or so back at the hotel, see you later".
Angela got out of the taxi, and walked very slowly along the pavement on the opposite side from Steve Temple's drive. There were about twenty people mostly from the immediate surrounding houses standing in attendance, opposite the entrance to Temple's house. She hadn't stood for long when the hearse came out of the drive, followed by the limousine with Steve Temple and four old ladies, who wore black lace veils over their heads. Then another two limousines. Angela got a good look at both of the men Carla had described. From her policing days, Angela had learned how to take in the description of a face and memorize details of that face that would make it easy to identify at a later date. Dougan was easy, with his long prominent nose and narrow untrustworthy eyes. Crane, with his shaved head now, and square thick set chin, complete with designer stubble. "Carla was right though, he is indeed, a very attractive man".
As the cars all left for the church, Angela began walking in the direction of the city centre. Across the road, there was a woman who she had failed to notice. *She* had been watching Angela watching the men. If she had got there three minutes earlier, Deborah Knowles would have seen Carla Paganni in the taxi.

MORNINGSIDE.

Three armed police officers guarded the house that the locals were now calling, 'The House of Death'.

John Hillman sat with his radio on watching the policemen coming and going in and out of his father's house.

He was, in fact, almost fifteen feet under the ground, in a safe house. One that his father had built by different builders who had built his house, and of course, there was a safe house in there as well. Now that both of his parents were dead, he was the only person who knew of this safe house's existence.

Outside, above his head, there were tiny lights staggered all over the wooded area. The policemen who had all seen them, failed to notice that one of them was not a light, but a camera, which was attached to a telescopic tube, that could be raised or submerged into the ground. In this safe house which measured thirty feet by twenty, there was a toilet, a small cooker, a fridge, a freezer, all fully stocked. There was a T.V, and a microwave oven, all mod cons.

He could live here indefinitely.

He spun the camera back round to the house and watched a policeman sitting on the top step, lighting up a cigarette, and enjoying a cup of tea. "I'll tell you what Lord, I've pissed those guys off now, really, I mean, I don't usually kill men as you well know, but all said and done Lord, that's still my father 's house, and it should be mine, and they're all just wandering in and out of it, like it's a bastard motel Lord, and I'm just not having it any more. What? Listen, I don't give a fuck what you think, it's my lying bastard father's house, and I'll decide who comes and goes in it thank you very much! What? Bring that police lady down here and violently bugger her?

Well, I could try Lord, if it be your will, I'll fucking do it, you know I will. She looks a sweet bit of pussy right enough.

I suppose I could trap her in the safe house, inside the house, and I could torture her for being such a whore, kidding everybody on that she's a police lady. Its sound proof in there as well Lord, nobody would be able to hear her scream as I buggered her savagely, I suppose I could do it Lord".

The schizophrenic disorder that Hillman suffered from was worsening by the day. He was in total confusion to everything and

everyone around him. The only person in the world communicating with him, was his god. All of his concentrations were placed purely on the orders given to him by his master, the voice. god.
He sat now looking through the camera at the house that should have been his home, rubbing his tongue over one of the occlusal cavities the hospital dentist had worked upon. The handy-work of the bastard whore who'd been his wife. As he looked he mumbled; "Fucking skipping rope bastard".

HARRINGTON POLICE STATION.
SHEFFIELD.

Deborah Knowles sat with Terrance Davis, each drinking a cup of tea, Deborah with a cigarette, much to the annoyance of Mister Davis. He got up from the table where they were seated and opened a window. "Will you be alright Deborah, to continue I mean"?
"Yes, I'll be fine, I told you".
"Good because I've arranged for another detective to join you in your hunt for your killer".
"Killers" said Knowles. "There is more than one person committing these murders".
"Well, whatever Deborah, I have to get back to London I have an appointment with the prime minister this afternoon".
"When do I get to meet my new partner, and what's his name"?
"Her name, and before you say anything, she's smart, she's proved her salt on many an occasion, so please, no complaints, we've got to get this case sewn up as soon as possible".
"I'm not complaining, is she pretty"?
"Very, but don't worry, she's blonde, but she's not blonde, if you know what I mean, she won't have any blonde moments, I can assure you".
"What's her name; it's not Snow white is it"?
"Her name Deborah, is Karen Jones, she's coming over this morning from Manchester". Davis looked at his watch. "She should be here by now actually. Right, I have to go, good luck Deborah, and remember, if at any time you feel it's getting too much, you just take that break, and I mean it Deborah, I don't want to come back up here from London and find you lying on one of Ashley's slabs down there". He pointed in the general direction of the mortuary. "Right, I'll see you Deborah, and be careful, whatever you do".
"I will" she replied, as Davis left the room. She went over to the window, and watched as the rain hammered down upon it. It was raining so hard that the water began to roll down the glass in waves, driven on by an unrelenting wind. In the quiet of the room she whispered. "You rest in peace John Crosby, I'll get that bastard if it's the last thing I ever do". Tears rolled down her face. Suddenly she was brought out of her little moment, with two loud knocks on

the door. “Come in.” shouted Deborah, wiping her face with her handkerchief.
“Hi, I’m Karen Jones”.
“Terrance was right, she is very pretty”. The young woman stood about five feet nine, shoulder length blonde hair, an immaculate figure, which could be noticed even though she was wearing a trouser suit. Her makeup was perfect. Beautiful green eyes, and immaculate teeth. Deborah poured her new partner a cup of tea and explained everything that had happened in the case, including the loss of John Crosby.
One hour later Deborah Knowles and Karen Jones were heading down to the mortuary. “If you don’t mind Karen, would you wait in the car while I go in here, it’s nothing personal, it’s just that my ex - partner was going out with a woman who works here, she might be a little emotional when she sees me”.
“Not at all, I’ll just wait in here until you get back, I understand, and that’s really nice of you to do that for her, you know, save her from any embarrassment”.
“Thank you Karen”.
When Deborah entered the mortuary she was surprised to see Ashley Barnes going about her business with her usual professionalism.
“Ashley”.
“Deborah, it’s nice to see you again”.
“It’s nice to see you Ashley, are you coping alright”?
“With what”? asked a bemused Ashley.
“Well with, you know, with what’s happened to John and everything, you two were going out together, and-”.
“Deborah, let me put your mind at rest. John and I were going out, yes, but I go out with lots of men, John wasn’t, we weren’t bloody Romeo and Juliet you know. We would meet for a night of sex now and again, that was it, there was nothing serious. I’m really sorry for what’s happened and everything, but I’m afraid I didn’t have any feelings like that. John and I were never an item Deborah, but he was a lovely man, If I was ever going to settle down then it would be with a man like him”.
“You missed your chance there kid” said Deborah, “men like John Crosby don’t come along with every bus I can assure you”.
“Oh” said Ashley. “Are you here for John’s things”?
“Well, I wasn’t, but now that I’m here, I can take them, has no-one been here yet”?

"No, I'll just be a minute Deborah".
Ashley disappeared through a set of double swing doors. She returned less than thirty seconds later with a polythene bag. Straight away Deborah saw the tape that John had had in his possession on the day of his murder. "Oh thank you" said Deborah. Ashley had missed the sarcasm.
She said goodbye to Ashley and returned to the car with the polythene bag. "Everything alright Deborah"? said Karen, as she got back into the car.
"Yes Karen, everything's fine, I needn't have worried about Ashley's emotions, the girl fucks with anyone it would seem. Oh, me and John weren't bloody Romeo and Juliet you know, I go out with lots of men, me and John only met to have sex, there was nothing serious, we weren't an item, Christ's sakes, the girl's a tramp, a bloody nymphomaniac if you ask me, she'd fuck a leper".
"Did this John seem happy enough with the arrangement Deborah"?
"Yeah, well, yes he seemed happy enough, but bloody hell,"
"There you are then, she must have made the situation clear to him at the start, and he's obviously accepted it".
"What a bloody way to go on though Karen, mind you, If I were a man, I'd go along with anything she said, if it meant I could get a fuck at her".
"Is she that pretty then"?
"Huh, she's that pretty Karen, and then some, I'll bet that's broke a few hearts in her time, and rules, you'll meet her soon Karen, because at the rate that people are killing each other around here, we'll be due to go back there in less than forty-eight hours".
"Where are we going now Deborah"?
"We, my new friend and colleague, are off to my house to watch a film, a rather nasty film I'd imagine. I think this tape contains footage of the prostitute being murdered, the one I told you about. If I'm right Karen, then what's on this tape is what started all these tit for tat killings around here. John and I had just discovered this tape on the day that he was murdered.
He was far too good for that little tramp anyway. "Oh I go out with lots of men. What is it Karen, with these beautiful young women, they're not content having a lovely body, they have to bed as many men as they possibly can.
Much too good for her, little bitch, cock teasing little scrubber"!

“It’s none of my business Deborah, but did you have a crush on John”?
Deborah smiled at Karen. “Is it that obvious Karen”?
“Just a bit, I take it you had plans of your own for you and him”?
A tear rolled down Deborah’s face. “I think I loved him Karen, I just never got round to telling him how I felt about him, I think I was frightened of the rejection you know, and then, that would be the end of our working relationship as well, there was so much at stake, I was trying to play it safe you know? Just a little at a time, now, it’s too late. I was doing fine until he met Ashley, look-at-my-legs Barnes”. Deborah sighed. “I’m being unfair to the girl Karen, it was jealousy, she’s a very beautiful young woman is what she is, and if I’m honest, I don’t blame her one bit for her life style. Wait ‘til you see her Karen, she’ll even have you drooling at the mouth, you think I’m kidding, she’s a hotty”.
Fifteen minutes later the two detectives were in Deborah’s living room sipping coffee. You see Karen, this tape, if I am correct, contains all the evidence we need. There’s a few guys going down here for a long time. There’s this drugs ring you see, and the main man, as far as I can tell was a certain Mister John Hillman”.
“What, the lunatic”?
“No not him, but his father, anyway he’s dead now, and his wife. But I think that all the killings around here, started off as a result of what we’ll see happening to this girl on this tape. Now, if I’m right, then it would seem that he ran, or was part of running the local prostitutes as well, hence, this revenge thing they’ve all got going on. Now then Karen, there’s a little madam that we need to have a talk with, named Carla Paganni, she’s a little demon, you know, martial arts and all that kind of stuff. Well, I think it’s been her who’s been doing all the executions on behalf of John Hillman senior. This tape may enlighten us a bit more, as I say; if it’s the tape I think it is”.
Deborah connected her camera to the television, then rewound the tape to the beginning. At first there was only snow on the screen, but then it flickered into life. “Here we are Karen. Bingo! That’s Susie Monk’s flat, you know the prostitute. Deborah cursed as she saw the men appearing with masks on their faces. “Oh look” she said, “there’s that poor little girl, just a slight little thing wasn’t she? They watched in horror, as the men began to torture the innocent young girl. Her hands being drilled to the table.

"Oh my Jesus" said Karen Jones, as they watched the girl being whipped with the heavy duty electrical cable. They watched as the girl on the screen was buggered and beaten beyond recognition.
"Fucking bastards Karen, I can't believe they would do that to anyone. That poor little girl, she had nothing to do with anything that was going on, the poor little bugger, what a mess. How can men do that to a little girl like that Jesus, it beggars belief it really does".
"No wonder Deborah, no wonder you want them so badly. It will be my pleasure to help you in any way I can to find these bastards. These demons need to be punished Deborah, really punished, severely".
At the end of the horror the beasts had passed on their threat to Carla Paganni, and then just left the camera still recording the last moments of Susie Monk's life. The girl looked to be unconscious, but it was hard to tell. Her skin hung off her body like crimson paper strips. There was no part of her upper body that had any unbroken skin. As Deborah and Karen watched the girl's life ebb away, they could see fresh rivulets of blood bursting out from various parts of her body. Bubbles of blood poured out from her feet where the bullets had gone straight through. Her hands lay helplessly by her sides, oozing blood onto the already bright red carpet.
"Never in my life Deborah, have I seen horror on this scale, never".
"When I saw that Karen on the night, I emptied my guts. I had just been in the flat next door, looking at the result of another sick bastard's work. At least he was merciful, he done it quickly. Do you know Karen what's made this execution so painful for me? It's the way those bastards were clowning around, as these things were happening to that girl. What's happening to Britain Karen, what's happening to people that they can inflict such brutal atrocities onto their fellow human beings? Kill the girl for revenge for the life of someone else, fair enough, but like this? Do all this to a defenceless girl. This country has problems Karen, this country has big problems, and they're only going to get worse. If you have any faith in the Lord, then you hang on to it, because you're going to need it girl. You can clearly see what kind of people we are dealing with here. Do you know this? The government are so concerned with teenagers messing about with bolts and fittings on our railway tracks, that they are about to put it on T.V., that soldiers will be patrolling stretches of the railways at random. Anyone caught now

fucking about on the railways will be shot. You listen out, you'll see. It's the last resort, but there's been too many derailments lately, and they're sick of it. I tell you Karen, this country is going absolutely mental.
Did you see that in the papers the other week? Whatever happened to boy meets girl, boy and girl break up, no, not now. The girl splits up with her boyfriend, two months later, not two days or two weeks, but two months later, she goes out with another lad. What does ex-boyfriend do? He and four of his pals ambush the couple. Tie their legs up and dangle them from a fucking railway bridge. Then they proceed to film the London to Brighton express battering into the poor kids. She was eighteen he was nineteen. That's their lives wiped out. Jealousy? no that's not jealousy that's demonic. That's driven by evil. You know what? Only one of them was found guilty. One gets life, the rest are back out in society in no time at all. That's what we're up against Karen. We have to catch them, and they let them go again, that's the way it is. If you're ever in a situation Karen, and you have one shred of doubt about the safety of your life, or mine for that matter, you shoot to kill Karen, whatever you do, shoot to kill, and regardless of what age they are".
"I'm sorry Deborah, not just for us, but for the decent people of this country. How the hell do you bring up your kids these days, it's getting like they have a one in a thousand chance of bringing up their kids unharmed by this poison that runs through our societies".
"What do you say Karen, we spend our first day right here. We can have a couple of drinks, maybe run over that disgusting tape again, see if there's any clues as to who those bastards are. One thing for sure though is that unless Carla Paganni has taken off somewhere, and if we don't get to her first, then I'm afraid she hasn't got long to live. You heard their threats Karen".
"Yes, and what frightens me is, if that's what they do to a innocent little hooker, then it makes me shudder what they'll do to that Paganni girl".
"If they do get to her first Karen, I hope it's not us who discovers the body, and when I say body, well, just look at the tape".

John Hillman watched through the camera, as the two policemen left guarding the house got into their car and headed down the drive, and out of sight. "Hungry boys"? He said, as he came away from his spy glass, as he called it. "You bloody should be boys; you've been here since four o clock". It was now twenty past eleven. One of the policemen had locked the doors before joining his friend in the car. Hillman now had a bunch of keys in his hand. He would have to be careful, and he would have to be fast. Maybe another two policemen were on their way maybe, maybe not. "Huh, there's one thing Lord, there's none of them in any sure fire hurry to come to this house now".

He took one last look through the camera. Satisfied that there was no-one else around, he switched off one or two appliances and then made his way up the ladder. Outside, it looked like the ground was moving as he opened the three foot square trap door. As he lowered it he ruffled up the ground a little, to hide any straight lines that may have appeared. Swiftly and silently, through the wind and rain, he made his way up to the house. Once he got in there he could retreat to the safe house and watch from the cameras everything that was going on in the house. There were hidden cameras in every room. He reached the edge of the woodland and was now crouched down behind a hawthorn bush. He listened, but it was hard to hear anything with the wind blowing so strongly. He made a run for the front steps, but as he did, he dropped the keys. He stopped and searched frantically on his hands and knees on the gravel, the place was almost in total darkness, all the security lights had been switched off. Through the gravel he groped, panic setting in by the second. Then, he looked to his left, it was the unmistakable glare of headlights coming up the drive. The police were returning. Then, just when he was about to give in and run for cover, he grasped the keys. It was still a risk, but it was fifty- fifty now, whichever way he ran. He headed for the steps. The car was coming round the corner now, he could see its nose. "Wrong key, fuck!!!" He desperately tried the next key. It fitted. He had only just got into the house and closed the door behind him, when the full bore of the headlights shone on to it.

He stood getting his breath back for a few moments, listening to what the policemen were doing. For the time being, they were staying in their car. “What are *you* doing here”? Hillman’s dead mother asked him, standing with her head blown to pieces.
“Christ”! Hillman gasped, talking to his ghost. “What the hell do you think I’m doing, I’m trying to save your house”.
“You can’t stay here son, your father says you’ve got to make your own way in life now, he says it’s time you were fending for yourself”.
“Mother” he hissed, “You’ll have to keep your voice down you’ll get us both caught”.
“Well, if you’re going into the kitchen son, watch out for your father lying on the floor with his head burst wide open, oh and you might find me there lying beside him, good luck son”.
“Yeah, good luck ma”`. “Love you son”.
“Love you too ma goodnight”.
Hillman made his way silently and stealthily, looking around him as he did so "Made it”. He slid a painting on the wall to one side, and exposed one little hole in the wall, in the shape of a key, almost like the figure eight. He put the key into the lock and turned it. There was a loud clicking noise, then he pushed the whole wall. It swivelled around, allowing him into the secret room. As he stepped inside, he stopped and turned. “No, go back down stairs ma you can’t come in here, go back down, and lie in the kitchen, don’t give the show away, go and lie beside dad”. He pushed the wall back around and it closed with a bang, just as the two police officers were coming in the front door. It took them only a few seconds to find the light switch, just enough time for the picture on the wall to stop swaying to and fro. John Hillman was home, and he was home for good.

MAIN STREET. (SHEFFIELD.)

Rachel White stood looking over the potatoes and the rest of her vegetables she had so caringly prepared for Heather. The roast was in the oven smelling delicious. This was the first meal she had actually cooked since moving in with Heather, and she felt really proud that she was, for once doing something worthwhile. In between customers Heather had been teaching her how to cut hair in various styles, how to use dye, and how to apply different lotions, for perms and loose cuts. For the first time in a long time, Rachel felt good about herself. She was off today and Heather said she was only going in to work for a couple of hours. Rachel knew why Heather was going in today, and it wasn't anything to do with work, not that kind of work anyway. She had witnessed it before. Once every two weeks Heather would go into the room at the back of the shop. There was an emergency door in that room and Heather would open it.

One by one the girls would come in through that door, and talk to Heather for a while. None of them ever stayed longer than ten minutes. Anything from ten to twenty girls would come in between those two hours. Occasionally, one or two of them would come through to the shop for a haircut, or some beauty treatment. After a couple of hours Heather would come back into the shop and then head straight to the bank. They were all Heather's working girls. This was the day that they all paid Heather their money.

Rachel opened the oven door and took out the tray with the roast. "Mmm! Maybe another ten minutes". She looked up at the clock on the kitchen wall, it was almost three thirty. "Heather will be in, in a few minutes, I hope she likes my cooking". She heard the front door opening. "Ah, that's her now, perfect".

"Mmm, what a delicious aroma Rachel, have you been busy"?

"Trying to be Heather, I hope you like it, it's just a roast beef dinner, I've just got the gravy to make, would you like a glass of wine while we wait for the roast"?

"Come here my little cream pie, that dinner smells just about as delicious as you.

The two women kissed passionately for more than three minutes. "Oh Heather" whispered Rachel, you make me feel so good".

"And you make me feel good as well Rachel, my little angel. Tell you what honey, I'll pour the wine, you make the gravy, and then we'll eat. I thought maybe tonight Rachel you and I could go out for a couple of hours. There's one or two of the girls I know going out for a couple of drinks, do you fancy joining them? You and me, what do you say"?
This was Heather's way of introducing Rachel to her working girls.
"Sure, yes, if you think it'll be fun".
"Of course it'll be fun, but first, after we've eaten, we'll have a bit of fun ourselves in the bedroom, do you fancy that"?
Rachel smiled. "I'd never tried anything like that before Heather, until I met you, I really enjoy it". The two girls kissed again, until Rachel broke away and said, "I really will have to see about this gravy".
Heather poured more wine. The timer on the cooker began buzzing.
"That's it ready" said Rachel.
"I can't wait" Heather said.

"Neither can I" said Paul Crane standing by Heather's living room door. "Well, come on missy, set another place for your newly arrived guest, we have lots to discuss over dinner so we do".
"Like what" said Heather, "And how did you get in here"?
"I simply opened the door, you should learn to lock doors behind you. You never know who could drop in. Sit down Heather, well, no, don't sit down, help your little lover to dish out the dinner". Rachel's face went red.
"Why are you here, I made a deal with you, and I've kept my word, we haven't seen Carla Paganni. I told you I would get in touch with you if she came here, and so far, she hasn't't".
"Now now Heather, you are jumping to conclusions, who said I was here about Carla Paganni. I'll tell you what, after we've all eaten dinner, I'll tell you why Mister Temple wants to see you".
"Wants' to see me, why? I don't know anything about what he wants' to know about".
"Oh yes you do Heather, and what do you think Mister Temple wants to see you about"?
"Bloody Carla Paganni, that's what"!
"Wrong Heather, now come on ladies, let's eat".
Five minutes later, all three were sitting at the dinner table. "I'll tell you something Missy, you sure as hell cook a good dinner, I've not

tasted anything like that since I lived with my mother. The two girls picked away at their dinner, both of their appetites completely ruined.
"I'm sorry" said Heather, but I've completely lost all notion of eating".
"Me too" whispered Rachel.
Paul Crane sat with his pistol lying where his desert spoon should have been. "Come on girls" he said, in between mouthfuls of meat and potatoes. "You've got nothing to worry about; he wants to make a deal with you Heather. Now when Mister Temple says he wants' to make a deal, then you just know you're going to be quid's in, so come on, eat up all this lovely nosh that you're beautiful little girl friend has made us".
"Rachel, her name is Rachel".
"Sorry, I couldn't help hearing Rachel, that it was Heather here who turned you on to pussy. Well." He said, again, between mouthfuls of food, "now you know why us guys make such a fuss about eating it, it's delicious, don't you think Rachel"?
Rachel placed her fork and knife onto her plate and pushed it six inches in front of her. "Tut tut" Said Crane, mockingly, do you know what my old mother used to say when I done that? She'd say, Paul, someday you'll be glad of that, that's what she used to say, anyway Missy, sorry Rachel, if you're finished you can pour me another glass of wine".
Twenty minutes later Crane said, "right ladies, it's time to go and see Mister Temple".
"We'll have to change first; we can't go over to see Mister Temple dressed like this, especially Rachel. Rachel wore a bright yellow vest top which was rather on the tight side, and making it painfully obvious that she had no bra on underneath. A tiny white mini skirt, and white ankle socks, a thong, that was it, that was her complete attire.
"No no girls, you'll do just the way you are". Crane lifted up his gun and said "Just you put on a pair of shoes Missy, and that'll do". Heather wore a dress top with a pair of jeans and shoes.
"I need the toilet" said Heather. "Fine, just hurry up, and don't be trying to do anything stupid, if you're not back down here in three minutes, I'll shoot your little girl friend here, now move it, no funny stuff do you hear"?
"I hear"!

LONDON ROAD. SHEFFIELD.

"Well well Paul" said Temple, as Crane and the two girls entered Temples study. "I see Heather has brought a little piece of the merchandise with her".
Straight away, Heather knew what the deal was going to be. He wanted a cut of the profits which Hillman had been receiving.
"She's not merchandise; let me make that clear to you right from the start".
"Now now Heather, let's keep it nice shall we, I mean, I'm being nice to you, even after your friend has killed my brother".
Heather looked at the floor. "Have you seen our pal Carla lately Heather"?
"No I haven't Mister Temple, as I've already told your friend here". She hooked a thumb behind her knowing where Crane was standing.
"You're absolutely certain about that Heather"? said Temple getting up from his chair. He walked over to his unit and took out a king Edward cigar from a hand carved cigar box.
"Absolutely".
"Good, good, just as long as we keep our deal Heather".
"I will sir" she said, knowing that Temple loved authority.
"Ok Heather., take a seat, you and your friend have a seat".
Amanda Pearce, who was sitting on the sofa, with a pair of white shorts on and a navy blue vest top jumped up when Temple said, "Come on Amanda, get our guests a drink, you too Paul, get yourself a seat, after all, this involves you as well. "Get yourself a drink too darling" he said to Amanda. She blushed at the tone of his endearment.
Five minutes later, they were all seated around the table. "Could you pardon me being blunt Mister Temple, but, how much do you want? What's your price"?
"My price Heather"?
"Yes your price, your cut".
"My dear girl, I'm afraid you've got the wrong idea as to why you're over here. I'm not Mister greedy bastard Hillman, excuse my French" he said to Rachel. "I'm not after any cut Heather. Let me ask you some straight questions Heather. Who owns the apartments from where your girls work"?

"You know Mister Temple, Mister Hillman does, well did, I'm not quite sure now to be honest".
"Has your girls been paying you rent since Mister and Misses Hillman met their maker"?
Heather looked down to the floor again.
"Come on now Heather, have they"?
"Yes".
"Yes? Well then, if Hillman is dead, which Mister Dougan assures me, he is, who's taking the rent money Heather, who's putting that money into their bank account. Hmm"?
"I am".
"You are, and yet you snap at me, what's your price? What's your cut? Let me tell you something young lady, you are not in any position to point the finger at anyone".
Heather looked into her glass on the table. "You are lucky that you still have a shop, a business from which to make a living. Now, how much did you pay Hillman, for your girls I mean"?
"He took thirty five per cent".
"He was a very greedy old man Heather was he not"?
"I suppose".
"Yes, I suppose too. Now then, more drinks Amanda. This is what I propose to you. You give me twenty five per cent and the girls give me the rent money, how does that sound? I've bought a few properties you see. Everything will remain the same, you'll run the show, but you'll keep books and I'll want to see them every month, along with my twenty five per cent. I intend to buy some of the houses that Hillman currently owns. As a treat, providing all the girls behave themselves they'll get a month's free rent every three months, provided your books all add up sensibly. Now, for that twenty five per cent you'll receive full protection, you'll have nothing to worry about, any problems, and you just let Paul know about it, or Amanda or Joe. Amanda's face lit up at the prospect of her being involved with any business transaction concerning Steve Temple. "Any questions"?
"Yes Mister Temple, just one. Why are you doing this for me, you could take all this over by yourself, and have all the money".
"I'm doing this Heather, because I respect you, you know what you're doing, you seem to know how to keep those girls together, working as a team, why should I try and fix something if it's not broken. Oh and the money? I'm not greedy like Mister Hillman

was; I know those girls have to earn a living. With the extra ten per cent you'll be getting', maybe you can give them a little extra".
"I will sir". Again, trying to patronise Temple. It seemed to work.
"Come on now Heather, we're going to be business partners, from now on, it's Steve. Oh, and if Joe or Paul here, or Amanda for that matter fancy a little rough and tumble, there'll be no charge right"?
"Right you are sir, just as long as they don't beat up any of my girls".
"Oh they won't, don't worry about that Heather, anyway they're my girls now as well, they're making money for me. If anyone hurts them, they'll have me to answer to, oh, and before you go Heather"?
"Yes"?" That threat concerning Carla Paganni"?
"Yes"?
"I'm afraid it still stands".

STATION HOTEL. SHEFFIELD.

Angela and Carla sat in their room unpacking their clothes. "How long do you think we'll have to stay here"? said Carla.
."As long as it takes, there's no way we're leaving here until it's all sorted out, one way or another. Heather says he's building his numbers up Carla, we don't know who we could be talking to so we'll have to be careful. I think if we just hang around here for a couple of days, relax a little, then work out a plan. You won't be able to leave here Carla, unless it's with me, and at night. The first thing we have to do is get your hair dyed a different colour, and get it cut, maybe wear a pair of non- prescription glasses".
"Fuck, I'm going to look pretty am I not"?
"Be that as it may Carla, do you want to look pretty or do you want to look alive, it's up to you".
"I know, I'm just joking Angela".
Angela picked up her mobile and began pressing digits. "Hello Tracy? Yeah, we're in Sheffield, did you get my note? Right, so you're at Sharon's sister's ok, how's the girls. Yeah I know, we'll get them settled in to a school just shortly, any trouble? Ok now you stay there Tracy with Sharon, until I come back down with Carla, she sends her love, bye babes bye, oh by the way Tracy, don't call this number after today, I'm getting a new phone, bye, yes I'll phone you or text you my new number, yes I will, you too, bye".
"Fancy a drink Carla"?
"Yeah, I think I could use one".
"I'll phone room service".
"Hell Angela, that'll cost a fortune, I can walk down to the bar".
"No you can't Carla, just relax girl, for once in your life someone is treating you and they don't want anything in return, I know it's strange Carla, I've been there myself. As I was saying to you in London, I look upon you as a friend, and I don't have too many of those right now, so I plan to look after the ones that I have. That's why I'm up here with you, so as we can sort this mess out.
You know I'm attracted to you Carla, don't you"?
Carla smiled, looking rather shy. "Well, I kind of thought that, I mean, I haven't done anything with a woman before, but, well, if I were to try it, I wouldn't mind if it was with you, does that sound alright to you"?

“That sounds more than alright Carla”.
“The thing is Angela, I like men, you know, I like to be with men, they will always be my preference, I think”.
The two women lay back on the bed and began to kiss passionately. After a few moments Carla sat up and said “Whow, I think I can safely say that I am by-sexual”.
“Everything starts with just friendship Carla…everything”.

MORNINGSIDE. 2. Am.

The two, armed policemen sat in their car outside of the house. John Nash and Chris Tanner sat listening to the radio, or at least, attempting to. “This is fucking crazy John” said Tanner.
“What”?
“Sitting out here in this fucking thing, while there’s a perfectly good house with all mod cons just sitting there empty. There’s no fucking way that loony is coming back here now, he may be mad, but he’s not totally fucking mental, besides”. Nash lifted the pump action shot gun from his lap. “I don’t fancy his chances much if he does return. What do you say we go inside, make ourselves a nice cuppa, maybe have ourselves a game of snooker, it’s a long time until six in the morning, anyway I can hardly hear what the guy on the radio is saying for all this fucking wind and rain, we’ll be needing a pluviometer if this keeps up”.
“We’re not supposed to go in there Chris we’re only supposed to guard the place”.
“Look John, if anybody does come we’ll just say we heard a noise and so we came in to investigate. Come on John, nobody will come, not at this time of the morning, it’ll be better than sitting out here in this fucking thing, who’s going to know”?
Nash rubbed his chin, weighing up the situation. “Yeah you’re right Chris, fuck it, let’s go”.
As the two men got out of the car, John Nash felt the full force of the wind and rain on his face. The wind blew his hat off, sending it spinning across the car park. Chris Tanner was laughing as he entered the house. Nash had ran over to the far side of the car park to retrieve his hat. As he picked it up, he looked up at the house. Something didn’t feel right. It wasn’t just the fact that they were not supposed to go in there, it was more than that. There was something not right about this, it was a gut feeling. The house looked sinister from where he stood. Chris had put two or three lights on down stairs; the rest of the house was in complete darkness. As the wind pelted his face again, he felt a fear he could not explain, because, after all, like Chris said, who would come here at this time of the morning. He squinted his eyes, struggling to see through the rain. Was that a light he saw flicker upstairs in the house in one of the rooms? “Come on” he told himself. “Chris will have the kettle on,

you'll feel better with a nice hot cup of tea". Even so, his instinct was telling him not to go in to that house.
Chris came to the door. "Come on, hurry up so as I can get this fucking door closed, I'm going to put the heating on". Once more John Nash looked up at the house, the bushes either side of the front door were almost bent right over with the force of the wind. The trees across the way even seemed to be warning him. He made his way up the steps reluctantly.
"Chris, where are you"? Said Nash as he entered the hallway.
"I'm in here" He could barely hear Chris's voice.
"Where"? Suddenly Nash heard the doors click behind him.
"Shit!!! Chris? Chris, where are you? This isn't funny; if you don't answer I'm going back outside to the car".
The lights suddenly went out. "Shit!!! Right that's it Chris, I'm going back out to the car, you're a fucking sick bastard, this is not funny, fuck you man". Nash turned around and tried to open the front door, although he somehow knew it was going to be locked. He had no torch with him; neither had he brought in his gun. "Chris"?
He could hear fumbling noises coming from somewhere down stairs. Then the sound of a hammer banging, hard. Bang bang bang bang bang. Silence. Then, bang bang bang bang, silence. "Chris!!! Please"! More fumbling noises, then silence. Bang bang bang bang bang bang. Silence. Nash did not know what to do. His mind was telling him that Chris Tanner did not seem to be the type of guy who would play practical jokes. He never had in the past, and he'd known him now for more than two years. This inside information was not doing John Nash any favours whatsoever. Bang bang bang bang bang bang. Silence. His eyes were slowly adjusting to the darkness, but still nothing like good enough to walk about. Silence. He listened intently. It even seemed like the silence was listening to him. He could hear footsteps. They weren't tip-toeing either. These were deliberate steps they were getting fainter though, as though they were heading away from him, they were. Then whistling. Someone was whistling a tune.
Then CLICK. The locks behind him clicked loudly again. He turned instinctively, and as he did, the lights came back on. "Fuck!" John Nash opened the door and ran down the steps and across the car park to the police car. He opened the door and picked up his rifle, checked it was loaded, and then ran back over to the house. There

was a giant-sized plant pot just inside the door, which he dragged over to wedge the door open. Then, feeling a bit more courageous now that he had his shotgun, he began to make his way through the house.
Nash had already made the decision that there was something wrong and that his partner wouldn't play a trick on him as bad as this, not here, not at a time like this. "Chris, Chris if you're ok, give me a shout man, are you ok"? Nothing. "Chris just make a noise man, anything, just let me know if you're alright. Chris, Chris I've got my gun, I don't want to be shooting you by mistake, now please shout!!" Silence. "Ok then, don't blame me if I blast you're fucking guts out, you've been warned". The warning was not for Chris, but for anyone who happened to be in the house. He knew something had happened, something bad. "Ah fuck this" said Nash. He walked through the hallway and into the lounge. The light in the lounge was off but he could see a light on further down the passage way. He found the light switch for the lounge and switched it on, then he made his way down the corridor towards the other light. Because he had wedged open the front door, he could hear the wind whooshing through the house, making flowers that were in vases flutter slightly. Then he heard a car pulling up outside. "Oh thank fuck" he gasped, "I don't give a fuck if I do get into trouble". More confident now that he would have company, he made his way down to the kitchen. As he entered the kitchen, he stopped in his tracks. After a few seconds, he began to cry, like a child would cry. A kind of helpless pitiful groan. The full length kitchen table had been turned up on its end. The banging he had heard was his friend's head being battered through his brains, and through the eye sockets, and ears. Five giant sized nails that must have been a foot long had been hammered into Chris Tanner's head. The nails in his head were all that was supporting his whole body. His feet were about ten inches off the floor.

John Nash stood crying for a few minutes, and then, like a zombie, he made his way back through the house, at least to try and explain to his superior what had happened. When he got to the door he started crying some more. He hadn't heard a car coming up to the car park at all, he had heard one leave, his. He flopped down on the top step with his rifle in his arms. He was crying in convulsions now, shaking sobbing bitterly. "I told you Chris, I told you we

should have stayed in the car. Someone's took the car Chris, I'm soaking now". The wind and rain pelted his face. Still he held on to his gun, he had to, because whoever had taken the car was coming back for him. As he sat on the steps, he heard something in the wind. It was footsteps on loose gravel, and they were coming up the drive. Whoever it was, they were whistling. He heard the crunching of their feet on the gravel getting louder and louder. Then, through the rain, he saw the silhouette of a person walking around the side of the house, the gable end. "Halt!!" He shouted through his tears. "Halt, or I'll blow your fucking brains out, I don't care who you are. You'd better stop now"!!! He fired the first shot. There was a scratching ruffling sound on the gravel. The rain pelted relentlessly on his face. He strained his eyes, trying to see if he'd hit his target. "You fucking sick bastard, I hope I got you". The wind blew more rain into his face. A sudden gust almost blew him off balance. "You sick fuck"!! He stood and listened, he could only just make it out, but he could definitely hear it, it was the sound of footsteps on the gravel again, but this time, round the side of the house.
He wasn't familiar with the lay out, but he was trying to reach the back entrance. He ran through the lounge again and down towards the kitchen, there was a patio door in there, right beside the upended table and his dead colleague. "Where else, there must be another door somewhere". Suddenly, just to the side of the kitchen, at the bottom of the passage way, a door blew open. Nash turned and instinctively fired a shot in that direction. He went to the door and looked out at the surrounding trees, which went all around the house. "I know you're out there sicko, but guess what, you've met your match tonight, I'm not scared now fucker. Now I'm hunting you. If you're in these bushes fuck head, then take your best shot, go on, cause I've still got four in here, and at least one of them is for your fucking face, that's a promise freak"!!
He closed the door and locked it. Just then, all the lights in the house came on, every one. Then piped music, all around the house, very loud. It was Cher's voice. "THEY SAY OUR LOVE WONT PAY THE RENT, SOON AS IT'S EARNED OUR MONEY WILL BE SPENT". Nash looked behind him, all around him, more cautious now than ever before. Then it was the turn of Sonny's voice. "WELL I DON'T KNOW IF THAT IS TRUE, BUT YOU'VE GOT ME, AND BABY I GOT YOU, BABE, I'VE GOT YOU BABE, I'VE GOT YOU BABE, I'VE GOT"-.

Silence again. Nash listened for footsteps in the house. He could hear something, what was it. Then he realized what it was. The giant sized flower pot had been moved. He heard the door closing. He cursed himself for not bringing his torch, for he knew what was going to happen next. He began to make his way back to the front of the house. Click, darkness. Silence. Then the whistling again.
"I'll whistle you, you sick fuck, I'll make you whistle you mental fuck! The wind will whistle right through your head, there'll be a hole in it, fucker"!!
Silence.
Nash moved slowly, ever so slowly, gun at the ready. He was now standing on a wooden floor. He would be able to hear if anyone came into this room, unless… John Nash had just had that thought when he heard three loud footsteps coming towards him. A sharp pain in his head, and then complete darkness and silence.
Hillman had been waiting. He hoisted the hammer and brought it hard down on Nash's head, cracking the man's skull as he did so. "Use that language in here young man". He pulled Nash's unconscious body through to the hallway. Then he went to the lounge and pulled an easy chair through, and sat it about eight feet from the front door. Hillman disappeared once again, returning this time with the stand of his father's telescope. Back and forth he went, fetching rope and string, masking tape and rags. Eventually he had it all set up.
He had tied the policeman to the chair, gagged his mouth, and set one of his shotguns on the stand, aiming it straight at Nash's head. The string led from the door handle to the trigger. Another shotgun, the one that belonged to Tanner, was on the floor, connected to a small tripod. It too was aiming directly at Nash's head. The string from that trigger was connected to the other trigger.
"There now". Nash's eyes flickered. "Ah, you're awake; I thought I'd killed you there for a moment. Good, you'll be awake when the cavalry arrive. Anyway who taught you language like that young man, that was awful it really was, I think it's time somebody washed out your mouth with gunshot to teach you a lesson.
Right, I'm off to bed, it's nearly ten to three. Six o clock they come isn't it? To change shifts. I'll set my alarm for five forty, I don't want to miss any of this, although I will be recording through the security cameras, three different angles, should be interesting. You've guessed by now officer, but when you came in here the first

time, it was me who answered you, that was why I whispered. Hillman sighed. “It seems a shame to leave you here unoccupied until they get here, wait a minute”. He returned with the mash hammer, and set about Nash’s knees, smashing them both into pulp, then, just before he put the hammer down, one more on Nash’s mouth. “There, that’s it officer, good night, and goodbye”.
Hillman had been humming religious tunes all the time as he inflicted these sickening wounds onto the officer, supervised by his almost ever-present mother. His hallucinations were becoming more and more idiosyncratic.

HARRINGTON POLICE STATION. SHEFFIELD.6.30.Am.

Deborah approached the sergeant's desk. "How many Tom"?
"Mam"?
"How many officers are dead"?
"We don't know, we don't know for sure if there's any dead. Officers Henry and Metcalf went to take over from Nash and Tanner, but when they arrived there, they weren't to be seen".
"You've got me out of my bed because two officers fucked off home early from their shift"?
"No Mam, the patrol car is still there, there's just no sign of the officers. The doors of the house are locked as well".
"Sergeant, if they've went into that house last night and fallen asleep. If I go over there and find that they've slept in that house then it would be better for them if they hadn't been born, I swear. Right, get me two armed officers. They can come over with Karen and me, although I think that this is a case of Henry and Metcalf getting the jitters, has anyone got spare keys"?
The sergeant handed Deborah the set of spare keys that were hanging up on the wall behind him. "Right Karen, let's go".
"Em, Mam"? Said the sergeant.
"Yes"?
"I'm afraid you'll have to sign for those keys". Deborah looked at the sergeant straight in the eye. "Do I look like one of your constables sergeant"?
"It's the rules Mam".
"Yeah sure sergeant, I've got news for you, there are no rules out there, so I sure as hell won't be abiding by any in here, make yourself a cup of tea sergeant, I'll close the door on the way out so as you don't get a draught".

Deborah and Karen came to the entrance of the drive which led to Hillman's house. Sure enough, there was the police car. She pulled up a few yards up from it. They got out of their car and walked back down the few paces back to it. "Now then Karen, why would they leave the car like this, facing up hill, it's quite a steep climb up to the house, so they haven't got out here to walk up to the house, even they are not as stupid as that".

"It doesn't make sense" agreed Karen.
"Unless Deborah, they've been on their way up here and they've spotted something in the woods and, well, if they've done that I fear for them".
Knowles nodded, lighting up a cigarette. "That's it Karen, you brighten my day up, that's the spirit".
Karen smiled at Deborah's perspicaciousness.
As the two detectives stood wondering what could have happened to the officers, another two armed officers pulled up
beside them.
"Good morning boys" she said to the two men in the van. I take it you're here to find our two absent friends are you"?
"Yes Mam".
"Well then" she said to the driver, "If you find those two sleeping up there in that house, then you have our permission to give them a damn good thrashing, clear"?
"Clear Mam" said the driver, laughing.
"Here you are" she said, handing the driver a set of keys. "Don't lose them boys, or you'll be signing papers for the rest of the year. On you go, we'll be up in a minute or two".
The police van pulled away and began climbing the twisting path up towards the house.
Hillman was in hysterics as he watched the van with the two officers coming around the bend. "I could have given those other two officers the fright of their lives Lord, but I thought they looked too nice. I could have unlocked the door automatically, but that would be less fun". He switched on the cameras that were facing Nash. His trousers looked like someone had stuffed small cushions at the knees. His mouth was just red pulp. Hillman looked at his victim. I know how that feels, don't I, you bastard Lord. Don't I know how that feels, having pulp for a mouth, oh yes, fucking child's skipping rope you nasty bastard , never mind, all's well' that ends well. Those knees look like they could do with some attention Lord. Hillman had all his cameras ready. "I'll tell you this my Lord, this is going to be nice and messy".

He looked through the security camera which was mounted above the door. The two officers did not notice the camera swivel slightly as they got out of the van. Now, Hillman was watching Nash's bloody face. His eyes were filled with fear. "I don't know" said

Hillman, impatiently, “some people Lord. You’d think he would be grateful for to be put out of his misery wouldn’t you Lord? I think the pain he is suffering with those knees must be just about unbearable.
He’s a tough cookie Lord, I’ll give him that. Many another man would have passed out before now, or even had a heart attack. Look Lord, look at him writhing and blinking right to the end”. Hillman switched on the microphone. “I’ll just say boy, before they turn the key, well done, very brave, very brave indeed. Now then, I’ve had a word with the Lord, so, after your friends have blown out your brains all over my walls, well, there’s every chance that you will land up in Heaven, what’s that Lord? Oh yes, he said you must stop that swearing though”.
Nash heard the key being put into the lock. It was the wrong key. “Oh look Lord, he’s pissing his pants, see that Lord? Nothing to be ashamed of officer, goodbye now”.

As Deborah and Karen pulled up behind the police van, they were just in time to see the driver of the van, who was at the front door, being shot in the face with the pump action. The force of it had thrown him from the top step to a good metre beyond the bottom step. There was a half second delay, and then a second gun shot fired off in the house. The driver was already dead. No nose or mouth, and only smoke coming from where his eyes should have been. His body was juddering as if he were holding an invisible jack hammer. The other officer dived for cover, then he crawled marine like on his elbows across the gravel, reaching the gable end of the house. “Well, we know he’s here now” said Karen.
Deborah got on her phone as quick as she could and asked for back up and plenty of it. “Yes Karen” she said”. He’s here for sure this time”. The armed officer had now cautiously approached the front door, and was now peeping round it. Eventually, he entered the house, with his gun at the ready. Two minutes later, the two detectives were looking at the body of Officer Nash. The manner in which Hillman had tied up the guns had been a complete mess. When the door opened, instead of jerking the trigger, it had swivelled the telescope stand right round so that the gun was facing the door. The shotgun on the small tripod had been set up perfectly though. Any movement at all would have set that trigger off, which was why, Mister John Nash’s body sat in a perfectly relaxed

position, and his head hung upside down, half way down his back, being held on only by his spinal cord. Now it was Karen Jones's turn to be sick on Mister Hillman's steps. A couple of minutes later, Deborah had discovered the body of Chris Tanner. "I swear Mister Hillman, when I get you, I'm going to cut off your cock and ram it down your throat, you sick, sick bastard that you are! God knows who'll get this house, but you will die intestate, I'll make sure of that".

Deborah left the officer standing staring at the unfortunate Chris Tanner. As she approached the corpse of officer John Nash she smelt the coppery aroma of fresh blood. As she looked at Nash's body, this time taking the time to overlook him thoroughly, she noticed the smashed knees. "Doctor Hillman" She said. "What on earth has happened to you? From a quiet well-mannered father of two, a man who has spent most of his life helping others, being kind and considerate, putting other people first, to, to this". She looked again at Nash. "You weren't satisfied with just killing him, were you Doctor, no, you had to inflict pain on to him first, and for how long, God knows, before that gun went off and put him out of his misery. You are indeed a sick bastard Doctor, and even though I personally think that death is too good for you, they'll get you, and they'll kill you".

Outside Deborah could hear Karen coughing and retching her guts out. "Poor Karen" she thought to herself. "You've never seen anything like this before have you, never seen this kind of maniac at work, poor girl. Deborah even wondered if it would be enough to make her pack in this profession once and for all. As the coughing and retching continued outside, she looked at the upside down face of John Nash, or what was left of it. As she stepped outside of the house, and went down the steps, Karen was now sitting on the bottom one. Her face was drained of all colour, and she was crying. "I know" Said Deborah, as she put her arm around her colleague's shoulders. "It's not very nice babes is it. I'll tell you what, you take some time off and-".

"No Deborah, that's not how it's done, you said it yourself when Davis told you to take time off. I'm in this with you, and I'm not resting until we've got that bastard, I want to see him behind bars".

"Well" Deborah sighed. "You just do what you feel is best Karen".

Knowles stood up from the steps looking over at the trees. “Well, we can say this for sure Karen, anyone who visits Doctor Hillman these days can be assured of one thing, they won’t ever be ill again”.
Only a few feet from where the two detectives sat, the body of another young police officer lay, gun-smoke protruding from what used to be his mouth.
Knowles had joked with the man only moments before about giving the missing officers a thrashing, and now here he was lying dead on the gravel, another victim of the infamous doctor Hillman.

OLD MILL ROAD. EAST LONDON.

Joe Dougan sat in his nineteen sixties bottle green E Type Jaguar. He had just got into it after spending the night in a cheap hotel, and an even cheaper bed. His back was paying the price for his scrimping now. It ached as he climbed into his car. As he drew his tongue long the sticky strip of the cigarette paper, he looked up, something catching his eye, movement. He saw a young lady coming out of a house. Nothing unusual about that, except that this young lady happened to look to her left and right like you would do if you were crossing the road. Dougan decided he would watch her movements for a couple of days or so. She fitted the description of a certain young lady who happened to be a friend of a certain hair-dresser. "You never know." He watched the woman walk down to the end of the street, and then disappear round the corner. Dougan lit up his roll up and drove off. As he turned the corner Sharon Hartley had no idea that she was being watched.

Dougan was missing his army life. He loved the discipline and all the physical training that went with it. He was too old now though, for that, although he was still a very fit man. He had loved being in the SAS and training the would-be new arrivals. Not many passed the strict regime that was required to be an SAS soldier. Some would say that he was sick in the head at the way he treated some of those men, and what agonising punishment he'd inflicted upon them, but those who made it would be respected by every other regiment in the entire armed forces, and they would rank, second to none.

He sighed. Now, here he was doing 'jobs' for a two-bit fucking wanker who thought of himself as a gangster.

He smiled to himself as he smoked his cigarette, at the thought of Steve Temple attempting some of the assault courses he'd put those men through. He remembered his sergeant. Sergeant McGeorge, and how he had introduced himself by sticking his face into his bowl of burning hot porridge and daring him to rub the porridge from his face, and then making him do fifty press-ups while the men were made to walk over him on their way to the sink to clean their breakfast bowls. Then he was made to eat his potatoes and mince without any cutlery, and given only ten minutes to eat the piping hot dinner. "Oh happy days" he sighed. "Temple would have had a nervous breakdown.

MORNINGSIDE. SHEFFIELD.

Deborah looked down onto the corpse that was Bradley Kemp. "Poor bugger". Karen was nowhere near ready to look at him again. "The wrong place at the wrong time I guess". Then she said to Karen, "That could have been you or me Karen, and if we hadn't stopped to look at the police car, it would have been". Deborah cursed as she brought out her cigarette pack, only to discover that it was empty. "Shit!!"

A white faced officer came down the steps of the house. "Mam"?

"Yes"? answered Deborah, crushing the empty cigarette box.

"You've been left a note, well, a poem. It's got your name at the top of the page".

"She sighed, he's not written the twenty third Psalm again has he, the sick bastard".

"I eh, I don't know what it is, it's a poem I think".

She took the piece of paper from the officer. In the distance she could hear the sound of sirens blaring through the city. "Do you smoke officer"?

"No Mam, but Bradley does, did, he's got some in the van, would you like one"?

"Yes please".

In less than a minute, she was inhaling deeply on the cigarette.

She glanced at the sheet of paper.

"Did you ever go to Sunday school officer"?

"No Mam, never".

"Ah, well if you had, you would have known what this was. This was written by someone in the Salvation Army, for the kids, to keep them interested in Jesus. Karen looked up from where she sat, as Deborah began to read out loud. "WE'RE GOING TO THE MANSION.

"What, does that mean, here"? said the officer.

"No the mansion means heaven, you know, our Father's mansion, ON THE HAPPY DAY EXPRESS. The happy day, to any Christian, is judgment day, you see? They have nothing to fear. THE LETTERS ON THE ENGINE. I like this, because many kids, up until they took the steam trains off the railways, used to write down the numbers of the engines and the company. For example, 84227G.N.E.R. That would stand for The Great North Eastern

Railways, you see. Now then, THE LETTERS ON THE ENGINE, ARE J.E.S.U.S. In other words, if there's no engine, then the train is not going anywhere. Unless you believe in Christ. The passport to heaven of course is the crucifixion of Jesus, he's the answer, He's your guarantee to heaven, without Him, if you don't believe in Him, entry to Heaven is impossible, THE LETTERS ON THE ENGINE ARE J.E.S.U.S. THE GUARD SHOUTS OUT FOR HEAVEN. The guard of course, is God. We gladly answer yes, usually with gusto, YES we are going to Heaven, WE'RE GOING TO THE MANSION, ON THE HAPPY DAY EXPRESS".

"That's amazing" said Karen. "How do you know all that"?

Deborah drew on her cigarette, looking down onto Bradley Kemp. "I know all that because my father was a minister."

Up round the bend of the drive, came a police van, an ambulance and an unmarked B.M.W. "Here they come" said Karen. "Nearly the next day, but never mind, they're here now".

Deborah was more interested in the occupants of the B.M.W. to make any reply to Karen's remark. Out of the van, eight armed policemen stood like soldiers awaiting permission to enter the house. A tall man in his mid- thirties Deborah guessed got out of the back of the B.M.W. along with Terrance Davis. The tall man wearing light grey trousers and brown brogues, and a raincoat that could have belonged to Clouseau himself approached Deborah.

Terrance Davis spoke first. "Deborah? This is chief inspector John Drummond from the Thames Valley Police Department. He's here to give us a hand to capture our villains".

Drummond spoke. "Villains that you seem to be having some trouble apprehending". He looked behind him as two paramedics were putting the body of Bradley Kemp into the back of the ambulance.

"I see" said Karen. "So they've sent you up here then, simply because there's nothing to do in London"?

"Listen" Said Davis. "You might as well all start getting on, because you're all going to be working together".

"No we're not" Said Deborah Knowles, I'll resign first, before I work with a cockney bigot like him".

"Deborah, I meant that you and Karen here will be working on one case, and, John here will be working on another, either way you look at it you'll both be working as a team. Now, Deborah, what do you want to work on"?

"We'll work on the drugs gang, and the murders connected with that".
"Fine" said Davis. "John, you'll be working on this here, this bloody Doctor Hillman case, and believe me, he is a case".
"Fine" said Drummond as he walked away and up the steps of the house. He looked behind him, and then at the ambulance, and then at the corpse of John Nash. Then he shouted down to the armed officers. "Right men, search the house thoroughly, and I mean thoroughly". Then he looked at Deborah Knowles and said to his men, "mind you don't trip up over all the dead bodies".
"Hope you find your Doctor Hillman soon John" said Deborah.
A few minutes later, after John Drummond had inspected the body more closely of Nash, he emerged from the house spewing his breakfast onto the top step.
Deborah looked up. "You ok Mister Drummond"?
Even Terrance Davis smiled at Deborah's sarcasm.
"I wouldn't go in the kitchen just now if I were you. Let's go Karen, let's go and see if we can find Carla Paganni". She raised her voice again and said, "I can see we're just going to get in the way of the professionals here. Good luck Mister Drummond in your search for Doctor Hillman". In between his vomiting, he managed,
"Go and fuck yourselves!!!"

"Well Karen, that'll keep us away from this bloody house for a little while anyway. We will be back though, there's no way that Clouseau there will deal with Hillman on his own. There's some connections here Karen I'm sure of it. Carla is on the top of our list, we really need to talk with her. She could set us right on a few things I'll bet, she'll certainly know who killed Susie. Carla has a lot to answer for as well; I think she's committed a few murders of her own, anyway, the sooner we speak with her the better. Oh and don't forget Karen we're still looking for John Hillman as well, don't think that I'm just going to let that cockney twat step in here and take over like he knows all there is to know. Just give him a few weeks, and Hillman will have him demented".
"You don't think he'll capture him then Deborah"?
"No way will he Karen, Hillman will do his head in, he's far too clever for the likes of that big head. Drummond is too busy looking at his own ego, that he wouldn't see Hillman if he walked right past him, and he probably will. I just hope we don't come back here

shortly and find our friend Mister Drummond lying in a heap on the floor".

"Those poor officers" said Karen, as the two detectives made their way through the city. "He is a mental case right enough" she continued.
"Who are you talking about Karen, Hillman or Drummond"?
Karen laughed.
"I've seen what he's capable of doing Deborah, he's a sick man".
"No Karen, you've seen what he's done, we've seen what he's done, what he's capable of doing is another thing altogether. It's a mystery how he's getting in and out of that house so easily though".
"Yes and where the hell does he go in between"?
"There's an answer for everything Karen, and we'll find it. As my friend Leonard Cohen informs us, there's a crack, a crack in everything, that's how the light get's in".

HEATHER'S BEAUTY SALON.

Angela Phorbes sat outside the salon in her rented car, watching Paul Crane get out of his car. He was parked across the road, and Angela knew where he was heading. She walked into the salon ahead of Crane. Heather was both surprised and panicked at the sight of Angela. There were two seats available in front of large mirrors. "Quick" said Angela. "Put a shawl over my shoulders".
Rachel, who was sweeping the floor, was told to gently comb Angela's hair. "You've got a visitor coming Heather, don't worry. Two old ladies, who were being seen to by two other girls, were totally unaware of what was going on. Paul Crane entered the shop. As it turned out, he was not here on behalf of Steve Temple, but was intending to have a good time with one of Heather's working girls. "We have to talk Heather". He said, pointing to the room at the back of the shop.
"Sure" said Heather. "Carry on girls".
As soon as Heather had gone through to the other room with Crane, Angela got up from her seat. "Can I borrow this for a minute Rachel, she said, as she took Rachel's overall. "I won't be a minute; I'm just going to play a joke".
Angela put on the overall and walked up to the back of the shop. She knocked on the door marked private.
"Just a minute" Came Heather's reply, and then the door opened. Angela walked into the room closing the door behind her. "Where do you keep your towels Heather"?
"In here" said Heather, looking rather confusingly at Angela and opening the door of a cupboard and handing her a bail of freshly washed towels, not quite knowing where Angela was going with this.
"Hello" said Crane.
"Hello" replied Angela.
Paul Crane looked at Heather, who shook her head and said,
"No, she's not one of my working girls, Angela only works in the shop".
"Pity" said Crane.
"Pity?" said Angela. "Pity about what"?
"It's a pity you don't work at nights; you'd make a lot of money so you would".

"Not from you I wouldn't, you see I suffer from bufonaphobia, I could only make love to men who were attractive, you know, men who act like men and not like baboons, full of themselves because they go around and bully people who are weaker than they are, you know the type Heather, the ones who go around making threats on the other side of a gun, big hard men, no I couldn't make love with them, fucking idiots so they are, fucking dead beats, with their skin head haircuts and their skin all fucked up with various skin diseases, like you, you fucking leper. Tell Heather you're sorry for being a fucking leper and for disturbing her at her work to go and get you a fucking woman, because you can't get one on your own you fucking pig, now tell her you're sorry!!"

Crain looked at Angela, completely taken aback at her verbal pugnaciousness.

Crane swung round with his clenched fist attempting to catch Angela on the jaw. Angela saw it coming and easily ducked out of its path. She pulled out her gun, and fired the first shot into his left arm, then another into his groin. It was done so quickly, he hardly had time to realize what had happened. She fired one last shot into his brow.

"Get some sheets Heather, I'll get the car".

"Oh God Angela, now I'm in the shit with Temple, what have you done"?

"No you're not, quick, get some sheets, get him wrapped up".

"Rachel!" Angela opened the door slightly, could you come through here for a minute please. Three minutes later, the three girls had Crane's body all wrapped up and bundled into the boot of Angela's hired car.

They had no sooner done this, when one of the hairdressing girls tapped on the door. "Heather"?

"Yes"?

"There's two police ladies here would like a word with you if that's alright".

"Won't be a minute" said Heather.

"Fuck in hell" she said, panic setting in by the second. Quick as a flash, Angela noticed hair dye, bottles of it sitting on one of the shelves.

She opened the bottles and poured them onto the floor, on top of the blood spilled by Paul Crane. "Smear it everywhere Rachel, Heather, you go and talk to them, I'm off, I'll see you later".
Angela left by the emergency door at the back of the shop. Heather came through to the front of the shop. "Good morning" She said to the two women.
"Good morning" Knowles and Jones replied.
Heather smiled at the two women. "What can I do for you"?
"Well actually, is there somewhere private we can talk"?
Again Heather smiled. "There usually is" said Heather, pointing to the back of the shop, but today, one of my staff has decided to rid me of a few bottles of hair dye, it's all over the floor".
"I see" said Knowles. "How bad is it, we could really do with a word with you, it's about one of your friends".
"Could you just wait a minute please, I'll see if she's cleaned it up yet".
Rachel had done an amazing job; She had cleaned the blood from the wall and then smeared hair dye on it. Then she had put another bottle of dye on the floor and spilled it everywhere, including over the blood lying there as well. Heather opened the door. "Oh for fuck sakes Rachel!! Blasted Heather at her employee, well I'll tell you this madam, that's coming off your wages, I can't afford to lose stock like this, fuck sakes you silly mare!!" Heather, once more turned to the police ladies. "Please, could you come through, you'll have to watch where you're putting your feet, but we can talk in here". Heather held the door open for the two police women. "Mind your feet, it's everywhere, Rachel, put the kettle on, do you think you can do that without scalding anyone Jesus Christ girl!!"
After Rachel had put the kettle on, Heather said. "Right, away through there Rachel and sweep the floor".
"I'm sorry "said Rachel, actually playing a blinder Heather thought.
"It's ok, I'm sorry for snapping at you, on you go darling, and sweep the floor".
Heather looked at the two police women. "I'm so sorry for that outburst but that's bloody dear stuff, I can't get that at cost price".
"I see" Said Deborah, who couldn't care less if she could or not.
"So, what was it you were saying about a friend of mine"?
"Carla Paganni", said Knowles, have you seen her or heard from her lately"?

"No miss, I haven't, and if I do see her again, she'll be getting a kick between the legs from me. She borrowed money from me about five weeks ago roughly, and I haven't seen her since".
"How much did she borrow?" said Knowles.
"Oh, let's see now" said Heather, "Oh yes that was it. None of your business that's how much. I've lent her money before, but she's always given me it back, of course, she was working for John Hillman then. Now, God Knows where she is or what she's doing, spending my money I guess".
Knowles looked at the floor. "Well if you hear from her you let me know, and remember Miss Bradley, it is an offence to with-hold evidence from a police officer, if you are found guilty you will face a custodial sentence".
"Don't you bloody worry about that, I'll be telling you if I set eyes on her, make no mistake about that, little Italian bitch that she is".
"Quite" said Knowles.
"Let's go Karen".

"What do you think, is she telling the truth Deborah"?
"Who knows Karen. The point is, she's been warned by us, and she's been warned by other people, the difference being, if she lies to us, we won't hunt her down and kill her. So, we just keep a close eye on the shop and the people who come and go there. If she's lied to us, and she thinks she's got away with it, then I think it's just a matter of time before we see Carla Paganni, and her close friends no doubt. It's like this Karen. Heather has a team of prostitutes, maybe twenty girls. Heather takes a percentage, and John Hillman took a percentage. Now then, John Hillman senior is now dead, but all the prostitutes are still working. The girls paid Heather for their houses and flats. That means that with Hillman out of the way, somebody is making money from the rent, because, rest assured, they'll still be getting charged rent by someone. Also with Hillman gone, there's an extra percentage up for grabs, now this city being what it is, I can't see how Heather has not been approached or threatened in connection to all this money floating around. So, what we do Karen, is like I say, just keep an eye on Heather's activities, and pretty soon things will start falling into place.
"I've been keeping an eye open Karen, all around the city, having a drink here and a coffee there. I even went round to London Road a

couple of weeks before you arrived. There's a petty gangster called Steve Temple, someone shot his young brother to pieces, and just dumped him in a ditch somewhere. I happen to think it was Carla Paganni, although forensics say there was nothing in the car connecting her with it. Anyway, I went along to London Road to watch the funeral procession leaving from Temple's house. I saw this woman, maybe in her thirties, just guessing. She was very beautiful though, and she seemed to be going out of her way to see the occupants of the first three cars, the chief mourners. I've never seen her around these parts before and I've never seen her since, but I could almost swear Karen, I saw her coming out of Heather's hair salon four or five weeks ago. I can't be absolutely certain, but I'm sure it was the same woman. Now, as luck would have it Karen, there's a café straight across the road from Heather's salon. At least twice a day we'll be in there Karen, watching. Drinking coffee and keeping out of this pissing rain and wind, and watching. Keeping nice and warm, gathering information Karen and"?

Karen burst out laughing. "Watching"?

"You got it in one kid. There's an old saying in life Karen, good things come to those who wait".

"Yes, and hopefully, good things come to those who watch as well".

"Yes" said Deborah, "Let's hope we're not struck with a sudden bout of prosopagnosia Karen".

"What the hell does that mean"?

Deborah smiled. "It's a disability Karen, and if you suffer from it, you will not be able to recognise even familiar faces".

HARRINGTON SQUARE.

“Now then Misses Miller”, Joseph Miller said, as he opened up all the bundles of the morning newspapers. On every national newspaper there was a giant sized picture of Doctor John Hillman. “What are you going to say about your lovely Doctor now? The most wanted man in Britain Nancy, huh? It just goes to show you hell, you and all your bloody gossipers around here, you called that poor wife of his everything from a whore to a Shanghai rooster, when all the time it was that beady eyed skinny shit of a husband of hers that was the bad bugger. I knew it, I knew it all along Nancy, but you lot around here, you called her to the bloody dogs hell and-”

“Give it a rest Joe, will you? You’ve went on and on about Hillman since the ten o clock news last night, and besides bugger lugs, I seem to recall you sticking up for him on one or two occasions. I told you something was happening in that bloody square that morning the police drove by, but you said, “Oh it’s probably a message for Doctor Hillman to go to the hospital, so just shut up your cake hole for five minutes and get those papers put on their shelves. I’m not one for swearing Joe, but you’re getting me close to it”.

“Swear if you want to hell, see if I care, stuck in here all day with you, you and your bloody gossip troops, I think that that’s all that keeps you ticking, and guess what Nancy, I won’t be making any bloody tea for you tonight hell, you can cook yourself something for a change, you’ve never cooked a bloody thing hell for more than twenty years, it’s your turn now”.

“You’re taking the bloody huff Joe, because I made a point”?

“It’s not just a point with you though, is it Nancy, you make a point, and then you take that point, and you stick it up my arse Nancy hell, that’s what you do!!”

“Is it now, is that-” CLANG. “Good morning Misses Macdonald”.

“Good morning Mister Miller, good morning Misses Miller. Who would have believed that Misses Miller about Doctor Hillman”?

“I know Misses Macdonald, Mister Miller and I were just discussing it before you came in, weren’t we Joe”?

"Yes we were Misses Macdonald, bloody awful, hell, good morning to you sweetheart".

MORNINGSIDE.

John Hillman watched the monitors as forensics, photographers, policemen, newspaper reporters, just about everyone in the city, came in and out of the house, his house. It had been going on now for three days. At last, as far as he could tell, it was all starting to calm down. It was down to two pairs of police officers. One pair in the house, the other two patrolling the perimeter. After an hour or so, they would exchange places.
"Huh, that'll be a lot of fun for them tonight Lord, when I knock out the lights. They'll soon stop roaming around when I do that, we'll just see how brave they are when it's dark".

Hillman put on the T.V. to watch the news. Half way through the local news, his name was mentioned. The newsreader began by saying, whilst they displayed a picture of him on the screen; "If you see this man, whatever you do, do not approach him, he is highly dangerous and is likely to be carrying firearms. Just phone or go to the nearest police station, and inform them of where you sighted him. There is a substantial reward for anyone who can lead the police to him. We repeat though, do not approach this man". The newsreader went on; "There was a meeting today at Downing Street, between the prime minister and Terrance Davis, the chief of police along with other major politicians about whether or not to bring back capital punishment". Two leading newspapers had done a secret survey around the country, from Scotland, England, and Wales. Both surveys conveyed that the public's view was most definitely in favour of execution being a more effective method, and that lengthy prison sentences were just a waste of the taxpayer's money.

The leader of the opposition said in an interview after the meeting. That it was time the rules in Britain were changing. For far too long now, innocent people's lives have been taken, by terrorists, by thugs, and by gangsters, looters and rapists, scum in general. We are hoping, that with the help of public opinion we can get this through parliament, and start protecting the innocent people of this country, by exterminating the beasts who inflict so much pain into our lives. It's time for the old traditional method of, an eye for an eye. We've tried all the alternative punishments, and they simply don't work. Personally, this was something I hoped I would never see, but needs be as needs must, and I'm afraid it is a case of a necessity, rather than a case of wanting to do this. Something must be done to protect the good people of this country, and to send out a message to these heartless murderers, that their actions are no longer going to go unpunished. There will be a price to pay. If you take someone's life now, then you can expect to lose your own".

Hillman watched the pretty newsreader with the low cut sweater complete the news. "Lord, you can see it as well as me; we've got whores reading the news now. I can't concentrate on what she's saying, for looking at her cleavage Lord. No wonder this once great country of ours is going down the shit pipe, no fucking wonder. I think I'll go for a walk tonight Lord and see if I can get all of this shit out of my mind".

He was just about to switch the T.V off, when a photograph of Tracy and his two daughters came on to the screen. The news reader said; "Concern is growing for the safety of the wife of Doctor Hillman. Tracy Hillman and her two daughters have not been seen now for more than six weeks. Their clothes and their belongings are still in their home in Harrington Square, in Sheffield. Police are appealing to Misses Hillman to contact them if at all possible, even if it's just to let them know that she is still alive. A spokesman for the Yorkshire constabulary said that they were beginning to fear the worst for Misses Hillman and her children; however, there is still a substantial reward for anyone who can lead us to her and her children. Hillman sat looking at the photograph of his two little girls on the T.V. He could no longer hear the words of the newsreader. "Daddy's coming girls, daddy's coming to get you, I'll find you, I'll give you cuddles again, wont I Lord? Yes I will".

STATION HOTEL. SHEFFIELD.

Carla pressed the digits for Angela's new phone, from her room in the hotel. "Hello? Angela"?
"Hiya Carla, listen, I can't speak right now, I'll call you as soon as I can, don't worry, I'll be back in about an hour or so".
"You're sure everything's alright Angela? You're not in any trouble are you"?
"No, I'm fine Carla, don't go out though, stay in your room, use room service for drinks or snacks, see you later babe".
"Love you Angela".
There was a short pause, and then Angela's voice came back. "Love you too Carla, bye".

Angela was driving towards Rotherham. In between Rotherham and Barnsley, on the A616, there was a quarry signposted. Two things she was hoping for. One, that the quarry would be unmanned, and two, that there would be a drop to the quarry, somewhere she could let the body fall without any chance of it being seen with the naked eye. She turned off the A616 when she saw the sign reading, Fenwood Quarry 1Mile. As she drove on she began to think about her dead passenger, and wondered what kind of a man he'd been before he got himself involved with criminals like Steve Temple, where was the turning point in his life, where he says, fuck it, I've had enough of playing by the rules. She thought about it, and realized how very quickly life could make you callous. You could be sailing through your life, minding your own business, good job, nice husband, a couple of kids, and then bang, along comes another woman and tempts him away from you. A woman you may never have met in your life comes along and just takes your husband away, and in some cases, the kids as well, just like that. Ten years, twenty years, even thirty, bang, just like that. They wake up one morning to a perfectly normal day, but by the end of that day, they have nothing.

All the things you and your husband or partner have worked for, all the dreams you've shared, all the hopes, special things, private things, things that you both swore you would cherish for the rest of your lives, the commitments, the secrets, the fantasies, everything. One day, it's gone. Taken from under your nose by a woman who,

at the end of the day, is only looking for the same as you. Maybe someone has done it to her in the past, this is her turn now, callous. She does not know you, so you do not matter.
Tough, callous, love...or lust.
Angela saw the sign for Fenwood Quarry. There was a man about fifty years of age standing at a pole gate, similar to that of a railway crossing. This one was worked manually. The man kept the bar down. Angela opened the car window. "Excuse me, do I drive through here to get to the quarry"?
"Get out of the car and come and speak to me here, I can't leave this pole gate, fuck".
Angela got out of the car and walked over to the scruffy man.
"Do I have to drive through here to get to Fenwood quarry"?
The man looked at Angela as though she had the bubonic plague.
"You'll have to wait until they come back out".
Angela looked beyond the man and saw all the skips, all standing in a neat row, and all labelled with large white and red signs. Household. Glass. Wood. Metal. Garden refuse. This was not what she was wanting, far from it. She looked at the scruff.
"Where about is the quarry"?
The man did not even look round to her and managed only a grunted answer.
"Fucking quarry closed down years ago, there's only skips now, can't you see"?
There was a young couple at one of the skips. They were putting old floor boards into the skip marked, Wood. "Hey"!! The scruff shouted. "You make sure you've taken all the nails out of that fucking wood, ok? You! He looked at Angela, what have you got"?
"I beg your pardon"?
"What kind of rubbish have you got to tip"?
"Oh it's em, garden rubbish".
"Garden rubbish? There's no metal or fucking glass in it is there"?
"I don't fucking think so" said Angela.
The man glared at her. "Hmph, call yourself a lady"?
"No I don't" said Angela, "Call yourself a quarry"?
"There was a quarry here at one time" he snarled. "There was a lady here at one time as well". Said Angela, her patience coming to its' limits.
"You'll have to move your car back to let these people out".

“Oh they’re people now, a minute ago it sounded like you were referring to dogs”.
“Hmph, move your car!”
“What a lovely man.” thought Angela to herself as she put the car into reverse. I should have let him meet you Mister Crane before I put you in the bag, huh, any more out of him and he’ll be joining you. You’d have some company whilst you both rotted away in the compost heap. The young couple moved up to the gate. Probably first time buyers thought Angela to herself. Doing as much D.I.Y. as they can to save money. The young man put his hand into his pocket and handed the gate man something. Angela could hear what the scruff said.
“Hmph, fucking fiver”. He lifted the gate bar and the young man drove through, with the driver’s window down. “Thank you” He said, as he drove past. “Yeah right” said the scruff. Angela began to drive forward, slowly. He put down the pole again. Then he dug deep into his bib and brace overalls, pulling out his wallet, and putting the five pound note into it, muttering something about a fucking scrooge. He then took out a small tin from his pocket and pulled out a ready-made cigarette and a lighter. He lit up his cigarette. Then, and only then did he raise the bar. “Don’t be long” he said, “We close in fifteen minutes”.
“We”? Said Angela looking around the compound.
“Alright then, don’t be long, I close in fifteen minutes, fucking fancy mouth”.
Angela drove in through the gateway, glancing into her rear view mirror. “Now then, stay where you are Mister nasty; don’t come over to the skips. She pulled up and reversed so that the back of her car was only just a metre off the skip, marked Garden Refuse.. He was coming. “I’ll manage” she shouted, as he approached the car.
“Huh, you’ll have to, I’ve only came up to switch off the shredder.
She could hear the noise of an engine purring away somewhere behind one of the skips and containers. She watched the scruffy man going into a small shed. “That must be his hovel, where he eats and wanks off”, she thought to herself. She was just getting the bundle out of the car when he came roaring out of his shed.
“For fuck sakes, what the fuck are you doing? I’m closed in ten minutes, Jesus Christ, you’re fucking useless, I pity your poor man, if you have one, what a fucking life he must have with you, I hope you’re not as slow as this when you’re taking your fucking knickers

off!!!" Without knowing, the scruffy man had just sealed his own fate.
Right next to the bag in the boot, there was a jack. She picked it up in her hand, her mind made up. "Could you give me a hand please; it's too heavy for me".
"Come on" he sighed "absolutely fucking useless".
"It's the shape of it you see"? Said Angela, suddenly smiling. "It's a dead body, and it's all crumpled up, plus, there's blood now, spilled out and swirling around, it's from all the bullet holes, there's liquid dancing around in the bag, its soggy".
Before the man had time to register what she had just said, Angela cracked him hard on the face with the jack. Automatically, he put his hands up to his face, and so the full force of the second blow got him right across all of his fingers. Angela whacked the man, time and time again over the face. Then she kicked and punched him on the head, on the ribs, in the stomach, and in the testicles. There was a small half square of glass lying near one of the skips. She picked it up and jammed the corner of it into his left eye.
Almost unconscious, she pulled him round to the back of the skips, where she was going to leave him, until she saw the shredder. It wasn't a small garden one; it was a huge industrial- sized machine, powerful enough to take large tree trunks and tree limbs. "Fuck you" she hissed, as she picked up his body and carried him over towards the lethal machine, as if she were carrying a baby. "Are you sorry, you horrible bastard man? Huh? Are you sorry for being alive, for being one of God's accidents, are you"?
"Yes, I'm sorry".
"So am I".
She put his body head first at the top of the shoot.
"Please, please I'm begging you".
"If I ever come back here and find out that you're still being a nasty bastard, then I'll kill you, do you hear me"?
"Yes I hear". The man stopped struggling.
She pushed him down the chute, head first. His head was mangled in a split second. The rest of his body was swallowed up by the blades and crush wheels, up to his backside. A huge tree trunk which was much too big even for this shredder, had jammed the mechanism. The machine had stalled or ran out of fuel. "Perfect" Said Angela. "What an unfortunate accident". She threw the remains of Paul Crane onto the compost heap, covering him with

grass and other garden waste that was in the skip. Soon, his body was completely hidden from view. “There now”. She walked over to the shredder again and looked down. “Thank you for your help sir; I’ll close the gate on the way out, good day now”. She then looked quickly around the area to see if there were any hidden cameras.

Just over forty minutes later, she had returned to the hotel, had a shower, a glass of wine, and was now making love to Carla Paganni. Callous.

MORNINGSIDE. 7.30. pm.

John Hillman sat in the safe room, watching and listening to the two officers who were in his home. "I'm bursting for a pee" one of them said, and then made his way up the first flight of stairs to go to the toilet. Hillman looked through the outside monitors. The other two officers were at the far end of the house, at the gable. Hillman casually opened the swivel wall, and walked out onto the hallway. He came down stairs to the bottom and onto the downstairs hall. He could hear the television playing in the lounge. As he approached the front door, he took the keys from the lock. Once outside, he began to press a number of digits on a remote control he held in his hand.

There was loud clicks and bangs, as window bolts, door locks, lights, electrical appliances all began to switch off. When he had crossed the gravel and gone into the wooded area, he then switched off all the outside lights. Once again, Morningside Manor was plunged into complete darkness. Hillman made his way through the trees and bushes, to the outside safe house.

He would cut his hair, maybe even shave it off, put on his reading glasses, shave off his moustache. He looked around to the house as he opened the hatch to climb in.

He could hear panicked shouting, running about, banging on doors. "Four men Lord, with four pump action shotguns, trained up, expert sharp shooters, trained to deal with the most dangerous situations, and there they are, in the dark, frightened to death of a general practitioner. Pissing their pants Lord like scorned school boys. It'll take them goodness knows how long, to realize that there is a set of keys in the back door.

Fear is a powerful thing Lord".

CITY CENTRE. SHEFFIELD.

Deborah and Karen sat with their coffees looking across the road at Heather's beauty salon. "Nobody seems to be in any hurry to open the shop Karen, do they"?

"It would seem that way" replied Karen. No sooner had they said this when two young women came along and tried the handle of the shop door. "Employees"? Said Karen.

"I think so" said Deborah, taking out a cigarette from her packet and then remembering where she was, and reluctantly replacing it back in the packet. The girls across the road each carried an umbrella, trying their best to shelter from the driving rain and wind. One of the girls' umbrellas blew inside out with a sudden gust. "Poor buggers" said Deborah, "goodness knows how long they'll have to wait there. It would be so different Karen, if the shop was open and they were the ones who were late, there would be deductions from their wages. That's how it goes, that's how it works, it's just the way things are, do as I say, not as I do". Deborah sighed, looking out of the window. "I could do with a smoke but I'm not going out in that bloody weather". It was now nine fifteen, and there was no sign of anyone coming to open up the shop. One of the girls pointed over to where Deborah and Karen sat.

"They're coming over" said Karen.

"Quite bloody right" said Deborah, "the poor buggers are soaking wet".

"I wonder if they'll recognise us from the other day".

"I doubt that very much Karen".

"Pros and magnolia Deborah? Is that what you called it"? said Karen, smiling.

Deborah smiled. "Prosopagnosia Karen, pay attention".

The two girls entered the shop, shaking their umbrellas before they came in.

"Bloody hell" said one of them, "what a bloody day". Outside, the weather was so appalling, that even though it was now nine twenty am, every vehicle still had full headlights on.

"I'll tell you what, Karen, let's go and see Ashley the slut, see what she's found out about these dead officers".

"Ashley what"? Said Karen.

"Ashley the slut. I told you about her, you know, the one who used to go out with John, in between going out with the rest of the men in Sheffield, you know, the pathologist? Ashley"?
"Oh yes" said Karen, "The one that we're so jealous of"?
"That's the one" said Deborah, smiling as she drained her coffee cup.

Deborah and Karen had just walked into the police morgue, in time to see Ashley going hammer and tong with one of her employees.
"I don't care Mister, how you do things in London, this is Sheffield, and I'm in charge of what goes on in here. Did I tell you to move that body, did I"?
"No".
"No I didn't, and if you ever pull a stunt like that again, I swear, I'll be doing a post mortem on you, now get back in there and finish what I told you to do. Don't you ever try that again! You come up here, and just because you've spent some time with the Met, you think you can go anywhere and call the shots, well not here Mister, over my dead body, you fucking twat, now move your arse, and I want you finished with that by eleven o'clock!!"
The young freckled faced student, whose face was now as red as his hair, said, "I'm sorry, I-".
"Yeah, you're sorry now, don't you ever, I fucking warn you for the last time!!" Ashley saw Deborah and Karen standing, and began walking towards them. "Morning Miss Knowles".
"Morning Ashley, this is my new assistant, Karen Jones. Karen, this is police pathologist Ashley Barnes".
"How do you do" said Ashley, offering Karen her hand. The two women shook hands, and then Ashley said, "You know the procedure by now Deborah".
"Yes, we'll see you in a couple of minutes". Deborah led Karen up the stairs to Ashley's office.
Karen said, "I wouldn't like to be working her ticket, she seems a fiery one".
"Yeah she is, but she has a point though Karen, you know with that guy down stairs, you let them off lightly, and then the next thing you know, they're pulling rank over you. Look at that bastard the other day, what do you call him? Drummond. Comes up here from London, and suddenly, everyone in the Sheffield Police department are incompetent.

The cockney bastard. Anyway, on a brighter note Karen, just wait till you see this, when she comes up here".
"What"?
"Just wait and see" said Deborah, smiling. They didn't wait for long. Three minutes later, Ashley came into the office wearing a mini skirt, a bare midriff, and a red v necked top which clung tightly to her body enhancing her ample breasts.
Karen almost burst out laughing, and could see straight away why Deborah had made all the comments she had. The girl looked like a hooker.
Deborah, who was pouring cups of tea, turned around and couldn't help herself. "Wow" She said, when she saw Ashley. "What"? Said Ashley, smiling at Karen, and knowing full well what Deborah was referring to. "Twenty-four seven darling" Deborah said to Ashley.
"Twenty-four seven what"?
"Twenty-four seven, you'll be working constantly with stiffs". The three women laughed as they sat down at the table.
Suddenly, everything was deadly serious. "Now then ladies, Mister Hillman is getting just a little bit more gruesome with each killing".
"Sorry to stop you Ashley, but we're not on the Hillman case anymore, not officially anyway. We are currently dealing with those bloody drug gangs, and all the murders connected with that, oh, and by the way Ashley, you were perfectly correct in your assumption in connection with the murders of the two prostitutes, remember"?
"Well, I don't see what that has to do with anything now", said Ashley, "so if you're not wanting information about the Hillman murders, then what are you doing here"?
"To be honest Ashley, we only came for a cup of tea, and to shelter from that bloody nasty weather out there, and for me to let Karen see just how beautiful you are, in case she didn't believe me. Do you know something Ashley, you've got me wishing I was a man, do you know that"?
"Karen" said Ashley, "get this crazy bitch out of here will you"? The three women laughed.
"Just for the record Ashley, if you've been watching or listening to the reports, how do you think he's getting away so quickly, do you have any theories about that"?
"Deborah, you've just heard me ripping the guts out of a man for trying to do my job, do you think for one minute that I am going to try and tell you how to do yours"?

"I'm asking Ashley, that's the difference, you're not interfering".
"Get her away Karen, I'll be in touch if any more information should arise about the drug killings, and stop staring at my legs will you"?
"Never" said Deborah, as she left the room and began walking down the stairs. Even when I was your age Ashley, and my legs weren't bad by any means, I was never gifted with anything like those".
"I think she's falling in love with you Ashley" said Karen, laughing once again.
"Out" said Ashley. "Come on, out, some of us have work to do".
"Dressed like that"? Said Deborah.
"I'm finished at lunch time today, I've got a half day off. I'm meeting a friend for drinks this afternoon".
"Lucky friend" said Deborah, "we'll see you Ashley, bye".
"Bye, you crazy cow, come again when you've got time to kill".
The freckled faced man looked up from his work as he saw Deborah and Karen coming down the stairs.
"Come on!!" said Ashley, you haven't got time to look at women you little pervert that you are, come on, do as I say, not as I do".
As Deborah and Karen drove back to the city centre, Deborah's phone rang. It was the desk sergeant from the station. Whatever he was saying to Deborah, Karen could see that she was very displeased. "What? No I haven't, well how the hell do I know. What? No I didn't, I left them in the door when I left there. What? Well you can tell Mister Drummond to take a run and jump, no I haven't, and tell him from me, that he stands some chance of catching Doctor Hillman when he can't even secure the fucking house". She switched her phone off. "Can you believe that Karen"?
"What's that"?
"That fucking clown from London, he's only gone and lost the keys of the house, what a fucking prick. Come on Karen, let's get over to Piccadilly mansion, and see what's been going on".
"Why did you call it that"?
"Well Karen on the twenty-first of September, nineteen sixty-nine, a mansion in Piccadilly was invaded. There were over a hundred squatters living in it, illegally. Police stormed the building, and put them all out. There'll be a hundred police officers here at Morningside, and they can't fucking get in. I am going to love this Karen, just wait until I see Drummond, the cockney twat that he is, losing fucking keys indeed".

"Where did he say he was going Amanda"? Steve Temple asked the young lady seated across the table from him. Without looking up from her magazine, she replied, "He didn't". Amanda continued, "Steven, you know what he's like, him and Joseph, they won't tell me any of their business". Temple looked at the girl, accepting the facts she had just given him.
"I still think it's strange though, he hasn't looked near since yesterday morning, he's not even phoned. I've called him, and his phone rings, but he doesn't answer it". Temple got up from his chair and walked over to the window. "When was the last time you saw him Amanda"?
"Same as you Steven, yesterday morning".
"And you're sure he didn't say where he was going"?
Amanda sipped her coffee, but gave no reply. Temple stood at the window, but could see nothing but the driving rain hammering against glass and rolling down in sheets. "Get dressed Amanda; you're going on a little errand".
"Mmm"? Amanda had one hand turning the page of her magazine, the other arm rested on her elbow, holding her coffee cup. Temple strode over to her, swiping the cup of coffee out of her hand.
"I said, get dressed, pay attention you fucking junkie little slut!! Now move your arse, and get dressed and do as you're fucking told, fuck, don't you forget yourself you little scrubber that you are, now fucking move!"
Amanda went upstairs to get dressed. Temple lit up one of his cigars, and poured himself a large brandy. He picked up his mobile, and texted Joseph Dougan, telling him to return from London, and that there was some more important business to take care of. He felt disappointed with himself now, about how he had snapped at Amanda. He had grown to like the girl, and, if he was honest with himself, she had kept him sane with everything that had happened recently, concerning the murder of his brother, indeed, he was very grateful for her comfort on the day of his funeral. His brother had been his only real friend, and now, he was gone. Amanda was helping him through it.
Twenty minutes later, when she came down stairs, he apologised to her, kissing her on the cheek. "I understand Steve" she said, "all this

stress you're having to cope with. I'm trying to help you through it the best I can".
"I know darling, I'm sorry".
He handed her a drink. "I want you to go into town to Heather's salon, and ask her to phone me. Ask her if Paul has been there, and watch her Amanda, watch her face for any kind of nervous reaction, you got that"?
"Yes Steven, I will. I'll tell you if she's hiding something"."Good, I'm really sorry for snapping at you Amanda. When all this shit is over with I'm going to make it all up to you, I don't mean to snap at you Amanda, God knows you're one of the very few people left in my life that I can trust".

STATION HOTEL. (SHEFFIELD.)

Carla Paganni sat watching the news channel on T.V, as Angela came out of the washroom. "Angela, come and see this, fucking hell!"
"What? What is it"?
"They've passed it Angela; they've only gone and passed it".
"Passed what"?
"The death sentence, that's it finalized. From now on, if you're found guilty of murder, then it's the death penalty".

The prime minister appeared on the screen, looking rather solemn faced. "We have been left with no choice, but to take this action. For too long now, the decent people of this country have had to take it on the chin. They have lost loved ones to callous murderers and rapists, and have witnessed the same marching straight through the British legal system, and coming out at the other end practically unpunished. It is with deep regret, that I have to make this decision, but we have to put an end to all this gang violence and hatred, that we are so familiar with in our streets today. Also, we have imposed a curfew on all teenagers to be off the streets by ten o clock each night. If this curfew is ignored, then they will be lifted and taken to a hard labour prison especially devised for unruly youths.

This prison will be run by ex-military personnel. There will be no outside interference of any kind. Prisoners will not be allowed any access to the outside world, once committed. There will be no newspaper reporters allowed in any of these prisons, and there will be no visitors allowed, whilst the youths serve out their sentences. There will be no dividing groups of various religions. Whether you are a Catholic, a Protestant, Jew, Muslim, Hindu, anything at all, you will not be exempt from serving your sentence. Pay attention, youth of Great Britain, things are going to be very different from now on. Discipline will be applied in these prisons, and it will be applied with the utmost severity. Once you end up in these places, I repeat, there will be no contact with the outside world for the duration of your sentence. I repeat to all the youth of today, take heed of what I have said this evening, because this message will not be repeated. If

you abide by the rules, you'll be fine. If you choose to disobey the rules, then you know what to expect, from midnight tonight.
Furthermore, if there be any adults causing obstructions in public places, or in any way causing a disturbance through violent behaviour, or urinating or vomiting on the streets, fighting, or shouting at the general public, or just generally making a nuisance of themselves, they will be placed under arrest and an automatic sentence of thirty days upwards will be imposed. Again, we care nothing of colour or religion. From midnight tonight, you are all equal, there will be no exceptions. In closing I would say to the young people of this country, think twice before you commit the crime, because the consequences now, are so different. I might add that these measures that have been taken are in place to keep the good people of this country safer than they have ever been. No doubt, through time, there will be complaints from human rights activists and the likes. I can tell them now, they will be wasting their time. Prisons henceforth shall be run by the authorities, and not the inmates.
Anyone caught taking illegal substances will also face an automatic sentence of thirty days upwards, depending upon which substance has been taken. In summing up, I would like to wish the decent people of this country a very good night, and a very pleasant future. To the ones who think that they are above the law, then, this is your wake up call, you will not get another. Good night Britain, and sleep safe". The news reader came back on to the screen, explaining how a paper would be put through the door of every household in Britain, and making the changes of the law clear to everyone.

"It was only a matter of time Carla" said Angela, as she put her arm around her shoulder. "It doesn't concern us babe".
"It bloody does Angela, everyone".
"No Carla, that rule we've just heard about only applies to the idiots, the ones who are stupid enough to get caught. we won't be caught".

MORNINGSIDE.

John Drummond stood on the top step of Morningside Manor with his hands in his coat pockets, staring out at the beautiful trees surrounding the house, as Deborah Knowles and Karen Jones pulled up in their car. The sun shone beautifully through the trees, a welcome sight after the wind and rain of the past few days. A cold breeze blew from the North, making Drummond keep his hands where they were. "Good morning ladies" the Londoner said.
"Good morning, both Knowles and Jones replied. As the two women began to climb up the steps, he said. "Ladies, I have an apology to make, I deeply regret my behaviour the other day. Miss Knowles, I could not have been more wrong about this case, please accept my apology, I'm afraid I began to shout my mouth off before I had been told the full story".
"Apology accepted" said Deborah, as she reached the top step."He is one clever bastard is this Mister Hillman".
"Aha" said Deborah casually, "he's all that".
"Last night Deborah, May I call you Deborah"?
Knowles shrugged her shoulders.
"Last night he was in here".
"Did he kill anyone"?
"No, that's just it, he didn't, but, he had the men who were here panicking, I can tell you that. It was he who took the keys from the front door. Three of the four officers who were here, all said that they'd seen the keys in the door at one point or another during their shift".
"What exactly happened"?
Drummond explained to Deborah and Karen, all the events of the previous evening. "He's playing games now; he's taking the piss constantly". Drummond took his right hand from out of his pocket and scratched his chin, a kind of nervous reaction. Deborah thought. The first sign of someone under pressure. "How though" he continued, "how the fuck is he just appearing and disappearing at will, hell Deborah, you know how thoroughly this house was searched, and it was searched from top to bottom. We even had men up in the attic, and the basement, nothing". Drummond looked into

the woods again, now scratching his chin with all four fingers of his right hand, then rubbing his brow with the back of his hand. He looked at Deborah, still rubbing his brow. "Does he have a shed or something out there do you know"?
The police woman lit up a cigarette. "Nothing, just the trees John, right down to the perimeter wall".
Drummond frowned. "Bastard, it's as if he's hiding somewhere out there".
"Obviously" said Deborah.
"No I know" said Drummond. "But it's as if somehow he can watch us, even now I mean, somehow watch, and know exactly when to strike, he knows it all".
"Maybe he's hiding up one of those trees" said Deborah grinning.
Drummond frowned again, "Miss Knowles, I said I was sorry didn't I"?
"Yes" said Knowles, realizing just how much she'd offended him. "Now I'm sorry John, I just couldn't resist, sorry".
"All I'm saying Deborah, is, that he seems to know exactly when to strike".
"I know " said Deborah, "I was only joking, and I know before you say it, this is hardly a subject to be joking about. The day I was here with John Crosby, I was in the study, I was checking the contents of the safe. He was here, he was in here. I had given John a tape, a cartridge. He left the room to look for a camcorder. He was only out of my sight for no more than two minutes. When I came back through to the lounge again, poor John, he lay there, practically filleted. I swear, I never heard a sound, not a thing. He could easily have taken me, but for some reason, he chose not to, and that's the worrying thing, he chose John, so where do you go from here"?
"Goodness knows Deborah, they are doubling the watch officers at night now, but somehow, I think he'll still strike when he wants to, he made sure those last two officers were killed with their own guns, the callous bastard".
"Callous and clever John, how does he disarm two trained officers, who, by the way, are looking for him"?
"Bastard's got me beat, just now, but he's bound to fuck up, you can't go on like that without making a mistake sooner or later".
"You would think, wouldn't you"? Said Deborah, "but up until now, he's not put a foot wrong".

Fifty-two yards from where the three police officers stood, John Hillman sat on his chair, head shaved, moustache shaved off, and a Sheffield United football supporter's hat on his head. He was whispering on his mobile phone to someone. That someone was his daughter Angela. "I know darling" he was saying, "but you mustn't tell mummy you were talking to me, ok? What?
Yes darling, that's right, it's a surprise. Where's mummy now darling"?
" She's down stairs talking to Sharon".
" Sharon? Is that the same lady who lives across the road from you and mummy"? " Yes it is" "Well, this will be a surprise for mummy, won't it sweetheart". "*I KNOW ,HOW FUCKING THICK DO YOU THINK I AM, LORD*!!
Now then Angela, I want you to help daddy play this game that will make mummy laugh and laugh, yes, that's right, now, go to your bedroom window, and look outside. Tell me if you can see any big buildings, buildings with names on them sweetheart, or names of shops, anything like that".
There was a pause, and then ruffling sounds in Hillman's ear. "I can only see one daddy; it says Williamson's Timber products".
"Oh, that's excellent my little angel, that's a help for daddy".
"Daddy? Are you alright? Mummy says you're not very well".
"Yes, I em, I'm fine darling, I'll see you very soon, and remember, you mustn't tell mummy you were talking to me, and spoil the surprise, do you promise daddy"?
"I promise daddy, I won't say a thing".
"Good girl, oh, and don't tell Amy, Amy's too little to play this game, see you soon darling, right daddy has to go now".

Hillman looked at his watch, then he looked through the camera. The two women were leaving again. "I'll wait until night Lord, then I'll make my way down to London. In the meantime, I'll phone the operator and see if they can tell me what part of London Williamson's Timber Products is located. A glass of wine, I think. What? You didn't say much to that whore wife of mine and her whore fucking friend did you, when they were getting all stewed up, huh? Imagine coming into your own home, and your own wife beats you up, right in front of her whore friend. You really do work in mysterious ways, don't you, you two faced Lord that you are, I'm having a glass of wine ok? That's a new whore detective with

Knowles, isn't it Lord? I wonder what she will taste like, anyway, she'll have to wait until I come back from London, plenty of whores down there who need to repent, but there are a certain two who are top of my list, priority, you might say Lord".

Inspector Drummond remained on the top step after Karen and Deborah were gone. He looked into the woods, rubbing his chin again.
"What is it? What is it that keeps making me look out there", he thought to himself. "Something, the answer's out there". He was sure of it. "What the hell keeps making me look out there? There are woods all around the house, so why over there all the time. His thoughts were interrupted.
"Sir, would you like something to eat? Two of us are going for something for lunch".
"It takes two of you to go and get fish and chips? Sorry, I'm sorry, yes, get me some fish and chips son".
"Right you are sir and what would you like to drink sir"?
"A bottle of Scotch".
"Coca cola sir"?
" Yes, coca cola son".

HEATHER'S BEAUTY SALON. (SHEFFIELD.)

Amanda Pearce walked into the salon. "Heather"?
"Yes Amanda, can I help you"?
"You can help yourself, can I have a word please, in private".
Heather put down the scissors she held in her hand. She had a good idea what Amanda was here for. "I've been sent by Steve".
"What's wrong, he knows the deal, I know my part of it, so what's the problem". Heather tried her best to sound as innocent as possible.
"The problem is, he hasn't seen Paul Crane for over two days, and he's worried. He's wondering if you've seen him lately".
"Yes I have" said Heather, "he was here yesterday morning, hunting for free fun from my girls, now you tell Mister Temple from me, I don't mind giving him, or his boys a free girl every now and then, but no-one gets anything in the mornings or afternoons, the girls need some time they can call their own. You can also tell Mister Temple that five minutes after Crane had left, the police were here asking questions about him. I told them the truth, I told them that Paul Crane had been here, and that I hadn't got an appointment available for him. He wanted his head shaved. Tell Mister Temple, I'm not happy about the police being here. A deal's a deal Amanda, I didn't figure on any trouble tell him".
"I'll tell him" said the young lady. He's just a bit wound up these days Heather. Crane will probably be doing one of his secret drug deals, well; he thinks they're secret, he thinks that Steve doesn't know about them".
"Amanda, I have the greatest respect for Steve Temple" Heather lied, "and you, I think that you are good for each other". The stupid girl blushed. "But these monsters he has running around for him" Heather continued, "I have no respect whatsoever for them. Amanda, as a friend, you are welcome in here any time for a free hair do, all I ask is that you are honest with me, that's all. Maybe, I. I, oh, it doesn't matter".
"What? What is it Heather"?
Well, I was just thinking, that, if you and Mister Temple were ever to get married, that you might eh, consider me for your bridesmaid"?

“Huh, I wish Heather, that’ll be the day that Steve Temple wants to marry me”.
Heather smiled, softly. “Amanda”?
“Yes”?
“I saw the way he looks at you, I know that he’s probably let one or two, maybe even three or four, maybe five of his men fuck with you in the past Amanda, but I saw the way he looks at you. I’m a lot older than you Amanda, and I can see things, so, would you consider me if Steve did happen to pop the question Amanda”?
“You’ve got it Heather, if he asks that is”.
“Oh he’ll ask Amanda, it’s just a question of time. Now, I’ll have to get on Amanda, I’m running late, now you remember to tell Mister Temple to tell Crane, not to come around the shop during the day, hunting for girls”.
“I will Heather”.
“Bye Amanda” said Heather, as Amanda closed the door, “You stupid little trollop that you are” she said under her breath. A few minutes later, Angela phoned the shop. Heather took the call in the back room.
“Well”?
“What’s wrong Heather?”
“What’s wrong? You may well ask Angela, you storm into here with no warning, take down one of Temple’s main men, only feet away from customers, and then get me involved by helping you bundle up the dead body, and Rachel too. Then you leave me to talk to the police, with a pool of blood at my bloody feet, and you ask me what’s wrong”?

“I had to do it Heather, before long, Temple intends to take everything that you and those girls have worked for, away from you. Try and understand Heather, Temple is not like Hillman, he does not think that you matter. After a while, once he’s seen the books and how you run the show, then you’ll be out on your arse, to say the least. You may even be found at the bottom of the river or in some building site skip, you have to believe me, Carla has told me everything, it’s a wonder he hasn’t sent one of his bimbo bitches to befriend you. After you become friends, she’ll hang around the shop more and more, listening Heather, listening and watching every move, don’t be fooled. So now that Crane has gone, that’s one less for you to worry about.

Carla says there's another called Joseph Dougan, I'll take him next, and don't worry, it won't be anywhere near you're shop Heather. That was just unfortunate the other day, but you and Rachel, you handled it quite well, from what I heard".

"We had no choice; we had no fucking choice Angela, did we"?

"Heather, one day you'll thank me, and just remember this, if you think I was a bit brutal the other day, well, every strip of skin that was lashed off that poor Susie Monk's body is going to be avenged, whether you like it or not, and for the death of Rose too, they were both your girls Heather. If I were to let you see the mess of those girls, or let you see Susie's execution as it happened, then you might not be so keen to make deals with this Steve Temple, I'm only protecting you because Carla cares for you, if she loses interest in you, then so do I, goodbye".

Sharon and Tracy sat at the kitchen table, having just finished their evening meal with the kids. Amy and Angela had gone upstairs to play computer games. “My sister will be back in a couple of days Tracy” said Sharon, “and although she and her husband will make us feel more than welcome, I just feel it will be a bit much for everybody, what do you say we find somewhere else”.
“I know, I’ve been thinking about that Sharon. Where though, most of the country will be looking for me and the kids”.
“I’ve already thought about that Trace. What if we book into a hotel, I mean individually, you check in with one of the girls, and I’ll check in with the other a couple of hours later. Angela is blond Tracy, Amy is dark haired they don’t strike off as sisters at first glance”.
Tracy thought about it for a few moments. “Ok Sharon, but sooner or later I’ll have to get these kids into a school; they’re going to be falling way behind their grades”.
“Don’t tell them though Tracy, don’t tell them we’re going to a hotel. It’ll cost a bit of money Tracy, to stay in a hotel, a decent one”.
“Don’t worry about that Sharon, I already owe you much more than money could pay you”.
“You owe me nothing Tracy”.
“Well, there’s one thing for sure, even though we’re going through all this, it’s still better than living the way I was, staying with that madman. It’s hard work keeping those girls off the telly though, that’s why I’m just letting them play all these video games all the time”.
Angela came down stairs into the kitchen. “Can Amy and I have a biscuit please mummy”?
“Of course you can my little princess, do you want juice as well”?
“Yes please”.
“You’re my little angels, you really are”. Tracy grabbed her eldest daughter and hugged her, much to the child’s annoyance.
“Mum, I’m not a baby”.
“I know that darling, but I still love you”.

“I know that mummy, so does daddy”.

"Yes he does darling, and that will never change, it's just that daddy's not feeling very well these days".
"That's not true mummy, daddy's just fine".
Sharon looked at Tracy.
"Daddy isn't fine darling, he needs to go to the hospital and get medicine Angela".
"You're just saying that mummy".
"No I'm not darling, mummy doesn't tell lies, and you know that".
There was nothing more said until Sharon handed the child the tray with the biscuits and juice. As Angela walked out of the kitchen, she stopped and looked round at her mother and said, "I know something that you don't know".
"Oh, is that a fact young lady"?
"Yes".
"Well now Sharon, I wonder what Angela knows that we don't know, can you guess"?
"I'm afraid I can't, so I'm afraid I'll have to give in, what is it that you know"?
"I can't tell you."
"Why, why can't you tell us"?
"Because daddy told me to keep it a secret, that's why".
"When, when did daddy tell you this secret"?
"Yesterday".
"Angela, now you're telling fibs, you didn't speak to your daddy yesterday".
"Yes I did mummy, he phoned my mobile when you and Sharon were down here talking, he said I wasn't to tell you and spoil the surprise, he said he had a nice surprise for you and Sharon, he said he was coming down soon, there, you've made me tell a secret, now I'll get bad luck".
Tracy's face changed from that of light humour, to sheer terror, as she dropped her cup onto the floor.

FENWOOD QUARRY.

The lorry driver stood crouched over with his hand against the wall for support, spewing out the contents of his stomach after the sight he had just seen. The remains of Charlie Sprake had been visited by hoards of rats, all feeding off the open red flesh that was splattered everywhere throughout the shredding machine. The driver had called the police when he discovered the remains of the man. That had been almost fifteen minutes ago, and still he was retching his stomach. He could still hear the rats screaming and squealing, fighting for the raw flesh. After twenty minutes the vomiting subsided, but still the retching, nothing in his stomach now but bile. Another twenty minutes and then the police arrived.

In Sheffield these days, every death was being investigated thoroughly. Deborah Knowles and Karen Jones decided they would come out here and take a look at this body. "You never know Karen" she said, as they drove past the pole gate which was pointing upwards. The two women laughed when they saw the driver leaning against the hut. "He looks white as a sheet doesn't he" said Deborah.

"Yeah, but I can't laugh at anyone Deborah, look what I was like the other day over at Morningside".

"We've all done it Karen" laughed Deborah, "It's just, you know, these hard men lorry drivers, and here he is look, he's seen a dead body, and he's absolutely fucked, look at him".

The two women got out of the car and approached the driver. The driver had his back to them, on his hunkers. Deborah tried to keep her face straight.

"Are you alright"? She asked the man.

Instead of trying to answer her, he pointed to the shredder.

As the man let out another loud convulsion, Deborah couldn't help but let out a burst of laughter.

The two women could still hear the man retching in the distance as they approached the machine. They were still laughing as they approached and looked over the shoot to see what the driver had seen, and then they stopped laughing.

CROMPTON ROAD. LONDON.

"We already may be too late Sharon, how could I forget about the kids' mobile phones, how stupid am I, oh fuck Sharon, I'll never forgive myself if this goes wrong".

Forty minutes later, Sharon, Tracy and the kids were all boarding a taxi. "Marble Arch" said Tracy, as they all were seated.

"Where are we going mummy"? Said Amy. "We're going to a hotel darling".

"Yes" said young Angela, "because *she* doesn't want us to see daddy any more".

MORTUARY. SHEFFIELD.

Ashley Barnes stood with her overall on and her disposable gloves inspecting the body of a certain Mister Charlie Sprake, or, what was left of him. Helen Stevens, her assistant, stood with a pen and notebook as Ashley dictated the details of the corpse before them. "Helen" She said, "I think we'd better call for Deborah and her friend to come over here and take a look at this. You see this here Helen"? She pointed to some bruising around the man's testicles. These marks they have nothing to do with his other injuries, these marks were caused by physical blows, and very hard ones I might add. Whatever has happened over at Fenwood, well, God knows, but it's looking more and more likely that Mister Sprake here, was thrown into the shredder, in fact, there's no doubt about it. The other bruises around the ribs, four of which are shattered, could also have been caused by violence, but it could also have been caused by the grinding of the wheels of the shredder, but not the testicles, those injuries were definitely caused by physical bows". From the middle of the stomach upwards there wasn't much left of the man. From just below the chest, the rats had burrowed through the flesh, and had begun to eat him from the inside. As one of Ashley's assistants walked past, he couldn't help thinking to himself that the place looked like a scene from a horror film. The remains of Mister Sprake looked horrendous, to say the least.

Half an hour later, Deborah and Karen walked through the front door of the mortuary. "Is Ashley here"? said the police inspector to the young lady who was typing something onto her computer. "You've just to go straight in" replied Helen Stevens, without looking up from the screen. When the two police women entered Ashley's office, she was standing putting coffee and milk into three cups, dressed only in a tee shirt and shorts.
Deborah's face lit up. "Hello Ashley, what news have you got for us today, my sweet little bundle of fuck".
Ashley didn't look round as she stirred the coffee cups. "Sit down and I'll tell you, you bloody lemon that you are". She sat the cups down on the table for her two visitors, and then sat down. "You see that mess down there that used to be a man"?
"Yes"?
"I'm afraid it's murder, there is no doubt".
"Murder? At a rubbish tip. We ran through his records Ashley, and he doesn't have one. The man was married in nineteen seventy-five, divorced in ninety-one, he's lived on his own since then. He's worked for the council for thirty-seven years, never been in court in his life, clean driving license, nothing, and he gets murdered at his work"?
"Well, I don't know about all that shit Deborah, but the man was in a fight before he died, his balls are swollen up like plums, all black and blue".
"Well then Karen" said Deborah, after we've had this coffee we'd better get back over to Fenwood, see if we can find anything lying about, you're sure he was in a fight Ashley"?
Ashley sipped her coffee. "I'm not even going to answer that, you cheeky bitch that you are".
"Who the hell would go to a rubbish tip, bloody miles from anywhere, and kill a fucking gateman Ashley?
"Just for the record Deborah, and again, I'm not trying to tell you your job, but, just supposing someone arrived at the tip with a bundle to dispose of, and let's just say that our Mister Sprake down there saw that bundle, then that person would have a problem would they not"?
"Well, if that happened Ashley, then that would mean that there would be another body lying at Fenwood".
"Well" said Ashley, "Did you search the tip thoroughly"?
"It's not a tip; it's just a bunch of skips".

“Did you search them then, clever bitch”?
“No we didn’t Ashley, but then, it just looked to be an accident, there was no cause to be suspicious or anything was there Karen”?
“No, there didn’t seem to be anything unusual, just an accident like Deborah says”.
“Well, there’s reason to be suspicious now ladies, I would get some officers over there as soon as, before they take those skips away to empty”.
“You’re really quite sexy aren’t you Ashley, sitting there with your shorts and tee shirt, you’re a regular little flirt aren’t you”.
Ashley smiled as she said; “I would go and search your skips Deborah, take a couple of men over there with you, and get them to dig in the shit for you, and then get one of them, or maybe two, it’s entirely up to you Deborah, to give you a bloody hard seeing to, because you need sex lady, now get her to fuck out of here Karen”.

MORNINGSIDE. (OUTSIDE SAFEHOUSE)

John Hillman was preparing to leave, under the cover of darkness, when his mobile phone beeped. Someone had sent him a text message. He lifted his phone from the small table and pressed the digits. The message read; MOVED ON JOHN, NO LONGER IN LONDON, CAN'T LET YOU TALK TO THE CHILDREN ANY MORE, PLEASE TURN YOURSELF IN, YOU NEED HELP. GET HELP. YOU WILL NOT SEE THE CHILDREN AGAIN UNLESS YOU GIVE YOURSELF UP, I'M SORRY. TRACY. Hillman's hands began to tremble, his head was dizzy with temper. He began to throw different objects around the room, cursing and swearing to his Lord, and asking Him why He had allowed him to marry such a fucking whore, and then let him get beat up by her. "I'll see my kids again, if it's the last thing I ever do, with or without your fucking help, you bastard Lord that you are. You opened up that fucking sea quick enough for those fucking Jews, didn't you, and yet you can't even see to it that I can see my own fucking kids, you're just a fucking prick, you are, don't even bother to talk to me for the rest of the fucking night, fucking whore, telling me when or where, or if I can see my kids or not"!!

"Kill those bastards John, kill them" said his mother, suddenly appearing at the table in front of him.

"It's not as easy as that mother". In Hillman's mind, Misses Hillman sat with her brains spilling out of her head, and her mouth gaping wide open. "You see ma, they're getting wise to me, they're going to catch me soon, I just know it".
"Listen son, you've got the Lord on your side, now you get yourself out there, and have yourself a fucking good time, get stuck in to those filthy women, and then rip their fucking sins right out of them. Make them die for their sins son, just give yourself a good time before you do it, and just keep killing them son, you're doing the Lord's work, He'll be so fucking pleased with you. Deal with them son, deal with them and kill them, you prove to yer da that yer not a fucking queer boy, go on, and you prove him wrong. You know he always thought you were a bent boy, now you just show him son. Give those whores some meat son, and show him you're not a bent

freak after all". Hillman began to be sick on the floor. After a few minutes, his breathing had returned to normal. He looked over to the table. His mother was gone. "Thanks Lord" he whispered, "I didn't mean to say all those nasty things before, I'll just leave it to you if I see my kids again or not, because Lord, as it states in your bible, "If the Lord is with us, then who can be against us"?

Hillman sat back down at the table, and poured himself a drink.

"Son, you're doing it all wrong". His mother.

"Look, just fuck off you, right? Just fuck off, interfering bitch!"

"John Hillman!! Language".

She grabbed her son by the ear, and banged his head off the corner of the table.

What actually happened was, he felt a stabbing pain in his head, got up from the floor and cracked his head on the corner of the dining table.

"Now, I'm going back to lie beside your father where we were both shot dead, and I won't be coming back to see you for a while, not until you learn to talk without using that kind of filth, you'd better get your act together, and start hammering those little whores, and prove to everyone that you're not a fucking frock boy".

"I'll show you who's a queer boy, you little Irish cunt, go on, go and die in the fucking kitchen". He had picked up the local phone book and was now flicking through the pages frantically looking for a taxi company. "Thompson's Taxis, perfect Lord". He looked up at the house through the security camera. "I'll phone a taxi Lord, that's what I'll do, I'll say it's for one of the evil pigs up there, I'll give them another fright Lord, they're so fucking brave aren't they Lord". Five minutes later, he had phoned the taxi company telling them he was a police officer and that he would need the driver for an hour. The young lady on the other end of the line informed him that that would cost more than two hundred pounds, and more than that if the time exceeded the hour." If it comes to more than that, then you'll be paid the extra cash at the end of the hire".

"Right you are sir" said the gullible receptionist.

"Tell your driver that I'll be waiting at the bottom of the drive of Morningside manor, Detective Inspector Robinson, I'll show I.D. of course".

"That's fine sir, about fifteen minutes, is that ok?"

"That will be fine my dear, thank you". He lifted the gun from the floor where he'd thrown it in his fit of temper.

At the far side of the room lay the silencer sleeve. "Better not forget you my little beauty, we don't want to be disturbing the cavalry up there, not yet anyway". He took one last look through the security camera, to make sure there was no-one wandering outside of the house, then he made his way up the steps and out of the hatch.
A strong wind blew through the trees, making branches creak and groan under the strain. He wore a black leather jacket and jeans, with a plain pale blue dress shirt. It was hardly the attire of a police officer, or a detective, but then he would not have to fool them for long. He stood now, just about ten yards off the bottom of the drive. Where he was standing, he knew that the cameras mounted on the roof of the house would not be able to detect him. Twenty-two minutes after making the phone call, he saw the headlights of a car swing into the drive. He was just going to step out from behind the bushes when he suddenly realized that it was a police car. "Fuck!! That was close". The two policemen in the car hadn't spotted any movement in the bushes.
"Careful son" his mother's voice. He did not answer her this time. If he didn't speak to her, she sometimes went away. The police car had just disappeared round the bend of the drive when the taxi did arrive.
The twenty-four year old young lady who was driving the taxi, shouted over to John Hillman, "this is a fucking wind up is it? A policeman, needing a bloody taxi? Don't detectives get their own cars any more"?
Hillman smiled at the young lady, as he approached the car. "I know, I know, it does look a bit odd doesn't it, but it's just that there's been a massive cock up in the office, and I can't get my car until the morning".
"Well, where are we going first" said the driver, as Hillman climbed into the cab, "I'm yours for the hour".
"You're mine for more than an hour my dear".
"Well, so be it, but you'll be charged more, anyway, I was told I'd be paid before we set off".
"Indeed you will, you little whore that you are". Hillman swung with his left fist, but much to his surprise, the young woman blocked his punch, and caught him with her closed fist across the nose. In a split second she was out of the car and running up the loose gravel drive towards the safety of the house. Hillman, whose nose was now bleeding heavily, gave chase, half crying with the pain in his nose

and with temper, and with sheer frustration. As she rounded the bend, she had about a hundred metres to go. Hillman knew he had no chance of catching her. He ran into the bushes and through the trees, hoping he could cut her off. Where he was now, was dangerous, he knew. He was coming out of the bushes near the steps of the house. If anyone came out of the house now, he was caught, or he'd be shot. He practically ran into the girl as she almost ran past him. She fell onto the gravel, screaming as she did. Hillman raised his fist, and this time he made no mistake, as he reigned punch after punch onto her head and face, until she lay before him, unconscious.

He grabbed the girl by the hair and pulled her through the woods. The girl's arms and legs trailed loosely by her side, dead weight.

"Is that sore queer boy"? His mother said, walking beside her son. Did the wee girly belt my little queer boy then, did she? Do you want your Ma to give her a belt on the ear for you Joan, is that yer fucking name now is it? Joan? Letting the little whores belt you now huh? Bleeding nose, just wait till I tell yer da, fucking woozie boy, eh Joan"?

Hillman got to the hatch. He let go of the girl's hair. Her head hit the ground face first. He opened the hatch then began climbing down pulling the girl by the arms, and dragging her down the steps. Once in, he wasted no time in putting a blindfold over the girl's eyes. He then tied her hands and feet together, and then climbed out of the hatch again. He closed it behind him and then made his way back through the woods again, towards the taxi. The engine was still running when he got there. Both doors of the car were still open. He had just got into the car and closed the passenger door when a police car came round the drive. The car stopped just behind the taxi. He saw the two policemen get out of their vehicle and approach him. Both of the officers carried guns. "What are you doing here"?

"I'm sorry officers, somebody must have played a trick with our receptionist, she told me to come here to Morningside and pick up a fare, but one of your officers told me that no-one has ordered a bloody taxi from here".

"Why is your nose bleeding sir"? The officer pulled out his pistol.

"Hey" said Hillman, "fuck, take it easy boys, I get nose bleeds, big deal, one of your guys gave me some tissues, for Christ's sake, I'm a fucking taxi driver, you're gonna fucking shoot me"?

"Why is your car facing up hill then sir, if you've been up there"?
"I never said I was up there, look, one of your guys pulled in behind me as I came in, so I pulled over to let him past. He stopped, and told me no-one ordered a taxi, he saw my nose bleeding, and he gave me some tissues, that's it. Go up there and ask him, and he'll verify what I've just said, please, I need to be getting back to base, my boss will be kicking up holy hell".
"Ok then, on you go sir, and don't be hanging around here".
"Not bloody likely sir, I've heard too much about what's gone on in that bloody house, and just for the record sir, I had no intentions of going in there".
"Right then sir, we'll reverse out and let you out, and be on your way".
"Yeah thank you".
The two police officers got back into their car, and reversed out of the drive. Hillman reversed out right behind them, stopping in the middle so that the police car could not get by. He switched off the ignition. The police car reversed into the side of the road. The wind was icy cold as Hillman got out of the car.
"Problem"? One of the officers shouted.
"Yeah, fucking thing's stalled again".
Once more, the two policemen got out of their car. Hillman had the bonnet of the car up placing the support bar into position.
"Fucking bastard thing, I'm fucking sick of this. Could one of you sit in the driver's seat, and switch on the ignition when I tell you please, fucking dodgy carburettor, I'm fucking sick of telling him about it, I'm bloody frozen, bloody nose bleeds, bastard".
"Take it easy sir, we'll soon have you up and running, try and control your language sir".
One of the officers got into the car. The other came and stood beside Hillman. Hillman pretended to fiddle with something in the engine.
"Do you need a torch sir? We have one in the car".
"No, it's alright officer, I've got it. He huffed and puffed and said, "anyway, your friend's eyes won't be able to see anything just shortly, that's it".
Hillman looked round to the driver. "Try that now officer". The car started first time. "Keep revving the engine". Hillman said to the policeman standing beside him, "Here's the problem look". He pointed down to a certain part of the engine. The officer bent down to get a look at what had been the problem. Hillman shot the man in

the back of the head. With the hood of the car still up, the driver could neither hear nor see his partner being shot, and his body slumping to the ground, with half of his brains and most of his face missing. Hillman cocked his head round the bonnet and said, "That'll do, silly cunt, are you going to rev that all fucking night"?
"Is that it sorted sir"?
"Yes it is thank you officer, I can't thank you enough for your help. I can't thank your friend either, because I've just shot him in the face". As the policeman looked up at Hillman, he looked into the barrel of his gun. "That's right son, Doctor John Hillman at your service". The young policeman, in a sitting position, made the mistake of going for his gun and got his hand blown off. He screamed with shock. "Out, come on, out of my taxi, I don't want blood and brains all over the seats, come on, out. He grabbed the officer by the collar and pulled him out of the car. "On your knees". The policeman, still in shock got down onto his knees. "Sorry son" said Hillman, and pulled the trigger. The whole of the man's face exploded in front of him onto the grass. Two minutes later, the two officers were back in their car, being held upright by their seat belts. They sat there, with only pulp for faces, spilling blood and matter down on to their uniforms. The taxi was driven seven hundred yards down the road and parked neatly into someone's drive, as if the car belonged there. Hillman walked calmly back towards the grounds of his house, his gun tucked neatly into his jacket pocket. "That my Lord was a bit too close for comfort, if you don't mind me saying, you wouldn't mind making it a bit less stressful next time would you? As he walked through the bitterly cold night, he began to think about the next stage of his essential work. "Time to sort out the whore now Lord, and please, when I'm banging away at her, could you please keep my mother out of the room, could you, bless her, but she gets in my way sometimes Lord, she'll get me caught one of these times I swear it, then what would you do, who would take care of all the cheap whores for you then, tell me that"?
The cold wind blew into Hillman's face as he made his way back to his retreat. As he walked, tears began to roll down his face. He was remembering images of himself and his two little girls playing in their garden at Harrington Square. The smiling laughing angel faces of innocence. "What happens Lord? What happens to us that we grow into people with very different ideas? We turn into money hungry people who care not a jot for our fellow human beings. We

will steal, we will lie, we will cheat, we will deceive, we will fornicate, with anyone, against any one, just to get richer. Money Lord, money, and do you know what? Even when we are comfortable and our families are secure, we still go looking for more. Innocence is a thing of the past. We were even born out of sin, like this greedy little whore I'm going to see now. She fucks for money Lord, well, she used to".

John Drummond had been down at the mortuary talking with Ashley Barnes. He remembered the girl from her training days down at the Thames Valley Mortuary. The girl knew her job now alright, he thought to himself, looking at the list of murdered people's names lying before him on the coffee table in Morningside Manor. A police officer came into the room and asked him if he wanted a cup of tea. "No thank you, I'm going back into the town in five minutes".

"Sir"

Yes? What is it"?

"We were just wondering sir, me and officer Kerr sir, well, we've been here since five o clock this morning, and well, we were wondering if you could phone in and see when they intended to send the relief officers sir, we're just about sleeping on our feet, it's nearly a quarter to eleven sir".

"Bloody hell" said Drummond, "Yes I'll call in and see what's happened, better still, I'll see to it myself, I'm just going back there now. How many more men are here"?

"There's eight of us sir, but six of them have just came on duty tonight".

"Right, I'll tell you what, I will have that cup of tea after all, I'll phone now, from my mobile, what's your names"?

Blackley sir, Officers Blackley and Kerr".

"Right, I'll see to it right now". Drummond went outside and stood on the top step of Morningside. He pressed the digits for the local police station. It was Deborah Knowles he got on the phone. After talking about Hillman for a few minutes, he then made inquiries about relief for the two officers.

"Oh, I don't know anything about that John; I'll have to ask about that, I won't be a minute. There were some crackling noises in his ear, and then Deborah came back on the phone. "They should be there John. The desk sergeant says that they left here at nine o clock,

they should definitely be there". Drummond looked at his watch. It was five minutes to eleven.
"Ok then Deborah, God knows what's happened to them, but I'm relieving these two officers as of now, Blackley and Kerr, they've been here since five o clock this morning".
"Well, I'm coming over John, two bloody hours to get to Morningside, no way, something's happened, oh Christ don't tell me"
Oh I hope not Deborah, I bloody hope not".
Officers Blackley and Kerr were at the bottom of the drive, on their way home, at last, from a long and very boring day. They came to the bottom of the drive. "Ok that way"? said Kerr, as he was just about to pull out.
"Yeah, oh, no oh fuck, take a look at this Steve".
"What"?
"Stop, look".
Steven Kerr looked past his partner over at the two men slumped in their seats in the police car parked just across the way.
"Wait here Steve, I'll go and see-".
"Wait fuck all, we're driving back up there to tell the chief and bring more men down here, fucking hero, wait here my arse. Steven Kerr swung the car round and headed back up the hill towards the house.
Drummond, with one hand cupped around a mug of tea, and the other hand nursing a cigarette, stood on the top step. He knew, by the way the car came scraping around the bend, that something was wrong. "Here we go again John" he said to himself.
"How many this time boys"? By the time Drummond and four of his officers were back down to the bottom of the drive, Deborah Knowles and Karen Jones were already there. Drummond walked up to the car and looked at the corpses. He shook his head and sighed, looking at Deborah and Karen as he did so. "Deborah? I may as well get myself back down to London for all the good I'm doing up here. Is this bastard just standing here at the gate and just waiting for policemen to come along, bloody armed police as well; "Oh, hold it, are you policemen? Then just sit still please while I blow your fucking brains out from here to Loch Lomond, thank you".
"How the fuck, I mean, yet again, not a single shot fired Deborah, not one. Two armed policemen, still in their car".

Karen had been wandering around the immediate area. “No Mister Drummond, come and see this”. Karen walked about ten yards up the path. “Here”. She switched on her torch again. “One of them was shot here” she said, as she pointed the light to the grass verge, and then onto the hedge. There was a spray of blood about four feet along the grass, and up onto some of the bush. Drummond took out a cigarette, and offered one to Deborah and Karen. Deborah took one, Karen declined.
Drummond puffed furiously on his cigarette. “He must be hiding in these fucking woods Deborah, he must be. Where the fuck does he go though, after it? We combed the woods, nothing. Then he kills again, in the same fucking place, almost the same fucking spot”.
“Forensics are on their way John” said Deborah, “They’ll be able to tell us more”.
“I’m not on about that, I’m on about where he retreats to. His photograph has been on national telly now for weeks, every night just about, for weeks, with a handsome reward being offered, and still, he disappears and reappears at will, he’s one smart fucking cookie ladies, I can tell you that”. Drummond looked directly into the eyes of Karen Jones, as if she alone had the answers to his questions, “Where the fuck does he go”?
Headlights appeared from the top of the hill, heading down from the house. A police van. “Here we go ladies, the bastard has probably killed another officer while we’ve been down here talking”.
The van came to a halt. A young officer got out of the van and approached Drummond. “Yes”? said Drummond, rather flustered.
“Sir, someone’s just phoned the house and asked where their taxi driver was. Thompson’s Taxis, they said a detective ordered one about two hours ago, and that the taxi was to be on hire to him for about an hour, they were wondering if we were finished with the taxi sir, send it back”.
“Send it back”? John Drummond looked at the two women. “Can you believe this, as if I haven’t got enough on my, send it back? Officer”. He put his arm around the young man’s shoulder. “How long have you been in the force huh”?
“About twelve year’s sir”.
“Twelve years eh? And in all that time, have you ever heard of an inspector or a detective to phone for a taxi, and then make their inquiries regarding drugs or violent crime or whatever; to solve

crimes, have you ever heard of that in your twelve years here, be honest now".
"No sir, I haven't". "No sir, I didn't think you had, it's a hoax son, somebody's just taking the cunt right out of you".
" Excuse my French ladies. Now come with me, I want to show you something, come on". He walked back down to the end of the drive, and along to the police car. Police photographers were now here. There were lights flashing from cameras, ambulances, police cars, all helping to illuminate the faceless officers seated in their vehicle. "See this"?
The young officer looked into the car and then looked away.
"Exactly" said Drummond, that's what I'm interested in, who done that to those two colleagues of ours, I'm not one bit interested where Thompson's taxi drivers are, now get back up to that house and pray that your pals have not had their throats cut, twelve years eh"?

Hillman sat huddled up against a large bush, less than thirty metres away from all the commotion around the police car. Flashing lights were spinning around the wooded area where he hid, as if trying to expose him to the police. Crowds of people were gathered around trying to catch a glimpse of the two dead officers. Other officers had been called in from their city duties, to assist their colleagues in what was rapidly becoming known as, 'The Death House'. Hillman peered through the bushes intently. He pondered on making a break for the safety of the hatch. He would have to move slowly, ever so slowly. He could see people looking into the woods, as if they were staring right at him. At one point, he saw someone pointing straight at him. Then he heard the loud roar of the DCI's voice on the megaphone. "Four of you get into the woods there, and if you see anything on two legs, then for the love of God, blow it to pieces. Search thoroughly men, take your torches. Comb the woods and see if that mental man is in there".

"Come on John" said Deborah, "Let me and Karen have a cup of coffee with you, get a bite to eat, come on". The three detectives walked up the gravel path towards the house. "I tell you girls, this, this sick pig is beginning to get to me. He doesn't leave any clues, nothing. He doesn't make any threats on the phone, he doesn't try to bargain with us, I mean, I don't even know why he's started all these

killings. For what reason is he committing these murders, is it revenge? Is it spite"?
"I'm afraid it's worse than that John" said Deborah, "It's worse than revenge or spite; you see Doctor Hillman has been called by God to do these things, he's on a mission".
"He's on a mission to kill cops"?
"No, it's just that cops keep getting in his way. He's on a mission to kill prostitutes. I have yet to discover why he has to kill them, what sparked it off, no-one knows that yet, but he's out to get them, although you wouldn't think so with the number of working girls still walking the streets of this city. All these warnings to them on the T.V. just seem to go in one ear and out the other".
"It's not just the prostitutes who are at risk either" said Karen. "Every girl or woman he sees in what he would call provocative attire is in danger as well. In his mind, any woman dressed scantily, or sparsely, are whores. If he stops killing the whores then he would be letting his God down, he has to carry on. On top of that, now that the death penalty has been reintroduced, he has even less to fear. He knows he's going to die, it's just a matter of time, and so now, it's just a matter of how many whores he can take out before he gets blown away".
Drummond looked at Karen and Deborah.
"I know John, it's not a very good situation to be in, but we're stuck with it. You're not alone here John, we want the bastard put down as well".
Drummond looked ahead of them to the house. "I've got a meeting with Terrance Davis tomorrow, what the fuck is he going to think now, after tonight"?

"Let him think what he wants, he's not going to get any better than us three to cover this, and he knows it".

Hillman crawled like a snake through the long grass and bushes. He was only about ten feet from the safety of the hatch. He could hear the men in the woods beating bushes and brush, and not saying anything to each other as they made their search. Yellow strips of light dances off trees and bushes, along with the continual spinning blue lights from the emergency vehicles over the perimeter walls. He heard feet striding confidently through the brush. He could feel the hatred of these hunters, the determination, and aggression. Now

he knew what it was like to be one of God's creatures. The men were getting closer. So was the hatch, but the hatch was in a clearing, they would easily see him if he attempted to open it. He had to make a decision, and fast, and he had only a few seconds to decide what to do, if not, then it wouldn't matter.
"Help me Lord." He whispered through the bitter wind. But God did not answer him, he was on his own. He saw a thicket of bushes just ahead of him, if he could make it to those, he could take out the man who came nearest to him. "Take a chance, take a chance, oh fuck, they're going to get me. Made it". He crawled into the evergreen bush. Sharp jagged holly leaves ripped and tore into his face and hands. He almost let out a scream. He sat waiting. Seconds later, an officer rattled the top of the bush with his rifle. Realizing it was a holly bush, the police officer moved on. Blood spewed from three different places on Hillman's face. One of the jagged leaves had torn into his mouth, and ripped open the soft flesh where his gums had been stitched. Totally convinced that God had rejected and abandoned him, he sat getting jagged all over his body, crying with rejection, and feeling like never before that no-one in the world wanted anything to do with him. His parents were dead, his wife was gone, his kids were gone, and now, after all this good work he'd done for God, even He had fucked off and left him in the shit. "Well" He thought, "It's time I moved on".

He sat there and watched the men getting further and further from him, their figures distorted with his tears. The four men were slowly making their way to the house. Now and then, one or two of them would stop and turn, shining their torches in the direction they had just came, keeping Hillman pinned in the agonising grip of the holly bush. He watched the men
eventually stepping onto the gravel path which surrounded the house, then they disappeared into the woods at the side of the house. Behind him, one of the ambulances pulled away along with one or two police cars. As he climbed out from under the holly bush, the thorns felt like the teeth of angry dogs, ripping and tearing away at his flesh one last time, as he got out. Tears rolled down his face, as once again, visions of his little girls came into his head. He could hear their voices now. "Happy Buffday tooo yooouuu, Happy Buffday tooo yoooouuu". Now he was actually sobbing as he crawled through the rugged grass, only feet from the hatch. "Happy

Buffday deeer daddy, Happy Buffday toooo yoooouu. Hillman was choking with emotion. "We loves you daddy, really really really love you". "We all love you daddy" said Tracy Hillman, whispering in his ear. "We love you like nothing else in this world Mister Doctor Hillman, don't you ever forget that". Tracy kissed him on the cheek. "No you don't" he sobbed. As he lifted up the hatch. "Blow your candles out, blow them out daddy". "I can't darlings, daddy won't be allowed to have any more parties with his angels, they won't let me, my angels. You'll have to have your parties on your own now my babies". "Blow out your candles daddy, come on".

Hillman managed to get himself onto the fixed ladder and close the hatch behind him. He only managed to climb down two steps, and then fell the rest of the way down. He sat sobbing on the floor, blood pouring from his mouth, and dripping from his forehead. His ears were scratched, and his hands, even under his jeans, he felt the tears, the stings.

The young woman was lying on the floor, petrified at the sounds she could hear. After a few moments, Hillman got up to his feet. This room had never seemed this quiet to him before, although he knew the girl was conscious. The room felt suddenly closed in, it felt almost claustrophobic to him. He walked over to a cupboard mounted on the wall and brought out a bottle of whiskey and two glasses. He walked over to where the girl lay and sat down, cross-legged beside her.

"Please Mister, I'm sorry for what I've done, I was only frightened, that's why I hit out at you, please, I'm so sorry for what I've done".

"Sshhh" said Hillman, "don't worry, I'm not going to hurt you any more, you made a mistake, and I made a mistake, let's leave it at that shall we? Now, will you join me in a little drink, will you"?

"Oh, if you say so, I-".

"I didn't say you had to, I asked you if you'd join me in a little drink".

"Yes, if, yes".

"Good, now what's your name"?

"Jenny, Jenifer".
"Jenifer, nice, nice and plain, Jenifer, it sounds like honesty to me" said Hillman, as he cut the ropes from the young woman's hands. "You know? Honesty, genuine, Jenifer, something like that".
Now he cut the ropes from her ankles. "Now look out" said Hillman softly, because when I take this blindfold off the light will stab your eyes, ready"?
"Yes sir, ok".
He gently pulled the blindfold from her eyes. "Keep them closed, and then open them gradually". Hillman could see the black eyes and the swollen cheeks of the girl before him. Her mouth was swollen too, as was his own mouth. He gently touched the girl's cheek with his fingers. "I don't think your jaw is broken Jenifer, but I would get yourself over to casualty in the morning, get it x rayed just to be sure".
"Yes sir, I will".
The girl felt a glimmer of hope. It was only a glimmer, but it was better than total darkness.
"Now then Jenny, can I trust you to behave in here before I let you go, can I"?
"Yes sir, yes you can".
"Good, now could you bring me out a bottle of soda from out of that cupboard up there, oh, and if you don't like whiskey, then there's vodka or wine in there".
"May I have a glass of wine sir, instead of whiskey"?
"Indeed you may Jenny, now, come on over and sit beside me and tell me a little about yourself".
She sat down next to Hillman, both with their backs against the wall.
"Do you drive taxis for a living Jenifer" said Hillman, pouring himself his first whiskey.
"Just part time sir, I-".
"Hey!!" Jenifer jumped.
"Stop with the sir Jenny, it's John, alright? John, not sir".
"Ok John, I only work part time, I've got a little girl, who's just started school".
"Really? What's her name"?
"Amy, her name is Amy, John".
John Hillman's head swung round. "Amy? I've got a little girl called Amy".
"Have you John"?

"Yes, and I have another little girl named Angela".
"That's a beautiful name John, is it not"?
"Come on, drink some wine, we're having a party here, a kind of belated party, it was my birthday three days ago".
"Oh" said Jenny, still a bag of nerves as she poured herself another glass of wine. "Yes Jenny, forty-two, do I look forty-two to you, do I? I mean it's hard to tell with all these bruises, but, come on forty-two? What do you think"?
Jenny sipped her wine. "Well, if you want me to be honest, I would have taken you to be around thirty, thirty-six maybe".
"You're just saying that so as I won't fuck you for my birthday aren't you"?
"No John, no, I'm eh, that's what I think".
"And do you think that I'm going to fuck you Jenny? What do you think"?
Jenifer bowed her head and looked into her wine glass.
"I don't know, I, think you'll do whatever you want".
"You're right Jenny, I will do what I want from now on, but don't you worry, I'm not going to fuck you, anyway, I don't feel like fucking you right now, but please. don't be offended sweetheart, because you are a very pretty girl, there is no question about that, no doubt at all, none, no, you're very pretty, very".
Jenifer was petrified again. She raised her glass and said, "Happy belated birthday John". The glimmering light of hope kept flickering on and off.

MORNINGSIDE.

"Will you be alright to drive tonight John"? Karen said, as she lifted the empty coffee cups from the kitchen worktop. "Deborah and I can give you a lift no problem, just leave your car here, get it tomorrow".
"No, I'll be fine, I'll be ok".
"Are you sure"? Said Karen, "You don't look too clever".
"With all due respect Karen, I look an awful lot better than those two men of mine down there in that car".
"Fuck"! Said Deborah, "I wish to Christ you'd stop beating yourself up about all this, listen, these are all fully trained officers with firearms, they have been trained specifically for situations such as these, now, no-one is more frustrated than me, to know that an untrained ordinary G.P. can take them out two at a time, but the fact remains that he can. Now, that's not your fault, and it's not Karen's fault, and it's not my fault. He took my partner out, only feet away from me John. I didn't hear a bloody thing. The fact remains though, that when all is said and done, he is only a general practitioner, and sooner or later his luck is bound to run out. So, stop with all this down talk John, because your negativity will pass on to your men, and you'll have them scared to death rather as have them all fired up for when that bastard does show his face again".
Drummond sighed and nodded his head. "You're right Deborah, I'm sorry, I'm sorry Karen, I haven't been very professional have I".
The telephone rang in the hallway. "Got it" shouted an officer. Less than a minute later, the officer came through to the kitchen. "Sir"?
"Yes"? Replied Drummond.
"It's about that phone call from Thompson's taxis sir, it wasn't a hoax. That was them on the phone there sir, they're wanting to know where their driver is, a Miss Jenifer Sadler they're saying that she came to this house last night to pick up a detective Robinson, and they say that that was shortly after nine o clock last night. She hasn't reported back in".

Drummond looked at his watch. It was now Two forty-one am. "Ah great" Drummond said, "He's gone he's took the piss, and he's took off. He's away now; he's away for good this time. I want to speak to the person who took that call, fucking detective Robinson indeed". Hillman was on his fourth glass of whiskey.
"That'll do me" he said, "After this one Jenny, I don't want to get drunk". Jenifer had only started her second glass of wine. "What is your opinion on tramps Jenny, I mean prostitutes".
"Prostitutes"? She knew she had to be careful with her answer. "Well, I suppose they don't bother me really, but then John, I only live with my little girl, I don't have a man to worry about, you know, being seduced by them, but I still think it would be a better world if we didn't have them. I would imagine they've broken a few marriages up".
"Oh they have Jenny, and you're right, it would be a better place without them. I've killed one or two of them Jenny you know. I can tell you this, because I'm going away from here in the morning. I'm going to where the streets are paved with those painted women. You won't see me again, not up here in Sheffield. I'm going South Jenny; take a few out down there, in the filthy city".
"London? You mean John"?
"Yes London Jenny, the place, is, drink your wine Jenny, the place is crawling with them, disease carrying sluts that they are".
"I wish you luck John, when you're down there". Wherever she was, at least she knew she was still in Sheffield.
John Hillman got up to his feet and walked over to the mirror on the wall. He opened his mouth gently, and with his pointing finger, pulled it open. "That was bloody sore Jenny; I think the whiskey has soothed it. Come over here Jenny".
"I'm sorry John, for lashing out at you, I am".
"Relax Jenny, anyway you didn't do this, it was a holly bush, I told you, I'm not going to kill you, didn't I tell you that"?
"Yes sir. John, I mean".
"When Doctor Hillman says something, then he keeps his word. Now, when it's time to go, I have to blindfold you again, you understand"?
"Yes".
"Right, well don't be panicking, I swear I won't hurt you anymore. You see, I'm doing what I want to do from now on Jenny, not what *they* tell me to do, I do all the dirty work for Him, and then when I

need His help, where is He? Nowhere, that's where. He just leaves me to get shot like a dog".
"They"? She thought to herself. Who were they? Demons"?
Jenifer looked at the floor as Hillman stood beside her. "You don't know who I'm talking about do you Jenny"?
"No sir, John, sorry John".
"I'm talking about God Jenny, that's who. He asks me to kill these whores for Him, but when I need a favour from Him, it's a different matter, "Go and fuck yourself Doctor John Hillman, fuck, help you, you fool, you must be joking doctor. Now Jenny, from now on, I do what I want, not Him, nor *her* either for that matter, interfering old bat". Hillman looked around the room, as he pulled an open razor from a drawer under the mirror. "Now relax Jenny, go and bring your wine over while I talk to you and have a shave".
Jenifer done as she was told. "Now then". He looked around the room as if there was someone else in there with them. With shaving foam over his face, and the razor pulled open wide, he said, "It's her I'm bothered about".
"Who"?
He looked once more from side to side, and then leaned over to whisper. "My mother Jenny, that's who".
Jenifer Sadler distinctly remembered hearing on the news, that Anne Hillman had been shot and killed in her own home along with her husband. She pushed her luck. "Your mother's dead John".
"I fucking know that!! It doesn't stop her though, coming in and out of here telling me what to do, don't worry, if she comes now, I won't listen to her". He began shaving with the lethal blade, and using it like it was a butter knife. "That's why I'm hurrying Jenny it's in case she comes in before you get a chance to get away".
Jenifer let out an involuntary groan, which sounded like a little girl when she's just discovered a large spider in the bath.
"Sshh, for fuck sakes, she'll hear us, I'm not supposed to bring girls home, not to stay the night Jenny. Mother said they're just whores John, you're not a whore Jenny are you"?
"No I'm not a whore John, I've got my wee Amy remember"?
"Oh yes".
"You make sure that no-one ever takes her away from you Jenny".
"I will John, if you let me go John, I promise I won't let anyone take her away".

Hillman continued his shave saying nothing. Jenifer was unsure what to do. Should she talk to him, or wait for him to speak to her. She realized that he could be unhinged very easily. It was a dangerous situation to be in. After all she'd read in the papers about him, she couldn't be sure he meant what he'd said about letting her go. How could you trust a man who claims to be talking to God, and to his dead mother? If any of these voices came into his head right now, he could easily snap and kill her. Her only hope as far as she could tell, was the fact that she happened to have a little girl with the same name as his daughter. He connected with that. She tried her luck. "How old is your little Amy John"?
He stopped shaving, and turned to look at her. "What do you want to know that for"?
"No, I eh, no, I, I was just wondering, my little girl is nearly five John, my Amy".
Hillman stood, with the razor being held just underneath his Adam's apple. "Let's see now, oh, my Amy will be nearly eight, and my other girl will be nearly eleven, now. In fact, Hillman was now so confused, he had no idea what age his children were. Don't you talk any more to me Jenifer, until I tell you, go and sit back down over there, no more questions, anyway, I know you're going to tell the police that I've changed my appearance, and try to give them an insight into what kind of person I really am".
She wanted to reassure him that she wouldn't, but she knew when he said, don't talk any more, he meant it. He washed the remaining foam from his face. "Finish your glass of wine; we'll have to go in a minute. Jenifer downed the glass of wine wondering where her destiny lay. This was it, she would soon find out. "Put that blindfold on, and don't be cheating with it or you'll die. She tied it securely around her head making absolutely sure that she couldn't see a thing through it. She wasn't sure if she wanted to see anything. "Now listen carefully" said Hillman. "Do as I tell you and you'll see your little girl again". He guided her to the wooden steps which led up to the hatch. "Wait here, don't move!!"
Hillman looked out at the house from his camera. There were two police cars and an unmarked car in the car park. There was no-one walking around the grounds. He spun the camera around and checked the woods. All clear. He lifted his mobile phone from the table and put his leather jacket on. Two minutes later, they were both out into the open air. He placed a couple of branches over the

closed trap door. Then he led her through the trees and down a slope. They came to the boundary wall which stood about eight feet high. Hillman explained to her about the wall. “I’ll lift you up and then you wait until I get up ok”?
“Yes John”. He levered her up onto the top of the wall, then he climbed up himself. He jumped down, and then supported her weight as he took her down from the wall. They were now on a public pavement. “Now then Jenny, we walk. If you hear a car approaching, then you put your arm around me and you bury your head under my jacket, do you hear”?
“Yes John”. The couple walked along the pavement entering a residential area. So far, so good she thought to herself. In less than ten minutes they were at the house where Hillman had left the taxi. The occupants of the house were not out of bed yet. It was four forty-one am.
“Ok” He whispered, as he opened the door of the car. “In you get Jenny”. The keys were still in the ignition. It started first time. Hillman reversed out of the dive and drove off in the direction of the station. “Get down on the floor please Jenny, in case anyone sees your blindfold. Less than fifteen minutes later, he pulled up outside of the railway station. There was a packet of cigarettes on the dash. “Are these cigarettes yours Jenny”? “May I have one”?
“Of course John”. The car park was completely deserted. “Would you like one Jenny”?
“Yes please, if that’s alright”.
Hillman looked around. “Ok you can sit up now”. He lit them both a cigarette up, and handed one to her. As he exhaled he said, “You know you’re a lucky girl don’t you”?
“Yes I do John, and I appreciate the fact”.
“Good, good, cause I’ll tell you something Jenny, there aren’t many people who could punch John Hillman on the nose these days, and live to tell the tale, you do know that don’t you”.
“Yes I do John, I honestly do”. There was silence for a while as they both smoked. Both of them very quiet for very different reasons.
At last Hillman said. “When I get out of the car, you keep down on the floor. Count in your head up to five hundred. After that Jenny, take off your blindfold, and go home to your little girl. Now, you will appreciate your life even more than you did before, won’t you”?
“Yes” she whispered, “Thank you”.

They sat in silence again. Then the rumble of a train could be heard coming into the station. "Five hundred Jenny, and remember, go straight home to your little girl, at least give me that much of a start, and maybe?"
"What John, anything".
"Maybe, you might not mention the fact that you know I'm going to London, after all, I'm only trying to see my little Amy".
The car door slammed. "John, John, are you still here"? Jenifer sat in silence. He really had kept his word. "John"? She started to count. When she got to three hundred, she heard the train pulling away. Was he gone, really? She sat up on the seat, and pulled the blindfold from her head. As she was about to change seats, she saw an envelope lying on the driver's seat. She put the light on in the car and opened the note. It just simply read: *Good luck Amy, may God bless you and your mum.* Inside the envelope there were two one hundred pound notes. Jenifer lit another cigarette and got out of the taxi. She stood listening to the sound of the train getting fainter and fainter. She was indeed a very lucky woman; it could have so easily gone the other way. As it turned out, she was now going home to cuddle her little girl and let her baby sitter away. "Thank you John Hillman" she whispered, "But I hope I never see your face again".
A delivery came down the hill into the car park. A little chubby man got out of the float carrying two cardboard boxes and heading into the station. "Good morning Miss" he said to Jenifer, "It looks like it's going to be a lovely day".
"Yes it is" she replied, "It's going to be a beautiful day".

MORNINGSIDE.

Drummond awoke on the armchair where he'd fallen asleep. He could hear voices coming from the kitchen, and he could smell toast. Someone had thrown a quilt over him. He looked at his watch. It was just after six o clock in the morning. He got up and walked down the long hallway to the kitchen. One of the officers had obviously been to a paper shop. As he entered the kitchen, four of the six officers on duty were standing reading their dailies. "Good morning lads" said Drummond. There was panic among the men, shifting around uneasily. "Relax boys, take it easy, is there any toast on the go"?

"There's muffins sir".

"Muffins will do fine guys, I take it nothing else happened through the wee small hours"?

"No sir, it's all been quiet".

"Hmmnn" said Drummond, "even the devil takes a breather, what time did Miss Knowles and Miss Jones leave"?

One of the officers said, "They were talking away to you, and you just drifted off, it would be about three o clock roughly sir".

Drummond looked at his watch again, "Huh, three hours sleep, I'm becoming a real slugger head in my old age".

"Here you are sir" said one of his officers, putting down a plate containing two toasted muffins, and sitting down a mug of tea next to it.

"Thank you officer, thank you".

"It's all over the front page sir, about last night".

"No doubt" said Drummond, as he munched on his muffin, "They're going to have a field day with me today, it's a wonder they're not at the front door now. They were sir, but we put them out of the gates, we've got police tape closing off the grounds now sir. There are two men down there monitoring the gates sir.

"Thank you lads, thank you indeed. I have to meet with Terence Davis later today. He left me in charge of this case, and since I've taken over we've lost four men, and now a taxi driver missing. Not a bad start in three weeks lads eh"?
"It's not your fault sir, the men were obviously off their guard and so they have only themselves to blame. Whatever happens sir, we're all standing by you, we will get him sir".
"I'm not so sure about that boys, really I'm not. He's hijacked that taxi now, he's got the girl, I don't think we'll see him again, he's off boys, I just know it, and God help that poor taxi driver. They must be wondering what the hell they've done to have this inflicted upon them, that's to say, that they're still alive of course. No-one who encounters this madman lives for very long. He or she may stand half a chance if Hillman requires them to drive him around for a while, but that's it, it'll only be for a while".

MADELY COURT. HEATHER BRADLEY'S HOME.

Heather sat with Rachel watching a DVD, having just finished their evening meal. Both girls had a glass of wine and were discussing hair styles and colours when the doorbell rang. "I'll get it Rachel; I think it might be the paperboy for his money. Heather picked up her purse from the table on her way past. Just before she got to the door, the bell rang again. "I'm coming" she said, as she unlocked the door, fastening the chain as she did so. On her step stood Steve Temple, Joseph Dougan, and a young man she did not know. "Hi Steve" she said nervously as she took the chain off, "Come in", though she knew they were coming in whether or not she invited them. "How are you Steve, is everything alright"?
Temple did not answer Heather, instead he walked past her and walked into her living room, taking a seat beside Rachel on the sofa. "Hello Rachel". Sitting straight up but with his knees open and his arms resting on his knees, he bowed his head towards the floor. "Alas Heather, no, everything is not alright, oh you know Joe don't you girls, this is Joseph Dougan, he's the last loyal man I have left, Heather, somebody keeps bumping my men off"."Yes Steve" said Heather, "we were sorry to hear the news about your brother, have they got anybody for his murder yet"?
"No, no they haven't. They haven't got anyone for his murder Heather because there's no-one even looking for his murderer, just the same as they're not looking for Paul Crane's murderer or Harry Felder's, or any of my men".
Heather tried her best to remain cool. "Would you like a glass of wine gentlemen"?
"Wine"? Said Temple. "Yes please, we'll have a glass won't we Joseph"?
"Certainly Mister Temple".
"What about you kid" said Temple, "would you like some wine"?

"I don't mind" replied the teenager.
"He doesn't mind Heather, three glasses of wine for three thirsty gentlemen. And how are you Rachel, do you like living here with Heather"?
"Yes sir" she replied. Rachel knew there was trouble coming. "I'll bet you do, do you like tasting the eh, the wine, huh, Rachel"? Temple smiled and winked at Dougan.
"Do you like tasting Heather's, wine mm? Is it good"?
Heather brought the three glasses of wine over as fast as she could.
"What can we do for you gentlemen" she said as she found a seat.
"What can you do for us Heather, that's a good question, because I was just thinking to myself, I wonder what Heather and Rachel could do for me. Do you know what I'd like you to do for me, can you guess what I would like
Silence.
Temple sipped his wine and then lit up one of his cigars. He puffed a few times and then blew smoke down onto the carpet. "I would like you to start telling me the truth".
"We do tell the truth Mister Temple".
He smiled, sarcastically, shaking his head, still looking at the floor between his feet, his leather jacket making squeaking noises in the quietness. Temple looked up at Heather. "Do you know who this boy is Heather"? He nodded to the youth.
"No, should I know him"? She was trying her best to remain calm, but it was becoming more and more difficult.
"This Heather is young Thomas Crane, not Paul's son, but his nephew. He has an interesting story to tell, go on son, tell the nice honest ladies your story.
"Well" began the young lad, "I was short of money, and I met my uncle Paul. He was in a hurry, but he told me to wait, he had a message to deliver. He said he would be back soon and that he'd give me some money and take me for a beer".
"What does that have to do with me" said Heather.
Temple said nothing; he just waved the boy on with his cigar, still smiling sarcastically.
"Well, I watched him go in".
"Go on son, it's alright, tell the honest ladies what you saw".
"I saw my uncle Paul go in to your hair dresser's shop, so I waited for him across the road, like he told me".
"And"? Said Temple.

"He never came back out".
"He never came back out Thomas, are you sure"? Said Temple.
"Positive".
"Now then Heather, listen to this, tell the nice ladies what happened next".
The youth pointed to Heather; "I saw a blonde woman coming out of the back of the shop with you, carrying a very large bundle in what looked like bin bags. Both of you put the bundle into the boot of the blonde woman's car; I couldn't tell what kind of car it was. The woman drove away. At the same time, I saw two other women going into the shop by the front door".
Temple, smiling directly at Heather, said, "Tell me Thomas, what did your uncle think of all this carry on".
"I never saw him again; he didn't come back out of the shop".
"How long did you wait Thomas"?
"About an hour".
"An hour? Well now" said Temple, "this is strange Heather, don't you think, very strange, because I know that you girls tell me the truth all the time, I've lost count how many times you've told me. Now then Heather, do you know what I'm going to do, I'm going to ask you one more time about Paul Crane". He took a drag of his cigar, his leather jacket once more creaking in the quietness of the room. "If you insist Heather that you're telling me the truth, then Joseph here is going to get out his big knife and he's going to hack off this boys fingers, one at a time, right here, right now, in front of us all, because if he's calling my girls liars, then he'd better be prepared to face the consequences. So, what's it going to be Heather"?
Heather picked up a cigarette from the coffee table and lit it. "Ok Steve, I'll tell you everything".
"So you *have* been telling lies"?
"Yes, but only because Rachel and I were roped into it, we had nothing to do with it, it was one of Carla Paganni's friends".
"What's her name Heather"?
"I only know her first name, I don't know her surname, I swear to you Steve". There was total silence in the living room. Sirens could be heard in the distance, wailing away.
Temple sighed. "What am I going to do with you, I thought I could trust you, I really did, I thought I could depend on you, you seemed so genuine when we spoke".

“You can depend on me Steve, as I said; we were dragged into the situation”.
“I’ve asked you numerous times Heather, if you knew anything at all about the disappearance of Paul Crane, and you kept telling me no. Rachel, get your shoes on”.
“Oh no Steve please” begged Heather.
“Rachel, Get your shoes on now!!
“Rachel’s coming with us Heather. Now, you listen to me you lying little whore that you are”. He looked at the clock on the wall. “This is the deal; you’ve got forty-eight hours to find out where Carla Paganni and her blonde friend are hiding. If you can’t tell me, or if you do something really stupid like going to the police, then I tell you now, that the next time you see Rachel, she’ll be lying in a long box with her arms folded across her chest. Tonight is a warning, your last warning, if you fail to heed this one, well, that’s up to you. Forty-eight hours, tramp, and your time starts now, I swear!!”
They let Rachel put a pair of shoes on her feet, then they turned to leave. Before they got out, Temple turned and said, “Thanks for the wine”. Then he nodded his head in Rachel’s direction. “Forty-eight hours Heather”.
Three hundred and twenty yards from her door, Heather’s beauty salon was burning to the ground.

CLEAVLAND TERRACE.SHEFFIELD.

Jenifer Sadler lifted the phone and dialled the number for the police station. It had been six hours since herself and John Hillman had parted company. She didn't know why, but she found herself feeling obligated to give him a head start. She supposed she felt this way because he'd shown her mercy, and kept his promise, letting her go home to her little girl.

Somewhere inside that man there was a real affectionate person, but the world would never see again the gentleman hiding inside the monster who was John Hillman. He would be shot, or hanged or fried, or whatever way they would do it, but for crimes committed, John Hillman would die, there wasn't a shadow of doubt about that. She looked at her child asleep on the sofa as she waited for the phone to be answered. Every mother loves her children, although every one of us have different ways of showing it. She had always loved her little girl, and she always would, but, after her experiences with Hillman, somehow, she loved her just that little bit more, if that was possible. She certainly valued her life more. One thing she knew she wouldn't be doing from now on, and that was, driving taxis, again, thanks to John Hillman.

She stroked her daughter's hair, reliving the ordeal she had just been subjected to. How she had arrived at Morningside on what was, up until then, a very quiet night. Within two minutes of arriving, her whole life had turned around, or upside down. She remembered running up the hill towards the house, trying desperately to reach safety, Hillman in pursuit, her feet finding difficulty to gain any purchase on the loose gravel. Then, the first punch. His fists felt like stone, as he reigned punch after punch into her face, with the rhythm of a black-smith's hammer, and then of course, the unconsciousness, the blissful unconsciousness.

Jenifer Sadler began to cry as she stroked her little girl's hair once again.
"I love you so much Amy, she said. "Mummy loves you so very much".

HEATHER'S BEAUTY SALON. 7:42.AM.

Heather stood in the rubble and looked around in disbelief at what was her beauty salon. Almost everything had been destroyed in the blaze. The chief fireman approached her, wiping his dirty face with a handkerchief. "I'm afraid it was malicious Miss Bradley. We found where they've placed petroleum spirit; in fact, they've sprinkled it all over the shop. I'm afraid the place was well ignited by the time we got here. Do you have any ideas who could have done this thing to you Miss Bradley"
She knew fine well who had done this to her. Paul Crane and that long nosed Irish bastard Dougan had warned her. "No. I em, no, I can't think of anyone who would do this to me, I was not aware that I even had an enemy, this is a shock, I mean that's four girls out of a job, and myself, I'm sorry, I can't speak with you right now".
"I understand" said the fireman. He repeated what he'd already told her, rubbing salt into very open wounds for Heather. Why was he doing this?
"By the time we got here the place was well engulfed, you know, with all the petrol. We saved what we could for you. Your computer escaped, along with a couple of hair dryers, but both of your sun beds perished along with"-.
"I know!! I eh, I can see, thank you for trying your best".
"Ok Miss Bradley, we can talk later" said the fireman.
From behind her, Heather heard another voice, a female voice, a voice of authority.
"I know this must be a very difficult time for you Miss Bradley, but could we please have a word with you". It was Deborah Knowles and Karen Jones. "Let's go across the road for a coffee shall we, and before you say anything, we're not going to ask you any questions, we just want you to listen to what we have to say, just listen to us for

five minutes, ok? Come on Miss Bradley let's go and get a coffee. Heather followed the two police women out of what was once her shop, her pride and joy, her dream. The smell of singeing seemed to be trapped in her nostrils, even when outside in the fresh air. The sprinklers which she'd had installed a few months ago had come on, but were inadequate to deal with such a blaze. This had been well planned and executed she knew. The three women sat down at a table in the cafe. Deborah deliberately picked a table away from the window, so that Heather would not have to look over at the carnage that used to be her living. Deborah looked at the pale young woman in front of her. "Heather, I know there are people leaning down on you, I just know it. You would deny this if I asked you, so I'll say this as quickly and as clearly as I can. You don't have to take this you know, you really don't. There are steps that Karen and I can take to protect you, and your family. I know you're probably petrified of these people right now, I don't know how much they've threatened you, but I promise you this, if you give Karen and I one name, just one, then I swear we'll have you moved to a secret location, until we have got a result". Deborah looked at Heather. "If you still don't want to tell us, then I'm afraid there's very little, if anything that we can do. It was on the news yesterday, we found Mister Paul Crane's body in a skip, twenty-five miles from here. Both of his arms shot out and one shot right between the eyes. Now then, Karen and I came to see you one day, and you were giving one of your girls a telling off for spilling hair dye, remember? Heather, I've been in the police force for a long time, however, as far as I'm concerned, it was hair dye that was lying on the floor that day, even the small pool of hair dye in the corner which had a piece of bone in it". Heather looked up at Deborah. Deborah put up her hands. "Don't worry about it Heather, I couldn't do anything about it now, even if I wanted to. All the evidence has long since disappeared. Just shake your head or nod Heather, you're not going to be held to any statement or anything. Was Paul Crane's blood mixed in with that hair dye on the floor that day? Just nod your head, and then it's not an official answer".
Heather sipped her coffee and then bent her head down in shame. She nodded. Deborah hooked her thumb in the direction of the cafe window, but kept her eyes on Heather.
"Is that what that's all about"?
Again Heather nodded.

"Here's my card Heather, I've written down Karen's number as well. Now, if you want to tell us anything about this incident, or anything else for that matter, then you just call us, any time, night or day. Don't leave it too long though Heather, I don't want to be finding you in any skip, but, if that across the road is anything to go by, then it doesn't take a Philadelphia lawyer to work it out that it's pretty serious".

Karen spoke. "Heather, even if you are involved in something illegal, tell us now, and we can help you. But if you get deeper into something, then I regret to tell you, you will go down with the rest of them. Look what the bastards have done to your shop, get them back Heather, just one name!"

Deborah Knowles leaned forward and took Heather's right hand in hers. "Whether you believe us or not babes, we're here to try and help you. We are trying our best to bring down the people like the ones tormenting the life out of you and causing you so much misery. Just give us a name Heather. Karen and I have a good idea who it is, but if you tell us and are prepared to testify against him, we can put an end to his bloody heavy-handed games, but we need you to tell us Heather. Look what the bastard's done to your life there across the road. Tell us officially, and we'll burn *him*, I promise you that Heather. We'll fire two shots each into his cerebellum. Help us to demobilise this nasty man".

CLEAVLAND TERRACE.

Detective John Drummond sat on the chair with his cup and saucer, smiling at the little girl perched on her mother's knee. "You are a lucky woman Jenifer, very lucky indeed".

"I know" said Jenifer, cuddling her daughter.

"We'll need you to come to the station sometime soon, to give us a full statement of your experience with Hillman. You can bring your little girl along with you, and I know Jenifer it'll be the last thing you'll feel like doing, but believe me, you have the only means of letting us know how he works, how he thinks, his mood swings. It's important you tell us these things now, while they're still fresh in your mind".

"Still fresh in my mind Mister Drummond? I can tell you right now, that not one second of the time I spent with him will ever be forgotten, that much I know for certain".

"Phone this number Jenifer, when you're ready to come over, and we will send a car over to pick you up. I have taken the liberty of banning the press from speaking to you, until we have an official statement. After that, you can sell your story to the highest bidder, and I don't blame you if you do, you might as well come out of this with some kind of reward". Drummond put his hand in his trouser pocket, and pulled out a five pound note. "Here you are Amy, tell mum to get you some sweets after breakfast".

"What do you say Amy"?

"I've had my breakfast" the little girl replied.

John Drummond and Jenifer Sadler laughed. "I'll see you later Jenifer, now don't you be worrying about anything ok? You're nightmare is over young lady, mine, just keeps going on and on, but, with your help , we might be able to put an end to it, trouble is, when this nightmare is over, there'll be another ready to begin, I should have been a postman. Oh, by the way, those two policemen out

there are there to make sure the press don't hound you. If you wanted to, we could organise for you to stay in a hotel for a couple of weeks until all this calms down, if you like".
"Thank you, I'll see how it goes today, if they won't give me peace then I just might take you up on the offer".
"Ok then , I'll see you later today then maybe, bye bye Amy".
Drummond left Jenifer Sadler's house feeling like he'd soon have something to go on. She might even know where he's headed, but now wasn't the time to pick her brains. The girl was still very emotional from her ordeal. She was right as well, she would never forget a single second of the time she was in his company, and she could never have been certain at any point if she would have seen the light of day again..."and I've just told her she is lucky"?

Four hours later, Jenifer had surprised everyone and had given her full account of her ordeal with the infamous Doctor Hillman. She had also decided to take them up on their offer of staying in a hotel until things calmed down a little. Drummond had sent over a WPC to the station hotel to arrange Jenifer's stay. "Now remember, you stay there as long as you wish young lady, you are under no pressure whatsoever". Drummond smiled. "Now, I'll be off to London tomorrow, thanks to your information, but if you have any problems, then just ask for inspector Deborah Knowles or inspector, Karen Jones, they'll help you out any way they can. It's been a pleasure speaking to you", maybe I could come and visit you when all this is over"?

"That would be nice" said Jenifer, smiling.

EUSTON STATION. (LONDON.)

John Hillman stepped off the train and on to the platform. The first thing he would have to do was get some new clothes. He had a few thousand pounds on him, but he knew that that wouldn't last very long if he were to stay here for any length of time. He also knew they would be watching closely for any transactions he would make, credit card or cash withdrawals. He walked along the platform, his eyes taking in the sights. Hundreds of strangers bustling around, pushing and shoving, laughing, shouting. Old people, young people and people dressed like they didn't know quite what sex they were. Girls with trouser suits on, men wearing skirts, huh, fashion. This was the, anything goes city, this was the big one. This was the crazy city. People from every nationality of the world lived here, and nobody gave a fuck about anybody else. Hillman deduced, that if you fell on the pavement down here, they would just trample over you, like buffalo, and here indeed, was where the buffalo roamed. He headed to the underground, because he had to make it over to King's Cross. That's where the whores were, hundreds of them. Even though he and his god hadn't spoken to each other for a couple of days, he knew they would soon make up, they'd soon be friends again. As it was now though, he was alone. He felt, not vulnerable, but kind of, not protected, not watched over. He decided he would get himself some breakfast before he caught the tube. He thought about Jenifer punching him on the nose. He smiled. "Yes, that won't be happening again".

Then suddenly, he saw his mother waving to him in the crowd in front of him. Even through all the throngs of people he could clearly hear her voice booming in his head. "Over here bastard boy, your mummy's looking out for you as usual, useless focking frock boy".

"Tell her to stop Lord, make her go away, please, take her to Hell or somewhere. Why can't she stay dead Lord"?

One or two people glanced at him as he spoke out loud, to no-one, but that was all. No-one pays any attention to anyone down here.
To Hillman, everyone looked pugnacious, most of them staring sternly into his face, and in *his* mind, they seemed to know what he was up to, and that he'd been sent here by God.

MAIN STREET. (SHEFFIELD)

Heather had left the two police women in the cafe, having decided not to give them anyone's name. She thought too much of Rachel to risk giving those bastard's names to the police. If they hadn't taken her with them she would not have hesitated. She stood now, once more in the burned out doorway of her shop. She was hearing in her head what Karen Jones had said to her. "Get them Back Heather".
She turned, stumbling over a piece of rubble and exited what was left of her dream, then made her way home.
Deborah Knowles watched from the cafe window. "It's going to kick off now Karen, you see if I'm wrong".
"Trouble"? Said Karen.
"You bet, if she knows where Carla Paganni is, then you can guarantee that someone is going to pay for that, big style. All Hell is going to let loose now, especially if Carla has this mystery girl working with her. If the blonde is unknown to Heather's enemies, then they can spring any number of surprises on them".
"Did you see Heather's face Deborah, when you mentioned Paul Crane's name"?
"Yes, but we both know Karen, that Heather never killed him. Whoever did, that's the one she's protecting. All will be revealed Karen, in due course".
Heather picked up the phone in her house, and then put it back down again.
" It might be bugged" she thought to herself. She took out her mobile phone from her bag and called Sharon's number. "Please answer Sharon, please"
Sharon answered her phone and Heather told her everything that had happened and the situation she was in regarding Rachel. She wrote down Angela's new mobile number as Sharon read it out to her slowly. "Get in touch with her Heather, as fast as you can. I'm not

supposed to give anyone the number, but in this case, just get in touch with her. Carla and her will sort everything out for you. What are you going to do now Heather, now that the shop has gone"?
"What am I going to do? If I don't give them an address for Carla Paganni and Angela, then I'm going to die, that's what I'm going to do, and so will Rachel. I'm in it here Sharon, I'm in it up to the back teeth, and I'm waist deep in quick-sands".

STATION HOTEL. (SHEFFIELD)

As Carla Paganni and Angela Phorbes made their way out of the hotel, they could see crowds of reporters, all assembled in the car park awaiting the arrival of Jenifer Sadler, the girl who had escaped John Hillman's murderous hands. Carla had had her hair cut and dyed blonde with burgundy tips and it was now considerably shorter than she'd worn it before. She wore a pair of non-prescription sun glasses which were tinted, the palest of burgundy lenses. The two women made their way through the car park to the Mondeo which Angela had taken out on hire.
Heather had told them everything that had happened, and explained that the police were now watching her, so it was impossible for them to meet. Carla had reassured Heather. "Stay calm darling, I know it feels like you're on your own, but you're not. Angela and I will sort it out, don't worry, you'll get Rachel back alive, trust me".
"Carla, I have to trust you, I have no choice, I have no-one else I can turn to". She had begun to cry.
"Listen to me Heather, get some things together, and go and stay somewhere outside of Sheffield, it doesn't have to be too far away. Book into a hotel, maybe Nottingham, and I swear, we will have Rachel back with you in two days, now don't worry. Right, now, we'll keep in touch".
Angela looked behind her at the press. "See that Carla? That young girl, that Sadler girl, she would probably be moving in to the hotel to get some peace, some privacy. The only people, who would know she was coming here, would be the police. One of them have tipped the press off, see? We can all be bought for a price Carla. Where are we going anyway, Said Angela, putting the keys into the ignition.

"Oh, sorry Angela, we're off to a little street named Homewood Drive, where we will kidnap a certain Mrs Audrey Temple, and then trade her for Rachel White. They may have someone watching her house, so we'll have to be careful".

Less than one hour later, they had Audrey Temple in the back seat and making their way over to London Road. "I think you should know Mrs Temple that your son is a drug dealer, he also deals in prostitution; your other son Billy was shot dead doing an errand for his brother." Carla was smiling.

"I don't believe a word of it, you are both liars" said the elderly lady.

"I'm glad you don't believe me Mrs Temple, because you'll soon find out for yourself. You see, you are in here because he has kidnapped one of our friends, and if he has murdered her, then I am going to shoot your knees out and then your arms, so that he has to spoon feed you for the rest of your days. Your son is holding our friend in his big fancy house that he's purchased with all of his drug money. Do you still think we are lying Mrs Temple? Your son is scum, and that's being kind" She said, blowing smoke into the back of the car, knowing it was annoying Misses Temple. " His father, must have been one good fuck old one, that's all I can say, because his son is one ugly bastard".

The old woman frowned. "I don't know who you are, or rather, who you *think* you are, but he'll soon sort out you two in no time, you'll see!!"

"No, you'll see, you stubborn old twat, now shut your mouth, or I'll shoot you now". Mrs Temple went quiet.

Five minutes later, they pulled right into the drive of Steve Temple's house. "Ready Carla"?

"Ready".

Angela got out of the car and walked up to the house. There was one car in the car park, a Mercedes S.L. saloon.

She walked up to the giant patio window and looked in. She was completely horrified at the sight before her. Temple was raping Rachel White. There was another young lady sitting on the sofa , semi naked, watching proceedings. Angela felt the gun tucked behind her jeans. She tapped hard on the window and then tried to slide it open. To her surprise, the window slid open. Angela stepped into the living room. Steve Temple dived off Rachel. The girl, who'd been observing then sat red faced with her legs crossed on the sofa. "Get your clothes on Rachel" she said. "Don't you move" she said to Temple. "I'm sorry to barge in like this Mister Temple but

we have your mother outside in the car, she's pretty keen to see you. She doesn't believe what a scum cunt you are you see, and so we told her that we'd prove it to her. You sit still" she said to the young woman who had attempted to get her clothes. "You sit still you dirty little scrubber that you are. Now, I think that Mrs Temple is a fair deal for Rachel, don't you? Although you might find that Rachel is a better fuck, but that's for you to find out".
"Who are you"? Temple snarled.
"Listen! Mister big man, if you ever interrupt me again while I'm speaking, I'll shoot your dirty little cock off, do you understand me? I said do you understand me? I'm giving you permission to speak".
"Yes".
"Right that's better scum. Are you ready Rachel"?
"Yes, thank you for"-.
"It's ok Rachel, go outside to the car". Angela looked at Temple again. "You burned down Heather's shop, didn't you, you bastard".
"I'm not saying anything to you".
"You burned down Heather's shop and you tapped into her little business on the side, now, you're taking over, huh? Is that it scum? Well, I'm telling you now, you don't get one penny more from Heather, and just to prove how serious I am, I'm going to make an example of your mother. Carla, come into the room with Mrs Temple.
Carla walked into the room with Temple's mother. She said, "Hello Mister Temple".
Temple looked at the young woman who had caused him so much grief.
"Hello Carla". He said quietly.
"Tie him up Carla" said Angela, "and the girl".
Temple's mother said. "Aren't you going to tie me up you disgusting wretch that you are, what the hell's going on here Steven"?
"No, I'm giving you a sporting chance, the way that your scum son gives others a chance".
Carla tied both Temple and Amanda up. "Keep an eye on her Carla" said Angela, "I'll be back in a minute".
Angela went outside and returned moments later with a jerry can.
"Angela, no" said Carla.
Temple couldn't believe his eyes.
"Oh, hey, wait now, what the fuck"?

"Ssshhh" said Angela, "this won't take long". She began to sprinkle the petrol all over the defenceless old woman. Carla spoke again. "No Angela, no, you can't".
"Can't Carla? Who's going to stop me, Mister Temple here? I don't think so".
"Please" said Temple, "Please no, please, she's all I've got left".
"That little shop was all Heather had left, but it didn't stop you from destroying it now did it".
"I'll give her it back, I'll build her a new one, I'll rebuild it for her".
Angela stopped sprinkling the old lady. She put down the can and sat beside Temple. "I don't even know who you are cunt" said Angela, and believe me, you don't know who I am. Let this be a warning to you. Your mother burning before your eyes, because Mister Temple, you knocked on the wrong door here my friend, got it? You may pretend to yourself that you're in the big league, but believe me, you're just a pretentious piss pot, nothing more.
When she goes up in flames here, remember, it was you who done it".
"Please" his voice began to break, because he could see that this woman was deadly serious, he could see it in her eyes.
"Go to the car Carla, start it up".
"Please, please, no".
"You want to play in the big league then you be prepared to play big games". Angela got up and walked over to the defenceless old woman, who was now in tears. "You stink" said Angela. She flicked her cigarette lighter on. She looked at Temple, and switched it back off again, then said, "Last warning, you even mention Heather's name again, and you won't hear me coming, promise". Angela looked at the old woman. "Now, untie your son, and his fuck slut, and don't be dripping petrol over his nice
furniture, oh, and I wouldn't smoke in here for a while if I were you".
As Angela started the car and began driving down the driveway, Joseph Dougan was driving up to the house. Angela rolled down the window. Dougan, not knowing Angela, and not recognising Carla, stopped level with his car. "Excuse me" said Angela, "do you work for Mister Temple as well"?
"Yes I do, can I help you"?
"No" replied Angela, "you can't even help yourself". She raised her gun. Dougan tried to get his, but Angela was way too fast. In a

flash, she was out of the car and shot him in the shoulder. “Put that cigarette out Mister Dougan, before you go in there to phone for your ambulance, let’s go girls, let’s go and phone Heather. Are you ok back there Rachel”?
“Yes Angela, thank you”.
“You’re welcome sweetheart”.
“You were right Angela” said Carla, “they actually believed you were going to set her alight”.
“Of course they did Carla, they had every reason to believe it, I just about done it, I was tempted. There was no point in taking Mister Dougan out though, that would spoil the fun for you, although Carla, I’ve fucked his shooting arm up for you, that should give you a sporting chance”.

“Thank you, because when he dies” said Carla, “It won’t be with my gun, that would be too humane for him, when he dies, it will take a long time, and he’ll suffer every minute of it”.

CITY CENTRE. SHEFFIELD.
(New Law Enforcement)

Two police officers on patrol in the city centre. Sandra Lamberton and her colleague, PC John Tarrent. "How the fuck are we supposed to keep law and order, they laugh at us, we're a joke", said Lamberton.
"Not any more Sandra, these new laws open up all kinds of alternatives now, at least with the youths anyway, and that's where most of the trouble comes from, it all begins with the youths".
"Yes but we'll still be outnumbered in no time if anything should break out on the streets, they would beat us to death with our own truncheons". The two officers were passing a supermarket, when the security officer came out and approached them.

"Could you come in here a minute officers, we've just caught three shop lifters. Lamberton and Tarrent followed the security guard back in to the store and made their way with him through the shop and upstairs to the manager's office. As they entered, the manager got up from his chair. The man was in his fifties, completely bald and very overweight, at least seven stones overweight. His bald head red as blood, and he was sweating profusely. Obviously the youths sitting before him had been giving him a hard time. He looked exasperated.
"Good afternoon" he began," thank you for coming so quickly. These three here" said the manager, pointing to the youths, "were caught in possession of these articles you see on the table". He waved his hand towards his desk, where on display, lay fourteen DVDs. Ten CD.s and an assortment of deodorants, from various top-of-the-range manufacturers.
One teenage girl and two teenage boys sat at the opposite end of the manager's desk. Sandra asked the youths, who all looked to be

around seventeen, eighteen, what they had to say for themselves. None of the youths answered her. The girl shrugged her shoulders.
"Are you all deaf"? Said PC. Tarrent, "she said what have you got to say for yourselves"?
Still no response. "They've been like this with me for the past hour" said Mister Timothy Bryant, the store manager. "Have they been caught before Mister Bryant, stealing from here"? said Lamberton.
"These two have" he said, pointing to the girl and one of the boys, this one here, well, let's just say it's his first time being caught, he's probably done it as many times as they have".
"What did he get caught with"? Said Tarrent.
"Two DVDs, that's it, the rest of the items were stolen by those two". Again he pointed to the girl and the first youth.
To the first timer, officer Tarrent said, "What's your name? I would strongly advise you to answer my question honestly, for your own good".
"Jamie Blake" replied the youth.
"Where do you live"?
The youth told him an address. "Run that through the computer Sandra please. For your sake son, I hope you just told me the truth".
"I have" replied the youth.
"Good, because it will take officer Lamberton here about two minutes to find out".
"Would you like some tea officer" said Mister Bryant.
"Yes please" said Tarrent, staring intently at the youths. The manager went over to the small sink in the corner of the room and filled a kettle, while Lamberton set about working on the computer. Tarrent walked around the chairs where the three youths sat until he was at the end of the table. He looked at the girl. "What's your name"?
"Kylie Minogue" she replied, smiling and chewing gum.
P.C. Tarrent looked at the three youths who were all laughing at him. "What did you say Miss? Did I hear you correctly? I'll try again, what is your name Miss"?

There was some sniggering and laughing, and then, just before the final burst of laughter, "Kylie Minogue!" Again the roar of laughter. Tarrent brought a slap, from the side of his hip, up to the girl's face, full pelt across her jaw, which knocked her right off the back of the chair. The youth who Tarrent guessed was going out with girl, made a move for him. He grabbed the youth by the ears and butted him with his brow, full force on the nose, which burst open on impact, sending a spray of blood, five feet behind him. He then went round and helped the girl back on to her chair. She was so dazed by the blow that she allowed Tarrent to help her sit down. Once seated, he swung his hand round again, and struck her once more on the same side of the face. Again, she toppled over onto the floor. "Come on pet", said Tarrent, let me help you to your seat, I know, I know, it's bloody sore isn't it, I had a teacher when I was twelve, used to do that to me all the time. I tell you what though, it didn't half make me sit up and pay attention".

The youth he had head butted was now seated back on to his chair, groaning. "Let me see". Said Tarrent. The boy took his hand away from his nose, with the same trust he would give a general practitioner. Quick as lightning, Tarrent cupped his hand around the back of the boy's head, and cracked it hard down on to the table. "Is that tea not ready Mister Bryant, we're dying on a cuppa. Now then young lady. What's your name and address"?

This time, the girl answered straight away, but struggling to speak.

"You lad, what's your name? Here, your nose is a bit blocked; write it down, if you can write, can you"? The youth nodded. "Write it down then, no, not on there, that's got your blood on it, you fucking half-wit, get a clean piece, here! Hurry up! Now then Jamie Blake" said Tarrent, are you going to steal again"?

"No sir, no I'm not, never sir".
"And what about you little bitch, are you going to steal any more"? The girl shook her head, and sniffed a sob. What about you, fuck nose, have you learned your lesson? He looked at the two youths he had struck. "Are you two junkies? Answer me, Kylie? Are you a junkie slut, answer!!?" He stood up.
"Yes".
"Yes what"?
"Yes sir, we're registered addicts".

"That's better, you little bitch. Fuck with anybody for money or drugs, won't you, huh? You cheap little piece of shit that you are,

well, I'm going to tell you something, and you bone heads better listen up. This time I'll let you go, one last time, one last chance. Now you tell all the other junkie trash out there who are poisoning my country with H.I.V. that the rules have changed now, do you hear me"?
All three youths nodded.
"You pair". He pointed to the couple. "Do you get help"?
"Yes".
"You do? What do you get"?
"Methadone" whispered the girl".
"Methadone huh, isn't that supposed to wean you off"?
"Yes".
"Yes, but you two want the best of both worlds don't you, get your Methadone, and get the real McCoy from the money you make stealing, isn't that right? Isn't it!!"
Again the whisper. "Yes".
"Yes, well, no more, you dirty cheap little scamps that you are. If I ever hear, or I ever have to come back here, then say goodbye to your scum friends, because I'll personally make sure that you'll go to camp, do you know what I'm talking about, do you"?
"Yes sir".

"Right then, you make sure you wise up" he said to the girl, pointing to the youth he had head butted, "now get this dope to the hospital". He swung again, catching the girl, yet again, on the side of the face. This time, her skin broke and split. Tarrent picked her up and put her once more back on to her chair. He had noticed the chewing gum lying on the floor where it had lay since the first blow was administered to her. He picked it up and wiped it on the sole of his boot, then forced it into her mouth again, in between her sobbing. "There, there's your gum Kylie". Blood was dripping from the boy's nose onto the table. "Now, you apologise to Mister Bryant here for being such nuisances, and then clean up this mess from the table, and then fuck off out of our sights, and remember what I've just told you, don't let me catch you at this again, little bastards".

KINGS CROSS. (LONDON.)

John Hillman strolled through the crowds in a very busy Kings Cross. He watched the people in strange fascination, almost like watching the T.V. with the sound turned down. He saw different expressions on different faces. He saw all manner of Nationalities. Now and then someone would glance at him, as if they had recognised him from the photographs they'd shown on T.V. He felt ashamed in one sense, that he had become one of Britain's most wanted. He knew what his parents would have thought of him. They had leaned on him heavy when he was a teenager, making him stay in on Friday and Saturday nights, when all of his school friends were all going out to dances and parties. When he was in his second year at secondary school, he was the only guy in the class who didn't have a girlfriend. Swatting John was his nick-name, and all because his parents wanted him to do well.

He had heard his mother and father talking one night. "Well, he's our son John, and if he doesn't do well, then that will be a bad reflection on us, we will have failed as parents".

It had nothing whatsoever to do with what John Hillman junior wanted to do with his life. " If I had been a brick layer, I would have been a failure, they would have been failures. All those teenage years wasted, and then what? The very man who pressed me so hard to do well ends up dealing in drugs and prostitution, running around like a lord, thinking I knew nothing about it. The number of times I caught him with his hand up Carla Paganni's skirt, dirty old bastard, while my mother was in bed, or away somewhere for the week-end. And what a dirty minded little bastard she must be, I mean, how many young women her age, would want to sleep with ageing old bastards like him, the sick little slut".

He came out of his semi daydream as he walked. Outside of the station, there was a line of taxis. People were jostling around trying to get one, so desperate to get to their destinations. Across the street, he could see already, the ladies of the night coming out, dressed in as little as the law would allow. One of his turns. “Fucking disease infested dogs, ready to charge men for their services in return for infecting them with H.I.V. or at the very least, syphilis”. Because he knew, that very few of them insisted on the men wearing condoms. Competition was so high now; just about every young girl who didn’t have a job was doing this these days. He stood still for a moment, watching them. He stared at them, in the same manner that a lioness would stare at wildebeest, only, in Hillman’s eyes, all of the herd were vulnerable, every one, and he wouldn’t have to do much chasing either. He looked up at the darkening sky. Just shortly, his prey would come and pick him.

“You can be in the huff with me Lord” he said to himself, “but I’ll still do your work, I won’t desert you , the way you’ve deserted me. I’m no Judas Iscariot; I wouldn’t take pieces of silver”.

Suddenly, three police cars pulled up in front of him on the road, sirens blaring loud. He almost panicked, then he saw the crowds gather on both sides of the street. A police officer tied tape to a trestle, and then pulled the tape tight across the road. More police cars appeared. Drivers peeped their horns in frustration, as their journeys home were brought to an abrupt halt. He looked ahead and saw the crowds of people looking up, and there she was. A would be suicidal. She was about seventy feet up, standing on a ledge of a hotel or apartment. Hillman stood with the rest of the crowd, which was growing by the minute, as the girl looked down. Two men got out of a police car, plain clothed, and entered a building just yards from him.

“They won’t get to her in time Lord, if she really means it”. Another man got out of a car with a young woman, both of them carrying megaphones. The young lady shouted up that there was help on the way. She continued to tell the young lady that these people would help her with whatever it was that was making her feel this way.

"Easier said than done Lord" he said to himself. "Let her do it, please, I've never seen anyone doing this before, I've often wondered what it would be like to see the mess". As it turned out, Hillman was right. The two men sent to help the girl, would be no further than half way up the escalator, when the young lady stretched out her arms, as though she were a professional diver, and let herself fall forward. There were gasps and screams from the crowd as the young woman smacked and burst like a polythene bag onto the roof of a parked car. Hillman watched in ecstasy as the girl's body turned into a lifeless pulp. Hillman felt exhilarated.

Two shop windows which were decorated with Christmas lights were pelted with liquids that were, moments before, part of a human being. Hillman looked in astonishment, as the girl's blouse now lay on the roof of the car. A few feet away, the girl's skirt lay on the pavement. "To me Lord, it sounded like a child's water balloon bursting; you know, just a liquid thud, thank you Lord".

Then, to his complete horror, he saw his mother in the crowds across the street. Although she was about fifty yards away, he could hear her voice as though she were standing right next to him. "I hope you're ashamed of yourself frock boy, no son of mine would stand and watch that. You must have come out of someone else's womb, because there's no way I would give birth to you".

"Make her go away Lord, please".

"Just look at you, and you a church goer as well, good Christian my arse, and you've never fucked a girl in your life, have you frock boy. Those two little girls you have were fathered by your own father with that dirty little whore you called a wife, the one who belted you, like the little fucking timid frock boy that you are, spending all your time trying to suck up after me and attempting to please me, when you should have been out hunting whores, you fucking Patsy".
"Please Lord" he whispered, "please make her go away, I can't stand it anymore, I'm sorry Lord, whatever I've done to upset you, I'm so sorry".
"You should have killed and fucked that little whore called Jenifer Sadler, you sad little bastard that you are, don't you know what you are? No fucker wants you, not even your father's little girls".

Again, he watched in absolute horror and disgust as his mother broke through the throngs of people, past the police officers, and got down on her hands and knees and began to lap up, like a dog, the flesh and blood on the pavement which had been the young woman. He screamed out loud, as his mother feasted on the red flesh. "Please God PLEEAASSSEE"!! Hillman was lifted up by two paramedics and placed into an ambulance, where he was given a sedative, and then taken to a nearby hospital. Ten minutes later, the traffic along Kings Cross was flowing once again. The damaged car towed away. The onlookers or thrill-seekers all once again continued with their daily routine. Conversations would be had in cafes or pubs for maybe a couple of hours or so, and then the incident, that would no doubt break some-one's heart and or perhaps leave a mother-less child, or a broken-hearted parent, be forgotten.
Life, in the city, was already back to 'normal'.

ROYAL INFIRMARY. SHEFFIELD.

Joseph Dougan sat up in bed reading his morning newspaper. Hillman Still At Large. was the headline on the front page. He had a tray lying across his thighs, from which, he had just eaten his breakfast. Now, the tray supported his newspaper as he turned the paper with his one remaining arm. Surgeons had battled through a six hour operation to try and save his right arm, but the damage was so severe, that, in the end, they had no option but to amputate. Steve Temple entered the ward with Amanda Pearce. Temple gasped, as he saw Dougan's right arm missing. "How are you feeling Joe" said Temple, placing a large package of assorted fruit on the bedside cabinet.
Dougan shook his head, looking at Temple disdainfully.

"Oh, I'm fine Steve, you know, can't complain, won't be playing bowls for a while, how the fuck do you think I'm feeling!!" I should have listened to Paul Crane, he used to tell me how fucking useless you are at this game, and he was right, wasn't he, you don't have a fucking clue, do you? I told you when I took out those two old bastards, that I should get Paganni, but oh no, you just leave that just now Joe". Dougan looked at the young girl. "If you have got one ounce of brains Amanda, you'd get yourself as far away from that prick as you possibly can, because if you don't, you'll wind up as dead as him. I know he's a free lunch ticket darling, but you're very pretty, there are plenty more lunch tickets out there that you could obtain with your bedroom skills. This cunt here, is a walking liability, I'm telling you now Amanda, those bastards will be back, and you don't want to be anywhere near him when they come".
Temple looked at Dougan. "I know you're angry Joe".

"Angry? Angry"? Said Dougan, pointing to where his right arm used to be. " Listen to me Temple, you thick twat, I can't help you any more, got it? I can't help you, you're on your own now, and don't think for one minute that those brainless thugs of yours are going to take my place, because they'll be dead before you. Half of them spend most of their time snorting your merchandise, did you know that? They are even making their own deals with their own customers, with your gear, you fucking thicko, wake up idiot, and get to fuck while you can!!"

Temple sighed heavily. "Joseph, I'm sorry for what's happened".

"Listen" said Dougan, "you know what you should do? Buy your mother a house abroad somewhere, then, get yourself into town, buy yourself a big slap-up meal, followed by a bottle of the best wine you can get, go to bed with two or three whores, snort some cocaine, then go home, lie down in your self- purchased coffin, pull out your gun, put it into your mouth, and pull the fucking trigger, that way, you can say your life's been worthwhile. Leave your house to Amanda here, because she deserves a fucking medal for hanging around with you. Wake up and smell the coffee Steve, it's over, you lost. You pissed yourself on your couch, you were so frightened, don't try and kid yourself on. I'll tell you another thing, just in case you have any stupid plans, don't send any of those clowns after them; it'll only make things worse for yourself, if that is possible. If you'd let me take out Paganni when I had the chance none of this would have happened, fucking know all, and where Paganni's got this bitch from Hell, God only knows, but she is more professional than me, oh, you're in deep shit here boy, and it's all your own doing. Now, the police are coming here today to talk to me, don't worry, I won't say anything, although I should, so just get your thick fucking head out of here before you make me change my mind".
Temple opened a drawer of the bedside cabinet, and put a brown envelope into it, sliding it closed again.
"What's that"? Said Dougan.
"It's just a little gift for being loyal to me all of these years".
Dougan smiled broadly, and sarcastically. "Loyal? Steve, oh I looked after you, but I was never loyal, fuck, I've stolen more from you than you could ever dream, I made a good few quid out of your gullible nature, fucking thousands in fact".
"Well, you were there when I needed you, that's what counts, I em, I take it we're finished".
"You bet your life we're finished, I want nothing more to do with you. Final piece of advice Steve, in case you don't realize how much shit you're in. Apart from Carla Paganni"? Dougan pointed to the front page and the headline concerning Hillman. "He's still at

large Steve, and as far as he's concerned, you killed his mummy and daddy, I would take a train Amanda".
Temple got up from the chair beside Dougan's bed. "I'm sorry Joe".
"Yeah, you're sorry, sure, you haven't listened to a single word I've said have you, you stubborn fuck, well, don't say I didn't warn you. You'll deal with it your way, and your way only, with that bunch of junkie shit you call men. If you don't heed that warning Paganni gave you, then you're a bigger idiot than I took you for, and believe me, I took you for an idiot. Amanda, good luck darling, thanks for all the nice fun we had, get yourself away from him, do yourself a favour, because you'll just be committing suicide hanging around with him, it's not a question of if Amanda, only when, you saw that crazed bitch, now you get away darling, you can start again, he's fucked".
"That'll do Joe!!! Just leave it, you've said your piece, now just leave it will you. Yes, Paganni's good, and her friend, but you're blowing things right out of proportion".
"Am I"?
"Yes you are, now, no-one feels more sorry for you than me Joe, but I think you're so annoyed at yourself for being caught out like that, that's where your anger is coming from. She could have taken you out Joe, but she spared you, you should look on the bright side, and remember, you were one of the gang who skinned her hooker friend alive, and buggered her skinless body. You poured sperm down her throat as she struggled to breathe, don't forget that, and then you sick bastards filmed it all, who told you to do that? Because when Paganni saw the tape that you nice people left her, well, that's what started all this tit for tat killing, don't you forget that my Irish friend. If you were as good as you say you are, then you would never have been caught out with that bitch in the car, and you know it. Now I can still find a job for you, you can still be useful, if you don't want that, then just say, and we'll be on our way, so, what's it to be Joe"?

"Dougan smiled. "You see that window there Steve, could you open it please, then take a few steps back, then take a run and jump, dead man"!!

"Very well" said Temple, opening the drawer and retrieving his money, "if that's the way you want it, goodbye Joe".

KINGS CROSS HOSPITAL.
LONDON.

"I'll be fine doctor, honestly, it was just a shock to my system, thank you for your help, I've never witnessed anything like that before, that's all it was".
Doctor Ali looked into Hillman's eyes. "Are you sure Mister Dixon? Are you sure you'll be alright. I would prefer it if you stayed in overnight, just to keep an eye on you".
"I'm fine doctor, I'm going to phone my daughter to come and get me, now please, don't make me have to sign myself out".
"Ok Mister Dixon, if you're absolutely sure".
"I'm positive doctor, and thank you once again for your help".
It was nothing less than a miracle, thought Hillman, that no-one had looked inside his pockets for I.D. When he awoke from his sleep, he was lying on a bed. His jacket had been draped over a chair. There had been another three people brought in as a result of witnessing the suicide. Hillman placed a coin into a vending machine on his way out of the hospital. He was now sipping coffee from a plastic cup as he made his way down to the busy Kings Cross station area. "No thank you Mister Ali, I have better plans on how to spend my evening" he mocked to himself. He lit up a cigarette as he walked, realizing, that if anyone had searched his jacket they would have found his gun and his knife as well as his credit cards. He knew he would never be as lucky again. As he walked, he noticed the area was getting busier. "This was more like it". There were two young women across the road who looked like they were whores, in *his* eyes at least , who were talking to two young men.
"Oi, yes you", one of the teenagers shouted. Hillman kept walking.
"You, I'm talking to you, fuck head!!"
Hillman crossed the road to the same side as the young men, but about twenty yards in front of them. There was a gate which led into a small public park and a footpath running through it. Hillman went through the gate and into the park, hoping that the two insolent youths would follow him. "They're bound to Lord, this is London, they think they're invincible down here".
As soon as he was through the gate, he began to run for about thirty yards. There was a mass of thick bushes which would be perfect for an ambush. He hid behind one of the larger trees and waited. Not

for long. He could hear the voices of the youths coming along the path. Then he stood where they would see him, pretending to urinate.
"You must be fucking deaf, are you"? Said one of the youths, although, now that Hillman could see them, they looked more like they were in their twenty's.
"How are you doing boys", said Hillman, "no luck with the whores then? Too expensive were they"?
"You are going to suffer for that Mister" said one of the young men, "one of those girls is my sister, are you calling my sister a whore"?
"Well, she was certainly dressed like one, wasn't she"?
"THAT'S MY JOHN, YOU TELL THEM SON".
"Shut up mother! I'm dealing with this!!"
"What"? said the youth.
"I said, she was dressed like a whore, or does she dress like that just because she likes cock so much, is that it"?
One of the young men pulled out an eight inch blade from his pocket.
"What are you going to do with that"? asked Hillman, smiling.
"It's going in to your guts, and then up your arse".
Hillman turned around, finished with the mock urination act. In his hand was his magnum. "Is that a fact" he said, as he pulled the trigger. He heard the leaves rustling in the distance, thinking he had missed the young man's hand, but in fact the shot had gone straight through, leaving just a bloody stump at the end of the arm. The other youth made a run for it, but Hillman caught him in the back of the knee, making the front of his leg explode. Down he went, rolling and writhing around with the pain. Hillman picked up the knife. "It's a beauty son, it really is, I like the handle". He drew the blade across the boy's good wrist. "Did you order this especially; he thrust the blade into the young man's stomach, and began a circular twisting motion, like he was stirring something in a bowl. "It's certainly sharp son, you keep it well. How many people did you manage to mug with this before you died, five? Ten? Whatever, no more kid, goodnight".
The other lad was trying to get up and hop away. Hillman soon caught up and pulled him from the path into the bushes. "Here, let me help you son, I'm a doctor, doctor Hillman's the name. Again, he drew the knife along the youth's wrist. "Fuck, this is sharp, got right through the main arteries there; give me your other hand". The

youth was in complete shock, and actually held up his arm to Hillman, crying as he did so. "No use crying now son, if I didn't have my gun with me, you were going to stick this up my backside, weren't you"?
He drew the knife across the boy's other wrist. Hillman heard the spray of blood rattle on the dry autumn leaves. "Well now, let's see what it looks like sticking out of your arse, shall we"?
He cut the youths jeans so that the lad was standing on his one good leg, then he rammed the eight inch blade inside the boy's rectum, right up to the handle, and then out. Then back in, then out, then back in, and then out. The boy, to Hillman's amazement, was still standing on his one good leg, and his shattered one, when he was finished. In a husky hopeless tone for a voice, the youth, through his tears and pain, attempted to say sorry, then he fell to the ground. Hillman pulled the other youth from the public path and into the bushes. He was still alive, just.
"I suppose you're sorry too"? The boy was unconscious. "Oh well" said Hillman, "I hope you're still able to feel this. Again, he cut the jeans from the youth's legs, and began ramming the blade in and out of the boy's rectum. In and out, he rammed it for a full minute. The knife was then taken out, and then rammed into the boy's ear. He rammed it so hard that the point of the knife threatened to come out the youth's other ear, the bone handle stopping it going any further. He wiped the blood from his hands on the boy's jeans, and then continued walking in the direction he'd been walking when he came in. He picked up his coffee carton from where he had sat it down upon the footpath. His heartbeat had not gone one beat above normal. "I wonder if there's somewhere I can get a meal at this time of the evening. Maybe I'll be lucky Lord, maybe one of the whores will take me home with them"

FOREST HOTEL. NOTTINGHAM.

“Well” said Carla to Angela, as they sat with Heather and Rachel in the lounge of the hotel. “That’ll be Temple riled up now, for sure” Angela said. “Really? I thought that little warning would frighten him off, at least for a while”.
“No chance Angela, now that his main man has been maimed, he’ll see that as the ultimate insult, and with us threatening his mother right in front of him. Before Angela, it was just me they were after, or maybe Heather here, but now, he’ll be wanting you dead as well, and he won’t be bothered how it’s done either. As far as I could tell, Crane, Felder and Dougan were his main men. Now that they are no longer around, he still has others, no more than dog’s bodies, but could still be dangerous, even monkeys with guns can be dangerous. I think it would be better if you stayed down here Heather, with Rachel, at least until Sheffield’s all clear. Do you have enough money for two or three weeks stay in here”.
“I think so” replied Heather.
“Don’t worry about money” said Angela, “I’ll get some down to you in a couple of days”.
Rachel said, “I could get a job here in the hotel, maybe help a bit”.
Heather took hold of Rachel’s hand over the table, and smiled at the other two women.
Carla and Angela could see that Rachel and Heather felt the same way about each other.
“You’re already doing a good job” said Angela to Rachel, you’re keeping our friend and yourself out of harm’s way, don’t you be worrying about any job sweetheart, you’ll be ok for money just shortly, I guarantee it, trust me”.

SWEETWATER RECOVERY HOME.
(SHEFFIELD.).

Audrey Temple sat by the patio window on her wheelchair, staring out at the sparrows and starlings feeding on the scraps of bread that had been thrown out for them in the garden. She had suffered a stroke and was paralysed down her left side. She had also lost her speech. Angela and Carla walked calmly up to the reception desk and spoke with the head nurse, knowing how to win people over, and using their kindness and sympathy to their gain. "Excuse me miss" said Angela, even though the woman she spoke to was more than fifty years of age. "I can see that you are extremely busy in here, but I wonder if you could do us a favour. You see, my brother phoned me a couple of days ago, and told me that our mother has had a stroke. I got up here as quickly as I could, but my brother is off on business somewhere, he left me a note in mum's house saying she was here. Could I sit outside with her for five minutes please, I'll wrap her up, please, because after today, I'm on duty again, I'm an air stewardess, and they won't give me compassionate leave until there's a death".

Before the woman had time to reply, Angela pulled out an envelope, marked, Recovery Home. "I thought I'd donate a little something to your cause, but then, you never think about things like that, until it happens to a member of your family".

Nurse Gladys Richardson, was going through a cash flow crisis at this moment in time. She had to act quickly before any of the other members of staff saw the envelope. The nurse looked at Angela. "Miss"?

"Miss Tracy Temple".

"Miss Temple" said Gladys, "I don't think there'll be a problem with that, so long as she's wrapped up. Were you informed Miss Temple, that your mother is paralysed down her left side"?

"Aw" said Angela, almost bursting out with laughter, holding her hands up to her face.

"Oh dear" said the nurse.

"What, tell me what?"

"I'm afraid she's lost her speech as well."

“Ha!! Oh no” said Angela, placing her hands up to her face, and on the verge again of bursting out into laughter. “Come on Jeannie; let’s take my mum outside for some fresh air. Thank you so much nurse, I hope that five hundred pounds comes in handy”.
Nurse Richardson’s heart skipped a beat. “Oh now come on Miss Temple, you poor thing, what a shock for your system you little darling, come on, I’ll take you to mum. Would you like some tea or coffee”?
“Oh, I don’t think I’ve got any change for the machine”.
“Oh now, don’t you be worrying about any machine dreary, I’ll get you a pot of tea. Tea for you as well Jeannie”? Gladys said to Carla.
“Yes please”, Carla managed to mumble through her hands without laughing, “Thank you”.
“You’re welcome my angels, so you are, little angels. Gladys made her way towards a set of swing doors.
“Angela, I swear, I’m going to kick you in the ass, I can hardly keep my face straight”.
“Shut up Jeannie, and let’s have tea with mum.
Angela and Carla sat outside with Audrey Temple.
“Bet you didn’t expect to see us again old one, eh? Your worst fucking nightmare returns, huh? And it’s so convenient isn’t it that that stroke’s fucked up your speech, now you’ll have to listen to me without interrupting me, drink your tea you fucking hag, I should have set you on fire you stubborn old bint!!”

KINGS CROSS. (LONDON)

It would be morning the next day, before the two youths would be discovered thought Hillman to himself, as he strolled down towards the station. The working girls were out in their droves. "Fuck Lord, where do I start, there are filthy evil bitches everywhere, whow, you've sent me to the right place this time Lord. "The harvest is plentiful, but alas, the labourers are few, well, you won't hear *me* complaining Lord, no way, oh Lord, look at the tits on that. Hillman's pulse began to race as he scrutinised woman after woman who came into his view, and, of course, most of them were smiling at him which did not help their case. He saw them all as evil manipulating demons from Hell, sent up to destroy mankind. Just about every girl who walked passed him tried to entice him into some action.

Then, about fifty yards in front of him, he saw the one he wanted. A small petite blonde with a beautiful complexion which got better and better, the closer she came. He didn't even hear the others who were trying to score him. His eyes were fixed on his target, like the lioness and the wildebeest. "Excuse me" he said, "Do you know where I could get something to eat"?

The young blonde woman, standing in a denim mini skirt and white crop-top, said, pointing down to her groin, "I sure do honey, but eating is twenty quid extra. The girl who was with her burst into laughter, "Yeah baby, how's about we shout on one of our friends and you can have a three course meal".

They were about to walk on, when Hillman said, "How much would that cost"?

"What"? said the young blonde, incredulously. "How much, for three of you, for say, four hours, how much would that cost"?

"Three of us for four hours? Honey, you couldn't afford us, not three.

How about us two for two hours say two-fifty".

Hillman smiled. "How about you two for four hours, four hundred".

The two girls looked at one another. "Honey, you've got a deal".

"Yeah, but I do need to eat, really. I'm starving".

"Listen baby, if you're serious about this, then we'll knock you something up at our place".
"Are you sure"?
"Of course we are, but we want the money up front first, you understand".
"Of course, but I want to see your place first".
"Just follow us babe, about twenty yards behind us, so that the filth can't pick you or us up for kerb crawling".
"Lead the way ladies".
"Ooh ladies, do you hear that Tracy, we're ladies".
"*I know Lord, another fucking whore called Tracy*!!"
The two girls climbed up the concrete steps into a block of flats. As he climbed the steps he could see up their skirts.
"*Evil fucking bastards Lord, I'll learn them a lesson*". The two girls stopped outside one of the doors.
"Right, money please".
"Not out here girls, I'll give you the money when we're inside, look, you can leave the door open if you don't trust me".
The girl who Hillman wanted the most, pulled out a key from somewhere in her denim jacket, and opened the door. They all stepped inside. The door was about three inches thick. "Bloody hell" said Hillman, "Fort Knox".
"Yeah well" said the blonde, "This isn't exactly Kensington honey, money please".
Hillman pulled out his wallet, and peeled off some notes. "Tell you what babes, let's count this in the kitchen shall we, close the door Carol, I think he's ok, "you're ok right"?
"Of course I'm ok, what did we say, four hundred"?
"What if I gave you five hundred, would that entitle me to some extra's"?, It mattered little to Hillman how much they intended to charge him. He was going to retrieve the money however much they charged. The dark haired girl said, "Five hundred will get you a whole load of extra's, won't it Tracy". The two girls began kissing and playing with their most fruitful score since the German supporters had been here playing a friendly football match with England. "Let's be having this jacket off, shall we"? Said the girl named Carol. "We have to make you as comfortable as possible don't we"?
"I'll take care of the jacket!" said Hillman," no offence intended, I'm just-."

"It's ok, we understand perfectly" replied Tracy. Tell you what, you take him upstairs Carol, and I'll be up very shortly, you two get the party started. Hillman slipped his jacket off, and draped it over one of the kitchen chairs. One of four kitchen chairs, each of the four coming from an entirely different kitchen set. The young girl lifted up her top and pulled it off, exposing her ample breasts to Hillman, and making him forget his jacket completely. "Take him up Carol, come on, the gentleman's paid good money, we don't want him to be disappointed now do we"? Food was now the last thing on Hillman's mind.
Carol led him up the small set of stairs. The flats consisted of only two flights, which surprised Hillman, who had expected them to be much higher. He wouldn't have far to run, when he was finished his task in hand.
"Is there no-one else here"?
"No, no-one" said Carol, "come on up".
There had been another door Hillman noticed, which would be the living room, he guessed, but the door was closed. He would just have to trust them. He wasn't thinking straight because he'd been beguiled by the blonde's beauty. He was aching for her. In less than two minutes, upon reaching the one and only bedroom in the flat, Carol had him undressed and lying back on the bed, performing oral sex on him.
"Are you two ok up there"? shouted Tracy, "I won't be long".
"We're fine," replied Carol, taking him out of her mouth to speak, "Take your time".
"No don't" shouted Hillman, "Please hurry up".
Eventually, the girl named Tracy joined them in the bedroom. Hillman's hunger seemed to have disappeared completely, taking the girls in turn, he began to enjoy himself. He was relaxed now, and was totally oblivious to anything else in the world. Each girl performing their favourite sexual position on him, he was in a state of bliss. After half an hour or so Tracy said, "Wow, I'll have to take a break, would you like a beer eh, what's your name"?
"John".
"Would you like a beer John, Carol and I are going to have a little drink, and you're not going to forget us in a hurry, I can tell you that babe, you'll be back to find us, you'll see, we'll get you addicted to us".
"I already am" said Hillman, smiling, "I'm addicted to you all".

"Ok Carol, keep John happy while I get us our drinks, and don't be making him cum yet, do you hear me, you greedy bitch".
Hillman had lost track of the time. He was in a state of confusion as well. Carol had gone to the toilet, and Tracy was down stairs getting drinks. He lay there completely naked and suddenly feeling very vulnerable, exposed. He lay, smoking a cigarette awaiting Carol's return. He hadn't heard the toilet being flushed yet. Tracy shouted up from down stairs, "I'm just coming now".
"Ok" shouted Hillman, as he lay in almost complete darkness. Then he heard muffled voices from down stairs. "*I might not Lord, I like these two, they're not like whores. Oh I know what I'm doing is wrong*, encouraging them, *but I really like them, they taste lovely Lord***".**
From the light in the hallway he could see enough to make out the shape of a wardrobe. He rose up from the bed and opened it. There was nothing inside, not a single garment of any description. If this was where they both lived, then where in God's name did they keep their clothes? He sat at the end of the bed and put on his pants, and then his socks. Then he put on his jeans. He was feeling uneasy. "Coming" shouted Tracy.
Hillman sighed with relief." Just for a minute there Lord, I thought-".Darkness.
He sat bolt upright on the bed. "Girls? Tracy? Carol? Girls"? He tried to stay calm as he fumbled for his shirt and shoes in the darkness. "Girls"?
Silence. He put his shirt on, and began fastening the buttons, with very shaky hands. His shoes had been kicked off, and so he had to untie the laces before he could put them back on again. "Has the lights fused Tracy"? He shouted.
He finally got his shoes on and fumbled his way to the bedroom door, his eyes still not adjusted to the darkness. He took a draw on his cigarette. There was a pale orange glow in front of him, but still not enough to see anything clearly. He managed to fumble his way to the top of the stairs. "Tracy? Girls? Where are you"? There was no reply. Except for the deep, vicious growl of what sounded like a very large dog. He started to shake violently. "Shit!! How do I get to the kitchen? Come on" he told himself, "think".
His jacket was in the kitchen, along with his gun and his knife. He made his way back into the bedroom.

“I know what to do John, it doesn’t matter about the whore bitches, just get to your jacket and let this be a lesson to you, paying money indeed for to fuck whores, goodness me John, paying indeed”.
“Mother, not now.” He could see his mother clearly in the darkness, standing there with the bullet hole in the front of her nose.
“Ok John, listen, grab that quilt off the bed”.
His eyes were starting to adjust to what light was in the room. He picked up the quilt and walked into the hallway. Then, slowly, he began walking down the stairs. Then the animal appeared. From what he could make out, it looked like a Doberman. He could see the shape of its large head. It began to growl again, this time somehow sounding more vicious than a few moments ago. “SHUT UP!!!” The growling grew louder. It was about to pounce. Hillman held the quilt up and then made his move down stairs. The dog lunged for him. He threw the quilt over the dog’s head and then dived on top of the bundle. Then he began punching as hard as he could, the dog snarling underneath the quilt. He kept punching what he thought was the dog’s head. He rolled the quilt over yet again, trapping the animal completely. He then began kicking. He could see into the kitchen. He could see the chair. His jacket was gone. Then he saw it draped over another chair. There wouldn’t be much time. A few seconds and the beast would be on him. He prayed that the whores had not taken his gun. He jumped up from the snarling bundle and made a dive for the kitchen chair. His gun was there. Hillman pulled it out hoping that there was still a couple of bullets in the chamber. If there wasn’t then he would be in some mess from the fight there would be between himself and this hound from Hell. Just as the dog struggled loose from the quilt, he pulled the trigger. He hadn’t time to aim at any particular part of the animal’s anatomy; he just pulled the trigger and hoped for the best. His shot caught the dog in the throat, it fell down whimpering. He looked at the animal, lying helpless. “That was a close one Fido, wasn’t it? You nearly had me fucked there boy, hard luck, good try kiddo”. He aimed the gun at the animal’s head this time with precision.” Just going to fuck you out of your misery boy, Jesus that was close, goodnight buddy”.
The bullet cracked into the dog’s head, and the animal lay dead. Hillman was still panting, his heart racing. Now he had time to check what the whores had stolen from him. They had taken his

wallet, which contained most of his cash. They had left his credit cards, but they were a bit risky to use. The police would
be waiting for him to make a transaction so they could trace his whereabouts. He slipped his jacket on, and tried to open the only outside door of the flat. The door he had came in. It was locked, and there was no key. He aimed his gun at the lock of the door and pulled the trigger. The lock shattered, in fact, he could have punched the door open; it was so flimsy and cheap.
He would have to work fast. Those whores had not just taken his wallet, they knew exactly who he was and he knew where they were headed. He was just heading out of the flat when he thought he heard sirens.
"Oh no Lord". He ran back up the stairs to look out of the hall window. Then he saw his escape route. A hatch for the attic, but it was too high for him to reach. Behind the door in the kitchen he'd seen a floor mop. He ran back down stairs to retrieve it. As he reached the top of the stairs he heard the heavy outside doors of the flat being opened, and lots of feet pounding on the concrete floor and steps. He thumped the attic door twice with the mop handle. The door opened. He leaped up as high as he could and just managed to catch the edge of the sill. He pulled himself up and closed the hatch behind him, just in time to hear the broken door being pushed open.
"Oh, he's killed my dog." He heard Tracy's voice, "He's killed my baby".
Hillman flicked his cigarette lighter. He saw a pile of old blankets lying in the corner of the attic. Slowly, and as quietly as he could, he made his way over to them to hide underneath them. As soon as he had got the attic door opened, he'd thrown the mop back down the stairs, and so, he surmised, if they saw the dog shot, and the quilt, and the broken door, plus the mop lying on the floor, surely they would think that he'd made his escape. All there was to do now was wait. He'd done everything he possibly could to get away. God could not blame him for this, if he was caught.

As it turned out, Hillman was right. They thought he'd gone. They thought he was away. Anne Hillman sat, with her hands tapping John's shoulders, consoling him like a child, as a proper mother would.
"There there now John, it's over. I won't let them hurt my boy, you just cuddle in and wait for your chance to get those nasty girls. Did

you enjoy yourself with them, did you? Was it nice? mmm? The next time John, you put that gun of yours somewhere where the sun doesn't shine, and you pull that trigger my boy, do you promise me"?
"I promise mum". "*Good boy, that's my little frock boy".*

LONDON ROAD. SHEFFIELD.

Steve Temple sat with Amanda, and two young men he used as runners. "Do you think Dougan will talk Steve"?
"He can't afford to talk Amanda, just the same as if the police were questioning me, I couldn't put anyone down, unless I was prepared to go down with them. No, it's just that he's pissed off with himself, and he has every right to be. Ten years in the S.A.S. and another six or seven working as a mercenary, and then he goes and drops his guard to a blonde with a nice pair of tits. It costs him his arm, fuck no wonder he's pissed off".
The telephone began to ring.
"Answer that Amanda please, and if it's the old folks home tell them that I sent them the money in the post yesterday morning, ok? Honest to God, you'd think I was going to leave the country, fuck, a grand".
Temple got up to pour more drinks. Amanda's eyes followed him across the room. "Steve, I think you'd better come and take this".
"Who is it"? Amanda did not answer, she just held out the phone for him to take. Temple looked at her, and then whispered as he took it in his hand, "who is it"?
"Hello? Who is this"?
"Have you dried your couch after pissing it the other day, I think you can guess who it is now"?
"What do you want"? He could hardly contain his temper.
"What do I want? Well, I'll be honest Steve, I could do with some money, say, maybe three grand, oh no but wait, it's the weekend, so four, sorry Steve, yes four grand, and the thing is, I want it in less than two hours, now I know, a man of your means probably has that lying around the house but"-
"You're getting nothing!! Nothing but a bullet that is, along with that little Italian bastard, that's what you're getting!!"
"Oh yes, I forgot about her Steve, eight grand, you're right Steve, thanks for reminding me, oh, and Rachel says you owe her four

grand for the privilege of using her body, as pathetic as your attempts were, she still wants paid, so, that's twelve grand Steve. Now then, there's a children's park, just about one hundred and fifty metres away from the nursery centre, do you know where I mean"?

"You're getting nothing bitch!!"

"I'll make sure, there's a bin as you go in the gate, I'll make sure that the bin is empty. Now, send one of your dopes with the parcel. After Carla and I have counted the money, we'll send her back to you in a taxi".

"Who, may I ask, crazy bitch, are you talking about"? Said Temple, with a tremor in his voice.

"Why, your mother of course Steven, who do you think I'm talking about, Carla Paganni"?

"For a kick off slapper, you do not even know where my mother is, so give it up, you're getting no fucking money off me, not one penny" There was silence for a few moments, a few moments where Steve Temple thought that he'd got the better of this crazy woman.

"Steve? Phone the home up, and ask them how your mummy is doing, and then call me back, but hurry, you've got one hour and fifty minutes left, I wouldn't fuck around if I were you, talk to you soon Steve, bye sweetheart".

Temple knew in his heart, that the bitch wasn't bluffing. Four minutes later, the truth was confirmed. He would kill them himself. He would pay the ransom, but he would hunt them down, and he would execute them personally. And he would make their deaths as painful and long suffering as he possibly could. "Amanda, get your coat, we're going to the bank".

Thirty-five minutes later, Temple was back on the phone. "Ok, where do I put the money"? He said to Angela.

"I've already told you, now, if you do as you were told, everything will be alright. If the person you send as much as ties their laces after placing the parcel in the afore-mentioned place, then your mother will be taken out, and abandoned somewhere in the Yorkshire Moors, have you got that Steve? Nice and clear? Because you know that I'm not joking, and we both know it can get pretty cold out there in the Moors, especially for a seventy-eight year-old naked woman".

"Right, I've got the message, but some day bitch, I swear, I'm going to gun you down and rip out your fucking throat, I swear!"

"Well, good luck with that Steve, just bring the twenty thousand, and we'll say no more about it, ok"? Angela switched her phone off. "Now then Carla, let's go and find a good vantage point".
"He'll be absolutely raging" Said Carla. "Yeah, he will, and he'll be off round to take his temper out on Rachel and Heather, that's what he thinks, he'll be sick to the back teeth when he finds that Heather and Rachel have gone".

KINGS CROSS. LONDON.

"When are they going to leave"? Hillman asked his god. "They've been talking to those whores for three hours now Lord". He could hear their voices, only just, through the loft insulation. "Goodness knows Lord how many people are in here now". Policemen had been up the stairs looking in the bathroom and bedroom. One of the two policemen must have looked at the attic because Hillman heard his partner saying to him; "Oh yeah Joe, he kills the dog, then he shoots out the lock in the door, then after he gets the door open, he comes back up here and traps himself in the fucking attic, he's a maniac, not a fucking idiot. We've searched thoroughly up here, ok, and don't you be bringing the subject of the attic up when we're back down stairs right"?
"Right"
"He's probably on a fucking train now as we speak, or at least the other side of London, fucking attic, don't be such a prick Joe".
"It was only a thought Frank, fucking hell man".
"Yeah, here's a thought Joe, we're finished our shift in an hour, how's that for a thought. You know what Beverley's like fuck sakes, it's my anniversary today, and dare I fuck *this* up this year. Fucking forgot last year, never heard the bloody end of it. Going out for dinner with those two bastards, bloody in-laws, so no more talk about attics, fucking eighteen years, bastard".

HEATHER BRADLEY'S RESIDENCE.
SHEFFIELD.

Temple knew that the blonde and Carla Paganni would be somewhere in the vicinity of the children's play park. It would be useless to try and ambush them just now; especially when they still had his mother. He would deliver the ransom and then, when he'd got his mother back he would set about finding them. He had sent two of his runners round to the park to place the money in the bin as instructed. He was now pulling up outside Heather's house with Amanda and a young man nick-named butcher. "Wait here" he said to Amanda and the young man. "If anybody pulls up here while I'm in this house, shoot them, Amanda, you know what those bitches look like right"?
"Right Steve."
Temple could see that the house was in darkness. He tried the handle, and then knocked on the door. Nothing. He knocked again, harder this time. Still no reply. He knocked loudly for a third time. This time a light came on in a downstairs room in the neighbouring house. Then Temple heard a voice. "What do you want, who are you looking for, there's no-one in there".
"I'm so sorry to bother you, I'm Heather's brother. Our mum has taken ill you see, and she was asking for Heather, the trouble is, I don't know her mobile number, and when she wasn't answering her telephone, I thought I'd come round. She's going to be awfully upset, I doubt if mother will make it through the night. As if Heather hasn't had enough bad luck lately, with her shop burning down".
"Wait a minute" said the old gentleman who had come to the door. "I'll be back in a minute".
"He could be calling the police" thought Temple to himself. But he would just have to take that chance. After a couple of minutes, the old man returned. "Here" he said to Temple, handing him a piece of

paper. “There’s no phone number, but that’s where she’s staying. She’s gave the missus a key to get in and out of the house to feed her cat, I can give it to you if you wish to phone the hotel from here”.
Temple looked at the old man, smiling. “No thank you sir, you look after her cat for her. It won’t take me long to get down there and pick her up. Tell me, did she have her little friend with her when she left”?
“Oh yes, they both left together”.
“Splendid” said Temple, “Well I won’t keep you any longer sir, thank you once again”.
“You’re welcome, I’m glad I could help”.
“Oh you’ve helped alright, more than you could ever know, good night sir”.

Half an hour later, Temple was back home. He was just sorting out one or two details when the taxi pulled up outside of his house. He and Amanda walked out to the car, where they could see Audrey Temple sitting in a world of her own in the back of the cab. It took Temple all his might not to break down and cry at the pitiful sight before him. He spoke to the driver, asking him how much for the fare. “Oh, it’s already been paid for” said the driver, “plus a tip”.
“Huh, they’re all fucking heart” Temple mumbled to himself. Once back in the house, he left instructions with Amanda. “If anyone comes Amanda, anyone at all, you tell them that I’m out with my mother, and tell them I’ll be back in half an hour or so, got it? Don’t whatever you do, tell them I’m out of town. Make her some tea. If that Paganni bastard or her friend calls, tell them I’ll talk to them as soon as I get back with my mother, tell them, tell them I’m grateful for them keeping their word”.
“Ok Steven will do”.
Temple looked at the girl. “Amanda, you keep those thieving little bastards out of my drinks cabinet do you here? Bad enough those bitches blackmailing me to the tune of twenty grand without those fuckers helping themselves to anything I have”.

Amanda knew where Temple was heading, and therefor took the opportunity when he had left, to help herself to some of his best brandy and cigarettes, and proceeded to bed one of 'Those Fuckers" just to get her own back on her very ungrateful boss, and sitting Audrey Temple in her wheelchair by the side of the bed and allowing her to witness proceedings. She just hoped Misses Temple's speech didn't return.

KINGS CROSS. LONDON.

It was coming on for twenty-four hours that Hillman had been trapped up in the attic. At one particular time of the day, he had to lie flat under a pile of stinking old blankets because one bright spark officer had decided to have a quick look around with his torch. One of Hillman's feet had been sticking out and he'd thought he would be caught, but thankfully, the torch light hadn't focussed long enough on him. The house was now quiet, but he couldn't be sure if there was anyone in the house or not. He had heard the whore called Tracy answer the phone earlier on, talking to some newspaper, wanting to hear her story no doubt. "More money for the whores Lord, I made a big mistake, and I'm sorry, now please give me the courage and wisdom to violently slaughter the bastards Lord, in your name of course. A harsh lesson must be dished out to them, so that other whores may see the error of their ways". He listened intently for sounds around the flat. He could hear none. Then, he heard the telephone ringing. It rang eight times, and then the caller hung up. This was going to be tricky. At any moment they could arrive back, or the police could. Maybe it would be safer to wait a little while longer, but he was very hungry.

He was just making his way over to the hatch, when he heard someone coming in the door. "Carol"? Came the call from Tracy, "Are you back yet"? Then there was a knock on the door. It was the joiner, who'd been told to come and fix the door. Hillman could make out his voice.

"It's knackered, just as cheap to put on a new one than to try and repair that nonsense, won't be long miss".

"Ok" said Tracy, "I'm just making a cup of tea, would you like one"?

"Oh yes please" replied the joiner.

"Yes please? You fucking bastard Lord, she steals five hundred off me plus she empties my pockets of all loose cash, and this bastard gets tea for changing a door? I hope she starts fucking him Lord, I'll give her a bullet up the arse, and him, fucking cup of tea indeed".

Hillman sat at the hatch listening. He couldn't make out exactly what was being said, but it sounded like small talk. "See that Lord? During the time that they're off the streets they pretend to live like normal people. It’s a wonder she doesn’t charge *him* for putting the door on, and for the biscuits. A couple of minutes later he could hear drilling and banging, then he heard a plain being run over the wood, then more drilling, then more banging. “Lord please, I’m starving, could you make this man hurry up a bit, my stomach is going to collapse if I don’t get something to eat soon”. Next, he heard Carol coming in. He couldn’t be certain, but it sounded like she’d came in alone. More small talk. More hammering, drilling, tapping. “Fuck sakes Lord, I could have hung Ned Kelly quicker than it’s taken that clown to hang that door. Of course, the whores will be looking to do some business with him, if at all possible. “Watch out buddy, they’ll have the money out of your wallet quicker than you can say fucking slut, oh but they’ll pay for that Lord, oh yes, and dearly”. Eventually, the joiner left. Hillman heard the girls talking, opening the door and closing it, again and again and again. He heard a chain being put on the door, then he heard Tracy’s voice as she came up to the toilet. Still Hillman sat by the hatch, patient as a cat. He would have to wait for his time, and his time was not yet here. He would only get one chance to escape and it would have to be timed to perfection. He had a burning need though, to inflict as much suffering onto these ungodly bastard whores who had made a complete fool out of him. They would soon learn about ruthlessness. Hillman had had to defecate in the corner of the attic, and now the stench of his own excrement was beginning to fill the small confined space which had been his home for the best part of a day. He could feel his skin starting to crawl with the glass wool insulation which had been rubbing constantly against his legs and arms, and now, his face. He had been as patient as he could, but the combination of hunger, and the eagerness to inflict pain onto the two women was beginning to ware out that patience. He would have to make his move soon…very soon.

HEATHER BRADLEY'S RESIDENCE..

The two police women watched with intense interest, as Steve Temple drove away with a young man in his car. Deborah Knowles and Karen Jones got out of their car, fifty metres or so from Heather's house. "I wonder what that was that the old man gave Temple Deborah".
"We'll soon find out" said Deborah, as they made their way across the road. They knocked on the old man's door. The old gentleman answered the door almost immediately. With the chain on the door he said, "Yes? What can I do for you"?
"Please sir" said Karen, holding up her I.D. card. "We need to speak to you urgently, may we come in"? He opened the door and let the two women in. "The man you spoke to a couple of minutes ago".
"Yes"?
"Who did he say he was"?
"He said he was Heather's brother, and that he had to get in touch with her, Heather's my next door neighbour you see and-".
"Yes, we know who she is".
"Well, he said their mother was in a bad way, and she wanted to speak to Heather before she died, it was something like that".
Yes, we saw you giving him something sir, what was it that you gave him"?
"Oh, it was the address where Heather and her friend are staying, she gave it to my wife and I, just in case there was an emergency, my wife's been looking after her cat for her".
"I see" said Deborah. "Well, could you please tell us where she's staying, it's very important that we speak to her before that man does, you see, he's not her brother, and we think that there's a possibility that he intends to hurt her, so where is she"?
"Oh dear, it's Nottingham, I can remember that much, what the hell was it, oh that's it, it's the Forest Hotel, that's it".
"Are you sure about that, absolutely sure"?
"Yes that's it, I'm afraid I don't have a phone number".
"That's alright sir" said Karen, as the two women began walking away, thank you sir, thank you so much, sorry to disturb you".
Deborah was already punching digits on her mobile before they reached the car. "Who's this?" She said, just before she got into the

car. “Ok sergeant, listen carefully now, I need you to find out the number of the Forest Hotel in Nottingham for me would you, and could you do it as quick as possible please, what? Deborah Knowles, now please hurry”. She gave the sergeant her mobile number and then waited. As she lit up her cigarette she said to Karen. “This Temple character is quite obviously bigger than we gave him credit for. Whatever Heather has done to him, well obviously him burning down her shop is not sufficient revenge it would seem. Now she has taken off, and that innocent old bugger there, thinking he was doing her a favour, may just have sealed her fate, and her friend. Carla Paganni as well Karen, I don’t know what it is just now, but I’ll find out, because I have a feeling that all this is connected. Someone’s annoyed this Temple for him to come out of his mansion and start looking for people himself, in person, usually he would get his dogs to do this for him”.

Deborah’s phone began playing ‘Dancing Queen’ by Abba. Much to the amusement of Karen Jones.

“ Hello? Right. Just a second”. She wrote down the number given to her. “Ok thank you sergeant. Now then Karen, I wonder if we’ll get this message to them in time. I hope they haven’t gone out for the night.

She heard the ring tone. Four times it rang, and then,

“Piss off, just piss off, and if you don’t stop this bloody stupid prank we will call the police!”

“I am, we are the, this is the police, now please listen carefully, you have a Miss Heather Bradley staying with you, I need you to put us through to her room, or bring her to reception so as I can speak with her”. The receptionist was convinced she was speaking to the police. “I understand Miss; can you give me a number I can call you back on”?

Deborah gave the girl her number.

“Now please Miss, do not think that this is a prank, this is of the utmost importance”. The young lady acknowledged the importance of the situation. Eight minutes later, Deborah’s phone played its tune. “Hello? Heather? No time to explain its D.C.I. Knowles, check out Heather, now, get out of there as fast as you can. Don’t come back to Sheffield yet, but just get out of there as fast as you can, your life is in danger, and Rachel’s. I can’t explain everything just now Heather, but please, for the sake of your lives’ get out of there, like right now. Throw your things into a suitcase and leave”.

POLICE MORTUARY. KINGS CROSS LONDON.

Pathologist Roger Healy was speaking on the phone with Ashley Barnes. "How are you doing babe, we miss you down here Ash, when are you coming down to work with us". Roger and Ashley had been students at the same time, both of them attending 'The Thames Valley Police Department for Criminal Pathologists'.

"Jesus Christ Roger, you actually passed your exams, you became a pathologist? You used to spend all your time shagging and smoking dope; how the fuck did you ever manage to pass"?
"I slept with the head pathologist, she passed me, after that I picked everything up as I went along. It wasn't easy Ashley either, she was about fifty-nine years old, but boy could she move her hips. She didn't seem to mind that I closed my eyes".
"Well, she wouldn't would she, not with what you've got between your legs. I'm coming down in about two weeks' time to visit my parents, perhaps we could get together for a bit of fun, that's if you've not got yourself engaged or anything have you"?
"No no, nothing like that, and anyway, it wouldn't have made the slightest bit of difference to me, you know how much I like having fun with you Ashley".
"Oh, flattery will get you everywhere, anyway, why are you calling"?
"Well, you know that Hillman is down here now"?
"Yes"?
"Well, he's been at it down here; he's left us a bit of his handy work to be going on with. I've got two young guys lying on the slabs here. They were found behind some bushes in a public park around the King's Cross area. By the looks of them they must have lay there for a couple of days. Both of them have had their wrists cut open, one of them have had his knee shot out, they're a mess".
"And"?
"No nothing, I was just saying, when he does them, he does them good".
"You phone me to tell me that? You think I haven't seen his handy work for myself? You should have seen the state of some of the victims I've had to perform upon. I seriously doubt if you could have taken it Roger, without spewing, like when you saw that junkie

with his ears cut off, and placed neatly in his mouth along with his eyes".
"Yeah, ok Ash, that was a long time ago. No, I called you up to tell you something that could be handy to know, if you tell whoever is in charge up there on the Hillman case".
"What, what is it"?
"Well, it might be nothing, or it could be something".
"Come on Roger, I'm busy!".
"Well, I heard this guy talking in the pub the other night, and he said he was friends with the guy who rebuilt John Hillman senior's house. He said the man who built the house was called Billy Waite, said he used to go some days and get casual labour off him. This Mister Waite has since emigrated to Canada. Now then, he used to tell this bloke that he couldn't come on certain days and labour to him, you're going to love this Ashley"
"I know, I'll see you in three weeks, just get on with the story will you"?
"There's a secret room in the house".
"What"?
"What do the Americans call it? A safe room, a room in the house where it is completely-"
"Yes I know what a safe house is Roger".
"Now, I don't know if that guy in the pub was just bull-shitting, but I'll tell you what Ashley, it fits in with the manner of ease that Hillman has been able to pick these trained armed men off, don't you think"?
"Yes I do Roger, but don't you be repeating this to anyone else ok,
I thank you for this information, I will pay you in kind the next time I see you. Thanks Roger seriously thank you for that information, good boy".
"No problem Ashley, I hope to see you soon".
"Oh you will, make no mistake about that, you will, bye".
Ashley Barnes smiled to herself, for more than one reason.

FOREST HOTEL. NOTTINGHAM.

Heather and Rachel were making their way to reception to check out of the hotel. "I don't think Deborah Knowles would bull- shit us Rachel, she just said leave, now, and don't come back to Sheffield. She must know something to warn us like that".
Heather paid the bill and then said, "We'll call a taxi to take us to the station Rachel".
"Where will we go"?
"I don't know, we'll decide that when we get there". Heather put her bags beside a table and went over to the phone on the wall to phone for the cab. She looked over to Rachel, who was now sitting at the table protecting the luggage. "Fifteen minutes Rachel, can we, I mean, do you think, will that be alright do you think"?
"Eh, yeah, I think so".
Two young men sat at the table immediately next to the one where Rachel sat. They had been sitting there for some time. They both wore pin-striped suits, one black, and one dark grey, and both of them wearing collar and ties.
They looked like respectable young men to Rachel. "Mummy's boys, without a shadow of a doubt". Heather came over and sat beside Rachel.
"Excuse me" said one of the yuppies, I couldn't help hearing you were booking a taxi to the station. Well, Kevin and I are going there, we could give you a lift, but you would have to come now. He looked at his watch. "Kevin's train arrives in twenty minutes, you are welcome to accompany us, please don't think we are trying to come on to you, I can assure you we are both happily married men". Both men held out their hands revealing wedding rings. "This is merely an act of genuine Christianity" the young man smiled.
"No thank you" said Heather, "we've ordered the taxi anyway".
"Oh well" he replied, leaving a twenty pound note on the table for the waitress. "No harm done ladies, goodnight".
"Goodnight" replied Heather.
The two men left the lounge and were heading for the revolving doors in the lobby. "What do you think Rachel, I think they were genuine, I mean, a bit snobby, but they're married and they don't seem to be trying their luck, what do think, do you think we should take them up on their offer"?

"They look alright to me Heather" said Rachel, "and they'll be quicker than the taxi. Deborah Knowles did say, as quick as we can".
"Come on then Rachel, go and stop them, I'll bring the bags and I'll go and cancel the taxi, quick, catch them. Tell them I won't be a minute. Rachel got up and made her way through the lounge to catch up with the two kind gentlemen.
Someone was already talking at reception. "Excuse me" said Heather, could I just leave this money for a taxi I ordered, for Bradley, my friend and I have obtained alternative transportation. She handed the receptionist a ten pound note and apologised to the elderly lady she had interrupted. She picked up the luggage and hurried outside. The car sat waiting in the centre of the car park ready to go. The driver revved the engine a couple of times, indicating to Heather that he was in a hurry. She could see Rachel already in the car. The gentleman who had left the tip for the waitress was now nervously looking at his watch. "Hurry miss". He came round and opened the boot, and took Heather's bags from her. Rachel was in the front seat. The other man who was sitting in the back seat offered Heather his hand as she climbed in. "This is really kind of you" said Heather.

The man who had held the door for her got in behind her as quick as lightning and put his arms around her neck, and squeezed. Heather passed out. Rachel was already unconscious. Heather simply hadn't noticed. "Right, off to Sheffield Terry my man that's the easiest two grand each we'll ever make, tie them up. "Steve said we could fuck them if we want to, on the way up, just as long as we keep them alive, he doesn't care what we do. I don't think he's very happy with them, whatever they've done".

Rachel and Heather had been gone for half an hour when Angela and Carla pulled into the car park of the Forest Hotel in Nottingham.

KINGS CROSS. LONDON.

There was silence in the flat now. Hillman listened at the hatch for any sign of anyone still going around. He could hear nothing. Now, he very slowly and carefully opened the hatch up. He could hear only faint steady breathing coming from the bedroom. He pulled himself over to the edge of the hatch into a sitting position, his legs dangling through into the hallway. He was just about to jump down when there was a very loud knock on the door. Impatient knocking.

He quickly pulled his legs back up and placed the hatch lid down just in time for Tracy to come padding bare-foot back into the hallway. "Who is it"? She shouted down.

"Open the door you fucking stupid bitch", the man shouted through the letter box.
"Who is it"? repeated Tracy.
"Open this fucking door now!!"
"Just a minute" cried Tracy.
"I'll just a minute you, you stupid fucking whore you".
Tracy shouted up the stairs, "Carol its Ash, come on get up he sounds pissed". Tracy got to the door and opened it. "I'm sorry Ash I thought"-
"Get me a fucking drink bitch" said the coloured gentleman. He was the girl's pimp. "And what the fuck you dooin' here anyway bitches, don't you got your own places to go, you know this place is only used for the Johns, you know that! I got girls out there, they gotto fuck with their Johns wid dare asses against the fucking walls, what jew dooin"?
"Ash, we had to stay here, the door was wrecked, and we had to wait until the guy came to fix it, otherwise the place would have been filled with junkies and alkies, they would have taken over the place and we wouldn't have got it back off them".
"Where's the dog"?
"It's dead, that Hillman creep killed it".
"Motherfuckingcunt! I get my hands on that white sun-bitch and he's one dead dude, I tell you that for peanuts, it woulda' been better for *his* ass if his motha' had fucking swallowed him".

"We're sorry Ash, but we didn't know where you were, you weren't answering your phone, so we thought we'd just stay here and guard the place until you showed up".

"Yeah well, that's ok, but you should keep in touch bitches, you know am ner` fah way, fuck you know that. How much you gonna make off that mental man anyway"?

We made three hundred, even, we've got your hundred here Ash".

"Ok, ok. Let's go and have a drink in the living room, just get worried that's all, I mean, girls like you don't grow on trees you know". Ash's last statement would be the closest any of his girls would ever get to a compliment.

Hillman listened intently again, as he heard the living room door closing. He would have to make his move now. He collected the blankets he'd lay under in the attic, and the quilt. He threw them onto the floor directly under the hatch, checked his gun, making sure the silencer was screwed on properly. It was now or never.

He hung from the hatch, holding on to the edge with both hands. He dangled for a few seconds and then let go. He hardly made a sound. Quickly, he picked up the blankets and the quilt and carried them through to the bedroom, where he threw them onto the floor behind the bedroom door. The lounge door opened and he could hear someone coming up the stairs. He pulled the gun from his pocket. The man went into the bathroom. Ash was whistling as he urinated, just as he had been as he'd come up the stairs, and just as he was when Hillman opened the bathroom door.

"It's just me nigger" whispered Hillman. Ash spun round, his free hand already going for the gun hidden in his jeans. Thud!! Thud,Thud. The three bullets from Hillman's gun had gone straight through the man's throat and head. He was dead before he hit the floor, rivulets of his blood running down the bathroom mirror and wall. "It's just me boy, you know, the mental man. Too many for you though, pimp boy, if I'm mental".

Hillman emptied the man's pockets, taking his wallet and a bundle of notes. He then began to whistle as he made his way down stairs with confidence. "*John Hillman you get back up those stairs and clean that mess up*". He was too focused on what he intended to do with the prostitutes to be bothered with his mother. He opened the lounge door and could not believe his luck. Carol had fallen asleep on one of the easy chairs, with one of her arms supporting her chin. Tracy had her back to him, watching a music video on T.V.

Hillman was delighted; he could not have planned this any better. Tracy was tired, but she knew it would be useless to try and sleep while Ash was here. Hillman lit up a cigarette.

Your mind, when you are tired can play funny tricks on you. It can make you think about things you wouldn't normally think about, Tracy thought about how she was not allowed to smoke while Ash was here, because he didn't want his lungs polluted with any white trash whore smoking. So why had he just lit a cigarette up. She turned around in the chair to look, and then she was fully awake. She gasped with shock and fear. She began to urinate uncontrollably and cry. Hillman took a draw of his cigarette and blew smoke up towards the ceiling. "Why Tracy"? Said Hillman. Tracy was now gushing urine onto the chair through her jeans. "Why? Tracy, please answer me". Tracy couldn't speak for fear. "Who's idea was it Tracy, hers"? He pointed with his gun to Carol. "Or yours, although it doesn't really matter to me because you're both going to die you know that don't you"?
Tracy nodded, still urinating. "I'm so sorry Mister Hillman" She sobbed.
"I'll bet you are. You were sorry enough that you were going to sell your story to the newspapers weren't you. Weren't you"?
"Yes" She sobbed again, "Mmm"?
Carol awoke. "Tracy? What's wrong"?
"PEEK A BOO!" Shouted Hillman.
Carol turned around. "Oh my God!!"
"Do not, young lady, take the Lords name in vain, do you hear me"?
"Oh, Mister Hillman. I eh. We-."
"Oh I know, Tracy's already told me, you're both so sorry. Now then, before I go, you both owe me a refund and a fuck, but I'll skip the fuck if you don't mind, just the money then ladies.
"We haven't got it here Mister Hillman, I can go and get it for you, it won't take me long".

Hillman smiled and shook his head. "Do you honestly think Carol that I would trust you to do that after what you've just done to me, hell, I wouldn't trust you to go to the toilet you silly fucking whore that you are". "IF I HAVE TO TELL YOU AGAIN ABOUT YOUR LANGUAGE, IT'LL BE WITH THE BACK OF MY HAND NOW CUT IT OUT!! Hillman's mother suddenly appeared on the sofa next to Tracy. The two girls were petrified as Hillman began to have an imaginary conversation with his mother.

Suddenly, he spoke to Tracy. "Take your clothes off bitch, and sit beside your slut friend, move it! He looked at Carol now. Now while Tracy's taking her clothes off, you go and get me a cup of coffee, and I fucking dare you to make a move for that door, because I happen to know that you whores would sell your granny to save your own arses. Don't even give it a second thought, now fucking move yourself, two sugars and milk as fast as you can, I've not got all day, been up there for an eternity thanks to you bitches". Carol looked at the door as she made her way through to the kitchen. She couldn't leave her friend alone with that maniac, she just couldn't.

She put the kettle on and began to make up the coffee. Then she had an idea. She would throw the coffee into Hillman's face and then try and somehow overpower him, hoping that her friend was not too overcome with fear. It was a long shot, but it was the only shot they had. He was going to kill them soon, and God knows what he'd do to them before he killed them. She had to try something. Even if she'd tried to make a run for it, she would have been sickened, because she could see from where she stood that Hillman had removed the door key, the sick fuck. He was hoping she'd make a break for it, the nasty bastard. Carol decided that she wouldn't put any milk in his cup, so that the liquid would be piping hot, and would scorch his eyes, allowing her time to get the better of him. Hillman's voice roared through from the living room. "Hurry up with that coffee you fucking two faced little bastard that you are, and don't try anything stupid!!"

Tracy was now naked and shaking like a leaf, with her knees tucked up on the chair under her chin. "What the fuck are you doing Tracy, hiding everything away, come on, you're a whore, let me see the goods, Lord knows I've paid enough to you, come on get those legs open you tramp, let me see that tasty pussy of yours that you used to beguile me. So fucking good at that aren't you, you tramp. Stole all my money as well you fucking little bastards that you are.
Don't you understand? You'll have to answer for your actions someday. What are you going to tell Jesus on that day of judgement, regarding ripping off poor old Doctor John Hillman of all his money,

when all he was trying to do was help you out a little, what are you going to tell God? Would you hurry up scrubber with that coffee?"
Carol entered the living room carrying a mug of piping hot coffee. Hillman laid his gun on the sofa and reached out with his left hand to take the cup from Carol's hand. Just as he reached out for the mug, Carol threw the near boiling liquid straight onto his face. Hillman screamed and put both of his hands up to his face, but as luck would have it, he rolled over on top of the gun so there was no chance of her grabbing it. Instead, she grabbed Tracy by the hand and the two girls made a break for it. Hillman had removed the key from the door, but Carol had a spare one in her handbag. She searched frantically at the door trying to retrieve the key. She found it, and quickly put the key in the lock, but in her panic, she could not get the key to turn. "Hurry up" Roared Tracy. "Hurry".
Then Carol felt the searing pain in the back of her left knee as her leg gave way. Tracy felt a burning sensation in the small of her back, and was suddenly unable to stand. She collapsed to the floor with absolutely no feelings whatsoever in her legs. Hillman had shot her quite deliberately in the spine. Another wave of pain for Carol, this time in her stomach. She slid down the wall with her hands holding her midriff.
She looked at Hillman as shock set in, and her breathing became short and laboured. Blood seeped through her fingers and down onto jeans. "I'm, s-sorry John, I didn't w-want t-to do it". She began to cry and shake her head in disbelief at the amount of blood seeping through her fingers. "Am I g-going to d-die"?
Hillman stood looking at the two prostitutes, pain still etched on his face from the burning liquid. He walked through to the kitchen and rinsed a cloth in cold water placing it on his face, the cold liquid immediately soothing him. He aimed the gun at Tracy and pulled the trigger and saw the girl's chest bone completely shatter. Tracy breathed in deeply, sounding like someone having an asthma attack. "We are all going to die my dear; it's a question of how and when, that's all. Your time just happens to be here and now. This is not how God had probably planned your time, he probably had something much nicer than this in store for you, but because you decided to be such a slut and use your pussy to make money instead of working like the rest of us, he's just said fuck it, you die your own way. He's asked me to hunt you all out and learn you a lesson for tempting men away from their wives and families, and for dressing

like you need cock constantly, so, you see Tracy, you have no-one else to blame except yourselves for ending your lives like this. Even if I called you an ambulance now, I doubt if they could save you, you're losing too much blood lady.
Look at your friend, she's passed out already. Hillman pulled Carol by the hair roughly and threw her out of his way. He then loaded his magnum three fifty-seven with another three bullets
and then aimed the gun at Carol's head. "Please John, don't k-k-ill me". Hillman pulled the trigger and the young lady's head exploded all over her friend's face and shoulders. Hillman emptied the two girl's hand bags of the money that was in them, and then left the flat, locking the door behind him. A minute later, Tracy momentarily came to, but her vision was fading fast, and her breathing almost non-existent. She saw the remains of her friend lying beside her and she tried to touch Carol's hand just before she died. She could hear her mother's voice clearly in her head. "I'm telling you Tracy, London is not all that it's cracked up to be, it's been the ruination of many a poor girl, believe me, stay at home and enjoy your life Trace, please, you'll have plenty of opportunities closer to home".

"I think that concludes business gentlemen." said Temple as he counted out the last of the notes to make up his new friend's reward money. "Now here". He handed the man named Terry, an envelope. "Give that to your boss, and tell him I'm very grateful for his assistance, it's been a pleasure doing business with you gentlemen. Amanda, could you go to the cellar please, and give these gentlemen a good bottle of scotch each please. Well, goodbye. Are you sure you don't want to participate in some sexual pleasures with these scoundrels before you go"? He pointed to Heather and Rachel, who were sitting petrified and bound on the sofa.
"No sir, we'd better get back thank you".
"As you wish. Amanda will bring your whiskey out to your car for you, and once again, many thanks for your help". The two men left the room and made their way out.
"Now then ladies" said Temple, walking over to his cigar box. He snipped the end off one of his cigars with a small pair of scissors, and lit it. "Do you remember Heather, our first meeting in here, a business meeting no less, Miss Bradley. We sat and discussed figures and facts, we had drinks Heather, hmm? Do you remember? Young Rachel, you were here too. At that time Heather, I thought I'd made the perfect partner decision, but that was then, this is different isn't it?
"We could still be partners Mister Temple, we could".
"Could we? Tell me, how am I supposed to conduct business with a partner who constantly lies to me when I ask them perfectly simple questions, how could I run a business like that, under those circumstances? Do you know what you're lying done to me Heather, have you any idea how much suffering you've caused me. Let me tell you, I've lost my brother, I lost a good man, in your shop by the way, and of course, you two were accomplices, I've been humiliated in my own home, by some peroxide blonde I have never met in my life, I've had my mother doused in petrol and threatened to be ignited before my very eyes, causing her, days later to suffer a stroke, which has left her paralyzed and speechless, and to cap it all, the afore-mentioned peroxide blonde bitch goes and kidnaps that same old woman and then dangles her for bait, and forces me to

make a ransom payment. That's what your lying has done to me Heather".

There were genuine tears rolling down Temple's face.

"And you say we could still be business partners? I really don't think so lady, our days for business transactions are well and truly over". Temple sighed heavily. "We had something good going Heather, and we both stood to make lots of money, but, you had to start lying didn't you, and don't say that the blonde bitch had you over a barrel because I could have sorted her out along with that little Italian bastard, I could have sorted everything out for you, but no, you choose to be loyal to that greedy little whore who, as you well know, only thinks of herself. Well, it was your decision Heather, not mine. Now, you have to live with the consequences of your actions".

Just at that moment, the lounge door opened, and Amanda came in.

"Sorry to interrupt Steve, but the mini bus is here with your guests".

"Thank you Amanda, but they're not really my guests are they? They are guests of our two friends here aren't they". Temple looked again at Heather. "Like I said Heather, you have to live with the consequences of your decision. It's time for your punishment".

"Steve, we could work this out, I promise you, I'll do anything that"-

"Too late Heather, save it. You've done all the damage you're going to do to me, it's my turn to inflict some kind of pain onto you now, and your little scrubber friend there. Thank you Amanda, tell them I'll be down in a few minutes babe, meanwhile, tell a couple of those lads down there to clean out the big shed, there's going to be one hell of a gang bang taking place in there shortly. Give me a shout when the other mini bus arrives will you".

Temple sighed and walked over to his drinks cabinet. He poured himself a generous glass of whiskey. "There are winners and there are losers, and you Heather, I'm afraid to say, will always be a loser, and why? One in ten thousand losers, at some point in their lives, get a chance, a once in a lifetime chance to make it, and they don't even see the opportunity, it goes right over their heads, Losers. So, as you were saying before, how could we be partners again, I'm curious as to how you're going to answer that question".

The two girls said nothing. There really wasn't anything Heather could say. She'd lied to him, and that was that. He wasn't interested in why she'd had to lie, that was of no concern to him.

"Oh dear Heather, do I detect fear among you two? Well, you have every right to feel fear, because I am going to teach you both a lesson. My bloody throat is hoarse asking you to be honest with me, I'm so sick of being the nice guy and being shit upon, time after time, well, you chose the path you're on, you chose to continuously lie to me, and so now, you must both face the consequences of your actions, and I wouldn't be looking for your super stars Carla Paganni or the peroxide blonde to be bailing you out, because, just for once, they haven't got a fucking clue where you are. You are completely at my disposal".

He sipped his whiskey and smiled at his two prisoners. "Ever had a gang-bang Rachel"?

Heather tried to save her friend. "Steve, this is all my fault, leave her out of this please, I'm the one who lied to you not her, let her go, she's just a kid, she doesn't deserve to be punished".

"Since when did I need you Heather to tell me who needs to be punished or not, you shut your mouth girl, you've had enough chances to save your arse. Now you're going to see what it's like for those poor whores who work for you, having to fuck beast after beast just to make their target, and just to pay your fucking bills. You're going to find out what it's like to be sexually humiliated in all kinds of ways; you're both going to be very busy girls, very busy indeed".

Again, he sipped his whiskey. "You only have yourselves to blame, remember that when it starts to get uncomfortable out there in the barn. Sixty odd men, Heather, and most of them fuck heads and losers, drinkers, wife beaters, bi sexual, oh, you're in for some time of it. Don't say you weren't warned".

FOREST HOTEL. NOTTINGHAM.

Carla and Angela were at the main desk, talking to the receptionist.

“How long have they been gone? said Carla, looking at her watch.
“Not long” replied the young smartly dressed girl. “Maybe twenty minutes, half an hour something like that”.
“Did they say where they were going”?
“Nope, oh, the station, they were heading for the station, in fact, one of the girls had phoned for a taxi. Then they were talking to two gentlemen in the lounge, that’s all I can tell you”. Angela looked at the girl, waiting for her to continue. “Well? What did they look like, were they old men, young men, what”?
“About thirtyish, I would say, well dressed”.
“What are their names are they registered”?
“Oh no, they weren’t staying here. They had only been in here about an hour or so”.
“Shit!” hissed Angela. Carla smiled at the receptionist and thanked her for her help.
“They could be anywhere” said Carla, as both women made their way down the sandstone steps of the hotel
“Try Heather’s mobile Carla”. Carla pressed the digits for Heather’s phone, but there was no reply.
“What’s going on”? said Angela, I told her to wait here, they wouldn’t be stupid enough to go back up to Sheffield, surely”.
“No they wouldn’t Angela. I’m just wondering about the guys who gave them a lift. What if they’ve been sent here by Temple”.
“They wouldn’t have had time to drive down here unless, unless he has associates down here”.
It’s possible. God I hope not Angela, not after us just taunting him with his mother, oh shit”.
The two women sat in the car, rain now hammering down on the roof. Angela sat tapping the steering wheel looking at nothing in particular. “I’m almost frightened to phone Temple, Carla, something tells me he’s behind this, and if he is, then God help them. I saw the state of poor Susie Monk when they were finished with her”.
“Oh Christ I hope not Angela, and by the way, I don’t think we should call Temple, because if he has got them, and we phone him,

it'll just make him worse, and maybe make their ordeal worse, and believe me Angela, if he has them, then they're in for a torrid time".
Angela sighed, looking at Carla. "Yeah, maybe you're right Carla. Maybe we'll just go back up there and try and take a look for ourselves, see what's going on". She started the car and drove out of the car park. The rain began to batter down even harder on the windscreen.
Angela attempted to lighten the mood and try and take their minds off what was frightening them by the minute. "Ever thought about living in Caribbean Carla? Ever thought about it"?
"Many times Angela, but I've never really wanted to leave Britain to be honest".
"Yeah me too Carla, we would miss all this rain and wind, and snow and fog wouldn't we"?
"Yeah, yeah we would, we would have nothing to moan about, or talk about, because that's all we do in this bloody country, talk about the weather".
Angela had to put the windscreen wipers on full speed to cope with the torrential down-pour. Carla laughed as she said, "Yeah, who the fuck would want to live in the sun every day".

EUSTON. LONDON.

Hillman had boarded the London to Glasgow express, and was sitting on an inside seat in one of the carriages, looking out at the people on the platform. He had decided to disembark at Preston and take a connection to Sheffield from there. He would feel safer back home in his little box, as he called it. "Couldn't live here Lord". He said to himself, "no way. Look at all these lost souls, too many to save Lord". Hillman had taken a taxi across the city from Kings Cross, just in case Tracy the prostitute had alerted the police before she'd died. He need not have worried. Tracy was now dead, with loss of blood. She had tried her best to reach the front door, but her shattered legs had been trailing, and losing blood at an astronomical rate. And even if she had made it, she would not have been able to open it. Hillman had locked the door and threw the key away into a skip more than fifty yards from the flat. He had also taken their mobiles.

Before he had left, he had gone through Tracy and Carol's hand bags, retrieving three hundred pounds. He searched Ash's clothes as well, who's name turned out to be Samuel Cook of all things. If Hillman had searched deeper into the coat pocket of Samuel, he would have discovered a set of keys, one of which would have started the red Porsche outside of the flats, and which would have saved him the trouble of the train journey.

The carriage where Hillman sat was filling up fast. People coming on with bags and suitcases shoulder bags, and bloody unruly children, screaming and crying and generally making a noise. A young woman sat down beside him. "Is this anyone's seat"? She said.

Hillman was slightly startled. "I beg your pardon"?

"Is anyone sitting here"?

"No, no, there's not".

Across the table, a woman with two small children squeezed in. The young woman, who had sat down beside Hillman, began making conversation with the mother of the children. "Thank you Lord, fuck." Said Hillman, to himself . I'm tired, I just want to rest and have a sleep, huh, not much chance of that is there, not with this fucking lot".

Hillman, with his elbow on the ledge of the window stared out at the busy station, as the train finally began to pull out. On and on the two women chatted as the two of them began to make friends with each other. As the train began to build up speed, the people on the platforms began to blur. Then, suddenly, in the reflection of the window, his mother appeared to him, wearing the same clothes she had worn on the day she'd been murdered. He jumped and looked away from the window, startling the two women sitting at the table with him.

"Are you alright"? The woman in front of him asked.

"What? Yes, yes, I em. I thought I saw someone, sorry".

The two women continued their conversation. He glanced at the children around the table, and smiled at them. The girl stuck her tongue out at him, while her slightly older brother silently mouthed the words" Fuck Off".

"Do you like going to school?" said Hillman, still smiling.

"We're on holiday, stupid".

"Stop that Danny." Whispered the boy's mother, tapping his arm with enough force, Hillman thought, to seriously wind a fly.

The train, still picking up speed entered a tunnel. It would be safe now to look out of the window again. All he saw was his own reflection, and the woman across the table with the rebellious children. Then his mother's face again. She seemed to be tapping at the window and pointing at the children, gesturing to him, to give them the back of his hand. He felt a nudge on his arm.

"I'm saying, do you have children"?

"Oh sorry what? Yes, I have two daughters, and a son, yes and a son" He repeated.

"I see" said the woman, "I'll bet they don't behave as badly as this lot, eh"?

"No, no they don't, they are all well behaved, well, when I'm there anyway".

The little boy was once more mouthing his favourite obscenity, only this time adding the famous two fingered salute.

"Cunt!! Can't think of what they'll be like when I'm not there though".

"Danny!, I'm warning you for the last time. I'm sorry for the way he's behaving; he's got like that since his daddy's took off".

"You're on your own then"?

"Yes, I'm afraid so, and believe me, they run me rugged".

"Yes I do see, but then, that's the law now isn't it, we're not allowed to touch them are we".
"Sorry, touch them"?
"Yes, leather them you know? Teach them a lesson. When I was a child, I wouldn't dare speak to an elder like that, they would have banged my head into next week".
"Yes, well, some of us don't believe in hitting children".
"Yes, some of us think that" said Hillman, "and the rest of us have to suffer for it".
"I'm so sorry that I don't agree with hurting children, and maybe, when you're not there, your children are not angels", said the woman looking across the table for some moral support from her new friend.
"Yes and maybe they do behave when I'm not there, and I know which one my money's on".
"People like you make me sick, bullying your children into how you wish them to behave".
"And people like you have helped to put our country onto its knees".
"And just how do you make that out"?
"You let them grow up without any discipline, they get none at school. If the police stop them for anything, then they just tell the police to eff off".
"Do you mind"?
"Yes I do, and then they grow up and get into drugs, and then they go out and attack pensioners to feed their habits, stealing their savings, yes I do mind, because people like you couldn't care less what your children get up to".
"Hey! That's enough!" A man sitting on the other side of the isle was looking straight at Hillman.
Hillman leaned forward and looked over at the man. "Shut your fucking mouth, who was talking to you, and don't you dare open your fucking nigger mouth to me again, because if you do, I'll throw you and your can of fancy energy drink right out of that window, now, shut it clown!".
The young lad, who'd been giving Hillman a bad time, began to cry.
Hillman looked at the child, his face right up to his.
"FUCK OFF!!!
The child cried in complete terror.

"Keep away from my children!!" The woman shouted. "That's it, I'm not sitting here, come on kids, come on Danny son, we'll go and

find another seat". She collected her luggage and began walking down the isle of the carriage, bumping into elbows and heads as she did so. Hillman slid over to the edge of his seat. The coloured gentleman said to him, "You made a big mistake brother".
As quick as lightning, Hillman replied, "No you did, and I'm not your brother, my mother never slept with shit".

"Mister Temple, I can understand perfectly you feeling this way, but let me assure you, this will never happen again, we are so sorry".

"It should never have happened in the first place, you fucking pricks that you are"!!

The four men and two women responsible for the running of Peaceful Meadows old folks home, all sat with their heads bowed. Temple looked at them all, shaking his head. "You say you understand how I feel? Do you know how I felt, when I learned about those two whores marching into here, and then walking away with my wheelchair bound mother, just don't tell me you know how I feel! You people are paid bloody good money to look after these elderly people, there's never any fuck ups when it comes to charging for their accommodation is there? Just think yourselves lucky I'm not closing you down you incompetent buffoons that you are!"

Giles Mercer, the manager of Peaceful Meadows, who also owned three more retirement homes throughout the country, straightened his tie and cleared his throat. "Mister Temple, we would be honoured indeed if you would accept, as a mark of respect to your mother and yourself, that her first year here with us be completely free of charge. This is a most humble apology on behalf of Peaceful Meadows and our staff. I swear sir, that this is the first time that anything like this has happened to us, we have an excellent record here, and we will guarantee you, that this will never happen again".

Temple got up from his chair. "It had better not Mister Mercer, I can tell you that, because there won't be a home here anymore if it does, do I make myself clear"?

"Yes sir, perfectly, now please, have you eaten, we would like to invite you for lunch today".

"No thank you, I have business to tend to, I suggest that you all attend to yours, I would start with security if I were you, good day".

"Good day sir", replied a red faced Giles Mercer.

THE KING'S ARMS SHEFFIELD.

Karen Jones came back from the bar carrying two plates of chips and buttered rolls. She was smiling to herself. "What's so funny" said Deborah Knowles.

"Up there, at the bar. I heard three or four young guys talking about some gang bang. One of them was trying to convince his pals, that when he comes, he can fill a half-pint glass".
"Did you bring any salt Karen"? said Knowles, smiling.
"I'll get some". Karen got up from her seat again and made her way through the crowded bar. Deborah sat wondering if Heather and Rachel had been taken and held captive, or even if Temple had done anything worse. If only she could get the chance to speak to Carla Paganni, she could maybe get some evidence from her that would help to put Temple away. He was obviously a much bigger fish than she had initially given him credit for.

There was also a very sinister side to Deborah Knowles. She had her own plans for building up her career, and she wouldn't let anything or anyone stand in the way of what she had planned for herself. She had managed to keep her dark side hidden from view from her fellow officers. No-one knew exactly what she was thinking, and that's the way she would keep it. It did not matter to her who she was working with, she would make it to the top, whatever it took, and God help anyone who stood in her way.
Karen came back to the table with the salt. She sat down, smiling. "Deborah? Stay calm, bingo".
"What"?
"Bingo, I've just heard where the gang bang is".
"I see." Said Deborah, "Well then, tell them to hold the phone I'll go and get our Ashley, she might want to trade places with the girl".
Karen looked at Deborah and said, "Girlzzza".
"What"?
"There are two girls Debs, and they are being held against their wills".
"Are you sure Karen"?
"Yes I'm sure, and guess where they are going to get raped"?

"Karen, if you say London Road, I'm going to get up from this chair and kiss you". Karen smiled. "They're all talking about it among themselves at the bar. They've been told to bring masks, as it's going to be filmed".
"Yes just the same as they filmed that poor Susie Monk. So it *was* that bastard who set that up. No wonder Carla Paganni was going to town with them. The thing is Karen, we can't get support in yet, we'll have to keep an eye on the place, and wait until they are just about to start. Then we can jump in. First though, we'll finish our snack here, and then we'll head over to London Road, and watch from a safe distance. We'll see the numbers quickly descend upon the house as it gets closer to the time".

Deborah and Karen pulled up thirty yards away from the entrance of Steve Temple's gate. "This is perfect Karen, we can see as they start to arrive". Deborah Knowles had already phoned John Drummond who was now back in Sheffield, that they would need back up at some point. Fifteen minutes later, there were a further twenty officers on standby, and were now positioned in and around London Road, just waiting for the signal from Deborah Knowles
"What the hell is that"? Said Karen, as a cattle truck pulled into Steve Temple's drive. "This is bloody crazy Deborah, are they bringing a bull"?
"Don't know" said Deborah, not even smiling at Karen's joke. Less than five minutes later, the lorry pulled out again, and drove off.
"Want to follow it Deborah"?
"Best not Karen, those two girls are our priority, we'd better not leave here, just in case". As she spoke, three cars, one after another, began to pull into Steve Temple's drive. "Here we go Karen, I counted about fifteen men in those cars". Two minutes later, another two cars pulled in, carrying a further eight men.
"Right, we'll give it five minutes Karen, and then we'll swoop. We'll get him this time, we'll have all the evidence we'll ever need to get him put away. We have had a stroke of good luck today Karen, and that makes a nice change for us babe. I think we'll walk up to the house Karen".
"I wouldn't Deborah, if they see two women approaching the place, they'll get suspicious. If we drive up, they'll think that we're spectators, at least we can get there before they realize that we're not with them".

"You're right Karen, I'm just a bit excited, that's all, come on babes, let's see what we can do".
The two police women drove up the drive slowly, looking around the grounds as they did. All of the vehicles were round the back of Temple's premises, except for one red sports car. They got out and began walking around to the back of the house. As they walked, they could hear cheering and shouting. "Oh God, they've started Karen; call the back up in quickly".

Karen took out her phone and called in the back up. In less than two minutes, the vans moved in, deliberately blocking the drive and any other escape route. Some of the officers went into the house, some of them went around the back of the premises. Suddenly, the cheering stopped. Deborah and Karen walked in between the crowds, who had formed a circle. Every one of the men still had their clothes on. In the middle of the ring lay a dead rooster. An old man stood with a battered cockerel in his hands, the obvious winner. Karen and Deborah looked at each other. They had been well and truly stitched up, and there was nothing they could do about it, except arrest the two old men for illegal cock fights.

Roughly twenty miles away in Buxton, Steve Temple awaited the arrival of three mini buses he had personally paid for to bring about fifty or sixty men who were going to participate in a free for all gang bang. Temple had had two wooden crosses made and erected in the old barn of the farm where they now were. He had stripped Heather and Rachel naked and now had them tied on to the two structures. The structures were in the form of the letter X, and so their arms and legs were spread as wide as could be. Rachel was crying.

"Now now little Rachel, it's a bit late for tears girl, don't you think? If only you had spilled the beans on Heather, I would have let you go, in fact, you could have been in charge of all the street girls, you would have been a very well off young woman, but, alas, you decided to stay loyal to this lying bitch here, and now look where it's got you. There's a whole lot of ugly nasty men coming to use your body for their own pleasure. They're going to turn you upside down and every which way, bite you, nip you, squeeze you, and generally use your body for about three or four hours. Do you think you're going to like that Rachel? It'll make a difference from you eating

pussy all the time don't you think"? Temple gently slapped her thigh. "Never mind Rachel, your friend here is going to get the same treatment as you, you'll both be a pair of slappers together. Temple then gently spun the wheel where Heather was tied, until she was upside down, her legs parted wide as could be.
"You are nothing but a sick inadequate bastard, do you know that Temple"?
"I know a lot of things Heather. I know I gave you no less than ten chances to come clean with me about Paganni and co, and their whereabouts, so you just spit out your sour grapes as much as you like, it's not going to change anything, unless, of course, Rachel here has the guts to shoot you, right in front of everyone here, then I would see that as justice done, and I would call off the gang bang. She would not endure the unpleasantness of all these men taking advantage of her. That's the best that I can offer you, what do think Rachel? Would you like to set yourself free girl"?
"Fucking do it Rachel" said Heather, " Please, fucking do it babes, shoot me, he'll let you go, just fucking do it Rachel, shoot me in the head babes, I love you, I love you with all of my heart, don't let them do to me what they done to Susie Monk, please Rachel, please shoot me darling, I'm begging you!!".
"Shut up! Shut up, shut up!! I can't Heather, I love you too, but I can't, why can't you let us go Mister Temple, we haven't done anything wrong, I swear to you, we didn't know that Angela was going to kill Paul Crane, we had nothing to do with it, Heather told you the truth, why won't you believe us, we're innocent Mister Temple".

"Tut tut Rachel, nice try girl, but you know as well as me, that she is a manipulative cunning bitch, who would defend Carla Paganni to the death, and besides, she's had enough chances, now, here is my gun, if you can shoot her, you'll be a free woman, do you want to be a free woman, or would you like to be gang banged, I'm afraid these are your only choices young lady". He spun the wheel round so that Heather was now upright again.
As soon as Heather was upright, she spat on Temple's face. "You don't fucking frighten me you creep, and Carla and Angela will cut your fucking balls off, if they can find them, you snake that you are, they'll fucking burn your mother next time, and then they'll burn you, you fucking rat that you are!!"

"Ah, so you did know about that Heather, you knew what they done to my mother, you see Rachel? nothing but a lying whore. Once a whore always a whore". Temple turned to one of the men standing near him. "Give me the bullwhip".
"Oh please Mister Temple, I'm begging you" Cried Rachel.
"Too late Rachel, much too late, time for punishment Heather".
"Go and fuck yourself creep show!!" said Heather.
"Is that camera ready to go"? said Temple, to another of the men, and the woman who was going to be filming it for him.
"You're a fucking sick bitch as well" said Heather to the young woman who was testing the camera.
"Stand back" said Temple, "and close those doors now, is everyone in? Remember boys, as rough as you like, up the arse, in their mouths, anything you fancy, they're all yours for the next few hours, now get your masks on before we start rolling the cameras".
Temple stood back and lashed the bullwhip into the air. "Just a practice shot ladies". He turned the structure once again, so that Heather was once more upside down. He stood back and lashed the girl across her breasts, using all of his strength. The crack of the whip was deafeningly loud in the small concrete barn. Heather screamed out in agony. Rachel began to cry again, this time sobbing. "One last chance Rachel, will you shoot her like the dog she is and put her out of her misery, or will you suffer along with her, what's it to be Rachel, it's your decision, but remember, once you decide, there's no turning back".
Rachel did not reply, she couldn't shoot the girl she loved, she just couldn't.
Temple turned the cross around so that Rachel was now upside down. "Last chance Rachel. Ok then, have it your way".
Once again Temple stood back and unleashed a tremendous crack onto the young girl's chest. Rachel did not scream. Her body had gone into complete shock with the sudden burning pain, from her right shoulder blade, down to the front of her vagina. Temple handed the whip to another man. "Give them one or two of them every now and then while they're being serviced".
"Enjoy yourselves boys, there's cans of beer there and meat pies, help yourselves to the pair of lying whores, no knives though, their executions have already been arranged, tuck in boys, they're all yours".

BIRMINGHAM NEW STREET.STATION.

The coloured gentleman got up from his seat as the train pulled into the station. He took his bag down from the luggage net, and turned to look at Hillman, who was looking out at the people on the platform. “Some other time man” said the coloured man.
Hillman didn’t even look round at him, but answered, “I look forward to it”.
“Yeah” said the man.
“You’d better look”.
Hillman smiled. “You have a nice day now”.
The man walked down the aisle behind the few people who were getting off here in Birmingham.
The guard’s voice came on the loud-speaker system, telling everyone that the train would be stopping here for fifteen minutes.
Hillman smiled at the woman sitting opposite him, who hadn’t spoken a word to him since his falling out with the woman with the unruly children.
“Excuse me” He said. “I’m just nipping out for some chewing gum, would you like anything while I’m at the shop”?
“No thank you” came the cold sharp reply. Hillman got up from his seat and walked down the carriage, noticing for the first time, that there were two children accompanying the woman. As he stepped off, he noticed the coloured gentleman going in to the public latrines. People were coming and going out of the busy toilets. He just managed to see the red top and baseball cap disappear into the last cubical. The other three cubicles were taken. He stood waiting beside the coloured man’s cubical. He tapped the door and it moved. It wasn’t taken at all. He got in and snubbed the door. The sections were more than a foot off the floor. There was more than enough room to slide under. The noise in the toilets was horrendous. There were football supporters shouting, there was music coming from someone’s music player, railway announcements coming from the system out on the platform. Morton Phillips sat on the toilet seat, with his jeans down to his knees, rolling his joint. He was just licking the paper, when a piece of clean toilet roll was pushed under his cubical. “What the fuck man, I’ve got toilet paper”, Came the reply. The toilet roll was pushed back through with his foot. Hillman lay on his back and pushed himself through as far as his

waist, aiming the gun at the man, he said, “You stink nigger” and then the top of the man’s head came clean off, spraying the white wall with blood, and covering an enormous painted warning sign, spray-painted there by a local gang, of the danger you’d be in if you confronted them. The joint had fallen from the man’s mouth onto Hillman’s chest. He retrieved it, and put it into his pocket along with his gun. He left the latrines and still had enough time to go and purchase cigarettes and gum at the shop before boarding the train. As he came back on to the train, he noticed some young men sitting on the seats where the coloured man had sat, all of them wearing football scarves. He also noticed that they were saying things to the woman who was sitting at his table. The two children looked frightened . One of them had sat himself down on his seat, and was now talking to the woman. Hillman approached.

“Move, move now”.

“What”? said the teen.

“I’ve already told you twice; now, if I have to tell you again, I’ll take out your teeth and your pals can play cards for them. Now, I am going back outside for a smoke, if any of you even look at this lady or her children, while I’m gone, and I’ll ask her when I get back, then I’ll drag the guilty parties, out into the hall-way and I will throw them onto the tracks. If you choose to sit there, then you behave yourselves like proper human beings, even though your fathers were probably your mother’s pet mongrels. If you don’t behave then you’ll get fucked in public, because I’m not scared to do time for justice, even if that means killing all you scum, got it”?

“Hey, what’s wrong with you, who said anything to you”?

Hillman sat down on his seat, and without looking at the youths, he offered the woman and her children a piece of chewing gum. The woman accepted. Still looking at the woman, he said “You can say sorry to me now for speaking to me like that, or, I swear, I’ll beat you all up here and now, so when you’re ready. I’ll count to five, ONE, TWO, THREE”

“Ok ok. Keep your hair on” Said the youth, “Hell we didn’t do anything wrong, we were only talking to her”.

“You were making her feel rather uncomfortable, now I do not wish to speak to you anymore, so please don’t even look my way, or I’ll throw you out of the window”. Hillman turned to the woman’s children and said. “Do you know this song kids. We’re going to the mansion on the happy day express”.

The youths got up and left the carriage, looking back at Hillman rather disdainfully.

"You just keep moving gentlemen, and no-one will get hurt. You have yourselves a nice day now".

Hillman looked at the woman and smiled.

"Are you alright? These young people now, they don't have any consideration for anyone but themselves do they. They go around intimidating people and frightening children. It's a different story when they're challenged by someone who means business though, they're not so cocky with themselves then. Not so pugnacious then are they"? said Hillman, smiling at the woman's children.

"I'm sorry Deborah, I'm so sorry; I should have known they were throwing me a red herring".
"It's not your fault Karen, I would have fallen for it as well, there's no denying it, they took us in hook line and sinker. I pray for those two girl's lives babe, I dread to think what will become of them now Karen, I have to explain to Terrance Davis, why I have taken thirty odd active officers away from their duties, just to stop a cock fight. As if he's not under enough pressure, I have to go and make things worse for him. Ah well Karen, the worst he can do is sack me, and right now, I'm not so sure if that would be such a bad thing".
"We can't think like that Deborah, we'll get a result one of these days, you'll see, and anyway, it was my fault not yours, you were only acting upon information given to you by me, so if there's anyone should be sacked, it's me, for being so fucking naive, and getting taken in by a bunch of teenagers, bastards!".
"I've never heard you swear before Karen, do you know that"?
"Get used to it Deborah".
The two women walked by the house and down the drive. As they were crossing the road, one of the officers shouted after them. "You have to report to Chief Davies mam".
"I know" said Deborah, wearily climbing into her car.
"Somebody must know us Karen, I mean as police officers, somebody must have tipped Temple off, that's why they said those things in the pub. We were meant to hear, and now that's our cover gone. I don't know Karen, where we go from here, I really don't. We've got John Hillman running around, killing at will, and at random, whilst preaching the fucking gospel. We've got a petty gangster turned pro-kidnapper and threatening people, we've got gangs roaming around on every second street, killing and raping. We have pensioners being attacked and raped by junkies who don't know what day of the week it is. We have kids at the age of ten getting drunk and young girls getting pregnant a couple of years older than that, and I could go on Karen, the list is endless. And what do the general public think? They say the police aren't doing enough, and they're right. That fucking idiot in Downing Street cutting everything he touches. He expects us to perform the same level of service when he's cut nearly half of our work force, the

stupid Tory bastard. Of course Karen, we all know that it's just headlines he's after, everybody knows that's what he's all about, cutting people's money and hours, cutting Police forces, scrapping bloody perfectly good ships, cutting army regiments, he's not even been voted in by the people, and yet he speaks with such arrogance, no wonder the majority of the British people hate his fucking guts".
"Oh look at me; I'll get them back out to work. Where Karen, where will he get them back out to work, there are simply no jobs to obtain, or certainly not enough jobs to go around, and of course, we have to let our foreign cousins have first pick. The lying bastard Coalition government my arse, will tell us different, but you ask some of the factory workers Karen, and you'll see, there are foreign line leaders in the factories, who can hardly speak coherent English fucking politics Karen, but don't worry, that bastard will have to answer for his actions someday, and it's my bet that it will be at the other end of a gun, well, all I can say is, God speed".
"Yeah, for someone not voted in by the British people, he sure has a lot to say".
"He's trying to make himself headlines Karen, the thing is, when he makes his biggest headline, he won't know anything about it, won't that be beautiful". The two detectives laughed.
"Yeah" Said Karen, He's just another Spencer Percival, waiting to happen I would say".
Deborah Knowles smiled at her colleague.
"He's the cheesiest Prime Minister we've ever had, bloody repeating himself time and time again. He sounds like fucking Ethel Jane Cain".

SHEFFIELD GENERAL HOSPITAL.

Carla Paganni had an idea that the man Angela shot would still be in hospital. When they arrived there, she went straight to the administrator's office. "I'm sorry to bother you" She said. "But I was wondering if you could tell me which ward my cousin is being kept in. He came in three weeks ago; he'd been shot in the arm".
"You will have to ask at reception about that, and who let you in here, you're not supposed to be in here" said a grumpy old man in a navy-blue suit.
Fifteen minutes later, Carla came out of the hospital with the information that she required.
"Is he still in Carla"? Said Angela, as Carla got into the car.
"No, he was released two days ago, but I got his address".
"Ok where to Carla"?
Carla looked at her phone. "Eighty-two Westbrook Road".
Another ten minutes and they were there. "This is going to be tricky Carla, he was looking for you to kill you, he hates you with a vengeance".
"Oh and you're his favourite girl of the month aren't you Angela, you shot his fucking arm, which, in case you might be interested to know, he's lost. He's not exactly going to go running for the kettle, no matter which one of us goes to his door. He'll still be able to shoot with his left hand, and I'll bet he's practicing every day".
"Ok" said Angela, we'll both go, and we'll have to be quick, we'll have to render him helpless". They crossed the road and climbed up the four steps to his door. To their amazement, the door was opened almost immediately.
"What the fuck do you want"?
The two women pushed him inside and quickly closed the door behind them.
"Mister Dougan" said Carla, "We're not here to kill you or hurt you, I am here to make a trade with you. Temple came to the hospital to see you, twice; now, he's holding two very dear friends of ours. We need to know what he intends to do with them, now".
"I'm telling you nothing you little Italian whore, and the first chance I get, you're going to die. Don't think, that just because this bitch here shot my arm off, that-"'Crack'. Angela smacked him across the

mouth. “Look, just answer Carla’s question, or I’ll shoot your other fucking arm off, now where’s the girls”?
“Let me explain Mister Dougan” said Carla. “The police are hunting frantically to try and pin all these gun crimes onto someone, anyone. Now, I happen to know that you killed Mister and Misses Hillman with one of your fancy long-range sniper rifles. Now if someone were to go into the police station with that kind of information, well, life could become, how shall I say, a little uncomfortable for you, so, for the last time, where has he got the girls”?
Dougan sighed. “He’s been keeping them at his house; he’s planning some big gang rape, that’s all I know. Whether he’s got them at his house, or whether he’s got them in an old farm in Buxton, who knows, now, that’s all I can tell you. I warn you two now, keep out of my way, do you hear me. I didn’t give you that information as a favour, I gave you it because I hate Temple, almost as much as I hate you, now fuck off slags, don’t ever come back here, unless you plan to die”. With that, he slammed the door behind them
“Where’s Buxton from here Carla”?
“It’s not far, ten, maybe fifteen minute drive, twenty at the most. Let me drive, I know the way”.
“Do you know where this farm is Carla”?
“Yes, it belonged to John Hillman senior actually, he bought it some time ago, it needs a lot doing to it. I don’t think anyone’s lived in it for over three years now. If you didn’t know where it was Angela, it would be pretty hard to find it, which is handy for what Temple has planned”.
Twenty-five minutes later, they were driving up the winding path which led to the courtyard at the back of the farm. Fifty metres from the top of the track Carla stopped the car. They could see a cattle truck with the back doors down. There were no other vehicles in sight. They walked up the winding path until they were at the house. They cautiously approached the front window, and looked in. No-one, nothing. Only a very old three piece suite and a couple of tables. They walked slowly and stealthily around the house until they came to the back. It was then that they spotted the two girls, pinned to two wooden crosses.
“Oh dear God” said Carla. They walked slowly up to them. Both of the girls were bleeding from various parts of their bodies. Heather

seemed to be bleeding heavily from the vagina. “Oh God, its Heather” said Carla.

Upon inspection, they discovered that the other girl, Rachel, was still alive, but was in deep shock. “What the hell have they done to them Angela”.

Even though her arms were securely tied, Rachel’s arms and legs shuddered in spasms. Carla looked at the blood which was dripping from her friend’s vagina. The two women were in a similar condition to that of Susie Monk. Heather was dead. There was not a single part of her body which had skin intact. The loose bloody skin rippled in the breeze. Again and again, Carla tried for a pulse, but to no avail. “She’s gone baby, she’s gone, she’s out of her misery now babes, they can’t hurt her any more”. Angela put an arm around her and tried her best to console Carla, but it was useless. Carla collapsed to the floor sobbing uncontrollably.

Just as Angela was about to untie Rachel, they could here sirens wailing in the distance, getting closer all the time. She grabbed Carla by the arm and pulled her up to her feet. “Come on girl, we have to move, come on!!”

“What about Rachel”? cried Carla.

“Leave her, come on they’ll help her, she’ll survive now Carla, come on girl, we have to get to fuck out of here. Angela reversed all the way back down to the bottom of the hill. She drove in the opposite direction from which they came. Higher and higher they climbed up. Sitting up on the hill again, they could see right down to the main road. They could see the blue flashing lights of the police vehicles coming up the hill less than three quarters of a mile away. The road which Angela had taken was a dead end. If the police continued up the hill, they would be caught.

“Quick” said Angela, “Into the woods”. Pulling Carla by the arm the two young women made their way into the heavily wooded area. They had only got about thirty metres into the woods when they heard the police vehicles pulling into Buxton farm. “You see Carla? Do you see what I mean”?

“How did you know Angela”?

“Mister Dougan, Carla, still choking on sour grapes. Let’s see how they taste when I take one of his legs off. He set us up Carla he knew fine well that Temple and his gang would be well away from here by the time we got here. Now we have a long walk, we can’t go back to the car. I think the police are at it now Carla, guarding it.

Angela relit the cigarette she had previously attempted to smoke. “Well, at least we know that they’ll save young Rachel Carla. Those bastards have left her for dead, if she survives this, then those bastards are in for it. If she can recognise any of them, they’re fucking dead. Her pulse must have stopped at some point, either that, or it must have been so faint that it was untraceable, it’s a bloody miracle, she must be stronger than she looks, but, poor Heather, they’ve really gone to town with her”.
Carla sat shaking her head. “She didn’t have anything to do with all the troubles poor girl, she was just minding her own business”.
Weren’t we all Carla, life can get very dangerous or precarious, in a very short time. We’ve just had a very narrow escape, no thanks to Mister Dougan, but we’ll soon sort him out Carla”.

THE TRAIN.

The youths had disembarked at Sheffield. "Off, to cause misery and discomfort to some other women and children, no doubt", thought Hillman to himself. The woman before him with the two children had at least warmed to him slightly. She was now answering him in a much nicer manner than she had been, since his falling out with the other woman. "Are you going all the way? To Glasgow I mean".
"No, we're getting off at Stoke; my husband is meeting us at the station".
"Good, it's not safe for women travelling alone these days, especially with that maniac running around, killing people".
"Quite", said the woman, looking at her children, and wondering why he should bring a subject like that up in front of them. In case he was going to continue on the subject, she said to him, "Are you going much further"?
Hillman smiled at her. "Well, I paid the full price for London to Glasgow, but I think I'll get off at Manchester. What does your husband do for a living"?
"He's a surgeon".
"A surgeon? And he lets his wife and children travel on one of these, in this day and age"?
"It's not by choice, he broke his leg in a skiing accident, and he can't drive just now". I can't drive".
"Oh I see, so he's going to be at Stoke standing there on the platform with his crutches, how are you getting home"?
"His brother is driving us home. James, tell the gentleman who's meeting us at the station". The little boy said " Daddy and uncle Charlie".
"There now, do you see? I don't tell lies, and if you don't mind me saying, you were starting to come over a little rude again".
Hillman raised his arms up. "I'm sorry, I apologise, I do, you see, I'm a medical man as well, I'm not a surgeon, I'm only a general practitioner, it's a habit I have, talking too much, and I assure you, I never once doubted you, besides, it's none of my business where you're going to, or what you do, I apologise".
"It's alright, forget it".

Hillman looked at the kids. "Who wants a sweet"? Hands up, hands up for Jesus".
"It's ok" said the woman, "We're nearly home thank you".
"Oh go on mum" said Hillman, "I'm going for a coffee, let me get you a coffee. Chocolate kids"?
"Can we mummy"? Before the woman had time to reply, Hillman said, " Good boy, good boy, that's what I like to hear,
you would like a bar of chocolate, but you still asked mum first, that's a good boy".
Hillman nodded and smiled at the woman. "I like that see? He knows who the boss is. I didn't mean for anybody to have to hit their kids, that woman before got the wrong end of the stick, I'm afraid, and so did that coloured gentleman".
"Thank you all the same, we will soon be home".
"Ok" said Hillman, "as you wish". Hillman got up and walked down the carriage, heading for the buffet car. The woman at this point, rather regretted not taking him up on his offer for a coffee, after all, he was only trying to be polite, and besides, what could he get up to in here, the carriage was jam-packed full. It's not as if he were trying to molest her or anything.
Five minutes later, the carriage door slid open and Hillman came through carrying a large white paper sack and two cartons of coffee.
"Please don't think badly of me, it's just, when I tell children I'll do something, then I usually do it, I like to keep my word you see. Now, if you don't want to give them it just now, then give it to them when they get home, ok? Also, I took the liberty of buying you a coffee, in case you should change your mind". He handed the bag to the young mother.
"Oh, sorry kids, our milk and sugar is in that bag, for our coffee, the rest is yours".
This time the woman sat shaking her head, smiling. "Thank you, you are very kind".
"Listen to your mummy, kind, goodness me, it's only a cup of coffee". Hillman made a funny face for the children.
They both laughed. "He's funny mummy".
"Yes he is" said the woman, still smiling. "Thank you". This time it was almost a whisper. It was only for him to hear.
"You're welcome my dear".
She opened her coffee carton. "Are you married"?

Hillman looked at the woman. “Yes, well I was, we split up a few months ago, I live on my own now. I travel the country now though, instead of just working from the same practice, that way, it takes my mind off things”. He smiled. “Also, I get to meet new people. Last week I was working in Edinburgh, this week I’ve been working in London”.

“Do you miss your wife? Oh I’m so sorry, I shouldn’t”.

” No, it’s alright, yes I miss her, I miss my kids”.

“I’m sorry for asking that, really, I shouldn’t delve into other people’s business, I had no right to ask you that, especially the way I’ve been treating you in here”.

“Please Misses, it’s alright, don’t fret yourself. My wife left me to go and be a prostitute”.

The woman almost chocked on her coffee. “For God’s sake”.

“HEY!! I’m sorry, but please don’t use the Lord’s name in vane like that!”

“I’m sorry, I’m just so shocked, what on earth possessed her to go and do that? You poor man”.

Hillman’s eyes welled up. It had been a long time since anyone had spoken to him with genuine pity. “She em, she started to hang around with one who lived in our street you see? Then it was just a matter of time. I’m eh. I tried to”.. He got up from his seat. “I’m sorry, I’m going for a cigarette, please excuse me”.

The woman felt so sorry for him.

“What kind of a woman could leave a life like that to get into prostitution” the young mother thought to herself. “No wonder he snapped at that woman before, and to be honest, those children were behaving badly, hell, he was only making his point”.

“Now then kids, when that gentleman comes back, you remember to say thank you to him”.

“Yes mummy, he’s nice isn’t he mummy”.

“Yes he is kids”.

“He chased those bad men away didn’t he mummy, and he told that lady off for her children swearing at him”. The woman smiled at her children. “Bloody hell, even the kids were sticking up for him”.

Hillman returned, blowing his nose on a piece of toilet tissue.

“I em. I’m sorry for that Misses, I’m just being silly, it’s just. Sometimes it just gets too much for me, her leaving me, for to do that, I mean, people split up all the time, but usually it’s for someone else, but to leave you to go and do that”?

“I’m sorry” said the woman, “I am so sorry for treating you the way I have”.

“Thank you Mister” said the young boy. “Thank you Mister” repeated his little sister.
“You are most welcome, but remember, I want you to make a promise to me and your mummy, will you do that”?
“Yes”.
“Now remember, when you make a promise, you must keep it ok”?
“Yes sir”.
“Right, I want you two to promise your mummy and I, that you will never, ever, never, never, never ever take sweets or money from a stranger, will you promise me that? That was ok today because mummy was here, and you asked her, but if mummy isn’t there, you won’t take sweets from someone you don’t know, promise? Not ever, never ever, never ever never ever, ok”?
The children burst into laughter.
“We already know that silly”.
“Ah uh, do you promise me, because the train is going to stop soon, and I may never see you again, so do you promise”?
“Yes mister, we promise”.
“Good, because now I know of at least two boys and girls who are going to be safe in the world”.
The train began to pull in to Stoke. The young mother sat smiling at Hillman. “Doctor”?
“Doctor Thompson”.
“Doctor Thompson, may I say sir, that you are quite a remarkable man. Believe me sir, when I say, that you will find love, I swear, and please don’t take this the wrong way, but if I weren’t married, you and I would be having drinks tonight”. She leaned over the table and kissed him on the cheek. “May God bless everything you do Doctor Thompson”.
He smiled at her. “He already does my dear, he does”.
As the train pulled up to a stop, Hillman saw the man, sure enough standing on the platform with his leg in plaster, along with uncle Charlie. He watched as the young woman ran to him with her children, and kissed and cuddled him. As the train was pulling away, she turned, just in the nick of time to wave at him. As the train began to speed up, she found herself running to keep up with it, just so as she could wave to him, one last time, and blow him an

enormous kiss. On the train, a young woman came and sat down opposite him with a young child about the age of four, who was carrying a plastic machine gun.

As she sat down with the boy Hillman said to him,

"Ooh please don't shoot me".

The little boy's mum laughed.

"Hi" said Hillman, and then continued to play with the little boy.

"Please, please don't shoot me with that alien-blaster gun mister".

The little boy laughed as he aimed the plastic weapon at Hillman.

"Hi" replied the young mother, taking off her jacket and then sitting down, crossing her legs with her pretty floral mini skirt.

Karen Jones looked at Deborah Knowles having both surveyed the sight before them. Two separate ambulance's had been sent to transport the girls to hospital. Karen fought to keep down vomit. She had seen the mess of the little girl called Susie Monk, on the film that Deborah had shown her, but to see this, right here in front of her. She watched as the paramedics lifted the helpless little slip of a girl into the ambulance. Flakes of skin hung off her body, making it look like she was wearing some kind of red woollen sweater. Her legs looked like they were hairy, like red fluffed wool. There was no part of her body that had escaped their tortuous treatment. She looked like she was wearing rags and feathers, red rags and feathers. Knowles stood smoking and staring into space, trying yet again, to come to grips with what she had just witnessed. Deborah shook her head. "I've had it Karen. Really. I can't. I'm. I'm stuck for words, those poor girls". Karen was down on her hunkers now, sobbing like an infant.

John Drummond came over to the two women with a flask and two cups. "Here you are ladies" he said, himself having to stifle a sob, as he handed each of them a cup of tea. The man did not know where to put himself, he felt awkward and lost. He had just seen the mess of the two girls in the ambulances. He stood with the flask of tea in case the two girls wanted a refill, but he was at a loss as to what he could possibly say to them.
Deborah put her arms around his shoulders and cuddled him. "I know" she cried, "I know John, it's alright, we feel the same as you".
"No, it's much worse for you women, who the hell could do that to a young woman and still be able to sleep at night this horror it's.. it's beyond belief".

Forensic officers were here now; with their polythene gloves, and their powders and sprays and whatever else they had in their magic bags. Three of them assembled in the ambulance at Heather's side.

Even though the girl was dead, they could still obtain a lot of information from her, valuable information. The other three forensic officers were gathered at the place of torture, where the two girls had been tied up. There were rivulets of blood still running down the wooden structures, where pieces of flesh stuck to wood. Drummond stared in silent fascination, as the team began their work, their expressionless faces concentrating on the job in hand.

They had been working around the clock these days, working on murder after murder in and around Sheffield. So now, they did their jobs with the cold heartless efficiency that comes only from years and years of professionalism in situations such as these. If they were to do their jobs to the best of their ability, then there was no time for emotional outbursts. Police officers go out and arrest the criminals, true, but it's these guys who most definitely point the way for them. "Do your stuff guys" said Drummond, "And help us to find the utter inhumane bastards who did this to those two beautiful ladies, give us a piece of vital evidence".

TILLER ROAD. ISLE OF DOGS.
LONDON.

In room 107 of the Bellgrove hotel, Tracy and Sharon sat watching T.V. with the children. "Come on kids, time for bed".
"Oh mum, can't we just watch the end of this, we haven't got school to go to" said Angela.
"I know you haven't" said Tracy, "but that's going to change soon, so come on". Half an hour later, when Tracy had settled the kids in their beds, she said to Sharon, "I'm going back up".
"What, to Sheffield, you mean"?
"Yes, I've had it down here; I'm so sick of hiding, living like a fugitive, when I haven't done a thing wrong".
"That's not why we're hiding Tracy, your ex-husband is still at large you know".
"I know, but I can't take this for much longer, these girls are missing school Sharon, I have a responsibility to them, for them to be educated, I'll have to do something soon, I'll crack up".
"Tell you what Tracy, what if I go and look at the property market, maybe put a deposit down on a house, and start from there, start somewhere new, afresh, what do you say"?
Tracy sipped her coffee. "It's a thought Sharon".
"Look" said Sharon, "You can change the girl's names by deed pole into your maiden name. We'll find somewhere, no matter where you want to live, even Sheffield".
"The thing is, I have a perfectly good house up there, but because they can't catch that madman, I have to stay away from it, surely to goodness he's not that hard to find, hell he leaves dead people behind him wherever he goes, I'm just sick of it Sharon. These kids are going back to school soon, no matter what, and no matter where I'm living. They found a man's body in the toilets in Birmingham yesterday Sharon, killed by John, now does that mean he's on his way South, or is he heading back up this way, why can't they find the bastard"?

“I know Tracy, but hey, they don’t know for sure if that was your ex-husband who done that or not”.
“It was him alright; I just don’t know where to turn Sharon”.
Tracy’s mobile phone buzzed. She had a text message. She read it, and then slumped to the floor, her back sliding down the wall. She sighed. “Heather’s dead Sharon and young Rachel is knocking on death’s door. Carla says to stay down here until we’ve heard from her or Angela”.
“Oh my God Tracy, what the hell’s happened”?
“She didn’t say. She only said that the other girl was still alive, but she was in a bad way, there’s no guarantee she’ll survive. Oh my God Sharon, what the hell is happening”.

SHEFFIELD.

John Hillman walked steadily through the cold rain, rather confused with himself. He had decided to board a bus when he'd got off the train at Manchester. He had taken the bus from Manchester and had disembarked for some reason at Dronfield. He could not remember why he'd got off, but now found himself walking along the A.57, two miles South of Sheffield. His mind was now completely blank, other than the fact that he had an overwhelming urge to get back to his safe house. London had turned out to be too dangerous to live in. The unfortunate incident with the prostitutes, the boys in the park, it was all too much. He had decided to move, knowing that he would surely have been caught if he'd stayed there.

Then he remembered the coloured man on the train. One thing had escaped his attention, until now. His Lord had not been with him. His mother too, had made fewer appearances as well.
In his mind, he heard himself asking a question. "Does this mean that I'm getting better"? Better? Better from what? "What the fuck's wrong with you. Don't you fucking start getting soft now! You know the whores and their pimp deserved to die don't you? Yes but. "Yes but nothing, serves them right for taking off with your money, it could have been worse too, imagine if they'd taken your gun, where would you have been then, don't you start getting soft with me now, and don't worry if the Lord has stopped talking to you just now, he's got more than you in the world to think about. He's blessed you with the brains to look after yourself hasn't he? Your very own lying bastard father couldn't even do that, could he? No. No, he went and got your mother killed as well, didn't he? Yes, so just stop your fucking whining and get on with walking home. Anyway, don't you think you should lay your mother to rest? Because that's why she comes back and curses you. "Why,

Why? You thick man, you have to find the bastard who shot her, find him and torture him, kill him whichever way you please, but until you do, your mother will always come back spitting rage at you, and whoever you are with. I know it might take some time, but you can do it John. You'll have to find out first who you're lying bastard father's enemies were. Now, how are you going to do that? I don't know. "You don't know? Yes you do John, who used to run around delivering messages for him all fucking day and night in her fancy fucking car, and who used to fuck with him when your poor mother's back was turned?
"Carla Paganni"? "YES JOHN, CARLA FUCKING PAGANNI!!"

Hillman walked on through the rain, discussing matters of importance with himself. Of course Carla Paganni. Ever think it strange John that she was one of the first people to be there, the day your mother was shot? You never know John, you see? How do you know it wasn't her who killed her? Yes, but she wouldn't kill that lying bastard though would she? That would be like biting the hand that feeds her. I'll get into hiding first, then, after a couple of days relaxing, I'll work something out, of course, I'm going to have to be real careful with Carla, she's a tricky one, she could end up giving me a bigger beating than my wife did, you fucking bastard that you are!!"

The wind was driving the rain in sheets onto his back. It was right through his jacket and shirt and his tee-shirt. The skin on his back was frozen, as he walked steadily through the night. "Go on, keep it coming down, fucker" he shouted out loud, looking up to the night sky. "Be a cunt if you want to, who cares? "I know what he said about having other people in the world to look after, but don't you think you might, just might give me a break now and again, huh? Look at all the things I've done for you, and what have you given me in return, eh? Oh yes, the girl in London, jumping to her death, but that's it, that's been it, the one and only thing, after all I've done for you. Look at me now, look how wet and cold I am Lord, I'm fucking frozen here, and wet and cold and I'm wet". Tears rolled down his face." And I'm wet and cold Lord, and wet".

"I'll bet she's not cold Lord, the whore with my children, bet she's alright. Nice and warm, and snuggled in to those little angels of mine". He walked on, crying to himself, at the thought of not seeing his children any more. As he walked, he noticed he was walking through a tunnel of trees. He could just make out two eyes, ahead of him in the distance. "Setting me up now? Lord, is that it? Is that what you have planned for me next? Maybe a fight with Satan himself? Well, you've thrown just about everything else at me."

As he got closer, he saw that what he was seeing was the back reflector lights of a parked car "Police? Who knows? I'm not walking back now, for anyone. He kept walking, and realized that the car was parked on a bend, on a hard shoulder. As he approached the vehicle, he could see that the windows were steamed up. He put his hand deep into his jacket pocket and pulled out the magnum, complete with silencer. The car was rocking back and forth, and he could here noises coming from within. He approached the back side window, and cautiously looked in. He could see nothing. Quietly, he walked around to the other side and noticed that the window of the front passenger side was open about one inch. With gun in hand, he looked inside. He saw a man on his knees pounding away in sexual activity. He walked back round to the back window and tried the handle. The door opened. "Sorry to spoil your fun boys and girls, but I need to know. FUCK!! No. Oh no, Lord Jesus fuck no, oh hell never oh no JEEESSUSSS FUCK NO NEVER CHRIST IN HEAVEN FILTHY BASTARDS, NEVER FUCK!!"
Two men sat up and tried to cover themselves.
"Oh my sweet God why the fuck, you dirty bastards". Hillman began to vomit. "Gaaa Bastards OH MY BASTARDS, AAARRGGGHHHH. His mind now in complete turmoil. This, in his mind, was the biggest insult a human being could give to God.
The two men quickly closed the door and snubbed it. Hillman was still spewing when he heard the ignition being started up. As quick as lightning, he fired a shot into the driver's side window. Hillman opened the door to find that he'd hit the driver on the upper shoulder. "Come on, out, the both of you, I want your car, come on". The two naked men got out of the car. "Get over here by the woods".
"Please Mister, we don't want any trouble".

Hillman pushed them both into the bushes. "Down on your knees, bugger boys, come on, I'm soaking. "Now, I'm going to shoot you in the back of your heads, because I can't stand to look at creeps like you, you'd better pray now, if you're going to. Hillman waited only two seconds. There were two soft thuds, as each man was shot in the back of the head. Both men fell face forward into a small stream running through the forest. Their bodies rolled down the small embankment into the shallow water, but it would be enough to conceal them for more than ten days, when Flapper, the ground-man's Cocker Spaniel would discover them.

Hillman wiped the seats with one of the men's shirts. "Dirty bastards Lord, yuck! Anything I get from you boy, I've got to work for it, right Lord? No matter".
Hillman still retched involuntarily as he drove, thinking about the disgusting human beings he had to dispose of.
"Did you *have* to let me witness that? Couldn't you have just pointed them out to me somehow. You've got a fucking sick sense of humour so you have, making me suffer that sight".
Another retch.

POLICE MORTUARY. SHEFFIELD.

The body of Heather Bradley lay on the pathologist's table, as Ashley Barnes explained in great detail exactly what the young woman died from. "You see Deborah, there would have been a point where Heather's body went on shutdown, and therefore, she would have felt no pain whatsoever from that point on. She would have lapsed into unconsciousness, and from that point on, she would have been out of her misery. Her blood loss was severe, and God bless her. Have you any ideas ladies, who could have set up such a sick show"?

"We have" Said Karen, looking away from Heather's body, "but we can't prove it, at least not yet, but we're waiting to hear from forensics later today". Deborah was walking slowly down the line of tables, looking at the dead bodies, some of them with sheets draped over them, and some of them zipped up neatly in body bags.

"By the way Deborah" said Ashley," I have a useful piece of information for you and Karen, if you want to have a cup of tea I'll tell you about it".

"Haven't got time Ashley, there are so many people out there that we have to find and question. The prime minister has been at Terrence Davis to get our fingers out and get these murderous villains imprisoned and out of society. Karen stood shaking her head in disbelief at the crimson shape lying on the pathologist's table, which used to be Heather Bradley, now an unrecognisable hideous shape. The whipping inflicted on the poor girl was so severe, that she could plainly see a couple of Heather's ribs poking through the torn flesh. Even the girl's feet had been whipped so badly that she could see her right ankle bone.

Ashley laid a hand upon Deborah's shoulder, and said, "go and put the kettle on Deborah, believe me, you have time to hear what I have

to tell you today, and I would even go as far as to say, that I'll be on top of your Christmas list this year".
"You are anyway, Ashley, after Karen, of course".
"Go on up girls, I'll be up in a minute or two after I've cleaned up here".
Five minutes later Ashley entered her office dressed in jeans and tee-shirt. "A bit over dressed today Ashley, if you don't mind me saying", said Deborah. Ashley just smiled and ignored the comment. Deborah set the cups down in front of Ashley and Karen.
"Come on then Ash, what's this bit of information you have that you think I'll be interested in".
"You know the Hillman house"?
"Yes, what does the Hillman house have to do with Heather and Rachel"?
"It's got nothing to do with, did I say it was about them? Just let me finish will you. Right, the Hillman house, ok"?
"Right Ashley".
"Well I think I know how he was killing people so easily, you know, in and around the house?
"Yes how"?
Ashley sipped her tea. "Because he was in the house, all the time, hiding, in his room Deborah".
"In his, what room"?
"His secret one, there's a secret room in that house somewhere".
"How do you know this Ashley"?
"A friend of mine in London phoned me the other day, a guy called Roger Healy, a pathologist".
Deborah shifted on her seat. "He's down in London Ashley, and we're up here, and yet he obtains this information, how on earth is this possible"?
"He was out having a drink somewhere one night, and he overheard this guy talking about the man who built Hillman's house for him. He was saying he used to labour to this man. Anyway, he said there were some days when he wasn't allowed to work, because of a separate project, a secret project, it was the safe room".
"I see" said Deborah, "but, of course, even though this man worked for the guy, he can't for the life of him remember the guy's name, isn't that right Ashley, huh? Am I right"?

“What’s she like Karen? What a pessimist you are Deborah, no wonder you can’t catch the bad guys”. Ashley immediately put up her hand. “Sorry Deborah”.
“It’s alright”.
“I did get his name Debs, well Roger did. The gentleman who built the house was called”. She looked in her desk drawer for her sheet of paper. “Ah here it is, his name is William Waite. On the down side though Deborah, I’m afraid the man has since emigrated to Canada, I made inquiries, but at least you know there’s a safe house in there. It won’t be hard to find out where in Canada he’s moved to. Once you’ve been in touch with him, then you’ll know exactly where in the house the safe room is”.
“It must be bloody well concealed, that’s all I can say” said Deborah, “Hell; it’s been searched more times than a dictionary. This Roger, Ashley, he hasn’t told anyone else about this, has he”?
“I told him not to, it’s just with this Hillman down in London now, everyone is talking about him, and this guy just happened to be telling his work mates, and anyway, by the way Roger was talking, they didn’t believe the guy anyway”.
“Well, all we’ll need to do is get in touch with the Canadian government and get them to speak with their immigrations department, then we’ll know if this guy was talking rubbish or not. Mind you Ashley it would explain a lot of those killings”.
Abba’s Dancing Queen began to play on Deborah’s mobile phone. She pulled it out. “Yes? Hello? What? Could you repeat that please”? Deborah held up her hand signalling to the girls not to talk. “Hello? Who is this? Hello? Hello”?
Ashley couldn’t resist. “Who is it, Lionel Ritchie”? She was referring to hit song. Hello.
At first Deborah did not even smile, and then, gradually a broad grin formed on her face, until she was almost laughing. “I don’t know who it was” she said, “But whoever it was, has just informed me that Carla Paganni and her friend are staying in the Station Hotel”.
Exactly twenty-nine minutes from the moment Deborah had received the tip off, Angela Phorbes and Carla Paganni each sat in separate interview rooms in Harrington Police station Sheffield.
“So, we meet at last Carla” said Deborah Knowles. “I’ve been looking for you longer than Bow Peep has been looking for the sheep. I have a list of questions to ask you Carla, longer than a

mariner's memory. Now, we can do this the easy way, or the hard way, it's up to you, either way though, I'll get my answers".
"You'll get nothing from me" said Carla, "not until I have a solicitor in front of me, I am entitled to a solicitor".
"No, you used to be entitled to a solicitor Carla, not any more, the rules have changed girl, you're out of touch, no solicitor, so, you may as well start telling me what you know, but first, let me tell you something. I know of at least three men that you have killed, at least three, and if I wanted, I could have you executed, and I'm not joking".
Carla said nothing.
"Do you want me to prove it to you? Don't make me do that Carla, because if I prove it to you, then you'll have to be tried for it, and I do not want to do that. I happen to admire why you killed those men, I really do, so, please, don't make me carry on."
Right, now we've got that out of the way, maybe we can cut to the chase. Has Mister Steven Temple got anything to do with the murder of your friend Susie Monk"?
"Yes".
"Ok Carla, can you give me any information as to who was involved that night".
Carla sighed. "I had a list of names that were known to have been there, I was, em. I was."
"I know Carla you were working your way through the list, until Temple retaliated".
"That's right".
"Ok, you see Carla, how easy this can be when you cooperate"?
"What are you going to do with us"?
"What am I going to do Carla? I'm going to keep my word, that's what. If you and you're friend give us the relevant information then I'll probably see to it that you walk free. Fuck me up Carla, and I'll fuck you up, got it"?
"Yes".
"Right then, let's get down to business, and don't worry if Temple has got anything on you, because between Karen and I, we'll make sure that nothing he says, holds up, I swear".
"How do I know you're telling the truth Deborah"?
"You don't Carla, but I'm afraid at this stage in the game, you simply don't have a choice".

MORNINGSIDE.SHEFFIELD.

The car belonging to the two male lovers had been parked one hundred and fifty metres from the perimeter wall of Hillman's grounds. The wind was in Hillman's face now, pelting hard cold rain into his eyes as he walked.
"Lord, it's bad enough that women are turning themselves into fucking tarts these days, and going to bed with anything that looks remotely like a man, but, when I am confronted with a sickening sight like that back there, then my guts heave, that wasn't funny Lord, there was no need to make me see that. There's pussy going about now, in absolute abundance, yet those dirty bastards prefer to stick their cocks up each other's arses, well no, I'm not having that. Why do you let them live anyway, you should be taking care of business a bit better than you do you know. Never mind, I'm home now, thank you for seeing me safely home".

Hillman jumped up and scaled the wall. As he landed on the other side, he looked up at the large house at the top of the hill. His house. In the darkness he could see that there was only one light on. Outside of the house, there was one police van, and no other vehicles. What Hillman hadn't noticed, because of the rain pelting in his eyes, were the two policemen sitting in an unmarked car across the road from the perimeter wall. They had watched him climb the wall and disappear on the other side. Now, they were radioing the station with their new information.

They had been told to sit tight, and do nothing but observe, and to warn the four officers in the house to be on full alert. "Shoot to kill" they were ordered to inform the officers within.
Hillman pulled down the hatch as the rain battered him one last time, before he finally reached the sanctuary of his safe house. "Thank fuck for that Lord, I'll have to get out of these wet clothes".
First he would need to switch on the power, and then the water heater. He fumbled through the complete darkness, and made his way over to where he knew the power box was. "Fucking soaking wet Lord, Jesus fuck!" I'm going to catch my death one of these days". He stood searching his pockets for his lighter. Found it. He flicked it. Nothing. "Even the lighter is soaking wet Lord, this isn't funny".

"NOBODY'S LAUGHING" came the voice in the darkness.
"Who's there!!?"
Silence.
He tried the lighter again. "Shit!!"
"WHAT A BRAVE BOY YOU ARE!"
Who's the who, Who is it, tell him, who's there"? His words were now jumbled and panicked as he stood in the complete darkness. Right back from his childhood, he had been petrified of the dark, but he thought he'd conquered his fear of it.
"HOW MANY MORE HILLMAN"?
"What? Who? Just What!!"?
"HE HAS AN ENEMY YOU KNOW, YOUR FRIEND GOD, DID YOU KNOW THAT BRAVE BOY"?
Flick flick flick flick flick. Nothing. "Jesus Christ!!!"
YES, HE'S AN ENEMY TOO, MY MASTER REMEMBERS HIM BUBBLING AND CRYING IN THE GARDEN OF GETHSEMANAE, WHEN ALL HIS SO CALLED DICIPLES LET HIM DOWN. FIRST JUDAS BETRAYED HIM, AND THEN IN HIS HOUR OF NEED, HIS OWN FATHER TURNED HIS BACK ON HIM, RATHER LIKE YOUR FATHER TURNING HIS BACK ON YOU, FOR BEING SUCH A PANZY".
"Who the fuck *are* you!!"?
"WHAT DOES THAT MATTER TO YOU, YOU'RE A BRAVE BOY, GET SOME LIGHT ON IN HERE, THEN YOU'LL FIND OUT WHO I AM".

Even through his panic, he suddenly remembered there was a box of matches lying on the table. He groped around in the darkness, knocking over a bottle in the process.
"CAREFUL".
"FUCK!!" Eventually, he found the matches. He opened the box and heard the soft ruffle of the matches falling on to the floor.
"Ha ha ha ha ha ha, WHAT A BRAVE BOY WE HAVE HERE, LOOK EVERYBODY LOOK AT BRAVE JOHN HERE".

He managed to pick up a few matches. He lit one up, frightened of who he was about to see. Cupping his hands, he made his way over to the power box. He lit another, and then quickly put down the main switch, and then the power box for the heating system. The lights flickered for a couple of seconds, and then everything came on full power. There was no-one here. "Fuck". The quilt still lay on the floor where Jenifer Sadler had lay, and her wine glass.
He looked slowly around the room. "Mother? Oh please Lord, not her again. Mother! Was that you"? He looked around the room and up towards the ceiling, as if she were floating around in the air. Silence.
He could feel the warm air already blowing through the room from the heater.

Up in the house, in the kitchen, a young police officer was making a cup of tea for his comrades. The other three men were in the lounge.
"You guys"? The young man said, as he came through with their cups.
"Yeah".
"Did any of you three switch an appliance on just now, did you"?
"No, we're all playing cards, why"?
"Well, because a green light just came on through there, followed by two amber ones".
"Well, it's not on in here, there's no heating on in this house".
The young officer looked at his friends, confused. "Well, something's just came on. Something has just switched itself on".
One of the men's radios buzzed and crackled. An officer answered.
"Yeah".
"Full alert, repeat, full alert, he's home, Hillman's home, repeat, full alert, shoot to kill".

The officer put his phone down. “Right boys, this is it, he’s home, Hillman’s home, and we have to shoot to kill. Take your positions, Hillman’s home, he’s just been spotted. Make sure you’re all loaded up boys, and stick together, somebody hit the lights, we’ll see better with the lights off, we’ll see him coming”.

John Hillman had poured himself a glass of whiskey and turned on his T.V. He sat on the quilt looking up at Carla Paganni’s face, along with one of the women he had seen playing with his children. “What did Tracy say her name was again? Angela, that was it, Angela, remember Lord? She was the one I wanted to fuck with the most, remember? So, she knows Carla Paganni does she? I wonder what they’ve been up to, helping the police with their inquiries indeed. That Carla wouldn’t be helping the police if my lying bastard father was still alive. Well at least I know where they are Lord”. Hillman’s head went fuzzy again, he became dizzy.
“Can’t trust them Lord, women, no good lying fuck bitches that they are”.
“EVEN THE OLD ONES?” Hillman spun round, to see Nancy Felder, standing with her head lopping to one side.
“Shit, fuck!!”
In her hands she carried the severed head of her kitten. “WHAT A BRAVE BOY YOU ARE DOCTOR HILLMAN, IT MUST HAVE TAKEN SOME STRENGTH TO KILL A DEFENCELESS OLD LADY LIKE THAT, SUCH A BRAVE USELESS TWISTED FUCK THAT YOU ARE BOY. NEVER MIND, THEY’LL GET YOU SOON, AND I DON’T MEAN THE POLICE”.

HARRINGTON POLICE STATION.

SHEFFIELD.

"That's all I know Deborah, I swear to you, that's all I know". Deborah Knowles had requested to Karen to bring Angela through to the same interview room as her friend. "What about you Miss Clark, can you think of anything else to add to what Carla has told us"?
"I'm afraid not" said Angela, "this was all up and running by the time I got up here".
"Up here, yes" said Deborah, "Up here from London, is that correct"?
"You know it is".
"Yes, tell me again, where is the address that is written on your driving licence"?
"Eighty-seven Carlington Road London W.1.".
"Yes, that's it" Said Deborah.
"Well ladies, it's a good job Karen and I are no gold diggers, isn't it"?
"Why"? Said Carla.
"Because your friend here is not who she says she is. Karen and I have scanned the computer, and guess what, there are only thirty-two Angela Clarks, living in this country, or was living. Twenty-one of them now live under their married names, eight of them are pensioners, one died a couple of years ago, and there are two at the ages of ten and four respectively. I hope for your sake Carla, that you've been telling me the truth, because I think I know who your friend here really is".
Deborah lit up her cigarette and handed the packet to Carla. "Tell them to bring us some coffee Karen, four cups.
"Thank you" said Carla.
"You're welcome Carla". Deborah walked over to the window, looking at the rain hammering hard against it. Without turning round Deborah said, "They never did find your body, did they Miss Phorbes, up there in the Lake District? Oh I know they made one or two dives up there, in Coniston Water, another couple in Lake Windermere, but then it was called off, you were presumed dead, am I right"? Deborah turned round now. "Am I right"?
Angela knew she was found out. "Yes Miss Knowles, you're right".

"Ok then, now, is there anything else you wish to tell me Carla? Or have you been telling me the truth, because now, right now, is your last chance to change it. I am going to haul Mister Temple's arse, and his friend's arses in here, and with the D.N.A. we've taken from Susie Monk and Rose's body's and also from Heather and Rachel's body's, we will find out. If this all works out, then we'll start to clean up this city. If you have been lying Carla, then I am going to receive one almighty pat on the back for capturing one of Britain's most ferocious killers that there has ever been. Now, do you wish to change anything you've said to me, last chance"?
Straight away and much to Deborah's delight, Carla and Angela said, "No".
"Good girls" said Deborah, "I was hoping you were telling me the truth".
Knowles looked at Angela. "What was it like Angela, running around with that gang"?
Angela sighed heavily, she was completely helpless in the situation, and was now at this woman's mercy.
"Dangerous, very dangerous, half of the time I was out of my face with drugs, but it was exciting too, and contrary to what the papers said, no-one was killed without reason".
"I see" said Deborah, even those fellow police officers of yours"?
"Apart from them, but at that stage, I was as much at risk as those two were. I was raped and abused for several days before I…before they-."
"What? Converted you? It doesn't matter Angela, because I am a person of my word, and, it was so long ago now, I was just curious, that's all".
"It was only a matter of time" said Angela.
"Why thank you Angela" said Deborah. "Now we'll have our coffees, and then you're free to go for now Carla. I'm not telling you *don't* leave town, but I am telling you to let me know where you go, it's for your own safety as much as anything else".
An officer brought a tray in with four mugs of coffee along with a milk jug and a packet of biscuits. "Thank you Paul" said Knowles. The man left the room. "Well, I must say, this was a lot easier than I had anticipated".
"Who told you where we were"? Knowles looked at Carla. "I don't know that Carla, but we can assume that it was one of Temple's men. He'll not want you two around, after what he's done to another

two friends of yours. He gives us your whereabouts, and then that's you two out of his way, and of course, to his way of thinking, he knows exactly where you are".
Carla looked at Angela, and then back to the detectives.
"Deborah"?
"Yes Carla"?
Carla looked her straight in the eyes. We could arrange it for you to get the biggest pat on the back, ever".
Deborah smiled, knowing that she had these two here now under her control, no matter what Carla said to her".
"And how might you be able to do that Carla"?
Deborah's facial expression changed immediately, as Carla said, "We can deliver Hillman right into your hands".
"Do you know where he is"?
Carla sipped her coffee.
"No, but we know where his wife and kids are".

MORNINGSIDE.

The four armed police officers stood back, slightly away from the window which looked on to the wooded area at the front of the house. It had now been twenty minutes since they had received their message. "Where the fuck is he then"? Whispered one of the officers, in the semi darkness. "It's been ages". Just as he spoke, he saw the headlights of a car turning into the drive at the bottom of the hill.

"At last, back up" one of the other officers whispered.

"It's not back up, it's only a car, they wouldn't send back up in a car would they, get a fucking grip man, it's probably D,C.I. Knowles and Jones, or Drummond".

Two minutes later, Deborah Knowles and Karen Jones walked up the steps and into the house.

"Lights!" She shouted, as she entered.

The leader of the officers said, "Mam, with all due respect, we had the lights off in order to see him more easily, we were told he was spotted scaling the perimeter wall half an hour ago. So far, he has not been spotted, which means that he is still out there, hiding somewhere in the trees".

"Half an hour ago"? said Knowles. "Forget it lads, he's probably in here now boys, all tucked up in bed, he would not wait half an hour to enter his home, believe me, and no disrespect to you lads, but you wouldn't delay him for more than two minutes if he wanted to come in here".

"Miss Knowles, I can assure you he did not enter this house" the police officer insisted.

"Well" said Deborah, "Mister Drummond is talking to the two officers who spotted him climbing the wall, you take your orders from him when he gets up here".

The young police officer who'd noticed the lights coming on in the kitchen said to Deborah, "Mam, could I show you something in here please, it might be nothing, but I'm confused".

"What is it" said Knowles, following the young officer to the kitchen.

He pointed to a panel on the wall. "Yes"? Said Knowles, "It's a central heating system, what's confusing you about that"?

"The heating is not on in this house mam".
"So"?
"Well, just before the officers radioed in about Hillman, well, you see these two lights here, and this green one, they both came on".
Knowles looked closer at the panel. There were six rows of small lights, each with a button underneath. All of the other
lights were off, apart from one, marked (Lights) and the three that the officer had shown her. "I have been on duty in this house mam, for three weeks, every night for three weeks, and that has not happened before. I just thought it strange, after those lights on the panel came on, that we got a message telling us that doctor Hillman was back home.
"So".
That was it mam, I just thought-".
Deborah put her hand cautiously on the teapot, deciding that it was still hot enough for her and Karen to have a cup. "Well done officer, I do think it strange, but we know that the heating has not came on in here, don't we, so what do you think"?
"Mam, I think he has a secret place or something, somewhere close to the house, where he can watch, and keep an eye on what's going on in here".
"I see" said Knowles, smiling at Karen, "And do you think he's in that secret place now officer, watching us".
"Mam, I am only saying that it's possible, I'm not trying to be smart, but it feels like I'm making a fool of myself".
Deborah smiled at the officer. "Don't feel embarrassed officer Bell, it turns out that you are perfectly correct in your assumption, and I must say, that you are to be congratulated because you worked this out for yourself, well done. He does have a secret place, and it is in this house somewhere. I wasn't kidding, nor was I being sarcastic when I said to your friends that he would be tucked up in his bed. What did they say when you told them about the lights on the panel"?
"They just, nothing really".
"There you are you see? That's why some of us get promoted, and some of us get killed, well done Bell".
"Thank you mam. In the house you think mam"?
"No, in the house I know, now, that will be all for now officer Bell thank you".

"He's on the ball" said Jones to Knowles.
"Yes he is Karen, he'll go a long way, that boy, using his brains Karen. Makes you wonder why we didn't think of the safe room doesn't it".
Karen smiled, "Yes".
They sipped their tea. Deborah checked her watch. It was one a.m. "Two hours Karen, and then we get Temple and his band of merry men. As soon as John gets up here, we'll get back to the station, and then, once we've rounded up the scum, we can get off home for a few hours sleep, make a start on them tomorrow. We may not need Mrs Hillman and her kids for bait if this turns out alright, you know, with this secret room thing, I think we may have him where we want him Karen".
The telephone rang in the lounge. "That'll be for me gentlemen" said Deborah Knowles. It rang four times before she reached it. "Hello"?
It was the Canadian immigrants department, confirming that there was indeed a Mister William Waite with his wife, now living in Montreal. "I have him here with me now, would you care to speak with him"?
"Yes please" Said Deborah.
Ten minutes later she had all the information she required to obtain access to the secure room. On the panel on the kitchen wall, she was to push, button number seven. This button activated the switch on the panel on the wall at the top of the stairs. Once activated, she was to remove the picture and push the small lever. The whole wall would spin round, and she would be in.
John Drummond was now standing beside her. "Have you got it Deborah"?
"We sure have John; we've finally got his hiding place".
"I'm not totally convinced that it was Hillman the two police officers saw out there, it could have been anyone".
"Anyone John, you surprise me" said Knowles. "A fucking night like this, and someone just happens to scale an eight foot wall, and probably thinking that the grounds were being patrolled by God knows how many armed officers, who are looking to shoot to kill, I don't think so, it was him alright".
"But where did he go Deborah, those boys in there said that no-one came in here". "Well, it's not very likely he could get in here and up the stairs without at least one of them hearing him, but I do think it

was him alright that those two officers saw". She looked outside and said, "He wouldn't hang about out there all night, surely".
"Well, if he did slip in here unnoticed, then we're about to find out".
Deborah ordered the armed policemen to wait at the top of the stairs for her orders. She pressed the button on the panel on the wall, and began to walk up the stairs, slowly, with Drummond and Jones directly behind her. They came to the picture. "Get ready boys" Said Knowles. Deborah pushed the lever in and pushed with her hand to the right of it. The wall swivelled round. With guns at the ready, the officers stormed the room. "Don't touch anything boys, we need forensics in here. The room was filled with small screens, monitors. Drummond was breathing heavily. "He must still be out there, search the woods boys".
Deborah and Karen left Drummond in the house, as they prepared for their raid on London Road.
John Drummond felt an icy eeriness about the place. He stood contemplating all the lives that had been taken in this house. A house which had not existed for that long, just an ordinary house, and yet, even in its short existence, some gruesome tales its walls could tell. His men out searching in the woods, and he, alone in here. He began to think to himself. "It would not be impossible for him to have crept in here", no matter what his men had said. He looked down the long hallway again, down towards the kitchen. The hall lights were off, but the kitchen light still burned brightly at the bottom of the corridor. He began to walk slowly towards the light, not quite sure why he was doing so.
His men had left the door open and he could hear the whispering hiss of the sheets of rain hitting the door and tiled floor. He was now almost at the kitchen door. He could feel cold shivers running down his back. "Why? Why was he feeling like this? There's no-one in here". As he turned into the kitchen, he looked once more to the kitchen floor where the silhouettes of Mister and Misses Hillman were still visible. The table had been put back into its place. This was where a police officer had been nailed. He stood shaking his head, as he looked at the marks on the table where the nails had been hammered in.

There were silhouettes everywhere in this house of dead bodies the young man at the front door who'd been tied to the chair, the other young man who had opened the door, only to be blasted in the face with a shotgun. Then there was poor John Crosby, Deborah's ex-partner, the poor bugger had been practically filleted in the lounge. "Fuck in Hell, who would be a policeman these days, we must be fucking mad". He turned and made his way back along the hallway towards the lounge. Every doorway in this house made you feel that there was a very unpleasant experience waiting for you on the other side of it, like you were about to be attacked ferociously. You just did not wish to be in here, and even though you knew that it was a sick man committing these crimes, you couldn't help feeling that the house had something to do with it as well. It was as if Hillman and the house worked as a team. If one of them didn't frighten you, then the other most definitely would. At this moment in time, Drummond thought to himself, the gruesome partnership was working perfectly.

He heard the footsteps of his men crunching up the gravel towards the house. He felt a sense of relief as he heard the men entering the house. One of the officers approached him. "Nothing sir, it beats me how he does it. If that was him that those two officers saw, then, just where the hell did he go"?
"It beats me as well" said Drummond, "but at least we know he can't take us by surprise any more, not in here anyway, now that we've found his little cubby hole up there. Well, I have to get back lads, what time will your relief arrive".
"Six o clock sir".
"Well, not long now, and stick that bloody heating on for yourselves its bloody freezing in here".
"We were told not to sir".
"Were you indeed, well, I'm telling you to put it on, it's like bloody Siberia in here, how the hell do they expect you to stay alert in conditions like this for eight or more hours at a time, get it fucking on, my orders. Now, be on your guard boys, whatever you do, don't fall asleep, make sure you have company wherever you go in the house, because you just never know, he is one clever bastard is our doctor. Goodnight lads".
"Goodnight sir".
Drummond drove slowly down the drive, glancing into the woods. "Where are you Mister Hillman, where are you hiding? I'll find you, one day soon, I'll find out where you are. He began to think about the doctor again, wondering what it was that had sparked this off, his killing spree, and why suddenly he had found this urge to kill young

women. Was he schizophrenic? Did he hallucinate? Did he hear voices in his head? Was some-one telling him to commit these murders? He remembered reading something about schizophrenics and how sometimes they suffered from frightening hallucinations, Idiosyncranicity. “No matter mister Hillman, I’ll find you soon, I’ll fucking hallucinate you my friend, don’t you worry about that”. Drummond smiled to himself in his car as Mister Buddy Holly sang to him from the radio, (That’ll be the day)

MORNINGSIDE. UNDERGROUND SAFE HOUSE.

John Hillman sat looking through the camera as the Jaguar rolled silently down his drive. He sipped his whiskey as he watched the car disappear. He had watched the armed policemen combing the woods again. "I wonder what sparked that off Lord". He said out loud. "Why should they come out here on a night like this looking for me, when they think I'm in London? Has someone spotted me Lord? Is that it? Seems very strange to me. Something's been going on". He lay down on the quilt on the floor, and pulled it over himself. "Sleep Lord, I need to have a sleep, charge my batteries". He lay his gun on the quilt next to him. "Goodnight Amy, goodnight Angela, wherever you are, your daddy loves you very much. Bless them and keep them safe Lord, from all the evils in this wicked world. In the name of my Lord and saviour, I ask these things, Amen".

HARRINGTON POLICE STATION.

SHEFFIELD.

"I demand to speak with my lawyer before I answer any more of your stupid bloody questions" said Steven Temple to the police officer. The officer smiled at Temple and said, "I would strongly advise you to shut your mouth, or I'll kick it so hard, that you won't be able to talk at all. Now, D.I's Knowles and Jones will be in sometime today to interview you, I suggest you keep it shut until then, and get this through your thick skull, whosoever is brought through these doors, or any door in any British police station, they will have no rights whatsoever, got it? Now it's the law's turn to hit back at you scum. For years you bastards have taken the piss out of the legal system, with your fancy lawyers, getting away with all kinds of atrocities, well, no more. Now it's our turn to take the piss. When you're eventually allowed a lawyer in here, then, if he steps out of line, he's just as likely to receive a smack on the mouth as you are. Now then, if you make any more noise in here, shouting off your mouth like that, any noise whatsoever, then I swear, I'll come in here and beat you up good".

Across the city, in London road, a team of detectives and forensics were going through Temple's belongings. Deborah Knowles was just getting out of bed. She'd had three hours sleep, although she had been in bed for nearly six hours. Her mind was racing, thinking about the death of poor Heather Bradley, and her friend Rachel White, although Rachel was still alive, just. As Deborah made her way to the bathroom, she wondered if the young girl would ever make a full recovery from such an ordeal. The poor girl would have witnessed Heather's horrendous execution. She would have heard her screams of pain and agony, and probably begging for mercy. Then, her own ordeal. Man after masked man raping her, buggering her, being spun upside down on that contraption that Temple had erected. Then the spitting, the cursing, the hair pulling, the whole degrading acts from supposedly, human beings. As Deborah showered, the image of poor Susie Monk's skinless body flashed in her memory. "Rest in peace little darling".

Deborah sat in her kitchen with her breakfast, which consisted of one mug of coffee, and one king sized cigarette; she listened to the news on the radio. A couple had fallen out over something to do with a lover. The end result was, that the woman had been thrown from the kitchen window which happened to be one hundred and forty feet from the ground. Her husband had then taken a gun and killed his two daughters, aged three and one year, before then turning the gun on himself. "What the hell is happening to our society? What's happening to our people? It seems like we're all going mad, committing crimes we just wouldn't have heard of twenty or thirty years ago. Mister Hillman for example, the murders he commits. Bloody hell, if that's what he does when God's voice is in his head, then Lord help us if the Devil decides to have a chat with him". She stood with her coffee cup looking out at the grey laden sky, which promised without fail to deliver yet another deluge of water once again upon the city, within the hour. "I hope to Christ boys, you've found something worthwhile in Temple's house. Something, anything, that Karen and I can throw at him. She also knew that, although Carla had cooperated with her, she would not rest until she got everyone who had inflicted those terrible atrocities upon Susie. And now, of course, there was Heather, even closer to Carla than Susie had been, even more of a friend. "Well Mister Temple, if you are found guilty and convicted, then the government will kill you humanely. If you walk free, then I'm afraid for you. Afraid, because I could not possibly imagine what Carla Paganni will have lined up for you, let alone what her new friend will do. And I'm afraid Mister Temple, that because of what you done to Susie, that I, as will my colleagues, be turning a blind eye on the whole course of events. Go with dignity Mister Temple, rather as begging for death".

Deborah drained her coffee mug and then rinsed it. "Right, let's go and get Karen, and then find out which way Mister Temple and co are going to die". She switched off her radio and then left the house. Outside, the thick dark rain clouds began to keep their promise.
Deborah Knowles had another plan in her head, a plan which excluded any of her colleagues. A plan that would make her the complete heroin and that would open up all kinds of opportunities for her. She had not, at this point, decided how she would execute her plan, but it would happen, and she would have her glory. And no-one, but no-one would get in her way.

MORNINGSIDE. OUTSIDE SAFEHOUSE.

Hillman looked through the camera, up to the house, where four armed policemen were climbing out of a van, and making their way up to the front door.. They exchanged words with another four armed officers who had come out and were making their way to their van. “Something's up Lord, I don't feel good about being here. Something doesn't feel right about this”. He rubbed his chin, and felt the thick beard on his face. He had never grown a beard in his life, condemning them to be unhygienic. He watched the four officers climb into the van and drive off down the winding road. He sat back down at the table with the cup of tea he had just made. He took out his wallet and pulled out a photograph of himself and his wife and children, when they had been to Blackpool. “What happened Tracy? Where did I go wrong? We were so happy. so happy. How could I lose something that was so precious to me”?

“What did I do to make her start hating me Lord? Yeah, I know, I know it only too well. The Lord giveth, and the Lord taketh away, I know, but what you don't seem to understand Lord is, that some of us just can't withstand that pain, it becomes too much to bare. When a man loses everything he loves in the world, he loses himself. He has no identity any more. His children are his life, he is them, they are him. When something or someone comes along and takes them away, then they may as well kill him, because all that is left of that man is the shell. He can neither think straight, nor act normal, his very life has been taken away from him, nothing matters any more, nothing is important to him. He loses his self- respect, his dignity, his self-esteem, he loses control Lord. If a man loves his wife and children, then they become everything. If you lose everything, then what have you left to lose. I have lost everything Lord, these two little girls here and their mother, they were my everything”.

“For the first time in my life Lord, I have no-one depending on me. Even that house up there, should be mine, but no, you saw fit to take that away from me as well, and now I can't get it, because of all those things I've done for you. Did it ever occur to you Lord, just how hard it is for us mere mortals, huh? Do you know what it's like to lose? Of course you don't, you're God, you're the one. Those people I've killed for you, you didn't need me to kill them for you.

You could have done them yourself, but you saw a way, that could make me lose my home as well. I should have two homes, but no, here I am, hiding in this, this hole in the ground, unable to go back and live some kind of life out there. I have nowhere to go. I have only the money I carry with me. I can't even draw out money from my own bank account, after what I've done for you. I keep asking for your help, but you never do reply". He sipped his tea, still looking at his children in the photograph. "You've just used me like a puppet. You pull my strings down here, and make me dance for you, I'll bet you're having a laugh up there. Then you send those ghosts to torment me. Take that old Nancy Felder, I would never have done that to her if you hadn't made me. I never get rewarded for anything I do for you, do I? I've only been put on this earth for to be made a fool of, Look".
He held the photograph above his head, aiming it at the ceiling.
"Can you see those two? How could you see fit to let them be taken away from me? What kind of a God are you? And don't you think that they won't be missing me, because they do. I'm beginning to doubt you, do you know that? All these years of service I've put in for you, and what was my reward? My reward was, to get beat up by my wife, you lousy bastard, in the presence of a whore if you don't mind. Get beat up by my wife with my little girl's skipping rope, you ruthless bastard, utter bastard that you are. You've never liked me have you? Have you? Well why did you make me kill those people, why couldn't you keep your fucking booming voice out of my head. Why couldn't you just leave me alone, you should have left me alone! Right back from my childhood you picked on me. You knew fine well, that I never stole the money from the teacher's desk, but you had to see to it that it looked like I was the guilty party. I bet you laughed when my lying bastard father leathered me for stealing, you fucking twat that you are. He beat on me with that fucking leather belt for ten minutes. Stripped me naked and beat on me until he got tired, and my mother fucking laughing at me and encouraging him to beat me some more. *"Make sure the little bastard learns a lesson John before I throw him in the focking dark cupboard with no dinner or anything, the thieving little bastard"!*
"Mysterious ways my arse"! Roared Hillman.

HARRINGTON POLICE STATION.
SHEFFIELD.

Steve Temple sat at the table where he had been sitting for almost four hours. He had only been allowed up to use the toilet and to stretch his legs. He was a very worried man indeed. This was the last thing he'd expected, after getting one of his men to reveal the whereabouts of a certain Miss Carla Paganni and her friend to the police. He thought that the police would have enough on them to keep them occupied for a while, and out of his face. He was obviously wrong. The door opened and Deborah Knowles and Karen Jones entered the room, each carrying a cup of coffee. There were two chairs opposite the one he sat on. Not one word was spoken to him at this point.

"Is there an ashtray in here Karen" Said Knowles, sitting directly opposite Temple. She pulled out a photograph from a folder and then said to Temple, as she showed him Heather Bradley, proudly standing outside of her new shop. "Do you know this girl"?
Temple looked at it and said, "You are wasting your time. I have already stated, that I am answering no more questions until I have my lawyer here with me". Knowles ignored his statement and pulled out another photograph of Heather Bradley. This one showed her naked and dead, just a mass of red flesh, her body almost completely skinned. "Do you know this girl"?
Temple shifted on his seat. "Listen, you can't, I'm not, I'm not saying anything until-".
"Tom!!" Shouted Knowles. Thomas Martin the desk sergeant came bounding into the room carrying a stun gun and a baseball bat. Deborah Knowles looked at Temple again. "Do you know this girl"?
At this point, Steve Temple done the worst thing he could have possibly done. He smiled at Deborah Knowles and said, "Try and frighten me all you want, it won't work, now give me my fucking phone call".
Knowles's face was expressionless. She rose to her feet with Karen, and the two women left the room. In the canteen Deborah said, "What bloody weather Karen, pissing down again". "Yeah, it's been

pouring down since seven o clock this morning, but you know what the old wives say don't you, if it's raining at seven, it's dry by eleven".
Deborah looked out of the canteen window. It was coming down in torrents. She looked at her watch. "Well if that's true Karen, it's got about eight minutes to stop. Stick that kettle on babes, I'll be back in a tick". Deborah entered the interview room again. Temple sat with his head bowed, blood spurting from his mouth and nose. She gently pulled his head back and showed him the photograph again.
"Now then" she whispered, "Think carefully. Do you know this girl"?
Temple snorted through his blood and tears, "You're going to pay for this when I get out of here".
Deborah put the photograph back into the folder. "Carry on Tom, come on, you're batting for the Yankees, if you score a home run you win the series, let's see you Tom".
Martin picked up the baseball bat once again and swung it to and fro, like a professional baseball player. "Ready"? He called to Deborah.
"Ready when you are champ". Temple's nose cracked like a twig in the woods, echoing round the room. The bridge of his nose was shattered. His head buckled right back and then forward again, so that his face landed on the table. Deborah pulled out the photograph one last time, and again pulled his head back. "Careful now, don't get blood on my nice clean photograph. Do you know this girl"? There was no reply. She let his face drop once more onto the table. "Better get our own doctor to sort that out, reset the bone if he can. See you later Steve" she mocked, as she began to leave the room.
"Oh by the way Tom, Mister Temple gets nothing but water until he answers that simple question I asked him, not that I think he'll be in any condition to eat, he's got a bloody sore mouth there I would say, not to mention his nose".
"Okey dokey Miss Knowles, oh, did I win the series with that hit"?
"Hard to say Tom, how about you try again after the doctor's been" said Knowles, closing the door behind her.

"Mister Temple" Said Thomas Martin, "let me be quite honest with you here. Deborah Knowles is only playing games with you, she's only toying with you, as indeed I am. I would rather snap your legs first, your ribs, your arms, things that are going to hurt for a long time. You see Mister Temple, although you don't show yourself in

the farm yard where Heather Bradley was brutally murdered, you overlooked one thing didn't you, and that was your own incompetence, after all, you're only a fucking novice at this game, aren't you, and my goodness, it doesn't half show. You see, our forensic boys and girls took samples of mud from the Buxton farm. When you got home that day, there was still mud on your tyres.
Also, there were several photographs taken at the farm, before, during and after the girl's executions. Guess who's car is parked in the background, can you guess? I don't know if you noticed all the porta-cabins outside when you came in. Well, we have eight of your friends in there, six of which are prepared to testify in court, that it was you who set up that horrible gang-bang and murder at Buxton farm. Six of them. You might make history here Mister Temple, because you are, without a shadow of a doubt, going to die. It depends how quickly we can get this to court. There's a guy down in London, shot a taxi driver and then his own girlfriend, he might get off if he pleads temporary insanity, but you, you are as sane as the day is long".

Temple's whole face, including his two black eyes, were puffed up and swollen. His mouth looked like he had cotton wool stuffed inside and under his top lip. "They've all grassed you in Steve. Not just with this, but with the drugs too, every one of them, oh, except for Amanda, she didn't turn you in with the drugs, she just grassed you in for the murder of Heather Bradley, and for the gang rape of Miss Rachel White. So Steve, are you still going to make us suffer when you get your phone call? The bottom line is, you're not getting any fucking phone call, and you'll be given a lawyer of our choice, to defend you". Tapping the baseball bat in his hand, which was dripping with Temple's blood, the sergeant said, "For what you had done to those two poor girls, you are going to hang, although, like many other people, I happen to think that hanging is far too good for scum like you.
Now, I have to get the police doctor to help you, put that nose back into place, huh, this will be interesting, he just lost his fourteen year old daughter last year to a drug overdose, he'll straighten your nose all right. Oh, by the way, Carla and her friend were asking for you the other day; they dropped in for a chat with Deborah and Karen. I'm sure Deborah said something about a list of names Carla had, and addresses she had to hunt down, concerning the slaughter of

Susie Monk. Deborah said to Carla to come in any time for a chat, I think Carla was keen in catching up with events concerning you. I think Deborah told her that you and her can have a little chat in here, nice and cosy like. We'll lock the door of course; we wouldn't want you two to be disturbed now would we, you both have so much to catch up on. She is rather pissed though about her friend Heather. She and her were the best of friends you know, they were like sisters. I think Deborah said she cried for hours when she heard the news. Carla was secretly saving money to put towards Heather's boutique that she so wanted you see. I think she had plans on working with her, they were ever so close. To cap all this, Deborah had said that whoever had done this to Heather would be punished by Carla, as she felt it was only fair. It was the least she could do".

WESTBROOK ROAD. SHEFFIELD.

Joseph Dougan was getting used to life with just one arm. At first, everything felt strange, putting a kettle on, making a bed, washing himself. The hardest thing for him to do was what he was doing now, shaving. Up until the day he was shot, he had always used an open razor. He was nowhere near ready to try that yet. Instead, he was using an electric shaver. His suitcase lay packed and ready to go on his bed. He needed a break, and had decided to go over to Cork in Ireland to visit his sister. He was thinking to himself that things could have turned out a lot worse than they had. Losing an arm was nothing, he reasoned, compared to what had happened to some of his friends over the years. Being a mercenary carried it's risks, and there was a price to pay if you were caught.
It was 7 am. His taxi was coming for him at eight o clock, to take him to the station. "It will be nice to see Martha". He hadn't seen her in over twelve years, and even that had been a flying visit. This time he was going to spend ten days with her, spend some real time with her, and catch up on things, like families were supposed to do. Martha had only been married for two months when her husband was killed, working in Belfast. A bomb. Wrong place at the wrong time. She was carrying his child at the time, but had lost the baby later on in the pregnancy. "Poor Martha" said Joseph out loud, as he lit up his first cigarette of the day. " You've never seen anything, have you darling, never had anything, never pushed the boat out, to taste life on the wild side. Still, she seemed happy enough, with herself, if her letters were anything to go by. "Post office clerk in a village shop for over thirty years, some life kid".

Joe put the razor into its pouch, and then made his way back into his bedroom, to pack it into his case. "Hello Joseph" said Carla Paganni, sitting on his bed. "Off on holiday somewhere are we"?
"How the fuck did you get in here"?
"Never mind that Joe, the point is, I'm here now, fancy another cup of tea Joe"?
Dougan turned and put his shaver on the dressing table, and began walking back through to his kitchen. "How have you been Joe"?
"Look, what do you want Carla"?
"Ok I'll tell you, revenge".

"For what"?
"Hell Joe, you've got a nerve, asking me a question like that".
He sighed. "This isn't about that whore again is it? I thought that was all done and dusted".
"One sugar and milk please Joe. Did you now, think it was all done and dusted".
She took the mug from Dougan.
"Carla, I had nothing to do with that, and you know it, that was Temple's plan, all that stuff, and it was just to get to you. Why don't you go and ask Temple all the names of the people you need to see".
"I can't Joseph, you see, he's in jail just now, helping the police with their inquiries, that's why I'm here to see you".
"Well, I'm afraid I'm catching a train just shortly, in just over an hour, so I can't be of any use to you".
"Oh but you can Joe, you see, I have a police car waiting outside, and both of those officers would like you to come down to the station and give a D.N.A. sample if you wouldn't mind. Those clever people have taken D.N.A. samples from Susie's house, you know, the furniture the carpets, her body, everywhere. The trouble is there are three different samples that they can't account for. Now, if you are certain that you had nothing to do with Susie Monk, then you won't mind coming down to the station will you, it'll only take you twenty minutes, we'll even bring you back over here, how does that sound Joe? Fair"?
"Fucking bastard Carla, come on then, and then they can give me a full apology for wasting my fucking time".
"You sound confident Joe".
"I am, because I don't have anything to fear".
"I hope not Joseph, for your sake, I sincerely hope not, because if your D.N.A. matches any of these samples, then you can take it from me, losing your arm will be like having a heat spot".
"Carla, little tom-boy Carla. Do you know I could have taken you out on three different occasions, do you know that"?
"Let me guess, you felt sorry for me, or you liked me too much, or was it because you thought you had a chance of getting me into bed before you done away with me".
"Don't flatter yourself, you little Italian fuck that you are!".

"I wasn't, I was flattering you, because Jack the ripper would stand a better chance than you of getting me into bed. Anyway, enough of this stupid banter, let's get down to the station, so as I can make my apology to you in front of everyone. You make a shit cup of tea Joseph, did you know that"?

Deborah, Karen and Carla made no attempt at any conversation with Dougan on the way down to the police station. Neither did Dougan make any attempt at having a conversation with them. When they arrived there, Deborah Knowles said, "Wait here until I come back out".

Knowles was gone for less than three minutes, then she appeared at the top step and waved them all in. "This way Mister Dougan" said Jones, as she led him up the steps. They all walked down a long corridor to a room at the very end. A room that Tracy Hillman could have told them a few tales about. Knowles tapped twice on the door and then walked in. Two men wearing white coats sat at a small table in the middle of the room. One empty chair sat opposite the two men. Both of the men looked to be in their late fifties Carla guessed. One of the men reminded Carla of Adolf Hitler, minus the moustache. "Come in come in Mister Drennon" said Hitler.

"It's Dougan" barked the Irishman.

"I do apologise".

"Right you are ladies" said the other man, "You can go back through now, we won't be long with these tests, we'll give you a shout when we're done".

"Good luck Joseph" said Carla, crossing her fingers in a mock gesture, "Good luck".

"Fuck off Paganni" replied Dougan.

Deborah, Karen and Carla made their way up to the canteen. "What do you think Carla"? Said Knowles.

"I don't know Deborah, at first I was one hundred per cent certain he was in that gang, but now, I'm not so sure. It's the way he is so confident that his D.N.A. won't match with those samples. Anyway, how is Mister Temple doing Deborah"?

"Not so well Carla is he Karen".

"No I'm afraid not, he em, he slipped off his chair yesterday, and broke his nose in three places, he's lost teeth as well".

"Ah", said Carla, "those chairs, so dangerous, how is he"?

Karen smiled. "As well as can be expected Carla, let me put it that way".

Carla pointed back down to the room they had just left.
"What will you do with him, just supposing his sample does match"?
"What would we do Carla"? Said Knowles. " Susie was your friend, maybe we could leave that up to you. You wouldn't have to leave any clues though Carla, you know, you'd have to do it right, professionally, ok"?
"Yes, thank you Deborah, you know I would do it right".
"Well, let's just see if he's been there first. Oh, by the way Carla, did you tell Angela to get in touch with Tracy and her friend"?
"Yes, she told me she was going to phone Tracy, and let her know that we were working with you now, and that after she speaks to you she can move back into her house".
"Brilliant Carla, you see what we can achieve by working together? I don't know why you didn't contact me before, we could have had all these bastards in here now, never mind, they're here now, that's the main thing. Did you give Angela my number to give to Tracy"?
"Yes, and Tracy will be so pleased. Those little girls of hers will be missing out on their education".
"Exactly Carla, although we can't risk them going back into a public school. They'll be taught by a personal tutor. Their mother will have full police protection, twenty-four seven, just as long as Mister Hillman gets to know that his wife is back home. I'll bet he's at that house in less than a week, and then Carla, that'll be that. You and Angela can be on your way, keeping on the straight and narrow I hope".
"Deborah, I have had enough of this kind of life, I just want a quiet life now".
"Good Carla, because you've got all your life in front of you girl".
"Travel the world" Said Karen, "See places you've always wanted to see, do the things you've only dreamed about doing".

The canteen door opened, and in walked Hitler with a piece of paper flapping by his side, as he marched up to Deborah, looking rather pleased with himself. He bent down and whispered something in her ear and then walked back out the way he came in.
Deborah lit a cigarette up. "You're not supposed to smoke in here" said Karen.
"We're not supposed to do a lot of things in here Karen.
Carla"?
"Yes"?

"You should have been a police woman, do you know that"?
"Does Dougan's sample match"?
"Yes it does, another one bites the dust. Come on, let's go and see if he's as cocky with himself now, shall we"?

As the three women made their way down to the interview room, at the front door, Angela was being brought in, escorted by four armed police officers, kicking and struggling.
"Before we go in here Carla, may I suggest something"? Said Knowles.
"Of course, what is it Deborah"?

"Well, it could be that Dougan here can point the way to finding some more of the culprits of the gang rape and murder **concerning Heather and Rachel. If we offer him a deal, let's say,** for the sake of arguments, that we let him walk, if he gives us a few more names who were present at the Buxton farm, because, I don't think that Temple actually knew any of the men there, give or take one or two of his main sidekicks, which we will extract from him later. Now, if Dougan went out drinking with some of those hoodlums, then he's bound to be on first name terms with some of them, what do you think"?
"What do I think Deborah" Said Carla. "It's you, it's what you think, you're the one calling the shots here, I'm only doing this to help you. If you want to let Dougan walk, then that's up to you, anyway, he's kind of paid back for what he's done by losing his arm, he's already handicapped for the rest of his life, you decide Deborah".

"Yes I know Carla, but I promised him to you for what he done to Susie, and of course, now we know for certain that he was there, he is guilty. I'll tell you what Carla, Karen and I will go back to the canteen, you go in there and break the news to Dougan. Don't go berserk, but kick his arse a bit, you know, a couple of black eyes or something, but see if you can get any more names out of him first, and don't be feeling sorry for him. If you feel guilty, then just remember the state of poor Susie Monk's body when you found her".
"Remember Deborah, I'll never forget it".
"Well then, there you go, but don't kill him, we may need him as a witness".
"What if he won't give me any names"?

“Tell him that it's his life we're offering him here, not a reprieve, but a total pardon, his freedom. You can also remind him Carla, that if he fails to cooperate, then he faces the death penalty along with his boss, it's as simple as that. I'll explain all that to him when I come in there in about fifteen minutes. Just make sure that he's still conscious when we get back, though I'm sure Carla that he'll listen to you, he doesn't really have much choice. If he doesn't believe you about the D.N.A, then give him this”. It was a copy of the results of the test. “Go get him Carla, go and get us some more names”.

Carla walked into the interview room. Sergeant Thomas Martin stood with his arms folded and his legs apart, staring into the face of Joseph Dougan. Carla approached Martin and asked if she could have ten minutes with the prisoner on her own.
“Certainly Miss, I'll just be outside the door if you need me. Would you like some tea brought in Miss, it's no trouble, I'll give them a shout, Miss Knowles has told me what you're doing, and we're very grateful”.
“Well yes, I would like some tea, a cup of tea Joseph”?
Dougan gave no reply. “Oh never mind him” Said Carla, “he's in a huff, he'll soon come out of it when I give him the good news, two cups please sergeant”.
Martin left the room.
“Well? Are you going to say sorry now Paganni, or are you waiting until they're all present”.
Carla looked down at the table as she sat down with a rather sad smile on her face. It was a smile of sympathy. She looked at the rugged hard features of the Irish mercenary. “Joe, Joseph Dougan, what the hell possessed us in our lives to get involved with the things we did. Before you even knew me, you were out to kill me. Orders given to you by a man, who, himself is going to hang in less than a month”.
“Look, I don't give a fuck about that idiot, so cut the emotional shit Carla, I'm just not buying it”.
“Joe, you -”.
”Don't Joe me, you little piece of Italian shit that you are, working for the filth, you little scum bag, you think you're so clever don't you, you just wait and see how clever you are, they've been hunting for you for a long time, do you really think they're going to let you walk away from here, you surprise me you really do.

There was a time when I respected you, but"...
The door opened and an officer brought in a tray containing the pot of tea she'd asked for. "Excuse me Miss, Miss Knowles says to take your time, have a good chat with Mister Drogan".
"It's Dougan! Dooogaaannn. Is that so fucking hard for you to remember!"?
"Thank you" said Carla, "tell Miss Knowles thank you".
The policeman left the room. "You can't see it Carla, you soppy cow, can you? I mean, I hate you, I hate you with bells on top, but I hate gullibility even more. They've got you".
"Here, have some tea Joe this looks marginally better than the piss you poured at your place".
"Hmph, you'd better get used to it Miss Paganni, because I'll bet you a pound to a penny you won't be leaving here today, how's that, do you fancy a bet on that scum bag"?
Dougan sipped his tea, and lit up a cigarette.
"The test proved positive Joe".
"Mmm"?
"The test, the D.N.A test Joe, you were there, it matched".
"Fuck off Carla, go and fuck yourself".
"Drink your tea Joseph, and I'll tell you how they got you, you thick Irish twat that you are. You took great care Joseph didn't you, to cover up your faces, and all in black, like professionals, gloves, condoms, but do you know Joe, do you know how they got you? You all may as well have taken off your masks and waved hi mum to the camera. the sperm Joe. All you sick fucks forgot about that, or probably, as the case may be, did not even see the danger of depositing your vile liquid into the girl's mouth or into the tumbler. Do you see now Joe, why people take the piss out of thick, the very thick Irish cunts like you? They'll catch them all Joe, through their sperm, every one of you. You all left your calling cards. How the fuck could you be so stupid Joe?

You say you once had respect for me? Huh, once I had respect for you Joe, but then I saw what a gang of men were capable of doing to a defenceless little girl like Susie Monk. Fuck, you've got a nerve Dougan, sitting there condemning anybody like you're in a position to do that. I saw the film remember Joseph, and I don't need any D.N.A test to know you were there".

Carla slid the results of the test across the table. There it is Joe, all done and dusted".
Dougan drew hard on his cigarette. It was the end. There was no more denying it, he was caught
Carla let out a heavy sigh.
"I'm here Joe, to save your life. They want to make a deal with you. They are prepared to let you walk if you can give them any names concerning the death of Heather Bradley, and the gang rape of Rachel White. It's as easy as that. Give Deborah a few names, and you walk Joseph".
"I don't know any names".
"Bull shit!! And you know it. Listen, you were in the S.A.S, you served your country. These fuck head junkies will only laugh at you when they string you up Joe, do you think they'll give you a second thought. Half of them will be out of their faces when they put the noose over your head. Laugh at *them* Joe, do your country one last favour, by delivering this scum to the police. Go on your holiday Joe, do us all a favour by delivering this scum to the authorities.
"Carla, I would, but you can't see it can you? I'm not going anywhere, you're not going anywhere. Fuck, take your time, have a chat, have some tea, Carla, they've got you. They had you already, they've used you to bring me in here. We're both going to hang Carla, no matter how many names I give them. Ok, I'll do as you ask Carla, I'll give you some names, I'll give you six names, ok? Then watch what happens. They won't be letting me go anywhere, except into one of their cells, and Carla, you'll be in the cell next to mine. If the Irish are thick girly, then the Italians are fucking dense".

Dougan wrote down a half dozen names with his one remaining hand. "I've been practising, but it's still untidy".
"They can read it Joe, and don't be such a pessimist, Deborah will keep her word".
"Will she now" said Dougan, stumping out his cigarette.
The door opened and Sergeant Martin walked in. "Miss Knowles asked me to ask you if you had a deal yet, Miss Pagannі".
"Yes sergeant, tell Miss Knowles that Mister Dougan has given us some names". Martin left the room, closing the door behind him.

"Carla, I know you think I'm crazy, or hell bent for revenge for this". He pointed to where his right arm should have been. "But I'm not.

You might get lucky Carla. They might get you to help them bring in those low lives I've jotted down. If they do, then you make a run for it girly, do you hear? If you can get your friend out, then all the better, if not, just run. Get your car Carla, and get as far away from here as you possibly can, these people are not stupid. They know it was you who threw that kid off the balcony over in those flats, do you think they don't know that? They're using you Carla, why can't you see that, wake up Carla, they're only playing games with you, they have no intentions of letting you go, believe me, they want to hang you as well, they want to make an example of us, wake up"!
"Joe, you'll see, Deborah Knowles is not as bad as you make out, she'll reward you for this, wait and see".
Dougan sighed. "Oh Carla you silly girl".
The door opened again. This time sergeant Martin was accompanied by Knowles and Jones, followed by a certain Mister Steven Temple, whose face resembled a turnip that had been used as a football. He was hand cuffed with his hands behind his back. Martin closed the door.
Dougan burst out laughing
."Is there something amusing you Mister Dougan"? Said Knowles.
"Yes there is Misses. This piece of shit here in a mess like this It's worth hanging just to see this fuck like this".
"Has Miss Paganni informed you that you have been found guilty of the murder of Miss Susie Monk, at least partly so"?
"Yes" He wheezed through his laughter. "Yeah she told me".
"Miss Knowles" Carla said, "I've told him if he gives us the names of -".
"Shut up Carla" said Knowles. "You think this whole incident is a laughing matter Mister Dougan"?
"Well, I do have some regrets about it all".
"Really"?
"Yes, I wish it was you who'd got all the skin peeled off your body, and fucked and buggered hard, I really do, you jumped up fucking dyke that you are!"
"Joe, shut up" Said Carla.
"No, you shut up Carla", said Knowles, "I won't tell you again. Tom"?
"Yes Mam"?
"Do your stuff".

Before Martin had even got a blow in, Dougan had sprung up from where he sat, and landed a savage blow with his foot, right between Martin's legs. As quick as lightning, he caught Martin again with his heel, square on the jaw. It snapped like a cane.
The door burst open and four officers came bounding in, and bundled Dougan to the floor, but not before he broke one of their noses with a lightning-fast head butt. In less than a minute, they had Dougan stunned and on the ground, stripped naked.
"Get over here Paganni" said Knowles, walking over to where Steve Temple had been seated.
"Take off your clothes".
"What? Deborah, what on earth"?
Take off your clothes; don't make me say it a third time".
Over the other side of the room, the four officers were now taking turns at aiming their hardest kicks, into the face and body of Joseph Dougan. As Carla began to undress, she watched in horror, as the men just kept kicking and kicking and kicking at Dougan's face. The man had been right all along. It was more than Carla could stand.
"Tell them to stop Deborah!"
Deborah did not answer. Instead, she locked the door and walked over to where Dougan lay. "Hold it!" She said. "My turn boys". She lifted up her right foot, and with the point of the heel of her boot, she stamped down onto the face of Joseph Dougan, inserting her heel into the man's right eye. "Carry on boys".
Carla, stripped now to her jeans, leaped over the room and began lashing out some fearful blows to the four officers.
Before she could be restrained, she grabbed one of them by the ears, and bit into his mouth, locking her teeth around his tongue.
His screams resembled a grizzly bear thrown into a frenzy.
Eventually, Deborah Knowles grabbed the stun gun and gave Carla a hefty dose of electricity. She fell back on to the floor where two of the four officers began kicking her ribs and face.
After a minute or so, Knowles said "stop, enough! Go and see to your injuries, and get Tom to a hospital".
Panting and heaving, one of the men said, pointing to Dougan, "What about him"?
"Leave him boys, hell, he was dead even before I kicked him, come on, get Tom out of here".

Blood was spewing from the mouth of the man who Carla had attacked, still groaning bearlike, as he left the room. Karen smiled at Deborah.
“What a noise he made” she said, referring to Thomas Martin.
“Yeah, fuck that must have been extremely painful”.
Knowles closed the door.
Carla lay unconscious.
“How's the nose Steve. “Did you get it put back into place? I'll bet it was sore” she smiled, as she wandered over the room to retrieve the baseball bat. “Ooh, it's covered in blood”. She opened one of the drawers of the desk and pulled out a packet of tissues, and wiped the instrument.
“How do you hold these again Deborah”?
“Two hands, right down the bottom of it, that's it, now swing, have a couple of practice swings. There, that's it, you've got it”.
Karen Jones put down the bat and lifted Carla Paganni's unconscious body up off the floor. She lay Carla down on top of the desk, so that only her head hung over the edge. Knowles lifted the cup that Carla had been drinking from, and sipped the tea. She then lit up a cigarette and pulled a chair up beside Temple.
Dougan lay dead only eight feet from where she sat, in a massive pool of blood. Carla's torso was purple from the beatings she'd received. Her face was badly swollen. Knowles lifted up Carla's head. “She's still breathing Steve; I'll bet you enjoyed watching that, huh? Did you see that film, you know, the one you had made, when all those men raped that wee girl, and whipped all her skin off in the process, huh? Did you? Did you!!?”
“No”.
“No? Well, you're fucking going to Mister Temple, and you dare look away, just once, just once, I fucking dare you. Before that though, I'm giving you a piece of paper, and you are going to write down every single name of the scum who were present at that sick fucking show, got it”?
“Yes”.
“Yes, and don't you go missing out any names, do you hear me”?
“Yes”
“Now Karen” said Knowles, taking out a coin from her pocket. “Carla is heads; Temple is tails, heads or tails Steve”? She spun the coin into the air. It landed heads. Your lucky day Steve” Said Jones, “Come over here”.

“I'll do it for you Karen, Steven's hands are bound”. Knowles lifted Carla's head up, so that it was level with her body.
By Carla's hair, she held her head. “Don't you miss Karen and smack my hands instead. Steve, pick a number from one to ten”.
“Oh please, no, please I beg you, no”.
“Pick a number!!”
“One”. Cried Temple.
Karen Jones hoisted the baseball bat high above her head with both hands.
Carla was just beginning to come round. Jones brought the bat down as hard as she could, onto the mouth of Carla Paganni.
“Fucking hell Karen, it nearly went through her face, fuck, look at the spray. Steve, you start writing, we'll be back in ten minutes or so”.
Knowles unlocked the hand cuffs. “You'd better not leave out one fucking name, do I make myself clear”?
“Yes Mam, please mam, help her, she's still alive”.
“I know she's still alive Mister Temple. If she comes round then help her, if she doesn't, Tough. All you scum have had your day, running around in this city like it belongs to you, now, come on, start writing before I have a shot with the bat”.
Knowles and Jones left the room, closing the door behind them.

“Oh God please” Temple whimpered. “Please make them stop it”. Temple's nose had been so badly broken, that it was almost impossible to fix. The bridge of it had a crook now, to the left. The police surgeon had put it back into place as well as he could, by tapping it with a claw hammer. He could see, that Carla's nose had been broken even worse than his. Her breathing now sounded like a kind of hissing. He broke down and cried, and held on to Carla's hand, begging her for forgiveness. This slip of a girl, who had murdered his men, who had brutally executed his young brother, who had kidnapped his mother and used her for ransom. “Please don't die Carla, please don't die, I'm sorry, I'm so sorry for everything”. Blood was flowing freely now from Carla's mouth, but, providing they didn't hit her again, he gave her chances of survival, about fifty-fifty.

MORNINGSIDE.

John Drummond was smoking his first cigarette of the day, as he surveyed the woods from his vantage point at the top of the steps. He had grown immune to the rain, accepting the fact that this is what the weather must be like in Sheffield continuously.
He was hyperalert.
He began walking down the steps towards the woods when one of his men came down after him. “Sir, we've found another camera”.
“Oh good” he sighed sarcastically, how about, you get all the men together and get them to stand on the top step there, and I'll take your photograph, how does that sound”?
“Sir, I don't mean. I think you should take a look sir”.
Drummond sighed. “Ok then, let's go and take a look at your camera”.
On the way up the steps the officer said, “I think this will explain the other night sir, when those officers spotted Hillman, and then he disappeared”.
“Is that what you think, is it”? said Drummond, as if the man was the least interesting person in the world.
“Well, let's see what we've got then”.
Underneath the tiled work top inside a cupboard, was indeed, the hidden security camera. To the right of it, there was an on-off switch. Underneath the camera was a white label, which read. Safe house number 2..
“So that's it boys, huh? He has two little havens. No wonder he's been making a cunt out of us, well done lads. Now, has anyone tried the switch”?
“No sir, we were waiting to see what you thought”.
“Right then, let's put the switch down and see what happens”. Drummond put down the switch and the small black and white T.V screen mounted on the kitchen wall came to life. Suddenly, they were all looking at Doctor John Hillman, sitting at a table with a glass of something in one hand and a cigarette in the other. Drummond felt a horrible tingle down his spine. He touched his faithful Browning pistol reassuringly in his shoulder holster.
“Who the fuck is he talking to” said one of the men.
“Don't know” said Drummond, taking in the surroundings of the room.

"Do you think it's in this house sir? The second safe house"?
"Don't know that either son" Replied Drummond.
"Did you say the officers saw him from outside the grounds, climbing in"?
"Yes sir".
"I see, and who was on duty that night"?
"It was us sir, us four here".
"And what, you stood here by the window"?
"Yes sir, we even switched the lights off so that we could see clearly if he was approaching the house".
"And none of you left the window right? I mean, there was no way he could have got in without at least one of you spotting him, is that correct"?
"Yes sir, that's right, unless of course he has some secret underground tunnel to get in".
John Drummond was about to walk away when he suddenly stopped in his tracks.
"That's it boys, camouflage".
"Camouflage sir"?
"That's right, between this house and that perimeter wall, I'll bet you there's a man hole or a trap door. I think he's out there, hiding underground. Look. Look at the room he's in".
"What about it sir? It looks like any other room to me sir".
"Yes, to you it does, but not to me, and do you know why"?
"No sir".
"There are no windows".
"Fuck, neither there is. Look at him sir, he keeps looking up at the ceiling and talking to it, and crying. Look, he's crying".
"Push that button there son, see if it will zoom us in a bit".
The young policeman pushed the button, and the camera did indeed zoom in on Hillman.
As soon as it did, Hillman immediately spun round and looked directly at the five men.
"Shit!!" said Drummond, "the camera must have made a noise. Hillman got up from where he sat and walked over to a work top. He came back to the table with a piece of paper and a pen.
"What's he doing sir"?
Drummond looked at his officer. "Fuck you've got problems kid if you don't know what he's doing". Hillman came over to the camera and held up the paper he'd been writing on.

It read; *God alone can forgive you, I can't..*
"He's cuckoo, sir he's fucking cuckoo".
"Oh, you think"? Said Drummond, again sarcastically, fuck you're quick boy.
Right lads; get your guns, because somewhere out there, there's a door, down to where he is. It must have sod covering it, or branches or something, so look carefully, we'll sort this bastard out once and for all, come on, let's go boys, let's hunt this fucking rat out. Now remember, if you spot him, only ask him questions after you've all emptied your guns into him, aim for his fucking rat bastard head. Take tear gas with you, throw a couple down his hatch, and then, you know, shoot, and kill". And you make sure you kill".

HARRINGTON POLICE STATION.
SHEFFIELD.

“Sorry about this Angela” Said Deborah Knowles, “There's been a bit of a misunderstanding you see”.
“These two idiots began to beat me Deborah” said Angela, pointing to the two culprits. “I tried to explain to them, but they wouldn't listen to me”.
“Did they now” Said Knowles, “which ones Angela”?
Angela pointed to the guilty parties.
“Come here” said Knowles to the two officers. “I want you to apologise to miss, eh, Clark here, come on, say you're sorry”.
“We're very sorry Miss, we weren't informed of what was going on, you see, we're sorry Miss Clark”.
“Apology accepted” said Angela, suddenly feeling slightly uneasy. “Where's Carla Deborah”?
“Oh Carla's coming through to you in just a minute Angela, but first, did you tell Tracy to come up to Sheffield with her pal and her children”?
“Yes, she sent me a text just before these officers came and, got me”.
“Splendid, now did you tell her to report here before she goes anywhere else”?
“Yes Mam, she said she would come and see you first when she arrives”.
“Aw, that's brilliant Angela, you're an absolute angel.
Well Karen, I think we've just about got everything in this case put together, now, all we need is Tracy, then we can help Mister Drummond to bring Mister Hillman's games to a close. Do you want some tea Angela”?
“Oh, yes please Deborah, and could I have a cigarette please, they wouldn't let me get anything”.
“Of course, It's the least we can do, for what you've done for us. You” said Knowles , pointing to one of the officers,” go and bring some tea for Angela here, and hurry up”. She pointed to another two officers. “You two go and ask Carla to come in here and join us”. She smiled at Angela. “ I know this is a bit inconvenient Angela, but we do have to go through the motions, as it were, but don't worry, Carla will be off to the hospital in no time, I even think she'll live, but Karen here says no, she doesn't think she'll pull through”.

Angela only half picked up on what Knowles was saying. “I'm sorry”? Said Angela, as she got a light for her cigarette.
“Oh, don't be sorry Angela; you see we made another mistake. You see, we left Carla in the same room as Steve Temple, well, we didn't think there'd be any trouble, but, there was. Temple got his hands on a club or something, and, well, he, eh, he gave Carla a terrible beating. Oh, speak of the devil, here she comes now”.
Two officers came down the corridor smiling, carrying Carla's limp frame. “She's still under” said one of the officers. “She doesn't even look like coming round”. One of the officers grinned at Deborah. “We took off her jeans Mam, thought maybe they were a bit too tight, so we removed them, try and get some air about her”.
As they turned into the alcove where the cell was, Angela let out a scream.
“Carla, oh my God Carla!”
“I know” said Jones, “That's what I'm saying Angela, look at the mess of her face, I can't see how anyone could survive this, and I'm being honest Angela, she looks fucked. Open that cell door men, come on, get her down on the bed, till the ambulance gets here, and Charlie, you keep your hands from between her legs”.
Angela was down on her knees now, looking at the red pulp that was her lover. Still on her knees, she turned round and stared at Deborah Knowles.
“You fucking bastards, you filthy scum bastards that you are, you dirty lying scum bastards, the pair of you”.
She looked at Karen Jones, who held up her hands, and said, “What”?
“You tricked us well, you scum, you stitched us up”.
“Yes Angela, that's right” Said Knowles, “what can I say; I want the glory for finding you.
Come on then boys, the ambulance is on its way for Carla, you'd better make a start on Angela now, before it gets here. You can start by shoving that cigarette down her fucking throat, lay into her a bit, come on, use the baseball bats. Let the bitch know that her time is up for threatening people. We've had enough of your fun and games Angela, come on boys, get stuck in about her, make her learn her lesson, let her witness first- hand what it feels like to have to be resuscitated”.

He had about two hours left before darkness would fall. Hillman had to act fast. He knew that they had found the safe room in the house, and of course, the other camera. He couldn't stand the thought of the policemen looking at him, and he certainly didn't want to turn out the lights. He also knew they would be combing the woods again, but this time with purpose. They knew that this place was outside of the house somewhere.

“Spread out men. Start from the widest points and work in towards each other. If you don't find anything, then start again, and work your ways back out. Look closely for anything unusual. The grass maybe slightly different in colour, to the other grass. Look for a patch of ground that may be disturbed. His den is out here boys, make no mistake about that. You find him, and you blow his fucking brains out from here to Ben Nevis, and then you question him, have you got that”?
“Yes sir!!”.
“Ok boys. Mister John fucking Hillman has taken the piss out of us for the last time, right”?
“Right sir!!”
“Ok then boys, now I'm nipping in to the station to see Deborah Knowles about something, I'll see if I can get some extra pairs of hands here to speed up the search, won't be long boys. Happy hunting guys”.
With that, John Drummond got into his Jaguar and drove away.
“It's alright for him” said one of the officers to his colleague.
“Leave us to comb the woods, let us hunt out the prick; put our necks on the line”. “Well, there's no use complaining about it is there? Let’s get on with it, while it's still light. Spread out guys, like Mister Drummond told us” said one of the leading officers. The men were about thirty yards apart. Each of them began disappearing and reappearing to each other as they began to search the grounds. They searched from the drive, right down to the perimeter wall. Then they turned and began searching in the direction of the house again. They searched again up to the drive, and then began to work their way back down to the wall. For three hours or more, they searched. It was dark now.

Robert Spencer, who had just past his fire arms tests the week before, was as keen as mustard. On his hands and knees now, with his rifle over his shoulders, he searched, feeling and patting with his hands. Suddenly, he looked up. There was a hatch door, and it was open. There was no light on, but he could tell that this was it. Slowly, he crawled, with his gun at the ready. Then his training kicked in, and he decided he would shout on his colleagues, rather than try and be a hero.
He was just about to shout on his friends, when, from ten feet above him in the tree. the magnum bullet took a journey through his skull and brain, exploding his face, down onto the floor of the safe house. From inside the safe house it would have sounded like someone tipping water onto a pavement from a great height. The young man's body fell down through the hatch and on to the floor.
Hillman watched for the rest of the men. He was safe for now.
He would have to kill another, and then make his escape over the wall. This time he had no choice, this time he really was finished with Sheffield. They had taken his wife, his money, his parents, his children, everything. Now, they were going to pay. Quickly, he climbed down from the tree.
In less than five minutes, John Hillman had put the dead man's uniform on, and was up and out of the safe house. His own clothes, he put into a carrier bag, and placed the parcel under a bush. It was dark. Now he could walk among them. He approached the widest man to his left. “Found anything”?
“No, not yet, and I'm fucking frozen, how about you”?
“Yes, I've found John Hillman”.
“What”? The man whispered. “You found what”?
“Look, I'm Hillman”.
The policeman looked up at the man's face.
“Aw fuck”.
“Exactly” said Hillman. Thud! The bullet went right through the man's head.
Hillman repeated the exercise twice more, and then made his way back to the bush, and put on his own clothes again. This time he made his way up to the back of the house, and climbed the hill, still under the cover of the trees, and made his escape over the wall.
Although he thought he was in full control of himself, his schizophrenia was dominating his actions. Had he been in his right mind, he would never had made such a daring move.

Laughing to himself he said, "Well, you found me boys. you won't ever find me again, I'll make sure of that. As for you up there, you can go and fuck yourself, that's what you can do, because now I'm on Satan's side, and I'll bet I get more help from him, than I ever did from you, and don't say I didn't warn you"!

D.C.I. John Drummond drove up the hill and on to the car park at Morningside.
Why was the house still in darkness? "Don't tell me they've gave up".
He got out of his car and walked up the steps, and into the house. He switched on some lights and walked down the long passageway towards the kitchen.
Even before he got there, he could sense that something had gone wrong. He had a bad feeling. The house was once more eerily quiet. "God, how I hate this place" he thought to himself, making his way back to the front door.
"Is anyone here"? He shouted for no other reason than to break the silence "Anyone"? He went to the panel on the wall, half way down the hall, and switched on the outside security lights. The police van sat parked where it had been and was as quiet as the house. "They must still be out there hunting. No, they might be keen, but they're not that keen".
He looked at his watch. It was nine thirty. Drummond began mumbling to himself. "No, something is wrong, but not this time Hillman, there's no way you took out four of my officers without reply, not this time, this time they were ready, they were hunting for you, no way you sick fuck".
He went back inside and switched off the car park lights, so that he could see properly into the woods. Once he was outside again he lit up a cigarette. He stood contemplating where his men could be. "Surely out there they would have heard me coming up the drive. They would see my car, see the lights of the house going on". He could see no torch-lights from the woods.
The detective stood rather puzzled as to what could have gone wrong. Rubbing his chin and staring out into the surrounding trees, he said out loud.
"Not this time doctor, surely not this time".
Drummond was frantic. He found himself shaking uncontrollably, and sweating profusely.

He remembered there was a megaphone in the back of the police van. "Maybe, just maybe, they're too busy, I'll shout for them to come back. Maybe they've found Hillman and gave chase, who knows"? His feet crunched loudly on the loose gravel as he made his way over to the van. Just as he approached the vehicle, a cat came scampering out from underneath it, making him jump almost out of his skin. "You little fucking bastard" he cursed, as the animal made off into the trees.

Drummond attempted to open the van doors. They were locked. The keys were in the ignition. He took them out and went back to the back doors of the van. The doors opened, but there were two cage doors. He found the key and placed it in, then turned it. Then he found his men, his dead men. All of them had been shot in the head. Where was the other though, there were only three men here?

"Fuck off Hillman, there's no fucking way, what the fuck. You had your guns boys, what the fuck has went wrong? How the hell"?

None of the men's weapons were with them in the van.

"I see" Said Drummond, "building yourself a little security in case things get tricky, huh"?

He went back over to the house to report what he'd found and to send for the ambulances to take away the corpses. "God knows where the other man could be. He went into the chilled living room and sat down on one of the easy chairs.

Another cigarette.

"Oh dear Lord. Another three men, maybe more. You've got me beaten Hillman".

He sat smoking listening to the rain outside.

"I'll get you; I promise I will get you.

You know your time is running out, you knew that we knew where you were, we were watching you. How the hell did you take out three men without reply? It's a mystery to me, but then every fucking thing you do is a mystery.

They tell me you're insane? Fuck, you're too many for us, but I swear, I'm going to fucking heel and hide you to a barn door".

EUSTON STATION. LONDON.

“I've tried three times Sharon to phone Angela, three times in the last two hours. Her phone is switched off. I've sent her three text messages, and she hasn't answered any of them”.

“What did she say Tracy, the last time you spoke to her”?

“She said that we were to come back up to Sheffield, and that we would be taken care of. A certain D.C.I Deborah Knowles, would see to it that the kids got private tutoring, and that we were to stay in my own house, and we'd be given police protection round the clock”.
“Tracy, forgive me for being a damp squib, but I smell a rat, don't you”?
“I don't know Sharon, Angela seemed so cheerful and confident about it all, so convincing, you know? And remember Sharon, she was the one who told us to stay down here until the heat was off, so when she says, come up, well, I believe her, I trust her, she wouldn't lead us into any trap”.
“I know that Tracy, not deliberately anyway”.
“What? Do you think this is some kind of trap”?
“All I'm saying Tracy is, that there's something not right about this situation, that's all. I mean, you know more about this kind of stuff than me. I don't know Tracy, it just feels, not right. Did you tell Angela what train we were catching”?
“No, well we didn't know ourselves until a couple of hours ago, did we”?
“No we didn't Tracy, but that could be a good thing. It means that there's less chance of the police putting a chaser onto us”.
“Mummy, can we get some sweets please”?
“As soon as we're on the train, I promise girls, I'll get you some sweets, the train is just coming”.
“Well Tracy, how does this sound. What if we were to get off at another station, and spend the night there? Now if we do that Tracy, then Angela is going to phone you and ask where the hell we are, don't you think”?
“Yes Sharon, brilliant, and if she doesn't phone, then we'll know that something has gone wrong”.

“Well, it would make sense Tracy, because if they are able to phone, then they will, one of them will”.
“And if they don't phone”?
“I don't want to think about that Tracy. Carla has killed people, and so has Angela. If they find that out, then, without a shadow of a doubt, they will both hang, you know how it works now Tracy, this is not the Britain that you and I grew up in”.
“No, and it's not the police force we grew up with either. Oh God, Sharon, you’re sounding xenophobic”.

“Well let’s just hope that my apprehensions are just that, and that nothing is wrong. If something *has* gone wrong Tracy, then our friends are in very deep trouble, and worse than that, there’s not a thing we can do to help them…we’ll soon find out”.

John Hillman had turned back, and was now on the perimeter wall of his father's property. He had only got half a mile onto the Marchfield Estate, when he'd had one of his brainwaves. Instead of stealing a car and taking a chance, his father had two perfectly good cars in the garage. “It's risky” he thought to himself, as he jumped down into the woodland once more. This was a quieter area round here. It was round at the front of the house where the greatest danger of being spotted was. He also had a key for the back door, it would depend if they had put a key in the door from the inside whether or not he could gain entry. From where he was he could not see how many vehicles were parked round the front. He would have to make his way round to the side of the house to gain a vantage point. And he would have to be extra careful. The keys for the garage hung on a wooden panel in the kitchen, along with the keys for both cars. If the keys were still there.

Stealthily, he made his way through the trees and shrubs, until at last, he could see the car park at the front of the house. He was surprised to see that there were only four vehicles parked there, a Jaguar, which he knew belonged to the detective who always seemed to be smoking. A Mercedes, which the two female detectives ran around in, an ambulance, which was just pulling away, and the police van, where he had deposited the bodies. The back doors of that vehicle were still wide open. He might have to stay here for a while, he told himself, until he could see what they were up to.

He had left the hatch door of the outside safe house open deliberately, so that they could find their man, naked, and his head in a terrible mess. He was also unaware of how much he was in control. As far as Hillman himself was concerned, he was always like this.

Schizophrenia has many forms. And with these different stages of the illness come different behavioural patterns. Unbeknown to him, Hillman was like a time bomb. Anything could spark his aggression off. Someone looks at him the wrong way, fear, panic, worry, stress, heartache, laughter, anger, or some old woman with a severely broken neck, sitting behind him now in the bushes, telling him how much of a coward he was, and holding up her dead kitten, and telling him what a big poofy softy he was, being afraid of the dark. Hallucinations, frightening ones. Idiosyncranicity.

"*What's wrong, is your mummy going to put you in the dark cupboard again frock boy*"?

MERRYFIELD MILITARY HOSPITAL.
SHEFFIELD.

The ambulance which had brought Angela and Carla to the hospital had been escorted by armed guard. Under no circumstances had these two women to be left unattended, even in their present condition, which was unconscious. The bone from Carla's nose protruded up about an inch, threatening to burst right through the skin. Her jaw bone was fractured in four places, and all but three of her top teeth had been destroyed. None of her bottom teeth survived the ordeal. She had several broken ribs and severe swelling to her right knee.

Angela's injuries were nothing like as bad as Carla's. She had a broken left arm, and swelling to the eyes, where one of the officers had struck her with the baseball bat. The police surgeon looked at Carla's x rays and tutted, shaking his head. "I've heard about the police getting tougher nurse Peterson, but this? Look at her, she must weigh all of seven and a half stones. They can't tell me that they can justify this" said Surgeon George Morton. "No way, I mean, where the hell do we start? God knows how much blood she's lost. Christ's sake, get her down to theatre nurse, I'll be down directly. I want to assess how bad this one is".
"Sir" the nurse came back into the room.
"Yes"?
"There are two armed policemen outside, and they're insisting that they follow me down to the theatre, I didn't think it was right sir".
"Send them in nurse". The two giant men walked into the room.

"Surgeon Morton, we have been instructed to stay with these women during their stay here", Said one of the guards.
"Even into surgery Gentlemen"?
"Yes sir".
"Have you two seen these girl's injuries"?
"Not really sir".

"Oh well, if that's what you have to do, then so be it, but I warn you, I am going to be carrying out some pretty gruesome surgery here, and if any one of you, cannot stand it, then I promise you here and

now, that I will jag your arses with something that will put you to sleep for a week, literally, do you understand me"?
"Yes sir".
"Ok then gentlemen, let's get this girl's teeth out ribs in, nose bone reset, jaw broken and reset, gums stitched, bowels drained, and of course those dreaded tubes down her throat. Oh, was it you two who put this slip of a girl into this condition"?
"Indeed it was not surgeon".

"Good, I'm pleased to hear it, by the way gentlemen, do you happen to know what blood type you are"?

John Hillman wiped the tears away from his eyes. Nancy Felder had left him alone again, after pouring on the scorn for over half an hour. He watched Drummond coming out of the house with the two female detectives. There was one other officer there who was wearing the same type of uniform as the armed officers had worn. The four walked down the steps and across the gravel into the woods. Both of the women held torches. Surely they would find the trap door, and inevitably, the other officer. He watched as they disappeared into the blackness. Only the dancing beams from their torches could be seen as they made their way.
"Now then, how many in the house? Are there any at all"? His brain was working at lightning speed. He got down to the gravel, knowing he was out of earshot from those in the woods. Whistling a tune, and with his gun at the ready, he walked boldly across the gravel and up the steps into the house. He walked down the corridor, still whistling, as he made his way to the kitchen. Humming and whistling, he turned into the kitchen, to see an officer making some cups of tea. "Fuck its cold out there", He said, as he lifted the keys for the cars and the garage from the rack, watching the officer all the time.
"I know sir, its bitter". The officer hadn't even looked at him. Hillman left the kitchen and walked back along the hall, still watching in case the officer should appear.
Amazing" he said to himself, "didn't have to kill him". When he got to the front door, he looked out at the woods. He could just make out the rays from the torches. He casually walked down the steps and opened the garage door. "B.M.W. I think, lying bastard father, may as well travel in style". To his amazement, the car started up first time. "That's B.M.W for you John; it's not been out in over three months, it starts first time, thank you my German friends".

As he casually drove down the drive, John Drummond said, "Who the fuck is that? I never heard anyone driving up there while we've been in here. Only fifteen feet from the hatch, they turned and headed back up to the house. As they approached they could see that the garage doors were open. "What the fuck's been going on"? said Drummond.

“We'll try and catch up with that car” said Knowles, but as she got to her car, she discovered that her keys were gone.
So was Drummond's, and the police van's. “Oh my bastard” said Drummond, “he's only gone and fucked us up the arse again, Jesus bastard, oh my fuck!!”
Words could not describe how detective John Drummond felt.
A combination of temper, and frustration surged through him like a tidal wave.

Fifteen minutes later.
“Another four Deborah, can you believe it” said a very depressed Drummond.
They had found the open hatch, and the missing policeman, and, of course, the missing safe house.
“Fucking four Deborah, right here in his own front yard. Religious? I'll tell you what; I'm beginning to think that He is working on his side”. Drummond looked up at the rain filled sky. He gritted his teeth and mumbled some kind of curse up to his maker. “ Why can't you give me a break”?
“John calm down, it's not your fault” Said Knowles.
“Not my fault? Fuck Deborah, I'm only looking for one man, I've got half of Sheffield's police force working with me, and I still can't find the bastard”. Again, he looked up at the sky, and gritted his teeth, pointing up there, but this time not cursing.
“Fucking hell Deborah, they lost less men at the Alamo. This keeps up Deborah, and Davis will hang me, I can see it coming. I can just see the headlines now. Detective chief inspector hanged, as four hundred and fifty men lose their lives hunting fucked up doctor”.
Karen Jones had to turn her head away.
“It's not funny Karen”.
“I know it's not John, it's just the way you say things”.
“It's just the way I do things as well isn’t it. I mean, there we all are, four of us, we've got our torches, and we're searching for his hide out, and what does he do? He walks up the steps and into his house, cool as you fucking like, passes the time of day with an armed guard, gets his car keys, takes ours and throws them God knows where”. Again, he looked up at the sky. “Opens the garage doors, and casually drives off into the night. How the fuck do I even start to tell that to Terrance Davis, tell me that girls, huh, Oh, and another four dead men to boot”.

“He drove past us as well John; he's not got a personal grudge against you”.
“Oh but he has”.
Once more, he pointed skywards.
“Fucking just taking the piss, Him and Hillman”.
He sighed and lit up a cigarette.
“Forty of these bastards a day now Deborah. I came up here from London, maybe ten a day, fifteen on a bad day...huh, forty”.

An ambulance pulled up outside of the house. “Where about is the body sir” the paramedic asked Drummond, who exhaled smoke, and pointed with his whole hand in the direction of the hatch.
“Down there, better get the girls to show you, I'll get fucking lost if I try to show you. Hey! Don’t laugh, there’s nothing to fucking laugh about”!

CHESTERFIELD . (TWENTY-FOUR HOURS LATER).

The black B.M.W pulled in to the forecourt of Marshal's Mechanics. Hillman got out of the car and walked into the garage. A radio was playing far too loud for him to engage in any kind of conversation. Three young men in green boiler suits stood looking at a calendar with pictures of semi naked women.

Hillman walked up to the radio and switched it off.

“What do you think you're doing”? One of the young men said, in a challenging tone of voice.

“Where's your boss”? Said Hillman.

“He's not here, I said what the fuck do you think you are doing”?

“What's your name creep”? said Hillman unmoved by the man’s aggressive talk.

“Never mind what my fucking name is, fuck face”. The other two men laughed.

“He's eh, he's gone for his lunch, is there anything we can do for you”? said one of the other men, tapping a spanner in the palm of his hand.

“I'm looking for a swap” said Hillman.

“The first young man said, “Have you got your wife there with you? We'll give you this calendar for her, that's if she's not made out of rubber”.

A roar of laughter.

Hillman stood patiently, until the laughter subsided.

“You!” He said to the young man. “Would you like to go to the toilet with that calendar, you may as well enjoy the last minute of your life”.

“Ooohhh, a threat”.

“Hillman turned and began to walk back towards the garage entrance.

All at once the young man began to sing in mockery, a rendition of Bobby Vee’s Rubber Ball. “And like a, rubber doll, you'll keep bouncing back to meee”.

More laughter.

Hillman pulled down the corrugated door, until it was only a foot or so off the floor. The three men began walking towards Hillman, until they saw the giant pistol coming out from his jacket pocket.

"You stand over there" he said to the only man who hadn't said anything nasty to him. He lifted the gun up, and began walking up to the other two.
"What's wrong boys"? He fired the first shot into the man's stomach. "Lost your guts"? The man fell back about five feet from where he'd stood, holding his hands over the tiny hole in the front of his boiler suit. To the second man he said, "On your knees, come on, I've not got all day". The man got down.
"Hey please Mister, we were only having a laugh".
As the young man who'd been shot in the stomach tried to get up, Hillman fired a second shot into his knee. He walked up to him and placed the gun against the man's forehead, and said, "Say sorry doctor Hillman".
The third man said, "Oh Christ!"
Hillman turned and shot him in the head, killing him instantly.
"Say sorry".
"I'm sorry sir".
"That's more like it, now; do you want your radio back on"?
"It doesn't matter, the young man managed to mumble.
"As you wish ". Hillman fired a second shot into the man's head. "And one more for the road". THUD.
Hillman walked back over to the corrugated door and lifted it back up to its' original height.
He got back into his car, reversed back, and drove back out onto the busy street. The young lady receptionist in the office hardly even looked up from her magazine, as the B.M.W pulled away and headed back into the traffic. He drove on further South from Chesterfield, until he came to Mansfield.
Hillman knew he had to get rid of the B.M.W, they would be looking even now for him. He was to have better luck here in Mansfield than he did in Chesterfield, although, as any car owner would tell you, luck has nothing to do with it when selling a B.M.W. He swapped his car for a year old Astra.
"You must be off your head sir, the salesman said. "This car is worth four of those".
"I know" Said Hillman. "The thing is, although the car is in my name, it belongs to my wife. I caught her in bed with my best friend last week, and we are splitting up. This he pointed to the Astra, is punishment for her, now, you're sure it runs alright"?

“Yes sir, I would love to say it doesn't, but it does, it runs like a dream”.
“That's good enough for me” said Hillman, “and oh, before you say anything.” He put the papers for the car on the man's desk, “I'm not *the* John Hillman, I get some weird looks these days, with that doctor roaming around the country killing people”.
The man laughed
As Hillman walked to the door with the documents for the Astra, the man said, “Hey”.
He turned slowly around.
“Here, I don't usually do this, but it's the least I can do, given your circumstances, there's a grand there, I hope everything works out for you Mister”.
“Thank you” said Hillman, “thank you very much”.
“You're welcome; now, get to fuck out of here before I change my mind”.
Hillman smiled, “Good day to you sir”.

WARRINGTON. (KINGS ARMS HOTEL.)

“Well, it's been two days now Tracy, and nothing”.
“I know, it's beginning to look like you were right Sharon, they should have phoned us by now”.
“I'm just glad we didn't go rolling into Sheffield and right into a trap”.
“Yes, but if you're right Sharon, it looks like Angela and Carla, have done just that”.
“They're not stupid Tracy, so it must have been a convincing ploy to catch those two out”.
“What though, what could the trap have been”?

“How about this Sharon, just supposing that this Deborah woman has something on Carla, you know, something concrete, they could have pulled her in, and Angela for that matter, and told them that she could have them put to death, and then offered them their freedom in exchange for information, names and such, you know, something to do with Temple or those lot. Then they could have made something up about putting me under police protection, while they secretly entice John into their trap. Only, when Angela and Carla have given them all the information they needed.”
“I get it Tracy; they give them all the names, and then they go back on their word”.
“Exactly Sharon, and now, for all we know, Angela and Carla could be locked up”.
“Well, it's not impossible Tracy, but if that were the case, then surely that Deborah woman would have been on the phone to you by now, asking where you were”.
“There's time for that yet Sharon, only if she does phone, we'll tell her we're in Nottingham, at least that'll give us a little time to work out what we're going to do next”.
“Unless of course Angela or Carla phones us, in which case, we're going to feel a little stupid, don't you think”?

“No I don't Tracy, there's nothing wrong with being careful”. Amy and Angela were both sleeping in bed. Tracy poured Sharon a glass of wine. “I'm going to do something soon about those two. We can't go on like this for much longer Sharon”.

“I know, I've been thinking about that, poor little buggers, they've been battered about from pillar to post these last few months, plus, their daddy is out of their lives, for good, no matter what the outcome.
“Amy keeps asking when can they go home and visit daddy. I haven't got the heart to tell them. Angela keeps asking when can they go back to school, and why doesn't daddy phone any more. It's all starting to get to me Sharon. Why can't they bloody well find him, hell, he's gave them enough opportunities Sharon. I can't help thinking that this was all my fault. I should have just grinned and bared it, hell, there's women a lot worse off than I was, I should have just carried on, for the sake of the kids, at least three out of the four of us would have been happy”.
“That's bloody rubbish Tracy, and fine well you know it. The man is ill, he needs help, hell Tracy, he could have killed you and the kids, probably would have done. You done the right thing Tracy, and don't you forget it girl. And by the way Tracy, he will still kill you if he gets the chance, you done the right bloody thing lady, don’t you be feeling guilty for those two children of yours, you’ve done them a huge favour Tracy, and yourself”.

HARRINGTON POLICE STATION.
SHEFFIELD.

John Drummond sat with Karen in the canteen, each sipping a coffee, and John, smoking his eighth cigarette. It was 9.40. a.m. Deborah came in with a piece of paper from the fax machine. "How did you get on John with Terrance Davis"?
Drummond had been summoned to Terrence Davis's office to explain what progress had been made concerning the capture of John Hillman, and why he was losing so many men.
"It wasn't him asking the questions Deborah, it was Richard Knight, the M.P.C. I think I said too much". Drummond had been summoned to Terrance Davis's office to explain the situation to him and to the Metropolitan Police Commissioner, Richard Knight.

"Why? Have they taken you off the case"?
"No, but they could quite easily, with all the things I said to Knight".
"And what about all the things you'll say tomorrow, I'm sorry John I couldn't resist that".
"I wish I could laugh about it Deborah.
What's that you've got there"?
"Oh, it's a fax from Merryfield, Carla Paganni has died". Karen looked at Deborah.
"Oh, don't you worry Babe Ruth; it wasn't your baseball bat that killed her. She died from internal injuries". She looked at the fax again. "Surgeon George Morton is ordering a full inquiry into how she obtained these fatal injuries. He's sending his report to the M.P.C.".
"Well, thank fuck I wasn't there, or that would be the end of me" said Drummond".
Knowles smiled and said, Mind you Karen that was some whack you gave her on the mouth; you nearly put the bat right through her face".
"Well" said Karen, "she won't be running around town in her sugar daddy's B.M.W, or her fancy Porsche sticking her finger up at everybody any more, that's for sure".
"Fuck her Karen" said Deborah, "you didn't hit her hard enough, anyway, the report will be thrown out, Knight will use it for toilet paper. We were told to clean this city up, and that's what we're

going to do, it's no good feeling sorry for these low lives, they're spreading poison right through this country, and I for one, take my hat off to the prime minister for putting his hands up and saying, enough is enough.

We have so many nationalities living in our country now, some of which carry huge terrorist threats to us all, and to our everyday lives. Before, they had some kind of diplomatic immunity, but not now. Asian, African, European, it matters not one wit now, they are all treated the same way when it comes to crime, and it's about bloody time, fucking bombs going off on buses and trains and aeroplanes, we've had enough of their shit too.

There's only one sure-fire deterrent, and that is execution. We'll see how fanatically they follow their religions now, when there's a rope waiting for the bastards when they're caught. We've made a good start getting rid of Paganni, and her nemesis, the one armed Irish terrier. Temple as well, he's off to London for his last supper, but make no mistake, some other drug dealer will be waiting to fill his shoes, and when they do? We'll be waiting to get them in here, and beat the fucking crap right out of them!"

"Fucking hell Deborah" Said Drummond, "is it the wrong time of the month?

"Sorry, I was just getting even". All three detectives laughed.

Five minutes later Karen said, "What have you got on today John"? as she drained her coffee cup.

"Well, I've been ordered to shut off the Hillman house, lock it up and close the gates".

"Do you think that's wise"?

"It's not my decision, it's Davis. He says it's to be guarded now, only by a skeleton staff, and only checked out now and again for squatters. He obviously thinks that there's not much chance of Hillman returning there, after the discovery of his two play-houses".

Deborah looked at Drummond. "I know, I know, you don't have to tell me, as long as it's there, it's always a temptation for him to go back there".

Karen started to laugh.

"What's so funny"? said Drummond.

“Well, I was just thinking, imagine if some junkies did move in and squat, and then Hillman returned to the house”. They all began laughing again.

“Yeah” Said Knowles, that would certainly help us to clean up the city, we could just let Hillman stay there until all the trash had been put out, talk about two birds with one stone”.

MANSFIELD

Hillman headed out from Mansfield, and made his way in the Astra onto the M1. He had changed his mind about not going back to Sheffield, because he knew they would be looking for the B.M.W. Until the police discovered what he'd done, he was perfectly safe.

As he drove past the junction for Chesterfield, he remembered the three men he'd killed in the garage. That'll learn the bastards anyway, trying to be hard men, tough guys, "Yeah tough guys" he said out loud. Tough guys until *you* show your pretty face. He touched his trusty Magnum 3.57..."They're not so fucking hard when you show your face, huh, they turned white, the three of them. Spend all their days with their hands in their pockets, bastards, listening to that fucking din they dare to call music, listening to shit, and looking at porn, meanwhile, some poor bugger is being charged by the hour".

The owner of Marshal's Mechanics had returned late in the afternoon to close the garage. He had walked in to find the corpses of his three employees. The girl in the office had been unable to give any kind of description of the man who had walked into the garage. She had no idea that the three men had been shot.

"You saw nothing Janis nothing? For fuck sakes girl, what were you doing? John, Dave and Barry are lying in there, shot to fucking ribbons, and you saw nothing"?
"I was busy Mister Marshal".
"Busy? Doing what exactly? Because since I've been away, there hasn't been a single customer. When the police get here, they're going to want to speak to you about this. They'll see this as a perfectly executed plan, and if you tell them that you didn't see a thing, do you think for one minute they're going to believe you? They'll kick your ass Janis, and I'll tell you this, I wouldn't blame them." Standing at the great height of five feet four, Mister Marshal, was at least four stones overweight from what his doctor had told him to be healthy. Marshal wiped sweat from his brow. "What the hell could those men have done to deserve that? Fuck, has one of them riled up some gangsters or what"?

The police arrived with two forensic officers, and began to set up equipment, to start taking prints around the garage. After another twenty minutes, an ambulance came to take away the bodies of Marshal's work force.

Bill Marshal stood at the entrance of his garage with his hands on his hips, shaking his head. He stood muttering in total disbelief at what had just happened.
"What the fuck? What's happening to the country when three men get wiped out just like that and nobody sees anything, fuck!!"
One hour and ten minutes from when the police had started their investigating, it was confirmed, that John Hillman had been here. Now, to Billy Marshal, everything became clearer. His men had done nothing wrong; they were simply killed by a lunatic, a madman. They were just unlucky, that's all, "Poor bastards just doing your day's work. Door opens, good afternoon, bang bang bang, that's it, your lives are over".
"You need to find this bastard fast". Marshal approached one of the policemen.
"I beg your pardon"?
"What steps are you taking to find this bastard? You're good with your dust and tape, and shit, and telling us *who* committed the crimes, but what are you actually doing to find this bastard, because it seems to me, he's just taking the fucking piss. He appears and disappears quicker than Count Dracula, and you boys follow behind him saying, oh yes, it was definitely him alright. Truth is, you're no closer to catching him than I am. Are you"?

"Sir, we are doing all we can, I can assure you. There are men and women working round the clock to try and catch him, now I know you're upset with the deaths of your employees, I can understand that, but don't push your luck, or I'll have to take you in, and you wouldn't want that, trust me. Now, I suggest that you get yourself down to the job centre and advertise for another three mechanics, or you won't have a business to run, and may I suggest, that you spend some money and get yourself to some security suppliers and install a camera in your forecourt, because if you'd had one here it might have saved you a lot of time. Just maybe your secretary would have spotted something on the screen, and perhaps could have phoned us earlier. Those men of yours have lay dead for almost three hours.

Do you know how far you can get Mister Marshal, in three hours? He could be anywhere, and all because you don't have a security system installed. Go and spend some money on protecting your garage Mister Marshal, while we go about the business of protecting your arse".

Marshal, a middle aged man, with greasy swept back hair, walked away from the policemen, shaking his head. His leather jacket had seen better days, as well as his shiny black trousers. He walked back into the small room he called his office. "Just go home Janis, I'll call you when I get this mess sorted out and when I've got some more mechanics and business can resume. I'll bring your wages round to the house when I've been to the bank. Better ask those fuckers out there, if they're finished interviewing you, fucking cameras in the forecourt, fucking pricks"!

HARRINGTON POLICE STATION.
SHEFFIELD.

"What do you think Deborah"? Said Jones, bringing in two cups of coffee over to where Knowles sat.
"About what Karen"?
"About Tracy Hillman, there's no sign of her showing up yet".
"No, I think she's been tipped off, but by who?
We took Phorbes's phone off her, and she won't get a phone in that military hospital, they're not allowed. All the calls from that hospital I've had monitored, she hasn't even made a call. We know Paganni hasn't made any calls from the time she brought Dougan in here, unless of course, that was the tip off, that if none of them phoned her, then it wasn't safe to come up.
I don't know Karen, but there's one way to find out. I was so certain though, that she was going to respond" said Deborah
"Yes, and so was I, just at the time when her husband is in the area".
"How do you know that"?
"Have you not heard Deborah? They're all talking about it in the canteen. Three men shot dead in Chesterfield, motor mechanics".
"Motor mechanics"?
"Yes, three of them, and a real mess he's made of them".
"Oh dear, that'll make Drummond's day".
"Why"?
"Because Karen, it would seem that mister Hillman was trying to trade his car in, you know, the B.M.W"? That was John's worst nightmare. He was hoping that Hillman would hold on to it long enough for one of our officers to catch a sight of him somewhere. Obviously, he's even more cunning than any of us give him credit for. Even if he didn't swap his car there, he'll swap it somewhere else, we can forget about him driving around in a B.M.W".
I hope John's put out the word to all concerned. I'll tell you something else Karen, he won't swap it in any of the larger garages either, he'll go to one of those grubby little shit hole garages where they do these underground deals with dodgy motors and fucked up number plates. He's out-witted John once more, fuck he'll be livid".
Deborah Knowles took a sip from her coffee as she punched in the digits for Tracy Hillman's phone.
"Hello?

This is D.C.I. Deborah Knowles, how are you doing Tracy"?
"I'm fine how are you Deborah"?
"Well, to be quite honest Tracy, I'm a bit frustrated, and a bit confused, you see, for three days now, you've been telling me that you're coming to Sheffield, and for three days we've had to make reservations for you at a good hotel, for you and your children, and your friend as well. We've had to pay for this, I mean; it's the tax payer's money after all,
so we were just, eh, we were just wondering if you're going to arrive, that's all, it's a lot of money Tracy".
"Oh I know, I'm so sorry about all this Deborah, but you see, there's been so many loose ends to tie up, plus the fact, that lunatic husband of mine is still running around out there, shooting people at will, so I have to be very careful. I'll tell you what Deborah, if you let me speak with Angela or Carla, I'll explain what the problem was, and I'll arrange a time to come up this afternoon".
"They're not in Tracy, they've gone back to their hotel, haven't they phoned you yet"?
"No they haven't, and guess what, that hotel receptionist must be a bloody liar as well, because she told me that they had been arrested by the police. Some kind of a raid or something, and that neither of them have resided in there since last week, what do you think about that Deborah"?
"Tracy that was a plan, Angela and Carla knew that. They had to make it look good, look I'll tell you. There were one or two men in that hotel, who had planned to kill them. Nobody knew who they were, ok? So, the only way to get them out of there safely, was to put on a show, make it look to everyone, that they were being arrested. Since then Tracy, with Angela and Carla's help, we have been able to bring those men to justice. You see Tracy, Angela and Carla have become, how shall I put it, kind of secret police if you like, they can't just phone you up now when they feel like it, their every move is monitored, so they have to choose their times very carefully when they can phone you. Wait, oh, here's Carla now, oh no it wasn't, it's somebody else, sorry, I thought that was her. Look, I'll get them to call you as soon as I see them, I've already told you that, but I can't emphasise to you, how much of an important job they are doing for us, your friends are going to be very popular Tracy, with all this help they're giving us, and I might add, that

they're none too happy about you delaying coming up here, they're concerned about you, they really are".
"And well they might be concerned Deborah, because I myself am concerned".
"Why? Tracy, why are you concerned? You are going to be protected even better than they have been, I promise you".
Tracy smiled to herself on the phone. She looked out of her bedroom window from the Alexander hotel, directly across the street from the police station.
"Well, the thing is, I eh, I panicked, and I'm back in London, and oh, you'll never guess who I ran into? You're friend, you know, the pathologist? Ashley? Ashley Barnes? Well anyway, I met her a long time ago when my husband had all of his marbles, and we became friends, didn't she tell you"?
Another sigh from Deborah Knowles. "No, she didn't tell me".
"Well, anyway, we got talking in Euston station, and she just happened to tell me, that the reason you couldn't let me speak with Carla Paganni, was because, you had beaten her to death, is that right Deborah? Anyway, just to let you know, that I'm safe and well down here in London, and when all the dust settles down from all this carry on with my ex-husband, you know, when you've finally caught him, I'm coming up there to kill you, and, of course, that other useless Welsh bitch. I'm dedicating the rest of my life to getting you two back for all this. A schizophrenic is taking the piss out of you all by the day, so it won't be long until you're taken off the case, and then I'll come and get you, I swear, that's a promise, and don't dare come down here to London, there's a lot of people down here, just waiting for you and the other whore to show your ugly faces. Now, what do you think about all that Debby"?

There was silence for a few moments, then Knowles said, "Can't wait for the hanging of your cousin Angela Phorbes. So, I will be down there in London, I'll be down to witness the execution. There'll be a large crowd Tracy, and if somehow through all the cheering, you hear laughter, then that'll be me, I'll be the one laughing the loudest, ok"?
"Yeah, just like the rest of the country are laughing at you now because of your incompetence, you and that scraggy Welsh bitch, oh, and not forgetting the cockney buffoon who's had more men with him than The Grand Old Duke of York".

There was silence again for a moment or two. Tracy was trying to contain her temper.

"When I get close to you Deborah, you won't know it, you won't hear me coming, so, until I kill you both, goodbye bitches".

"Hey Tracy I'll"-. The signal died.

"Stupid fucking bitch Ashley"!

"What"? said Karen.

"She's only gone and told Tracy Hillman that Carla's dead".

As it turned out, Tracy did not even know Ashley Barnes. Angela had called her from George Morton's phone and told her everything that had happened. Ashley Barnes was a friend of Nurse Peterson's.

Tracy now stood at her hotel window, looking across the road to the police station. From here, she could watch and know exactly when Knowles and Jones were out. It was a start. She would scrutinise their movements, very carefully. Her first priority would be how to get Angela out of that hospital safely, once her wounds had healed. It was going to be extremely difficult...Knowles was seeking glory, and poor Angela was an essential part of the evil bitch's plan. She would have Angela guarded round the clock.

SHEFFIELD.

Hillman walked from the car park, the short distance to the shopping centre, right in the middle of the city. It was the first time, since his troubles began, that he had felt safe enough to do this. He himself had no idea that he was schizophrenic, but he did sense that something was wrong, though he still viewed his killings, as justified.

People had to learn that John Hillman, doctor John Hillman had had enough. As far back as he could remember, he had been bullied, always told what to do, and when to do it. He believed that this was why God had chosen him to do this work. His mother and lying bastard father had even picked his friends for him. He wasn't even allowed the privilege of picking his own friends, even girlfriends, later on in years.

"No John, she's not for you, my goodness boy, can't you see she's as common as muck, no, not her. Her father drives the bin lorry for goodness sakes, don't bring her back here, I doubt if she'll be able to spell the word mortgage, no definitely no".

"But mum, I"-.

"Don't even bother John, she's not coming back here, and that's the end of it!"

"Dad"?

"Shut your bloody mouth, and go and get ready for church, your mother has spoken".

He was suddenly back in his youth, remembering a particular day.

"It's not fair".

"It's not fair? His mother cried," Of all the ungrateful little wisps in the world. John James Hillman, heavens above, don't make me lose my temper with you on the Sabbath day, my Lord, what are we to do with you. I know what this is all about, don't I? Yes I do, it's about those dirty girls you've been looking at, in those filthy magazines isn't it. I've seen them, oh yes. Photographs of them posing with their bloody pants around their ankles and their legs open, smiling at the camera man, can't you see it boy? They're not, for one minute smiling at you, you silly boy, they're smiling at the camera man John, for the money, for the blinking money John, they're not interested in you, who would be interested in any man pulling down his trousers, and taking out his penis, looking at dirty girls, hhmm? Getting himself all excited and spilling his seed into a handful of toilet tissue, so as not to get his mother's lovely sheets soiled. Like you done last Wednesday night John, when you thought I was down stairs, and don't deny it, because I crept down stairs and got your father and his friend, judge Millburn, and we all watched you.

So, tell me what girl would be interested in a man like that John, I've burned all your dirty books, for goodness sakes John James, you're twenty years old. Stop living in a fantasy world. The girls you bring home, are no better than the sluts you fantasise over in those dreadful magazines. They're after your money John. Someday, when you're a good man, a real man, you'll thank us for helping you become a doctor, you really will. In the meantime, you just stop bringing sluts home for dinner, because it won't wash with your father and I.

You become a doctor first, then you can make your own decisions, there now, I've said my piece, now, come on, church, look, you've gone and made us late. Bloody coloured pages of sluts indeed, blooming twenty. You have to think of Jesus more and more often. Stop being an abomination in God's eyes, you pathetic boy".

As Hillman made his way, with the rest of the shopping public up the escalator, he felt tears in his eyes. He looked at all the display windows as he ascended. "Why had she been like that to him"?Always making out that she was on his side, but always humiliating him as often as she could, especially when there were guests in the house.

Suddenly, he was in conversation with his God again. "Was that right Lord? Was that right, that judge Millburn and my mother and my lying bastard father could stand there and watch a grown man playing with himself? Was it? "I don't think so!" Hillman said out loud, as he got to the top of the escalator.

A young woman pulled her small child away as she went past him, looking at him disdainfully.

He walked along the isle, looking at all the different displays in the shop windows. All of them in full display of festive joy. He suddenly remembered as he came to a book shop, that it was a year ago, along this very isle that he'd been out shopping with his wife and family, how very different things had been then. He was happy,

his wife and children, like so many other families he could see around him now, were so happy. Not now, he was far from happy now. Tears formed in his eyes again, as he heard one little girl asking her mum if Santa would still come to her house, even if she didn't have a chimney.
He remembered Angela asking that same question when she was five. More tears. This time, they began to flow. In the distance he could hear a choir singing "Silent Night".
"They're singing for you Lord" He said out loud as he looked upwards. They're singing for you Lord. It'll soon be your birthday"."An old lady came out from the shop he was standing at. Seeing the tears in his eyes, and hearing the choir, she put an arm around his waist, and said, "I know son, I know, it's beautiful isn't it, it always makes me cry, that one".
John Hillman and an eighty-three year old woman, by the name of Esther Worthington, had never met in their entire lives. They stood now together, outside a toy shop in Hensley shopping centre in a full embrace, both listening to the soothing tones of the children's voices, both of them crying, Esther, for joy, and John Hillman for the fact that everything in the world that had meant anything to him, had been taken away from him in a matter of a few short months.

"Oh dear" said Esther, sniffing, "I'll have to be going son, Merry Christmas". Hillman mouthed the words but his sobbing made it impossible for any words to come out. Instead, he half waved at the old lady. As he tried to walk on, his sobbing continued. People were now looking at him, most of them feeling sorry for him.
"Are you ok"? A young cub scout asked him, rattling a collection tin at some other passers-by.
"No" sniffed Hillman, "I'm not very well".
"Would you like me to walk you outside sir, for some fresh air"?
"Yes I... Yes please, I'll be ok when I get to my car".
"Which way sir"?
"This way". He pointed over to the other escalator, "Over that way".
"Come on sir, can you walk alright"?
"Yes, I'm not well". More sobbing.
To all the people who looked at Hillman and the cub scout, the boy said, "He's alright, he just doesn't feel very well, that's all".
When they got outside, Hillman began to sniff in the cold air.

“Thank you” Said Hillman., “I’ll be alright now”.
“Merry Christmas sir”.
Along with his schizophrenia, Hillman also suffered bouts of Lethologica, a disorder that makes the sufferer forget key words in sentences.
“Yes, yes merry to you, merry Christmas to you, oh, here boy, here, thank you”. He took out some notes from his pocket, and without knowing the exact amount, handed the lad ninety pounds.
“Sir, no sir, it’s too much”.
“No it’s not, no it’s not, don’t, no it’s not, now you get yourself something nice for Christmas, because we both know, don’t we, that Santa Clause doesn’t exist don’t we”?
“Yes sir, I found that out when I was eight”.
“Yes, my mum and dad told me when I was four; they said he was just a lie and not to be such a stupid boy”.
“Merry Christmas sir”.
“Yes, God bless you merry, God bless you, I’m not well”.
The eleven year old Cub Scout counted out the money in one of the public toilets in the shopping centre.
“Fucking yes!!! Ya fucking beauty”!!
John Hillman made his way along the crowded pavements of Christmas shoppers, tears still rolling down his face. The icy wind cut through his thin clothing, and made his eyes sting. He was in a state of confusion, as he slowly made his way back to the car park. What was he going to do, once he got there? “Where can I go Lord, they’ll be out to get me, everywhere . The truth is Lord; you’ve never been on my side, have you? There was no point in killing those whores for you, was there? You were just toying with my emotions. I can’t even buy my kids a Christmas present, can’t buy my wife one either, because now I don’t have one”.

Someone banged into his shoulder, knocking him off balance for a moment. He was just about to say sorry to the man, when he looked straight into Hillman’s eyes, and snarled, “Watch where you’re going, you fucking prick, will you”?
A rage ran through Hillman’s body, making his eyes twitch. He had an almost overwhelming urge to shoot the man in his stinking beer breathed face, but something inside told him not to bother. There were children walking up and down these pavements.

"Deal with that bastard Lord, in your own way, just take him down a peg or two, it's time you done something to help me out, I've been on my own since I left London. No wonder I fall out with you Lord, no fucking wonder".
"*Still moaning lady boy*!!"
He spun round to see his mother walking just behind him.
"*Go on, you little imp that you are, keep moving, I need to talk with you, you stupid little bastard boy that you are, Santa Clause indeed, frock boy".*
His face turned white, and he began walking as fast as he could, almost breaking into a run. He turned again, she was gone.
"Come on Lord; keep her away, just fucking give me a break for once".
He looked round again to find that a crowd had gathered on the pavement about fifty yards behind him. He didn't turn back to see what had happened, but he would have rejoiced and praised his Lord if he had.
The ugly drunk man who had snarled and shouted at him, moments before, lay underneath the wheels of the double Decker bus, number eighty-seven. The man had died instantly.
Hillman reached his car. He lit up a cigarette and contemplated his next move. He would change his look again, maybe denims this time. He remembered buying his first pair of Levies. He also remembered his mother forbidding him to wear them, unless he was helping his father in the garden.

MERRYFIELD MILITARY HOSPITAL.
SHEFFIELD.

Angela sat looking out of the window, onto the immaculate gardens outside. The grass had a film of frost upon it, giving the false impression that a shower of snow had fallen. She sat watching the crows and starlings fighting and scrapping for the scraps of bread that the kitchen staff had thrown out for them. On the small table, which was between her bed and where Carla's had been, there was a photograph of Carla. Although George Morton had done his utmost to save Carla, there was, in the end, nothing more he could do, and through her internal injuries, Carla had finally lost her fight for life. The daily newspaper lay, with an old photograph of Doctor John Hillman, smiling up at her from the front page. 'STILL AT LARGE', was the headline. She had read the report of how Hillman had struck, yet again, this time in Chesterfield, killing three innocent, hard-working honest men, and that two of the men had left behind a wife and two children, all the children under the age of ten. "Steps must be taken to bring this homicidal maniac down, and fast".

Opposition from all the other parties were giving the Prime Minister a hard time, suggesting that the Sheffield police department were no more than incompetent dummies, and officers from The Metropolitan Police Department, who had been sent up to help deal with the situation, were no better.

One of the reporters was quoted as saying that, 'The Prime Minister is just not taking this situation seriously enough, while members of the British public are being gunned down, in their place of work'. "I put it to the right honorable gentleman that he needs to get his act together, and get this lunatic off our streets and into a body bag as soon as possible".

"They're all good at pointing the finger of blame at each other, but while they're all doing that, the madman continues his reign of terror inflicting heartache and misery into families with his continuous killings. Why can't they all just get their heads together and get on with the task of bringing him down. Bloody politicians, kidding themselves on that they're doing the public a service". Angela sighed heavily as she continued reading the newspaper.

"There's only one way to put an end to bastards like Hillman, and that's with a bullet, or a rope, that's it, that's the only real deterrent.

Directly underneath that report was another headline; FIRST EXECUTION IN BRITAIN SINCE THE NINETEEN SIXTIES.. The story read; A petty gangster and drugs dealer is to hang in forty-eight hours' time. He received the Death Sentence for arranging the gang rape and murder of a nineteen year old prostitute, named Susan Monk, and for arranging the gang rape and murder of another young woman, who, at this point remains nameless, but is believed to be a local hair dresser and beautician. If these acts had not been bad enough, the excuse for a man had also filmed the whole procedures on both occasions. Another young lady who survived the ordeal is in a secret location. Her condition is said to be comfortable and stable. It is thought that he'd intended to send the films of the executions to a rival gang. The Prime Minister has passed on his deepest condolences to both victims' families. Representatives from the government will attend both victims' funerals".

The prime minister went on to say, in a later interview; "It is exactly crimes like these that have persuaded me and my cabinet, to give our police forces back, some of the power they once had. This country has long been suffering the consequences of gang warfare. Innocent people being gunned down on the street, caught in the crossfire of these gangs and their ruthless killings. We have a situation where people are afraid to leave their homes after a certain time in the evening, for fear of being victimized by these violent gangs. Young girls being raped and beaten on their own streets and then threatened that if they tell the authorities, their families will be the next victims, well, no more.

Let the execution of Mister Steven Temple mark a turning point in British justice. This includes John Hillman. The opposition can say what they want, but the man is no fool. He listens to what's going on, he constantly changes his appearance, but the people of Britain can rest assured, that we are doing everything in our power to bring him to justice".

"Huh, bring him to justice"? Angela thought to herself as she watched a crow snap the crust of bread from a Starling's beak, "You haven't got a clue where he is. There you all go blaming each other as usual, but you lot live in a world of complete pretense. None of you have a clue what it's like in the real world, but you'll convince yourselves that you're doing your constituents a huge favour, and you're always pleading poverty aren't you, like you can hardly live".

She stood sipping her coffee, when surgeon George Morton walked into the room, slamming the door once more behind him. “Angela” he whispered, looking over his shoulder, as if the two guards would come into the room behind him. He got up close to Angela. “Here” He whispered again, “this is an old mobile phone of mine, it’s not a very good one, but it’ll let you talk to your friend now and again, just don’t let them hear you using it”. He pointed to the door. “I’ve put twenty pounds in it, and I’ve also phoned your friend, giving her that number, but be careful Angela, because if they find it, I’ll have to deny all knowledge of it, ok”?

“Thank you doctor Morton” she whispered back to him.

“Now then, I’ve got a little bit of good news for you. Tomorrow, there’ll be a nurse coming in here, a new nurse, she will take you from here down to another ward, to have some tests done. The tests will take about an hour or so. Those thugs there will of course be outside of the door, but once you’re in the ward, you can then go through to another room, where they won’t be able to hear your conversation”.

“Hear my conversation”?

“Yes, the nurse will be Tracy. I’ve been in contact with her. She’s coming here tomorrow, I’m going to pick her up in town. I’m taking a nurse’s uniform with me. She’ll walk into the staff entrance with me. I’ll try and arrange this a couple of times a week it’ll give you the chance of trying to work out some kind of plan to get you out of here”.

“Thank you doctor Morton, from the bottom of my heart”.

“You can thank me when you’re free Angela, you’re not out yet, and please, don’t be trying anything tomorrow, not on the first day”.

“No I won’t, don’t worry, but thank you doctor for helping us out, thank you so much”.

“You’re welcome, now, I’ll have to go, I’ll see you tomorrow”.

Angela kissed the man on the cheek. “Thank you”.

Surgeon George Morton turned and left the room.“Good afternoon” the two guards outside the door said as he passed them.

Without turning round, George Morton replied, “Go and fuck yourselves gentlemen”.

ST. JAMES'S PARK. LONDON. 10.55a.m.

A large crowd of people had gathered in the grounds of the park. People jostled around the scaffold, trying to get the best view of the execution. None of the mainstream television channels had been allowed to televise the execution, but there had been a one-off special channel set up, scheduled to run for an hour, to witness Temple's punishment if anyone cared to watch at home. At first it had been suggested that the execution would not be made public, but, as one politician put it, "It would be a deterrent to any would-be criminals out there, if they could see what it was like to hang by the neck until dead. Or to help them understand, that if they run around breaking the law dealing in drugs, or being found guilty of rape or beatings, then *this* is what they could expect. This will be the consequence".

It was then decided that the execution would be beneficial if it were to be made a public event.

There were, of course the usual protesters in the park accusing the government of going back to the dark ages, and for not being in tune with modern life in the British streets, but their protesting was to no avail, the execution would take place.

Temple sat on his bed, tapping his hands on the back of his head, with his elbows on his knees. He heard a buzzer ringing out loudly, and then the squeaky footsteps of the boots of the prison wardens coming down the corridor. There was a rattling of keys in the door lock, and then the heavy metal door swung open. A priest came into his cell carrying a bible under his right arm.
"Five minutes Mister Temple" Said one of the two tall prison wardens who had accompanied the entrance of the priest. He sat down on Temple's bed beside him smiling. "I am here" he began, but was abruptly interrupted by Temple.
"No no, get him to fuck out of here" he barked at the wardens. The priest began muttering in Latin, and then in English."Get him to fuck out of here!!"
He picked up one last cigar and lit it up, just as the priest was led out of the cell.

“Four minutes” said the warden, and then closed the door.
“It’ll be quick Steve” he told himself, there’ll be no pain, and there’ll be no more beatings either. He got up and looked in the mirror at his deformed nose. This was it then, this was what it felt like to be the condemned man. He drew heavy on the cigar as the door opened.
“It’s time Mister Temple”.
Steve Temple took one last drag of his cigar and stubbed it out in the ash-tray, then he picked up the photograph of his brother Billy, standing beside himself and their mother. He kissed the photograph and whispered to his brother’s image, “my turn Billy boy, it’s my turn; I’m coming to see you”.
“Let’s go Mister Temple, they’re waiting”.
Outside in the corridor they put hand cuffs on his wrists, he still clutched the photograph. They walked him along to the end of the corridor. He could hear the murmur of the crowds. There was a set of metal steps leading up to the scaffold.
An officer began to climb the steps first, followed by Temple, and then two more officers, then the priest, and then the prime minister himself. Up and up they climbed. The steps seemed to go on forever, his legs felt weak. Eventually, they reached the top.
The first officer led Temple out onto the middle of the scaffolding. “Stand here!” He said, “Don’t move!” Then he whispered into Temple’s ear “this is too good for you, you sick bastard that you are, I would draw and quarter you if I had my way”.
To the warden’s surprise, Temple whispered back, “You couldn’t have your own way with a willing woman, you sad fuck!”
The crowd began to roar and jeer at Temple, shouting all sorts of obscenities at him. The warden whispered again into Temple’s ear, “We’ll see how brave you are just shortly won’t we huh?”. Then he shouted, “Lower the rope”.
A rope noose was lowered down to the floor. The warden placed the noose loosely around Temple’s neck.
To Temple he said, “I’ll be back in five to tighten this beauty after the P.M. has said a few words.
The priest stepped forward and once again attempted to give Temple the last rights.
Once more Temple interrupted him. “Don’t waste your fucking time Father, you could be buggering a nice little choirboy just now, on you go, you fucking hypocritical bastard that you are”. The priest continued to mutter his Latin verse at Temple.

“Go and confess fuck face” he said to the priest. “Trying to save my soul, if there is a Hell at the other side of this, you can count on me to be waiting there to bugger you with a red-hot fish fork, you can count on that Father, now come on, let them get on with it, go and fuck your infants!”

The priest shook his head at the end of his sermon. “May God have mercy on your poor soul my son”.

“Yeah, right” said Temple, “and may Satan have mercy on your poor hole when I get hold of that fish fork, fuck off!!”

The scaffolding stood twenty-three feet from the ground. A P.A. system had been set up for the benefit of the crowd so they could hear what the prime minister had to say.

The P.M. stepped forward standing about five feet in front of Temple, and took hold of a microphone which was handed to him. He cleared his throat and began to speak.

No-one could hear a single word. “Switch it on you stupid fuck” cried Temple.

The P.M. pushed the small switch forward on the microphone and tapped it twice with his fingers. The sound of the two taps echoed around ST James’s park like two massive gun shots. People could be heard laughing all around the park. The P.M’s face was bright red. Again, he cleared his throat.

Just before he began to speak, the warden who had been talking to Temple earlier, walked up to the condemned man and said, “Oh I almost forgot Steven, give me that photograph, I’ve got a better one for you here, and Oh, your mother died four days ago, I forgot to mention that to you. She had lay for about six hours in total agony before anyone found her, two broken legs I believe, and some ribs, poor bugger, we’re burying her the day after tomorrow. I was told to give you the option of going to her funeral, and delaying the execution on the grounds of mercy, but me and the boys here, we thought, no, fuck him, we’ll give him the message on the scaffold”.

“Lying bastard” hissed Temple.

“Am I”? Said the guard, “have a look at these beauties then if you think I’m a lying bastard”. He pulled out four picture postcard sized photographs from his pocket. Audrey Temple lay naked on a mortuary desk. Both of her legs had been badly broken underneath the knees, her shin bones sticking out in a hideous fashion. All down one side of her ribs was a mass of black and blue bruises, and a swollen pelvis. Beside her lay a builder’s mash hammer.

“That’s mine Steven, that hammer, it belongs to me, and I have a rule that no-one but no-one else is allowed to use that hammer, do you catch my drift hard man? Not so fucking tough now huh? Six hours the poor old bint lay. Shame eh? I hope you take an hour to die you sick fuck that you are. Gag”!! The warden shouted.
The P.M. waited until the gag had been placed over Temple’s mouth.

As the prime minister began his speech, addressing the good people of this God fearing nation of ours, how much he regretted having to take action like this, Temple’s body began shaking with the severity of his sobs, thinking about how his mother had died.
The P.M. turned around just as the warden was tightening the noose around Temple’s neck.
“You see? Ladies and gentlemen, how sorry he is for his deeds, but forgiveness is in the hands of God almighty himself. He will decide the fate of Mister Temple’s soul. We have tried in vain to be tolerable with these hard core criminals, but still they persist in poisoning our country with their violence and their drugs, and their grooming of young girls into prostitution, and corrupting our children into that world of helplessness and hopelessness. Alas, no more. May God have mercy upon his soul. Let this be a lesson indeed, a warning, to drug dealers, murderers, terrorists, and all, that Britain no longer intends to tolerate your vileness. You have finally broken our temperament. Gentlemen, proceed”
The warden stepped forward, placing the black hood over Temple’s head, and making sure he was not standing on the one meter red square marked on the scaffolding floor. He tested the rope one more time, whispering into Temple’s ear. “Charlie said your mother’s arse was nice and tight, good ride, now, rot in Hell you bastard. Pull!!

Suddenly, the floor beneath Temple’s feet collapsed, and his body descended fifteen feet, as his neck took the full weight of his thirteen and a half stones. His neck snapped, making the sound of a thick dry stick breaking in the woods, underfoot. It seemed to echo in the frosty air. His spinal column completely severed. The body of Steve Temple kicked and thrashed for a final few seconds before he finally came to a permanent rest.
The enthusiasts in the crowd, all cheered at the first execution to take place in Britain for almost five decades. The more civilized onlookers muttered to themselves, “God help us”.

HARRINGTON POLICE STATION. SHEFFIELD.

"I can't give you any more men Deborah, and that's that, besides, you've got two armed officers standing by her door. To my knowledge, this Miss Clark, or whoever the hell she is, has got a broken arm and wounds to her knee, I hardly think she's in any shape to make a run for it, do you"?
Deborah Knowles sat at the table with Karen Jones and Terrence Davis. He continued. "There's no need even to think about her just now anyway. You should be concentrating in bringing in the rest of the drugs gang to face justice".
John Drummond was also at the table.
"Anything new on Hillman, John"? Said Davis.
"Not yet Terrence" said Drummond, "He's not been seen or heard of since his little visit to Chesterfield. We're doing all we can sir, I've even got men scouring up and down the motorways looking for his B.M.W. you never know, maybe he still has it".
"Davis frowned slightly, as if what Drummond had just said was the most ludicrous thing he had heard in the past decade. "Well I'll tell you something John, and this is not from me, this is from the M.P.C. They want a result, and they want it fast. They're saying that this has gone on for long enough and that this Hillman is completely taking the piss out of the whole police department, and we are becoming nothing less than a laughing stock. In a nutshell John, they're growing tired of excuses, and if you haven't got him by the week-end, then they're taking you off the case, and oh, by the way Deborah, what's the story with that Paganni girl, what happened exactly"?
Deborah cleared her throat, but before she could speak Davis put his hand up, stopping her.
"Hold on Deborah, it was a rhetorical question, I know fine well what happened. I went down to the morgue and I saw her body. I would advise you to use your powers with caution. Yes, be heavy-handed by all means, but when I see a seven stone girl lying on a slab in *that* condition, well I'm only warning you, watch what you're doing. Just get out there and bring that mental doctor in, dead or alive, just get him, and of course, you'll all become national heroes.
Deborah? I want you to forget about the girl in the hospital, you and Karen in helping John find Hillman.

You have until the end of the week, so I suggest you get cracking, otherwise, you just might find yourselves a little further down the ladder. Now, I have faith in you guys, even if they don't. Now you get out there, and prove them all fucking wrong and try showing a little more enthusiasm".

"I'm glad you think it's as easy as that" Said Knowles. "This is a very cunning man we're dealing with here, don't you forget that, and don't talk to us like we were bloody cadets, we'll get Hillman, don't you worry about that".

"Oh, I'm not worried" Said Davis, after all, it's your bloody jobs, not mine, they would just like it if you could prove to them that you are all capable of doing them".

MERRYFIELD MILITARY HOSPITAL.

SHEFFIELD.

Surgeon George Morton pulled in to his reserved parking place in his beloved Ford saloon, and it's V.8 engine, with a nurse who was new to the hospital.

"Now then Tracy, I've already told your cousin, no heroics today, alright?

Just walk round with me, and no-one will question you. I'll arrange it, so that you and Angela can have a little chat together without those bloody guards listening to anything you say. You'll be able to catch up with one another, and find out what exactly has been going on.

Did you know that Angela and Miss Paganni were lovers"?

"Well. I kind of knew they were close, but I didn't think..."

"Well they were Miss, so I want you to cheer her up, she's been on a constant downer since the death of Carla. If you play this cool, then I'll help you get her out of here, before long, but you must be patient, do you hear"?

"Yes sir, I hear, and thank you for what you're doing".

"Ok then, now remember, no tricks today Tracy, I mean it, because, as I've already told Angela, if you try anything, and you fail, and get caught, then I will, of course deny knowing anything about it, and then you'll be in as much trouble as she is".

"I won't, I promise".

"Good girl, right, let's get to work Tracy."

One hour and fifteen minutes later, Tracy was pushing Angela on a wheelchair down the ward towards the theatre, followed, inevitably, by the two security guards.

Five minutes later than this, and Angela and Tracy were sitting sharing tea and cakes, and filling each other in with the course of recent events.

"Here" said Tracy, handing her friend a Magnum 3.57 caliber pistol.

"Keep it safe Angela, ready for the big day, make sure you keep it out of sight.

There's six rounds in that thing, so be careful where you point it".

Angela placed the pistol underneath a pillow. She sighed as she said, "I'm going to miss her Tracy, I loved her deeply".

"I know, Mister Morton told me on the way over here".

"I'm going to be lost now without her. She and I have spent some special times together, God it feels like I've known her all my life. I think I'd found my soul partner Tracy".

"I know, it must be hard babe, but you have to be brave, think of what Carla would want you to do. Would she want you grieving over her, or would she want you to be devising yourself a plan on how we can get your arse out of here"?

"I don't know if I can walk out of here with a strong will Tracy. I've seen so much this week; I don't know how much more I can take".

"I know babes, but let's show them Angela, this one last time, that they can't fuck around with us, let's get this Knowles bastard whoever she is, and teach her a lesson for doing that to Carla, her and that other bitch she has with her. With Mister Morton's help, we'll get out of here, and we'll make those bastard's eyes water, we owe that to Carla".

"They beat her to an absolute pulp Tracy, you have no idea. The police now, well, don't trust them, I mean, really don't trust them. They'll kill you now and think nothing of it, the whole system has fucked up and gone mental, you should have seen the mess they made of poor Carla".

"Exactly Angela, but let's get out there, and show them just exactly what *we* can do. We'll show them just exactly what ruthlessness is".

SHEFFIELD.

John Hillman sat in his car about three miles outside of Sheffield, in a small wooded area. He was trying to put his thoughts together, as to what to do next. He looked at his reflection in the rear-view mirror, and noticed that the beard he'd grown was now getting rather neglected. He would have to trim it as soon as possible. He sat listening to two different parties arguing the toss about the public execution of Steven Temple, the day before. As he listened, he began to enjoy the two mince pies he'd purchased in the city earlier in the day.

Then, without warning, one of his turns. "You see Lord" he said, with his mouth full of pie, "This is always the reaction you get whenever justice is dished out, all those goodie two-shoes, babbling about human rights. Nobody gave those two girls any rights, when they set about whipping and raping them. They done well to hang the bastard Lord, they really did, I mean hallelujah and all that jazz Lord. "See"? He said, "When they catch me, you know, for doing your fucking dirty work, I'll make sure they won't get the chance to hang me. As soon as I'm cornered, old Betsy here will see me off, they're not stringing me up on any fucking scaffolding, for every fucker to see me pissing my pants, or coming in them, like my mother and lying bastard father did with that judge, fuck, how embarrassing Lord".

As he listened to the argument on the radio, and enjoying his pies, another vehicle pulled into the same lay-by. It was a people-carrier, one of those vehicles that he detested. It had pulled in, in front of him, having come from the opposite direction. They were parked now, directly in front of him, windscreen to windscreen, about a meter and a half apart.

"Hello Jesus"? Said Hillman, still munching happily, and now, for some unknown reason, completely relaxed.

Two young men, about the age of thirty he guessed, sat in the vehicle. In between them sat a young lady who looked to be of a similar age. The voice on the radio was saying "If these people think that they can just go around manipulating people, bullying them, and generally being idiots, then from now on, they can expect to be dealt with harshly, and can have no argument about it. It's time that the British people stood up for themselves and for each other, team up if you have to, to get the bullies, and kick the living daylights out of them"!

Hillman put the brown paper sack on his lap, and began applauding the woman on the radio. “Here here” he shouted, picking up the paper bag which contained his second pie. The driver of the people carrier burst out laughing at him, and began pointing at him, and mocking him by clapping his hands.
Hillman smiled.
The second young man began clapping, and then, curling his hands underneath his arm pits, in a mock gesture, suggesting that he was a monkey.
Still Hillman sat calmly, smiling, and opening his first carton of tea. If the young men in the people carrier had looked closely, really closely at the man in the car, they would have spotted the danger signs, and they might have had maybe a fifty-fifty chance of survival. As it was, they hadn’t noticed, and so now, it was only a matter of time. Hillman had ignored the ignorant gestures, because he was so focused on the young lady sitting in the centre of the vehicle, and once again, like the lioness hunting wildebeest, the eyes remained constantly on the intended target. The young lady wore a red blouse, with the buttons opened just one or two too many from Hillman’s point of view. In his eyes, those two unfastened buttons had condemned the girl into being a slut and a whore, and she would have to be dealt with accordingly.

One of the men began to roll a joint, whilst the other got out of the passenger side and walked up to Hillman’s car, and began urinating on the back of it, and on to the back windscreen.

Hillman, although aware of what was happening, still sat smiling at the girl, who was now in hysterics at her friend’s antics. The young man shook his penis and made his way back to the people carrier. The three of them sat in their vehicle laughing and pointing at Hillman. The driver switched on his window wipers and then off again.
Another roar of laughter.
John Hillman, still smiling, got out of his car, carrying in one hand, his carton of tea, and his bag with his pie in the other. Leaving his driver’s door open, he casually strolled over to the van. The driver rolled down his window.
Hillman sipped his tea, but said nothing, only staring into the driver’s eyes. He was careful where he stood, so as the driver couldn’t push the door into him.
“What the fuck do you want shit face” the man said.

"I need to punish the whore, so if you'll just hand her over, then she and I will be on our way, and we'll say no more about the urine incident, ok"?
"Johnny"?
The girl shifted uneasily in the middle seat, "watch out, he's fucking mental".
Hillman looked at the girl. "Me?" He said, "You're calling me mental? I'm a doctor you silly whore, a fucking good doctor at that, I'll have you know, mental indeed". He took a bite of his pie, and with his mouth full said, "So? Are you going to hand her over monkey man"?
"You're the fucking monkey man you stupid cunt".
The girl, who was far more aware of the danger than her friends, said, "Come on boys, let's go, come on, please Mister, we're sorry, we were only having a laugh, we didn't mean any harm, come on boys, let's be going".
The passenger door of the van opened up and the other young man got out. "Not before this creep tastes my fucking boot leather!"
John Hillman aimed the brown paper bag at the young man's groin, and pulled the trigger.
Although only a small hole in the front of the man's jeans gave any indication that he'd been shot, the whole of his stomach exploded inside his body, sending a stream of blood out through the back of his jeans and up his back, two feet higher than his head. He collapsed onto his knees clutching the small hole in the front of his stomach. Blood oozed out from his nose and ears.
"Out" said Hillman to the driver, "Come on, out!!"
The man got out of the van holding his hands above his head.
Hillman took another bite from his pie.
He said to the girl, "get out, and drag the pissing monkey over to those trees, and hurry, or I'll shoot your friend here, move!!"
The girl struggled to pull her friend by the arms, but only managed after two or three attempts.
"I'm sorry Joe" she said to the semi-conscious man.
"Get into the woods the pair of you, and start walking, I'll tell you when to stop".
Another bite of his pie and a sip of tea, "keep moving, come on, where no-one will find your bodies". "NOW" the young man shouted. He and the girl turned and intended to overpower Hillman, but he was much further behind them than they'd anticipated. Hillman simply raised his gun and shot the man's right knee to pieces. "Aaarrrgghhh"!!

The girl stopped, in tears.
"Now what"? said Hillman, mocking the girl. He pulled the trigger again, this time completely destroying the man's right shoulder.
"O K" said Hillman to the girl, this'll do here, take your clothes off, now".
Her friend lay on the ground, only feet from where she stood, unconscious, broken bones sticking out from where his upper arm should have been, his leg bent in a hideous shape from his knee down.
"Come on whore, a quick fuck, then you can be on your way, don't waste any more time, unless you want to die like him". He pointed to her friend. "Look, here's an idea, you take your clothes off honey, and I'll get that miserable bundle of monkey spunk and drag it in here where it can rot. Be gentle with me now, do you hear me? Gentle".
When Hillman returned, the girl stood, still wearing her underwear in the cold December air.
"Come on now, take them off, everything".
The petrified girl stripped completely, shivering and clutching her breasts with one hand, and trying her best to cover up her genitalia.
Suddenly, and what could only be described as a miracle, Hillman had a brain wave.
"I know" he said to the girl, "I know who'll hide me for a while, of course, why didn't I think of that before, how bloody stupid of me, Miss? What's your name"?
"Sandra".
"Sandra? Well Sandra, I'm sorry to say, I don't have time to have sex with you, I'm sorry, because I have to go now, I'm so sorry about this, but this is important. Now, when you hear me pulling away from the lay-by, then you start putting your clothes back on, do you hear"?
"Yes"
"Not until you hear me driving away, and if I may say so, I would choose your friends with a little more care if I were you in future. You're a lucky girl today, because I was going to hang you, after I fucked you. You're lucky I've just had a brilliant idea. Now you be a good girl in future ok? And don't be impertinent to anyone, now, open your legs up, let me put a couple of fingers in, just to let me see what I'll be missing".
The girl began to cry, but opened her legs up slightly as Hillman inserted two fingers.
"Mmm nice and sweet" he said, as he put his fingers into his mouth, and turned to walk back to his car.

Looking back over his shoulder, he called back to the petrified naked girl, "Merry Christmas".
He took out the keys from the van, and also the girl's hand bag. He had already taken the mobile phones from the two deceased young men. Now he took the girl's phone along with a spare set of keys for the van. He threw the phones as far as he could into the woods, along with the two sets of keys.
He then got back into his car, started it up, and drove back towards Sheffield.

"Why didn't I think of this before Lord, it's perfect, bloody perfect, and no-one would suspect this person of harboring a criminal because that's what I am, seeing as you won't do your own dirty work. Somebody's going to be a lucky man Lord with Sandra back there, it turns out Lord, she's not a whore, she just acts like one, but I've told her off, about her behavior, and her choice of attire. A dangerous game Lord, acting like a whore. You fly with the crows, and you'll be shot at"

HARRINGTON POLICE STATION.
SHEFFIELD .

The sergeant at the police station shook his head in dismay as he listened to inspector McRae's report on an incident that had taken place earlier that afternoon.

McRae looked at the sergeant and said, "Two men have been fatally wounded in a woods three miles south of Sheffield. Tell whoever's in charge to set up a rape crisis nurse, as there has been a female victim. Although she has no life threatening injuries, she is apparently suffering from shock".

The girl had tried to pull her friends from the woods, as she thought they were still alive, but the doctor who arrived at the scene of the crime pronounced them dead".

McRae continued, "The girl is pretty shook up Tom, she's rattled, she may even have psychological problems following this".

"Right sir, I'll get on to it straight away, are they coming here with the girl"?

"No Tom, I thought I might take her to the pictures first, maybe a candle lit dinner".

"Ok sir, I just thought maybe you were taking her to the clinic first"

"I'll see you in ten minutes Tom" McRae laughed.

Thomas Adamson laughed as well. "See you sir"

"Fuck, here we go" Adamson, whispered to himself. "This lot's just had their arses kicked the other day for not getting their fingers out, the last thing they need is this, they'll go fucking mental". He tapped on the door of Deborah Knowles's office, and walked in.

Drummond sat at the table with Knowles and Jones.

The first thing the sergeant thought to himself was, they might stand a better chance of catching this Hillman, if they actually got up from their backsides and looked for him, out there, not sitting looking at a map of Yorkshire. He kept his opinion to himself.

"Yes Thomas, what can we do for you"? Said Drummond.

"There's been another two murders sir, just three miles from here, two men".

"How were they murdered? Don't tell me, they were shot"?

"Yes sir. There's a survivor sir, a young girl, I am to inform you to send for a rape crisis-nurse, they're bringing the girl here now sir".

The three senior officers all rose to their feet at once, and began to make arrangements for the girl.
"Is she wounded"? Asked Jones.
Adamson thought to himself, "as if they would bring her here if she had a bullet inside her, silly cow.
"No mam but she may suffer mental health problems, there could be psychological problems.
"Right Thomas, thank you, you may go now" said Knowles.
"Too many chiefs" thought Thomas to himself.
"Right you are mam".
Adams couldn't for the life of him work out how they intended on bringing Hillman in when all they seemed to do was drink tea and discuss Hillman's victims. If they weren't careful, they themselves would become victims of Hillman. He would be the reason they all lost their jobs.

MERRYFIELD MILITARY HOSPITAL.
SHEFFIELD.

Angela sat reading her magazine. At least that's what the officers who looked into her room thought. She was actually looking at her mobile phone.

Tracy was once again in the building, and she and George Morton had devised a plan to make their escape.

George Morton made his way down the corridor towards Angela's room, completely ignoring the two officers standing at her door. The two guards had long since stopped attempting to pass the time of day with the surgeon. Morton closed the door behind him as he entered the room. Everything ok Angela"? He said, smiling and winking.

"Yes Mister Morton, Tracy's just text me, telling me what's going to happen".

"Good" he said. "Don't ask me how, but Tracy has managed to get hold of a Mercedes S.L.500, so you'll get off to a quick start in that thing".

"Tracy knows people Mister Morton, Tracy knows a lot of people".

"Ok then, now, in about four weeks time, not before, just take a good sharp pair of pliers to that plaster cast, there shouldn't be any problems. Your arm will feel weak and stiff for a few days, but it will soon strengthen. Now then Angela, you know what to do"?

"Yes Sir Mister Morton, and thank you".

He smiled and nodded at the grateful young woman.

"You're welcome Angela, but remember, if this goes wrong, I know nothing about any of it".

"I know sir, I just want you to know how grateful I am, you are an amazing man".

Morton smiled. "We won't have time to talk later Angela, so I've come to wish you and Tracy all the best for the future. It has been an honour meeting you Angela I'm just vexed that I couldn't save your Carla for you".

"You tried your best Mister Morton, and that's all anyone can do, thank you for trying sir".

"Well, this is goodbye then Angela, may everything you do flourish and prosper".

Angela smiled at the kindly gentleman who had helped Tracy and her forge this plan of escape, risking his own well-being in the process. If Knowles were to find out he'd assisted their escape, she would jail him.

“Same to you Doctor, and may I say something? She’s not coming back, your fiancé I mean. Angela was referring to the fiancé he’d lost all those years ago, and how he felt he could never love again because of the fact that her body had never been recovered from the avalanche that had swept her away. “Now, if she could, she would tell you to get yourself out there and find yourself a nice woman, some company. You need to share a part of your life with someone else, your soul is pining for it. Don’t deny yourself a slice of happiness you so deserve”.
Morton sighed and tapped Angela’s hand. “Maybe you’re right”.
“You know I am, now come on, give me a big kiss and a cuddle.
“Take care Angela” he said, as he got up from the chair at the side of the bed.
“Oh, you might want to thank Linda Peterson, you know, Nurse Peterson? She’ll be the one wheeling you down to theatre later tonight”.
“I will, thank you again Mister Morton”.
“George, just for once call me George”.
“Thank you from the bottom of my heart George”.
At eleven fifteen, just as Tracy had instructed her, Angela leaned over and pulled the emergency cord. Immediately, lights began to flash on monitors, buzzers rang out, deafeningly loud.
It looked to Angela, as though the computers and machines themselves were hitting some kind of panic button, and were reacting frantically to the alarm. Coloured lights flashed and danced on screens on machines of which, Angela did not even know the identity.
The two guards outside the door jumped up in panic as Nurse Linda Peterson came speeding down the corridor.
The two officers opened the door. Angela was looking like she could hardly breathe. “There now” said Peterson, “just try and relax, come on now, just relax, you’re going to be fine”.
Nurse Peterson had placed an oxygen mask over Angela’s mouth. She had also connected, what looked like a drip to her arm for the sake of the two officers in charge of her security. She made one of the officers push the drip trolley along beside Angela’s.
Nurse Peterson continued, “Come on now, just relax, take deep breaths, you’ll be fine”. The swing doors of the operating theatre burst open. George Morton stood in his full medical attire, complete with gloves and mask beside him stood a certain `Nurse Phorbes.

"Ok gentlemen, thank you for your assistance but I'm afraid you'll have to leave us now". They were the same two men who Morton had donate their blood. They were pleased to hear George Morton's statement, and did not have to be told twice to leave the theatre. They were also relieved that the surgeon, for once, had spoken to them in a civilised manner.

Wasting no time, Angela and Tracy gave George and Linda one final kiss and hug.

Tracy put an envelope into Nurse Peterson's hand.

"Here" Tracy said to the nurse, "buy yourself something nice". "Goodbye Linda and thank you".

Angela and Tracy slipped out of the emergency entrance door, and out into the night.

Linda had placed a student's practice dummy on the operating trolley where Angela should have been.

Morton and Peterson sat now drinking coffee.

After a few minutes, Nurse Peterson said to the surgeon, "Now then surgeon Morton, our turn to escape".

"Yes, see to it Linda".

Nurse Peterson stepped out into the corridor, feigning to wipe sweat from her brow.

The two guards looked at her as she lifted the mask from her mouth, and over her head.

"Are you alright Miss" said one of the officers.

"I'm not sure, I feel a bit dizzy, do you think you could walk me down to the canteen, I think I need sweet tea and a biscuit".

"Certainly nurse, how's the girl? Is she going to be alright"?

"Mister Morton has just finished the operation; he's gone outside for some fresh air. I'm afraid it's hard to tell if the girl will be OK, she's suffering from pneumonia, as well as her blood disorder, she'll be out for at least another three hours, you may as well have some tea with me".

SERVICE STATION. M.6.

If you were to ask any of your friends, or anyone at all for that matter, what their idea of their worst nightmare would be, we would, no doubt, be given some gruesome examples. So often we use the expression to make the listener a little more interested in what we're telling them. "Oh it was my worst nightmare". There are instances however, where nightmares become reality, living nightmares, which suddenly arrive without warning, and give no indication whatsoever, if they will ever depart. Such a nightmare was about to befall a certain young lady, travelling up from London with her boyfriend. She had been driving all the way up here, and had only fifteen minutes beforehand, swapped over to let her boyfriend drive the rest of the way up to the Lake District, and then to Morecambe to visit her parents.

"We're getting low on petrol" she informed her boyfriend, as she settled down on the passenger seat for a well-earned snooze. The Porsche Carrera GT guzzled petrol like a Camel guzzles water, the only difference being, the Camel would get nearly four hundred miles to its tank full.
What was strange about Gillian Payne's nightmare was that, it would not begin until she woke up, and she would never be certain if it would stop, unless death kindly intervened.

John Hillman pulled into the petrol station, having noticed his fuel light flashing. As he pulled in, there was one car in front of his, a Porsche Carrera.
"Fuck in Hell baby, look at this". The driver's door was open, and its owner was returning to it, placing a credit card back into his wallet. He acted on impulse. He got out of his car, and just as the man was getting back into the sports, Hillman said. "Excuse me sir, excuse me".
The young man looked behind him to Hillman. "Yes what is it"?
"Somebody's, do you know that your tail light is broken, the police will pull you up if they see it".
"What"? The young man said, frustratingly as he got out of the car to look.
Hillman glanced behind, nothing, no witnesses. "Here look".
The young man bent down to look, just as Hillman put the gun to the back of his head, and pulled the trigger.

The man's face sprayed over the forecourt. "There, do you see it"? Hillman took the man's jacket and draped it over the driver's seat. "Oh my sweet Jesus" he said, noticing for the first time, the beautiful blonde girl asleep on the passenger seat, "I take it all back Lord, oh my sweet fuck, I take it all back, help me Jesus", Hillman pulled away from the forecourt and turned back onto the road from which he had just came.
The girl in the petrol shop was pre-occupied with a bunch of unruly youths who were standing around the shop looking like they were about to steal something. She had already pressed the crisis button underneath the counter, so she knew the police were on their way
Hillman was in his glory. All of his life he had secretly wanted to own a sports car, and now, here he was, driving a Porsche Carrera GT, with a tramp beside him who looked like a model. Gillian Payne had done herself no favours in the eyes of Hillman, dressed in a very short skirt and a tight top which showed off her ample cleavage. Around her neck she wore a gold chain with the word S.E.X. boldly exposed. The girl and her boyfriend had been playing a game of dare with a pack of cards back at their hotel. Gillian had lost the game and so her boyfriend had dared her to dress this way all the way up to the Lake District.

As Hillman headed out onto the motorway, he kept glancing at her tanned legs. He noticed the girl's hand bag lying at her feet. He picked it up and opened it, keeping a careful eye on the road. A credit card was taken out, "Ah Gillian, Gillian Payne, ooh Kensington, she's a golden goose my Lord, she's minted, I'll bet lover boy back there was minted too, these kind Lord, the kind who are born into money, they're the mean bastards, oh, they'll spend money on themselves, certainly, but they'll part with fuck all for anyone else Lord, that's why, they tend to go out with their own kind, the ones who have money, that's so they can keep theirs, see? Tight bastards, well, I can tell you this my sweet Jesus, she won't be tight tonight when I'm finished with her. She has got one beautiful fuck frame has she not Lord"?

"The Lord giveth, and the Lord taketh away. Sure enough today Lord God, you have obviously decided that it is John Hillman's day, and I thank you!" Even the nagging pain in the back of Hillman's head had been forgotten about, now that his god had provided him with such an opportunity.

HARRINGTON POLICE STATION.
SHEFFIELD.

The front double doors of the police station burst open, and in strode Terrence Davis, followed by Richard Knight the Metropolitan Police Commissioner., and a Scottish D.C.I. named Terry Hanley. The three men walked past the unmanned reception desk, through the fire doors, which still badly needed their hinges oiled, and down the corridor towards Deborah Knowles's office. It was empty. Only a giant map of Yorkshire lay open on her desk. There had been red circles marked upon various locations as Davis glanced at it momentarily. "Oh well, at least they're out doing something worthwhile. They may even be out there looking for Hillman gentlemen. Who knows"? said Davis sarcastically.

The three men walked out of the office as Davis said, "We'll get some coffee gentlemen, and then I'll fill you in with the course of events so far Terry".

To his complete horror, as Davis opened the canteen door, over in the far corner sat John Drummond, Deborah Knowles and Karen Jones. The three men stood watching for a few moments. Davis, with his arms folded stood and listened to the three D.C.I's taking bets with each other as to how many men Ashley Barnes would sleep with whilst down in London.

Eventually, John Drummond, who was facing the direction of the men, looked up and saw them, tapping Knowles on the arm, who looked round.

"Ah, Mister Davis" she began "there has been another shooting, just outside the city. Two men have been fatally wounded. There was a young woman who has survived the ordeal, they're bringing her in, and that's why we're waiting here. We were-"

."Shut up Knowles" barked Knight. "Shut up and listen, the lot of you. I have a good mind to strike you all off the police force altogether, you are either lazy, or you are incompetent, that's your choice, now what are you? This here is D.C.I. Terrence Hanley, he is from the Strathclyde Police Department, and he, and he alone will be in charge of the Hillman case. If any of you have any problems with that fact, then there's the door.

You will answer to him, and you will do exactly as he says, when he says it, got that? If I hear of any rebellion whatsoever from any of you, then you'll be out on your arses for good. Up and down this country, we have police officers whose work rate would put any one of you to shame. There are people dying at the hands of a lunatic, and you three senior officers, who are, by the way, supposed to lead by example, are taking bets on the sex life of a pathologist. Well, I'll tell you this much, however many men she sleeps with during the course of her holiday, it has nothing at all to do with you. When she's here, when she's at her place of work, she is bloody good at her job, which is more than can be said for you lot, so don't sit there and mock her.
You'd all better get your thinking caps on, that's all I can say, because as far as I can see, we have cadets in training who would put you all to shame. All I can see progressing in this case, is the number of victims, so you'd better get your shit together and get some progress made here, because everyone is fast losing patience with your bloody excuses. As from today, Inspector Hanley is in charge, as far as Ashley Barnes is concerned, I'm sure she would very much appreciate it, if you could take some of the work load off of her shoulders. The bodies are stacking up over there, because you lot are not doing your jobs. If this keeps up we'll need a bloody osteoarchaeologist, not a pathologist. Well, here's the news people you're all going to start working, and conducting your behaviour like senior police officers, or else you're all out that door".
"Sir" said Drummond. "We are all doing everything we can".
"Are you? Are you really doing everything you can? Taking bets at a table. All you can? Let me tell you something Drummond, Mister Hanley here, will soon show you the meaning of the words, all you can, and I'll tell you this much, if he gets as close to Hillman as you were, I'll bet you any money on this, I'll bet Hillman won't throw *his* car keys away, from right under his nose, I'll take a bet on that. Now, get your arses up from there and go to Knowles's office, get what you need, and wait there for Mister Hanley to come and get you, and don't make any plans for this evening, because you've all got a lot of catching up to do, now move"!

M6. SERVICE STATION.

The police van pulled up directly in front of the petrol station / shop. P.C's John Pullman and Sandra Lamberton slid quickly out of their vehicle, and into the store. They approached the young lady at the till. "What's the problem" said Pullman, pulling out his stun gun. The girl pointed to the back of the shop, where three young boys and two girls stood, looking at the selection of DVDs.
"Right!" Said Pullman, as he and his colleague headed to the back of the store. The police officers approached the youths as Pullman said, "Ok people two questions, one, have any of you stolen anything? And two, what are you all doing out at this time of the night anyway? It's well past your curfew time". A curfew had been put into place demanding that all teenagers under the age of eighteen, should be off the streets after nine p.m.
One of the youths looked down to his feet smirking, and said "We're not *out*, we're *in* here".
The boy, about the age of fifteen, didn't even see Pullman's fist coming, as he was hit with the same force than if the policeman had been fighting a man. The boy went sailing back about ten feet, before landing on his back, unconscious, against a large fridge.
"Now then, young scum, empty your pockets".
"No" replied one of the other boys. "You can't make us, we haven't done anything wrong, and you're in trouble when we tell his dad, he'll kill you".
Pullman aimed the stunner at the young boy, and gave him a blast
of electricity. "There now big mouth", he said to the youth, now lying on the floor, "That has shut your big mouth up. Now the rest of you, empty your pockets, in fact, just take your clothes off, `till we see what's been going on here, come on".
"You as well" said officer Lamberton to the girls.
"No way" one of them replied to her.
"As you wish" said Lamberton, taking out *her* stun gun, and aiming it directly at one of the girls.
"Look, the easy way, or the hard way, we don't mind, either way though, it's going to happen, it's up to you".
Five minutes later, the two girls and two of the boys all stood in their underwear. Sandra Lamberton began searching the clothes of the youths, garment by garment.

“Who does this belong to?” She said, holding up a hooded jacket
“What have you got Sandra”?
“A torch and three C.Ds”.
“Ok, let’s go people, into the van, just carry your rags, come on, the lot of you. Don’t worry, I’ll bring that piece of unconscious shit out in a minute, let’s move, and faster than that ladies, come on, or I’ll zap your fannies, now move”.
Another five minutes and all the youths were in the back of the police van, including the unconscious youth.
“Right Sandra darling, let’s get this lot over to the youth prison, and locked up for the night, that’ll just about see us to the end of our shift”.
As Pullman closed the driver’s door, a man came round the side of the van, and tapped on the window.
“Yes sir” said Pullman, smiling, and what can we do for you”?
The man looked flustered.
“Is there eh. I’m sorry, is there an ambulance coming for that gentleman, only, people are queuing for petrol, and they can’t get in”.
“Gentleman”? Said Pullman, “where”?
“Over here sir by the petrol pumps”.
“Fuck in Hell Sandra, I knew it, I just fucking knew it, too good to be true, to get a quiet shift in. That’s my anniversary dinner down the fucking drain. Bastard! And I’ll be the bad one. Fucking Hell, twat!!” And I fucking promised her as well, aw shit!”
“He’s over here sir, lying by the pumps”.
“Yes, I know my way to the petrol pumps thank you, now get back into your car, before I give you a kick in the balls for spoiling my day, and anyway, how the fuck is an ambulance going to get in there, with all you silly twats blocking the way, tell them all to get to fuck out of here, and make space for this poor fucker to be taken away, come on!! Move your fucking arses, three years on the trot Sandra, she’ll go fucking mental, the savage bitch!!”

Three hours and seventeen minutes later, the police van pulled away with John Pullman, Sandra Lamberton, and five youths who were all sleeping in the back of the van. All except one, who was still unconscious, and had in fact, slipped into a comma. When Pullman reached the youth prison, he would discover the boy’s condition, and would be held up for another two hours, explaining in detail all the reasons why the lad had lapsed into this condition.

THE M.1.

Hillman had stopped at a roadside cafe, and purchased cheese burgers and cola on Gillian Payne's credit card.
When the girl in the shop looked at him strangely, Hillman said, "It's ok dear, there she is in the car she's sleeping, look".
The girl had glanced out of the shop window and saw the young lady sleeping.
She allowed the transaction and gave him a receipt.
"Thank you my darling" said Hillman, as he left the shop and got into the sports car outside.
The young lady who had served him thought to herself, "You're nothing but a fucking whore, so you are. Imagine going out with that old hairy bastard just to be seen in his fancy sports car. I'd rather go around in Colin's Metro any day than stoop to that level, fucking cow".

Just outside of Rugby, Hillman pulled in to a pathway, which wound up through a small forest. He drove slowly up the cinder path, until he came to the top of the hill. Just up ahead of him, was an old warehouse which had long since been abandoned. Beside the warehouse was a large house, also derelict. He turned the car around, so that it was facing the way he'd came in and switched off the engine.
Gillian Payne began to move, and slowly came round from her slumber.
She opened her eyes, blinking rapidly, stretching her long legs, and parting her arms wide, clenching her fists. She yawned and said "Are we there yet darling"?
"Depends what you mean by there" said Hillman, who had switched off the inside car light.
"Here, I got you a burger and a coke".
Again Gillian yawned and said "Thanks".
She sat upright and turned to take her burger.
Fear shot through her body, like an electric shock.
Immediately, her throat went tinder dry.
"Where's? Who are you? Where's Trevor. What have you done to, where is he"?
Having been jolted into full consciousness her mind began to take in the precarious situation she was now in. She'd read stories about young women who'd been abducted, and the horrors they'd endured. She felt even more vulnerable being dressed the way she was.

"Well I like that, you little trollop that you are, I go out of my way to get you something to eat, and the first thing you say is, where's Trevor? Fuck you Madam muck, now just eat your burger and drink your coke, and don't even speak to me, and pull that skirt up to where it was, or I'll fucking shoot you". He lifted the gun and pointed it at her. "Now, if you do as you're told, you'll be back with Trevor in the morning. If you don't, I'll hang you by the hair from one of those trees, now shut up and eat.
Gillian's nightmare had commenced, and it didn't look like it was going to end in the foreseeable future. She began to cry, as she imagined poor Trevor, lying shot to ribbons in a ditch somewhere.
"Look, it's no good crying like that because it's cold. If you'd eaten it when I gave it to you, instead of fucking moaning about where Trevor is, just let me make one thing clear to you, tonight, and maybe tomorrow, we are going to have lots of sex, now don't start sniffling again. After I've had my fun with you, and you with me, of course, and if you haven't been a sniffling bitch all the time, I'll take you back to Trevor, who I have locked up, nice and safe where no-one will find him. Now, depending upon how enthusiastically you give me your body, will determine whether or not I let him live, or die, understand"?
The petrified young woman nodded. She didn't know what else to do.
"Wouldn't you like to know who I am, before we have sex, or are you in the habit of taking em down for any guy who buys you a burger. My name, you lucky little nymph' is none other than Doctor John Hillman". The girl burst out crying again, with her face in her hands. "You're beginning to be pathetic lady, do you know that? You are in this situation now; you are not getting out of it. Now why don't you focus your mind on how you can save this Trevor of yours, and serving me some sensational sex? Here, you can start by sucking this, while I'm eating my burgers, come on, you're not really wanting your burger are you. Let's see if you're as good as your attire would suggest. Tell you what, you hook that necklace of yours around my penis, and start sucking, not too fast, I've still got to ram your pussy and your bum before I cum into your mouth, I do think of the women too you know, I like to give the ladies their fun as well. Now here" he said, "Blow your nose". He handed her a tissue. "Make sure your nose is not blocked. If you do as I tell you, then I promise I'll take you back to your, what's his name again, so just remember, you're performing for him. His life is hanging in the enthusiasm of your performance, now are you ready to suck me Gillian"?

Still sobbing, the young girl nodded.
"Are you sure"?
Again she nodded.
"Oh I don't know, I really don't, I'm not convinced. You don't look very enthusiastic to me Gillian".
"Doctor Hillman"?
"Yes Gillian"?
" I'm begging you please, I won't say anything". The petrified girl stammered, shaking constantly.
"Oh now come on my darling, you do your thing".
The young woman continued to cry.
Nothing could have prepared Gillian Payne for the ordeal she was about to experience.
She loved reading suspense and horror novels, but this was by far and a way, worse than anything she'd read…or could even imagine.

"Look" said Hillman, softly "this is getting nowhere, you can't possibly perform to the best of your ability with all this sniffling going on. Would you like a few minutes to let your mind grasp the situation? I know it's a shock to your system, but you really must understand what the situation is here Gillian. This is going to happen my little sex kitten, not because I particularly picked you out, no, it's just, well, you happened to be all dressed up for sex when I em, borrowed this vehicle from your boyfriend. You will agree with me won't you? That you are dressed for sex"?
The girl sniffed and rubbed her eyes with a Kleenex, and said, "I wasn't aware of-"
"Hold it! Just fucking hold it there madam. Would you repeat that please, you weren't aware, you were going to say, that you were dressed for sex, wasn't that what you were going to say"?
Again, she sniffed "honestly, I, I was doing it for my boyfriend, I-"
"Hey! Nobody said, did I say you were doing wrong? Did I? No, let me explain something to you Gillian, get out of the car, come on, I'm not going to hurt you, I'm going to show you something".
"Oh my god" she said to herself, "what's he planning to do to me. What on earth has he done to Trevor? How on earth hadn't she woken up when this lunatic had taken the car".
Gillian Payne got out of the car and stood with her hands by her sides, looking like an awkward schoolgirl awaiting and dreading the punishment that would be inflicted.

Her legs, felt like they were going to give way any minute. Hillman tucked his penis away. He got out of the car and came and stood in front of the girl, about two meters off her. He shook his head and tutted five times, "don't you tell me Miss that you were unaware of what you dress like. You dress like a whore, and no mistake. For a start, look at your make-up, it's plastered onto your face like a whore, even though anyone can see that you are beautiful, and that you don't need that muck on you. No, you put that on to enhance your already good looks, making your eyes look provocative, yes. Secondly, you wear that sex necklace to advertise to men, and perhaps women, who knows? that you are a wild bitch, and proud of it. Do you know what that says to a man, that word? It says that, no matter who you are, you have the right to come and chat me up, even if I'm with my boyfriend, because the chances are, you'll stand a good chance of getting it together with me, if not tonight, then some time in the future.
That's what that says".

Gillian's nightmare had slipped into overdrive.

“Tracy, I don’t know what to say darling, you’re an absolute angel”

Tracy smiled. “It was all down to that doctor guy, you know George Morton? Not a bad guy that Angela”.
“I know” said Angela, looking at her face in her compact mirror. “He’s sweet.
“Ow” Angela said, as she gingerly touched her cheek bone.
“They beat you up bad Angela, didn’t they”?
“Yeah, not as bad as poor Carla though, and I dread to think what they done to the Irishman, he just disappeared.
They were ready to use me as well Angela, I’m just glad that Sharon was sharp enough to know that something was wrong. I’ll get that Knowles though Angela, I’ll get her for what she done to you and Carla”.
“No no Tracy, Knowles and Jones are mine, the trouble is, she knows who I am, and now that I’m not in that hospital, she’s got a slight dilemma. Does she tell everyone that I’m still alive, and have everyone in the country looking for me, or does she keep it to herself, and take a chance on finding me herself, therefore taking all the glory for herself, tough decision”?
“Once your arm’s healed Angela, we’re going back down, right”?
“Not you Tracy, this is my war, it’s too dangerous, and besides, you have two little girls up here, who need their mum, don’t you forget Tracy, what that was like when those Hillman bastards took them away from you? Now you’ve got them back, and you don’t want to be parted from them again, do you?
You wouldn’t want those little angels subjected to anything like that again Tracy would you. They need you Tracy, they need the security of their mum, and you need them, hell I saw the state of you when they were away from you”. “I suppose” said Tracy. “You’re talking sense Angela, but I will never feel safe, I’ll never be able to relax with them for as long as their father is running about out there, killing. He’ll be looking for me as well Angela, but the girls are safe up there in Carlisle with Sharon”. Tracy and Sharon had arranged for Tracy’s girls to go and stay with Sharon’s aunt, up in Carlisle, which was handy on two counts. One, it kept the children out of harm’s way, and two, Sharon’s aunt just happened to be a retired primary school teacher.

After a few moments Tracy said, “Angela? I would rather be the hunter than the hunted”.
“Just shortly Tracy that will not be a problem, the police will get lucky one of these days darling, and then your troubles will be over”.

“Do you know something Angela? You fucking prick!!” Tracy shouted as a car pulled out in front of them to overtake. “I don’t think they will Angela. Every time they get anywhere near him, he always gets away, always. I’ll say one thing for the sick bastard Angela, he gets more attention and respect from me now, than I ever gave him when we were living together”.

“Is it any wonder Tracy? He wouldn’t have slit your throat when he lived with you, not like he would now”.

HARRINGTON POLICE STATION.
SHEFFIELD.

Terry Hanley sat with Sandra Crawley, the rape crisis therapist, talking to Sandra Kerr. The young woman had been in the police station now, for nearly an hour.

"More tea Sandra" said Hanley, picking up his empty cup along with Susan's and Sandra's.

"Yes please" the girl replied.

Susan looked into Sandra's eyes and took the girl's right hand into both of hers.

"Sandra, you're a lucky girl you know. I know how stupid that sounds at a time like this, but I'm referring as to how Hillman usually leaves his victims. I know you've had a pretty horrendous experience, and we really appreciate your cooperation, so soon after the attack".

Sandra looked down again, and began to cry, shaking with the severity of her sobs. Susan, once again took the girl by the hand, trying to reassure her that everything would be alright.

"There now, there now, I know, I know it must have been horrible, but soon you'll be strong again, I promise. Now then, when D.C.I. Hanley gets back, he's going to ask you a few short questions, not many, I'll see to that, but the more accurate and clear your answers are, the quicker we'll find this madman, who is such a dangerous nightmare to all women. You, my little angel, can help us put a stop to this maniac's reign of terror; do you think you could do that for us"?

"Yes, as long as he doesn't keep asking me the same questions over and over again".

"He won't, I promise, D.C.I Hanley is a good man Sandra, he wants to help you as much as possible".

Ten minutes later, Hanley began his questioning.

The first and most important question Hanley thought, was appearance.

"What did he look like Sandra, his physical appearance"?

"He em. He had scruffy curly hair, and a beard and moustache. His hair was curly I think because it needed washed and brushed".

"Ok" said Hanley, what was he wearing? Can you remember?

"Oh, he had a pale blue dress shirt, like the sort you would wear a tie with, a dress shirt".

"But he didn't wear a tie"?

"No sir, and he had the shirt sleeves rolled up to his elbows".

"Fine" Said Hanley, "What else"?
"He wore jeans, dark blue ones, and desert boots, sandy coloured desert boots".
"Did he have any marks on his face, any cuts, and bruises? Any indication of struggles he may have had previously to today"?
"No sir, none that I noticed".
"That's fine Sandra, thank you, you've been a great help, oh, what was his behaviour like, I mean how did he approach your friends"?
Sandra put her head down and said, "Well sir, John and Joe kind of started it. This Hillman man was already parked in the lay-by. He was eating pies or something when we pulled up. Joe started poking fun at him, making monkey signs at him, and-"
"What was his reaction to that Sandra"?
"Nothing. He just kept eating his pies, and smiling at me".
"Smiling at you, specifically at you"?
"Yes".
Hanley wrote something down.
"I see, carry on".
Sandra told Hanley the whole story, right up to where Hillman had left her naked in the woods, and wished her a merry Christmas.

Hanley stood up from his chair and walked over to the window. "I think what saved you Sandra, was, not just a brainwave, this thought, this idea, was so powerful and exciting to him, that he had to carry it out immediately, down tools and get on with it, this was his eureka, he said something like that to you didn't he"?
"He said he'd hit the jackpot or words to that effect".
"I think he thinks he's found the perfect hiding place. But where? Thank you Sandra, I think Susan's taking you to see the nurse".
"Yes" Said Susan, "We'll just take our tea along with us Sandra".

Hanley turned from the window. "Thank you once again Sandra, you've been very brave". He turned and looked once more out onto the colourless car park. Grey mist was now descending over the whole area, like a blanket of bad news covering up any hope that may have been built up. "Bloody hell, it must have been some thought he had to stop him in his tracks. Somewhere he could go, completely undetected, impossible. Unless, unless he knew someone who would protect him, even after all that he's done?

Surely there would be no-one foolish enough to do a thing like that. They would have needed to have known him for years to do something like that".
The mist was fast turning into fog. Hanley half expected Hillman to appear out from it, wave at him, and then disappear again back into it, which, in effect, was exactly what he was doing. Appearing, and killing, and then disappearing again.
"Ah, but Mister Hillman" thought Hanley to himself, "one of these times, you're going to appear, and I'm going to be waiting for you, and then I'll disappear back into the mist with you, and bring you back out, dead".
The door burst open. John Drummond came striding in with purpose.
"Ah, Mister Hanley, just the man, now that those two pricks are away, maybe I can fill you in with events regarding Doctor Hillman".
Hanley turned to look at Drummond.
"Mister Drummond isn't it"?
"Yes".
"Well, I think I can safely say that I'm well and truly filled in, as you put it regarding Doctor Hillman. As far as I can see, the man has been allowed to roam free, killing at will, whilst you and your colleagues play gambling games in the canteen. Now, if this is an attempt to put me in my place, let me assure you, if you had any doubts about who is in charge here, then be my guest to phone up Mister Davis or Mister Knight. You've had your chance Drummond, now you do as I say, ok"?

Hillman lit up his cigarette, offering one to Gillian. “No thank you” she replied, in an almost child-like voice, a child who had just been scorned. “Bloody hell woman, it was only sex, what’s wrong with you, it’s not as if I’ve taken your virginity now is it, and may I say whilst we’re on the subject, that *that* little play thing between your legs has received many visitors, has it not? But you just want the cocks with the big wallets don’t you, keep *your* money safe. Look, look at your fingers”. Hillman pointed to her diamond ring. “How much did that cost”?
“I don’t know. Trevor bought me it”.
“Bullshit!! I know he bought you it, but bitches like you go and make inquiries as to how much it cost, just in case he’s a cheap skate, in case you’ve gave him your pussy at an undercut price, now how much did it cost”?
“I don’t know I’ve told you”.
“Liar!, that’s what you are, I just saw your face when my cock was deep inside you, but you would tell your friends that you fought me all the way, you fucking slut that you are.
Oh I was unaware of how I was dressed, .Fuck, you’ve got a necklace on that reads *SEX.* A top which is practically see through, and no bra’ underneath, a skirt that’s shorter than a wash-cloth and you tell me that you’re unaware of what messages you’re sending out. No more bullshit, little Miss nothing, or *you* might not see the light of day, never mind Trevor, do you hear me”?
“Yes” Gillian said softly, sensing the danger she was in.
“Right, ok, don’t get me upset now, because I don’t want *her* to come. If *she* comes then you will die, so you best keep me sweet, alright”?
“Who” said Gillian, with perhaps a glimmer of hope, who’s *she*”?
Hillman drew on his cigarette. “You don’t want to know, and anyway, stop talking about her, *she* could come at any time, and I won’t be responsible for my actions, now, shut to fuck up, and smoke a fag, because we’re going again in a few minutes. This time, up your bum, we’ll see if it’s a bit tighter than that greedy pussy of yours, now here, smoke”.
There was silence in the car for a couple of minutes, while they both sat and smoked, their minds both filled with thoughts. Very different ones.

As they smoked, Hillman looked over to the trees. Something caught his eye. Long straight beams of light began to stagger and dance through the branches. It reminded him of the torches in the grounds of Morningside. Hillman grabbed his gun and opened it. There were five bullets in the chamber. He opened the gun and placed another bullet inside. He had lifted Trevor's jacket in the petrol station, but had left his own in the other car.

"Shit!" he said out loud.
"What *is* that" said Gillian.
"Come on, quick; let's get over to those trees, hurry!"
"What is it"? Repeated Gillian, running over to the trees with Hillman, and not really understanding why.
"You think I'm bad missy? There's a bunch of bikers coming up here, and it's my guess they're going to have some kind of party in that warehouse. Now you tell me now, do you want me to fuck you, or do you want them to, the choice is yours".
"Yes, I mean, no, you! You!"
"You're sure"?
"Yes, yes I'm sure". She could hardly believe her ears, what she had just said.

"Right, we'll play it by ear, let's see how many there are first before we do anything".
Hillman had Trevor's jacket on, Gillian had her own dress jacket on, but it was extremely flimsy, and it was a bitterly cold night. They couldn't stay hidden in here for long. Soon, they heard the roar of the bikes getting louder and louder, their lights now dancing across the derelict buildings, bouncing off the windows, and, of course, bouncing off the Porsche Carrera. Two bikes went by, then another two, then three. "Oh shit" said Hillman, "how fucking many more Lord".
Two of the bikers had passengers.
"That's their bitches, they've brought them here to gang-bang them. Oh fuck Lord, give us some help here".
Gillian looked at Hillman, bemused, because it seemed to her, that Hillman had spoken to Jesus, as if He were actually here in the woods hiding with them.
Eventually, all the engines were switched off. Only the voices of the bikers could be heard now, and the voice of one of the girls, who was obviously drunk.

The leader of the bikers wolf-whistled at the Porsche. ."Wow, take a look at this baby, boys, somebody's came up here with their chick to fuck her, I'll guess, now all we have to do, is find them!"
Altogether, there were seven bikers gathered in the disused car park, plus the two young women.
The leader spoke again, calling up to the warehouse and the house. "Nigel? Nigel, come on out man and let us see your little girlfriend, come on and have a drink with us, we won't harm you, we just want a shot of your nice Nigel's-been-a-good-boy car, that mummy and daddy's bought you!"
When no reply came, the biker said, "Where's the gun"?
One of the other bikers said, "Chad's got it, it's in his top-box".
Another biker said to the leader, "What are you going to do Ray"?
"What am I going to do? I'm going to have a fuck in this Porsche Carrera and shag Nigel's bird in it, that's what I 'm going to do.
It's not every day you get a chance to ride in something as fancy as this boys. That's these fancy fucking mummy's boys for you. I bet if we find Nigel, that there won't be a trace of a blister on his little smooth-as-a-baby's-bottom little fingers".
Hillman breathed a sigh of relief. "Phew, they've only got one gun, thank fuck, but it's only a matter of time before they come searching for Nigel, and his bitch. They'll come in here, but don't worry I'll be watching where their gun is at all times. You ever seen a gang bang Gillian? Well, you're going to see one tonight, you are about to see how a real slut performs".
The bikers all split up, telling their two female friends to get everything ready inside.
"Right boys let's go" said the leader.
Hillman and Gillian watched from the woods, as two men went round the back of the warehouse. Two men went in to the front of the warehouse and three went into the house. From where Hillman and Gillian stood, they could see torch lights dancing around the walls of the buildings, and they could hear voices, mocking voices, calling out for Nigel and his chick to come out from their hiding place. Outside they could hear the voices of the two girls, as they unloaded alcohol from the top-boxes of the motorcycles.
"Are you excited Carol"?
"Fuck yeah I've wanted this to happen for a long time, fuck, my husband never gives me enough attention babes, and anyway, it's hardly worth the trouble when he does".

After fifteen minutes or so, all the bikers were congregated outside of the warehouse. "Nothing, can't find them anywhere Ray".
"Ok then" said the leader. "They must be hiding in the woods; they can't stay in there all night. Toby, you keep guard out here with Henry, get the gun. If they make any attempt to come out here and escape in the car, stop them, shoot the bastard if you have to. Carol, bring the boys some beer out, after half an hour, we'll change guard".
Hillman whispered to Gillian. "Do you see what I mean? You see, you are dressed like you have an appetite for cock like that slut there, point taken"?
"Yes" said Gillian, deciding that this was not the time to upset Hillman.
He carried on "You see? She's dressed in trainers and jeans, and
you're dressed like-"
"I take your meaning, ok"?
He looked across the car park, studying the position of the men.
"Now don't panic when I make my move, I'll wait until they've had a couple of drinks and joints, I'll wait until their party's going full swing. Are you not tempted Gillian, you know? To get hammered like that girl is going to be"?
"I'm freezing, and anyway, I've already explained to you, I'm only dressed like this because my boyfriend"-
"Don't worry, not for long by the looks of it, they've got a nice fire going in there, fucking candles and everything, how romantic" Hillman was just not interested in hearing her explanation.
When I tell you to, I want you to calmly walk over to your car, like you're a bit drunk, stagger a little, jangle those keys. They'll come over. Don't worry, they won't attack you, you're too delicious looking, they'll only have one thing on their minds. Ask them to help you into your car. I will then pounce and kill one of them with the gun. If you fuck this up Gillian, then we both die, do you understand that"?
"Yes".
"Ok then, because it's your only chance of seeing Trevor again, remember, I have him tied up, so he can't eat or do the toilet or anything, so, timing is of the utmost importance".
"Ok, I'll do it".
"Ok then, don't be frightened, this gun does not make a noise, but it does make a mess, let's do it, go".
Gillian walked out from the bushes onto the gravel. She made a gesture to the two men, by waving at them, then continued across the car park to the Porsche.

The two men, upon seeing her, moved like two greyhounds from a trap.
"Hey, wow there honey, you've had a little drink then"?
This would be the one and only chance she would get to escape the madman, but Hillman had filled her with so much fear of the bikers that she found herself following Hillman's instructions. Had she been thinking straight, she would have realized that the bikers would have saved her life. She was still numb from being raped, and filled with fear of what Hillman would do if she tried anything stupid.
Here goes, Gillian thought to herself, "Zummbuddie's spiked my drinkz, and they've been and raped me the bastardzz, honestly, that's the truth and they even have".
"They've raped you? Well now, you come with us, you're frozen, you poor little thing you, we'll warm you up, where's the keys? Is this your car? Where's the keys angel"?
"They're here!"
The two men turned around. The first shot cracked right through the man's chin, and up through his brain, right out through the top of his head. It was so sudden; he stood there for a full three seconds, before the corpse crumpled to the ground, first onto his knees, and then falling face first onto the gravel. The biker named Henry, looked at the shotgun which had fallen from his friend's hands.
"It's up to you buster, do you think you're faster than Nigel?
Pick up the shotgun Gillian, and bring it to me".
The man raised his hands above his head.
"That's more like it Henry, now, let's all go inside and join the party, shall we? It's far too cold to be standing out here. Let's see how Carol is enjoying her gang-bang shall we.
Well done Gillian" said Hillman, as he took the gun from her.
Without realizing, Gillian had just given up the one and only chance she would get to execute the animal holding her hostage.
They walked in the door, Henry first, down a corridor.
"They're in here" said the biker, quietly.
"Ok you first Harry boy and no silly stuff". He opened a door which led into a rather large room which had once been someone's office, or maybe a conference room. One of the girls was kissing one of the bikers, whist the other girl was laughing and teasing the other bikers.
Gillian was unsure of what Hillman had in mind, he seemed to her to be confused, like he was trying to decide what he was going to do…like he was waiting for instructions from some-one.

"Total sluts Lord see? Do you see Gillian this is a proper slut, none of your pretentiousness here, my little kitten. Enjoying yourselves boys? Please, don't stop on our account, goodness me no". Hillman walked over to where three of the bikers were. "Having a good time Carol? Huh? This will do your reputation no end of good you silly girl you. Lowering yourself to this bunch of shit indeed, your parents must be very proud of you, with your achievements thus far in life". Holding the shotgun with one hand, Hillman looked down to the girl who was now trying to sort out her clothing. "I can plainly see who the hostess of the party is, but who is the host, where is *he*"?

A man stood up from the couch he had been sitting upon with Carol.
"*You*"! Said Hillman
"Yes me, who the fuck are *you*"?
"Oh, it's like that is it"? Said Hillman, he pulled the trigger of the shotgun and hit the man right in the middle of his stomach. "There now, you just die in your own time buddy. Now the rest of you, get yourselves gathered round this sofa here, get yourselves straightened out, there'll be no gang bang tonight ladies and gentlemen".
The five remaining men all sat on the sofa as instructed. Carol was now crying, realizing the danger they were all in.
Hillman said to them, "Now, I'm not going to kill anyone else unless they get silly, oh I know he's not dead yet, but that's only a matter of time".
The biker lay pinned against the wall, trying his best to stem the blood loss from his wounds. He managed to say, "Why"?

"Why?" Repeated Hillman, "I'll tell you why, while me and my girlfriend here were hiding from you nasty people, I heard you say you were going to ride my chick, and then ride my car, now that's not very nice, is it? That's why I've killed you, but you may go to your maker in the knowledge that it was none other than Doctor John Hillman who sent you to your rest".
Noticing for the first time the wedding ring upon Carol's finger, Hillman was further enraged at the thought of this young woman's adultery Except for you Carol, the bullet's too good for you girl, I've got something really special lined up for you babes, well, at least from the point of view of your hard working husband I'll bet. Come on boys, get yourselves seated in an orderly fashion.

Carol was crying now, knowing that her life and the lives of her friends were now in the hands of the gods. It was anyone's guess what this lunatic would do to them. Two of the men lost control of their bladders, as Hillman instructed them to strip to their underwear.

CARLISLE. 2.30. Pm.

Tracy pulled up outside of Sharron's Aunt's house in Upperby. She looked at the piece of paper she had taken from the glove compartment. "This is it" she said to Angela, "Number twenty-seven". They both got out of the car, stretching their legs and then made their way up the steps to the door, which had a beautiful display of ivy hanging over it from top to bottom.

Angela said. "I won't stay long Tracy, I'll go and book into a hotel somewhere".

"Well let's just see" said Tracy, "there's no guarantee that Sharron's Aunt can put me up, I may have to join you in the hotel later".

Sharron Hartley opened the door. The three women kissed and embraced each other in the hallway of the house. Tears of relief from Sharon, to know that her friends were safe, especially Tracy.

"My Aunt Joyce has just gone to the shops with the kids; she'll be back in a couple of hours".

"I've got money here for her, for doing this for me, I'll talk with her when she gets back".

"You needn't have worried Tracy, about the girls losing out from being at school; they're as sharp as tacks, the two of them. Joyce has had all her books out from when she was a teacher, and she's been giving them separate lessons. She says they are just fine with their math's and English. She says that Angela is a remarkably neat writer for a girl of her age".

Joyce returned an hour and a half later with the girls. It took Tracy almost two hours to get the girls settled into their beds, after the excitement of the return of their mum. The youngest insisting that Tracy read them both a story. When Tracy finally returned down stairs, Angela, Sharron, and Joyce were all sitting around the dining room table, each drinking a glass of wine.

"Ah, here she is" said Sharon, we thought you'd fallen asleep with the girls".

"I nearly did" replied Tracy, yawning.

For the next three minutes, the three girls explained in detail to Sharon's Aunt Joyce, the whole situation.

Tracy tried to explain the situation in such a way so as not to panic the pensioner.

Angela spoke now. “I feel it only fair to tell you Joyce, so that you know just exactly what has happened and who we are”. The girls had introduced Angela as Angela Clark. There was no need to go into any greater detail than that, and the fact that she was Tracy’s cousin.

They sat talking into the night, making plans for the near future. The outcome was that Tracy and Angela would stay until Tracy had decided what she was doing, or until her lunatic ex-husband had been apprehended.

Joyce said, “It’s a shame for those two little girls up there, their daddy turning out like that”.

“I know” said Tracy, “but thank goodness I left him when I did, God knows what could have happened to me if I hadn’t got out when I did”.

“Never mind pet, you’re safe now” said the pensioner.

Hillman stood looking at the bikers and the two young women who accompanied them. "Listen Caroline, it wouldn't have made you feel any better if I'd let these fuck-heads have sex with you, don't sulk with me girl. You intended to let all these men use your body? Don't you know that Jesus has a plan for every single one of us? He doesn't want to see you flashing your body off to all these fucking losers, and letting them use your body. He has a plan for them as well, only I'm afraid I'm about to fuck it up. They have sinned once too often for my liking, and I'm afraid they've shit in their own nest as it were, still, I'm not trying to save them, I'm trying to save your soul young lady, I mean look at them, take a good look at them. They have it in their heads that they are Hell's Angels, fuck me, my poor old granny was more frightening than they'll ever be, and that's the truth".
Caroline stood crying and shaking with absolute fear.
The leader of the bikers lay in the corner of the room, he had slipped into deep unconsciousness, his life slowly slipping away from him.
"See this everyone". Hillman pointed to the semi-dead man on the floor. "This is your leader huh? This is who calls the shots, and tells you all what you're doing, huh! Fucking dog shit! Why don't you all wake up? Nobody is frightened any more of gangs of motor cyclists, living out your fantasies at the week-ends. I'll bet you've all got regular jobs, you haven't got a clue what it's like to be born to be wild. I'll bet you've all got E-Mail addresses, you sad fucks you!"
All the motor cyclists were now fully dressed again.
"Get over there the lot of you, against the fucking wall where I can see you, and pay attention when I'm talking to you, try and learn something in your sad pathetic lives, you bunch of cunt-fucks, come on Caroline hurry up and finish dressing, you can wash your fanny when we get to a service station, and wash some of that sin away from your filthy mind."
Hillman took out a cigarette and lit it up. His voice was calm and level again.
"For your own sakes people, find a different hobby, because people are just taking the piss, they really are. I mean, if you genuinely like riding motor cycles, then do that, but for fuck's sakes, you don't need to wear a leather jacket with the words "Satan's best friend" written on the back of it, I mean, who the fuck is going to take you seriously? Can you tell me that?"

“Now, I want all of you to bring over your motorbike keys, and give them to Gillian here. Gillian, you take all the keys from the key-rings. Strip them of all the fancy Devil’s fucking heads and witchcraft shit they’ve got attached to them for fuck sakes, and then throw them into that empty cardboard box there. You see? Doctor John Hillman is not as ruthless as those bastards on T.V. would have you believe. All I’m going to do is loosen a few wheel nuts and the likes, just to make sure that you can’t follow us immediately after we’ve left, and report us to the police”.

One by one, the bikers handed Gillian their keys, who reluctantly stripped them from all the fancy attachments.

He pointed once more to the wounded, and now, dead motorcyclist, “Huh, he was going to ride my chick? Does she look like a chick? Does she? Does Gillian look like a chick? Who uses those stupid phrases anyway? They belonged in the sixties, and even then they only sounded good coming from an American, not in fucking Rugby, or wherever the fuck it is you come from. My girl is not a chick, she’s a rich spoiled bitch from Kensington I’ll have you know, London. She chooses to dress like a full time whore. She’s not a fake though, she’s got money. You people are fakes. Stand over here Caroline, next to Gillian”.

“Oh please” whimpered Caroline.

“Please what”? Shouted Hillman, “you’re getting no cock from me until you’ve washed out that sinful mind of yours, now get over here and do as you’re told. Hurry it up with the keys guys, come on, don’t get me angry now, when you’re finished with the keys, then just start again with the mobile phones ok, same thing, in the box with batteries disconnected. Caroline, fetch me a can of beer over please, Hell’s Angels indeed. I can tell you this my friends, if the day comes when your earthly life is over, and in the day of judgment you are passed over to the other side, then you will meet a Hell’s Angel. Angels from Hell, and then you’ll know all about fear, believe me, you’ll know, huh, Satan’s best friend? I don’t fucking think so mister!”

Everyone present in the room, with the exception of John Hillman, was feeling sick with fear.

MERRYFIELD MILITARY HOSPITAL.

SHEFFIELD.

Deborah Knowles looked out of the window from the same room in which they had held Angela Phorbes. "This is bad Karen this is real bad, fuck. The shit is going to hit the fan now, that's for sure".
"It's not our fault Deborah" said Karen Jones, sipping a cup of coffee. "We can't be blamed for this" she continued. "You even asked Davis for more men".
"You don't get it, do you Karen. "It doesn't matter who's fault it is, or how she managed to get out, the fact remains, she *is* out, and now, it's just a matter of time before she comes hunting for us. It's like having another Hillman loose, except this one has all her faculties. Make sure Karen that all your locks are secure and working properly before you retire at nights. Have your gun with you at all times".
Hanley walked into the room, followed by Drummond.
"What is it with you people" he said, in his strong Scottish accent. "You catch your target and then you let them go again. I think you're giving them keys, you must be, either that, or all our prisoners are escapologists, there's no other answer".
"That's a bit unfair" Said Drummond.
"Is it? Well, according to my report, Hillman let himself out with a key, am I wrong"?
"That was not our fault" said Knowles.
"No, it never is your fault. Someone get me the security tapes for the hospital grounds. At least we might see what kind of car her accomplice was driving".
Drummond did not think before he said his next sentence.
"How do you know there was an accomplice"?
"Jesus fuck! I'll tell you what, you fucking idiot, that had better be a fucking joke, are you taking the piss? How the fuck could this Angela woman drive when her left arm is in plaster from the wrist up to her fucking arm-pit, you stupid cunt, one more remark like that, and you're back down to London, you fucking clown. How do I know, fuck!!"
He looked at Drummond, shaking his head.
"At first I thought maybe Davis was exaggerating with frustration, but I'm beginning to wonder. Now get me the tapes".

Hanley could hardly contain his temper, “ No, never mind, I’ll go and get them, you lot go and have tea somewhere, there’s bound to be a canteen in here somewhere, they maybe have a map as well that you can all study whilst you’re having your refreshments, meanwhile, I’ll go and try and be a detective, that’s what they pay me for”.
He looked at Drummond and mocked, “how do I know there was an accomplice, you’ve got problems boy! You’d be better suited, clipping tickets in a fucking railway station somewhere!”

Hillman had marched all of his prisoners outside and lined them up against the wall of the mill, whilst he let the air out of their tyres or loosened wheel nuts. "There now gents, back inside please". As soon as they were all back indoors, he made them empty their pockets and strip off out of their jeans, including the other girl. "Now, all sit down cross-legged and relax. Caroline, give me the mobile phones please".

Three minutes later, Hillman had destroyed every one of the phones. "Right, before we go, check out the pockets of that dead rat Caroline, and retrieve the phone from its' pocket if he has one".
Caroline was crying again, as she attempted to search the body of her friend.

"For fuck sakes, it's only blood". Hillman marched over to the corpse and retrieved the phone from his pocket and then destroyed it in seconds. "There now, that's us. It's been nice meeting you all, nice robbing you, watching you all nearly shitting your pants here. Don't know if we'll ever meet again, but if we do, I'll probably kill you, so it's best if you don't approach me, unless of course, you're armed. Now remember what I said about being Hell's Angels, and how you are all making fools of yourselves, because tonight, you have been held up, showed up, and fucked up, by a general practitioner. Now I know for a fact, that a real Hell's Angel wouldn't get turned over like that, and so do you, Goodbye folks and good luck to you all. Remember, wait until you hear us drive away before you come outside, I don't want to be killing anyone else today".
"Right, come on Gillian, Caroline, let's go, things to do". Hillman let the two women go out in front of him, keeping his eyes on the bikers at all times. He followed the girls outside, and made his way to the sports car. "Now then, who's sitting on whose knee? I would advise Gillian, that you sit on Caroline's knee, let me look at those lovely legs of yours Gillian, the ones that you're so unaware of how sexy they are, filthy little whore".
Hillman drove the car slowly down the twisting drive, down onto the main road, and headed for London. "I know just the place for you Caroline, where you'll feel right at home, you'll feel right at home with the other whores".

Caroline said nothing. She knew the man was deeply unhinged. Fear had gripped her so badly now, that her body shook constantly.
“It’s funny isn’t it”? said Hillman lighting up another cigarette. “One of you is dressed up in T-shirt and jeans, with a hooded jacket, and is attracted to cock like a blue-bottle to cow shit, and the other is dressed up in a skirt, right up her fucking arse, a see-through top, with no bra`, and even a chain around her neck, proclaiming the word S.E.X., and she would have me believe that she’s not interested in cock, one bit. Now, you’ve got to agree with me girls, one of you is a fucking liar, wouldn’t you say? Where does your husband work Caroline? If you lie to me I’ll take out your pretty knees and leave you in a ditch”.
“He works in a warehouse in Rugby called Milligans, he unloads freight all night”.
“Okay Caroline, change of plan, it’s time to get you home”. Hillman turned the car less than a mile further down the road, and headed back towards Rugby. After a couple of minutes, he broke the silence.
“Will you tell him Caroline, what you’ve done tonight? Or what you nearly done”.
“I don’t know, if I...if you don’t kill me”.
“Who the fuck said anything about killing you, did I say anything about killing her Gillian? Chick, my chick. Did I”?
“No” said Gillian, softly.
“No, so stop being so stupid. Do you have any kids Caroline”?
“No, I can’t have any”.
“No, you see? The Lord knows what chicks are going to be cock hungry sluts, so he decides to inflict some malfunction in your works, so that you can’t have any children, saves them growing up to be sons of whores you see”? He slid his left hand up and down Gillian’s legs, “so you might not tell him, huh”? He drove on in silence, and then, “I might”.

Nothing else was said until he asked Caroline for directions to the warehouse. Once there, he said, “If any one of you as much as moves in this car, I swear to God, you will die, and so will your boyfriend Gillian. Now, I won’t be long, what’s his name”?
“His name is John Miller”.
“Right, don’t move!”
The two petrified women discussed whether or not to make a move, and to gamble. They couldn’t do it with the thought of one of them being caught, and what torture that would mean to the unlucky one.

Hillman walked calmly up to the reception desk at the offices, where a young lady sat reading a magazine. Much to Hillman's disgust, the girl sat with a white vest-top on, which deliberately showed off her cleavage.

" Another one Lord with a mini-skirt I'll bet she loves all the attention she gets from all the truck drivers, fucking cock teaser".

Hillman rapped on the office window, hard, startling the girl.

"Fuck!!What!? Round the back if you're a driver, round the back!" She pointed as she shouted.

Hillman rapped the glass again, smiling at her. This time, she got up and made her way to the window.

"Yes? Can I help you"? She said, sarcastically.

"I need to speak with John Miller".

"He's busy!"

"You can see from here he's busy"?

She looked at the clock on the wall. "This is our busiest time of the shift, I know for a fact that he's busy!"

"Well, Miss, I know for a fact that his wife has been in a serious accident, now go and get him, and don't be long".

"Why didn't you say it was an emergency? I'll go and get him straight away".

"Yes you will".

Less than a minute later, the girl reappeared back in her booth. "He's coming out of the door marked 'STAFF' at the side of the building. I'm sorry about that, I didn't realize-".

"It's ok teaser, relax".

"I beg your pardon? What did you say"?

"I said I could have made it easier, thank you Miss".

Hillman walked around the corner. Sure enough, a man came out of a store room and stood waiting. He approached Hillman. "Are you, Where's Caroline is she alright"?

"Hey, calm down, she's fine, she's not badly hurt. A bit saddle sore I expect, but then, I suppose that's to be expected when half a dozen men or so has just been through her".

John Miller was still in shock with what the receptionist had said about 'Serious Accident' and so he wasn't picking up on what Hillman was actually saying to him.

"Where is she, is she in the hospital"?

Hillman looked at the man as if he'd grown horns.

“No, she’s not in the hospital silly, for a gang bang”? “Wait here Mister Miller, I’ll go and get her, I won’t be long, wait here now, don’t be moving”. Hillman returned to the car and signaled Caroline out of the car. “Come on, Caroline, let’s go and see John, he’s worried sick”. Hillman and Caroline walked around the corner. “Here she is John, safe and sound!”

Caroline ran to her husband. “It’s *him* John, it’s Hillman!”

“What”?

“It’s *him*, it’s Hillman, the lunatic”.

“Well, I like that John, eh? I bring her over here to you, safe and sound, after her gang bang”.

“What the fuck!”? said Caroline’s husband.

He lunged at Hillman, but was stopped in his tracks, as his left knee shattered.

“Aaarrgghhh”.

“Take off your jeans Caroline, take them off now, or I’ll kill him, I’ll count to three”.

She quickly opened her jeans, and pulled them down over her hips. “I’m doing it, please, don’t kill him”.

“Hurry up then. Now then, Mister Miller, let’s get one thing straight here, Doctor John Hillman does not tell lies. What were you doing last night Caroline? Tell him. Were you going to get gang banged, tell him”. He aimed the gun at Miller’s good knee.

“Tell him, were you wanting to be banged by a half dozen men last night, by request, were you”?

“Yes, I was going to-”

Hillman fired another shot into Miller’s good knee.

“Aaarrgghhh”

“There now, you two sort your lives out, Caroline? Stay loyal, and live a healthy normal life, look after your husband, and stop fucking about behind his back”.

Hillman walked around to the window at the reception booth, and rapped hard against it.

Again, the girl jumped.

“Would you please stop doing that, there’s no need to rap the glass as hard as that for goodness sakes”.

She rose up from her seat and came straight to the window. “Is everything ok? Did you find him alright”?

“No, everything’s not ok you little whore, you got too good a look at me, you’d be able to identify me easily, no hard feelings”. He lifted the gun, and fired a single shot straight into the girl’s head. She died instantly.

Gillian Payne had thought long and hard about making a run for it. She had no way of knowing, that there were in fact several routes she could have taken which would have led her to safety, but to get to any one of them, she would have to have turned the corner, and she wasn’t about to risk that scenario, and besides, she was still trying to keep her boyfriend alive. She decided not to take the gamble.
Hillman suddenly appeared round the corner and jumped into the car. He reversed down the long straight road he’d driven up, until he reached the perimeter of the industrial estate.. He straightened the car, and then drove back down towards the main road.

Nothing was said in the car for a few seconds, then Gillian said, “Did you find Caroline’s husband”?
“He’s dead” Hillman lied, lighting up yet again. “And so is she. And that little cock teaser at reception, fucking whore, the whole country’s full of whores. You’re all playing your part to bring this country down to its knees, going around half naked. You sit and cock tease half the night, and then you entice the poor buggers into bed with you. Before he knows it, he’s cunt-struck, meeting you again and again, behind his wife’s back. Then, she either finds out from a friend, or, he confesses, and that’s that, they break up, kids or no kids. Then guess what you do. You’ve had your fun, so you break up with him, leaving him a penniless wreck, and in some cases, homeless. Then you move on to your next victim, and so on, fucking cock teasing bastards that you are, that’s it, that’s how it works. No remorse, none of you, none whatsoever. That’s what you spend your life doing, and don’t deny it, because it’s true. Meanwhile, the wives who have been wronged, who have been loyal up until this point, suddenly think, fuck this, so they get all dressed up, and then they start playing the same game. Different men home with them every week, not caring if they are married or not. They join in the game. It’s only a matter of time before marriage is a thing of the past in this country. It will get to the stage, where no-one will trust anyone, no-one will be stupid enough to get married. Too much hassle getting out of marriage. See, See what going around half naked does, destroys families, you little tease, that’s what it does.

Look, look at your skirt, look where it is. Do you have any idea what that does to a man, have you? For me, you dress like that, you want fucked, and you'll get fucked, but that's all you are to me, a cheap fuck, nothing more than that!! So you can go around with your head in the clouds for as long as you wish young lady, because you and your kind do not fool me, not one bit. You actually think you're so much better than everyone else, don't you. You think that we should feel honoured if you as much as speak to us. Well, I just want you to sit there quietly until I decide what we're doing next, fucking whores. No more interrupting me, or you just might not see that yuppie bastard Trevor again, got it!?" Hillman took a deep breath. The nagging pain once again, drilling into his head.

He switched on the radio and began to think of his next move. It would only be a matter of time before those bikers alerted the police of his whereabouts. As much as he hated the thought, he would
have to get rid of the Porsche sports car, it was too risky. It was hardly an average car; he would be spotted easily if he didn't change it.

Gillian had the fingers of her left hand in her mouth, chewing her knuckles, and wondering if there was any way she could survive this ordeal. Tears rolled down her cheek as she thought of her boyfriend. She found it harder and harder to believe that Trevor was still alive. "Hillman either killed you on the spot, or he took you with him. He hadn't brought Trevor along. He was dead".

"How much money do you have on this card? I mean, is there enough money on it that we could get another car to run around in"?
Gillian took her knuckles from her mouth.
"Yes".
"What!"?
"Yes, there's enough. There's about twenty-five thousand on that card".
Hillman whistled in mock admiration.
"You see that? What age are you"?
"Twenty-six"."Twenty-six, Huh, twenty-six, and you can run around with that kind of money. Huh, twenty-five grand, just like that, plus, the value of this thing. He tapped the steering wheel twice, and then whistled again. He looked at her legs and rubbed his chin. "I'm going to need to fuck with you again, and then park this up, get another one. You won't object to me having sex with you again Gillian will you"?

Tears rolled down her face again as she nodded her head.
"Good, because that's all you're here for, to fuck for your man, you're my, em, chick, my fuck chick, don't you ever forget that, bitch! Understand"?
On numerous occasions in her life she'd heard the expression, *Hell On Earth.* She could now, without the slightest hint of exaggeration, say that she knew exactly how that felt. So helpless and hopeless her situation now, she even began to think about suicide.

HARRINGTON POLICE STATION.
SHEFFIELD.

Terry Hanley walked into Deborah Knowles's office, where Deborah and Karen sat with a young woman who had claimed she had been attacked by John Hillman the previous evening. "Excuse me, I need to talk with you two, it's important". Knowles told the young woman that someone else would be through to take her statement.

"What's this about"? said Hanley, as the three officers made their way down the corridor towards the front desk.

"She said she was attacked last night by someone who fitted the description of John Hillman".

"Well, she wasn't, Hillman is heading back up here, he was spotted by a petrol pump attendant, who said he was travelling with a young woman who did not look very comfortable. They are travelling in a Porsche Carrera Cherry red. Also, we've been informed that a motor cyclist and three other people have been shot dead in the Rugby area. Rugby constabulary are going to give us more details as they get them.

Now then Deborah, *your* friends, they were spotted travelling in a blue B.M.W. Saloon, we don't know the registration. You and Karen could maybe go out on a little run today. Your friends were spotted just outside of Rochdale. It's my guess, they're heading further North, maybe even as far as Cumbria, maybe even further, like into Scotland.

Anyway, it would do no harm Deborah, to inform Carlisle constabulary and one or two others, say, between Manchester and Carlisle to look out for a B.M.W. Saloon, and, of course, the two women, one of which has a plaster cast on her arm. Right, I'll let you two get on with that, where's John"?

"I don't know" said Karen, too quickly.

Hanley looked at her. "Is he in the canteen"?

"Yes".

"Right, that's all I asked, I'll see you later, good luck ladies".

Hanley walked into the canteen. Drummond was looking at the list of Hillman's victims. "Let's go John, you and I are going to look for a sports car, the bastard's heading back up this way. He's got another female prisoner with him, they're travelling in a Cherry red Porsche Carrera. Mister Hillman is coming up in the world".

Drummond whistled through his teeth.

“In a Porsche Carrera? He repeated “Well, we won’t catch him in a chase, that’s for sure Mister Hanley. That’s all we need, as if he isn’t hard enough to catch as it is, he goes and gets himself one of the fastest cars available to mortal man. We’ll never catch the fucker now, no fucking way”.

“That’s it John, optimism, that’s what we need”, said Hanley, shaking his head.

NOTTINGHAM.

John Hillman parked up the Porsche in the multi-storey car park, with deep regret. He gave the keys back to Gillian Payne.
"Very nice to drive Gillian, very nice indeed. You'll remember where it is, won't you, so that you can pick it up, maybe tomorrow"?
"Yes" she said softly, not entirely sure if she'd even be alive tomorrow.
"Now then Gillian, I need you to be my woman this last time ok, link arms with me as we walk, you know, cuddle up and smile, look as if you're happy, look as if we're a couple, it's in your best interest, and Trevor's. Now, I'm giving you your credit card back, do you have your driving license with you"?
"Yes, it's here".
"Right, ok, let's go and find a garage. If you try anything foolish Gillian, then those pretty legs of yours will be numb for the rest of your life, and you'll be stuck in a wheelchair, do I make myself clear"?
"Yes".
"Good, now you do this for me, and I swear tomorrow, you'll be free, and you know that doctor John Hillman does not tell lies, don't you"?
"Yes"
"Ok then, let's be a nice couple until we get something to eat".

An hour and a half later, they were over on to the M.6. via Manchester, in a three year old Volvo estate.
"I tell you Gillian, it's like driving a fucking tractor compared to that Carrera of yours, but never mind, it'll take the heat off us for a while, at least".
He glanced into the back seat in the rear view mirror, where his mother sat, alongside Nancy Felder, who was stroking her headless cat.
"FUCK!!"
Gillian almost jumped out of her skin, fear suddenly gripping her, making her skin prickle all over.
Hillman looked again cautiously to the back of the car. The seats were empty once again.
"Fuck, I'm sorry about that Gillian, I thought she was back again, fuck in hell, shit!"
"Who"?
"What"? said Hillman.
"You thought *who* was back"

The searing pain was back in his head as he tried to steer the car. His vision blurred from time to time as well, he was sweating profusely.
“Her, fucking her, you don’t, fuck no, you don’t want her with us, mother, no, not mother”.
Again, he looked over his shoulder onto the back seats. There was no-one there.. “Have you ever been to Scotland Gillian? It’s beautiful up there, if you behave yourself I’ll take you. They say Loch Ness is bottomless”.
His pain had receded as quick as it had arrived.
He began to hum some Scottish tune as he drove along.
“So much for me returning to the Porsche tomorrow” she thought to herself.
The sight would have been pitiful for any onlooker, if they could have seen Gillian sitting there helplessly in the car with tears streaming down her eyes, while Hillman drove singing heartily, a rendition of some Scottish song; *SPEED BONNY BOAT LIKE A BIRD ON THE WING, OVER THE SEA TO SKYE...”* Come on Gillian, my chick, my, come on sing along…be happy, sing, *CARRY THE LAD WHO IS BORN TO...*

ROTHERHAM.

"No sign of any Porsche Carrera" Terry Hanley said to John Drummond, as they sat in Drummond's Jaguar, sipping tea from plastic cartons.
"No" Replied Drummond. "Nothing surprises me now with Mister Hillman. He's probably came off the motorway, and heading in the opposite direction.
"I've alerted the patrol forces up and down the country, one of them is bound to spot him, somewhere".
Terry, don't take this the wrong way, but you think this bastard is going to be easy to catch, don't you? Well, you'll see, just wait, I know he's been certified insane, but I'm telling you, he has outwitted everyone and everything that has been thrown at him".
"John, you had him locked up, and you let him go, it's not a question of anyone outwitting us. He got a key, and simply let himself out of there, he walked out of the door, you and Deborah would have been in the canteen I'll bet at the time".
"No, that's where you're wrong. Deborah and I would have been in our beds at the time. You see, he wasn't being held at the police station, he was being held at the Institute for Mental Health, that's where he was. Oh, did Terrence fucking Davis not tell you that"?

"No he didn't John, he made out to me that he'd been kept in the police station".

"Fly bastard. No, he wasn't, he was in the Institute, they were the ones who let him go. We knew nothing until the following morning They were going to be moving him. You see, that's mister Davis for you, he loves painting pictures to people, you know, telling them things the way he wants them to see it".
Hanley looked at Drummond.
"So, everything he told me was lies then?" Not everything, he just informed you of things a certain way, to make Deborah and Karen and I to look incompetent, that's all, and by the way, if you haven't got Hillman under lock and key, or lying somewhere with a few bullets in his head, he's going to make you look the same way, make no mistake about that.

You'll see, just how slippery this bastard Hillman is, believe me Terry, we had him cornered at one point, in the grounds of his own house, bastard got away. He put on a uniform and joined in with the team who were searching for him, one by one, he took them out. End result, Five dead policemen, he even walked into the house, took a set of keys from the kitchen, opened the garage door, took out his father's B.M.W. and drove away.
On another occasion he was being hunted by twenty odd men, all armed and keen as mustard to blow the fucker away, you know where he hid? In the fucking police car, Insane? Yes, most definitely, stupid simple? No fucking way. And do you know what I think? I think that we'll never catch him, he'll die in his own way, he'll put the gun to his own head, he won't give us the privilege of killing him, he's on a mission for God, remember, he thinks he's got God on his side. And what is it, one of the prophets from the Old Testament says? If God is with us, then who can be against us?
That is what you're up against here Mister Hanley, and, even though you've alerted all the forces up and down the country, none of them will spot him, and do you know why? Because he's not fucking stupid, he'll have dumped that Porsche and he'll have himself another vehicle now, that's why they won't catch him. That's what you're hunting Terry. Have you read the history on this guy? He hasn't got one. He's never once been in trouble in his whole life, not once. Even you and I would have minor offences Terry, when we were younger, not this guy though. I doubt if he ever threw a stone. But, one day in his life, a few months ago, snap, he's insane, the rusty wire gives way. Today, a very quiet hard-working well-meaning general practitioner, tomorrow? The most ruthless killer this country has ever seen. These crimes he's committing, they match those serial killers in the states, the ones they make all the films about, well, I'll tell you this much, when he's finished, or when we get him and bring it all to an end, then they'll be able to make some film about our friend here, a bloody blockbuster. But we'll never catch him; he'll do it himself Terry, when he's good and ready, not before".

Hanley looked at Drummond, and sighed heavily. "There's that enthusiasm again John, that's the spirit, positive thinking bud".

M.6. PRESTON.

"Here we are Gillian, Preston, do you know how it got that name, do you"?
Gillian was staring out of the passenger seat window. She didn't acknowledge the question. Instead, she said, "Trevor's dead, isn't he"?
"Yes he is, I killed him at the petrol station, when I got into your car, do you know how Preston got that name"?
"I'm not interested in how it got its name, could you just kill me now please. I would rather be dead than travel with you, just shoot me, please, because I'm not scared any more, just have the decency to put me out of my misery, because I'm embarrassed to be seen with you, you are a state, and you're a scruff".
It was the biggest gamble Gillian Payne had ever taken in her life, but she needed to know how he would react to insult. Up until now, it had been he who had been calling names and pouring insult on to women, she wanted to see his reaction, even if it meant gambling her own life, her life was not her own now anyway, there wasn't that much to lose.

"Now now, come on, it's only because I killed your yuppie boyfriend that you're talking like that".
"No, it isn't, it's got nothing to do with Trevor, I kind of knew you'd killed him anyway, it wasn't a great shock, now, why can't you kill me? Have you not got the guts to kill me? Or is it because you want to rape me again? Because we both know, that that is the only way you'll be able to get sex these days, don't we? You hate beautiful women, because you're frightened of them, and because you know that they'll have nothing to do with you. They'll laugh at you. You are intimidated by them aren't you"?

Hillman lit up a cigarette, and decided to give Preston a miss. He drove past the junction for Preston and remained on the M.6 heading north.
"Is this how you treat women? I haven't had a bath or a shower for two days, is this how you treat your girlfriends, is it? Fuck, you're a real romancer aren't you"!
"Nice try Gillian, and just for those comments, I'm going to give you some real treatment".
"Boo-hoo" she mocked, "I'm so fucking scared"!

He pulled out her address book and waved it in her face.
"Embarrassed, would be a more fitting description Gillian, being fucked in front of your parents, while I make them watch their slut daughter perform her specialty.
Has your mummy ever saw you taking cock for England, and gagging on the sperm has she? Little miss nothing"!

CARLISLE.

Angela Phorbes lay in the bath with her head resting on the rim. Her left arm was being supported by the rim of the bathtub. She had lay here now, for nearly twenty minutes. Her mind had wandered back to Sheffield, and the course of events which had taken place there. She felt it was her fault for Carla dying. She should have taken more care. She should have known that the police would not do deals, especially these days. They have all the power they need, and they don't answer to anyone. As she felt the comfort of the warm water on her back, she recalled one evening when Carla and her had lay in the bath together, making plans for their future. Now? She wasn't even sure if she had a future.

Deborah Knowles knew who she was, and so now, there could never be a future, not a planned one anyway. Her future had been beaten to death in a police station, by the woman who would now be hell-bent on finding her. Knowles would make a fortune as well. Newspapers would pay highly to hear her story, and how she managed to find out that I was still alive after all these years.

Angela lay back, enjoying the soothing comfort of the flannel on her brow and eyes. Suddenly she thought of something. "The greedy bitch". There had not been a thing mentioned in the daily newspapers, or on T.V. about Angela Phorbes. Deborah, it would seem, was keeping the information to herself. She obviously wanted all the glory, and all the royalties that went with it, for herself.

Of course, If she had disclosed the information to the public, then they would all be out there searching for me, to gain their reward, and Deborah would not want that. One thing was certain now though, Knowles had unwittingly made it a personal affair, and because it was a private affair, then it would be a fair fight, just she and Knowles. Angela had the advantage though. Knowles had killed her future, now, she would kill Knowles. From underneath the flannel, she heard the voice in her head of an old friend of hers, named Tools, "It's about fucking time, is it not"!
Angela smiled at the memory of her fiend, the one who had raped her at the beginning of all this. How terribly strange, life.

Gillian was defeated. She had forgotten that Hillman had her address book. Now, because of her gamble, she had put her parents' lives in jeopardy. On her left, there was a signpost showing the miles to Heysham, and, of course Morecambe where her parents now lived in retirement.
"Are you finished with your little outburst madam, Are you? Because if you're not, I can soon drive over to Morecambe and let them see just what a little slut they have for a daughter, do you want me to do that? Do you"?
"No" Gillian whispered.
"What? What was that"?
"Please, no, don't take me to Morecambe".
"No, because I'll bet that they don't know that their one and only snobby little daughter, goes around like she's begging for cock all the time, do they"?
"No" Gillian whispered again.
"No, I'll bet they don't, you'd make them feel ashamed wouldn't you? Did they make you go to church when you were younger, did they"?
"Yes"
"Yes, you see? Good people, bringing their child up the proper decent way, until you got into your evil ways of the flesh. Satan educated you in how to get what you want, by using your body,
And by fuck, he's learned you well".

"Doctor Hillman, can I explain something to you, the reason why I happen to be dressed like this, can I"?
"Come on then, let's hear your excuses
"It was all just a bit of harmless fun, we had played cards in the hotel the night before, my boyfriend and I, and instead of playing for money, we were playing dare, Trevor won, and, he dared me to dress like this as we drove up here. I would not normally go out with clothes like this on, these clothes are usually only worn when we were having fun in the bedroom. I wouldn't dream of going out like this, not for one minute. I know all the things you said about being dressed like this are all true, but I would never go out like this, never, I am not a whore, doctor Hillman".
It was as though Gillian hadn't said a word.

"All you do is go around cock teasing, and you know your stuff, don't you. You've had plenty of practice, sucking all the toffee-nosed little mummy's boys' cocks, haven't you? Never done a day's work in your life, just cock teasing and sucking off toffee-nosed nice boys, that's all you've done. I'll bet they were all crap in bed as well, but because they buy you nice shiny diamond rings, well, you'll suffer it until another nice boy comes along, and then they can have a big fight and try and make the other one's nose bleed a bit, or scratch each other's eyes, or nip each other until one of them cries, and then they'll be your new champion, now no more of your shit, do you hear me, or mummy and daddy will see you taking this right up the back door, do you understand"?

"Yes doctor Hillman".

"Ok then, friends"?

"Yes".

"Yes, that's more like it, playing fucking cards indeed.

Ok then, take out my cock and suck it until I work out what we're going to do next, you little whore that you are. Now you suck nice whore Gillian".

As she reluctantly performed oral sex on this monster she realized where he drew his strength from. He took his confidence from other people's fear. As she performed he said, "Did you mean all those things you said about me"?

She pulled away from him momentarily.

"Sometimes we girls say things, to hide our true feelings".

"Is that so"?

She would try another approach.

"Yes, you know it is, because you're a doctor, you know us women, and how we work, better than we know ourselves. If truth be known Doctor Hillman, you are the first *real* man that I have had sex with". Gillian was trying another way to win him over, using an alternative method. She had to try and keep him calm. If she could do that, then she stood a better chance of survival. Praising him and complimenting him seemed to be the thing to do, although she had to be careful not to overdo it, or it would have the opposite effect. If he thought for a minute that she was patronising him, it would spark him off on one of his fits of temper. She had to try her best now to think about someone else as she performed this ungodly act on this deranged madman.

The one thing in the forefront of her mind now, was the safety of her parents. She would have to try and keep him from talking about them, because, if she didn't, he would undoubtedly visit them, and make her perform more acts like this, in front of them. She had to somehow convince him, that she actually liked him. Probably the most difficult thing she had ever attempted in her life.

HARRINGTON POLICE STATION.

SHEFFIELD.

John Drummond and Terry Hanley sat in one of the offices, each with a burger and a coffee. They had returned here after giving up on spotting Hillman in the Porsche Carrera.

“Told you Terry, I told you. He’s probably nearer the South coast than here” said Drummond, with his mouth full of burger.

“Give it a fucking rest John, will you? Ok, so he’s a slippery bastard, point taken, just don’t keep on about it, every second sentence ok”?

Drummond took another bite of his burger, then mumbled, “I wonder which way he’s headed now, and that poor young woman with him”.

“Yeah, I know” said Hanley, he must have a reason for keeping her with him”.

“Yeah, he’s keeping her for his own pleasure Terry, that’s why”. We’ve made inquiries and she’s from London, Kensington to be precise, and from what I can gather she’s quite a looker”.

Terry sighed and said, “She must be wondering what on earth she’s done to deserve this, a living fucking nightmare John, God help her”.

“If she’s still alive, he can change like the weather, and twice as fast. That Sadler girl, she says he hallucinates, he see’s certain dead people, his mother, and someone else who’s obviously dead”.

“Let’s hope he fucks up soon John, before someone else dies”.

“I know. He’s killed more people than the plague. It makes you wonder though, doesn’t it? You know, living a normal decent life. A general practitioner and a very good one by all accounts, and then, snap. Bang! Something gives in his brain, gives way, and suddenly, he becomes a ruthless mindless bloody killer. Over the course of three months, he becomes Britain’s most wanted serial killer, since Harold Shipman”.

“A bloody mystery John” said Hanley, “but who cares who or what triggered him off, that’s not our concern, our concern is to bring him in to face justice”.

“Justice”, Said Drummond, “If I get the chance, he gets three rapid shots straight to the fucking skull, that’s the justice he’s getting from me. He’s taken the piss out of me since the day I was put on the case. Oh no Terry, you can try and bring him in alive if you want to, just don’t expect me to, I’m giving him half a chamber to the brain before I even ask him a question”.

There was silence between the two policemen while they both finished off their lunch. Eventually, Drummond said, "So what now Terry, what do you think we should do now"?
"Don't know, if I'm being honest. It would help us if someone phoned in with a sighting of him. What the hell *can* we do"?
"Do you see what I mean Terry? The bastard will get to you; he'll get under your skin".
Drummond held out his cigarette packet. "Do you see these bastards? When I came up here from London, I was smoking maybe ten a day, fifteen on a bad day. But now, I'm on to thirty a day, and rising. If Hillman doesn't get me, then the fags will"
"Or I will" said Hanley, "If you keep blowing smoke into my face, there's a rule about that you know, you're not supposed to be smoking in here".

CARLISLE. 23RD DECEMBER.

Tracy and Angela had been out doing Christmas shopping. The little girls had been constantly questioning their mother throughout their shopping trip, about how Santa Clause was going to get down the chimney when there was no coal fire. Amy particularly, being the youngest of the two girls.

"Of course he will, after all, he manages to get all the presents to all the boys and girls who live in those big high flats doesn't he? So I don't think he'll have a problem getting your presents to you, do you"?

"He'll find a way down, won't he mummy" said Amy. "Yes, cause Santa Clause is clever mummy, isn't he"?

"He certainly is" said Tracy, opening the door of her temporary home. "Now you girls go and play upstairs while I talk to Auntie Angela and Sharon, here, take your juice and sweets up with you".

"Would you like some tea Tracy"? said Sharon "looks like you need a cup".

"Thanks Sharon, I think I must have the most inquisitive children in the whole country.

Angela had gone for a sleep.

"I think she's missing Carla", Sharon sighed. "She keeps blaming herself for Carla's death. I've told her, but she won't listen, she keeps saying she should have protected her better than she did".

"She's pining for her Sharon, that's what it is. They'd built up quite a strong relationship in the short time they'd known each other. I'll have this cup of tea, and then I'll have a word with her.

"Coming up from Sheffield, she kept going into spells of quietness, almost trance-like. And then she would cry".

"I'm worried Tracy, because she says that all she wants to do, is get even with the evil bastards who killed Carla. She said that, as soon as she puts an end to their lives, she'll be quite content. She said that once she puts an end to their lives, she doesn't care what happens to her, but for as long as they breathe, they are taking the piss out of Carla and her. She keeps moving her arm about in the sling. Tracy, she'll damage it, the doctor told her at the hospital to leave it on for at least another four weeks. She's on about taking it off in a couple of days".

“I’ll go and have a chat with her Sharon, I’ll take her a cup of tea up, but I’ll tell you one thing, once Angela decides to do something, then that’s it, wild horses wouldn’t stop her. If she says she’s going to kill this Deborah Knowles and Karen Jones, then she will, and guess what Sharon, I’ll be going back down there with her, to help her do the job. Carla Paganni helped me out Sharon, in my time of need, it’s the least I can do

LANCASTER.

John Hillman sat on the double bed with a mug of tea watching television. Gillian Payne was taking a shower in the cubicle at the far end of the bedroom. Hillman had booked them in as Mister and Misses Payne, and had specifically asked for a room with an en-suite shower and bathroom, so as he could keep a close eye on her. His eyes shifted from the television to the frosty glass door, where he could see her silhouette.

In her travelling bag, she had a few pairs of briefs and a couple of skirts. As she turned off the shower, she knew he would be watching her. She also knew that he had his gun underneath the pillow. He would surely drop his guard, just once. One thing she knew for certain, if he did drop his guard, it would only be once, she would only get one chance, and if she blew it, she was dead.

“Come on” said Hillman, patting the bed beside him, “I’ve poured you a cup of tea, it’ll be getting cold”.

“I won’t be long” said Gillian, “I’m just going to dry my hair, they’ve provided a hair dryer”.

“Listen” said Hillman, “I’ve been thinking”.

“Wait for it” said Gillian to herself, knowing that he was probably going to say something to shatter her. She was right.

“I think it would be best if you came up to Scotland with me”.

Her heart sank, but she tried to sound as if she would cherish the idea.

“Oh, that would be nice. That’s where Trevor and I were, em, that’s where we were heading, after we’d been to the Lake District”

.“Well then, you can see Scotland with me, how does that sound”?

“Fine ,I mean, great, yes”.

“Look Gillian, I know that you’re worried that I’m going to kill you, but I can promise you here and now, that, as long as you’re sensible, and don’t try anything stupid, then I have no intention of hurting you, ok”?

“Yes John and I won’t try anything stupid. I told you anyway, I have feelings for you, I’m not going to try anything”.

“Gillian, please don’t try and make me out to be a clown, I know that you have as much feelings for me as you would have for a scorpion in your shoe, now, don’t insult my intelligence, do you understand me”?

“Yes”.

“Right now no more bullshit ok? Now come and get your tea, you can dry your hair shortly”.

Gillian sat on the bed beside him. She had put on the only dressing gown she'd brought. A flimsy little thing which Trevor had bought her especially for their nights of fun, and it was see-through. Much to her surprise, Hillman didn't make any moves towards her semi-naked body, instead, he had put one arm around her shoulders. In his other hand was his cup of tea.
He pulled her head, so that it was nestling on his chest. Her cup, in her right hand, rested on the bed.
"What are you watching"? She said, as she sipped her tea, and trying to sound interested.
"Some crap about antiques, absolute rubbish, this is what we pay our license for. I'm waiting for the songs of Praise Christmas
Special to come on; it's on in ten minutes".
After a few moments, Gillian said, not knowing about Hillman's obsession with God. "Do you believe"?
"Do I believe? Do I believe what"?
"That there's a God"?
Hillman took his gaze from the television and looked at her. "What sort of a stupid question is that? God is my life, He is my breath, He is my hope, and He is my salvation and yours too, if you would only stop dressing and acting like a whore. He is the reason you're still alive, or else I would have rid the world of you. One less piece of fuck temptation, for decent men not to be tempted with. Look at the way you lie there!"

The lion had been aroused, and Gillian knew it.

"Dressing up especially for me in your see-through bloody night dress and all covered in that provocative oil, you are temptation; you are the very meaning of the word!"
"Look, doctor Hillman, I have already explained to you that I was only dressed like this for my boyfriend, I'm not in the habit of going around dressed this way, like a whore, as you say".
"Is he here now? Your boyfriend. Because I don't see him, and yet you have this bloody provocative clothing on, and whore perfume cream, how the hell am I supposed to resist temptation like this? Come over here and do your stuff, do I believe in God indeed".
Gillian had no choice than to begin performing oral sex on the monster again.. It was the only way she could give herself half a chance of survival.

Fifteen minutes later, Hillman got up from the bed and walked over to the kettle.
"More tea"? He asked, as if the last fifteen minutes had not existed. "No? Suit yourself, but don't ask me to make you a cup when Songs of Praise begins, because I won't be moving lady".
"I wouldn't dream of it" she said, sarcastically, as she rose up from the bed.
"Where are you going"?
"I'm going to clean my teeth, and my filthy fucking whore mouth, if that's ok with you and God, is it"?
Hillman did not look round from making his tea, instead, he just replied in an extraordinarily calm voice, "If you ever get flippant or sarcastic again, to me or my Lord, I will kill you so painfully and slowly, that you will *beg* God for death. Now, go and clean your teeth, and then get back in here, and if you speak one more word to me, unless I ask you a question, then believe me, you will regret it, now go and get cleaned up, and while you're doing that, pray to God for mercy, because my patience is fast running out with you. Until I tell you different, you are with me to do exactly as I tell you, got it? So don't try and be sarcastic with me again. I have been placed on a mission to rid the world of as many whores as I possibly can. Whores like you. I am going against my Lord's will, by just keeping you alive, so, for the last time, I'm telling you, be very careful fuck bitch, because you're walking on extremely fragile egg shells, now go and clean your mouth, bitch!"
"I'm sorry".
"Yeah, you're sorry. You will be, if you come away with any more of that shit".
Gillian went into the shower room. Hillman walked back over to the bed, carrying his cup of tea, and sat back down on the bed with his head against the head-rest.
Five minutes later, he shouted, "Hurry up Gillian, it's starting" as though it were the beginning of a major block-buster film.
"I'm coming" she shouted back, as enthusiastically as she could. She came through and sat on the bed beside him.

"You should listen to the words of these songs Gillian; they will bring you closer to God. Help you understand why we must trust in the Lord, and love Him with all of our hearts and souls". Sipping his tea, he said, "slide over Gillian, and start sucking my cock again until it's hard, good girl, oh, here's my favourite coming on, In The Bleak Mid-Winter".

Gillian lay on the bed beside Hillman. Tears rolled down her face, as she suffered, yet again this madman's depraved actions. She even began to pray to the same God that Hillman prayed to. The same God who was telling him to do these things to women. The same God who had allowed this sick sick man to totally ruin her life, and take the life of her boyfriend. "Please" she prayed in her mind, "please let me get away from this, I promise I'll be a better person". God, it seemed to Gillian, was not listening, at least, he was doing nothing in a hurry to help her in her plight.
The choir on the T.V, were mid-way through the Carol. Hillman sang heartily, as Gillian continued performing to his sickening request, his right hand pressing down on her head, making her almost choke. "IF I WERE A WISE MAN"
There was no God. How could there be? If He were a caring loving God, then these things just wouldn't happen to innocent people, no way. I would be just as successful if I asked that wardrobe to help me. God only exists in the minds of the people who want him to exist. Hillman needs Him to exist to atone for all these evil things he does, he needs to blame someone on all of this irrational behaviour. And God does truly exist in his mind. The man is convinced that God has ordered him to do all these things. So God, because He's in Hillman's mind, is therefore on Hillman's side. He can't possibly be on my side, because I know that He is a lie, he's not there, so how can he help me"?
"EARTH IS HARD AS IRON"
Still the tears rolled down her face.
"I'll be my own God; he's bound to fall asleep after this, surely, "just you doze off; sicko, when I've drained you again, then you can find out whether or not your God exists. You can go and fucking meet Him".
Suddenly, without warning, his hand lifted off her head, then he quickly pushed her head away from his penis, which had gone limp.
"Sit up" he said, "I'm sorry Gillian".
Gillian looked up at the T.V.

A little girl, about the age of seven, was singing a solo verse of the Carol. She remembered Hillman saying something about his two little girls, and thought for a moment, that maybe this was his daughter singing. Whatever it was, it sparked a sudden change in him. He looked now, as though he were genuinely embarrassed about his behaviour, ashamed even. He pulled the quilt over his groin to cover himself up, and stared at the screen, as the child sang out her little heart.

Tears now rolled down Hillman's face, as he watched, in awe, this little angel give a performance that would have made Satan smile as the rest of the choir joined in again for the last verse, Hillman climbed down from the bed and went down on his knees. He knelt down naked in front of the T.V., and placed his hands together underneath his chin, and began sobbing for forgiveness. Most of his words were incoherent, but she could pick out some of them. Something about Angela and Amy, and their Papa John, and then Tracy, Papa John and Nanna, Merry Christmas up in Heaven, and then Amy again, then Papa John and Tracy. Still sobbing, he muttered something about a skipping rope, and vodka. Papa John again, and lying bastard father, and my mummy is dead." I tried to be good mummy, I didn't mean to spill the sugar, please don't mummy, please no, not the dark cupboard again".

Gillian was trying her best to fight her fear. She was just about keeping it together, but it was a struggle. She had to do something, something that looked like everything was normal. She picked up her mug and Hillman's, and walked over to the small wash-hand basin and washed them out. Then she walked past Hillman, who was still kneeling, still sobbing, and put the kettle on. She washed out the tea pot and brewed a pot of tea. She then carried a mug of tea over to him, and sat it on the floor beside him.

He had stopped crying now, but was sniffing involuntarily, like a child.

"Thank you" he managed, still with his hands under his chin.

Gillian tapped him twice on the shoulders as she walked past him. "Everything will work out fine John, you'll see. Maybe I have conducted my behaviour in a provocative manner, I don't know, but I do know this, that God does indeed love you very much, any fool can see that, and He knows all the good things in your heart, all of them. He knows all our secrets, good and bad, and He knows every thought in our minds, so, if I can see how great your faith is, don't you think that He does? Don't you worry doctor, He'll take care of you, you'll see". Gillian sat on the end of the bed with her hands around her mug, watching Hillman.

He knelt there almost trance-like, watching the choir's performance, still muttering incoherently, mumbling about some Nancy Felder and a cat.

She couldn't think of what to do. Should she console him, or would that spark off yet another attack. If she didn't keep control of her fear, she would cry out involuntarily, and strengthen him further, because she knew he fed off the vulnerable and the helpless, which is exactly what she was.

For a further five minutes, he remained in the same position, silently praying. Then he got up from his knees, lifted up his mug, and put it on the dressing table next to the bed. “I, em, I’m sorry about that Gillian, I eh, it was always my hope, that eh, Amy or Angela would sing for the Lord on T.V. Whoever that little girl’s parents are, they must feel very proud, very proud indeed. They must have done good in God’s eyes, they em, they must have found favour in God’s eyes. Me, I’m eh, I, well, I don’t know what I’ve done wrong, can’t tell, really. Perhaps taking my girls away is eh, it’s maybe punishment for something, I don’t know. Maybe one day soon He’ll let me see them again, maybe, maybe not, who knows? He does work in mysterious ways you know, don’t you think? Eh Gillian”?
“Yes I do Doctor Hillman, and who knows indeed, maybe you will get to see your little girls again, but in the meantime, think positive. They’re alive and healthy, and if they’re with their mum, then at least you know, they’re happy, even if they do miss their daddy”.
Hillman looked at Gillian. “Do you think Gillian”?
“Of course Doctor”.
She thought she would press on this opportunity while she had the chance.

“You see Doctor, those little girls of yours; have been made by you, God made them from a part of you, and from your wife. You know that better than me. So it doesn’t really matter where your wife is just now, because lump it or like it, she is stuck with you. Those children are part of you; therefore part of you is with her constantly. When she kisses them goodnight each evening, then she is really kissing you goodnight as well, she can’t get away from you, God saw to that. That is why, when we take our vows at the altar, the minister says, what God has brought together, let no man break apart, or words to that effect. If there is anyone present who knows of any reason why these two people should not be wed, let them speak now, or forever hold their peace. God has brought you and your wife together, and through His handiwork in the creation of your children, she can never leave you, you will always be there with her, as long as she has your children with her”.

Hillman took a sip of his tea and walked round the bed. He sat down beside Gillian. He took both of her hands in his, and squeezed them gently. “I am truly amazed at your knowledge young lady, I really am. Where did you learn about all of these things”?

"When I was younger, I went to Sunday school, and then later, I went to bible class".
"My goodness girl, I've never heard anyone of your age, able to speak about issues like that, I am flabbergasted, I really am". He rose up from the bed and walked around to his side and picked up his cup. He took a sip of tea and then lit up a cigarette.
"Tomorrow, I'm going to let you go Gillian, not here though, a little distance from here. I need a head start".
Silence.
Eventually Gillian said "Thank you."
"You're welcome my dear. Do you think you could make love to me, just this last time, just for me to remember you by, you are so beautiful."
"If you must" she replied, her heart sinking yet again.
She tried to sound cheerful. "It won't be adultery either, because.-"
"Yes it is Gillian, yes it is adultery, but I don't care. I have had so little comfort lately, that I just don't care. Being with you has been the only comfort I've had, I can't help it. When I look at you, I just want to make love with you, I can't help it". He took another sip of tea.
Gillian looked at him. "I won't say anything you know, I mean, I'll tell them all the wrong information, I'll say you're driving a, a Ford or something, and-".
"Yes you will Gillian, you will tell them, I know you will". Putting his pointing finger up to his mouth, he said, "Let's not spoil this nice little moment I'll let you go, about thirty miles from here, that should give me enough time".

Hillman put down his cup and made his way to the bathroom. Moments later, Gillian could hear him splashing water onto his face. She looked at the pillow. She would have to be quick, very quick, because, if it went wrong, she would die; there was no doubt in her mind about that. As fast as she could, she pulled back the pillow and took the magnum. She pulled the safety off, and walked towards the bathroom. It felt heavy in her hands, powerful, lethal. Even though she was nervous, she could feel a certain kind of power running through her body. She had never fired a gun in her life, but she knew she was going to now. It wouldn't be hard to do either. She would not have to think about it. Gillian entered the bathroom with her two arms straight out, the left hand underneath the right, supporting the hand she held the gun with. She spoke to Hillman, who was still splashing water onto his face. "Hey! God man, turn around!!" She pulled back the hammer.

Hillman knew she was there but did not hear what she had said. He groped for a towel and found one. As he dried his face and hands he said, "Pardon. What was that you said"?
"I said, turn around, God cunt! I want to see your face, as I splatter your guts onto the wall, you sick bastard that you are. You've screwed with the wrong bitch this time, you ugly bastard!"
Hillman's face seemed to go into shock. "Gillian, please"
"Don't please me sicko, get down on your knees you fucking half-wit that you are, putting people through hell, to fulfill your sick depraved needs. No wonder your wife left you, sicko, don't you get it? You are mental. You are sick in the fucking head, God man. Huh, God, if there was a God, do you think he's going to talk to you? You? A very sick general practitioner like you? You think He's going to unfold some great plan onto you? Keep your hands behind your neck, sick man, until I tell you different!"
"Please, Gillian, I was going to let you go, really I was".
"Sure you were, probably going to let me go over some cliff-top around here somewhere!"
"No, I was going to, honestly".
"Huh, you've never been honest about anything in your entire life, God man!"
"Stop saying that, stop using the Lord's name in vain like that!"
"Like what? God cunt, don't you like it? It's not nice, is it, when people make you do things you don't want to do, and then, when they rape you, time and time again, huh? And kill the person you love?
Here's the news, God man. God does not exist. He only exists in your feeble pathetic sick fucking head, keep those bastard hands behind your head!"
Hillman whimpered, "Please Gillian, don't do this, I love you".
"Well, I despise you, you fucking freak that you are!"
Again, he whimpered, "Please, my arms are aching, I-".
"Oh are they now? Well, my body was aching and stinging when you raped me time and again, did you do anything to help me? No, you pounded me harder, you bastard that you are.
Now don't you move your hands.
Get up slowly, and walk to the bedroom"
"What? What are you going to do to me"?
For the first time she saw fear in his face. His eyes were flickering and his head was twitching, and he was crying again. He looked petrified.

“Something I probably shouldn’t, I’m going to phone the police. I’ll let them deal with you. They can take you from here, get you hanged. All the misery you’ve caused to so many people, now move your arse God cunt!!”

“Please, not the police Gillian, you shoot me, please, not the police. Shoot me, go on you shoot me, go on, pull the trigger, please, not the police”.

Hillman got up, and began walking towards Gillian, smiling. “You can’t do it, can you? You can’t shoot me, you love me too much!

“Don’t bet on it, pig!”

He kept coming.

“Stop!!”

Still, he crept closer.

“One more step, and you’re dead, freak!!”

He took another step.

Gillian felt fear again.

She knew now, it was *him* or *her,* there was no choice, the police would understand.

She aimed the gun at his stomach, and pulled the trigger. Click.

“AAaarrrggghhh, Hillman roared, in mock pain

“Bastard!! Click, Click, Click, Click, Click.

Hillman, smiling, said, “You should have checked the top drawer. You see Gillian? I knew you would tell them everything, I just knew it, whore”!

CARLISLE.

It was inevitable. Sooner or later Tracy knew that the girls would overhear something, or see something in a newspaper somewhere lying around. That day had come. Angela had just had her bath, and Sharron's aunt was upstairs, bathing Amy. The child was sitting at the kitchen table colouring in a Christmas scene in her colouring book, when the woman on the portable T.V. made the horrific statement.

"A police spokesman said today, that they had made considerable progress in finding the serial killer Doctor John Hillman. In a statement to newspaper reporters, they said that the net was closing in on him, although they couldn't clarify on his whereabouts, for obvious reasons. They also stressed to all women, particularly, prostitutes, to stay indoors at nights, or at the very least, make sure you have company if you must leave the house. This man is, as I'm sure you're all aware of by now, extremely dangerous. It is thought that Doctor John Hillman, until recently, a very quiet man, is responsible for the deaths of as many as sixteen people, although that number could rise as more and more bodies are being found each day. He was last seen driving a cherry red Porsche sports car, and is thought to be holding the owner of that vehicle, a Miss Gillian Payne, as hostage. News has just came in that the car has been found, deserted, in a multi-storey car park in Nottingham, but there is no trace of Hillman or the girl at this time.
Once again, we would warn all women to be on their alert, and not to speak to strangers in bars or clubs. This man is a callous, cold killer".
It took Tracy, Angela, Sharron, and her aunt, a full hour and a half to calm the child down. Angela loved her daddy very much indeed. He was her hero until a few weeks ago. Obviously the child knew nothing at all of why her parents had split up, only that mummy and daddy didn't love each other anymore, and so they couldn't live together.
To hear the newsreader talking about her father like that sent the girl into a state of shock. How could this be? "My daddy is a doctor, he helps people to get better, he doesn't kill people. He teaches the bible class on a Sunday afternoon, this lady is telling lies. God will punish her for that, my daddy is a good man, he buys us bikes and presents."
The child was deeply distraught, she had never in her life heard anyone saying anything bad about her daddy. She sobbed, knowing her daddy was hiding somewhere from the people who were coming to get him.

"Oh dear Jesus Lord, what am I going to do"? Tracy sat at the kitchen table with her elbows supporting her hands on her chin. Tears streamed down onto the book with the half-finished picture of Santa Claus looking at her, smiling.
"Here" said Sharron's aunt, "take this, it'll make you feel better". The elderly lady handed Tracy a glass of brandy.
"It's my own fault, they shouldn't be up at this time of the night, anyway, I should have had them bathed hours ago. It's just that we were all talking, I lost track of the time. Hell, it was nearly seven o clock when we got back from shopping, I'm so stupid".
"No you're not, now come on Tracy" said Angela, "You said it yourself, it was only a matter of time before they found out".
"Yes, but two days before Christmas? Fucking Hell. This will scar them for the rest of their lives, what kind of a mother am I"?
"Now that's enough" said Angela, "don't you dare question your motherhood? It's only because of your bravery that you got those two angels out of that house, and away from that bloody lunatic. He nearly caught up with you, didn't he? When he phoned Angela's mobile, he was coming to get you Tracy, and Sharron, by the sounds of it. Then where would those little girls be, taken into a home? Huh, scarred for life? Seeing their father kill their mother right in front of their eyes? Don't you forget Tracy, he will still come and get you if he gets the chance, he still wants to kill you, don't you forget that.
That Mister nice-guy stuff down in Sheffield was just to win your confidence back again, to make you stay put, so that he knew where you were. I wouldn't mind betting that he's even tried that house in Harrington Square, just to see if you were back there. Now you explained to young Angela, that her daddy is sick, and that he doesn't really know what he's saying or doing and that God won't punish him because He knows that he's ill. Now I know it's heart rending Tracy, but you had to tell her, because in her heart of hearts, she knows that the news-reading ladies on T.V. do not tell lies".
Misses Hartley" said Angela, "If I open a window would it be ok to smoke a cigarette"?
"Of course" said the pensioner, there's ash trays underneath the sink in that cupboard somewhere".
Tracy half laughed, half snorted, remembering where Hillman made her keep *her* ash trays when she lived with him.

She took a swig of the brandy and accepted the cigarette offered to her by Sharron.
“Well girls” said Misses Hartley “I’m off to bed, I expect you all have things to discus, help yourselves to the drinks cabinet, there’s plenty”.
“Goodnight Misses Hartley” said the girls.
“Goodnight Aunt Sarah” said Sharron.
“Don’t you be worrying too much now Tracy” said the pensioner, “Worrying never gets us anywhere”.

SHEFFIELD POLCE STATION.
DIVISION STREET.

Deborah Knowles sat with Terry Hanley, John Drummond, and Karen Jones in one of the interview rooms. All of them were looking at the newspaper reports. It was response from the T.V. interview, given by the chief of the M.P.D. Jack Knight.

"What the fuck did he go and say that for? The net is closing in, what a fucking prick!" Said Drummond

"He has to say something John, what else can he tell the public? Oh no, we haven't got a clue as to where he is, so just lock your doors and windows, and good luck".

"He may as well have said that, because it's the fucking truth".

"Well" said Hanley, "he was last seen, or rather, we know for certain that he was in Nottingham, that's what we know. He swapped vehicles. Karen had made enquiries and discovered that a silver-blue Volvo estate had been purchased by a 'Misses' Gillian Payne.

"How long ago was that? Said Hanley.

"Three days ago" said Karen.

"Does every police sector in the country have that information"?

"Yip" said Karen.

"Ok then, that's all we can do for now, is look for the Volvo. Deborah, Karen, you two go into Nottingham and speak to the person who sold her the car. John and I will try our luck up and down the motorway. Let me know if you find out anything important.

If we could have had his wife back here, we could have perhaps lured him into some kind of a trap" said Knowles.

"Yes we could" said Hanley, "but you decided to batter fuck out of her friends, thus, ending any hope whatsoever of that happening".

"I know" said Deborah, "haven't you ever made a mistake in your career"?

"Yes I have" said Drummond, "I left you in charge of the people who could realistically bring Hillman in, better be on your way girls".

"Those two bastards Deborah" said Karen, "did you hear the sarcasm from Drummond as well? He loves to unleash that vicious sarcasm doesn't he"?

Deborah smiled. "Mister Hanley there, Karen, he thinks that Terrence Davis is going to be licking his arse forever. Just wait until this time next week; if we still haven't found Hillman, then we'll hear sarcasm".

It mattered little to Deborah Knowles how sarcastic mister Hanley was. He would be put in place at the first opportunity, and so would anyone else who happened to stand in her way. The hardest part would be to get Karen Jones on the same wavelength as herself. If she refused to cooperate with her, then she would have to be dealt with accordingly.
Nothing, but nothing would stop her reaching the top, and at this moment in time, there were lots of them trying to. Terrance Davis for one, but he was very vulnerable to attack. It was *his* job that appealed to her the most.
Knowles had her own ideas about where Hillman would strike next. She had been the first to have any correspondence with the Paynes. She had even gone up there to Morecambe to interview them and warn them that Hillman may come to visit them. No-one else who'd been up there to see them had taken the time to keep in contact with them, at least as far as she knew. Maybe *they* were keeping quiet about the search for Hillman as well, leaving *her* out of the equation
It mattered little to her. She would win in the end…she would get the glory, of that there was no doubt.

LANCASTER. CHRISTMAS EVE.

John Hillman came down the stairs whistling the tune of ``*In the Bleak Mid-Winter*``, carrying Gillian Payne's black leather bag. "Good morning" he said, to the middle-aged woman who was carrying a breakfast tray into the dining room.

"Good morning Mister Payne, I trust you slept well"?

"Like a log my dear. I was wondering if you could do me a favour"?

"Certainly, I'll be with you in just a jiffy I'm just taking this plate of bacon through to the guests".

In less than a minute, she was back. She lifted up a hatch, in the corner of the hall, then replaced it, as she stood behind a small desk, with a massive ledger opened up in front of her. She looked to be around fifty, although the dyed white hair done nothing for her to disguise that fact.

"Now then, what can I do you for"? She smiled.

Hillman thought to himself, if he ever heard that corny phrase again, he would scream.

"Well, it's like this, my wife and I were wondering if it would be possible to stay here until boxing day, maybe even the day after that, only, the plans that we'd made have been cancelled. We're willing to pay extra".

"Oh I don't know if-."

"Please, oh please, you see, if we can't, then I'm going to have to drive all the way down to Cornwall, and to be quite honest, I am absolutely sick of driving".

He pulled out a bundle of fifty pound notes from his wallet.

Misses Kerr saw the money, and said, "just a minute, I'll go and have a word with my husband".

"Oh, I hope you can, we'd be very grateful, really".

Misses Kerr, once more lifted up the hatch and made her way through to the kitchen, where her husband did the cooking. Moments later, she returned with a man who looked to be in his sixties.

"Now then, Mister Payne" said Kerr, as he stood now, where his wife had stood behind the hatch.

"Till boxing day you say" said Kerr, studying the ledger as though it were some great battle plan, tapping the red pencil he'd picked up, on his teeth. Mmm, I wonder, I wonder" he mumbled.

Hillman was becoming bored and very impatient with the man's attitude "It's not the fucking Ritz I'm in here" he thought to himself.

Hillman placed eight fifty pound notes on the desk, in front of Mister Kerr.
"Oh, it's not the money Mister Payne, you understand, goodness no, it's just that we eh".
"Oh well then, if you can't do it, you can't do it" said Hillman, gathering up the money.
"Oh now wait, yes". Kerr turned the page. "Yes, that will be alright Mister Payne. Now then sir, enjoy the rest of your stay with us".
He lifted up the hatch, and headed back to the kitchen.
Misses Kerr said, as she picked up the money, "Oh, you'll be wanting some change Mister Payne".
"No no, you keep that, and thank you once again. Now then Misses Kerr, I have to go to Carlisle, it's to pick up a late Christmas present for my wife. Can you keep secrets? Misses Kerr."
"Ooh, of course sir, I won't say a thing".
"Thank you Misses Kerr, now there's just one more favour I need to ask you. My wife didn't sleep so good last night, she told me, so, she's sleeping now. I've put the DO NOT DISTURB sign on the door, is that alright"?
"Why certainly Mister Payne, I'll see to it, that she's not disturbed".
"Thank you very much, now, if she has not awoken by two-thirty this afternoon, would you wake her up please, she asked me to ask you, I mean, I should be back from Carlisle by then, but if I'm not"?
"That's not a problem" said Misses Kerr.
Another one of those phrases he hated.
"Thank you Misses Kerr, thank you so much, you have no idea how grateful we are, you are so kind."
"Not at all Mister Payne, that's what we're here for, isn't it".

Hillman felt the biting wind and rain on his face, as he threw the leather bag into the back seat of the car.
"Money Lord, they can all be bought for a price".
He climbed into the Volvo and reversed back a few yards, to make room for himself to drive out of the small car park. There was sleet pelting onto the windscreen. Now then, I'll have to get rid of this car as soon as possible. He pulled out of the car park and headed off to Carlisle, because he knew Misses Kerr was watching from one of the windows.
He had no intentions of going to Carlisle.

"I'll have to change the car Lord, I can still smell the perfume from the whore. What a silly girl Lord, huh? You know I was going to let her go, don't you? There is some good in me isn't there Lord? Well, she didn't trust me that was *her* problem. She missed the chance to escape as well. She couldn't say she wasn't warned. Anyway, as nice as she was, it's one less trouble-making bitch off your hands Lord".
"They all get a chance Lord, they can't say that about me. It's their own stupidity Lord that lets them down in the end. It was the same with the armed policemen in the grounds of the house; they all had the chance to take me. Mind you Lord, I'm not complaining about that. Very handy indeed that one of them carried a Magnum," he said out loud, as he once more loaded the lethal pistol.
He left Lancaster and drove on the A.683, and headed for a place called Kirby Lonsdale. He would find another car there he could use. As he drove, he touched the inside of his jacket pocket, reassuringly touching the Magnum, fully loaded once more.
"What a silly girl Lord, she could have been heading off back home now. Ah well, too bad, too bad, her last mistake".
He drove on, wondering if he would spend Christmas in Sheffield, or if he would drive further south. Maybe he should drive way down South, to Southampton, or Brighton. Yes, somewhere far away from Sheffield. Sheffield would be pushing his luck. He pulled into a lay-by, and lit up a cigarette.
No, this was a bad idea. Kirby Lonsdale would be a small village, or town, at best. A stranger would stick out a mile up here. He switched the engine off and leaned over to the back seat to get Gillian's leather bag. He took out various things belonging to the girl. Make up, lipstick, condoms, "Ah, here we are, address book, this is what we want. He flicked through the names and addresses of various people, and then came across the address for her parents.
"Ah, now this could be useful". Hillman was looking at the address of her parents, again.
This time, he *would* go and visit them, they're bound to be worried sick about their one and only daughter, their only child. "I'll go and put them out of their misery, it can't be much fun for them."
He wondered if they were aware of the fact that their daughter was nothing but a raging nymphomaniac dressing provocatively and teasing men everywhere she went, and advertising herself for sex to all and sundry.

As he took out the map from the glove compartment, a seething pain shot through his head. He could feel it at the back of his eyes, and both sides of his temple.

"Aaaarrgghhh.

"It was so painful, he shouted out loud, and threw his cigarette out of the window. The pain stayed with him for a full five minutes, before eventually subsiding. "Fucking Hell Lord, what the fuck was that for? What did I do to deserve that? Fuck!!

"He lit up another cigarette and stared at the address for Gillian's parents. The words were blurred as he read the details. "Seafront Cottage Morecambe.

"Well, that won't be hard to find Lord, will it"? As he smoked, he began to think about his daughters again. This would be the first Christmas he would spend alone, completely alone. He wondered what they would be doing. Would they even take the time to think of him? "Ah, they're children John, they'll be too busy thinking about what Father Christmas is going to be bringing them to be worrying about you, that whore they have for a mother will be seeing to that, no doubt, and that other whore, if she's still going around with her.

"*Never mind John, it's no less than you fucking well deserve, you son of a bastard that you are*!!"

Hillman spun round to see his dead mother sitting on the back seat.

"*I tried to warn you didn't I*? *Way back, would you listen? Would you fuck listen. Little gold-digging bitches, of all the girls in God's sweet world, you go and lose your virginity to a, a, fucking whore, You stupid bastard boy that you are!*"

"Shut up!! Get out of my car, you're dead, you are fucking dead!!! Leave me alone!!"

"*Your car? Cunt boy, your car*"*? I have as much right to sit in here as you have, You thieving little bastard that you are*"!!

"Get out! Right!

"Hillman got out of the car and opened the back door, he reached in, and pulled his mother out, and threw her onto the ground. "Now leave me alone, please, please, just fucking leave me be". Doctor John Hillman, was now on his hunkers, sobbing bitterly. All he had thrown to the ground was Gillian's bag. The two right hand doors of the Volvo were wide open as he sobbed into his hands, now covering his face. The sleet had turned to snow, and was now beginning to lie. A car pulled up, just to the side of him.

The woman passenger rolled down her window. “Are you alright sir”? Hillman, thinking it was his mother’s voice, replied, without looking round, “What do you care? One minute I’m your bastard boy, the next you’re all nice as nine-pence, and by the way, you can’t talk, because you knew all along, that that lying bastard was banging Carla’s arse!!”
“Drive on Tom”.
The car drove off and disappeared into the distance.

Hillman gradually regained his composure and got to his feet. He closed the back door of the car, glancing into the back seat. “Right Lord, Morecambe it is”. Another sigh, “Ah well Lord, maybe Gillian was right, maybe someday you will reward me for my faith, but please, take her away somewhere, stupid mother. Take her to heaven, if you’re going to, or Hell, it doesn’t much matter to me, just keep her to fuck out of my face, and anyway, she’s supposed to be on the fucking floor with a hole in her head at Morningside, lying beside that lying bastard father of mine. She’d better not appear at Morecambe Lord, and fuck up my Christmas dinner, she has no manners whatsoever”.

LANCASTER. 3pm.
CHRISTMAS EVE.

Mister and Misses Kerr employed two girls to clean and change bedding. There were only sixteen rooms in the hotel, and so the girls would do other duties as well as cleaning. Bar work, or running errands. Whatever was needed. Today, Arlene had one more room to do before she was finished until the day after Boxing Day.

She was excited about sharing Christmas with her boyfriend. She looked at the tag hanging on the bedroom door handle. "You must be joking" she said to herself, "It's three o clock in the afternoon". She left her vacuum cleaner and dusters outside of the room and decided to go down and speak with Misses Kerr, who was busy serving customers in the small bar.

"Oh, is Mister Payne not back yet Arlene"?

"I don't know Misses Kerr, I've just saw the sign on the bedroom door".

Misses Kerr looked up at the clock on the wall.

"Just wake her up Arlene, she wanted to lie in today. Mister Payne told me, in fact, I'm sure he said two thirty to wake her up. Never mind Arlene, wake her up now, it's alright".

"Right you are, is there anything else you want me to do when I've finished the room"?

"No, I don't think so darling, oh, you've to go and see Mister Kerr, I think he has a little something for you, a little Christmas bonus I think Arlene".

Arlene Hannah knocked on the bedroom door.

"Misses Payne" she softly called, as she gently tapped on the door again.

"Misses Payne, it's after three. Misses Payne? Misses Payne, chamber maid, Misses Payne? Huh"

Arlene said to herself, "She might have taken the tab off the door, let people get on with their work.

Arlene brought the vacuum cleaner into the room and plugged it into the socket next to the bedside cabinet. Before she started, she looked at all the Christmas parcels lying neatly assembled on the floor.

There were nine parcels, all neatly wrapped in various colours of Christmas paper, all lying neatly placed along the floor. She looked at them. They were all quite big and bulky.

"Humph, somebody's spoilt rotten by the looks of it" she said, as she switched on the vacuum. As she went about her chores, she couldn't help noticing a strange kind of musky smell. She opened the bedroom window to let some fresh air in.

Outside, the snow was falling thicker than ever, driven on by an almost gale forced wind. How romantic this Christmas was going to be. She couldn't remember a white Christmas in her life-time. She began dusting the units and wardrobes, spraying furniture polish here and there as she did so. The rooms were never bad to do. They were done on a day to day basis. She sprayed some more polish around the room, in the air, just to prove that she'd been cleaning in here.

"Right, just the bathroom to do, and then that's me". The wind was now blowing the curtains and almost knocking over some chalk ornaments, of various cheerful looking animals. She closed the window and placed the curtains and ornaments back into position. She then entered the bathroom, closing the door behind her, as she set about cleaning the taps and shower units. Less than half an hour later, she was finished. "Right, that's me" said Arlene, placing her dusters and cleaners back into her wooden box, especially made for her by her boyfriend. As she entered the bedroom again, she smelled the musky odour once again. "What the hell *is* that"? She wandered around the room, sniffing the air. "It seems to be coming from the bed? Oh no, don't tell me someonc has soiled the bed". She pulled back the sheets. "No, there's nothing wrong here". She walked towards the wardrobe. The smell was getting stronger again. She opened the two wardrobe doors. Nothing. "What on earth is it"? She collected her cleaning things, and made her way down stairs. Misses Kerr was making her way to the kitchen, when she saw Arlene coming towards her. "Everything ok Arlene? She asked, as the young lady put away her cleaning products.

"Well I, don't, is Misses Payne down here in the bar"?

Misses Kerr looked at Arlene, "Misses Payne"?

"Yes, is she down here, because she's not in her room."

"I don't think so" replied Molly Kerr, rather confused.

"I'll go and check in the resident's lounge, she's not in the bar because I've just came from there.

Are her clothes in her room Arlene"?

Arlene looked at her employer as though she had just asked her the most stupid question of all time.

"No, there are no clothes, only, a strange kind of smell, and a whole load of wrapped up Christmas presents. A strange kind of smell, I don't know what it reminds me of. Come up and smell it for yourself, see what you think. I've smelled something like it before, but I can't for the life of me remember where".
"I'll just check the resident's lounge pet, and then I'll come up, won't be a minute".
Arlene went back to the closet in the hall and put away the rest of her cleaning equipment.
Molly Kerr glanced around the door of the resident's lounge. There was no-one at all in the room.
Her husband came by. "Who are you looking for Molly"?
"I'm looking for, have you seen Misses Payne John"?
"Misses"?
"Misses Payne, you know, the couple who have asked to stay until Boxing Day"?
"No I haven't. Didn't he say something about letting her lie in; wake her up this afternoon or something"?
Molly sighed. "John, it's ten past four, that was nine o clock this morning he said that. He said his wife was sleeping, *then* how much of a long lie does she want? Anyway, she's not in her room, and she definitely did not leave with her husband, because I watched him driving away.
The thing is John, Arlene says there's a strange kind of smell in the room, and she can't seem to find the source, and, although Misses Payne is not in her room, the do not disturb sign is still hanging on the door, and that was three o clock or there about when Arlene entered the room".
"That's strange" said John Kerr, "Maybe she's nipped out for something at the shop".
"I'm going up to take a look John, have you got Arlene and Mary's presents"?
"Yes, I'm just going to give them to them, when they're finished. Mary is just finishing off in the bar. I've given them fifty pounds each and a bottle of Scotch, what do you think"?
"Fine John, I just hope we don't go bankrupt before next year".
"Well I don't know, how much do you think I should give them"?
"Give them a hundred each John, goodness knows, they work like Trojans".

John sighed. "Right, I'll see to that, you go and see what's wrong with the room".
As John Kerr was walking back to the bar, he stopped, suddenly remembering something.
Mister Payne had come down the stairs around nine o clock last evening, and ordered two rounds of sandwiches. While he was talking to him, he had asked if he could take some of the large polythene wraps, used for storing large cuts of meat. He had handed John a twenty pound note, and grabbed a bundle. They were the large industrial sized bags, used for all types of food storage, meat, poultry, salmon etc.
"Why the hell would he want them"?
He hadn't given it much thought last night because they had been so busy, and he wasn't quite sure why he was thinking about it now.
Molly Kerr tapped on the bathroom door at the top of the stairs.
"Are you in there Arlene"?
"Yes, won't be a minute Misses Kerr".
"Right you are sweetheart; I'm just going in to Misses Payne's room now".
Arlene had changed from her work clothes into casual wear. She had put on a black velvet jumper, and jeans with suede boots. She was just putting the finishing touches to her makeup, when an icy chill ran through her body. "Oh Christ no".
She had suddenly remembered where she'd smelled that horrible stink from. It was when she was just a teenager. She had been sent down with her brother's packed lunch to his place of work, because he'd slept in that day. Her brother worked in the abattoir.

MORECAMBE. SEAFRONT COTTAGE.
3pm. CHRISTMAS EVE.

Harold and Beverly Payne sat on their sofa, listening to the man in the easy chair opposite them.

"So you see Mister Payne, it is of the utmost importance that you tell no-one you were talking to me, it could ruin the whole operation. You see, I happen to think that your daughter is alive and well, that's why I'm here talking to you now. It is my job to go over every possibility, every clue, with a fine toothed comb. "Now, you say you've had a visit from Deborah Knowles"?
"Yes" said Beverly, "But that was about three weeks ago. Then we had a call, or rather, a visit from a chief inspector John Drummond, and chief inspector Terrance Hanley".
"I see, and do they phone you"?
"Yes, about three times a week, just to see if Gillian has got in touch with us or if Hillman has demanded ransom money".
"Has he"?
"No sir, no he hasn't".
"He won't either, Misses Payne that is not what he's about".
"Let me pour you some more tea Mister Phillips".
"That would be lovely . All this must be tearing you apart".
"It is Mister Phillips, you have no idea, its agony, waiting for the phone to ring, and then, when it does, you dread to hear what you might hear".
'Phillips' without asking, lit up a cigarette.
Harry Payne was in the habit of smoking a King Edward now and again, but thought it would have been manners to have been asked permission first before he just lit up.
Phillips rose to his feet and looked out onto the sea. The snow was falling thicker by the minute.
"You can rest assured Mister and Misses Payne that I will do everything in my power to bring your suffering to an end. I really feel it for you both, I do".
"Have you got far to go Mister Phillips"? Said Beverly Payne, "because the snow is getting deeper by the minute, it's a blizzard out there".

"It's even worse further South" said Harold Payne. "They say there's one or two rail networks closed down completely already".

“Well, I haven’t booked into a hotel or anything, but I’m going to have to try, there’s no way I’m going to make it back home if the snow keeps on falling like this. I may not even get a room in a hotel, you know, with it being Christmas. I’ll have to do something. failing that, I’ll just have to sleep in the car, that’s all there is to it, it won’t be the first time”.
“Indeed you will not Mister Phillips, you can spend the night her and tomorrow, if necessary”.
“Oh, I couldn’t, haven’t you got guests coming tomorrow”?
“No, we haven’t, Harold and I usually spend Christmas alone anyway. Sometimes we spend Christmas with Gillian, whenever we can. This would have been the first for three years that she’d spent with us. She was going to the Lake District with Trevor, and then to Scotland. Then, she was supposed to be coming here, we were *so* looking forward to it. I don’t hold much hope of spending it with her now” said Misses Payne, with tears now rolling down her face”.
“Now now then Misses Payne”, said Phillips, “you know what they say about times like these, no news is good news, and that’s the way we must think, we must try and be positive”.
“Yes, but if she was able to call us she would, she wouldn’t keep us in this agony”.
“Yes, but if she’s being held captive, then she won’t be allowed to call you will she? It’s psychological torture Misses Payne”.
Harold said, “According to the chief of police, he said that the net was closing in. He seemed to be implying that he knew where Hillman was, although he couldn’t say it on T.V.”
“Really” said Hillman, “well there you are then, that must give you hope, does it not”?
Beverly Payne said “I won’t feel any hope until I at least hear her voice on the phone”.
Outside, the snow was thicker than ever.
“Goodness me Mister Phillips, you may end up having to stay here for a week if this keeps up”.
“It certainly is getting worse” said Hillman”.
Misses Payne went off to the kitchen to prepare their evening meal.
“Do you like roast beef Mister Phillips”?
“Oh now, just a sandwich will suffice Misses Payne, please”.

“Nonsense” Said Harold, you will have dinner with us Mister Phillips, and most welcome you are, after all you’re doing to help find our daughter”.

"You are too kind Mister Payne".
"Rubbish, there is no such thing, and please, call me Harold"
."Thank you, my friends call me John", Hillman smiled.

"FUCK FRIENDS? YOU DON'T HAVE MANY OF THOSE, DO YOU, DOCTOR FROCK BOY!!"
Hillman's mother suddenly appeared on the sofa next to Mister Harold Payne. Hillmans face went red, as she said to Harold Payne,
"DON'T LET THIS LITTLE BASTARD BOY FOOL YOU FOR ONE MINUTE, HE'S BEEN STICKING HIS COCK INTO YOUR DAUGHTER'S BUM AND MOUTH, DISGUSTING LITTLE BASTARD THAT HE IS, AND PROBABLY UP SOME MAN'S ARSE AS WELL, IT WOULDN'T SURPRISE ME, BASTARD BOY THAT HE IS!"
Hillman momentarily lost control. "SHUT UP!!

Harold Payne dropped his cup of tea with fright. He stood bolt upright.
"Mister Payne, I do apologise for my outburst, I, I suffer from a severe type of migraine. It comes in sudden bursts, almost unbearable it is sometimes".
"Good God man, I nearly jumped out of my skin, blast, my trousers are soaking, Jesus Christ".
"Hey!! Now I've said I'm sorry, there's nothing more I can do, I'm sorry ok"?
"Yes, of course, it's alright, I'll eh, I'm just going to change, excuse me, I'll just be a couple of minutes. Oh, do you have any luggage Mister Phillips, because I would get it out of the car while you still can".
"Yes, yes I'll do it while you're changing".
"Well, if you come up now, I'll show you where the guest room is".
"Thank you Mister Payne, Harold, I mean, thank you, and once again, I am terribly sorry".
"Forget it" said Payne, waving his hand. "Think nothing of it, please".
Misses Hillman sat smiling at her son, rocking backwards and forwards with her hands around her knees, whispering, "BASTARD BOY. BASTARD BOY, YOU'RE GOING TO DIE SOON, THE NET IS CLOSING IN. CLOSING IN. CLOSING IN. BASTARD BOY!"
"Are you alright Mister Phillips, you look quite shaken"?
"I'm, eh, she's, I'll be fine, thank you".

But just as the two men began climbing the stairs, Hillman could hear his mother shouting; "*Misses Payne, that dirty little weasel frock boy of mine has been doing despicable things to your daughter. Don't give the dirty little bastard any roast beef. Phone the police, phone the focking police, he's going to kill you both, because his focking whore wife belts him with skipping ropes, drinks vodka, and focks his Da*".

LANCASTER.

THE RED LION HOTEL.

Arlene Hannah made her way along the hall towards room number six, which was the Payne's room. When she got to the room, Misses Kerr was already there. Molly Kerr stood by the double bed and sniffed the air, with her face turned up towards the ceiling. She walked towards the double wardrobes. "It seems to be stronger over here Arlene" still facing the ceiling.
"Misses Kerr" said Arlene, "I think I know where it's coming from, I hope I'm wrong, but I think I know. May I have permission to open one of those Christmas parcels"?
"Arlene, I"-.
"Misses Kerr, if I'm wrong, and I sincerely hope that I am, then I will take full responsibility and answer to Mister Payne. The trouble is, Misses Kerr, I don't think he's coming back, ever. Misses Kerr, if I'm right". She pointed down to the Christmas presents once again.
"You think he's took off and left his wife"?
"Misses Kerr, I think that those parcels are the cut up remains of Misses Payne".
Molly Kerr looked at Arlene as though she had just grown a pair of horns.
"Arlene, you can't be serious child, what on earth are you saying"?
"Misses Kerr, how else would you explain the smell? Smell those parcels".
Molly walked over to the parcels, bent down slowly, and smelled them.
"Let me open one Misses Kerr you have a right to, you know. You can wait outside the room if you wish".
"I think I will" said Molly, "my goodness me. Oh Arlene, you don't think"?
"Well, we'll soon find out".
Molly left the room, and waited outside the closed door.
In all of her twenty-two years in the hotelier business, Misses Molly Kerr had experienced a few incidents in some of the places where she and her husband had been proprietors, and some quite violent, but what Arlene was suggesting was preposterous, surely.

“Surely nothing like this could happen, up here in Lancaster, surely not. There would be some other explanation to all this, there had to be. But the fact that it was now almost four thirty in the afternoon, and Mister Payne had not yet returned, only made Arlene’s theory more possible.
The bedroom door opened, and Arlene came out into the hall.
“Well.” Said Molly Kerr, hopefully, “what is it”?
“Phone the police Misses Kerr”.
“Oh my sweet Lord in Heaven”.

Molly Kerr phoned the police, and told them of Arlene’s discovery. The Red Lion was situated almost two miles North of Lancaster. The snow was now so thick that it would be impossible to reach here until the snow plough had been through the town, whenever that would be. She was told to lock the door of the room in question, and under no circumstances was she to let anyone else into that room. There would be police inspectors there as soon as possible. She was also told to tell no-one else of the discovery in the hotel.

“As if I would, bloody stupid man” said Molly, replacing the phone back onto its cradle. “He must think I’m crazy or something”.

Arlene had been through in the kitchen informing Mister Kerr of the gruesome discovery. She was carrying a newspaper under her arm. She looked around to see if anyone else was present, then she said, “Misses Kerr, this just gets worse, look”. She opened the paper up to page five. “It’s *him*, minus the beard and the moustache, but it’s *him* Mister Hillman”.

Molly grabbed the newspaper, and studied the photograph for a few moments.
“Good God, you’re right child, we’ve had a bloody serial killer staying with us. And he could have killed...oh my Lord”.
Mister Kerr said one of his carving knives are missing, as well as six rolls of Christmas paper”.
Molly looked up at her husband. “Oh John, my God”.
“I know, I know pet, take it easy, he’s away, he won’t be back here, what did the police say”?
Molly told him.

“Well, I’m going to call them again, and tell them just exactly who we’ve had here for breakfast, that’ll get them moving a bit quicker, snow or no bloody snow. I’m going to phone the national hot-line as well.

When the officer in charge of this case hears about this, they’ll bloody walk up here if they have to.

Judging by this weather Molly, he couldn’t have gotten very far, not in this”. He pointed outside to the thick flakes of snow”.

“Yes, but John, he left shortly after nine this morning, it didn’t start snowing heavily until a good hour and a half after that, he could be anywhere, he could come back here”.

“He won’t come back here pet” said John Kerr reassuringly. “Why do you think he’s put the do not disturb sign on the door. It’s because he knows fine well that we’d discover his handy-work, he just had to give himself some time to put some distance between himself and us…he won’t be back Molly”.

Darkness had fallen and all the down stairs lights were now all shining brightly.
Hillman sat at the dinner table, as Beverly Payne dished out, mashed potatoes, roast potatoes, roast beef, peas, carrots, and runner beans.
"There now Mister Phillips, you tuck in, and there's plenty more where that came from".
"More" said Hillman, "Misses Payne, I'll be lucky to finish what's on my plate and that's the truth".
Harold Payne poured three large glasses of red wine. "Come on now Beverly, come and sit down to eat, before it gets cold".
Hillman looked cautiously around the room.
"Is anything wrong John"? said Harold.
"Mmm? Mother, eh, no, no, no, Mister Payne, eh Harold, I was just admiring your decor that's all, it's beautiful, you have a beautiful house, it's lovely" said Hillman, once more looking over his shoulder.
"Thank you, we didn't do it of course, we got tradesmen in to do it, you understand".
"Of course" said Hillman, "It's lovely" he repeated.
Beverly had taken her cooking apron off, and was wearing a lemon blouse, which happened to show off her ample breasts, and a knee length cream skirt, which hugged her hips. She was still a very beautiful woman at the age of fifty.
"This is amazing Misses Payne, it really is" said Hillman, in between ramming potatoes and chunks of roast beef into his mouth. "Mmm, you're a lucky man Harold, absolutely delicious".
Harold looked at his wife, and smiled.
"What?" Said Hillman, "What"?
"Oh nothing Mister Phillips" said Beverly, "we just like to see people enjoying their food. Gillian used to do that all the time".
"No she didn't" said Hillman, "I mean, did she? She sounds like quite a girl".
"Oh, she is Mister Phillips, she'd do anything for anybody, so she would", said Beverly Payne, as she put the smallest amount of mashed potato onto her fork.
"Yes, I'm sure she would" replied Hillman, still glancing around the room.

Outside, the snow was coming down even thicker than before. "Well, Mister Phillips, we haven't had a white Christmas up here for years, looks like nothing is going to stop it this year".
"Yes, nice and romantic it'll be for you two".
"Are you married Mister Phillips"?
"I was, not now, and certainly never again, really".
"Did you have a bad experience then"?
"Yes, you could say that, Misses Payne, you could say that".
Whilst they all ate their meal, they discussed things concerning Gillian.
"Poor Trevor" sighed Beverly, "I really feel it for Tom and Sarah, his parents, Mister Phillips he was their only child. Sarah couldn't have any more after the birth of Trevor, there were complications at the birth you see. He was their only hope of carrying on the family name". Another sigh, "I'm very sorry Mister Phillips, please excuse me". Beverly wiped her mouth with the tissue and threw it onto her unfinished meal, and then left the room.
Harold cleared his throat. "You have to understand Mister Phillips, it's an awful strain on us, this business with Gillian".
"I fully understand Harold, my heart bleeds for you both, but there is a greater power than us, who is watching over our deeds, and He knows what we do and what we don't deserve, have faith Mister Payne, and all things will be revealed. You see Harold, I can't let my emotions interfere with justice, believe me, I have had to kill people, who would seem to society, to be perfectly good people."
But you knew about them? You knew what they were up to? Mister Phillips"?
"Exactly Harold. Old men, young girls, even old women would you believe".
"Good grief".
"Yes, so you see Harold, I cannot get emotionally involved with victims, or perpetrators. God watches over me, He keeps me safe from harm's way, although sometimes He puts my patience to the test, more often than I would desire, actually".
Once again Hillman looked around the room somewhat nervously.
"Quite" said Harold, listening to every word from Hillman's mouth, intently.
He wasn't sure if Beverley had picked up on his signals. If she had she was playing an absolute blinder.

“Help yourself to the wine John, I’m just going to see if Beverly’s alright, it’s the time of year as well, I must admit, it gets to me as well John, I spill a few tears as well these days, huh, before this, I think the last time I cried was when my father died”.
Hillman was pouring wine into his glass.
“Really” said Hillman. “Not had much sadness or heartache in your life then? Making up for it now though, Mister Payne”.

Harold Payne made his way up the stairs to see if his wife was alright. How would he go about this? There was no way of telling her this, without panicking her. If she hadn’t picked up on his signals then he had some job on his hands. She was an emotional wreck as things were, without informing her that they were playing host to a certain Doctor John Hillman.

DIVISION STREET POLICE STATION.
SHEFFIELD.

John Drummond and Terrance Hanley stood in one of the interview rooms in the police station, awaiting the decision on whether or not they were going to be flying up to Lancaster.
It was snowing in Yorkshire, but nothing remotely as bad as it was further North in England. Cumbria, Northumberland, and Lancashire had been hit with the worst blizzards since records began. Parts of Cumbria were under a foot of snow. “It’s pretty bad up there John, they say there’s a foot of snow lying and getting deeper all the time”.
“Well, there’s one thing” said Drummond, “If that was Hillman up there who has committed this murder, then he’s still up there, because there’s no way he’s drove anywhere in that, all the roads are blocked. He’ll have to stay put, until this lot thaws, of course, it would depend on what time he set off. How much of a start he had, before this storm set in. Are Deborah and Karen coming with us up to Lancaster”?
“No”.
Terry Hanley made no attempt at explaining why he wasn’t letting them come up.
Drummond said no more about it.
The desk sergeant came into the room.
“You’re wanted at the front desk sir” the young fresh-faced officer said to Hanley.
“Wanted”? Repeated Hanley, “Sergeant, Doctor John Hillman is wanted. My presence is requested at the front desk, sergeant, not wanted”.
He followed the young policeman out of the room.
“I am required”.
Drummond smiled to himself as he loaded his pistol, and took out a notebook from his desk.” Your own English isn’t exactly perfect mister Hanley”. He said to himself.
“Bloody hell Terry, you could do with a course on phonology yourself bud, never mind correcting police cadets. He smiled to himself imagining the Scotsman volunteering to do just that, although he had noticed when Terry was trying to put a point forward that he suddenly began speaking more politely, and leaving out his usual swear-words.

Yes, the Scotsman and he had got off to a bad start, but as time had gone by, he had grown to like him or, at least, respect him. He was good. Whether or not he was as good as himself would remain to be seen. They would find out in due course. He could still hear him down the corridor, correcting the young sergeant on his pronunciation, “Huh, and *him* a Scotsman, like he could talk about pronunciation”.

Harold Payne tapped on the bedroom door. "Are you alright in there Beverley"? He opened the door and walked in. His wife sat at the built-in wardrobes in front of the mirror.
"She's dead Harold, I just know it. Don't ask me how I know, I just know".
She hadn't picked up on his signals.
"Beverley, I need to speak to you, it's very important. I need you to be in full control".
"Important?
What, may I ask could be more important than the welfare of our one and only daughter? Tell me that Harold. That gentleman down stairs seems more interested in Gillian, than the rest of them put together, and I've only known him for a few hours. They are just not interested. At least he seems to have some kind of knowledge of the character who's holding our daughter".
"Yes, and the reason for that, is because". He bent down and whispered. "Beverley, it's because he's-"
"Because he's what Harold"? Hillman's voice seemed to boom, like he'd spoken through a Public Announcement system.
"Because he's what Harold. Do you want your wife to have a nervous breakdown? Because I can tell you, she's about ten minutes off having one. Now I think that you and I should go back down stairs and finish off our conversation, don't *you* Harold"?
Harold sighed. "Of course, Mister Phillips, you're right. Forgive me dear, for interrupting your quiet time. Mister Phillips and I will be down stairs, join us when you're ready Beverley, take your time".
"That's right Beverley, you take your time, you're husband and I have lots to discuss".
"No" said Beverley. "Answer Mister Phillips' question, the reason he knows the character of the man who holds our daughter, is what? Harold, you were going to say something, that's because what"?
Harold Payne looked down at his feet.
He was in a situation now alright. If he said the wrong thing now they were dead. Why hadn't she picked up on what was becoming painfully obvious. Christ you just had to listen to him talking for a couple of minutes and you could tell the man had a screw loose.

"It's nothing Beverley, I confess, the man is on the ball, I must admit. It's just that sometimes I think that I could do better myself, but Mister Phillips here, he seems to be, well, a cut above the rest, I'm just jealous Beverley. He's a good looking man, and I thought that you were, well, kind of looking upon him as some kind of hero. I'm sorry Beverley, sorry Mister Phillips, I most humbly apologise to you both".

Beverley shook her head.

"Harold Payne, you have some weird ideas floating around in your head, God bless you. How on earth can you think about subjects like that when Mister Phillips is here to help us find our daughter"?

Harold Payne lifted his eyes, ever so slightly, and caught Hillman's eyes briefly.

Hillman stood smiling over Beverley Payne's head.

"Honest to goodness Harold, you're like a high school student, you really are, but the fact that Mister Phillips, is indeed a handsome man, should give you no reason to doubt me, now should it. Have you ever doubted me before? Or should I say, have I ever given you any reason to doubt me before. Have I ever let you down"?

"No dear, you haven't".

"Go down Harold, with Mister Phillips, and think shame on yourself. Mister Phillips? I am so sorry for the way Harold has conducted his behaviour, please make yourself at home, you are most welcome in our house, it'll be nice to have some company on Christmas Eve, especially with two handsome men".

Beverley smiled at Hillman.

He smiled back, and blew her a kiss.

Harold Payne was almost sick with fear and dread. This was one Christmas Eve he was not looking forward to, because there was no guarantee, that he or his wife would see Christmas morning.

"Are you going to kill us"? said Payne as they made their way down the stairs.

Harold Payne felt numb on his feet, as if his legs would give way any moment. He knew almost for certain that his one and only daughter was dead. No-one survived this monster. He clambered laboriously down the stairs to face God knew what. He could have quite easily just spoken the last words he ever would to his wife, and what would he do with his wife after he'd killed him. He was shaking involuntarily.

"That all depends on you Harold me boy", Hillman mocked. "If you had told your wife there, then yes, I would have had no choice but to kill you, but it's like I said before, me old mate God does look out for me. For some reason He put it into my head, that you were up to something, so I followed you up the stairs. Now, very soon, you will receive a phone call from one of those detectives. If you hint to them, in the slightest way, that I am here, then I will make sure that your wife dies in the most agonising fashion you could imagine, and then I shall kill you, in an equally agonising manner. Now, are you crystal clear about that Mister Payne"?
"Yes".
"Good. Right, let's have another glass of wine Harold, after all, tis` the season to be jolly".
As Harold poured another glass of wine for Hillman, he said "Put me out of my misery, is she still alive? You owe me that".
"Owe? Mister Payne? I owe you nothing, however, I shall tell you everything in due course, now you just concentrate on keeping Misses Payne happy, and make sure that you behave normally, because if not, I will kill her in front of you, I swear, as God is my witness, so be very careful, you just act like everything is ok, do you hear me, Or else".
"Can I go and get my box of cigars"?
"Don't be stupid man, act normally I said, just don't be going near any phones, that's all".
Payne got up from where he sat and walked over to the cabinet where he retrieved his mahogany cigar box, with the inscription; THE BEST DAD IN THE WORLD, engraved on the lid.
"Oh, fancy", said Hillman.
"It was a gift from my daughter if you must know".
He opened the box and took out two cigars, handing one to Hillman.
"King Edwards, a good smoke Harold".
Payne sat down at the table again, and lit his cigar, then gently threw the lighter to Hillman.
Outside, the wind had picked up, but the snow was not falling as heavily as it had been.
"Kind of wild out there Harold, is it not"?
Harold did not answer, but poured himself another glass of wine.
"How long do you plan to stay here, If you don't mind me asking".
As soon as he had spoken the words Harold knew that he'd upset Hillman, asking him a question like that. It was too late.

“I don’t know how long, and I *do* mind. Look, you never mind how long I intend to stay here, but I’ll warn you, if you ask me any more stupid questions like that, then I’ll sweep my hand across this table, and I’ll fuck your wife on top of it, and make you cry, now, any more stupid fucking questions? Bastard? Huh? Spoiled bastard? That’s your last fucking warning, now behave yourself, else I’ll take her knickers off right in front of you. Anyway, let’s go into the lounge and watch some T.V. there must be one or two good films on”. Hillman got to his feet. “Come on, let’s go through, bring your wine”.

Hillman sat down on an easy chair in front of the T.V.

“This is lovely, ah, just fine and dandy, fancy Misses Payne thinking I was handsome, she’s got a good taste in men, I can tell you that, ah, here she is now” said Hillman.

“Beverley? Do you like lots of sex, good sex? Does Harold pay you enough attention Beverley”?

DIVISION STREET POLICE STATION.
SHEFFIELD.

Terry Hanley was sitting in one of the interview rooms with Deborah Knowles, John Drummond, and Karen Jones, when his mobile phone buzzed. Knowles had been arguing her case why Karen and herself were not permitted to go to Lancaster.

"Look Deborah" Hanley had said, "It's got nothing to do with efficiency or anything like that; it's just a case of numbers, that's all. I mean, what the hell is Terrence Davis going to say, if we all traipse up to Lancaster and meanwhile, while we're all up there, doctor John Hillman decides to pay Sheffield another visit, huh? How would we look then?

Oh sorry sir, we all went up to Lancaster to view a dead body, we didn't stop to think that Hillman would come back here, sorry.

And don't forget Deborah, you still have to find Carla Paganni's friend, *and* Hillman's wife, you know? The ones you said were being watched around the clock by armed guards? The ones who drove away from the Merryfield Military Hospital"?

"I know, I know, I fucked up, ok? Have you never fucked up in your time"?

As Hanley's phone buzzed, he looked up to the ceiling, as if to think about the question, and then said, mockingly, "Nope". He glanced at the screen on his phone, and began pressing buttons as he did so.

Karen Jones said, "Is that Terrance asking you to *his* place for tea and bum licks is it"?

The two women were nearly at the door when Hanley spoke out.

"Wait ! Oh shit"

"What is it"? Said Knowles

"Oh shit, fucking hell!"

"What is it Terry for goodness sakes".

"It's Hillman. This text is from Beverley Payne; Hillman is in their house at Morecambe. People, we've got the bastard this time. We know for sure that he isn't going anywhere this time. I think he must be planning on staying with them until the weather breaks. I just hope he's feeling festive and he spares their lives until we can get to him.

Change of plan Deborah, you are coming up there with us, you and Karen. Now, right here and right now, we take a vote. Do we four handle this ourselves? Or do we alert everyone, who by the way, would steal all the credit, all the glory.
Hands up, those of us who think we should handle it ourselves"?
All four put up their hands, including Drummond, although rather hesitantly.
"Right, that's it folks".
Terry Hanley was pressing buttons on his phone, as Deborah Knowles was calling the helicopter base.
"What are you doing Terry"?
"What do you mean? What am I doing, I've answered her text, that's what I'm doing. I'm letting the poor woman know that we're on our way, and not to panic".
Deborah stood with her phone resting on her hip. "You haven't sent it yet, have you"?
"No, I thought I'd wait until *next* Christmas, and keep her in suspense of course I've sent it!"
"Oh Terry, fuck Terry, what have you done? Why do you think she sent you a text? She obviously can't use her telephone, if that bastard hears her phone, when she reads your text message. You might just have sealed their fate for them Terry. If that bastard hears the phone, then we can forget about ever seeing Mister and Misses Payne alive again. Chances are, he'll confiscate their phones. If he looks at that message"…
"Also" said Karen, "who the fuck is going to recognise him wading through the snow with an overcoat, after he's killed them"?
"Oh Terry" repeated Knowles, dear God man, what were you thinking? What was that you were saying a minute ago about not fucking up"?
Hanley put his clenched fists up to his brow, and began thumping.
"He wouldn't hear her mobile would he? He said, hopefully. Surely not".
Deborah sighed. "Well, if you ask me, I think we should inform the Lancashire constabulary, and the Cumbrian constabulary, give them some warning, at least". She was bluffing when she said this, knowing full well that Hanley would never agree to such a thing, he was a glory hunter, just like herself, but the fact that she'd suggested this would look good on her, even if her own plan failed. She smiled as Hanley answered.

“No, no way Deborah, no chance, now listen you guys” said Hanley. You three have been on the trail of this bastard longer than me, ok, I fucked up, right, but there’s an equal chance that that bastard didn’t hear the text, and that’s what I think we should assume, and carry on ourselves.

I know I may have executed the Payne’s, by answering the text, but we’ve got to give it a go. If he’s heard the phone, then he’ll have fucked off anyway, all the King’s horses and all the King’s men, wouldn’t find him in this weather, so I say, we take the chance, what do you think, Huh”?

“Ok” said Knowles, but if this fucks up, then it’s your arse, ok”?

“Ok” said Hanley. “It *has* to be *us* who captures him though, right”?

“Right” they all agreed.

Karen Jones spoke up. “Don’t worry Deborah; because if this fucks up, we won’t be here to answer to anybody, you know how this ruthless bastard works”.

“Right” said Hanley, “I’ll send a couple of officers up to Lancaster, we’re all off to Morecambe”.

“Fuck, I hope we’re doing the right thing here” said Drummond.

“Don’t worry John, this time tomorrow, you’ll be a national hero, you’ll have done the people of this country, a huge favour, and when we do get there folks, you have my blessing to hit him with everything you have in your guns, empty a whole magazine into him, if you want, then reload, and empty another one into him.

I think Doctor Hillman has earned himself the right to an on the spot execution. I’ve lost count on how many people he has taken out now, the number just keeps growing and growing, but not after today. After today, Doctor John Hillman is history, are we all in agreement with that”?

“Here’s to Hillman’s execution” they all replied.

Deborah Knowles smiled to herself as she poured herself another cup of coffee.

MORECAMBE. SEAVIEW. 7pm.

Hillman had ordered Harold Payne to get his wife to sit in the lounge with them, while he sat thinking. He had turned off the T.V. as the din on the Christmas shows were hurting his head. After five minutes of complete silence, Hillman spoke up.
“Ok, listen up everyone, here’s the deal, the brass tacks Misses Payne. It may come as quite a shock to you, but I am in fact, none other than Doctor John Hillman. Your husband already knows.
Now, as far as your daughter is concerned, I’m afraid I have bad news, she didn’t make it. I told her to behave, and I would set her free, but, alas, she went for a gun. This one”, he said, as he pulled out the Magnum from his inside jacket pocket.
Beverley Payne sat bolt upright on her chair at the dining table, hands clasped together between her knees, her bottom lip trembling, and tears rolling down her face.
“You might want to get your wife a drink there Harold, they say brandy’s the best for shock, come on man, move, and get me one while you’re there”.
Beverley Payne stood up.
“I’ll get my own drink, thank you, and so will you Hillman, you mental bastard, God is not with you, you stupid man, you are ill, don’t you know that? Don’t you know why you are killing all these people? It’s not God, it’s your sick mind, you need to get treatment, only, it’s too late for that now, you’ve gone too far. Do you think if God loved you, that He would make every person on this Island hate you, because they do, every person who has heard about you? The nation is going to cheer, when you die, imagine that, everybody laughing and singing at the joy of your death? Now, Mister murdering innocent people Hillman, do you think if God loved you, he would allow that? God hates your guts, just like the rest of us. You kill my one and only child, for no reason? No reason, Doctor Hillman, and you order my husband to get you a drink? Get it yourself, you mental bastard, steal it, because you’re a thief, you’re not welcome anywhere, except in a lunatic asylum, so don’t think you can frighten me with that gun, because we all know, that without that, I doubt if you’d be able to give a school girl a decent fight, you fucking weed, get the drink yourself, you piece of shit that you are!”

"Your wife is suffering from shock Harold, it's a natural reaction".

"Fuck off Hillman, you don't know the meaning of the word natural, nothing in your sick life happens naturally, it's not God making these things happen, it's *you*, you sick fuck, do us all a favour, and turn the gun on yourself, if you've got the guts, God wants that to happen, you can be sure of that"!
"Take your clothes off slut! Let's see how brave you are. If you don't, I'll kill your husband here and now!"
"I'll take my clothes off, don't worry Harold, this freak won't be capable of an erection, he's full of shit, fucking coward that he is killing defenceless people that's all he's good for, because, without that gun, he's not even a man".
She lunged at Hillman attempting to punch him on the face, but he simply grabbed her hand, twisted her round, and threw her onto the sofa.
"Now get undressed bitch! Or he's dead"!
Beverley began taking her clothes off, crying as she did and regretting her outburst.
"Drink Harold please, I've already told you once, now move it, and get yourself one, you might need it, while you watch me entertaining your wife. In fact, bring the bottle over here; we can all have a drink. Hell, we can even take turns with your wife, and I'll bet this is not the first time that this has happened, eh Bev? Have you and Harold here had a few swinging parties, have you"?
"Shut up, stupid man". She managed, between her sobs.
Hillman smiled as he lay the gun down on the chair beside him and began to take off his trousers.
Even through her heartache, Beverley Payne felt the fire of anger raging inside again.
"Oh, by the way Mister Phillips" Beverley mocked, "we knew who you were from the minute you walked in the door, just for the record, just in case you thought you were smart or something".
"Take your pants off as well Beverley, how do you expect me to service you with those on, huh?
When you get over here Harold, get your face in between her legs, soak her up for me, wet her pussy up for me, will you pal"?
Hillman hadn't noticed Harold picking up the ice pick, and tuck it down the back of his trousers.

Harold knew, he would get one chance at this, maybe, and if he messed it up, he and his wife would die a horrible death. But he would give this his best shot, for Gillian, he would kill him for her, he had to.
"You!" Hillman snapped at Beverley, now standing naked. "Get through there, and sit your whore arse on the couch, me and Harry will be through in a minute. Harry? Bring the drinks through here".

Hillman stood, with only his shirt and his boxer shorts on. He picked up one of Harold's King Edward's and lit it up, blowing smoke up into the air.
"Do you like what you see Bev? Huh? Want this, do you"?
Beverley avoided his eyes, and now showing her fear, as she sat down on the sofa, with her hands clasped around her breasts. Her flames of anger had been extinguished.
"Trust me, you'll love it, your daughter did, in fact she gagged for it constantly, took it good as well, she knew how to use her body, yes, very experienced, very. Oh, before we start, do you like to spit or swallow Bev"?
Beverley Payne said nothing, still looking at the floor.
"Good, that's good that you leave it up to me, because, you're going to do neither, you're going to gargle, and choke I know that for a fact".
Hillman's mother appeared to him, smiling, and mouthing the words, "FROCK BOY"
As Harold came into the living room, Hillman said to him, "did you hear that Harry boy? Did you hear the plan"?
Harold said nothing, only nodding.
Harold Payne sat a tray down on the coffee table, with a bottle of brandy, a bottle of whiskey, and an ice bucket.
"I've forgotten the glasses" he said, as he returned to the kitchen.
"Yeah, you've forgotten an ice pick as well Harry, I'll tell you what, you bring a rope in here as well, and bring that ice pick you have tucked into your trousers there, and wash it first, I'm not breaking ice with anything that's been anywhere near your pansy arse".
Beverley cried out hopelessly.
Not only had Hillman subdued her anger, he had put the fear back into her, even more than before. She silently prayed that the detectives had got her text message and were responding. She cried again, the sickening truth refusing to go away, Gillian was dead.

“Now now, bitch, nobody’s even touched you yet, and anyway, where’s the brave whore who told me I was a sick man, huh? Where’s the brave tramp who informed me that God did not speak to me? I’ll tell you something, fucking rich whore that you are, He’s not saying much to *you* at this moment in time to make you feel any better, is He? I don’t see Him coming to *your* rescue right now. You think you’re so much better than everyone else, don’t you? You think you can buy your way through life. Fancy house, fucking fancy cars, parties, fucking fancy clothes, sleeping around with each other’s husbands, the most expensive hotels, yeah, you think you’re really something, don’t you.
Then you wonder why God let’s something like this happen to your daughter, your spoiled, rich, filthy minded daughter, who travelled around in a brand new Porsche Carrera, with her skirt up her arse, begging for cock, constantly, fucking see through clothes, I love sex necklaces, fucking high heeled shoes, slut make up, and a never ending credit card to go with it all. Why do you think God chose her, huh? Why was *she* there at that petrol station, at the exact time that I pulled in? One minute later they would have been away. One minute earlier I wouldn’t even have seen them.
Fate, rich slut, fate. Just as it’s *your* fate that you are going to have the pleasure of having sex with me. Where’s those clean glasses Harry”?

Harold Payne returned with the glasses and the ice pick, and a roll of washing line, still in its wrapper.
“Right, it’s party time” said Hillman.
“Sit down on that chair Harry. Bev, tie his hands up, real tight. I’ll inspect it when you’re finished, and if *he* can get his hands out, I’m going to destroy his knees, now tie him up”.
Hillman poured himself a whiskey.
“What do you want Bev? Whiskey or brandy? Come on, you’re having a drink with me whether you like it or not”.
“Brandy” she managed to mumble.
“What about *you* Harry? Whiskey or brandy”?
“No thank you, nothing”.
Hillman picked up his gun and pointed it at Beverley.
“I can fuck a dead woman just as easily, now, what do you want”?
“Whiskey”.
“Whiskey, right, coming up sir, ice”? Said Hillman.

“No thank you”.
Hillman looked at the ice pick on the table. “No, me neither. Right, here you are Bev, and give this one to your husband, give him a drink. Right, put his glass on the floor; keep tying him up, nice and tight”.
Two minutes later, Harold Payne sat on the chair, his hands completely bound.

“Now then Beverley, get yourself sat down on the sofa.
“Come on now everyone, its Christmas time, come on, nice and cheerful like. You’d better make a more convincing attempt at smiling Bev, or else I’m going to kill your husband right here and now.
Do you have a camera Harold? I would like to take a photograph of your wife, now get those legs open Bev, nice and wide. Beverley began to cry, but for the sake of her husband, she done what she was told.
Hillman held the camera. Right, I want you to put on a great huge smile Beverley, like this was the best Christmas ever, ready?
One, two, three, merry Christmas everybody!!”
Hillman drained his glass and stubbed out his cigar.
“Now then Bev, time for the time of your life”.

“Doctor Hillman”? Harold Payne spoke softly.
“Yes”? Replied Hillman getting onto his knees in front of Beverley. “What? Are you getting jealous there Harry boy. I think I know what you’re going to say, you don’t want to be in the same room. Me and Bev here can go into the bedroom, if that’s what you want, I can understand”.
“Doctor Hillman, before I say to you what I’m about to say, I fully understand that it’s not money that you’re after, I know that now, but please, here me out, before you refuse my offer

“Your offer of what, as far as I can see, you’re in no position to haggle Harry boy” said Hillman, still kneeling in front of Beverley. “Come on then, let’s hear it, but don’t be long, your wife needs a good seeing to”.

"Doctor Hillman, I have never begged for anything in my entire life. I'm begging you now, not to take this situation any further. As far as our daughter is concerned, yes, we screwed up there, we gave her far too much, we spoiled her, but I feel God has punished us both for our sin. She was our only child, and now, we have paid the price for our misjudgement. I can't undo anything that God has put before me, but I can assure you Mister Hillman, of one thing, He has obviously sent you here to teach us a lesson, which my wife and I have most definitely learned. We can help you Doctor Hillman, because I know that the law will not understand anything that you are attempting to do here in the name of our heavenly Father, but I do. I can get you out of this country with a clean passport, immaculate, and money, I can get you money, name your price, only, please, spare us any more pain and indignity.

As a man of healing, that you are, I'm asking you now to give Beverley and I the chance to repent to God, and to do some works of good for Him. I know that we have splashed money around in our lives, and yes, you're right, we probably *did* think we were better than everybody else, but please John, believe me, we have learned our lesson, we know now, that we are no better than anyone else, the value of a person is their soul, not their bank account. It has cost us the life of our daughter, but God has spoken to us through you, so please sir, on this holiest of nights, please have mercy on us, and let us live to serve God"

Hillman stared trance-like at Harold Payne's distraught face. Then he looked at Beverley Payne, and the indignity she was suffering.

"How do I know you are telling the truth Harold"?

"I know Doctor Hillman, because God knows I'm telling the truth, and if He knows, and you work through His word, then He'll find a way of making you see that I am truthful".

Harold Payne knew he was taking a risk, but he had to tell Hillman what had been said.

Hillman got up to his feet.

He looked at Beverley and said, "Put your clothes back on, hurry up".

"Doctor Hillman, before all this started, my wife sent a text message to inspector Terry Hanley. They know you're here".

His wife could hardly believe what she was hearing.

There was silence while Hillman and Beverley put on their clothes.

Hillman walked over to the table and poured himself another drink.
"Sit down!!" He snarled at Beverley.
"Well now Harold, why would you be telling me that, huh? You should be buying time until they get here".
"I'm telling you that doctor, because if I am to be a good Christian, then I must tell the truth, and that means every detail".
"How long ago did she text them"?
"About three quarters of an hour ago".
"Well then, they should be here any minute now".
"No" said Payne. "You see I heard them talking in here one day, and they said they weren't going to pass on any information on to any other police force in the country, should they find out where you are. They want all the glory for themselves. They say they want to capture or kill you themselves, there are four of them, you see, Inspector Drummond, Inspector Hanley, Inspector Jones and Inspector Knowles. They four alone are the ones who have all the information on you. Hanley's in charge of them, he's the main one".
"And what makes you think they won't inform the police here in Morecambe"?
"Because they are in Sheffield, look at the weather, the Morecambe constabulary would be here long before they could get to you, and then *they* would take all the glory. They won't want that. That would mean you beat them again. It's my bet doctor Hillman, that they'll summon a helicopter, if the weather clears up enough, and land as close as they can, to here, without us being able to hear it of course. They would walk the rest of the way here, and then try and storm the building, hoping they could take you by surprise".
"I see" said Hillman, relighting his cigar.
Beverley Payne sat on the sofa with her head bowed to the floor, too afraid to look up.
"Untie your husband" said Hillman, blowing smoke up towards the ceiling.
"After that, go and get your mobile phone, and bring it here. Get your drink Harold when she's untied you, you might as well make yourself comfortable while you can".
Hillman lifted the Magnum up from the table and checked the chamber. He snapped it shut again, making Beverley jump.
"Come on, hurry up, untie him and get your phone. And no more of your smart-mouthing lady, your daughter was good at that and look where it got her".

Hillman walked over to the window and looked outside. The snow had virtually stopped. Only pellets of sleet were being driven by the near gale-forced wind. "I don't think they'll be flying around in any helicopter in that wind Mister Payne, do you"?
"I wouldn't think so doctor Hillman".
"Hmm" sighed Hillman, without looking round. "And there's not much chance of them driving up here, they'll be lucky if even the motorways will be clear, and even then, there's no guarantee of that, I've never seen snow like this before, in this country, which means Harold, that if they want to be guaranteed to catch me, they would have no choice but to inform the local constabulary round here".
"Either that, doctor Hillman, or they're thinking that they've got you where they want you.
They'll be thinking that you can't move either, you can't drive anywhere, there are no trains, and there wouldn't be anyway, because of Christmas, so, they'll be praying for the wind to die down, and then fly here as soon as possible, they'll all be on standby, and we can rest assured that none of them will be having a Christmas dinner, they'll be waiting, thinking that you're trapped here".
"Am I not Harold? I don't have much option *but* to stay put, I would hardly get very far wading through knee deep snow now would I"?
"Yes, but they don't know that do they".
"Don't be so stupid Harold, and tell her to get down here with that phone before my patience runs out!"
Beverley came into the living room. She walked slowly over to Hillman, and handed him the phone.
"Go and sit down on the sofa" he said, pressing a couple of buttons on the phone. He clicked a few more buttons and then said "ah, here we are, Received message" *'ON OUR WAY AS SOON AS POSSIBLE, TRY AND KEEP HIM THERE, DON'T PANIC, HELP IS ON THE WAY. HANLEY'*. Hillman looked up from the phone to Beverley. "You've not to panic" he repeated, taking a draw from the cigar, "you've not to panic Bev, you've to try and keep me here".

Hillman waved the phone in the direction of the window. "Huh, that won't be hard to do".
"What do you think doctor Hillman"? Said Harold Payne.
"What do I think? I think that you are very lucky to be alive, that's what I think, don't you think that Bev? Do you think he's lucky to be alive"?

“Yes I do”.
“Yes sir, so do I” repeated Hillman. “And so are you Bev, now, you go through there and knock us up something that resembles a Christmas dinner, while I sit here and think this over, and while your husband shuts his fucking mouth, unless I speak to him, ok? That’s what I think”!

Hillman sat back down on the chair, opposite Harold Payne. His phone beeped.
“Well I never, I wonder who that could be texting me”.
He pulled his phone out from his inside jacket pocket and clicked it on. The message read; “*MERRY CHRISTMAS DADDY FROM AMY AND ANGELA. XXX”.*

Hillman took a draw from his cigar, and exhaled smoke.
“It’s from my little angels Harold, you see? I was wrong, they didn’t forget me, I thought they would have forgotten about me, but they haven’t. Their mother has allowed them to send me a text message, isn’t that wonderful Harold? My daughters, they remembered me. Come on, this calls for a celebration Harold, toast a drink to doctor Hillman and his little angels, who would have thought it huh? I’m a very lucky man Harold”.

Harold Payne looked over to the photograph of his own daughter. The photograph was taken on her first day at school. He raised his glass to the man who had taken her away from him.” Yes you are a very lucky man Doctor Hillman…very lucky”.

DIVISION STREET POLICE STATION.
SHEFFIELD.

Deborah Knowles sat with the rest of the team around the table in the interview room. So we just wait? We just wait here and do nothing, until something happens"?
"Deborah, I know it's frustrating but there's nothing that we can do, they won't go out in those choppers in gale force winds like that, and that's the end of it. I know you're keen to nail this bastard, I know it, but we have to wait until these winds subside, remember, he isn't going anywhere, he can't move, he's stuck as well, and, even if he *does* know about the text message, he can't move. He's probably waiting for the Lancashire constabulary to kick in the door any minute. He doesn't know that we haven't told anyone of his whereabouts, so, just sit tight Deborah, and pray for the wind to die down. We *will* get him; he won't get away this time".
"I only hope that Mister and Misses Payne's luck holds out, though I can't see it myself" said Deborah.
"Well" Hanley said, rubbing the stubble on his chin, "I must admit, I haven't helped their cause there, I messed up bad, I only hope he didn't hear the reply on Misses Payne's phone".
Drummond stubbed out, yet another cigarette in the already overflowing ash tray. "I think we should alert everyone, tell them, and then if this goes wrong, we will all be in the clear".

"And what John, let some country bumpkin cops, who have just learned to shoot last week, take all the glory? How many men did you lose at Morningside? Right under your nose, He took the piss out of you, he even walked in the house, straight into the kitchen, took his car keys off the rack, opened the garage door, while you lot searched the grounds for him, and quite calmly drove away. Now, surely even that should be enough John, to make you want to cut off his balls. For the honour of those men you lost. Don't even think about telling anyone else about this. We found out of his whereabouts by means of our own sources, so we will finish this, within our own sources, and besides, we took a vote, and we decided this was the way we were going, agreed"?
Deborah, Karen, and eventually, John Drummond, all nodded their heads.

"I know" said Drummond, I just want this all over and done with, I want this bastard to die, and as soon as possible. He has plagued my life, and has driven me to the depths of despair; I want to see him dead".

"You will John" said Hanley. "I promise you, you will, just as soon as we can get up to Morecambe, but get that idea out of your head about informing anyone else. They've given you nothing but grief since you started hunting this lunatic, calling incompetent even. We'll show the bastards who's incompetent John".

MORECAMBE.

CHRISTMAS NIGHT.

The wind had calmed down now, to no more than a stiff breeze. Harold Payne sat on the sofa, next to his wife, who had fallen asleep, with sheer exhaustion. Payne had been watching Hillman throughout the evening. The man was tired. Harold Payne was tired as well, but he could not allow himself to fall into slumber, for a number of reasons. Earlier on in the evening, when he had come through to the kitchen, he had placed himself, a nice sharp carving knife underneath one of Beverley's tea towels, for an opportunity such as this. As Harold had loaded the crockery into the dish washer, Hillman had sat talking to his wife, making sure she never left his sight.

Now, he looked over to Hillman, who was once again, dozing off, with his gun lying diagonally across his chest. Hillman jumped up with a start, and made himself sit up.

Harold Payne had no desire to have any kind of conversation with his captor at this moment in time, so he pretended to sleep, hoping that Hillman would not "*wake him up*".

"That's it Doctor Hillman" said Harold to himself, when he heard Hillman moving. "You pour yourself another whiskey, you've had about half a bottle already, it's bound to put you to sleep sooner or later, you pour yourself another large one".

He carefully watched as Hillman lit up another cigar and walked over to the window.

"He's not thinking straight" said Harold, to himself. "We are up here in the living room, and the curtains are still open". From outside, looking into the light, a good marksman could take him out with one shot. "He wouldn't know anything about it".

Without turning round, it was as if Hillman could read his mind. He closed the curtains and turned.

Payne closed his eyes again.

He was struggling to stay awake. Exhaustion was taking over.

Adrenalin could only keep you going for so long.

Hillman was sipping whiskey again.

It would be better if he *could* catch forty winks" thought Harold, because he knew that Hillman's moods could change with lightning speed. Harold could feel the exhaustion creeping in. He knew he was going to doze off, he could feel himself drifting away, his body in desperate need of total replenishment.

He would sleep, and with any luck, he would awake to find John Hillman sleeping.

Three hours later, he awoke to total darkness, other than the glow of the gas fire. He felt his wife beside him on the sofa. Was it his wife? He carefully felt her face. "Thank God". It was *her.*

"Hillman must be sleeping, this could be my chance" he thought, as he slowly lifted himself from the sofa. It took only seconds for his eyes to adjust, but he could already see that Hillman was not in his chair. He walked over to one of the main light switches and turned it on. One half of the room lit up brightly. Beverley awoke from the glare, covering her eyes with her hands, and yawning.

Harold put a finger to his mouth and whispered, "sshh, he'll hear us". He walked over to the other side of the room, and put the other switch down as well. Now, the room was lit up nice and brightly for anyone outside to see. Then he went into the kitchen. He lifted up the tea towel, expecting to find the blade.

Instead, he found a note.

"Shit!!" He hissed, as he read Hillman's words.

Now now, Mister Payne, this is not what we'd call a good start to your Christian life, is it. Be careful what you promise God Mister Payne, because sometimes He'll hold you to it, I swear.

Bastard" whispered Payne. He looked at the wall where the knife rack was. All six blades had been taken. He returned to the living room, and then he and his wife checked all the rooms. Fifteen minutes later, they had searched the whole house, and found nothing.

"He's gone Harold, he's bloody gone, he has".

"Don't get *too* excited" he said to his wife. Harold Payne walked to the front door, and opened it. He looked outside. Then he walked straight through the house and opened the back door. He returned to the living room.

"Well? Is he gone"?

"No".

"No? Well then, where is he"?

"Don't know, but there are no marks on the snow at either end of the house, so we can assume that he's still here, his car is still outside as well".

."Where the hell could he hide"?

Harold turned to find another note, this time on the coffee table in the living room.

Didn't want to wake you up Harold, Thanks for putting me up and feeding me, I don't suppose we'll meet again, so ,if you want to serve God, just do it, just pray, He'll make you see what He wants you to do, oh, and by the way Harry boy, it would have taken more than a kitchen knife to see old Doctor Hillman off. Take care of your wife, and learn not to be so greedy with money, and to help other people in need. Do good things for one another, and for other people, and do it for no money. Do these things, and you'll find your life more fulfilling. Best wishes John Hillman.

Harold Payne held the note in his hands, staring at Hillman's words.

"What does it say Harold? Is it a trick? Is he gone"?

Harold gave his wife the note to read, as he poured a drink for the two of them. "It's a trick Harold, the bastard's playing another game. You said it yourself, there are no footprints on any of the steps. He can't fly away, the bastard is still here". Harold sat down on the sofa, next to his wife, handing her a drink. He put the pointing finger of his right hand up to his lips. "Ssshhh". He leaned over and whispered into his wife's ear. "If we sit quietly for long enough, then we'll hear him, we'll know where he's hiding. There is only one place he can be hiding, the cellar, I think you're right Bev, I think he's still in the house. Maybe he's waiting for me to phone the police, so that he can kill me for going back on my word". He tapped his wife on the shoulder, making her look at the carving knife he had tucked into his sock. Again, he put his finger up to his mouth as he handed her a small but very sharp kitchen knife. He smiled, tapping her once more on the knee. It was Harold's way of letting her know that everything was going to be alright. He had done this right through the thirty one years of their marriage, and he was usually right, only this time, he wasn't right. This time, it was not going to be alright. Their only child had been brutally murdered by a ruthless religious madman, and, the girl's fiancée. And this madman was still in their house, just waiting to pounce when the time suited him.

Even if the police in Morecambe had been alerted, there was at least, two feet of snow lying out there, their progress would be slow, very slow. She smiled at her husband, as she tapped him back a couple of times on *his* knee. Tears rolled down her face as she sipped her brandy, tucking the knife into the waistband of her skirt. As the clock on the wall struck midnight Beverley Payne spoke to her daughter, in her own mind. *Merry Christmas little darling, mummy and daddy loves you very much".*

At twelve twenty-two, Harold Payne jumped with fright as he was awoken from a semi-conscious slumber.
"What is it"? said Beverley herself jumping with fright because of the sudden movement from her husband.
"I don't know something woke me.
Wait here Beverley" he said "I'm just going to check something".
"Wait here nothing" said Beverley. "Wherever you're going, I'm coming too".
"I'm just going to the kitchen".
"Why? Was there a noise in there? Is that what stirred you"?
"Don't know, come on".
Harold pulled out the large knife from under his trousers, and made his way to the kitchen, his wife close behind. He was dreading seeing a space on the wall where the cellar key usually hung. The key was there. He sighed as he turned to his wife. "There's just one last place to look".
The couple made their way down to the cellar door.
"If this door is locked to the cellar, then it looks like he really *is* gone Bev". As they reached the door, Beverley said,
"You or me? Who's going to try the door handle"?

"I'll do it darling" said Harold, half expecting, half dreading the door to open, it did.
"Close it, and lock it Harold, close it and phone the local police, don't go down those steps, the bastard's waiting, come on, move Harold, there's no way out of there, he's trapped, he's trapped himself playing his sick games, come on!!"
Harold closed the door and turned the key. He and Beverley could hear footsteps coming up the concrete steps of the cellar, and then; Thump, thump, thump, on the door.
"Mister Payne"?

"Sorry Doctor Hillman, we're too busy phoning the police to be bothered with you" replied Beverley. "How does it feel to be trapped like the dog that you are, has God turned His back on you? Oh dear, what a shame, never mind. I hope it takes them three days to get here, because there's no way you're getting any food or water from us".

"Misses Payne, please,"

"Oh, Misses Payne now, is it? Not Bev, or whore, now that you're a victim of your own sick games. Doctor Hillman? Here's the news, are you ready for this? God hates you!"

The thumping continued on the door.

"Mister Payne, pleasc listen, you have to-"

"We don't have to do anything Doctor, you're fucked, if you pardon my expression.

Tell you what, if you want out of there". Beverley cleared her throat and began to sing heartily, mocking; ASK THE SAVIOUR TO HELP YOU, COMFORT STRENGTHEN TO KEEP YOU, HE IS WILLING TO AID YOU, HE WILL CARRY YOU THR-"

The front of her husband's face disintegrated onto the cellar door, right before her eyes. She felt a sharp needle-like pain in her left knee, as it completely gave way, taking her breath away as she slumped to the floor, and as John Hillman began ripping her clothes off with one of her own kitchen knives, she noticed a card slipping through from underneath the cellar door, it read; D.C.I. Terrance Hanley.

It all began to register now in her mind. "Misses Payne, of course Misses Payne"

Her husband gasped his last breath, desperately trying to reach for his wife. One of his eyes lay on top of Hanley's I.D. card

More thumping on the door.

"Misses Payne? Misses Payne, please open the door, it's the police, its chief inspector Hanley, everything is going to be ok, it's alright".

"You're right there inspector Hanley" said Hillman, running the blade in his hand, right down Beverley Payne's back, digging into her, as he cut through her clothing.

She screamed with the burning pain in her back, as the knife tore mercilessly through her skin.

“Everything *is* going to be just fine, you’re right inspector” said Hillman, pulling off what was left of Beverley’s skirt. You shouldn’t have hid down there should you Mister Hanley? You and Mister Drummond, you only led Mister and Misses Payne here into thinking that *I* was down there. Never mind though Mister Hanley, better luck next time huh? You’ll get lucky one of these days”.
Hanley and Drummond began banging on the door once again.
Even if the police detectives attempted to shoot the locks out they would be out of luck. Harold had the builders install a metal heavy-duty door which was almost four inches thick.
“Please, Doctor Hillman, don’t hurt them, please, we can talk about this, we can work out a deal Doctor, there’s no need for any more blood to be spilled, please doctor, let them go”.
“Too late Hanley, I’m afraid Harold has moved on to the other side, he has an appointment with his maker, and I have been asked to learn his whore wife a lesson, before I send *her* on her way, to explain herself to God, and as to why she looked down her snobby fucking nose at other people, just because they weren’t as rich as *her*”.
“Please, Doctor”.
“She is going to be sodomized Mister Hanley, on top of her husband’s corpse, she will writhe in her husband’s blood”.
Hillman pushed the card back under the door.
“Your credit card is no good here Mister Hanley, you just listen to her crying out for mercy. This one’s on the house Mister Hanley, enjoy”.
Beverley Payne, although only half conscious, screamed with pain, as Hillman jammed his erect penis into her anus, causing her to lose her breath, such was the agony.
“Doctor Hillman, please don’t hurt her any more”.
Hillman ignored the police inspector.
“Is that not nice Misses whore? I thought you said you found me attractive? Didn’t you? What was that you were saying to Harold before? Oh yes, you said that you doubted whether or not I could get an erection, wasn’t that what you said, Bev? Fucking whore! It’s up now, my little slut whore, isn’t it eh”?

He pounded even harder as he spoke to her. Blood oozed out of her anus, as he pounded her as hard as he could. Once more, his mother appeared to him, and looking excited at what he was doing to the poor unfortunate woman.
"*That's it, that's it, you fock her hard son*" said Hillman's mother, "*you fock her hard and prove to your father that you're not his little frock boy, go on son, dig in to the little whore. The whole world is poisoned with little scrubbers like her, look, she's got the nerve to pass out on you, dirty little tramp that she is, that's my bastard boy, you give it to her*"!!
"I'M NOT A BASTARD, JUST FUCK OFF MOTHER, I'M NOT A BASTARD"!!
"*Oh but you are son, you're not John Hillman's son, your father is a priest, Father Thomas Mcreary. That's who your father is, that's why you're such a religious freak bastard, go on son, tan her focking arse for her, I used to love it when Father Mcreaery gave me one up the tail-pipe, go on frock boy, show the world that you don't play for the focking pink team after all, because that's what everybody thinks you know*"!!
"FUCK OFF MOTHER, JUST FUCK OFF!!"

Hillman's gun lay on the floor, just to his right.
Deborah Knowles quickly picked it up and pulled the hammer back. She placed the barrel of the gun against his cheek.
"Your time is up sicko" she said.
"That will do sick man. Pull out of her now, or your head is mince, pull out now, Karen, get those cuffs on him. Just nice and easy, bad boy, that's it, nice and steady. We've got ourselves a nice little blood bath going on here haven't we? I don't see your fucking mother here though sick man, where is she"? Karen Jones clipped on the hand cuffs, with Hillman's hands behind his back. "There now, that's better sick boy, nice and harmless now".
Deborah Knowles used her right foot to kick Hillman over onto the floor, making him land on Harold Payne's body.
"There, how does it feel doctor, lying in the blood that you've spilled".
Before he could move, Knowles swung with her steel capped wellington boot again, and caught Hillman square on the mouth. All of the dental work that had been done in the hospital, burst open again.

Beverley Payne sat huddled up against the wall, sobbing uncontrollably, and still bleeding from her anus.
"Is everything ok"? shouted Hanley and Drummond from the cellar.
At this point Hillman began to hallucinate again. He could plainly see his wife Tracy standing there, laughing at him, as she twirled the skipping rope round and round, and holding a cigarette in her other hand.
"It's not looking too good for you holy boy, I think she's really fucked your mouth up this time bud, more than I did I think, it's looking really bad bastard boy, shout for your mummy to help you like you usually do".
"It will be in a minute boys," replied Knowles, "there's just one or two things to sort out here, won't be long, get away from the door though, go back down the cellar steps".
"Is Hillman still alive Deborah"?
Deborah looked at Karen and smiled.
"Yes, he's still alive Terry".
"Deborah? Don't kill the bastard, whatever you do, don't kill him sweetheart, please, stay cool".
Deborah looked at Karen again, and again, she smiled.
Karen smiled back, and nodded.
Deborah whispered something to Karen that Hillman couldn't hear, and then she shouted; "Ok, you're the boss Terry. Are you at the bottom of the stairs"?
"Yes".
"Right Terry, you and John put your guns away; Misses Payne here is petrified, ok"?
"Ok Deborah, they're away, tell Misses Payne that everything's going to be alright, try and calm her down Deborah".
"Right you are boss" said Deborah, giving the cellar door the two finger salute.
"I'm opening the door now".
"Good girl, good work Deborah".

Deborah Knowles saw an opportunity to execute her plan, a plan that would gain her fame beyond any of her colleagues' wildest expectations. Her time had come.
"Stay here Karen" she said, as she opened the door and began walking down the cellar steps. As she got half way down, Terry Hanley said, "You're sure you've got him secured"?

"Yes, but the only thing is he shot you and John here, before we could get to him".

Deborah Knowles lifted the Magnum and shot Terrance Hanley in the head. Before Drummond could react, she shot him as well, first on the shoulder, and then, as she walked up to him,

quite calmly, she shot him a second time in the face.

"Sorry boys, it's just one of those things, Karen and I have worked too hard on this case for you two fly by nights, to take all the fucking glory, sorry".

She walked back up the steps and into the house again. Beverley Payne still sat huddled up in the corner.

"Never mind darling" said Knowles, "we'll learn this bastard a lesson for you, you just see if we don't". Deborah Knowles once again swung her steel capped boot into the face of John Hillman.

"Want a shot? Karen"?

"You fucking bet I do" said Karen. "Sit him back up again Deborah, I can't get a decent shot at him. Ready?" Watch this Misses Payne" said Knowles.

For a full five minutes, the two women took turns at kicking Hillman in the mouth, until his face was just pulp.

"There now, Misses Payne" said Knowles. "You saw us get him back for you, give me that gun Karen.

Karen handed Knowles the gun who quickly held it to Beverley Payne's head and pulled the trigger.

"There now Karen, that's that taken care of, fucking do this do that, you're not coming here, you're not doing that, and he's just the same rank as me, the Scottish fucking twat!!"

"What about *him*"? Karen said, pointing to Hillman.

"What about him? He's practically unconscious anyway".

Beverley Payne's body had slumped over Hillman's legs, her semi naked frame saturated with blood.

"Ah well" said Knowles, "we've only done what she would have done herself Karen, it would only have been a matter of time. The woman wasn't strong enough to live with that. Losing her daughter to a freak like that!" She kicked Hillman in the mouth again.. "Then being tortured and raped by that same FREAK!!" Another kick. "And then watching her husband getting his head blown from here to kingdom come, no, no way Karen, we saved her a lot of pain".

"Why didn't you interfere Deborah before he buggered her"?

"Well Karen, it's like this, if we had moved in too soon, then who knows what might have happened, as it was he began his sexual endeavours, I wasn't to know he was going to do that. Anyway, the only time a man's attention is completely occupied, is when he is inside a woman, we had to wait until he was completely pre-occupied, that's why Karen, anyway, now *we* take the glory my friend, you and I. As for those two fucks in the cellar, huh, we would have been lucky even to get a mention. This animal here had them running in circles".
"Us too" said Karen, aiming a full solid blow with *her* steel capped boot, straight into Hillman's genitals.
"Ooh, you nasty cow Karen, I felt that for him".
"He's still conscious though" said Karen, smiling. "It just shows you, I could have sworn he was out".
Deborah Knowles took out her cigarette packet and placed a cigarette in her mouth.
"Would you like one partner" she said, laughing at the thought of getting the better of the two dead officers lying in the cellar.
Karen smiled. "You know? I think I will, eh, partner".
"Come on Karen, let's go and get something to drink, after all, no-one knows where we are, except for the helicopter pilot, and even he dropped us off more than a mile away from here".
"Anyway" said Karen, "Hanley down there swore him to secrecy".
"So he did Karen, so he did".
The two detectives left Hillman to go and get a drink, after both women had sat him up and each of them given him another sound kick in the teeth.
"There now bastard" said Knowles.
"Just in case you were thinking about crawling away somewhere, now don't you dare move" she said,, "unless God comes and heals your wounds for you, and takes those cuffs off.
Don't hold your breath slime ball".
Hillman could just make out their voices in the semi-conscious daze he was in.
His mother appeared to him once again.
Hillman had never felt pain like this in his entire life.
His head was throbbing as blood poured from his mouth and his ears. His eyes were puffed up and almost closed. He knew he was very close to death, very close indeed.

"My poor little helpless bastard boy, what have the nasty ladies done to you. You should have been a girl my little frock-boy, you'd have done better as a girl...you fight like one, poor bastard boy. Misses Payne was right though son, God does hate you, and your father did too...so did I for that matter. Look at you lying there all helpless and hurt, crying for your whore wife and bastard children. Even they couldn't stand the sight of you. To be honest, not many people could, apart from old misses Semple, but she's not right in the head either. Well, I tried to make a man out of you, but now, you're lying there hurting like anything, and all because you're a useless focking good for nothing, frock-boy, goodbye little bastard, plague of my life".

"Just think Karen, we are going to be national hero's, we could make a fortune if we sell our stories to the papers, nobody will pull rank over *us* for a while, that's for sure".
The sinister plan that Deborah Knowles had devised in her head, was about to be put into place, and played out with the callousness that comes only from the overwhelming desire to achieve, and to be successful. Loyalty or faithfulness had no place in Deborah Knowles's career.
Their voices began to drift away out of earshot, until Hillman could no longer hear what was being said, only distant laughter, loud laughter, and then, thud!! It was the sound of a gun being fired. Then, all he could hear was a kind of scraping dragging sound.
Deborah Knowles could be made out, through his one, half closed eye, dragging the body of her female colleague up to where he lay.
"You know"? She said to Hillman, as she threw down Karen Jones's body next to him. "You really are, one bad bastard Mister John Hillman, do you know that? And I thank you for it. You have just made my life an awful lot easier".
Once again, Hillman's mother appeared to him, standing shaking her head in disappointment at her son, mouthing silent obscenities at him and pointing to Deborah Knowles, and continuously wagging her finger in his direction. Then his mother disappeared. Tracy once again appeared before him. She stood shaking her head also and continued to swing the skipping rope, smiling sarcastically. Hillman reached out to her, asking for help, but Tracy ignored his plea for mercy. "*It's time to die monster, your children hate you and loath you".*

Deborah Knowles aimed her own gun at Hillman's head and said, "Any last messages for Tracy, no?
Goodbye then John, thank you for everything, you've gone and made my life a hell of a lot easier, and an awful lot better fuck freak".
She took hold of the pistol firmly in her hand. Hillman had another hallucination. His children this time.
"*We love you daddy, happy buffday daddy, blow out your candles daddy...mummy's eating all your cake daddy. Happy buffday too yoo, happy buffday too yoo".*
"All those innocent people you've killed doctor Hillman, in the name of God, well, you'll just have to explain to Him now, why you chose to be a mental fuck head, and why you let your guard down long enough for me to take you out, goodbye sick man".
"*Happy buffday dear daddy, happy buffday too yoo...we love you daddy".*
And with that, Deborah Knowles pulled the trigger.

JANUARY. 10th. CARLISLE.

Tracy Hillman sat at the kitchen table with the daily newspaper opened out in front of her. Angela sat opposite her, reading hers.
Deborah Knowles had been praised and honoured beyond belief for nearly three weeks now. Every day, there seemed to be something new to add to her already courageous accomplishment, something she had somehow forgotten in a previous interview.
"Huh" mumbled Tracy, "her story seems to change every day, talk about gloat Angela".
"Yeah, it seems that way Tracy doesn't it".
"What do you think Angela"?
"About what"?
Angela Phorbes lit up her first cigarette of the day.
"Tracy, I've been giving that some thought, and,-"
"And"?
"And I don't think it's a very good idea, you coming with me".
There was silence for a few moments, while Tracy digested what Angela had just said. Then Tracy finally said, "May I ask why"?
"Tracy, do you really have to ask me that? Do you?
Those little girls of yours, should be your first priority, do you know that"?
"They are".
"No they are not Tracy, or else you wouldn't be wanting to be on the move with me. They need you here Tracy, or wherever you decide to live, they need to be with you, young Angela there, may need therapy to get over her father, do you know that? Those kids of yours have been through hell Tracy, since all this began with their father".
"Look!" Tracy snapped, "if you don't want me to come with you, just say so, there's no need for the big moral story, I know my kids need looking after, it's just that, that fucking lunatic of an ex-husband of mine, has taken so many people out, bloody top notch marksmen and all, along with the best detectives the country has to offer, and then, along comes heroin, Miss high and mighty Deborah fucking Knowles.
I've never heard such bull-shit in my life. She's a very dangerous bastard Angela, and you could use some help you know.

According to the report, John took out Mister Harold Payne, his wife Beverley, DCI's John Drummond, Terrence Hanley, and Miss Karen Jones, but not Deborah Knowles? There's something strange about that, don't you think? He can take out three men, two of them trained and armed, and an armed policewoman, also trained, but he fails to take out Deborah Knowles? She is one dangerous bitch Angela, and don't you forget, she's looking for you as well; it's not just one way you know? So I thought I could help out my cousin here you know, for the sake of old times, but if you don't want my help, then I'll just stay here and watch cartoons with the girls".
"Tracy, you're taking this the wrong way".
"Am I, am I taking it the wrong way? Don't make me out to be a fool Angela, I know why you're delaying your move, it's because when you *do* go, you'll be gone for good, that's why. No matter what the outcome with Deborah Knowles, you've got no intentions of coming back, have you? Go on, tell me I'm wrong".
Angela drew hard on her cigarette, then exhaled the smoke up into the air. "You're not wrong".
"I know I'm not, so why the fucking lecture"?
"Tracy, ok, I know you think the world of your kids, I know that, and it's for that reason I'm doing this".
"Doing what? Running out on the only people who love you, is that what you mean"?
"Tracy" said Angela, rising up from her seat. "Just think for a minute. Suppose you came along with me, right? And suppose, just suppose we tracked her down, and took her out. Do you *know*? Have you any idea how much the people in this country love her now? They would hound us down through hell and high water, until they found us, they would frog march us down to St James's Park in London and make a public execution of us. The people would hate us more than they hated Guy Fawkes. And then what would those two little girls of yours do? No, this is personal Tracy, I have to do this myself, and I may not get the chance for quite some time, so I need to get away, obtain a new identity, and lay low until all this publicity shit has died down. It's not about not wanting to take you with me, it's about the future of those two little girls, and you, and Sharon. I know you love each other, stay here and be happy Tracy, don't you think you've had enough shit in your life Trace"?

Tracy sighed, long and hard. “I’m not going to change your mind am I Angela”?
“No, you’re not Tracy”.
“But Angela, she’ll look for me as well, she’s already stated on T.V. that I should come out of hiding, and it’s a trap to catch you, you know it, so you see? I can’t move on with my life, not until she’s out of the way. If you take off Angela, I’m in a worse situation than I was in before all this began. Come on Angela, you know I’m right, at least think about it”.
“Ok Tracy, I’ll think about it”.
Promise, I mean think about it properly and fairly”?
“I promise I will”.
“Thanks Angela”.

SCOTLAND YARD. BROADWAY VICTORIA.

Terrance Davis sat at the long oak table, with a further thirty-one dignitaries gathered around it. Beside him sat Richard Knight the Metropolitan Police Commissioner, among others from various high-ranking positions in the police force.
Deborah Knowles walked into the room. Each and every one of the other thirty-one men and women gathered around the table, all stood and applauded her, as she approached the table.
Knowles's face was aglow; she loved it, all the attention, the praise, the dinners, the interviews, the T.V. appearances, the newspapers. The press had even found out where her parents lived, and interviewed them, even though Deborah Knowles had not spoken to them in over twenty years. They had said nothing bad about her though, she was happy to read. Only good things and how she had always had this bravery streak in her. She was a bit of a Tom-boy when she was young, choosing to climb trees and walls, rather as play with her prams and dolls and little girl things. It was easy for them to talk about their daughter this way, and say nice things. It was payback time for them. Deborah had stolen eleven thousand pounds out of her father's account, and just took off, never to be seen again. This particular newspaper were paying them thirty thousand pounds for her childhood story, it was a good deal. They would help to keep Deborah in the lime-light, and they would cash in on the whole thing, everyone was happy.

"Come, come and sit down Miss Knowles" said Terrance Davis, making a gesture for her to sit in the seat next to his. He took hold of Deborah's right hand with both of his, and kissed her on the cheek, "Just to think" he whispered in her ear, "I nearly took you off the case, how foolish would that have been" he smiled.

Deborah looked him straight in the eye and said, "Very".

"Indeed" he said, "but at least it's all worked out for the best".

"Yes it has Terrance I can forgive you, this time".
Some of the press had been allowed to attend this dinner, and were now listening intently to what she said, every word.

Davis found her reply to be intimidating, threatening almost, as if she were higher up than him. Maybe she was going to be. He let go of her hand and began applauding along with the others again. After an hour or so of questions to Knowles, about how she managed to corner this lunatic, who'd been terrifying half of Britain, and put him to death before he could do any more damage, they began the meeting, which was about how they were going to go about stopping anything like this happening again in this country.

They, of course had asked Knowles to speak first, and give them her valued opinion as to how they would go about this.

"Ladies and gentlemen, it is indeed a great honour for me to be standing here among you today, and to give you my account of what happened that day in Morecambe. Christmas day, I will never forget. It is so easy for me or for anyone" she glanced around at Davis, "to take the credit for something when it goes right. That Christmas day in Morecambe, did not go right, it did not go to plan. My superior here, Mister Terrance Davis had placed D.C.I. Terrance Hanley in charge of the Hillman case, now, it matters little to me, who is in charge of any particular operation, except, in this case, it was to prove a grave mistake. Mister Hanley, up until he came to Sheffield to join us, had been in charge up in Glasgow and Edinburgh, and had indeed done sterling work up there in keeping law and order. But this case with Hillman was different. Hillman was different. This wasn't just another average murderer, this man was a serial killer, and, no offence to detective Hanley, but *this* man was really clever.

Myself and D.I. John Crosby, whom I dearly respected, had been on the Hillman case from the beginning. Poor John met his fate with Hillman, and as a result, I was almost taken off the case". Again, she looked at Davis. This time, quite a few others in the room looked at him as well. "I was then given D.I. Karen Jones to work with, to try and apprehend this, this, madman. Then Karen and I were taken off the Hillman case and put on to another. Meanwhile, enter D.C.I. John Drummond, from here in London. Again, he had no idea of how Hillman was operating, how he functioned. He was adamant he would catch him though. Then, when that wasn't working, Mister Davis here then sent for detective Hanley.

Davis was getting the feeling, as numerous people around the table looked at him rather sternly, that he was on trial. It felt like it.

Of course, all the time, Karen and I were keeping an eye on what Mister Hillman had been getting up to. There wasn't much progress being made, and as you can imagine, Mister Davis here and Mister Knight were getting hell from the prime minister, so they were coming down hard on us. By us, I mean Karen and I. So we took it upon ourselves to work on the Hillman case in our own way. This meant taking orders from Hanley, and obeying them, but also doing our own investigating to find out where Hillman was. You all know the rest ladies and gentlemen, it's eh, it's just a pity I lost them, I lost a very dear colleague and friend in the process of capturing Hillman. I'll miss her, I'll miss them all. I'm still undecided whether or not I want to continue to stay in the force. I couldn't possibly if incompetent decisions were being made all the time, I really don't think I could go through all that again".

Davis sat with a wry smile on his face. She was literally tearing him apart. Everything that had gone wrong with the Hillman case, had been blamed on him. Every finger pointed to his corner. She *was* after his job, there was no doubt about it. What made matters worse was the fact that she had suggested that if he stayed in his post, then she would leave. Her, Leave? This national hero who had taken this murderous rapist off their hands? There would be an outcry if she left the force. Britain needed officers and personnel of her quality, not bungling half- witted idiots like himself and Jack Knight. There was no doubt about it, his head was on the block, and the executioner was wielding his favourite axe. "Nasty bitch" he thought.

Deborah Knowles continued to praise herself and Karen Jones, and to criticise everything the chief of police had done throughout the case.

Davis and Knight had no choice but to sit and take it. The situation they were in reminded Davis of a burned out boxer, who found themselves against the ropes in the corner, and hoping they had enough strength to take everything their opponent could throw at them. Maybe the bell would go, or maybe they would burn out themselves, thus leaving themselves open for a counter attack. But none of these things were happening. Knowles was boxing clever, and she was hitting hard at Davis. Without being able to defend himself, she tore into the open wounds.

"The time has come ladies and gentlemen, to clean up our country. To hit back at the hooligans and villains, and hit them hard. For first time offenders, we have to make their experience one they will never forget, and one they will not want to repeat. The government have gone some way in helping us deal with these thugs, I say, let them help us some more by allowing us to build special prisons, particularly for the worst offenders. It is my opinion, that we should do away with the methods of old, and fight fire with fire, and punish them with a sentence they're going to remember, in other words, a proper punishment, a realistic rehabilitation programme. We must also consider relieving the older generations from their duties, and replacing them with a younger stronger staff, who would be well able to inflict hard physical punishment, when necessary. More determined people who believe, that if a person commits a degrading crime, which affects their victim either physically or psychologically, then in doing so, they have automatically given up their rights. Those twenty-two people murdered by Hillman weren't given any rights, were they? Plus, there are all the officers who have left wives and husbands and children. Where were their rights? She took a breath and said in a more controlled steady voice, "Ladies and gentlemen, I've had enough of Britain being the laughing stock of Europe. Even if I *do* resign, I'll tell you this much, if any thug out there attempts to mug or rape me, after everything I've been through, and what I've seen happen to my friends and colleagues, I can tell them here and now, whether I'm in uniform or not. Whether I'm in the police force or not", another glance at Davis. "Then prepare to die, because if I'm carrying a gun, I'll shoot you right between the eyes, and the chief of police here, can send me to jail if he wants, or hang me, but at least I'll know that I've saved some other poor woman from confronting the sick bastards"!!
The applause almost took the roof off.

CARLISLE. JANUARY.30th .4am.

Angela Phorbes crept into her car, having put all of her luggage into the boot. She had thought long and hard about taking Tracy with her, but had decided for the sake of Tracy's children, to go without her. She knew that Tracy would be furious and that she would think that she hadn't given it any thought at all, but she had. It had taken her a long time to make this decision. Angela had been reading all the newspapers as well, about all the heroics of a certain Miss Deborah Knowles, and how she had outwitted the monster Hillman, and how she had done all the women, particularly prostitutes, a huge favour by ridding them of this callous cold bloodied killer. Tracy had been right when she'd pointed out something in one of the stories. Hillman had managed to kill two men. Drummond and Hanley, and D.I. Karen Jones, and yet Knowles was able, not only to survive, but to kill Hillman.

She remembered how Knowles had been able to trick her and Carla, and then, how she pounced. Now, her gut feelings told her, that something sinister had happened in that house at Morecambe. "Guess we'll never know" she said to herself as she started the car. "You'll be fine" she said out loud, as she looked up at the house where Tracy and her children lay sleeping. You'll be safer up here Trace`".

She drove down the quiet narrow street. This would be her last adventure. Just one last person to take off the face of the earth.

She looked to the passenger seat, where Carla Paganni's smiling face looked up at her from the photograph sewn onto the side of her hand bag.

"I'll get her darling, I'll get her, or she'll get me, but I swear I'll die trying.

You stay here Tracy and look after those two little girls of yours, you've had to fight tooth and nail to get them back.

They've already lost their daddy, I don't want them losing you babes".

As she drove out of Carlisle, she saw signs for various places in the area, including one for Kendal. Kendal had been where all of this had kicked off, all those years ago. It was where she was forced to kill her two friends Amy Smith and Linda Evans in order to save Tracy's life. Then she was forced to go into hiding. The whole of Britain thought, thanks mainly to Tracy's story to detectives John McRae, and Sandra Bellingham, that Angela Phorbes's body lay in one of the waterways up here in the Lake District. The whole of Britain, except for one person who knew different, and would now be looking to build upon her new found popularity. If she could prove to the people of Britain that Angela Phorbes was alive and well, and not only that, but capture her, then no doubt she would be receiving no end of awards and honours.

"We'll see about that, bitch".

LONDON. METROPOLITAN POLICE HEADQUARTERS. FEBRUARY 10th.

Deborah Knowles was informed by W.P.C. Elaine Birch, that the last of her luggage had been loaded into the taxi waiting outside. She had decided to accept the offer given to her, to be the Chief of Police for Yorkshire. She had also been informed, unofficially that she would be the Metropolitan Chief of Police in around a couple of years, if she so wished.

Terrance Davis had resigned, as had Richard Knight. Knowles had got her wish.

The two men had resigned voluntarily, two days after her last speech. Life was going to be a little rosier for her from now on.

The government had given their permission to build separate prisons for serious offenders, or at least one anyway. There was to be an experimental prison built in Sheffield where the Park Hill estate was situated. All the flats there were to be demolished and the new prison built in their place.

The younger generations had been warned, both in newspapers and on T.V. that if they stepped out of line now, they would pay the price for their actions. There would be no visits or any good behaviour rewards in these prisons, once placed in custody.

"You will be cut off from the rest of civilization for the duration of you sentence. You have been warned". The home secretary had said on television.

Numerous friends who were personnel from the M.P.D. wished her well as she headed out to the cab.

"Good luck Mam" said a twenty-year-old W.P.C. Birch, as she held open the door for the new Chief of Police for Yorkshire. A fresh-faced young lady, who Knowles could see was as keen as mustard.

"Thank you, and good luck to you too W.P.C. in your career, and remember" said Knowles, placing a hand on the officer's shoulder, "Not everything your superiors tell you is correct, remember that. Sometimes we have no choice but to do things, how shall I say? Not by the book".

"Mam" said the officer, smiling. Knowles had just made her day.

Knowles walked down the steps and into the taxi. Her own car, a brand new Jaguar, was being delivered to Sheffield, where she was now heading, A gift from the Police Commissioner.

“Sorry Miss Knowles” said the taxi driver, “there’s no smoking in the cab I’m afraid”.
Still smiling and waving to all of her well-wishers she said to the driver; “Shut your mouth and drive,” closing the window behind the driver’s seat, and then opening it again.
“Open your window, why don’t you. You should have taken a bath or a shower this morning before you started work, the whole car stinks of B.O, there should be a law against that. Tell you what cabbie; I’ll keep my smoke to this side of the car, if you keep that horrible sweaty stench to that side, now Sheffield. Drive!
No smoking indeed, who the hell do you think you’re talking to fat boy”!

THE CREST HOTEL.
ROTHERHAM.

“Come on Tracy, surely you can see my point of view”.
“Your point of view Angela” replied Tracy.
The phone call had lasted eleven minutes so far.
“What about *my* point of view, did you think about that? Did you hell”!
“Tracy, listen, I had to come on my o-”
“Oh yeah, on your own, that’s you, you always want to do *your* thing, *your* way, well let me tell you smart arse, what that bitch is saying in the papers. She’s only been promoted to Yorkshire’s chief of police, that’s all.
She says here, she’s going to look up one or two old friends with her time off. She says she can’t mention their names for publicity reasons. She says she’s going to come and give them a real surprise. ‘They won’t have a clue I’m coming’ were her exact words. She says she’s going to have her photograph taken with them and have it printed in all the daily newspapers. Now you know as well as I who the fuck she’s talking about.
She’s had a taste of glory, and she wants more, and that is going to be at the expense of you and yours truly, and Sharon, come to think of it. So don’t tell me to listen, like you know all the answers, because you don’t.”
There was a short silence.
“Tracy? I know you’re right, what you’re saying, I know, but her first priority is me, I’m the one she really wants, and that’s why I chose to leave myself. If this goes wrong, then I’ll be killed, but at least you’ll still be around to take care of your kids. I wanted to bring you with me Tracy, I really did, but I owe it to those little girls of yours to do this on my own. I know it was sneaky of me to take off like that, but I couldn’t do it any other way, I’m sorry Tracy, I really am”.
“Where are you Angela”?
“I can’t say where I am Tracy”.
“Oh of course not, can’t risk nosey Tracy coming to see you huh? Ah well, good luck loner, you just get on with things your way”.
“Tracy, please don’t be like that”.

"Like what? Like I don't care? Well guess what Angela, I really don't".
Angela sighed. "Tracy? Is Sharon there, I need to speak with her".
"I'll just go and get her for you, goodbye".
A few moments later she heard Tracy's voice.
"Sharon?
Here, there's someone wanting to speak with you".
"To speak with me, who is it Tracy"?
"God knows" said Tracy, sarcastically.
Angela knew Tracy would react like this. This was the very reason she had decided to sneak away from Carlisle. She loved Tracy, and she loved Tracy's kids, and she felt that they'd been put through the shredders enough lately, without their mother putting her life at risk and perhaps leaving them parentless. She couldn't do that to them, although if truth be known, she could have done with her helping to get Knowles.
No matter, she would find a way of doing it unassisted.

PARK HILL. SHEFFIELD.

Deborah Knowles stood and watched with great satisfaction as the massive crane swung the huge steel wrecking ball to and fro into the Park Hill flats. Some local people stood and watched with her, agreeing with one another that it was not before time that this hideous monster of Sheffield was torn down. The flats had gone long past the need for renovation, and now the only alternative left, was demolition. Most, if not all the locals knew that the empty flats were being used now by drug users and prostitutes.

Deborah stood watching with a smile upon her face, as the wrecking balls continued to batter down the buildings. This was to be the site for the largest prison in Britain for serious offenders. This would be the first of five up and down the country. This one though, was *her* brainchild, this prison would be the one remembered in future times, and although she was under no illusions that this whole project was an experimental one, she couldn't help feeling excited about the whole thing, because she knew, if the prime minister kept his word, and left her to run the prison *her* way, then she would bring the crime rate down considerably in Yorkshire, and eventually, the whole of the country. If you were sent here, you would be a very different person when you left, of that there would be no doubt whatsoever.

Knowles turned to a man in the small crowd. An old man of about seventy years she guessed. "How long have they stood there"? she said to the senior citizen, pointing to the flats.
"Oh, quite some time now Miss, I think it would be the nineteen sixties they were built. They were beautiful at one time believe it or not. They were actually built for Naval Officers. It had its own shopping mall at the start. Everything they needed in one large condensed area, oh yes, it was something to see in those days. They looked quite luxurious back in those days, but, before too long, they began to deteriorate, until they've got to the state they're in now".
Knowles looked at the man with interest. "How do you think the local people will react, when the new prison goes up, you know, having criminals living in their midst"?
"They'll be over the moon Miss".

"Really"?
"Of course they will, because they have to live with criminals living on their own doorsteps now, and with no-one to tame them, so when that gets built, and if the police do their job, then the bastards will be under lock and key, excuse my French".
"Oh they'll do their jobs sir, make no mistake about that".
"Good" replied the elderly gentleman, "because right now, they're getting away with murder, literally".
"Not for much longer sir, I can tell you that for certain".
Knowles turned and said to the man as she lit up a cigarette;
"Well, it's been nice talking to you".
"You too lass" said the elderly gentleman.
As he was walking away, he said; "When are they planning to start building"?
Just at that moment in time, they heard the screaming of a car's brakes along the main road. Knowles turned to see a red B.M.W. being pursued by a patrol car, with sirens wailing and all lights flashing.
"Bloody joy-riders lass, sick to death of them, we are. Even when they catch them, they only get put on probation and the buggers are free to do it all over again with some other poor bugger's car, pardon my French again lass".
"Don't you worry about your French, Mister"?
"Mister Braithwaite, Tom Braithwaite".
"Well Mister Tom Braithwaite" said Knowles, pointing up towards the construction site, "as soon as that building goes up, I can safely say, that this joy riding will stop, it will be a thing of the past".
"Do you think so Miss"?
"I know so Mister Tom Braithwaite" she said, smiling.
"What makes you think that this prison will be any different to all the others"?
"Because sir, this prison will be run by the authorities and not the inmates.
There will be no pampering in *this* prison.
This prison will be run with complete discipline, extreme discipline by a dedicated disciplinarian".
Knowles could see that the pensioner was taking a genuine interest in the progress of the prison and what it would mean to the local community. Even at his age, in the twilight years of his life, he was still concerned about law and order.

“And who might that be” said Tom, filling the drum of his pipe with tobacco. “You know, we’ve heard all these stories before Miss around here, everybody means well, but after a couple of years or so, they give up. Bloody yobbo’s rule again, they always win. Anyway, who’s the goody-two-shoes who’s going to be running *this* new prison”?

Knowles threw her cigarette stump onto the ground. “You’re looking at her Mister Tom Braithwaite”.

“*You*? You are going to be the governess of the prison? Ay lass, I’m afraid you have a lot to learn if you think you can tame these bastards, excuse me again, but that’s what they are lass”.

“I never said I was the governess now, did I. I am the chief of police for Yorkshire”.

“That’s right Miss, and I am Sir Stanley Mathews, how do you do, it’s nice to meet you”.

Deborah Knowles pulled out her I.D. badge and showed it to the gentleman.

“Well I’ll be... sorry for doubting you Miss Knowles, hell you’re the one who killed that bloody lunatic Hillman”.

Knowles smiled.

“I’m sorry Miss if I seemed rude, it’s just that, well, you’re just a slip of a girl, and you’re, well, you’re very beautiful. I would never have taken you to be a police officer, let alone a detective,
and now, Chief of Police? I read all your stories Miss, how you eventually got the chance to kill the bastard, oops, sorry Miss”.

“That’s quite alright Tom, and you can call me Deborah”.

He looked her up and down.

“Hell, Miss, there’s not much of you is there? Deceiving, bet you fight like a grizzly though Miss”.

“You bet I do Tom Braithwaite, oh, and to answer your question, next week”.

Tom looked at this beautiful woman before him. “I beg your pardon? Next week”?

“When they start to build the new prison Tom, next week”.

“Oh, yes Miss, yes, I em, Chief of Police eh”?

“Are you married Tom”?

“Me miss? I was married to my darling Mary for forty-nine years, until God called her up to be with the angels. I’ve been a widower now for nearly six years, miss her Miss, I really do, aye”.

Knowles could see that the affections and emotions this man had for his wife were right on the surface. Tom quickly bowed his head to light his pipe and to hide a tear which had rolled down his cheek.
"Well" she sighed, "I'm not married Tom. Nobody will have me".
"Huh" he said, between puffs of smoke, "I like a lass with a good sense of humour".
Knowles had taken to this old man. Here he was, with his whole life behind him, and a woman he had so obviously loved for the best part of that life. Yet, he still wanted to see discipline; he still wanted to see law and order, respect, decency.
"Are you doing anything tonight Mister Tom Braithwaite, because I could do with some company for dinner. Seriously Tom, would you like to have dinner with me tonight? Please don't embarrass me by refusing".
"Miss Knowles, I am honoured, really I am, but I wouldn't fit in with these fancy hotels Miss, it's not me".
"Did I mention hotels? Did I? We'll have dinner at my place. Now, where do you stay, and I'll send a cab over for you at seven thirty. Only you and I Tom, what do you say"?
"I say, thank you Miss, you have a date. Goodness me, imagine having dinner with none other than Deborah Knowles, you're probably the most famous person in the whole of Great Britain right now, thank you Miss, just wait `till I tell my pals in the pub tomorrow, they won't believe me".
"Where do you drink Tom"?
The old man took his pipe from his mouth and pointed with the stem.
"Just down there Miss Knowles, The Golden Egg. It's not a bad little place really, there's never much trouble in there, that's why I like it lass, peace and quiet you know, at least during the day".
She looked at her watch.
"Tell you what Tom, fancy a pint just now? My treat".
"Oh now Miss, it's one thing to accept a dinner invitation from a young lady, but to let a lady buy me a drink?
Well that's just not on Miss, no way. I'll buy you one though, if you wish".
Yet again Deborah Knowles saw an avenue of opportunity opening up for her. Publicity was a wonderful thing, and what a chance to introduce herself to the community. She had learned long ago that if you wanted to win people's favour, then all you had to do was be nice to them.

“Ok then Tom, just a sec though, I’ve just got to make a phone call”. She saw a perfect opportunity to get her face in the local newspapers. By mixing with the locals in their environment, it would go down well with the local people, especially with an old pensioner on her arm.
She phoned the local newspaper, informing them that she would be in The Golden Egg in about fifteen minutes, if they wished to take a photograph.

By the time the newspaper reporters got there, Knowles was in deep conversation with Tom and a few of his pensioner friends, about how she felt about discipline, and the importance of respect.

Tom Braithwaite had never had his photograph in the newspaper in his life, apart from his wedding photograph, but there he was on Friday’s Sheffield Gazette, standing with none other than Miss Deborah Knowles, Chief of Police for Yorkshire.
One of the reporters had taken him aside in the pub, and asked him his opinion of the new leader.

“This one is different son” he had told the reporter. “This one means what she says. I feel safer already, having her around. I would warn all those yobbos out there, don’t mess with *this* lady boys, she’ll tan your arses, she will”.

SHEFFIELD MORTUARY.

Knowles pulled up outside of the mortuary in her brand new Jaguar. Still officially off duty, she decided to pay Ashley Barnes a visit, a surprise visit. She walked down the corridor and through the swing doors into the chilled area, where she expected to see Ashley hard at her work, but instead, found the place deserted. There were only one or two lights on in the room today, giving the place a rather sinister look. She felt an icy chill running through her, and couldn't help feeling that she was being watched.

"Hello" she shouted "is there anybody here? Ashley"? She walked on until she came to the steps which led to Ashley's office. She remembered coming here with John Crosby, and how he had deliberately left his car keys on Ashley's desk, in order to ask her out. She also remembered coming here with Karen Jones, and the two of them joking about Ashley's promiscuousness.

"Sorry Karen" she said to herself. "I'm so sorry Karen that I was so ruthless, and took all the praise for myself, it's just one of those things I'm afraid, winner takes it all, and there are no rules how you win".

"Can I help you"?

Knowles turned around, almost jumping out of her skin. A young man of around twenty years of age stood a few feet behind her.

"Oh what a fright you gave me" said Knowles, "I was looking for Ashley? Ashley Barnes, is she here"?

"I'm afraid not, Ashley won't be back until tomorrow, she's down in London, can I help you with anything"?

"Em, no, I was just passing by, her and I are friends you see, and I thought I would surprise her, it doesn't matter, I'll come by tomorrow perhaps, sorry to have bothered you".

"That's alright, I'm sorry to have startled you, who will I say was calling"?

"Deborah, tell her Deborah was here, but I'll see her tomorrow anyway. Is she back at work tomorrow, or just back home"?

"Oh no, she's back at work, she'll be here first thing in the morning, I've been running the place on my own for the past ten days".

"Have you now"? Said Knowles, "Good for you, well, I won't hold you back from your work any longer, it's been nice to meet you".

"And you" replied the young man.

“What a bloody creep” thought Knowles to herself. The young pathologist reminded her of one of the members in a seventies rock band called Sparks. Ron Mael, that was him. The creepy looking guy who played piano, very thin faced, with a hideous moustache. She climbed back into her car and made her way towards the city centre.

She was pleased with the coverage the local newspapers had given her, letting them know that she was a kind caring person who was concerned for the community and their safety. Tom Braithwaite had been the prefect subject. The old bugger had enjoyed his treat. A well-mannered gentleman who knew how to conduct his behaviour in the presence of a woman. He was a rare jewel in this day and age. She began to think to herself, “I think *his* Mary has had a wonderful life with him. I’ll bet he was frisky in his time”. She drove on at crawling pace through the city traffic. As she was heading towards the city centre she looked up onto Park Hill. All the battered run down apartments were now down, every one of them demolished, much to the delight of the general public. It would just be a matter of clearing up the debris, and then the building could begin. Deborah had sat in the architect’s office, discussing the plans for the new look prison. Once the proposed plans had been drawn up, there had been a number of protests by one or two of the do-gooders. Questions had been asked.
“Where is the prison gymnasium?
Where is the T.V. room?
We don’t see a recreational room.
Where’s the library.
Where are all these essential areas”?
The architect could only tell them the truth, which was, that he was designing the prison on the orders and specifications put to him by Miss Deborah Knowles, who in turn, was questioned by the P.D.O. (The Prison Development Organisation). They had put it to her that there could not be a prison without these areas, and that it would be unacceptable to expect inmates to live under these conditions.
She had answered them in the city hall, which was packed to the roofs with locals who were not only in support of what she was proposing, but were eager for the building to begin.
She knew that there would be protests by human rights activists and had already worked out her plan in how to silence them, or at least, verbally disarm them.

"May I remind these well intentioned people that this will be a place of punishment, not a popular holiday camp, which I might add, seems to be the order of the day with the existing prisons in this country. No longer will inmates dictate how a prison is run, or be able to deal drugs, and various goods around the place, like it was some free market. Very soon, word will get around about the conditions in *my* prison, and that alone will act as a deterrent. If they are not happy with the conditions here, then do not become a guest. We have tried the soft approach, it does not work. So, we go this way. If you are involved with drugs, or you kill an innocent person, or you're involved in a gang, then please, don't expect corn flakes and cold milk in bed in the mornings. If you *do* have a stay in my prison, I personally guarantee you, right here and now, even before your sentence has begun, before even the first block has been laid, that you will not want to come back".

Everyone in the room rose to their feet cheering and calling out Deborah's name.

Park Hill, was no longer a pipe dream. It was going to happen.

As she drove on through the city towards her new home in Summerside, on the outskirts of the city, she began to think about the whereabouts of a certain Miss Angela Phorbes.

"You must be watching with interest young lady" she thought, as she drove.

"I wonder where you're hiding out my little gold mine. I nearly had you Angela, I did have you, but Mister Hillman took first priority. Now that he is out of the way, I must come for you, I told you that in the national press. This is between me and you girl. I can't even tell any police officers, because everyone in Britain thinks you're lying in your watery grave up in the Lake District. I have to be careful as well, because I know you're coming for *me*, you'll want revenge for what we done to your lovely Carla. I wish you luck Angela, because you're going to need it girl, last one standing and all that".

ROTHERHAM. THE CREST HOTEL.

"This is going to be easier than I thought" said Angela to herself in her hotel room.
She had read in the press about this new prison being built in Sheffield, having nipped across the road and purchased a paper. There she was, on the front pages, bold as brass. Knowles had been photographed outside of her new home in Summerside, with a pensioner on her arm. The headline read; Deborah Knowles, New Chief of Police for Yorkshire, Dines Old Tom". "This is too good to be true" Angela thought. "Or was it a trap? Was this what she was supposed to think? Surely, she couldn't be this stupid. Then again, she could be so caught up in this publicity thing, that she'd blinkered herself, therefore leaving herself vulnerable. Or, it was an insult. "I don't care if you know where I live Angela, because you don't pose a threat to me, come on, let's see if you can find me before I get you".
"Be positive" Angela said to herself. "You know where she lives, you don't have to do anything straight away, keep an eye on her. Just wait and see what her next move is. According to the newspapers, the prison was to be completed in less than six months. Deborah Knowles would never be away from the site. Angela lay back in her bed, looking at the woman she hated most in the world. Who would believe it that this smiling, innocent looking woman with an old age pensioner on her arm could have caused her so much grief? As Deborah Knowles's face smiled up at her from the newspaper, Angela once more vowed her vengeance. "We'll see Debbie" she said out loud, "we'll see who has the last laugh". She lay back on her bed, thinking about her friends from long ago, Tools, Amy, Linda, Paul Trent. Ten years she thought. "Hell, more than that".
If any of them were here with her now, the matter would be brought to an abrupt end. Deborah Knowles would be lying dead somewhere, and that would be that.
Alas, they weren't here though. There was no-one here but *her*.
She would have to be very careful indeed if she was to get away with this. Deborah Knowles was a very clever woman. She was also a very dangerous woman, a killer.

Angela had become a killer herself. She hadn't planned it, it just happened, and when it did, she found that it did not disturb her in any way, not like she thought it would. Deborah Knowles, on the other hand, seemed to enjoy it. She inflicted those wounds onto Carla with the help of some friends no doubt.

Angela remembered the sheer joy on Knowles's face when they'd brought Carla through to her cell, "Evil bastard. Now, you little bitch, you think you're going to do the same to me, don't you? I'll watch you for a few nights, to see if you have any company round, or friends, if you have any, real ones, that is. I'll watch out for your routine, you'll drive past me and not even know".

Angela rubbed her arm. It was still tender, but it was getting stronger every day. Tracy was right; she *had* taken the plaster off too soon. But it was ok now, and soon it would be strong enough to smash into Knowles's face time and time again, until the nose bone was beyond repair, and every last tooth was burst and broken in her mouth.

"Patience Angela, you'll get your chance, you know you will" she said, smiling at the newspaper. Just as Angela was drifting off, her mobile phone began to play her favourite pop song; she reached over her bedside table and picked it up. It was Tracy.

"Hello? Angela"?

"Hello Tracy, listen darling, if you've phoned me to give me another lecture about leaving you behind, I'm afraid you've picked a bad time".

"Oh, have I, I'm sorry, do you have company Angela"?

"No, I don't have company Tracy it's just that I'm knackered".

"No no Angela, this'll just take a minute, I'm calling to apologise to you. I'm sorry for the way I reacted".

"It's alright Tracy, it's understandable, I know how you feel, I suppose I would have reacted the same way if I were you".

"No, it was selfish of me Angela, I'm sorry, listen, have you read the papers yet"?

"Why"?

"Why? Because that bitch has just given her address away to you, and the rest of the country Angela, she's living in Summerside".

"I know Tracy in fact, I'm beginning to think that she's laying some kind of trap for me, what do *you* think"?

Angela was smiling, relieved in the knowledge that Tracy had accepted the situation and that she'd finally seen sense.

"Angela, that's why I'm calling you. I kind of thought it was too good to be true, I mean, surely she can't be *that* stupid, after all, you read what she was saying in the papers about her friends not knowing when she would call".

"Exactly Tracy, that's why I'm going to keep an eye on her from a distance, see what kind of company she keeps. She could have security guards all over the place; anyway, I'll deal with it. Right now Tracy, I'm just so very tired, I need to get forty winks, tell Sharron I send her a great big hug and a kiss, and tell those two nieces' of mine that their aunty Angela loves them very much".

"I will Angela, and listen, please be very careful what you're doing, she's a very dangerous bitch. All I have in the world is my kids and Sharron and you, if anything should happen to you lot, then I'd lose the will to live".

"I'll be very careful Tracy, and if I get in to any difficulties, then I promise I will get in touch with you straight away".

"Is that a promise Angela, I mean a real promise"?

"I promise you Tracy, I will".

"Then that's a deal Angela, take care babes, and stay in touch with us, we're rooting for you babes".

SHEFFIELD MORTUARY.

Ashley Barnes stood waiting for the kettle to boil. "So Deborah, you're quite the hero now, huh"?
Knowles sat at the table in Ashley's office, amazed at the young woman's figure.
"I wouldn't say hero Ashley, hardly a hero".
"Well I bloody would" replied Ashley, pouring the boiled water into the two cups. "Your name has made the headlines in every newspaper in the country. You got your bad boy Deborah, you always said you would get him, and you did, well done".
"The thing is Ashley, I just got lucky, that's all, any one of us could have got him, it just happened to be me, that's all".
Ashley put down the mugs of coffee on the table and picked up her cigarettes. As she lit one up, she looked straight into Deborah's eyes and said, "It must have been some fight he put up though, was it"?
"What"? Mumbled Knowles, taking a sip from her mug.
"John Hillman, Doctor Hillman, Deborah, he must have put up some fight, you know, struggle, resistance".
"Well. It was, it all, em, it all happened so, what do you mean Ashley, fight"?
"The mess of his face. They brought all the bodies down here from Morecambe Deborah. It was me who done all the post mortems".
"They brought the bodies down here Ashley"?
"Yes, didn't anyone tell you Debs? Of course, that would be before you became the Chief of Police for Yorkshire.
What's wrong Debs? You look a bit uneasy".
"No, I'm, I'm fine Ashley, I just eh, nobody told me about it".
"Didn't they? Well anyway, as I was saying, he must have put up one hell of a battle. His face was practically unrecognizable, honestly Debs, do you want to see him"?
"*See* him"? Replied Knowles, completely shocked.
"Yeah, he's in one of the cold store containers".
"He's not been buried yet, no funeral or anything"?
"Nope, I've been informed to keep him here until forensics are finished with him".
"Forensics"?
"Oh yes, they've been in and out of here looking at Hillman for the past month now. Deborah, don't worry".

"About what"?
"About why your prints were on Karen Jones's gun, and Hillman's. They found traces of your skin on Hillman's face as well. They reckon that Hillman was hand cuffed and then nearly kicked to death, by at least two people.
You and Karen Jones, would they be correct Deborah"?
"Yes, they would Ashley".
"I thought so Debs, those guys don't miss much. I've been out with a couple of them".
Deborah Knowles tried to smile.
"There was just one thing they couldn't connect, just one little mystery they couldn't solve".
"What was that"?
"Well, if you and Karen kicked Hillman practically unconscious, then how come Karen is dead, they couldn't work that one out".
"Ashley, look" said Knowles impatiently, there was a lot of shit going on that day, things happened so fast, there wasn't any-"
Hey! Wow, listen Deborah, you don't have to sit there explaining yourself to me, anyway, they were all told to bury the files on this case. The only story about the course of events from that day, is yours. Everything else had to be put asunder".
"Who gave that order"?
"Your old friend Deborah, you know the one you got to resign from his job? Terrence Davis? That's who passed that order; of course he's no longer with us is he. They may decide to keep Hillman here for a while longer, whilst they carry out some more, eh, tests".
"Why? Why do they need to carry out more tests Ashley"?
"Beats me" the pathologist answered.
"What is it Ashley? Is my word not good enough, that they have to keep coming in here poking and prodding a bunch of corpses who have been dead for over a month. Fuck in hell Ashley, they wanted Hillman dead, so he's dead, what the fuck are they hoping to find"?
This time Ashley did not reply. She just shrugged her shoulders, smiling.
"What's so funny Ashley? This is serious you know, there's nothing to laugh about here".
Knowles's face was burning. She hadn't been waiting for this.
She was still reeling from the shock of Hillman's body still being poked and probed. They were hunting for something. They couldn't be allowed to continue, one way or another. Or she was fucked.

Ashley Barnes drew on her cigarette. "I'm not laughing Deborah, not like that anyway. It's just that you are the Chief of Police for the whole area, and here you are, getting all worked up because a few forensic boys are doing some tests, hell Deborah, you got your glory out of Hillman, let these guys get theirs".
"No, it's more than that Ashley, and you know it, come on, tell me what's going on, you're bound to know, you've slept with half of them".
"Ooh, nasty Debs, did I feel the claws out there"?
"Fuck you Ashley, I'm not in the mood for jokes, I'm off".
"Ok Deborah, do you really want to know"?
"Yes".
"Right, well, in a nutshell, one of the forensic team, and I repeat, only one of them, thinks that they smell a rat".
"About what"?
"Well, he's convinced that one of the police officers was still alive after Hillman was killed, namely Karen Jones".
"And"?
"Well, he thinks you shot her in order to take all the glory for yourself".
"You're joking Ashley, tell me you're pulling my leg, Jesus Ashley"!
"Look, you asked me to tell you, I've told you, and that's off the record by the way".
"Who's in charge of them"?
"Well, *he* is, otherwise this lot would have been burned or buried long ago".
Stupid bloody man, I've never heard anything so ridiculous in all my life, what's his name Ashley"?
"Ah now Deborah, I'm not going to tell you that, now am I"?
Knowles shifted on her seat.
"Miss Barnes, I am, in case you have forgotten, the Chief of Police around here, how long do you think it will take me to find out who he is, now, what's the prick's name. And why didn't you tell me about this before Ashley, you've got my number".
"I didn't call you because I only found out about a week ago, and then I had to go to London".
"What for"?
"None of your fucking business Miss Knowles, that's what for".
"Sorry Ashley, really I am, I didn't mean to prise".

"Yeah well, I've told you now, I didn't have to tell you anything".
"I know, and I'm grateful, I am, but just tell me his name".
"Nope" replied Ashley. "As you so rightly said, you are the Chief of Police, you have the power and the authority, you find out for yourself, and anyway, I only know his first name, you would have to look it up anyway, even if I told you that".
"Fine, if that's all you know. I'll find out".
"Right then, I'd better get back to work" said Ashley, standing up and straightening her skirt.
"Can I ask you a favour Ashley"?
"Sure".
"If he persists with this stupid idea of his, I mean if he gets silly, you'll let me know, will you"?
"Yeah, I'll let you know Deborah. Now, will you do me a favour Deborah"?
"If I can, what"?
"Tell me what it was like to kick the teeth down the throat of Britain's most ruthless killer since Jack the ripper. I mean it must have felt like heaven, to hear the screams of pain as you smashed his face apart, the murdering bastard that he was, it must have been beautiful to see. He only had two teeth left intact, did you know that Deborah? Most of them were wedged in his throat. He was *some* mess Deborah, you did a good job".
"Thank you Ashley, it did feel good if I'm honest. Now, I have to go now Ashley, no rest for the wicked huh"?

As Deborah Knowles drove through the afternoon traffic towards Sheffield prison, she began to think about the consequences, if this forensic glory boy could prove she'd killed Karen Jones, or any of the other three for that matter. No-one up until now, had the slightest idea that she had in fact killed Hanley, Drummond, Jones and Beverley Payne. If this forensic twat could work that out and prove it, she would be in deep trouble. Something would have to be done about him. It had been over six weeks now since the killings. The bastard must be on to something or else the bodies would have been released for the families before now, for funerals or cremation, like Ashley said. That little whore knows even more than she's letting on, but, all said and done, at least she'd had the decency to raise the alarm for me.

As soon as she left the prison today, she would look into it. She couldn't take any chances. He would have to be dealt with, and quickly. Even if Ashley thought it was her who killed Karen, well, Ashley could be shut up, but, Mister Forensics would have to be dealt with differently, and immediately. She approached the prison for her meeting. There were two reasons why she was here today. The first reason was to interview some of the staff, to see if she wished to have any of them work with her in the new prison. The second reason was to put the fear of God into the inmates who would be unfortunate enough to be transferred to the new prison. Some of the inmates here were lifers. From what she could make out, they seemed to have the best facilities; they got that little bit more, as if society felt sorry for putting them there for such a long time.

"Huh, we'll see about that" she thought to herself. "What a shock they're going to get". She parked her car and walked up to the main gate, and pressed the button on the wall. Much to her frustration, there were some clanging and clicking noises, then she heard chains being rattled, and finally, the door built into the gate, began to open. The prison warden smiled at her as she walked past him. "I'm sorry I'm late for the meeting" she said, "But it took someone twenty minutes to open the gate".
"Afternoon Mam", said the warden, ignoring the sarcastic remark.
"Yes, afternoon" she said, as she walked over the compound towards the main office.
As she did so, she received a few wolf whistles from some of the inmates, high up in their cells. She smiled to herself, when she heard them, not for the compliments, but the fact that these men, were very soon, going to be living very different lives. They wouldn't be doing any wolf-whistling, that was for certain.
The prison governor greeted her as she stepped into his office. The prison warden smiled at her as she walked past him.
"I'm sorry I'm late for the meeting" she said, "but it took someone twenty minutes to open the gate".
He and four of his staff all rose to their feet as she entered the room.
"Good afternoon" they all said in unison, as if they had rehearsed.
"Good afternoon gentlemen, and lady" she replied.
The woman in question was a governor from another prison, and was here to find out information as regards to how Deborah intended running the new prison.

“Tea Miss or coffee” said Governor Yates, a fifty-five year old ex-staff-sergeant from the army.
“Tea please” said Knowles, “and then we can get on with the business in hand”.
Yates opened a door at the far side of the office and spoke to a young warden, and then returned to the table.

“As you know” began Knowles, “I am here to inform you of the new rules concerning inmates, and how they are treated. Now, I have done some intensive investigations, and I have discovered that more than ninety per cent of prisoners are reoffending when released. Now then, the people of this country want to know why this is, as do the government; after all, it’s the tax payer’s money they are giving us to run these places. The answer to this question is a mystery to some people. Some governors simply can’t understand why this is happening. They are telling me that they run their prisons with extreme discipline, and that they are doing everything within their power to stop people reoffending. This, my friends is absolute rubbish. The time has come for change. Some may say that my ideas are going back to primitive times, instead of moving forward. As you will have read in your papers, some of these do-gooders are saying that, with my proposals, I am taking away their human rights. Would they be so keen to knock me, I wonder, if it was their four year old who was brutally raped by two youths, or if it was their grandmother who’d been thrown forty feet from the top of a stairwell to her death, for the seventeen pounds and twelve pence in her purse? I wonder, and do you know this? Do you know what the two teenagers got for raping that baby, huh? Anybody? They got six years and four years.
That little girl now has mental problems, and will, for the rest of her life. One of those youths will be out of prison in four years; the other will be out in two, and the old lady? There were five of them, two girls, oh yes, and three boys. No-one could prove who actually threw her to her death, and so, they each received two years. Some of them will be out in months. All I can say to you people is if this does not make your stomach churn, then I’m afraid you’re all in the wrong jobs”.

Knowles looked at the sheet of paper she had taken from her bag, and then said. “A ninety-two year old bed ridden lady raped, and her head shaved, while his accomplice ransacked her house for her life savings of four thousand pounds, on her head, the words written in her own lipstick. ‘WAR TIME SLUT ’, Guess, guess what they received for their deeds? Four years. Four years each”.

Governor Yates and his staff, sat with grim faces, all shaking their heads.

Deborah Knowles continued. “Ladies and gentlemen, the government for the first time in years, are giving us the chance to turn this around.

Now, in order to be able to turn this around, each and every one of your staff are going to have to be able to inflict harsh punishment. Physical discipline. The reason my friends, that there is a ninety per cent reoffending percentage is that they have learned nothing. They have not changed their attitude about how they live their lives.

They have suffered nothing, and therefore they have nothing to fear, should they be sent back to prison. It’s a regular home from home. I even hear, that in some cases they are allowed their wives or girlfriends in, and if they have neither, then prostitutes are brought in for them, the poor souls.

From now on, anyone who comes in to my prison, is going to be subjected to the biggest shock of their entire lives, mark my words.

Now, is there anyone here seated at this table, who thinks that extreme discipline is *not* the answer, because if there is, I would advise them to resign now, because you are all going to be called upon to deal harshly with the scum that are in here. You will not be able to bluff your way through this. You will all be monitored. No offence will be taken if you happen to disagree with my proposals, and you wish to resign. Any employee who leaves will be paid full redundancies and given excellent references for future employment. While you think about it, I want you all to take a good look at these photographs, taken at the scenes of the crimes, just to remind you all of what we are dealing with here”. Knowles handed out the pictures, containing hideous scenes of violent crimes. She continued. “I for one am sick and tired of this bastard bred country we now live in. I’m so sick of the way society deals with these scum bags with kid gloves. Be assured of this, it will not be continuing, not in my prison. I aim to bring down the cost of running a prison, by at least fifty per cent, at least.

Now, you were all given details in writing when these changes were taking place, and that they would come into force, not as an isolated experiment, as some people seemed to think, but permanently, full stop, and in all the prisons throughout the U.K eventually".

Knowles pulled out another piece of paper, and read its contents to herself. She then looked up to Mister Yates and asked if she could see prisoner number 38724 a Mister Robert Finch.

"It says here Mister Yates, that Finch attacked a young girl and her brother because their pet dog attacked *his* dog. It also states, he punched the fourteen year old girl in the face, and punched and kicked her twelve year old brother, and then proceeded to kill their dog with his knife, right in front of them.

He got eighteen months, I don't believe it. How long has he been in here"?

"Eleven months mam," said Yates.

"Eleven months? And he's getting out today"?

"He's been behaving perfectly mam, it's his parole".

"Is it now, bring him in here so that I can speak with him, no wonder over ninety per cent re-offend, eleven months indeed, it's a joke, that's all.

Has this Finch been in prison before"?

"Yes mam, he's been in prison on four separate occasions, all to do with knives, or at least violence of some nature".

"Tell me Mister Yates, how do you feel when they send these scum bags back to your prison; do you think they are receiving the just punishments for their crimes"?

"Indeed I do not Mam, but it's the law, the rules, my hands are tied".

"Were, Mister Yates, were tied. If I get my way you could beat a man to death, and you would not even face an enquiry. As I said, the government have given us a free hand. After midnight Mister Yates, you answer to no-one, as to how your prison is run, absolutely no-one. We owe it to the decent people of this country of ours, to give them their lives back, take it back off the scum.

No more lawyers picking away at red tape, and getting these pigs out of here early. This is where we put our foot down, literally".

There was a soft tap on the door, and a young prison warden walked in carrying a tray containing two large tea pots and several cups.

"Thank you Jones" said Yates, "that'll be all for now, thank you".

Knowles was determined to put things right in these prisons. Discipline would be the order of the day, harsh discipline.

As they all sat drinking their tea, Knowles explained to them what was to happen to all prisons in the future. Renovations were to take place in every prison in the country eventually. Gymnasiums were to be turned into lecture halls. There were to be no more cinema rooms. All televisions were to be withdrawn. Inmates were to be allowed one hour of radio per week. This would be increased to one hour per day, pending on good behaviour. There would be no cigarettes or tobacco, no chocolate or sweets of any description. There was to be no family visits, only with the exception of an inmate awaiting execution. They would be allowed the luxury of one visit, from one loved one, on the morning of their execution.
"Excuse me Miss Knowles" said one of the young gentlemen sitting next to Yates.
"We will never get away with this, there will be a public outcry".
"Your name"?
"John Smedley mam".
"Well, Mister Smedley, there will be no public outcry, because, the public will no longer know what goes on behind prison walls, and anyway, every household in the British Isles have been informed about the changes in the prison systems. No-one, but no-one can say that they haven't been warned. They were given a firm warning on television by the prime minister himself, recommending ex-cons and would-be criminals alike, to shape up, and not land themselves in prison. Prison, is not the same as you remember it. Now I think that that was fair enough warning Mister Smedley, don't you"?
"I still don't think we'll get away with it".
"Mister Yates" said Knowles, "I think that Mister Smedley here has a hearing problem. Either that, or he thinks that I am a liar". She looked at the young man once more.
"Watch my mouth Smedley, we will, listen carefully, we will answer to nobody, got it, Nobody".
I will say this though, and I would advise you to repeat this to all of your staff. If anyone leaves these premises, and then attempts to sell their story as to how the prisons are being run, or mentions to any outsider what takes place within the walls, or any other prison walls in Britain for that matter, then they can expect severe consequences, and I mean severe. We are going to stamp down hard on these ingrates, once and for all. I don't care if I have to kill them, they will not leave with the attitude they arrived with".
Someone knocked on the door.

“Enter” shouted Yates.
Warden Jones walked into the room with prisoner Finch.
“Thank you Jones, you can leave now” said Yates.
“No, let him stay” said Knowles.
Robert Finch stood in front of the governor’s desk with his hands clasped together, a tall scruffy looking young man, with an unshaved face, and scraggly hair.
“Mister Finch” said Yates, “this is Miss Deborah Knowles, Chief of Police for Yorkshire. She wishes to ask you some questions”.
Finch looked at Knowles.
“Mister Finch” she began, “I understand that you are to be released today, is that correct”?
“Yeah, I was in the middle of packing up my things when the warden came for me”.
Finch looked at the clock on the wall, and said, “My taxi is coming for me at five o clock”.
It was now four thirty-three.
“Take a seat Finch” said Knowles, “this won’t take long”.
Finch looked at the clock again.
“You must be keen to get out, I would imagine”.
“Well, I’m meeting my girlfriend; we’re going to the pub”.
“Are you”?
“Yes Miss”.
“Tell me, what have you learned from your stay in here? I mean, do you regret your crime? Are you sorry for what you done”?
The inmate sat looking in front of himself, fidgeting uncomfortably.
“Well, yes, but my dog was a pedigree, theirs was just a mongrel”.
“Really, So you won’t go back out there and punch and kick any more fourteen year old girls, or twelve year old boys, and you won’t slaughter any more family pets with knives in front of them, eh, Mister Finch?
Tell you what, I don’t think you’re sorry for what you done, and I also think that if I let you go out there, you would do it again, as quick as lightning. So, Mister Finch, I’ll tell you what I’m going to do, because I’m such a decent person, and remember, I don’t do this for just anyone. I’m going to give you the chance to come in here another day, and convince me that you really are sorry for your crimes”.
“Another day”, the prisoner complained, looking at the clock on the wall once more and shaking his head.

“No no Mister Finch” said Knowles, “you misunderstand me. Another eighteen months, you’ll do your sentence again”.
There were gasps around the table at Deborah’s statement.
“You must be joking” said the stunned inmate.
Deborah Knowles pulled out her cigarettes from her hand bag, and lit up.
“No” she said, exhaling smoke into the prisoner’s face. “I’m not joking, and if you speak to me again, without me first asking you a question, I will add six months on.
So Mister Finch, your girlfriend will have to put the party on hold for a while, but, young Jones here is off duty tonight. If you wish, he can go and give your girlfriend a good time, how would that be Finch? It’s ok, you can answer”.
Finch stared into the eyes of Deborah Knowles. “I think you’re a sick bitch, that’s what I think”.
“That’s better Finch, that’s more like it, now, you’re doing two years extra, six months for being insolent to me, hell, your girlfriend is going to have enough time to get pregnant and give birth a couple of times before you get back out”.
Knowles looked at warden Jones and said, “I would advise you Jones to be very careful in future if you decide to have fun with Finch’s woman, it could be risky, because she’s got all the time in the world to play the field, so, be warned Jones.
Take him away” she said smiling at Finch.
“You’re a fucking bastard bitch!!”
“I know that Finch, see you in two and a half years”.
“Miss Knowles” said Smedley, “I really must protest, you cannot deal with people in this manner, when that man’s solicitor gets a hold of this, he’ll make our lives hell, you cannot just inflict sentences onto people willy nilly, just like that”.
Warden Jones escorted the prisoner back out of the office, and closed the door behind him.
Knowles jumped up from her seat and opened the door.
She shouted for Jones to stop.
“Jones, if that slime ball says anything to you on the way back to his cell, I want you to come back here and tell me. I will add another six months on to his sentence every time he opens his mouth to you, do you understand me Jones”?
“Yes mam”, Said the warden enthusiastically.
“Good man, carry on”.

She came back into the office and closed the door.
"What is it you do Smedley, I mean, what exactly is it that you do around here"?
"I am an assistant governor that is my post".
"That is your post is it, well then, why don't you act like an assistant governor, instead of being a pain in the ass nancy boy, with all your fancy talk, and let me tell you something Mister, if you ever, and I repeat, ever, interrupt me again, let alone in front of an inmate, then I'll slap your face in front of everyone present. Now, this time I'll let you keep your job, but I promise, once more, and you'll be slipping along down the ladder, am I getting through… understood"?
"Yes mam".
"No more shit Smedley, or you'll be the one to land in it! Ok, everyone leave the room please, I wish to speak with Governor Yates alone".
Two minutes later, the room was empty save Mister Yates and Deborah Knowles.
Frank Yates sighed and sat down on his chair. "Miss Knowles" he began.
"Deborah, please call me Deborah".
"Deborah, Smedley means well, he's just young and keen. He doesn't know about the kind of discipline you're talking about".
"I know that Frank, but he'll have to learn.
He has to learn that from now on, when these bastards come in here, they have chosen to, nobody forced them to steal, or to push drugs, or attack children, or rape old ladies, or kill innocent bystanders with stolen cars. Nobody forced them to do these things.
Now, it's our job Frank, to make sure, that when they are released back into society that they will not reoffend. In case you think Frank, that I was being cruel to Mister Finch, well I was. I'm giving him a shock to his system.
Right now Frank, his head is all fucked up.
He's preparing himself for a long stretch; he has had a massive shock.
Now, I am actually going to let Mister Finch go home later tonight, but first I need him to understand that it is *that* easy, for me or you to lengthen his sentence.

Hopefully, he's had a big enough fright, that he may leave here with a different attitude and that he might now have the sense to keep himself out of trouble, because, as he'll be told, the next time, there'll be no reprieve. Frank, they're coming in here and practically running the place, and I don't mean that as any insult to you or your staff. As you rightly said, your hands were tied, red tape, all sorts of shit. *Now*, if you want to get a message over to a prisoner, you can punch him in the mouth if you wish, no-one is going to question you, but for Christ's sake, you'll have to toughen up Smedley there, or these inmates will walk all over him, it's for his own good Frank".
"I know, I know, I'll deal with him".
There was another knock on the door. It was warden Jones. "Ah, go and get Finch Jones and bring him back here" said Yates.
Five minutes later, Warden Jones returned with prisoner Finch.
"Sit down Finch" said Knowles, "now then, have you anything to say for yourself"?
"Yes Miss, I'm sorry for speaking out of turn".
"Are you sorry for anything else"?
"Yes Miss, I deeply regret attacking the two youths and for killing their pet dog, I was *so* stupid, and I deeply regret my actions".
"Ok, I'll tell you what I'll do. You can go and have your drink with your girlfriend".
"Thank you Miss Knowles, oh thank you *so* much".
"Yes, that's all very well, but I'll tell you something right now, or rather, I'll give you a bit of advice, and I would strongly recommend that you take my advice.
Start again Finch, and don't ever come back here, I mean it, don't you ever come back here, because if you do, I promise you here and now, that you *will* regret ever being born, now, are we both on the same page"?
"Yes Miss Knowles definitely most definitely".
"Ok then Finch, go and have some fun with your trollop".

LONDON ROAD. SHEFFIELD.

Amanda Pearce's life had taken a turn for the better. Since the execution of Steve Temple, she had gone to a solicitor in the hope of obtaining some of Temple's money. To give herself a fresh start, as she had put it. She had done better than that. She had ended up with everything. The solicitor had published the proposed amount of money that he felt Miss Pearce was entitled to, and, of course, because she was a live-in partner of Mister Temple, she would therefore stand to inherit all of Mister Temple's estate, as there was no other relatives.

Not one single person had contested the decision. This did not surprise Mister Masterton, Amanda's solicitor, one little bit. He knew, that even if there were people out there who felt they were owed something, they would not dare step forward for fear of being dragged into something concerning Mister Temple. Amanda received everything. For the first time in her life, she was winning. The house, the cars, the property, everything, it was all hers.

She sat at the large dining table with two girls who had become friends with her. The three young women sat at the table dressed only in their underwear, and each of them snorting the neat lines of cocaine spread out over the table. They were awaiting the arrival of several young men who Amanda had invited round for some fun. The girls had started their party early. It was now seven o clock. The men had been informed to arrive at eight. As they all sat snorting, Amanda said, "I'm going to get some more tonic, won't be long".

As Amanda walked, somewhat unsteadily towards the kitchen, her front door bell rang.

"Oh brilliant" said one of Amanda's friends. "They're here early, the boys have arrived".

Amanda shouted through, "Answer that, one of you, and don't be using them all up before I get back through there".

"You'll have to hurry then" the girls replied, laughing. One of the girls got up from the table and made her way down through the long living room and into the hall, just as unsteadily as Amanda, and answered the door.

"Oh" said the young lady, "Were you invited? I don't remember you from anywhere".

"I'm looking for Amanda Pearce, is she in"?

“She’s in alright, but I don’t know if she wants to speak with *you*, we’ve got enough pussy here honey, and there’ll be barely enough boys to go around as it is”.
Deborah Knowles pushed past the young half naked girl and walked up the hallway, then up the carpeted steps and into the living room. She pulled out her I.D, card and said, “My name is Deborah Knowles, I am the Chief of Police for Yorkshire, I would advise you all to sit down while I read you your rights”.
Even through the daze of the cocaine, the girls said, “Shit!”
After she had read them all their rights, she told them to go and get dressed. Knowles then gathered up all the cocaine powder and put it into a plastic container, which was about the same size as a large coffee jar, and which was three quarters full.
“Oh fuck” said Amanda, realizing the desperate situation she was in.

“Well, Miss Pearce” said Knowles. “It would seem that you *will* be changing your address after all. Imagine that, after all you went through to get this. You are indeed, a silly girl”.
Amanda sat on the sofa, still only in her underwear, her head hung heavy, as she sat with her arms over her knees, her head slumped, nodding, “My life story” she mumbled, “One step forward and two steps back”.
“Come on Amanda” said Knowles, “You can’t go down to the station dressed like that put some clothes on”.
Knowles had come here with a plan in her head, it was a bonus to find the young women taking cocaine. Now, she had something to bargain with, and it wouldn’t cost her a penny.
“Please inspector” said one of the young ladies, “We’re not doing anyone any harm, I mean, we’re not pushers or anything”.
“That may be the case young lady” said Knowles, “but, the law is the law, and taking cocaine, is against the law”.
She pulled out her mobile phone and began pressing some digits. Then Knowles stopped pressing. She asked the girls their names and addresses, advising them, for their own good, to tell the truth. Then she called into the station and asked them to check out the names and addresses given to her.
“They’ll phone me back in less than ten minutes, I hope for your sakes you’ve been telling me the truth”.
This situation could not have been set up herself any better than this. She had Amanda Pearce over a table.

"We have Miss", the two girls answered with slurring speech. As all three girls began to get dressed, Deborah's phone rang. It turned out that the girls had been telling the truth.
"I'll tell you what" said the Chief of Police, "I need to speak with Amanda alone now, you two head off straight home, unless you want to go straight to jail now. Go home and stay there until I come and get you, now move your arses".
Ten minutes later, Deborah Knowles and Amanda Pearce sat in the living room, alone. Even the cocaine couldn't help the way Amanda felt just now, because she knew that everything she had obtained, would soon be taken away from her again, it was inevitable. Nothing could save her now. She was going to jail for a long time.
Deborah Knowles had her where she wanted her. She sat now, scrutinising the young helpless girl, knowing that she held all the cards she needed to win this game. She cleared her throat, and said to Amanda, "A bloody shame Mandy, you've landed yourself in a bit of a mess this time, have you not? And there's nothing I can do to help you out. Nothing legally anyway, you understand".
Amanda looked up. Was that a glimmer of hope?
"What do you mean Miss Knowles"?
"Well, there is *one* way to get you out of this mess and to keep you out of jail".
"What way? Anything, I'll do anything".
"Anything"?
"Yes Miss Knowles anything".
After fifteen minutes Amanda and Deborah shook hands, "Do we have a deal Amanda"?
"Yes we do"
"Good, remember, if you fuck this up, you're going away for a very long time".
"I won't".
"Good, now here's your cocaine, call your friends back, and enjoy your party".
"Are you sure that's the guy Miss Knowles, Stanley Spears, I have to be certain, I don't want to kill the wrong man".
"Of course I'm sure, now you just make sure the job is done, and we'll forget all about this cocaine business. Now, if this is done properly Amanda, you won't be hearing from me again. If you fail, then you can say goodbye to ten years of your life, and I promise you, each day will feel like twenty, so, you'll make sure"?

“I’ll make sure Deborah”.
“Right, here’s the gun, it’s loaded and there’s a silencer attached to it, so, no fuck ups Amanda. Now then, enjoy your party, and remember, not a single word of this to anyone, do you hear”?
“Like I’m going to say anything Deborah, please, give me some credit”.
“Right, I’ll see myself out Amanda, and just tell your friends you gave me some information regarding Steve Temple or something. Tell them to say nothing of my visit here tonight to the em, the gentlemen you have coming here, or I’ll be back to arrest the three of you, got it? Right, good luck Amanda, and if you want to do yourself a favour, then get off of that bloody powder, you’ll have nothing left in no time”.
Amanda nodded.
“Ok, goodbye Amanda, and good luck”.
Amanda stood by her window and watched Deborah Knowles climb into her car and drive away.
She was in a fix; there was no doubt about it. There wasn’t any choice. She would have to do it. It was either that, or spend the next ten years in jail. She didn’t fancy doing that either.
She looked at the photograph of Stanley Spears in her hand, and then at the gun in her other hand. “I’m sorry Stanley, whoever you are, or whatever it is that you’ve done, but it’s me or you buddy, that’s just the way it is my friend, no hard feelings. I’ve never killed anyone in my life before, but I’ve never done ten years in jail either”.
She made the decision there and then, that it would be easier to pull the trigger than to attempt to do ten years in jail, plus, Deborah had given her three weeks to complete the task. There was plenty of time. She called her friend’s mobiles and told them to come back, and that everything was alright, unless they were going to let her have the group of boys all to herself.
The girls were back within ten minutes.

HENSINGHAM AVENUE. SHEFFIELD.
24 HOURS LATER.

The rain battered relentlessly on the kitchen window as Linda Spears stood by the dish washer, loading it up with the crockery of the evening meal. Her husband Stan was putting the children to bed. This was more like it, having him home at a decent time. This was how it used to be before he'd taken the job of forensic investigator. When he was just an ordinary officer, he used to be home at the end of his shift, regular as clockwork. In those days, they could plan things, they could go places. In those days, they would climb into bed with each other, and they would wake up in the morning together as well. These days, her husband could receive a call at any ungodly hour of the day, and off he would go, sometimes not returning for three days or so, even longer sometimes. She could remember several occasions when she hadn't actually seen him for more than a week.
"Come on now Linda, count your blessings, there are people in the world far worse off than you are" she told herself. "He's home tonight, so make the most of him when he *is* home. The gale-forced wind continued to batter the rain against the kitchen window. It made Linda feel all nice and romantic, nice and cozy, homely.
Her husband came into the kitchen and said, "Emily thinks there's a ghost in her cupboard".
Linda smiled, "does she now, another one. What is it this time Stan, a boy or a girl"?
"It's a girl she says. She informs me that this girl wakes her up at nights and tells her to get food, chocolate biscuits and yogurt to be precise".
"Ah, a hungry ghost, I see, and what does young Johnny think of this situation"?
"He says that his sister is a big baby, and that he sleeps with his alien blaster gun by his side, she shouldn't worry".
"Are they both asleep now"?
"Yip, they both went out like a light tonight".
"Do me a favour darling would you? Could you take this bin bag out to the bin please? The only thing is Stan, it's out at the front gate, you'd better put a coat on, or you'll get soaked".
"Ok, give it to me, the things you do for love".

“Thank you my darling, you’re an absolute angel you really are. I’ll pour us a nice glass of wine each; I’m just nipping upstairs to change”.
“Oh, sounds good, into something more comfortable I hope”?
“Well of course my darling, I have to look after my one and only bin emptier man, don’t I”?
“Yes you do, my very own dishwasher lady”.
“Ah, but I have a dish washer who takes care of that for me”.
“Yes, and I have a bin bag man who takes care of the rubbish for me, but he’s up stairs defending his sister from ravenous ghosts with his alien blaster”.
The couple both laughed as Stan put on his overcoat.
“Won’t be long my darling” he said, “I hope I’m going to be rewarded for this when I get back in”.
“You’ll just have to wait and see, won’t you”.
“Good, I love surprises”.
Stan lifted the black plastic bag and headed for the back door.
“See you soon, if I don’t get blown away with that bloody wind”.
Linda went upstairs and looked in on the kids. They were both fast asleep, sure enough, with John nursing his rifle. As she began to change, she heard the sound of a bottle breaking, or glass of some description. She laughed to herself “He’ll be in some mood now. The bottoms’ came out of the bag and something has broken”.
He was always telling her about putting far too much heavy rubbish into those flimsy bags. “Never mind, my darling, I’ll soon take your mind off that when I come down stairs” she said to herself, pouting her lips, as she applied her lip stick. As she continued to dress, she couldn’t help noticing that there was an extremely cold wind blowing up the stairs. “The back door must have blown open, it was always doing that. Linda made her way along the hall and down the stairs, and then towards the kitchen. She put a hand up to her mouth and began to laugh. The door *had* blown open, and it was smeared with tomato ketchup, the broken ketchup bottle lay just inside the door. As the wind howled ferociously into her kitchen, she retrieved the small brush and shovel that she kept for small emergencies such as this, and the floor cloth. She placed an old cushion on the floor and got to her hands and knees to sweep up the broken glass. Then she looked at the sauce on the door, and the trail of it which led half way down the path, right to her husband’s head whose body lay slumped, face down on the path.

The alien-blaster gun on little Johnnie's chest, leaped up into the air and onto the floor in reaction to the sound of his mummy's screams. As Linda Spears sat on her knees with what was left of her husband's head cradled on her lap, she heard a car speeding off in the distance. The bag of rubbish lay by his side. He hadn't even made it to the bin.

Now, it was Linda's turn to jump with fright, as her two children stood at the back door screaming hysterically at the sight of their daddy's bleeding head.

THE GOLDEN BULL. SHEFFIELD.

"I'm fucking telling you Sophie, things are really changing in those prisons babe. I would think twice about what you're doing. That governess called Knowles or whatever her name is, just slapped another eighteen months on me, just like that".

Robert Finch sat opposite his girlfriend. "Don't be so bloody stupid Rob, they can't do that, and you know it, she was only trying to frighten you".

"I know she was Sophie, but I'm telling you, this chick is serious, she means business, I'm fucking telling you the truth, right? I said something, and because she hadn't spoken to me first, she added on six months, just like that, and then another six, for me calling her something".

"Rob, you're out aren't you? She was only playing with you".

Finch took a drink of his beer. "Yeah, I'm out, and I'm staying out Sophie, I'm not going back in there, that's for sure".

"Oh, and how are you going to do that? Are you going to stop being a runner for Sam? Are you? Kind of hard to do when you owe her three grand, are you just going to wake up tomorrow and land yourself a full time job? Huh? Are you going to wave a magic wand, and make everything happen are you, just like you said when you first started shagging me? Oh don't you worry Sophie you said, you and this baby will want for nothing, I promise you, remember Rob? I'll tell you how it is Mister Finch. We run for Sam. And the reason we run for Sam, is the fact that she provides food for us and clothes for our baby's back, that's what we do, and that's what we're going to keep doing, ok, unless you want me to go and tell Samantha Adams that you no longer require her business, and that you're breaking away from her, and oh, by the way Sam, I'll give you that three grand I owe you as soon as I get back onto my feet, See Ya. Do you want me to do that Rob, because I fucking will, and you know as well as me, that you'd be dead before daybreak if I did? Now, no more shit about packing this in. She looked at her boyfriend.

She could see that he was frightened. This Deborah Knowles or whatever her name was had done a good job on him. Sophie thought, like so many others in her position, that it was all bull-shit, all this toughening up in the prisons.

“You know what this is Rob”? Sophie Blair took out an envelope from her hand bag. “Do you? This is seven hundred pounds, and she gave it to us, not a loan, this is a gift, to help us get a start, now that you’re out of jail. Now that’s what I call a friend Rob, don’t you? We are changing nothing. We’ll just have to be a bit more careful that’s all, hell Rob, you would think they were going to kill you the way you’re talking”.

Right there and then, Robert Finch made his mind up. He would leave Sophie, and Sheffield, and make a new start somewhere else. He had a brother up in Scotland, in Aberdeen, he could try up there.

“You’re right Sophie, as usual”, He sighed, and looking like he was admitting defeat.

“Look Rob” she said sympathetically, “This is steady income, I know it’s not ideal, but it’s steady, plus, we can rely on Sam to help us if we’re in a fix”.

“Yeah you’re right Sophie, and anyway, where would we go, all our friends are here”.

“ Exactly Rob, you’re thirty-four years old, you’re not going to achieve anything now, you have no qualifications whatsoever, all you can hope for is minimum wage, there’s no light at the end of the tunnel, anyway Sam says you’ve to go round to her place in the morning she’s got an errand for you, and when you’re done, she’ll knock a grand off your debt”.

“What time”?

“She didn’t say, I wouldn’t leave it too late though Rob, you know what she’s like. Better go round about nine, ok”?

“Yeah, right, same again Sophie”?

“Yes please, vodka and coke please”.

“As Robert Finch stood at the bar, he looked at Sophie Blair sitting at the table studying her mobile phone. When he first met her, she was a beautiful young woman. But five years on crack had taken its toll. Instead of the twenty-six years she was, she looked more like thirty-six years old. She was moody, arrogant, selfish, and she slept with lots of guys behind his back.

In the eleven months he’d spent in jail, he’d been informed of nine different men who had visited his house, most of them staying overnight, some of them even longer. She didn’t even enjoy sex any more, at least, not like she used to. She was sleeping with them for drugs.

He also knew that if he left it would only be a matter of time before the authorities took the baby away from her. At least then, the kid would get a fair crack of the whip. Whatever, he had made his mind up he was off in the morning, because he also knew that if he didn't, it would only be a matter of time before he landed back in prison. He could still hear Deborah Knowles's voice in his ears. "*Whatever you do, do not come back here Mister Finch*".

LONDON ROAD. SHEFFIELD.

Amanda Pearce grabbed the bottle of vodka from the drinks cabinet. She had never felt so scared in all of her life, she was shaking so badly the neck of the bottle and the rim of the glass tinkered, as she poured herself a very large drink. She grabbed a couple of pieces of ice and placed them into her glass. Then she poured in a small measure of coke, gave the glass a quick swirl and then took two large gulps. She took the gun out of her coat pocket and placed it on the table, and then threw her coat onto one of the easy chairs topped up her glass with vodka, and then sat down upon the floor.

"Fuck, I've done it, I've killed a man. A man I have absolutely nothing against, a man I don't even know. God forgive me". Amanda reached into her coat pocket and found her cigarettes. "Oh fuck, oh good God, I'm shaking like a leaf".

As she sat in the quiet of the night, she listened through the window outside, half expecting her doorbell to ring, and then three or four armed policemen to burst in.

Hensingham Avenue was over three miles away, but it had felt more like three hundred. On her way back home every car which overtook her, was a police car, every vehicle's headlights, every car at a junction, finally, she was home. It was, without a shadow of a doubt, the hardest thing she had ever done in her entire life. She took swigs of vodka in between puffs of her cigarette. Then inevitably, she began to relive the whole episode again. Right from when she had pulled up a few yards from Mister Spears's house. She'd been approaching the house to gain a vantage point, when he came out of the house carrying a bin bag. She had been presented the perfect opportunity. Both of his hands were occupied as well, which made it that bit easier for her. He saw her coming in the gate and did not have the slightest look of concern on his face. And why would he? She looked just like any other ordinary girl of her age. He probably thought she was here to speak with his wife. She had taken out the gun, and fired one shot into his brow. The kick from the monstrous pistol almost broke her wrist. The man raised his hand instinctively. The shot had gone through the rubbish bag as well, and sent a red jet-line right up to the door.

Still no police.

She got up and poured herself another vodka. After this, she would snort a line of coke to calm her nerves. She picked up the gun. What the hell was she supposed to do with this?

Ten minutes later, she had snorted two lines of coke, and felt the comfort of having done so. Her mind seemed relaxed now. She felt in full control of her senses once again. She would hide the gun, and not in the house. It was over, she had done it. She had murdered someone, for reasons none other than to save her own arse.

She looked around the room at all the luxurious furnishings and fittings. All the beautiful paintings which she knew were worth quite a lot of money, they were all hers. That's why she'd done it, so that she could keep all these nice things. If Deborah Knowles kept her word, then she'd be left in peace to live her life now, and to enjoy her inherited possessions. If she kept her word.

SUMMERSIDE. SHEFFIELD.

Deborah Knowles sat on her easy chair sipping a glass of white wine, and listening to the local radio station. This area where she lived now was very tranquil. She could get used to this. Her neighbours, either side of her, were at least thirty yards apart. She could lie out the back on her sun lounger, and no-one would be able to see her. At the back of her house there was a small orchard which contained about twenty or so apple and pear trees. It was a beautiful little secluded retreat.

Today, however, she had confined herself to staying indoors, and listening to the radio. The wind had died down, but the rain still fell continuously. Then she heard it.

"*The whole community is in shock this morning with the news of the death of forensic officer Stanley Spears, who was shot dead last night at his home. Mister Spears had been taking out rubbish when he was shot at point blank range. Police are undergoing investigations and are appealing for any witnesses to step forward. They would like to make it known, that there will be a substantial reward for anyone who can lead them to the killer. Mister Spears leaves a wife and two children. Our thoughts and deepest condolences go out to his family*".

Knowles was smiling when her telephone rang. It was the local police station, "I want to know why I was not informed about this immediately after it happened, I have to hear about it on my radio? I'm coming right over!" As she drove through the city, she thought to herself, "*Well done Amanda, well done indeed, and no witnesses, very good. Of course, faced with the same situation that you were in, then I would have done it as well .Well, you live in peace now Amanda, enjoy your small fortune. Right, that's him out of the way. All I need to do now is get those bodies out of that morgue, and get them buried or burned as quickly as possible*".

As she drove past Park Hill, she could see building progress. "*Not long now, you bastards, until Auntie Debbie makes your lives a living hell. Clean up time is almost upon us boys and girls*".

On the national news on her radio, she was informed of two men in their forties, who had been arrested for the rape and the beating of a ten year old girl in London. "*I hope they don't take too long to build Park Hill. I'll have those two bastards up here before they can say their names. I'll show them what rape is just shortly, perverted sick bastards".*

By the time Knowles got back from the police station, it was ten-thirty. Having not eaten all day, she sent out for food, and then showered. Twenty minutes later, her meal arrived. She had the T.V. on to hear the local news, just to make sure that Amanda had done her job properly. Nothing had changed from the radio's report. Police were still looking for witnesses to step forward. All they had to go on, was a car speeding off. There were no details of what type of car it was. It was done and dusted.

"*I'll keep my word as well Amanda,"* She said to herself, "*I'll leave you alone with your nymphomaniac friends"*

Deborah smiled to herself. She'd had some wild times herself, in her younger days she recalled. She finished her smoke and her glass of wine and decided to go to bed with a magazine. She had a meeting at nine o clock in the morning, up at Sheffield prison. "An early night will do you no harm at all Deborah" she spoke to herself. Sheets of rain pelted her window, driven on by a ferocious wind which had picked up again. "Bloody weather" she groaned, as she picked up her wine glass, and took it through to the kitchen. While she was in there, she thought she heard something. She stood perfectly still to try and hear, but it was difficult to hear anything, other than the wind and rain. She walked back through to the living room and down the hall, to make sure her front door was locked, which it was. Then she went through to the kitchen again and checked the back door, which was also locked. She lifted her cigarettes and a magazine from the kitchen table and headed up the stairs. Once in bed, she fluffed up the pillows to support her back while she read. Her gun as always tucked neatly underneath the mattress. All her bedding was brand new. She felt something uncomfortable on her back.

"For goodness sakes" she sighed thinking it was a label on her pillow. It wasn't a label, it was a note.

"Dear Deborah, looking forward to taking your life, and doing the world a big favour. I still miss my friend Carla Paganni, you remember her? You and that Welsh tramp beat her to death remember? Well, you are going to die a slow death, bitch, I promise you but where am I. Am I in your attic, bitch? Or under your bed? Or in your closet. Lots of hate, Angela Phorbes".

Knowles looked around her bedroom. The window was locked, there was no way she got in through there. She pulled out her gun from under her mattress and got out of bed. She checked the other two bedrooms. They were all securely locked as well, then the bathroom, and then the shower room. All locked.

"Hmm, Miss Phorbes, that leaves only one place you could have got in. You may even still be in there, we'll see". She opened the back door and walked outside to open the garage. Once inside, she opened the boot of her car and retrieved her torch. The wind was now gale force again, catching her breath as she closed the garage door again. She locked her back door, hanging the key next to her note pad pinned to the wall. She then retrieved her front door key, and hung it beside the other. "There now Miss Phorbes, if you *are* in here, then you're not getting out in any hurry". Then, she heard it again, a definite thump.

"So, she *was* still in the house, but where did the noise come from"?

She slowly climbed the stairs and picked up the long pole for opening the attic door. As she gently pulled on the pole, a set of step ladders conveniently unfolded for her to climb. "Won't be long Angela" she shouted up into the pitch blackness. "Just coming up now my little scrubber". Then she heard the thump again. It was coming from above her. With gun in hand Deborah began to climb the step ladder. As she climbed, she shouted up, "I kind of wanted this to stretch out a little bit, you know, with so many things going on just now but, if you want to die now honey I don't mind".

She switched on the torch and took a quick look around. Her attic had been floored, and so there was no danger of her falling through the ceiling.

Another thump, louder this time.

"Ah, so you're over there are you, dead girl, won't be long". The attic was shaped like a giant L. She had reached the end now. There was only one place to look.

Another thump.

Knowles held the gun in front of her with both hands, her thumb hooked around the handle of the torch. She saw the source of the banging. The attic skylight had been closed, but not fastened down. The gusts of wind were raising it slightly, and then dropping it down. "So, you didn't have the guts to stay, after all Angela".
Outside, in the garage, the fire burned ferociously in the engine of her brand new Jaguar. As Knowles climbed down the step ladder, there was an almighty explosion. She ran down the stairs, and could see the reflection in her hallway. "Fucking bitch" she screamed, as she ran to get her keys. The keys were gone. "You fucking bastard" she tried the handles of the front and back doors, both were locked. Then she heard banging on her front door, then the sound of her lock being opened. "Hello"? The sound of a man's voice "Are you alright? Is everybody alright, it's your neighbour. Your car has blew up, I've called the fire brigade, hello"?

Deborah Knowles could hardly contain the anger inside her, as she watched the firemen dealing with the blaze. "So, you want to play games Angela, do you? I should have killed you when I had the chance, fucking bitch. No matter, your time is at hand".
A tall man in his early thirties tapped her on the shoulder. "Are you alright Miss"?
"Huh"? She turned around to see one of the most handsome men she had ever seen in her life. "Pardon? Oh yes, thank you, I'll eh. I'll be fine".
The young gentleman offered her a handshake.
"Phillip Krane at your service Miss Knowles I live just across the road there". He pointed over to a large white house nestled among the pine trees. "It's an honour to meet you Miss Knowles, but I would rather it had been under different circumstances than these".
"Yes, it is a bit of a nuisance having one's car blown up in the middle of the night".
They both laughed.
One of the police officers walked up to her and whispered, "Mam, it's malicious I'm afraid".

Deborah Knowles looked at the officer in total disbelief and hardly able to keep her face straight. "Do you think so constable? Carry on; I'll be over to talk to them just shortly. I'm just going to have a coffee with Mister Krane here, ok"?

"Are you sure you're ok mam, you look a bit, in shock mam".
"On you go officer".
"Yes mam".
As the officer walked away, Knowles said, "Would you like a cup of coffee Mister Krane, now that we're wide awake".
"You don't mind? Miss Knowles".
"Of course not, after all, it was my fault you were woken up, wasn't it".
After Knowles had spoken to the fire chief and one or two of her officers, she and Phillip Krane went into her house to have their coffee.
"I'd better not stay too long Miss Knowles, my wife will be demented with those three kids of ours"

That was it, as far as Deborah Knowles was concerned. She wouldn't have even bothered putting the kettle on if she'd known about him being married. Now it was going to be difficult just to be civil to the man. She should have known though, she thought to herself. "How many single men would be living in a house that size? Stupid bitch".
"Have you lived in this area long Mister Krane"? She said, as she put coffee granules into two mugs.
"No not really, about six months Miss Knowles".
She knew that the persistence of calling her Miss Knowles was his way of getting her to say, call me Deborah, but she did not respond.
"I see, and do you like it"?
"We love it, and there's so much space for the kids as well".
"The kids, yes" said Knowles stirring the cups.
"What is it you do Mister Krane"?
"I'm a doctor over at the Sheffield medical centre. I took over from the infamous doctor Hillman".
"Really"?
"Yes mam, I must admit I get some weird looks from some of my patients. They ask me if I was friends with the man, Christ".
"Were you"?
"What"?
"Were you friends with Doctor Hillman"?
"No Miss, I never even met the man, and from what I've heard about him in the papers, I'm quite glad".
"Indeed Mister Krane, he was a bit of a handful".

The young man sipped his coffee and smiled. “You were very brave Miss Knowles, to take him on, and win. I think the whole country was beginning to get paranoid about him”.
“Well, he’s gone now doctor, their wives are safe from him now”.
“Yes, thanks to you”.
“Not just me Mister Krane, there were others who helped to tackle him, and now that we are on the subject of villains, I wonder if you could do me a favour”.
“Certainly Miss Knowles, what can I do”?
“Well, when I’m not here, which is quite a lot of the time, do you think your wife could keep an eye on the place for me”. She tore off a piece of paper from a note book, and scribbled down her number.
“Night or day Mister Krane, you let me know if you see anyone around here, especially women”.
“Do you think it was a woman who did this Miss Knowles”?
“Now now mister Krane, you be a doctor, and I’ll be a police lady, ok”?

CARLISLE.

“Are you sure you won’t come Tracy” said Sharon’s Aunt, picking up the food hamper from the kitchen table.
“No, honestly, you go and enjoy your day out with Sharon and the kids, I’ve got one or two things to sort out in the city.
“Aw mummy you should come” said Amy, “It’ll be great fun, really”.
“I know it will sweetheart, but on you go and have a great day ok? Tell me all about it when you get back home tonight. Now, give me a big kiss and a cuddle, and maybe save me a cake?
Tracy kissed her youngest daughter and hugged her.
They were heading to the wild life Safari park.
“Now, go and tell Angela to come through”.
Angela came through to the kitchen, rather reluctantly, but gave her mother a kiss and a cuddle.
“Listen darling” said Tracy to her eldest daughter. “I know you’ve had an awful lot to deal with babes, but you’re being a very good girl, very brave. Very soon, you and Amy and me and Sharon are going to get a new house somewhere”.
“Where”?
“Well, we don’t know yet, but it will be happening soon, I promise. Then we can get you and Amy back into a proper school where you will both meet new friends, like it used to be, I promise”.
“I want a bedroom of my own I’m tired of sharing with Amy”.
“I know darling, I know, but just bear with me, just a little longer, it’s all going to be sorted out shortly. Now, have you got your money”?
“Yes mum” said Angela, with an air of exasperation.
“I love you babes”.
“I love you too mum” replied Angela, sighing.
“Right, off you go, and enjoy your day”.
“We will”.
Sharon came into the kitchen.
“Right, all aboard, let’s get ready to roll”.
“Aunty Sharon, you’re mental” said Angela.

Tracy and Sharon could see, that although young Angela would have them think she was not in the slightest bit interested in going to the wild-life park, she was in fact, as excited as her young sister. Angela's favourite animal just now was tigers, and today she was going to see some real ones.
"Yes I know that sweetheart, just don't go telling anyone ok. Now you go and wait in the car, I'll be out in a minute, and remember, I want *you* in the front seat, next to me, let Amy sit in the back with my mental Aunt, ok"?
"Ok" laughed Angela, see you later mum".
"Bye bye darling, see you later, now you be good, do you hear"?
"Mum"!
"Sorry babes".
Tracy stood up and she and Sharon kissed each other.
"I wish your aunt was taking them on her own Sharon".
"I know Tracy, but I thought I'd let you get your feet up for a few hours, give you a break".
"Thank you Sharon, you're a gem darling, you really are".
"So are you Tracy, now you take it easy today, because you and I are going to very busy all night".

SHEFFIELD PRISON.

What the hell is going on Deborah, trying to blow you up in your house" said Frank Yates, "this meeting is not even important, what the hell are you doing here"?
"It's ok Frank, honestly, I'm fine".
"It's not the point lady, you should be at home, resting".
"Frank, even if I wanted to, I couldn't, because even as we speak, I have forensics in, wall to bloody wall, and they're wasting their time".
"Oh now Deborah, I know these guys work a little on the slow side, but they always get results. If that person has left any traces, they'll find them".
Knowles lit up a cigarette.
"They'll find prints alright Frank, but they won't find a match on the criminal records".
"How do you know that"?
"I just know".
"Yes, but *how* do you know? It could be anybody".
"It could be Frank, but it's not. This goes back a long time, and to last year particularly. This person is going to try and kill me, and I will kill them if I get the chance, and they know it, there's no truce here Frank, it's just a question of, last one standing. I have to let the forensic boys do their stuff, but they won't find a match on any criminal files"
"Yates looked at Knowles through half closed eyes.
"Why don't you call in some help, get them that way, then you'll know you'll get in first".
"Can't, it's like I said, it's personal".
"Well" said Yates, picking up some documents from his desk and rising to his feet, if it was me Deborah I wouldn't be taking any chances, that was a bit too close for comfort for my liking. You do know that they could have killed you last night, if they'd wanted to, don't you"?
"Yes, I know that Frank, I dropped my guard, that's all".
"Did you hell drop your guard, you were out, and they managed to gain entry to your supposedly secure house, it's got nothing to do with dropping your guard, you be careful Deborah".

“Don’t worry, they won’t be back for a while, they were just trying to show off, trying to give me a fright that’s all”.
“For God’s sake Deborah, they blew your car and your garage to pieces, I think *I* would get a fright. Next time, they may go for your home”.
“No”.
“You sound sure of yourself”.
“I am, this person wants to see me die, anyway enough, I want to see a couple of inmates today, they’re going to get a good hard kick in the balls, that’ll make me feel better”.
After the meeting, which was focussing on cutting bills in prisons, chiefly catering costs, Knowles asked to be shown around one or two of the prison wings. As she and Yates walked through C wing, Yates informed her that some of the prisoners here would be coming up to Park Hill once it was completed.
“I’ve put a small yellow sticker outside of the cells of the prisoners that you’ll be taking. You’ll be getting the short timers, you know? The short sharp shock treatment. This place, will eventually take only the long term prisoners, the lifers, the ones who won’t be getting home”.
As they walked, Deborah stopped and pointed to a certain prisoner.
“What’s *this* in for”? She pointed to a young scruffy man sporting a skin head haircut, who was scrubbing the floor with a yard brush and bucket.
“Stand!” Yates barked at the man.
The young man stood straight up, with one hand on the shaft of his whalebone brush, amusing Deborah Knowles, who thought that he looked like a small child, playing soldiers.
Yates looked at the file in his hand.
“Let’s see, let’s see, prisoner Paul Morgan, 882216719 caught in possession again with coke”.
“How many times is *this* he’s been in Frank”?
“This is, his, three, three times now he’s been caught in possession”. Yates looked up from his folder.
“Are you *never* going to learn Morgan”?
“Sir” the man replied, smiling.
“How long is he doing Frank”?
“He got ten months, he’s done three, he’ll be up in front of the parole panel next month. He’ll be gone by the time your prison is completed”.

Knowles walked up to the young man, who was still holding his broom upright. “You must like it in here cunt, do you”?
“No Miss”.
“No Miss? repeated Knowles. “Well I happen to think that you are a fucking liar, because you keep coming back here”.
The man looked straight ahead of him and said nothing. He had obviously been warned about Knowles.
Knowles made to walk away, then turned suddenly and swung with her right foot, and caught the man right between his legs.
He went down, clutching his testicles, and writhing in pain.
“Now listen scruff boy, you get yourself off those drugs, do you hear me, because if you land in *my* prison you can expect two of those beauties, before and after each meal, every day, for the duration of your sentence. Please believe me when I tell you, that your life will be hell, complete hell, if I should ever set eyes on your ugly fucking drug infested face now, have you got that scum boy”?
“Answer the lady” barked Yates.
“Yes Miss”, the prisoner managed between gasps of breath.
“Good”. Replied Knowles, as she picked up the hard brush, and jammed it in the young man’s face. “You’d better”!

AMBLESIDE. A. 591. CUMBRIA.

Sharon's aunt sat with the small mobile draughts board on her lap, placing her white counter on to her selected square.
"Oh dear Amy, I think I've made a big mistake, I think you're going to beat me again, this will be four nil, you're too good young lady".
Sharon smiled, as she looked into the rear view mirror. "Is that Amy beating you again Aunt Sarah"?
"I'm afraid so, she's just too good for me, and that's that".
In her excitement, Amy dropped her draught piece onto the floor.
She unfastened her seat belt and bent down to retrieve the piece.
The articulated timber lorry heading for Penrith with a full forty ton load of Larch had taken the tight bend way too fast, and ploughed straight into Sharon's car, causing it to spin right around, in the opposite direction it had been travelling. The lorry went up on its side, causing the support bars to slip out, and allowing the giant logs, to tumble off, directly onto the roof of Sharon's vehicle.
Now, both lanes were blocked.
By the time the unsuspecting driver of the milk tankard rounded the bend, it was too late. The milk tankard smashed into Sharon's car, though all the occupants were already dead.
The driver of the milk tankard also died, as he was thrown through his windscreen and onto the timber and glass. The driver of the timber lorry would die later in hospital. Meanwhile, as he dangled upside down in what was left of his cab, he saw a draught board, and the severed hand of a child. He cried, as he realized that there was, at least one fatality.
He felt the warmth of his blood, flowing freely down from his stomach and around his neck. Maybe it was just as well that the unfortunate driver was trapped and that he couldn't see the insides of his stomach hanging out around his chest. Two more vehicles crashed into the carnage, before the fire brigade and police arrived, and leaving a total of six fatalities.
The A 591 was an accident black spot in one or two of its nooks and crannies, but had never been witness to one as bad as this.
In Carlisle, Tracy browsed through the property magazine looking for a suitable home for herself and the children, and Sharon, as she sat sipping her coffee and enjoying her break from the kids.

(FATE.)
THE RED LION. SHEFFIELD.

Sophie Blair sat in the corner of the pub lounge, curtains closed against the sunlight. The fact that the sun was shining was irrelevant. The curtains were always closed, night or day. Robert Finch, her boyfriend, had taken off two days earlier, leaving her a note explaining that he could neither tolerate her, or the kind of life he was living in Sheffield. The trouble was, he had also left a note for the local authorities, informing them that his girlfriend was a drug addict, and that she was in no fit state to look after their eight month old baby Beth.

The authorities had acted quickly and had paid Sophie a visit, examining the condition not only of herself but of the house as well. They decided that both Sophie and her house were both unfit for bringing up a baby. They took the child away.

Sophie had been drinking, almost constantly since they took her child from her. She had not eaten, and she had not slept.

The only customers in the pub were two young teenage boys, who were sharing a tin of coke and playing a game of pool, three old men studying the form in their newspapers for the next race, and a young woman sitting on the barstool at the bar, sipping a bottle of beer.

Sophie struggled to her feet and made her way to the bar, returning her empty glass.

Her eyes were burning from the tears she had spilled in the last twenty four hours.

"Same again please" said Sophie to the barman, with slurred speech.

"What? What was that"?

"Same again please, vodka and coke please", the words sounded more like fodka, and pleazze.

"One more! And that's it. One more, and don't you be wandering around the pub looking for takers either Sophie, you should be barred from here anyway, you little tramp, no wonder Rob fucked off. Excuse my French" he said to the young lady seated at the bar. He cupped his hand over his mouth, and leaned his head over to the woman, pointing his finger at Sophie and whispering, "*Sells herself for drugs you know, they've taken her baby away from her. Her man's took off and left her, and now look at her. I would ban her in a minute if I had my way, little dog that she is".*

"Here! Fucking junkie, no more, got it, little whore".

As Sophie was walking away from the bar, the barmen shouted after her. "Hey! You're eight pence short, bring that drink back until you've paid it in full, you little thieving bitch".

Sophie put down her glass on the nearest table she could find, and returned to the bar. She pulled out her purse from her hand bag and pulled out a ten pound note. As Sophie handed the barman her money, the lady sitting at the bar said to him, "give her her money back, I'm paying".

"I beg your pardon Miss"? Replied the barman, knowing full well what she'd said.

"You heard me, I said I'm paying for this, unless of course, you're calling me a whore as well, are you"?

"No Miss, it's just that she's"-.

"Get me another bottle of beer as well while you're at it".

"Certainly Miss. Here you are Sophie" said the man, as if Sophie had suddenly became his best friend. This lady here is buying you this drink, say thank you Sophie".

"She doesn't have to thank me".

Sophie heard what the woman said, and came over.

"Thank you" she said, her voice almost a whisper. "Thank you very much".

"You're welcome, now go and enjoy your drink in peace. I'll make sure he doesn't say any more nasty things to you.

The barmen rang up the price on the till. "That'll be seven pounds exactly please".

The young lady handed him a twenty pound note. "What do you like to drink"? She said to the barman.

"Thank you very much, I'll have a pint of lager please, if that's alright, thank you".

"Not with my money you won't, I only asked you what you liked to drink".

The barman's face went red, very quickly

The three old men sitting together had heard what was said, and now all sat laughing at the barman's expense.

Even Sophie smiled.

"There now" said the woman at the bar. "It's not nice to be made a fool of in public is it"?

"Look Miss, if you're referring to the way I spoke to her" he said, pointing his finger at Sophie, "then I'm afraid you're going to wait a long time for an apology, you don't know the bitch like me. She is nothing but a pest. She's a junkie, and she deserves everything she gets. They've taken her kid away because she's incapable of looking after it, huh, she's incapable of looking after herself, look at her! Fucking little junkie bastard that she is"!

The woman had turned her head away from the barman, half way through his sentence. "Having any luck with your horses boys"? She said to the three elderly gentlemen.

"No Miss, no luck today I'm afraid", replied one of the pensioners.

Turning round to the barman she said; " Get those three gentlemen a drink please, anything they fancy, and those two lads playing pool, get them a drink as well, I'm just going to your toilet, I take it you have one".

The barman pointed to the far side of the room. "Over there, Sophie will show you".

As the woman was walking away, he shouted "Mind you don't get any junkie needles up your arse when you're in there"!

When she returned from the bathroom, there was another woman sitting at Sophie's table.

Her hair looked long and dark, though it was hard to tell in this poor light the exact colour. She was dressed far too well to be a junkie. She passed Sophie and her friend and returned to the bar, where she found the two young lads, each with a pint of beer in their hands, and the three elderly gents with the same. As she reached the bar, the barman said to her, "Don't you want to buy Sophie another drink? I'm only asking before I ring this in".

"No, Sophie has company, can't you see"?

"Yeah, I can see alright. Sophie has trouble, that's what Sophie has".

The woman beside Sophie had no drink. She was obviously here on business. Then the woman raised her voice,

"Where the fuck is it then Sophie, you must know, and where is that thieving bastard; you must know where he is"!

Realizing that she was just a bit too loud, she controlled her voice again, and began to speak softly once again into Sophie's ear.

The young woman at the bar watched proceedings from the bar mirror. Whatever was up, the woman sitting with Sophie was not happy about something. The conversation she guessed would have something to do with drugs…or money…or both.

Now it was Sophie's turn to lose control, as she cried out, "I don't know Sam, I honestly don't know. I sent him round to your place, like you said, and that's the last I've seen of him, honestly. He even reported me to the welfare, and they've taken my baby away from me. I don't know where the fuck he's gone. He could be dead for all I know. His clothes are still in the wardrobe".

"Sophie" the woman called Samantha said, "That boyfriend of yours has stolen fifteen grand from me. Yes fifteen. I get a phone call this morning, and they're asking me for the money. That bastard Rob, has taken off with it, plus what he already owes me, and now, I'm afraid, it's you who owes me. Now, I don't give a monkey's fuck, where you get the money from, but you'd better get it"! You've got three days Sophie, either to deliver the money, or Mister Robert Finch. Sophie, if I find out that you and Rob have worked together on this, you will suffer like you've never suffered before in your life!"

"Samantha, I keep telling you, I don't know where he or the money is, you could give me three years Sam, I won't be able to get him or the money".

The woman leaned over the table and whispered in a menacing voice; "Well, in that case Sophie, I suggest that you start praying to your guardian angel, because that would be the only thing that would stop your certain death. You find that money, and that thieving bastard of a boyfriend of yours, you little whore, you have one week"!

The woman rose from the table and left the pub.

The barman smiled to himself smugly, as he wiped a pint tumbler with a tea towel.

"Everything alright Sophie"? He shouted out, still smiling. "Looks like you're in deep shit this time huh? Let's see you fuck your way out of this one. You've bitten off more than you can chew this time, junkie bitch. You finish your drink, and then get to fuck out of here, and don't come back here either, for a while, we're not wanting the place smashed up because of you, now you hurry up and get out of here!"

Sophie sat with her head in her hands, tears rolling down her face.

Angela Phorbes rose up from her barstool and walked over to her, taking a seat next to the distraught girl. "That woman who was just here, is that who you run for"?

Sophie looked at Angela, and eventually nodded.
"Do you owe her money"?
Again Sophie nodded.
"Tell you what" said Angela, "I'm leaving here in five minutes, what do you say we go to your place, get your things, and come with me, huh? It's got to be better than this has it not"?
Sophie looked into her face, and then said, "Ok, I haven't got any money though".
"Oh, don't worry about that, we'll soon sort that out, that's the least of your problems, just wait here a minute". She went into the lady's room, then came back out less than a minute later. She shouted over to the barman. "Excuse me, there's water running everywhere in here, there must be blocked drains or something, the stink is terrible, you'll have to take a look at this, hurry!"
"I'm coming, I'm coming, keep your hair on, fucking barman, cum electrician, cum cook, cum fucking plumber, I'm so sick of this shit I am".
The barman entered the toilets followed by Angela Phorbes.
The three old men and the two young lads all looked at one another, smiling. Two minutes later, the barman came out of the toilet and walked up to Sophie's table. There hadn't been any leak in the toilets.
"Miss Blair, I would like to take this opportunity to apologise to you for everything I've said to cause you insult or hurt. I swear I will never again refer to you as anything but the beautiful young woman you are. Please accept my most humblest apologies, and may I take this opportunity to wish you well in everything you do in the future".
Angela came over to the table.
"Sophie? Tell it, you accept it's apology, and to get it's arse back behind the bar and continue serving the public. Tell it Sophie. He knows he's only dog shit, don't you"?
"Yes".
"Tell him to fuck off from your table Sophie, he's fowling the air around us".
Sophie looked at her, then at the barman.
"Fuck off dog breath, get away from me".
"That's it Sophie" she said. "Now then, I believe you have something to say to the customers" she snapped at the barman.
"Yes" said the barman, looking at the floor. "Let me buy you all a drink, it's my way of apologising for being such a brainless wanker".

“That’s better” said Angela Phorbes, “but I’m afraid Sophie and I will have to decline dog shit’s offer of a drink, we have to go now, but maybe another time we might let it buy us a drink, we have to leave now, bye everyone” said Angela, waving at the few customers in the bar.

The three old men waved over to Angela and Sophie, as did the two youths.

“You’ll have to give me directions to your house Sophie, is it far from here”?

“No, it’s just a couple of hundred yards from here, and why are you doing this”?

“Doing what Sophie”?

“This, helping me escape Samantha”?

“Well, let’s just say, I know where you’re hanging, I know what it’s like”.

“It was that stupid boyfriend of mine who got me into this. He’s fucked off with fifteen thousand of Sam’s money. He said something about prisons changing, and something about taking off. He didn’t want to go back there, whatever the reasons, I don’t know, I think he got a fright. Oh yes, he said something about a nasty woman, a real nasty woman I think was how he described her. He said she’d slap six months onto your sentence at the drop of a hat, just like that”. Sophie went quiet. Then she began to cry. “They’ve taken my baby away, Rob, you bastard, how could you”?

Angela put her arm around Sophie’s shoulder as she drove. “You’re gonna be ok kid, I’ll make sure of that. You’ll be fine Sophie. *We’ll* be fine”.

Once inside Sophie’s house, the young troubled girl began to empty her drawers and wardrobe into a single suitcase. The whole house was a mess, and if Sophie was honest with herself, she would not be able to remember the last time she had taken out the vacuum cleaner , let alone use a duster or polish. As she closed the suitcase, she took a last look around the place. The only photograph in the entire house was the one Rob had arranged his friend to take. It was he and herself and baby Beth. She wasn’t going to take it with her, but then changed her mind, deciding that it would be of some comfort at least, if she could look at her baby from time to time. Two black polythene bin bags, and one small suitcase, that, was Sophie Blair. “The girl in the car was right, things could only get better than this”. “That’s me” Sophie said, climbing into the car.

“Are you ok? I mean, I know you’re a bit drunk, but other than that”?
“Yeah, I’m fine, just a bit tired that’s all, so if I fall asleep, don’t be offended, anyway, what’s your name”? I don’t even know your name”.
“Angela, Angela Clark”.
“Hi Angela, I’m Sophie, Sophie Blair”.
Angela smiled.
“What? You think my name is funny”?
“No I don’t Sophie, I think your name sounds like a pop star’s name. *And starring in tonight’s concert, that’s right folks, it’s the one and only Sophie Blair”.*
The two girls laughed together, something neither of them had done for a long time.
“Where are we going anyway”? said Sophie.
“First, we are going to Rotherham to pick up some of my things, and then young lady, we are going to meet a very dear friend of mine, and a very very dear cousin”.
“They live in Rotherham”?
“No, they live in Carlisle”.
“Carlisle? Where’s that”?
“Carlisle” said Angela, “is the last city in England as you head north, it’s only a few miles from the legendary Gretna Green, in some people’s opinion, the most romantic place in the world to get married”.
“Can I smoke in here”?
“Of course you can” smiled Angela.
As the two women sat smoking, Sophie suddenly said, “It doesn’t matter where you get married, it’s what happens after the day you get married that makes you romantic or not, that’s how I see it anyway”.
“Yeah, you’re right Sophie”.
“Have you ever been married Angela”?
“Nearly, engaged”.
“What happened”?
“I got kidnapped and gang raped”.
“Yeah, fuck marriage” said Sophie, not really taking in what Angela had said.
Two hours later, they were on the M.6, outside of Preston, heading for Carlisle.

Sophie Blair lay across the back seat, crashed out.
Angela glanced over her shoulder at the young woman. Sophie had not stirred since she fell asleep, fifty seven miles from Preston. A little under an hour later, they were entering Carlisle. “Did you enjoy your sleep”? said Angela, handing the girl a can of coke
“What the, where are we”?
“We’re in Carlisle; we’ll soon be at the house. Let me do the talking, I’ll explain everything to them, now, there’s two little girls in here, so, watch your P’s and Q’s Sophie. You’ll really like these people”.
Less than five minutes later, they were pulling into the street.
“Shit!!” said Angela.
“What’s wrong”? said Sophie, taking a drink of her cola. There was a police car parked outside of the house.
“Oh, don’t say they’ve found her”, said Angela out loud.
“Found who Angela? What do you mean”?
“It’s a long story Sophie, and I haven’t got time to explain it now”.
“What? Is there trouble”?
“Well, let me put it this way, you know your friend Sam”?
“Yes”?
“Well, if this is who I think it is, then double Sam, and multiply by ten”.
“Shit!!”
“Exactly Sophie. You know how you told me about your boyfriend, and how he had met an evil bitch in the prison”?
“Yes”?
“Well, this is her”.
“So Rob was right, he was right to be frightened of her”?
“You bet your life he was. He’s moved away Sophie, because he does not want to meet this woman again, he’s done the right thing, believe me”.
“What Angela? And she’s after *you*”?
“That Sophie, is the understatement of all time”.
“And you think she’s in your friend’s house”?
“Don’t know, but I’m about to find out”. Angela sighed heavily. “Sophie? If I’m not out of that house in ten minutes, then get out of the car, and forget you ever met me, can you drive Sophie”?
“Yes”.
“Then take this car. Take the car and get to hell out of here”.
“Where will I go”?

"Go anywhere Sophie, because if Deborah Knowles catches you with me, then believe me, hell would be like a summer vacation compared to what she'd have lined up for you".
"You're frightening me Angela".
"Good. Here, take this".
Angela opened her handbag and pulled out her purse. She handed Sophie a bundle of notes.
"There's about three hundred pounds there Sophie, it's all I've got on me".
"But you're coming back out though, right"?
"I sincerely hope so. If I don't, there's nearly a full tank of petrol. That'll get you far enough away from here where you'll be safe".
"You'll be alright Angela, everything will be alright, you'll see".

Angela stepped out of the car and walked over to Sharon's aunt's house. It was a deathly calm night, and she could hear voices in the distance. People laughing and shouting, probably on their way home from the pub or their local club. She climbed the steps up to the house and took a deep breath.
"Here goes" she thought to herself, "It's shit or bust". She tapped on the door lightly, and walked in.
A policeman was standing at the entrance to the living room.
"Who are you madam"? He said, in a soft affectionate voice.
"I eh. I'm going to be staying here for a while, I'm a friend of Sharon and Tracy, my name is Angela Clark".
"Well Miss, you'd better come through here".
The policeman pointed to the kitchen.
"What's wrong officer, is there a problem"?
The policeman walked behind Angela, into the kitchen.
"Miss Clark, there is no easy way to tell you this, there's been an accident, a fatal one".
"My God, who"?
The officer cleared his throat.
"At around ten fifteen this morning, Sarah Hartley and her niece Sharon, along with two little girls, were travelling in a motor vehicle which was in collision with an articulated lorry".
"Oh no, oh God no, not the girls, not Tracy's girls, oh my sweet Jesus".
"I'm afraid so Miss. I'm sorry to inform you that there were no survivors, I'm so sorry".

Angela felt numb, from her head to her feet.
"Oh Lord Jesus no, not the kids Lord, oh my sweet God have mercy". She slumped onto one of the kitchen chairs with her head in her hands. She began to mumble questions to the police officer. "Oh fuck, what on earth, where's Tracy"?
"We have a doctor in there with her now. I think he's giving her a sedative".
"Let me see her" said Angela, in desperation.
"That might not be a very good idea just now Miss".
"Let me see her. I am the only family that girl has; now you let me see her!"
"Let me talk to the doctor Miss, he'll tell you what's what".
Angela sat at the kitchen table. Everything that had been explained to her in the last two minutes or so, seemed, unreal, untrue, it was almost completely incomprehensible. This could not be happening. There was a packet of cigarettes on the kitchen table, she took one out of the packet and lit up, her hands shaking involuntarily, she inhaled deeply and looked around the kitchen. Everywhere she looked, there were examples of Amy and Angela's handy work. On the fridge door, there was a drawing of a clown's face with the slogan underneath reading; SMILE, AND LET THE WORLD SEE YOU'RE HAPPY".
As Angela sat waiting for the officer to return, she thought about Sharon, and Tracy. What would this do to Tracy? She was on edge as it was, this could finish her. Oh my God, her little girls, dear Lord.
The officer returned with the doctor and a police woman.
"Miss Clark"? said the doctor, laying a sheet of paper on the table.
He was a very tall man, about six three Angela guessed, tall and lean, mid-forties, with receding hair.
"Yes, I'm Angela Clark".
"Are you a relative of Misses Hillman's"?
"Yes, I'm her cousin".
"Well, as you can imagine, Misses Hillman has had quite a shock, devastating, as you have yourself. Tracy has had to be sedated, she's on the sofa sleeping. Are you going to be here for her, I mean, are you going to be staying here for any length of time"?
"Yes, I'll be here for about two or three months".
"Good, now, as regards to Miss Hartley and Miss Wells, we don't seem to be able to trace any relatives, do you know of any"?

"No, I eh, no, I'm afraid not. I've heard Sharon on about a brother, but I don't think she's had contact with him now for years". Angela sat shaking her head, still reeling from the shock of the bad news.
"Miss Clark" said the doctor, as he sat down next to her. "We'll need someone to identify the bodies, preferably within the next twenty-four hours, do you think"?
"Yes, I'll come and do it tomorrow, where do I go to do this"?
The doctor handed her a piece of paper with the address of the Carlisle royal infirmary.
"Thank you Miss Clark. Now, can I give you a little something to help you with -"
"No thank you doctor, I'll manage fine thank you".
"As you wish, Miss Clark, and I want you to know something. I was at the scene of the accident, and I can assure you, none of them suffered, it was sudden".
He handed Angela a card with a phone number on it.
"If you have any problems with Misses Hillman, or yourself for that matter, just call this number, and a crisis nurse will be here in no time. As it stands now, she'll be here around eight o clock in the morning to give you a hand, and to talk with you".
"Thank you doctor".
"You're welcome" he replied.
The police woman now spoke.
"Miss Clark" she began, "we need to ask you some questions. I know this is a bad time, but-"
"For God's sake!" said Angela, "can't it wait until tomorrow, I've just lost my two little nieces for crying out loud!"
The police woman looked at her partner. "Of course Miss Clark, we'll come back tomorrow, sure".
Angela rose from the table and saw the doctor and two police officers out.
She was just about to close the door when she suddenly remembered Sophie.
She watched as the doctor drove away, followed by the police car. She signalled Sophie to come over to the house. After fifteen minutes, Angela had explained everything to the young woman. She walked into the living room and looked at Tracy lying on the sofa in a deep sleep. How on earth Tracy was going to deal with this, was anyone's guess. Would she be able to handle this?
"Poor Tracy" thought Angela "always the bum deal Trace".

She returned to the kitchen, where she and Sophie sat drinking coffee.
After a few minutes of taking the present situation in hand, and thinking of all the complications that this had added to her own existence, Angela said "Sophie? I'm afraid this is where you and I part company kid. I'll have to watch that woman in there around the clock. She is going to need me more than she ever has in her entire life. If I should turn my back, she could quite easily top herself".
"I know all this Angela, but I wouldn't get in your way, I promise, I can clean the house, I'll make your meals, I can cook, I'll go for groceries, errands, please Angela, I will be a help, I will, I have nowhere else to go, I don't know anyone who could help me Angela".
"Sophie" said Angela, softly, "we can't stay here. I can't stay here. I'm just about to lift Tracy from the couch and put her in the car. If I don't, she and I will be in jail by this time tomorrow. We have to get out of here tonight. Now, you are only running from one woman Sophie. Her and I are running away from Deborah Knowles, there's a big difference".
"I know, I know that you're in a hell of a situation here, but aren't we all? And if you don't mind me saying, you were the one who offered me a way out of Sheffield, and now? You're going to dump me off? You should have left me there. I don't know why I bothered packing".
"Sophie, that's unfair, that was all before this, I didn't know that this was going to happen. I, look"
"Angela, give me three days with you, alright, and if you feel that it's not working out, then I'll leave, ok? You owe me that much, for taking me away from Sheffield".
Angela sighed heavily.
"Ok Sophie, we'll give it a week, and see how we feel".
"Thank you".
"Right, we have to think straight now Sophie. Help me pack some of Tracy's things, and if we get caught, and are confronted by Deborah Knowles, then remember, you asked to come with *me*, do you accept that? Because let me tell you something, this bitch is pure evil, she sleeps with Satan".
"I understand that Angela".
Less than half an hour later, the two women had the clothes packed and in the boot of Angela's car.

They were now carrying Tracy outside and placing her on the back seat of the car.
"There, that's it, get those lights out and lock the door, let's get out of here".
"Where are we going Angela"?
"Don't know, you better drive Sophie, I'll sit in the back with Tracy, in case she wakes up. I don't know what kind of sedative that doctor gave her, but it looks like she'll never wake up. God help her when she does, poor girl" said Angela, stroking Tracy's brow. "The whole shock thing kicks in again. It's almost as bad as being given the bad news all over again".
Ten minutes later, they were on the outskirts of Carlisle.
"Which way"? said Sophie, looking over her shoulder.
"Get onto the M6 and just head South Sophie, we'll think about where we're going as we travel".
"Thanks again, Angela, for letting me come with you".
"Don't thank me Sophie, we could have a very bumpy ride in front of us. Have you ever killed anyone Sophie"?
"No".
"Well, that may change over the next few weeks or so, in fact I know it will".

HARRINGTON POLICE STATION.
SHEFFIELD.

The office was not busy. There was only a new recruit in the front room, who was busy making Deborah Knowles her coffee. Deborah was on the phone to Frank Yates.

Sergeant Smith entered the room, whistling and heading to Knowles's desk.

"Do you mind" said Knowles, "I'm trying to talk on the phone here".

"With respect mam, I think you'll be interested in my news".

"Really"?

"Yes mam" said Oliver Smith, who had not long been promoted to the post of sergeant, and who now wore the permanent smile on his face which had been there since the day he'd received the news of his promotion.

"Sorry, I'll call you back Frank, apparently I have some good news to hear, speak to you soon, bye".

Knowles took a sip of her coffee. "Oh you fucker constable Lake. Go and take that back and put two spoonful's of sugar in there please. You'd better right that down constable".

Constable Lake's face was red with embarrassment.

"Now then Sergeant Smith, what's this good news you have"?

"Well mam, it's not exactly good news, but I think you'll be interested".

"Well, can I hear it please, before they come in collecting for the Christmas concert".

"Well mam, there was a fatal accident yesterday, up in Cumbria".

"And this is good news is it"?

"No mam, Carlisle constabulary have been in contact with us with information regarding two of the passengers killed in one of the vehicles. The two children killed in the crash, well, there surname is Hillman, two girls mam. They are the same age as John Hillman's girls. They done some investigating, and discovered that neither of the girls are enrolled at Cumbrian schools".

"I see" said Knowles, suddenly interested in what Smith was saying.

"The police are going back tomorrow to the house where the two little girls were staying with their mother, and two friends of their mother's".

"Names"?

"Sharon Hartley, and I've forgotten the other".
"What's the name of their mother Smith, can you remember that"?
"Eh, Tracy, Tracy Hillman".
"Is she dead"?
"No mam, she wasn't in the car with them".
"Where is *she* now"?
"She's in the house, the house in Carlisle. I've been informed that the doctors have her heavily sedated".
"Phone them back Smith, and tell them to keep her there, whatever they do".
"The officers told me that she had a friend arrive, she's looking after her just now. She said she was going to stay for a few months".
"Her name"?
"Angela, Angela Clark".
"Shit! You had to go and spoil it Smith didn't you".
"You know this Angela Clark mam"?
"Oh I know her alright Smith, believe me, I know her. I'll bet you your bottom dollar, by the time the police went there this morning that they were gone. How much would you like to bet, and I know that you're a betting man, because I saw you going into the bookies yesterday, in your work time. Do it again Smith, and you'll be demoted back to constable and I will also kick you in the balls, understood"?
"Yes mam".
"Ok then, go and phone Carlisle and ask them if Tracy Hillman and her friend are still at home. I think I already know the answer Smith".
"I'll go and phone anyway mam, you never know".
"Wrong Smith, it's you who never knows, now go, and tell that jerk to hurry up with my coffee, oh and bring my car round the front please".
"You're new car mam"?
"No, bring the one I take to the drag races, for goodness sakes sergeant".
Ten minutes later, Sergeant Smith returned to the front office, handing Deborah Knowles her keys.
He had just been on the phone to the Carlisle constabulary. "You were right mam. When the officers went to the house this morning, they were gone, and it was definitely the Hillman children who were killed".

"I thought as much" said Knowles.
"Ah well, at least it saves me the journey of going up there, I don't suppose anyone up there saw them leave"?
"I don't know mam, they didn't say. Do you still want me to leave your car out the front"?
"Yes, I'm going over to see Mister Yates".
Smith left the room and went back to the front desk. Lake entered the room carefully carrying Deborah's coffee mug.
"Well done Lake, but listen, you needn't have gone down to Exeter for the sugar, you should have just gone down to the canteen in here, it would have been much quicker".
"Sorry Miss Knowles, I'll try and be quicker next time".
"On you go Lake".
Deborah sipped her coffee, savouring the flavour, now that she had her sugar. "I wonder Angela, where you'll be heading young lady. Not down here, that's for sure. I'll find you though, no matter where you are, I'll find you, and when I do, Mister Yates and I will have a field day". Knowles picked up the phone again and called Frank Yates.
"Frank? It's me again Deborah, listen, I'll have to cancel our meeting today, there's something came up I have to attend to".
"That's alright Deborah, the meeting was only about the progress of the new prison being built, you won't miss much. Oh by the way, you've to go down to London sometime this week. I think they want you to accept that job, at the Metropolitan Police Department, this is the big one Deborah. The Chief of Police".
Yes, I've been thinking about that. I don't know if I want it or not, I'm quite happy where I am".
"Happy? Fuck sakes woman, they're trying to blow your house up and your garage, and you, how the hell can you be happy"?
"That's just it Frank I know who that was".
"You know"?
"Yes, I told you. Forensics can look all they want, they won't find anything".
"How do you know all this"?
"I just know Frank. Don't worry, if they had wanted me dead, I would have been dead, believe me. This person is just playing games just now. What they want, is a personal one on one situation, where it will be a case of the last one standing".
"Hell, you must have done something nasty Deborah".

"Oh, I did, myself and Karen Jones, God rest her soul".
"Yeah, and if you're not careful, it'll be God rest *your* soul".
"Oh, I'll be careful alright. Now then Frank, if the M.P.D. calls back, tell them I'll be down tomorrow to see them".
"Will do, take care, and I mean that. These people who are after you, just watch out Deborah".
"I will, bye for now".
Knowles sipped her coffee, and lit up a cigarette. What should she do? "Should I take this job in London?" But, if I do that, then I won't be running the new prison when it opens, and I *so* want to clean up this country from all these scum-bags. To inflict as much pain onto the vermin who inflict pain and heartache onto innocent people. I would make headlines again, because the scum who walked into my prison, would walk out, decent law abiding citizens, or they wouldn't be walking out at all. What to do Deborah, what to do" she spoke quietly to herself. "Whatever I do, my first priority is to find Angela Phorbes. She *will* feel pain before she dies".

“Where are we”? Tracy, with her eyes half closed squinted up at Angela.
“It’s ok Tracy, you just lie back down sweetheart, get some rest, it’s ok, it’s going to be ok”.
“Where’s my girls Angela, where’s my babies, they told me they were dead, where are they? Who’s driving Angela? Where’s my girls”?
“There now, you just lye back down and rest, everything will be just fine Tracy, there now”. Less than a minute later, Tracy had fallen back into a deep sleep.
Tears were rolling down Angela Phorbes’s face. “Pull in Sophie somewhere, until I get a smoke and a coffee, this is a nightmare, it really is. This poor bugger here has had no luck in her life whatsoever, and now this, Jesus have mercy” she sighed. “Fuck I don’t know Sophie if she’s going to pull through this, what a fucking mess. I don’t know what we’re going to do, I don’t know where to go, I, fuck, I don’t know what to do for the best”.
Sophie pulled in to the car park of the road side services.
“Go and get coffee’s please Sophie, a couple each, fuck. I need some fresh air”.
Ten minutes later, Sophie returned with four cartons of coffee, two plastic spoons, and a handful of small sugar bags.
Angela was leaning on the back of the car, almost sitting on it, on the back seat, Tracy lay sleeping, once again oblivious to everything in the world.
Angela exhaled smoke up into the night air as Sophie came around and joined her. “They were beautiful kids you know”.
“I’ll bet they were” said Sophie, looking at Tracy lying upon the back seat. “Their mother is very beautiful”.
“She is that” replied Angela, “in every sense.
All the bad bastards in the world Sophie, and this has to happen to *her*. There’s no fucking justice, that’s all I can say”.
“Yeah, you’re right, but then, that’s always been the way Angela, and it’s not going to change any time soon. This big old world will still be turning, long after we’re gone.
So, what now Angela”?

“God knows Sophie, God knows. The thing is, if Deborah Knowles wants to get nasty, she could involve Tracy in all this trouble I’m in, and believe me, I’m in deep trouble here. She’ll hang Tracy and I”.
“Hang? said Sophie.
“Yes, hang. Now do you see why I don’t want you being around me. It’s not because I don’t like you or anything, I happen to think that you’re a good kid, it’s just that being with me is putting your liberty in jeopardy, and I don’t want that. Once that bastard Knowles spots you with me, or even hears about you running with me, then your life’s fucked Sophie. You should have listened to your boyfriend, the guy has brains. He’s got himself far away from her, and making a new start for himself, good for him, full marks, and you should have gone with him”.

“I know I should, but I could never live with him. We were going to split up anyway. Angela, he used to beat me. Sometimes in front of his friends. He would go out with his friends, and then come home pissed and accuse me of sleeping with other men. He would pull me out of bed, beat me, then make me make him something to eat, then beat me again.
After he eventually calmed himself down, or he burned out from his temper, he would expect me to make love with him, he used to end up raping me, either way, he got his way. That was his idea of having a normal relationship. He thought there was nothing wrong. That’s when I started using drugs, and when I started seeing other men. I was getting beaten for it, so, why not? At least I got some proper attention from time to time. More than I ever got from him. You want me to be honest Angela?
Huh, my life has been such a shambles, that I would gladly hang with you and your cousin than stay in Sheffield with him, or any of the bastards like him, and believe me, most of them are. They’ve taken my baby away Angela.
You know as well as me, the chances of me getting her back.
You’ve told me the risk I’m taking being with you, fine, I’m prepared to take it, but don’t offer me a new life, and then take it away from me again, that’s not nice Angela”.
Angela knew from experience that most of what Sophie had just told her was untrue, but she knew the girl was just trying to win her favour so as that she could stay with them. She’d reacted similarly herself in the past, and if you were good at it, it worked.

“I’m sorry Sophie, I really am, but I don’t want you caught up in all this”. Angela glanced at Tracy in the car, and then looked at Sophie. “It could not be worse, this situation. I never expected to be put in a situation like this, never in a million years. Shit! This just gets worse Sophie by the minute. If I were you, I’d get away from me as far as you can, you’d be safer that way. At least then, you’d only have that, what’s her name, Sam, to worry about. If you stay with us, you’ll be running from Lucifer’s Lady, I kid you not”.
Sophie looked at Angela, as she sipped her coffee. “What the hell is it with you and this Deborah Knowles. What did you do to her to make her hound you like this? Did you take a shit in her dinner”?
Angela looked at Tracy, who was still sedated.
“It’s not what I did to *her*, it’s what I did to society, and to the police force. A long time ago, I was a police officer, just doing my job. I was engaged to be married to a very nice man, trouble was, he was too nice. I don’t even know if I would have went through with it or not. Anyway, we were called out one night. We, being, myself and two other male officers. We were called out to a domestic disturbance. It was a set up. It turned out, that one of the guys who had made the phone call to the police, had a friend brutally murdered in prison. Someone had given him a tip-off that it was the prison wardens who had killed his friend, and it had all been hushed up. This set up, was supposed to be revenge for that incident.
My two colleagues were shot to ribbons, and I was raped by four men, well, two men and young lads, and two women” Angela looked into the car again to check on Tracy.
“Anyway, the craziest thing Sophie, I ended up being friends with them. We ran wild, all around Britain, through towns, cities and villages. We stayed in caravan parks, deserted woodlands, you name it, just ducking and diving from the law. We killed some people on our way”.
“Did they never catch you”?
Angela looked at the girl incredulously.
“No, the two men were killed, through their own carelessness, and I had to kill the two girls in the end, or else they would have killed her”, Angela pointed to Tracy.
“What Tracy”? Why did they want to kill Tracy”?
“Because it was Tracy who shopped us to the police”.
Sophie looked at Angela, bewildered.
“I told you it was crazy, didn’t I”.

"But how come? You're both still good friends"?
"Long story Sophie, too long".
Sophie lit up a cigarette, and handed it to Angela.
"So where does this Deborah Knowles fit in to all this"?
As Angela opened her second carton of coffee, she said, "My name is now Angela Clark. It's obviously not my real name. My real name is Angela Phorbes, but she died.
She's supposed to be lying at the bottom of one of those water ways up in the Lake District. Angela Phorbes was on Britain's most wanted list. Like I said, I was supposed to be lying up there in the lakes. Trouble was, this up and coming new hero of the police force, has done some research of her own, and discovered that Angela Phorbes is very much alive and well.
To my knowledge Sophie, she has kept this information to herself, so as, when she captures me, or kills me, she will receive all the glory , just like she did with that Doctor Hillman".
"Oh yeah, that's where I've heard her name, she caught that fucking loony, didn't she".
"That's right Sophie, now remember Hillman, that killer? That nasty bastard of a man, do you"?
"Of course I do, the whole country does".
"Yes well" once again Angela pointed to Tracy.
"That's his wife".
"Oh my God" said Sophie.
"Now then Sophie, now that you know who it is that you're running with, do you still want to come along, because I'll tell you now, if she catches us, you'll be charged along with Tracy and I".
"I know Angela, but where can I go. I have no friends, other than you, and if I go back to Sheffield, then I'm dead anyway, so I would rather take my chances with you two, and besides, this Deborah Knowles, she doesn't know me, right"?
"Right, not yet Sophie".
"So, give me a gun, and I'll blow her away. If she hasn't told anyone else that you exist, then if she dies, no-one will ever know, end of story. Give me a gun and I'll rid you of her".
"You think it's as easy as that"? "No, I know it won't be, but, it's not impossible Angela. As far as I can see, this woman is going to haunt your every minute, she's going to kill you, or you're going to have to kill her. All I'm saying is, it's going to be an awful lot easier for me to get near her than you, or Tracy for that matter".

“Sophie, I really do appreciate the offer, but I couldn’t let you take the risk, and besides, it’s not going to be easy for anyone to get near her. Hell, she walks out of her door, and she’s got the press following her every move. She’s a national hero, no chance Sophie. Plus, I want to be the one who takes her out, it’s been my priority since...”Angela trailed off as she sipped her coffee.
“Since what Angela”?
“Nothing. Since nothing”.
“Since nothing? Come on, I might be”—
“Look, it’s got fuck all to do with you, just fucking leave it, right!”
Sophie exhaled smoke, and threw her cigarette stump onto the ground, and whispered, “Right. You’re right, it’s got nothing to do with me”.
She drained her coffee carton and walked back round to the driver’s side of the car, leaning her back against the door, with her head bowed and her arms folded.
Angela came round to her.
“Sophie, I’m so sorry for snapping, I know you were only trying to help the situation”.
Sophie said nothing.
“Ok, I’ll tell you what it is between me and Deborah Knowles. I’m bi-sexual Sophie. To cut a long story short, I fell in love with a beautiful young woman named Carla Paganni. She and I had big plans about living together. Deborah Knowles, eh, she...” Angela struggled not to break down. “She eh, they, they beat, they beat her, they beat her to death. They beat her to death Sophie”. Angela breathed in the night air.
“Sorry Sophie, I miss her, I really do”.
Sophie wrapped her arms around Angela and cuddled her. “Don’t worry Angela, one way or another, we’ll get that evil bastard. I’ll tell you something Angela” Sophie said, still cuddling her new friend. “I have never harmed anyone in my entire life, let alone kill anyone, and I know I haven’t known you for long, but already I know, I will do anything, anything, to rid you of this woman, I swear”.
Angela breathed in again, now patting Sophie on the shoulder. “I know Sophie, thank you”.
“Listen, Angela, let me stay with you and Tracy, she’s going to need all the help she can get, and so are you, and so am I Angela, so, will you let me into your lives”?
“You already are in Sophie”.

“ Good, now maybe we can start working out some plans now then. Let’s help Tracy out here first, then we can devise a way of taking out this super cop. Is that a deal Angela”?
“Deal” Angela replied, smiling.
Angela pointed once more inside the car. “It’s not going to be easy to pull her through this”.
Sophie lit up another cigarette, handing it to Angela. “I’m going to have to take a gamble here Sophie, we’ll have to go back to Sheffield”.
“Why”?
“Well because, in a little street called Harington Square, in a little cupboard, in a little corner, in the house that belonged to a friend of mine, who has just been killed, there lies a bag of cocaine.
If Tracy, or us for that matter are to get through this, then we are going to need it”.
“It’ll be a big risk Angela, don’t you think”?
“Yes I do, but it’s a big bag Sophie, and needs be as needs must”.
Sophie smiled at Angela.
“I meant what I said Angela, I will kill her for you”.
“I know what you said Sophie, but so did I, this is personal, and I will. I must be the one who takes her out. She took someone away from me who will always remain in my heart, and so Sophie, she is mine. Her death is all that I live for. I won’t be happy until I see her dead”.

SCOTLAND YARD.
BROADWAY VICTORIA.

Deborah Knowles sat before the three highest ranking dignitaries in the Thames Valley Police Department. Samuel Blake tapped his pen on the table, smiling at Knowles. "Are you sure Deborah, that you don't want this post? Because it seems to me that you are perfect for it".

"Mister Blake" she replied, "with the greatest respect sir, I am deeply honoured, that you have this opinion of me, but I am more than happy with my present position. The prison up in Sheffield, is well under way, and I am looking forward to running it, along with the staff that I shall personally choose. If it works out, and the crime rate falls to such an extent that I feel my presence is no longer necessary, and if you good people are still in your present positions, then, maybe I would reconsider".

The police commissioner looked at Knowles.

"You may not get this opportunity again Deborah, although, I do admire your enthusiasm towards this project of yours".

"Sir, it is more than a project, it is an essential act of decency towards the law abiding citizens of Great Britain. There is no question of this failing sir. This will not fail. I fully intend, if I am left alone, to rid the country of the vermin who have contaminated this Island of ours. When I am finished in Sheffield, car theft, armed robbery, rape, prostitution, drug trafficking, they will all be a thing of the past".

The deputy Chief Commissioner, a Mister William Mcnab, said, "Come now Deborah, I think you're aiming your sights just a little too high, don't you? How on earth are you going to stop all the crime, you can't stop it all".

Knowles shifted in her seat.

"Mister Mcnab, when these criminals come in to my prison, their lives will change. They will be given no therapy, or help in any way. They will be beaten, again and again, if that's what it takes to learn them. When, or *if* they walk out of my prison, they will cherish their freedom. They will never again, take their liberty for granted".

Knowles studied the three men's faces in front of her. They had no idea whatsoever what was happening to their country. They were protected from that world within their wealth.

They would never encounter situations that normal everyday people encountered. To them, there was nothing wrong with the country, other than a few minor problems within certain communities. Other than that though, there wasn't a great lot going wrong with the country. They would sit with their after-dinner-cigars and boast to one another that Britain was still the best country in the world to live.

Samuel Blake studied Knowles over the rim of his reading glasses. A man in his late sixties, more than a little over weight, with thinning grey hair, he reminded Deborah of an old history teacher from her secondary school.

"We had hoped Deborah, that you would be, how shall I put it, a little bit excited, to say the least, at the thought of being offered this job, after all, it's not every day, one gets offered a post like this one. Would you like a few days to think about it Deborah, I mean, it's a very, very honourable position you've been offered, although, I might add, that it was on merit that you were offered this post, your name wasn't exactly just pulled out of a hat. You're still a very popular young woman you know, after your heroics, disposing of our friend Hillman".

Knowles took a sip from her glass of water.

"Mister Blake and friends" she began. "As I have already said, I am deeply honoured, I really am, but I have already made my mind up, and I'm afraid I've put too much time and effort into what I'm doing in Sheffield, just to give it up like that. I know full well sir, that the day may come, that I may regret my decision, but that's a chance I'll just have to take".

Samuel Blake, once again tapped his pen on the table, as he looked at his two colleagues. "Well, if that is your final decision Miss Knowles".

"Yes sir, it is".

"Well then, so be it, we'll just have to look further down our ranks to find a suitable candidate for the post, though I doubt we'll find one with your credibility".

"Thank you sir, I'm flattered, I really am".

"Quite, and we are disappointed, but, on you go young lady, and rid the streets of Sheffield and the rest of Yorkshire of their crime".

"I fully intend to sir".

They were over doing it with their patronising, but it didn't bother her.

"Be warned though, Miss Knowles, I have heard about what happened to your car and garage. You don't want to be making any new enemies".
"With all respect Sir, any enemies of mine, will not be around for long".
"You sound so sure of yourself miss Knowles".
"*And so do you, you pretentious prick*".
"I am sure of myself sir, because I will be in full charge of anything and everything that happens within my prison walls. No-one else in the country seems willing enough to stand up and do something against these criminals who are running havoc on our streets, and in our prisons. As I say, if I am left to my own devices, then their day is coming to an end. They will answer for their actions".

HARRINGTON SQUARE.
SHEFFIELD. 10 A.M.

The black Mercedes rolled into the square, with Sophie Blair at the wheel.
"Which house is it Angela"? said Sophie, throwing her cigarette stump out of the window.
"Just go to the end of the road Sophie, I'll tell you when to stop".
She drove the car to the bottom of the road until she came to the end, and then turned the car around.
"Stop here, I just hope that no-one has had the locks changed.
Right, I'll be two minutes girls, if everything is alright".
Tracy was sitting in the back seat, just staring into space. Although she was sitting up, she may as well have been sleeping. She was numb from all the sedatives she'd been given, plus the amount of cocaine that Angela had on her. Her eyes were as red as could be, bloodshot from all of her heartache. She was numb with grief.
"Keep the car running Sophie, I won't be long".
Angela walked up the path to Sharon's house and put the key into the lock. It was no good, it didn't fit. "Shit!!" She hissed to herself. She took two or three steps back towards the car, and then thought she would try her luck at the back door, after all, she'd never actually used this key before. She approached the back door and placed the key into the lock. "Here goes" she sighed. The door opened. Less than three minutes later, she was heading back down the path to the car.
As she got back into the car, Sophie said, "Is everything alright"?
"Yes, let's go people".
"Where"? Said Sophie. "Where will we go, I'm knackered".
"Right em, I'll tell you what Sophie, just head for Rotherham, we can book into a hotel".
Angela had a large heavy-duty black plastic bag on her lap. As Sophie drove, she could hear clicking noises in the back seat, though she couldn't see what Angela was doing. "Here" said Angela, handing Sophie a Colt pistol forty-five caliber "I'll show you how to use it later, stick it in the glove compartment just now. Get us to Rotherham Sophie, and we'll get something to eat, and a good night's sleep. We don't want to be in Deborah Knowles's territory for too long".

As they pulled out of the square, a certain Misses Irene Semple was on her phone, talking to a police officer, and asking if she could speak with Deborah Knowles, just as Knowles had instructed her to do if she saw any strangers arriving in Harrington Square.
The old woman had thought the world of Deborah Knowles, who had been to visit her with some newspaper reporters who had been covering the story of the new chief of police for Yorkshire with great interest. Misses Semple was delighted that Knowles had chosen her house to have a cup of tea and a chat.
“I feel safer already” She had informed the young reporter.
“You can tell genuine people a mile off” she had said.

HARRINGTON POLICE STATION.
SHEFFIELD.

Thomas Adamson, the desk-duty sergeant was sitting scrutinising his crossword puzzle in his daily newspaper, when the telephone rang, making him jump slightly in his seat.
“Hello, sergeant Adamson speaking, how may I help you”?
Irene Semple explained to him, what she had just witnessed from her living room window. She told the sergeant about the blonde haired girl she had just seen visiting one of the houses that Deborah Knowles had told her to keep an eye on, and how the woman had arrived at the house empty handed, and had came back out carrying a large black bin bag.
“Well, thank you for your information Misses Semple, but Deborah is not here at the moment”.
“Well, you make sure young man that she gets this message as soon as possible, do you promise”?
“Yes, I promise Misses Semple” he replied, smiling.
“You won’t forget now will you”.
“No Misses Semple, I won’t forget to tell her, in fact I’ll phone her as soon as we’re finished here”.
“I would have told the two police officers who are usually here, but they’ve been away since eight thirty this morning. They left in the car and haven’t returned yet”.
“Been away since eight thirty this morning have they”? said Adamson, looking at the clock on the wall which was reading eleven fifteen.
“What time did the blonde woman arrive at the house Misses Semple”?
“Oh, I would say about an hour ago, something like that. I was waiting for the two officers to return, but they haven’t showed face since, so I thought I should just call you, at the office, I lost your number you see”.
“Was this woman alone in the car she arrived in”?
“No, because there was someone else driving, and there was someone else in the back seat, although I couldn’t give you an accurate description”.
“I see, and what type of car was it Misses Semple”?
“I beg your pardon”?

“What kind of car were they travelling in”?
“Oh, a black one”.
“A black one, could you be a bit more specific misses Semple”?
“Yes, it was black, with black windows”.
Adamson sighed, and smiled to himself.
“Right you are Misses Semple, thank you once again for your assistance, Miss Knowles will be pleased with you, I expect she’ll come and visit you when she gets back”.
“I beg your pardon”?
“I said, I expect—CLICK.
The old lady had hung up.
Adamson replaced the receiver back onto its cradle, laughing.
“A fucking black one indeed”.
At five twenty P.M, Deborah Knowles came in to the station, almost knocking the door off its hinges. Once again Adamson jumped up from his still unfinished crossword puzzle.
“Are those two useless bastards in yet Thomas”?
“Not yet mam, they’re due in at” he looked up to the clock on the wall. “In about half an hour mam”.

Deborah Knowles had searched the house in Harrington Square long ago, and had found the cocaine, along with the hand gun and the ammunition, but had decided to leave them there, in the hope that someone would eventually return to the house for them. For three weeks, nothing, no-one had arrived. Two men had been posted into the square in an unmarked car. Two shifts, four men, twenty-four seven, for three weeks.
Then, today, they came for their gear, and no-one was there to report them. God knows, it wasn’t as if she’d asked them to apprehend them. Just report back here with a car registration, that’s all, and they weren’t there to do the job.
She knew, by what the old lady had said to Adamson, that it was Angela Phorbes and co.
“Half an hour? Thomas”.
“Yes mam”.
Constable Lake entered the front room, just as Deborah Knowles was approaching the desk.
“Where are *you* going”? snapped Knowles.
“I’m finished mam, it’s five thirty”.

“Are you fuck finished, get coffee and don’t take all day, take out your notes and study them, so that you remember just how I like it, now move, fucking finished indeed.
Tom, I’m sick to the back teeth of these lazy incompetent bastards around here, calling themselves police officers, I really am, I don’t know how half of them get into the police force.
Most of them would need back up to stop a schoolboy fight”.
Adamson smiled.
“I know mam, but it’s just the way they are these days, we just have to grin and bear it”.
“Just wait until those two useless baffoons get back in here, I’ll show you grin and bear it alright”.
A little over five minutes later, constable Lake arrived back with Deborah’s coffee.
“Thank you officer Lake”, she said, sighing. She took one sip from her mug. “Mother of fuck!!!”

CENTRAL HOTEL. ROTHERHAM.
ROOM 14.

The three women sat in the room that Angela had booked for herself and Tracy. Sophie's room was down the corridor, four doors away, Angela had booked herself and Tracy in as Anderson, two sisters. Sophie was booked in under her own name. All three women had eaten, and all had snorted cocaine. Each of them sipped from a glass of vodka and coke, and were all smiling and feeling very chilled out. Before they had taken the cocaine, they had decided to stay here for a couple of days, to get their thoughts together. Tracy was finally accepting the situation, as to what had happened to her girls. She knew that Angela was right as well, they couldn't go back to Carlisle, no matter how much she longed to be at the girls' funeral. It was impossible, Sharon's aunt's house would be constantly observed in the hope that they would be foolish enough to return. Deborah Knowles knew, that if she found Tracy, she would find Angela.

Tracy lay back in her bed in the hotel room, smoking and completely relaxed. Angela had told her who Sophie was, and how they had met, and that she was now with them, on a permanent basis. Tracy looked up from the bed at Sophie. "You don't know what you've let yourself in for girl, you really don't't".

"Oh but I do know Tracy, Angela has told me everything".

"Everything Angela"? said Tracy, sitting up on the bed, and looking at her cousin.

"Everything Tracy, she knows what she's in with here, don't worry about that".

"Well" said Tracy, stubbing out her cigarette in the ash tray on the bedside cabinet. "You can see what a mess her and I are in here, running from the law for our lives. I can't for the life of me think why you would to put your life in jeopardy, I mean, according to Angela, you are only running from one person. Her and I are running from the entire police force".

Sophie smiled. "I could help you both though, if only Angela would let me".

"How can you help us Sophie" said Tracy, looking at Angela.

The cocaine was playing a huge part in how calm Tracy was. Angela had been giving her copious amounts.

"Well, as I've already said, Knowles doesn't know me. All I would have to do, is walk up to her and pull the trigger, and that would be that, she'd be out of your faces, and then Angela Phorbes could lie in peace, wherever she is meant to be lying, end of story".
Tracy began laughing at Sophie's suggestion.
"Sophie, have you any idea how protected this woman is, and how she's thought of? They would scour the ends of the earth to find you, and they would-"
"I know, that's what Angela said, but she doesn't know me. It would be easier for me to get anywhere near her than it would for you. From what I can make out, you two haven't got a cat's chance in hell of getting anywhere near her".
Tracy leaned over the bed and snorted another line of cocaine from the bedside table.
"Thanks for the offer kid, but forget it. You should fuck off now if you have any brains before Knowles catches you running around with us".
Tracy looked over to Angela with half-closed eyes, and with very slurry speech she said; "Tell her Angela".

CENTRAL HOTEL.
THE FOLLOWING MORNING.
ROOM 15.

John Sweeny, the site foreman for the new prison over in Sheffield, stood at the mirror, shaving, in the built in bathroom of his room. His friend and work mate, Steve Feld, a bricklayer, stood beside him. Sweeny tapped his friend three times on the shoulder.
"Some fucking night buddy huh"? What do you think Stevie"?
"I reckon she's the best ever, really. I've heard about women like her, but really, you think it's only fantasy don't you".
"Stevie boy" said Sweeny, "you and I have fucked women up and down this country son, but never, never in my life, have I came across a woman as beautiful as that, with an appetite for sex like that".
"Alright boys"? Came the voice from the bedroom, "did you enjoy"?
"Oh yes, we enjoyed alright honey, we'll never forget *you*, that's a fact".
"Well" said the young lady, "you must really trust me, allowing me to put our fun on film, both of you married as well".
"Darling, I couldn't give a fuck if she divorced me tomorrow, and that's the truth" said Sweeny, a forty five year old Londoner. "Both my kids are up now anyway. I only go home once a month now, and that's only to see my mates and have a drink. What will you do with the recording; you won't put it on the internet will you"?
"Of course not. I would never do that. It's for my own personal use, and I can assure you it will be erased within a month or so".
Sweeny dried his face with a towel.
"We'll have to get a move on Steve, the van will be here for us in a few minutes. Do you live around here pet? We could give you a lift if you want".
"No thank you, my car is in the car park".
"Right, well, we'll have to move, not that we're chasing you in any way you understand".
"Yes you are" replied the young lady. "You've had your wicked way with me all night, and now you're kicking me out of the door, you should think shame on yourselves, really" she said, laughing.
" Oh we do, we do, because if this was Sunday morning, you wouldn't be going anywhere. I can assure you of that.

It's just that we are building to a tight schedule, and we have to keep on top of the job you see".
"Oh, you manage that fine, the two of you, make no mistake about that".
She kissed the two men on the cheek and said "thanks again guys, I'll have to get my skates on myself".
"Do you work darling"? said Sweeny.
"Oh I work alright, I work over in Sheffield as well".
"Let me guess" said the man called Steve. "You work in the sex shop, don't you".
"Nope".
"Well, something like that then".
"Nope, nothing like that, nothing remotely like that".
"Don't tell me" said John Sweeny "you're a dental nurse"?
The young woman picked up her bag and hung it over her shoulder.
"I'm a pathologist".
"You're fucking kidding us!"
"No, I'm not boys, you have just had the privilege of having the hottest pathologist in Yorkshire, Miss Ashley Barnes, I'll see you guys, take care" she said, as she left the hotel room, closing the door behind her.
As Ashley walked down the hallway towards the lift, she heard another door closing behind her, and the voices of two women. Ashley didn't turn round, but instead, stopped and fumbled for nothing in particular in her hand bag.
As the two women passed her, she politely said good morning. The women responded with a similar greeting. She let them get three or four yards in front of her, and continued walking. The two women were now standing at the elevator door, waiting. As Ashley approached, she heard the dark haired girl say to her blonde friend, something about Deborah Knowles.
Ashley pretended once more to be searching for something in her bag, in the hope that they would continue their conversation. No such luck. The elevator clicked, and the bell rang, as the doors slid open. Two businessmen stepped out into the hall, and the two women, followed closely by Ashley, stepped into the lift. The elevator clicked once more and began the descent to the ground floor.
Just for a split second she thought she saw the blonde girl looking at her.

The women made their way to the reception desk. Ashley walked past them, and straight out of the front door.
She walked down the ten steps of the hotel and turned left, looking into the first shop window she came to, which conveniently happened to be bridal wear. She decided to wait there to see if the women would come out of the hotel. As she lit up a cigarette, a builders van pulled up, and stopped just outside of the hotel. At that point, the two women came down the steps, followed closely by John Sweeny and Steven Feld.
Perfect. Ashley walked up to the two men before they got into the van. "Thanks again lads, for a wonderful night". She kissed both men on their cheeks again.
The blonde girl looked round to Ashley and then continued walking with her friend.
"See you guys" she said, as she began walking in the same direction as the two girls in front of her. As the women turned the corner, she decided to hold back for a few seconds. If the blonde was who she thought she was, she'd be looking over her shoulder. After a few seconds, she turned the corner.
They were gone.
"Shit! Where did they go"?
Then she saw them, taking a seat on one of the local buses. The blonde girl did not even look at Ashley as the bus passed her. Either that wasn't who Ashley thought she was, or, she was aware that she was being watched, and was being extremely clever about the whole thing. Ashley Barnes was devising a plan of her own, concerning Deborah Knowles.

PARK HILL PRISON SITE.
SHEFFIELD.

"Excellent, excellent" said Deborah Knowles to the young female architect, and the site foreman John Sweeny, as all three looked at the building plan laid out before them.
"You are doing very well Mister Sweeny, very well indeed".
"Yes mam, we are, it's going well".
He picked up a diary and glanced at it.
"We are nearly two months ahead of schedule, and because we're having such a mild winter, I can see no reason why we can't finish this, three, maybe four months ahead".
"You are to be congratulated Mister Sweeny, you obviously know how to get the best out of your men, well done, keep up the good work".
"Just treat them with respect mam, that's all you have to do. Respect them, and they'll respect you".
"Really"?
"Yes mam".
"I see, so, what about the prisoners who'll be in here serving their sentences, how would you treat them, would you treat *them* with respect"?
John Sweeny lit up a cigarette.
"With respect Miss Knowles, you are a highly trained police officer, I am a lowly building worker. How I would treat these inmates would probably offend you".
"Why so"? said Knowles, herself lighting up a cigarette, and now more than a little curious of Sweeny's opinion.
She was glancing at his huge hands, his swollen fingers. Hard work, hard physical labour. The swelling coming from years of outdoor graft. The rough weather-beaten skin. A man's hands, a real man's hands, not these pretentious little college graduate-type who knew about everything by what they'd read from books. This man had the skills of civil engineering. He would know how to do all kinds of things around his home. He wouldn't have to phone for the plumber if the tap started leaking, or the electrician if the lights wouldn't come on, which was the case with sergeant Adamson the other day. The electrician just looked at Deborah when all he had done was in fact, change the light bulb.

"Miss, I grew up in Hendon, with three sisters and four brothers. We had nothing. When I was a kid, my father worked in a butcher's shop, my mother in a launderette. I can stand here and proudly state that not one of my family have claimed a day's benefit in our entire lives. We have all worked hard and paid our way through life. Some of the vermin who you will be dealing with in here will not have done a day's work in their lives. They rob from people like me and you, to feed drug habits, about which they were well warned, before they even left school. They murder elderly people, even, in some cases, rape them. They entice young girls into taking heroin, who are then left with a raging habit. They run for this scum and perform sexual acts in return for their fix. Then, if we are lucky enough to catch the bastards, they are brought to places like these, where we, the tax payers have to pay for their keep, as well as paying for the bastard's methadone. Would I treat them with respect? I would line them up against a wall and I would shoot the bastards in the back of the head, after I had grown tired of kicking them in the balls, and I don't tire easy".

Deborah Knowles smiled at John Sweeny, who held his hands up and said, "I'm sorry, I'm sorry, I got a bit carried away there folks, it's just the way I feel about it, that's all".

Knowles, still smiling at Sweeny, said "If you ever feel like a change in your career, then just come and see me, I guarantee you, there'll be a job there waiting for you. I wish some of my officers held the same view as you do; it would make my job an awful lot easier. So, you see no harm in beating the prisoners then Mister Sweeny"?

"Of course not. These days the prisons are like bloody holiday camps. I've even heard that in some prisons they get a menu for their lunch, T.V. Films, books recreation time, fuck it's no wonder they reoffend, sorry for my French ladies, but I give respect to those I feel deserve it, just as I strive to gain the respect of everyday people like yourselves. That's the way I see it, anyway".

"Well" said Knowles, "I can honestly say that you've already gained mine, without a shadow of a doubt".

Deborah's mobile phone rang. "Excuse me" she said to Sarah Fox and John Sweeny. After a minute or so, she said, "I have to go now, thank you for the coffee Mister Sweeny, thank you for your time Miss Fox".

John Sweeny smiled. "Have you been summoned to speak to one of the bad guys Miss Knowles"?

“No, Mister Sweeny, I have been summoned to go and speak with one of the bad girls”.
“A junkie mam”?
“No Mister Sweeny, well, if there’s such a thing as a sex junkie, then yes. It’s our pretty little pathologist called Ashley Barnes, with the body to die for. If you stay around these parts Mister Sweeny, then I’m sure it’s only a matter of time before you bang into her, literally I mean. She says she has some news for me”.
John Sweeny turned around, and pretended to study the plan again, smiling to himself.

THE MORGUE. SHEFFIELD.

Deborah Knowles entered the building, wondering why Ashley Barnes had requested a meeting. The creepy young man she had encountered a little while ago, greeted her as she entered the premises.
“Hello again” he said, with his usual creepy smile.
“Hello” said Knowles, “Is she here”?
“Who Miss”.
“Ashley Barnes, that’s who, your boss, is she here”?
“She’s up-stairs in her office. Is it something important? I’ll tell her to come down as soon as possible, you can wait in reception”.
Knowles pushed the young man slightly to one side, and headed up to Ashley’s office.
“She won’t like being disturbed Miss” he shouted after her.
“We’ll see” said Knowles, walking up the steps.
As she reached the top, she was just about to knock on the door when it was opened for her. Ashley stood wearing a black mini skirt and a white blouse, unbuttoned to almost her chest. Her ample cleavage looked dangerously close to escaping either side of her blouse.
“Ah, Deborah, glad you could make it, come in, come in, take a seat, I’ll get you a coffee. Oh, this is John Hunter, the new head of forensics, and this here is, well, you know who this is don’t you, this is Amanda Pearce, she’s the one who shot the former head of forensics, Stanley Spears, remember him Deborah? Sit down Deborah, I’ll get you your coffee, make yourself comfortable”.
“What’s going on Ashley”? said Knowles, staring at Amanda Pearce, who was sitting on a chair with her arms folded and looking at the floor.
“Oh, you won’t get anything out of her Deborah, she’s been told to be a good girl and keep her mouth shut.
No luck there Debs”.
“Ashley? What the hell are you playing at here”!

“Playing? No no Deborah, no-one is playing, this is serious Miss Knowles, this is deadly serious. Deborah, We know everything, absolutely everything”. John Hunter said. A man in his early fifties, slim, with thinning grey hair, dressed in T-shirt and jeans.

"We got a confession out of your friend Amanda, she's told us everything. It's unofficial just now, no-one else knows, except Ashley and I. How long it remains unofficial, is entirely up to you".

"I haven't got the slightest idea what you're on about, but I would strongly advise you to get your"-

"Shut up and listen"! Howled Hunter.

"We've got you Deborah, don't you realize that? If I wanted to, I could take this information further, and I guarantee, you'd be in jail before bed time. Just take it from me, that we can prove that you got this little junkie girl here to kill Stanley Spears, and if *that's* not enough to bring you to your senses, then we can also prove that you killed your partner Karen Jones". There was silence for a few moments, then Hunter spoke very softly.

"Deborah. Only we three alone here know about this".

Knowles looked at Amanda Pearce.

Hunter waved his hand in Amanda's direction to indicate to Knowles that Pearce didn't even matter.

"No-one else need know Deborah, it's up to you".

Again, there was silence, as Deborah finally realized that these two were not joking.

"What's the deal" she said, despairingly.

"That's more like it. See? Now we're getting somewhere".

"Don't, whatever you do Mister Hunter, try to patronise me, or I'll kill you here and now, so, what's the deal, and I don't want to hear any more of your shit talk, just cut to the chase, I'm a busy woman".

"Very well Miss Knowles, half a million each for Ashley and I, that's the deal".

Knowles looked at Hunter, and then to Ashley. "Is he for real Ashley"?

"Oh yes Deborah, he's for real alright, and so am I. Half a million each, and we could have asked for more with all the information we have on you, you should think yourself lucky".

Knowles lit up her cigarette. "And just where do you think I can get *that* kind of money? I'm the chief of Police for Yorkshire, not the director General of Barkley's bank".

"Oh, you'll get it Deborah" said Hunter, "because we all know what your publicity means to you, your self-esteem, your pride, your honour, your life, you'll get it".

Knowles inhaled deeply on her cigarette. "How long"?
"Three weeks" said Hunter.
"Three weeks? That's not long enough".
"It's all you're getting Deborah. This young lady here" said Hunter, pointing to Amanda, she might sell that big house she inherited, if she doesn't want to go down for murder. Take her away with you, and work something out".
"Why Ashley"? Said Knowles, "I thought we were friends"?
"We are friends Deborah, we are".
Knowles thought for a moment, and looked at Ashley and then Hunter. "If I get you the money, *if*, I get you the money, then what's to stop you doing this to me again, how do I know you won't come back to me again, with another threat, another demand".
"You don't know Deborah, I give you my word though, me and Ashley, we both give you our word, that's it, that's all you've got, but I really don't see what other choice you've got".
"What about *her*"? said Knowles, "where will she live if she sells her house"?
"Fine" said Ashley, "let her keep her house, get the money somewhere else, see if we care, just get it. Oh, and by the way Deborah" said Ashley as she adjusted her bra under her skin tight vest, "I happen to know where Angela Phorbes is hiding out, one good turn and all that you know. You deliver the money, and I'll give her to you on a plate, and before you think she's around these parts, forget it, she's nowhere near here. I have a friend looking out for her just now, watching her every move".
Hunter butted in, "just as we have someone out there watching *your* every move. Imagine the publicity Deborah, if you could pull *her* in, huh"?
"Glory or what!" Said Ashley, "That's all you've got to do, bring the money, and I guarantee, you'll be front page news again, within three days, see? We are friends Deborah, I'll scratch your back, and you scratch mine, hell, that's what good friends do".

"Bring the money Ashley? Just like that, bring the money, one million pounds, bring the money, and that's that, huh? No problem, I mean will one million do, eh? Maybe two? Three? Huh? Do you want three million, cause hell, I've got three weeks until my name gets dragged in the gutter, and I get thrown into jail".

"I know" laughed Ashley, "isn't it funny as fuck? The Chief of Police, the very first inmate in Park Hill, I think that's hilarious, don't you Debs? Hey, I bet you're hoping that the prison staff are a lot kinder than you are. Just get the fucking money!"

"I'm sorry" said Amanda, as she got into Deborah's car.
"Hmph, a lot of good sorry will do Amanda, we are both in the shit now sweetheart, we're going down, if we don't come up with the money, or rather, we are going up, as in strung. What the fuck did you have to confess for Amanda? They did not have a single thing on you. You should have just said nothing, and everything would have been fine, fuck sakes".
"I didn't say anything Deborah, honestly, I didn't, we were set up. I was set up".
"How"?
"Remember the night you came round to ask me, you know"?
"Yes, what about, oh, don't tell me one of those bitches was a plant, right"?
"I'm afraid so Deborah, the blonde one. She followed me, obviously unbeknown to me. She saw the whole thing. She even saw where I hid the gun".
"Which was where Amanda"?
"In the bottom of my garden, underneath the roots of one of the trees. She'd told me she was off home. I watched her leave through the front door, she must have come around the side of the house, and watched me bury the weapon".
"Is she a cop"?
"No, she works down at The Dragon's Den, she pulls pints and does a bit of pole dancing".
"I'll bet she does. And that'll be how she knows Ashley the slut. Birds of a feather right enough".
As Knowles drove through the city, she said "so, Amanda, how much do you value your life, are you prepared to sell the house"?
"I'll have to, won't I, if I want to live, I don't have any choice".
If Knowles was honest with herself, she wouldn't be surprised at something like this happening, she *was* surprised however that it was Ashley Barnes who was doing this to her. She thought the world of the girl if truth be known. There was a certain level of respect between the two of them, at least there used to be.

“Don’t you worry about somewhere to live Amanda, I have more than enough room, you’re welcome, and anyway, the house may sell at more than a million. I can lay my hands on maybe two hundred thousand, so, we’ll be alright, but, we’ll need to keep some money for this and that, as we hunt out our victims, I mean Angela Phorbes is mine, but I’ll have to pay a friend to take out Mister Hunter, and Miss Barnes, but it *will* happen Amanda, I promise you, pretty little Ashley has fucked with the wrong person this time, and as far as mister Hunter is concerned, well, he’ll soon be history,…another senior forensics detective murdered Amanda”.

CENTRAL HOTEL. ROTHERHAM.

Angela and Tracy had discussed the situation. It might have been coincidence Tracy, I don't know, but we are in no position to take any chances. It just seems to me she was paying us more attention than was normal. It was a stroke of luck that the local bus pulled up when it did. That's what convinced me, did you see her looking for us as she turned the corner. We're making the right decision Tracy, the more I think about it.

We'll tell Sophie, when she gets back, to get ready, I hate hotels anyway. They don't bring me much luck" said Angela, placing some garments into a bag.

"Where is Sophie anyway" said Tracy, pouring two cups of tea.

"I gave her some money to get some clothes, she said she wouldn't be long".

"As Tracy handed Angela her cup of tea, she said, "You know what's going to happen to her Angela, if she gets caught with us, she'll go down with us you know".

"I know Tracy, but the kid has no-one, she's on a death threat over in Sheffield, some Samantha woman, a drugs dealer".

"Fuck me" said Tracy, "is that all we Brits do now these days, push drugs"?

"Yeah, well, anyway, that's why I took Sophie out of there, she doesn't seem to mind the situation she's in with us, or could land in".

"Does she fully understand the situation though, does she actually realize that her life's in peril when she's with us, she's just a kid Angela, can't we just leave her a note and some money, explain it on paper to her, that we think too much of her to put her life at risk, I'm sure she would understand, anyway, we don't even have a plan, we don't know where we are heading".

"Tracy, no, I'm not leaving her a note. If she wants out, I'll explain it again to her, and if she wants to leave, then she can leave, I'll give her some money".

"What if she insists on staying with us what then? We'll feel responsible if anything should happen to her"?

"Tracy, I've been thinking. Maybe she *would* be prefect to take Knowles out".

Three hours later, the girls were packed and ready to leave.
"Right, let's go ladies, let's get out of here and back on the road, it's safer".
As they walked out of the room, they saw a couple kissing and cuddling at one of the room doorways.
Angela said, "young love girls huh? There's nothing like it".
Sophie said, "For God's sake, are they still here"?
"What"? said Angela.
"Well, I'm just saying, they were standing there an hour ago, when I came back from the shops, you would think that they'd get into their room wouldn't you"?
"Yeah you would" said Angela, as if she couldn't care less.
As they approached the lift, Angela heard the young blonde girl, standing with her boyfriend, saying to him, "You just go in to the room darling, I've forgotten something in the car I won't be long". Then she blew him a kiss and headed for the lift.
"Sorry" she giggled to the three women. "Just got engaged today". She held up her left hand to let them all see the engagement ring.
"Congratulations" said Angela, "have you picked a date"?
"Yes, this November, he's really nice, he is, and so are his parents, lovely people".
"Good" said Angela. "Always helps when the in-laws are nice".
The door for the elevator clicked and slid open.
All four women stepped into the lift. The door slid closed again.
"Who are you working for"? said Angela.
"Oh, I work over at the supermarket, and"-
"Who are you working for? If you make me ask you again, I'll scatter your teeth all over this elevator floor, don't make me do that, now who"?
The girl looked at Angela, and the other two women.
"I'm sorry, I think you've got me mixed up with someone else".
"Ah, I see" said Angela, "Well, in that case, I'm going to take you back up in this elevator and back into my room and then I'm going to drop you from my bedroom window, now, you know the question, I want to know the answer, and you've got five seconds. One, two, three four"-
"Ashley Barnes" said the young woman, realizing at the last moment, that this woman was not making an idle threat.
"What is she, and where is she"?
"She's a criminal pathologist over in Sheffield, that's all I know".

"Ok then. Now, if you want to live, you won't tell her we've had this chat, ok? Because if you do, you will not live any longer than twenty-four hours after you've told her. Now, *you* will be the one being watched. Is that man up there in this with you"?
"No, he doesn't know anything, honestly, we really did get engaged.
The lift stopped, and all four women stepped out.
"Right then if this Ashley Barnes asks you about us, what are you going to tell her".
"I'll tell her, no change, you're still staying here".
"Perfect, now then, you have a nice engagement, and an even nicer marriage, because if I see you again, I'll kill you, unless we meet per-chance, do you understand me"?
"Yes".
"Good, now goodbye, and good luck".
"Thank you" replied the nervous young lady.
As they were just about to walk away, Angela said "wait a minute. There must be more than one, there's someone else, who"?
"Eh, well the only other person she's spoken with, when I've been in her presence, is a forensics officer. Hunter, em, Hunter, John, that's it, John Hunter".
"She's spoken to you about me in front of him, has she"?
"Yes, over in her office yes".
"How did you meet her? How did you come into contact with this Ashley Barnes"?
"She em, I work in the Dragon's Den, it's a night club. I serve behind the bar, and I do some pole dancing. Ashley used to come in quite a lot. The manager asked her one night if she would dance, one of the girls were off. That's how I got to know her".
"When are you supposed to get back in touch with her"?
"She'll phone me, unless you leave the hotel".
"Yes, but we haven't left, have we"?
"No, no you haven't".
"Good, you'd better keep it that way for your own sake, and your boyfriend's".
Tracy said "I hope you believe that these threats that have been made to you, are genuine".
"I know they are".

"Right then" said Angela, "on your way, and remember, keep her sweet, or there won't be any wedding, goodbye".

The young lady stood awkwardly for a few moments, as if she were taking in everything she'd been told, then she re-boarded the elevator.

As Angela, Tracy, and Sophie checked out of the hotel, Sophie said, "How did you know that, how did you know she was spying on us"?

"You told me Sophie" said Angela. "How many young couples do you know, would stand outside of their hotel room when they had a key for a room.

Kissing for an hour Sophie? I don't think so. I caught her looking at us a couple of times as well, as if she were confirming to herself, that we were who she was looking for. Somebody has obviously informed this Ashley Barnes that we were staying here".

"You're good Angela" said Sophie.

"Yes I am, now, let's go and visit this Ashley Barnes over in Sheffield".

Tracy walked with Angela and her new friend, but her mind was elsewhere. The cocaine was wearing off again, and she longed to be with her daughters, but she would never be with her daughters ever again. Neither would she be with Sharon again. She was sliding into deep depression.

THE MORGUE. SHEFFIELD.

“Do you think she’ll get the money Ashley”?
“Of course she will” replied Ashley, to John Hunter, “We’ve got her on the ropes. She knows that if she doesn’t get the money, then her arse is going to hit the ground with one almighty bang”.
“Yes, but remember Ashley, she is a very powerful woman. We should make sure we lock our doors and windows at nights, I know I’ll be locking mine. You saw what happened to Stanley Spears”.
“She got away with that John, at least she thought she did, this is different, she can’t try anything like that this time”.
“I wouldn’t be too sure Ashley, she pulls a lot of strings in the force now. It’s not beyond her, for her to bribe someone else into killing us”.
“I know that John, but it’s highly unlikely”.
“You think so? because I sure as hell don’t. You know how rats fight when you get them cornered”.
The small speaker above Ashley’s head buzzed.
She put down her coffee on the table, and pressed a button.
“Yes Paul”?
The young man who had spooked Deborah Knowles, spoke.
“Sorry to bother you Miss Barnes, but there’s a lady down here, who says that she is the wife of one of John Hillman’s victims, she would like a word with you regarding funeral arrangements”.
“Right Paul, tell her I’ll be right down”.
“Begging your pardon Miss, she says she wishes to speak with you in your office, and she’s asking if she can have a cup of sweet tea, she says she’s a diabetic, she’s not feeling too well”.
“No problem Paul, see that she gets up the stairs alright”.
“Thank you Miss Barnes”.
“Right John, you’ll have to make yourself scarce, there’s a woman coming up to see me, I’ll be in touch if I hear anything from Knowles, and don’t worry, she’ll get the money, see you soon”. Hunter rose up from the chair and left the office.
One minute later, Angela Phorbes stepped into Ashley’s office. Ashley half turned around as she was making her tea, and then turned round to confirm to herself who she thought she’d glimpsed.
Angela stood with the Magnum pistol pointing directly at Ashley.
“Hiya. Two sugars and milk please” she said.

She watched Ashley like a hawk, as the pathologist proceeded to make a pot of tea. She didn't look much like a pathologist, dressed in a mini skirt and white blouse, but then again, everything's changing by the minute these days, and who knows, maybe it won't be long before the minister delivers his Sunday morning sermon, dressed in his bib and brace overalls, holding his boyfriend's hand.
As Ashley turned to put the tray on the table, Angela said, "you know who I am, obviously".
"Yes" replied Ashley.
"The gentleman who just left there, would that be, a Mister John Hunter"?
"Yes".
"Ok then, what are you up to Ashley".
"I'm looking to make some money, that's all, just like everybody else".
"By turning me into Deborah Knowles, is that what you mean"?
"Well, not exactly turning you in, I was going to give you a sporting chance".
"Really? That's very nice of you, and just how were you going to do that"?
"Well, I was going to tell Deborah where you were on the phone, and then I was going to tell Linda, that's the pretty blonde who you've quite obviously met, to give you a warning to leave straight away.
By the way, is Linda still alive Angela"?
"Don't worry, carry on".
"That's it, that's all I was going to do".
"I see" said Angela, smiling, "but just how were you going to make any money out of that? Knowles would give you nothing if I got away".
"I know that. Let's just say I found out one or two things about Deborah, that she would not want, how shall I say, em, published".
"I see, so it's blackmail then Ashley"?
"Yes it is, two sugars did you say"?
"Yes please, so why should I believe your story Ashley, I should just kill you now, and be done with it".
"Yes, but I've already told Deborah that I know where you are.
If she brings the money, I could set her up for you, if you wish, I could have her walk straight into your trap"
Angela watched the young pathologist with growing interest.

"And then, John and I would have our money, and you would be rid of that evil bitch, who, from what I can gather, has plagued your life for quite some time. It's up to you Angela, it's your call".
"You've got lovely legs Ashley".
"Thank you".
Angela smiled at Ashley. The girl was quite obviously used to getting compliments about her shape. It wasn't the first time anyone had complimented her on her legs.
"I'll tell you what Ashley, we'll give this a chance then, ok, and if it pays off, I'll give you back your Mister Hunter, you see, right now, he is presently unconscious in the back of my car I'll bet, with a great big lump on the back of his head, the size of a large boiled egg. You sort this business out with Knowles, and, like you say Ashley, you'll get your money off her, and set her up for me, and then you can have your Mister Hunter back, how does that sound"?
"That sounds fine Angela, the only thing is, I've given Knowles three weeks to come up with the money".
"Three weeks? How much did you demand"?
"One million".
"Fucking Hell Ashley, nice one, do you think she'll pay up"?
"Oh yes, she'll pay up, or they'll hang her, so to speak".
"Well, all I can say is, it must be something nice that you've got her with, for you to be confident enough to bribe the chief of police. Right, I'll be off then Ashley, I'll be in touch".
"So, it's a deal then Angela"?
"It's a deal Ashley, just behave though, no silly stuff".
"Oh I'll behave, you can rest assured on that".
"Good, I'll be off now".
As Angela got to the door of the office, Ashley said, "Angela"?
"Yes"?
"Nice ass"
"Why thank you Ashley".
Both women smiled at each other, then Angela left the office, gently closing the door behind her.
Ashley smiled to herself. Her friend Linda must have made it look a bit obvious that she was observing Angela's movements. She also knew just how lucky Linda was still to be still breathing, but everything had turned out well in the end. She knew that if she behaved herself as Angela had put it, she would get Hunter back in one piece. Angela would keep her word.

Ashley walked over to the window and looked down onto the car park. Wherever Angela had parked her car, it was out of view from where she stood. Ashley picked up the phone to call Deborah Knowles. She couldn't tell Deborah that Angela was in Sheffield, because that would jeopardise her payment. But she could dangle Angela in front of her, tease her.
"Hello Deborah? It's Ashley here. If you could get that money as soon as possible, I've got her trapped. She's there for the taking Deborah, but I would hurry if I were you, she's chomping at the bit to kill you".
"I'll have the money within four days, Amanda doesn't have to sell her house".
"Oh good" said Ashley, sarcastically, "I'm so glad to hear that Deborah, but remember, I can't promise I'll be able to keep Angela in this situation for very long, it will be nobody's fault but your own, if she slips the net, you get that as soon as you can, for everybody's sake".
"I'm working on it Ashley, as fast as I can".
"Good".
Deborah Knowles had worked out a deal with one of Steve Temple's associates. She was to make sure a blind eye was turned at a certain fishing port in Scotland. She made it very clear to a couple of friends of hers, who worked in Customs and Excise that they were to leave the fishing boat named Sarah-Louise alone. "Let it go through. There'll be a whole load, a van load of a certain illegal substance which is going to be used in a set up. Whatever you do, do *not* disturb the crew, let them unload in peace".

On board would be five million pounds worth of pure cocaine.
Deborah would collect one million pounds if she could guarantee this load getting through customs. She could.
Knowles looked at the clock on her office wall.
It was 10.15am. The fishing vessel was due in at the harbour of Oban in Scotland at 10.am.
Now, she sat waiting for a phone call from the dealer, to inform her that all had gone well, and that she would receive her payment as planned.10,20 am. Nothing. 10.25am. Nothing. At 10.40am her telephone rang. It had gone through. A messenger would be sent to her from London. He would bring the leather bags containing the used notes as requested.

"Now that we have made a deal Miss Knowles, perhaps we could do business again sometime".
"Yes, perhaps, she replied, replacing the phone gently back onto it's cradle".
She felt numb. The very people who she was trying her damndest to eliminate, were now doing deals with her. She was one of them. "No better, that's for sure. Ah well" she sighed, "What can you do when the devil himself pisses in your coffee, and you've fucking had it Ashley as soon as I get the first chance".
She did however, still have an element of admiration for the girl, after all, she'd worked out this plan with her accomplice, the bastard Hunter. It's not just anyone in this day and age who would have the guts to fuck around with Deborah Knowles.

DRONFIELD.

John Hunter regained consciousness in the back of Angela Phorbes' B.M.W. He had no idea where his attacker had come from. All he could remember was coming out from the morgue, after speaking with Ashley, and was heading towards his car, when he felt the bang on his head, then nothing.
As he came to, at first he panicked, thinking he was blind, but then quickly realized he'd been blind-folded. "This must be the work of Deborah Knowles" he thought to himself. He could hear voices in the car, women's voices, though he couldn't make out what they were saying. His hands were bound behind his back, and his legs were bound at the ankles. There was no doubt in his mind, he was going to die. It was as simple as that. The whole idea was risky. He and Ashley had discussed it on numerous occasions. Deborah Knowles was no fool, and the fact that they had threatened her with the information they had on her, only served to make her even more dangerous. Now, he would face the consequences of being brazen enough to threaten the chief of police. He heard the gears of the car coming down, until the vehicle came to a stop. Then he heard two of the car doors being opened and closed. Then the boot opened.
"Come on then John Hunter, let's be getting you out of there and into the woods".
"Deborah. Is that you"? He said. "Deborah, I can explain everything, honestly, she made me do it!"
"Mister Hunter!" shouted Angela Phorbes. "What a bastard of a man you are, really. Soon, you're going to collect half a million pounds, thanks to Ashley, and all you can do is grass her in, I've a good mind to tell her everything you've just said there, you wormy bastard that you are. Just shut up now" she said, as she untied his feet.
Tracy and Angela pulled him out of the car and frog marched him into the woods.
"Do you need a piss Mister Hunter"? Said Angela, "because you could be here for quite some time you know".
They tied him to a tree after sitting him down. "There now, Ashley shouldn't be too long, bye".
"Will, will he be alright Angela"? Sophie asked, straining to see into the woods. Angela turned her head to Sophie and said "who cares? He's not our problem now sweetheart, he's Ashley's problem.

Tracy had bound Hunter really tightly around a Birch tree.
"What do we do now Angela" said Tracy, herself peering into the trees.
"I think we'll just spin around in the car for a while Tracy, we don't want to be too far away from Sheffield, in case Ashley needs to tell us something. At the same time, it's best we don't book in anywhere around here. Knowles will have officers looking out for two women signing into hotels or bed and breakfasts".
Angela pressed the digits on her mobile phone. The number Ashley had given to her.
"Hello Ashley? It's Angela here, how are you doing? Good, good, only there's been a slight change of plan, what? yeah, he's ok, he's not saying much just now, anyway, being the suspicious bitch that I am, I eh, I took the precaution of eh, giving my friends and I, a little insurance. Ok Ashley, here's the deal. I've left your friend, Mister Hunter in the woods, over at Dronfield.
As you're heading out of the South side of Dronfield, there's a farm called Blackley's. About one mile further on, on the right hand side, there's a red gate. Fifty yards further, go into the woods, and it's not far into the trees, you'll come across your friend. The thing is Ashley, I've gone and put a note inside his jacket, explaining everything that you and he have been up to. Now then Ashley, for you to retrieve that note, and him, you'll have to bring Deborah Knowles to me. You call me on that number I gave you the other day, about an hour before you bring her here, and, of course, only you and her. Now then, you let me know what you're going to do. I would hurry if I were you Ashley, because Mister Hunter will be getting rather cold, tied up there where we left him".

THE WOODS.

Night had fallen, and it was bitterly cold. John Hunter had lost all feelings of his fingers, his feet, and his backside. A biting wind was blowing through the trees and stinging his already numb face. He began to ask himself some frightening questions. "*What if Ashley didn't come? What if that woman had just been bluffing him, saying that Ashley would be here soon? Maybe Ashley hadn't even been told. Also, if Deborah Knowles had come up with the money, and had given it to Ashley, then she would be tempted to take off with the lot, he would be left here to die.*

It was well into the night now. He was cold, he was tired, and he was hungry, and it felt like his bladder was going to burst. He had tried in vain to slacken the bindings, but it was useless. He was in trouble here, deep trouble. He was shivering now, having only a tee-shirt and a suit jacket on, a pair of jeans, socks and shoes. Suddenly, he heard rustling in the bushes just off to his right. It was pitch black.

"*Just some animal* "he thought to himself. Then he heard two or three footsteps, twigs snapping, silence again. "*It's probably a deer*". Snap! Close, really close.

From behind, a woman whispered right in his ear making him jolt with fear. "*Can you hear me alright, just nod*".

He did.

Still whispering, she said "*Right, you cooperate with me now, and no funny business, and I'll save your life. If you start anything stupid, I will not hesitate to shoot you in the back of the head, got it*"?

Again, Hunter nodded. He knew he had heard this voice before somewhere, but he couldn't remember where.

"*Ok, let's go*" she said, cutting away at his ties.

" *Now, we haven't got much time, we'll have to move quickly*".

" I'll have to pee".

"*Well, hurry up then, we need to get you to fuck out of here*".

The woman waited for what seemed an eternity.

" *Come on, hurry*".

They got to the edge of the woods and found her car. She opened the boot.

"*Right, get in*".

She helped him climb into the car.

Once again John Hunter was scrunched into the back of a car. Slam!! Darkness.
John Hunter found himself once more in a bizarre situation. The woman who had rescued him from the woods, had nothing to do with the women who had abducted him earlier in the day, at least, he didn't think so, he couldn't be sure. Whatever was happening to him, it had to be better than being bound up in those woods. He was dry, and he was warming up. His hands were beginning to thaw out. She had taken the binding from his feet, but she had left his hands bound. The gag had been taken from his mouth, but the blindfold remained. Who could she be? Was she working for Deborah? Was she a friend of Ashley's? No doubt he would find out in due course. "*One thing at a time John*" he told himself. At least you're warm and dry, that's a start, and she did say, if I behaved myself, that she would save my life, so she obviously knows who I am, by the sounds of it. She knows the trouble I'm in, therefore she must at least know Deborah Knowles, and she must know Ashley Barnes as well.
After about twenty minutes or so, the car slowed down. He guessed that they must have been in a town or city, he could hear traffic. Another ten minutes of slow driving, and then the car came to a stop. He heard footsteps on loose gravel. The boot opened, then the whisper again. "Are you alright"? Ok, I'm going to be about ten minutes, alright? Don't panic, I'll be back for you. Don't start kicking or shouting, or anything stupid like that, or else I'll shoot you, are we clear"
"Yes".
"Right, I'll be as quick as possible, lie still". Slam!!

The woman had been gone about fifteen minutes, then he heard the footsteps on the gravel again. Once more, the boot opened. "Let's go" she said, helping him out of the car.
Once inside the house, she sat him down on a very comfortable chair, and cut the ties from his hands.
"Now you leave that blindfold on, ok, because if you try one move, you're dead, now, would you like a glass of brandy"?
"Yes please".
"Right, you'll be safe here now".
"May I ask why you're helping me Miss"?
He was confused, but relieved. It seemed that whoever had brought him here had no intentions of killing him.

"None of your business, that's why, now you listen to what I'm going to tell you. I have made up a room for you. The room will have no windows, so you won't know where you are. You will be under lock and key at all times. If you need the toilet, I'll show you where the buzzer is in the room. I will come and get you. Whilst you are in the toilet, you will be under lock and key. There are also hidden cameras in the room, and so I will be watching you at all times. If you make any attempt to escape I will not hesitate to shoot you, do you understand Mister Hunter"?
"Yes, I understand".
"Good, now all being well, you should be out of here in about two to three days, pending on good behaviour".
"Is it to do with Deborah Knowles"?
"Drink your brandy up Mister Hunter, I'll go and make you something to eat soon, it couldn't have been much fun for you out there in the woods, I wouldn't like it, and yes, it does have something to do with Deborah Knowles, but, you've already worked that out for yourself haven't you Mister Hunter, don't worry, I'm not on her side, I hate her guts, I'm on Ashley's side, but I'm looking out for *me*, you are only a pawn in my little game. Now then would you like a nice fry up Mister Hunter"?
"Yes please".
"Ok then. I'll just go and sort it out now, and, for the last time, don't try anything stupid".
"I won't".
Twenty minutes later, the woman returned with a plate of bacon and eggs, mushrooms, tomatoes, sausages and baked beans.
"There now" she said, as she took off his blindfold.
The light stabbed his eyes, and it was a full minute before his sight adjusted, and was able to focus on anything.
When they did, he looked at the woman sitting before him, with the green face, horrible crooked yellow teeth, and the pointed hat, complete with white scraggly hair. The woman behind the Halloween mask said "it was all I could find, now eat up Mister Hunter, that is good wholesome food, there are no poisonous red apples".
They both laughed, although mister Hunter's laughter was more nervousness than anything relating to humour.
"Who the fuck *is* this? He thought to himself.

ROTHERHAM. TRANSPORT CAFE.

Just outside of Rotherham, there was a transport cafe, not far off the M.1. Tracy had been tearful, deep depression was once again looming. The cocaine was keeping the worst of it at bay but reality kept jolting her with the truth, the painful truth that her little girls were dead, and she wasn't even be able to attend their funeral. Amy and Angela had kept asking their mum that day to come along with them, and Sharon, poor Sharon, she had nothing to do with any of the troubles between herself and John Hillman. She had become a friend of hers, and a confidante, and then, a lover. "Now, thanks to me, she's dead, along with my two little angels, and Sharon's Aunt Sarah as well, all dead because of me".

Life for Tracy, was now empty and meaningless, a pointless void.

Angela and Sophie came out of the transport cafe, each carrying cartons of coffee and bags of food. Ashley had phoned Angela and informed her that she would be at Dronfield at noon the next day, and that Deborah Knowles would be with her. "She thinks that we're going to pick up John, and that he'd be waiting at the woods, as he didn't trust Deborah. "I don't know Angela, if she has anything up her sleeve or not, I'm hoping not, for my sake as well, that's the best I can do".

"Well" Angela had said, "I hope he has a strong will to live, because it's been a bitterly cold night Ashley. I'll see you tomorrow. Oh, has she got your money"?

"Yes she has".

"Well, be careful".

"I will".

Angela walked with Sophie carrying their parcels of refreshments heading to the far side of the car park

As they approached the car Angela said, "Tracy must be sleeping, poor thing, she's handling this better than I thought Sophie".

"She is" replied Sophie, "It hasn't been long since the accident."

Tracy in fact had been snorting cocaine four or five times a day. Her brain had become numb from the day the police had arrived at the door bearing the news of the death of her little girls and her lover. She'd had many a hardship to deal with in her lifetime, but this was, by far and a way, the hardest.

“Three weeks now, although it must seem to Tracy, like three hours. The fact that she couldn’t go and see them, I think that still bites at her. They’re buried, and she couldn’t even be at the funeral”. As Angela opened the front passenger door, she saw the black and red stain on the ceiling in the back of the car, where Tracy, had blown out her brains. The parcels fell out of Angela’s hands and onto the front seat.

Sophie just stared at the sight before her, completely numb. Angela got into the car.

“Drive Sophie, just drive”.

Angela had swept all of the parcels onto the floor. Sophie put hers down by her feet. She knew better than to ask Angela where she was to drive to. She just started the car, and drove off, heading for the M.1.

Angela began sobbing, shaking involuntarily.

Sophie could feel her stomach tightening, making her feel like she was going to be sick. She knew as well, that this was the last thing that Angela needed. Once Deborah Knowles had been sorted out, they would be alright, but then, that was Angela,

Tracy had different problems, would she have ever been alright. You can’t lose two children, especially like that, and think that you’d be alright. She glanced at Angela, who was still sobbing and shaking. This was going to fuck things up for Angela, there was no way she’d be going anywhere near Dronfield now. What made this all the more sickening is that Tracy seemed to be doing so well, she was even laughing from time to time, but then, that would probably have been the effect of the vast amounts of cocaine she’d been taking.

“Shit, this was bad, this could turn Angela either way. It could make her feel suicidal, or it could turn her into a woman hell bent on revenge”, because Sophie knew, that this would all fall on the head of Deborah Knowles. Nothing, or no-one else would be to blame for any of this, other than Knowles. Sophie drove on to the M1, and headed South. Where she was going, was anyone’s guess. She placed her left hand on Angela’s shoulder, half expecting her to shake it off. To her surprise, she took hold of Sophie’s hand and gently squeezed it.

“Please Sophie, help me, help me through this, I don’t know what to do any more. I’m all out of ideas. Everything” she sobbed, “everything just keeps blowing up in my face. I thought, I, she, I thought she was going to be alright Sophie”.

"So did I Angela, so did I". Sophie gently removed her hand from Angela's shoulder and placed it back on to the steering wheel. "Angela? I'm going to pull off the motorway as soon as I can, we need that coffee, you and me". Angela nodded, unable to speak.
"We have to carry on Angela, we have to move on. The car raced down the motorway with the two distraught girls in the front, and the corpse of Tracy Hillman lying on the floor in the back, the hand gun lying next to her, a thin line of smoke protruding from the barrel of the Magnum 3.57.

Sophie saw the junction for Stavely and pulled on to the A619. Before she got there, she pulled up at what looked like the drive up to a farm. It definitely wasn't a public road. She stopped the car and picked up two cartons of coffee which hadn't burst open.
"Here Angela, drink this and have a cigarette it'll help us, come on and don't look at Tracy, she did her best Angela. The woman could take any amount of this kind of pressure, but she couldn't deal with that, not her little girls. Don't be angry with her Angela, she did her best, and that's all she could do".
Again, Angela nodded, taking the lid off her carton of coffee, and taking a sip, her hands shaking. "I know Sophie, I know, but this was the very reason I didn't want her coming around with me, in case of complications, though I didn't think for one second that anything like this would happen to her little girls".
"I know Angela, and that's what killed Tracy, not you, or Deborah Knowles, or anything. Just the fact that she couldn't live without her daughters, that's all". Sophie lit up two cigarettes, and handed one to Angela. "After we've had our coffee, I'm going to take Tracy's body over there, into that wooded area, and I'm going to lay her down to rest. You just stay in the car, don't look at her, you just remember her the way she was, before the accident, do you hear me"?
Angela nodded. "She was some kid Sophie".
"I bet she was, a bit of a wild one was she"?
"Huh, you wouldn't believe it Sophie".
"Oh yes I would ".
"Sophie we need to, em, we have to"-
"Hey, just try and relax. Don't be worrying about anything just now, we'll get over each obstacle, one thing at a time, nice and easy".
Sophie was unsure how to keep Angela calm. She seemed to be accepting her efforts of support, she appreciated her concern.

"I'll help you Sophie, I'm alright now. I want to hold her hand just one last time, while it's still warm. There's a ring as well, that she's had for a few years. She was given it by a special guy. Tracy got the ring, I got this".
Angela pulled out the locket from underneath her jumper. "And oh, how I wish he were right here now".
"Was he one of your friends? The one you called Tools"?
Angela nodded, still looking down at her chain.
"Yes, that was the guy Sophie, I'll never see another like him, that's for sure". The two women sat smoking and sipping their coffee, not saying anything to each other, but both of them feeling grateful that the other was there.
Angela was wondering what she would do next. Ashley was too foolish to think that Knowles wouldn't set something up the next day. There would be an ambush of some description, even if it wasn't there and then. She would plan something so that Ashley and Hunter wouldn't be around for long, certainly not long enough to start enjoying their new found wealth. She would have to phone Ashley and tell her not to meet Knowles. Sophie interrupted her thoughts.

"Angela, I'm going to take Tracy over there now, while there's not much traffic".
"I'll help you Sophie".
"No, Angela, please".
"No Sophie, come on, I'll help you, we'll both do it, it'll be quicker, let's get her over now".
Five minutes later, they were both back in the car.
Tracy lay thirty meters or so from where they sat. They had covered her with dead leaves and branches.
"Where to Angela"?
"Head back to Dronfield Sophie, let's get that poor man out of there. He sure as hell didn't deserve that treatment, if anything, he deserves a bloody medal, anyone who can cause grief to Deborah Knowles should get a pat on the back, if he's still alive and hasn't frozen to death. I hope he's ok Sophie, really".
Angela picked up her mobile phone and pressed the digits for Ashley's phone, only to be greeted by the automatic messaging system. She hated using these bloody things..."talking to bloody nobody".

The person you have called is unavailable to take your call, please leave a message, after the signal. "Ashley, it's Angela, cancel tomorrow, keep away from Knowles, there'll be a trap. If you have arranged to meet her somewhere, then do not tell her you're cancelling, just don't turn up. Don't worry about John Hunter, I'm just going to get him now. I'll send him back to you, enjoy your money Ashley, and enjoy your life, take care".
Less than twenty minutes later, Angela and Sophie were at Dronfield woods, but, mysteriously, John Hunter wasn't.
"Now then Sophie, what do you think? Should we let this lie, or do we help Ashley, because she has got a problem now, a big problem".

LONDON ROAD. SHEFFIELD.

Amanda Pearce opened the door, after putting on the safety chain. Deborah Knowles stood on her step.
"Amanda, we need to talk, open the door".
Two minutes later, the two women sat, each with a drink in their hands.
"Now then Amanda, I've been fair with you, have I not"?
"Yes, Miss Knowles" Amanda lied'
"Yes, you still have your house, which, by the way, you obtained through the use of your pretty arse, right"?
"Well, I've eh"-
"Oh come on Amanda, you were Steve Temple's bed partner, that's how you have this place"!
"Yes".
"Ok then, you owe me Amanda, now all I want you to do, is tell me the truth here, aright"?
"Yes, I always tell you the truth".
"Do you promise? Because if I find out later, that you were lying, then I'll put you in a wheelchair for the rest of your days. Now, has Ashley Barnes approached you since the day she had you there in her office"'?
"No, not once".
"You're sure about that Amanda"?
"Of course I am, she told me to fuck off remember? when she said you and I could work something out about selling this house".
Knowles took a sip of her drink.
"Has John Hunter approached you then"?
"No, no-one has, and I've not been out anywhere, since you brought me back".
"Alright" sighed Knowles. "So what the fuck is she up to?
Why would she want to get me out in the countryside to get Angela? Why didn't she set it up in a town or a city, and how on earth could she get Angela out there without arousing her suspicions, no, fuck no, Angela Phorbes?
No no Amanda, they're working together, they have to be, there's no other explanation".
Knowles looked at Amada. "One last time Amanda, you haven't had any contact with any of them"?

“Miss Knowles, no, I haven’t seen or heard from them, since that day at her office”.
“I’ll take your word Amanda but I”-
“How many times do you want me to say it Miss Knowles, I haven’t seen any of them, I swear”.
“I’m sorry Amanda, I’m sorry, it’s just that I’ve got to know if they’ve spoken to anyone else since then, before I fucking learn them both a very harsh lesson”.
Amanda was getting good at lying to Knowles. She hated the woman. She’d spent most of her life looking out for herself, she hadn’t had much choice in the matter after her mother had abandoned her at the age of three. She couldn’t be classed as the brainiest person on God’s earth, but she was street-wise enough to be able to survive. The down-side to this was that she was very selfish and self-centred, in fact she thought of no-one but herself.
She was thinking of herself now, as regards to Deborah Knowles.

"Hello? Ashley? It's Angela here. Has John Hunter been in touch with you yet"?
"No, and how could he, he's with you isn't he"?
"No he's not. I went to the woods where I left him, and he's not there. There's no way he could have untied himself, not the way he was bound up, someone has released him. Now then, if he's alright, he'll be getting in touch with you soon, he'll want to know where his cut of the money is, if not, if he's being held against his will, you won't hear from him. Listen Ashley, where were you to meet Deborah Knowles"?
"I'm supposed to meet her on Division Street at eleven a.m. later today".
"Phone her at nine, and tell her I've moved on, you've lost track of me, right? You don't know where I am, and whatever you do, do not be in your office when you call her. Get your money Ashley, and get out of there. Now I know it's three in the morning, but move Ashley, I don't think you have a lot of time. If you *do* get out, do not try and leave the country, stay here in Britain, Knowles will have all the airports covered. Have you tried Hunter's mobile"?
"Yes, it's switched off".
"Right then Ashley, you get going, and good luck. If it turns out that Hunter *is* alright, he'll get in touch, if he doesn't, well that means that you are a millionaire".
"Right Angela, and thanks for the warning".
"No problem, just move Ashley".
Ashley switched off her mobile and placed it on the table.
She turned to look at the two leather bags on the floor, and exhaled a gasp of fear, as Deborah Knowles sat on one of the chairs.
"Come on Ashley, put the kettle on babes.
Who was that you were speaking to Huh?
Was it your new friend Angela, giving you advice, or was it instructions, because you know what Ashley?
I think you've done this blackmail thing with her, am I right"?
"No, no you're not.
John Hunter and I did it, and it's no less than you deserve Deborah".
Knowles looked at the pretty pathologist disdainfully.

"And who are you to decide who deserves what, you little slut that you are, you've slept with half of Sheffield in the short time I've been up here. You think you're the bee's knees, don't you Ashley? Well, we'll see how smart you are with a couple of bullets in your knees you little sperm bank that you are. They won't want to fuck you when you're stuck in a wheelchair Ashley, will they"?
Ashley tried her best to regain some composure.
"Well, at least when my legs were ok they *did* want to fuck me".
Knowles moved slowly around the table and filled the kettle.
"Still full of it Ashley, huh?
Still got that, I'm better than you attitude haven't you"? "Not for much longer though missy, you'll get your wings clipped just shortly, you'll see, little miss nothing".
Knowles picked up Ashley's phone and pressed a couple of digits.
"I wonder who this could be Ash? After a few seconds, Knowles spoke into the phone. "Hello"?
"Hello? Ashley? Are you alright"?
"Well, she is just now Angela, she is just now, although that could change soon, my little sewer rat".
"What are you going to do to her Knowles, don't you harm her".
"Huh, harm her? I'm going to do more than harm. The little slut had the audacity to blackmail me to the tune of a million pounds, huh, harm her? Oh, and buy the way Angela, nice one with my car and my garage, well done, but do you know what? The nice working class people all chipped in with their money and bought me a brand new one, a brand new jag, wasn't that sweet of them Angela.
Tell you what, I'll do a deal with you. I seem to be doing lots of deals with people these days, although none of them seem very beneficial to me, however, here's a proposal for you. If you turn yourself in, I'll let Ashley go, and she can keep the million pounds, how's that? What do you say Angela, because to be quite truthful with you, I'm tired of our little game.
I'm thinking about informing the whole country who you really are, and of course then it's just a matter of time before you're caught or shot, it doesn't make much difference to me, because you're going down, one way or another, so you may as well give a young lady a chance to live a little. Let her have some kind of a life instead of opening up her legs to anyone wearing trousers, she may even gain some self-respect, some dignity, so what do you say rat bag.
Have you got the guts?

Because if you don't I'm going to turn her into a cripple, plus, she'll spend the next ten years in prison. Do you think you could live with that on your conscience, huh. You could have saved her from becoming a cripple"?

The phone went dead.

"Oh dear Ashley, she doesn't seem to be very keen to help you out. Now that *is* a fucking shame. Now hurry up and make the coffee. Turn around, let me see those beautiful legs, lovely, nice arse as well. It's a shame it'll get all out of shape, sitting on that wheelchair, oh, and those lovely shapely legs of yours mmm, what a shame girl. If you'd only been honest, instead of turning into a greedy bastard, things could have been so much better for you".

Ashley brought the two cups of coffee to the table

"Now then Ashley, sit down here".

Ashley sat at one side of the table, Knowles on the opposite side.

Knowles, as usual, lit up her cigarette.

"When's he coming Ashley, mister sticky prints Hunter, when is he coming for his muck money"?

"I don't know, I haven't seen him since yesterday".

"Huh, what a fucking little liar you are Ash, really".

"Honestly I haven't, I don't know where he is".

"Do you think I'm going to believe that? Think of it from my point of view Ashley, if you were in my shoes now, honestly, would you believe that"?

"No, I wouldn't".

"Thank you".

"But it's the truth Deborah, I haven't got a clue where he is. Angela abducted him from here and drove him to Dronfield woods, and tied him up there. She went back for him earlier this morning, and he was gone. She said there was no way he could have freed himself. That was her phoning me, asking if he was here. I know how far out it sounds, but that's the truth, really".

"Hmm" said Knowles, who had heard Ashley saying *"I thought he was with you"*

"Why do I believe you"?

Ashley now, was beginning to panic.

She had been contemplating spending time in Park Hill, and knowing what Knowles would allow happen to her whilst she was in there. "It's true Deborah, look I've been foolish, and I regret everything I've done".

She pointed to the two bags of money lying on the floor.
"There has not been one penny of that money touched, I'm asking you, for all of our past friendship. Can't you take the money back and just forget all about this? I can make all this up to you Deborah, I can, I can set Hunter up, get him put away. I know he's been having an affair with an MP's wife. I could work it out that you could pin him with that. The MP's wife has been stealing money out of public funds, that's how Hunter got his new Audi. She stole the money to buy him it as a gift, please Deborah, I swear, I'll do everything you tell me, anything, just tell me, and it's done. Deborah, I've just made a terrible mistake, and"—
"Just stop it Ashley, God's sake, your crawling is making me sick to the stomach, and relax, I'm not going to shoot your pretty knees out, I couldn't, not unless I really had to.
Now then, Ashley, what are we going to do here, we have a problem.
Knowles rose up from the table and walked over to the sink, and looking out into the darkness.
"Where can our Mister Hunter be? Who could have rescued him? Someone who knows what's going on. Someone who knows he's about to inherit half a million quid or, *was* he Ashley?
You dirty little slut that you are, was he getting *any* of that money, or were you planning to fuck off with the lot, you're a very self-centred little bitch, aren't you, huh?
You're prepared to turn him in, and his mistress, just to save your own arse, huh? You little scrubber, you're not a very nice person at all, are you Ashley, and now, begging me to forgive everything you've done against me. I think you've got a fucking nerve, don't you"?
"Can I say something Deborah"?
"I don't know, can you Ashley? Can you say something that's the truth"?
"You were saying just now Deborah, who could have helped John Hunter. Apart from us, the only other person who knew about anything, was Amanda Pearce".
Deborah continued looking out into the darkness.
"Of course it was Ashley, how could I have been so bloody stupid.
But why did she rescue him, and more to the point, how did she know that Hunter was in the woods?
Unless, she saw Angela Phorbes putting him into the car, ah maybe, and then followed her.

I've just asked her if she'd spoken to you or Hunter, and she swore that she hadn't". The smile had now changed into a frown.
"If I find out she's been lying to me, I'll shoot her in the face. As for you Ashley, I don't know, oh I know how you feel guilty about everything now, but that's only because you're feeling sorry for yourself, you wouldn't be talking like this if everything had gone to plan. I'll tell you what Ashley, let's get you over to the prison, you can have a short stay there until I can lay my hands on Mister Hunter. I'll feel safer if I know where you are".
"Deborah, I can"-
"Oh don't worry Ashley, I'm not going to jeapardise your job, I'll tell them someone is stalking you or something, and that it's for your own safety. Then once Hunter has been taken care of, I will reconsider your offer to lick my boots for the rest of your career, that's the best I can do Ashley, and if you don't mind me saying, it's not bad, considering what you've been planning to do to me, bloody blackmail indeed. Don't play around in that game Ashley, unless you know exactly what you're doing. It's a bloody good job Park Hill is not ready yet, because then you'd have got a bloody rude awakening young lady, you'd have got your arse tanned.
Come on then slut, get your jacket on, let's wake up the sergeant at the police station, he'll probably look into you throughout the night, you know, just to make sure you're alright, if you catch my meaning. Of course, that won't bother you too much, will it Ashley, you'll enjoy all the attention won't you? You and your skimpy little skirts. Let me tell you, if you cock tease with these boys, then you had better watch out". Knowles picked up the two leather bags containing the money, and handed them to Ashley. "Here" she said, "you can carry these out to my car, I'll switch the lights off and lock up, come on, let's go, fucking blackmail, you silly fucking slut-bitch that you are". The two women walked down the stairs through the chilled room, where there were two rows of trolleys. Four on either side. One or two of the trolleys had dummies lying on them, for training purposes. Neither Ashley Barnes nor Deborah Knowles saw the last dummy get up and make its way to the back of Deborah. Amanda Pearce hoisted the four foot crow bar high above her head, and brought it crashing down onto the back of Deborah Knowles's head. The Police Chief came crashing to the floor instantly unconscious. Amanda lifted the bar above her head once more, ready to repeat her actions.

"No! No! Amanda, you'll kill her, don't!"
Amanda held the bar in her hands, looking like a baseball player at the plate.
"It wouldn't be a bad idea Ashley, I'm sick to death of her telling me what to do, making me shoot people to save *her* scabby arse, the fucking bastard, let me whack the bastard again!"
"No, no Amanda, keep your cool, come on now, give me a hand, help me get her tied up and gagged, she could have back up in the car outside, we don't know".
"So, what are we going to do? Just wait here until they come in for her"?
"That's exactly what we're going to do" said Ashley, binding bandages and body straps around Deborah Knowles.
"What? Just wait here to get caught"?
"Look, Amanda, if she's got anyone with her, they'll wait for a while, then, if they think she's taking too long, they'll come in looking for her, but they won't come in here running like lunatics, with guns, like they will if we go out there without her. So, we'll give them half an hour to come. If no-one comes in by then, then it would seem that she has come here on her own, hell, it's twenty past three in the morning. I don't suppose there'll be too many officers keen enough to come out with her at this time of the morning, especially to a morgue".
Ashley laid Deborah Knowles's crumpled body onto a trolley, and pulled a sheet over her. She felt the right hand wrist of the unconscious woman, and, much to her great relief, found a pulse. "She's still alive Amanda" Ashley whispered.
"Oh good" Amanda mocked, "I'm so pleased to hear it".
"Come on you" said Ashley, you can tell me what's been going on, up in my office, and if anyone comes in looking for *her*, then you leave the talking to me, right"?
"Right. I've got her gun Ashley"
"Ok put it out of sight, better still, give it to me".
"I'll keep it Ashley, because if anything happens, you won't shoot, I will".
"What the hell are you doing here anyway Amanda"? Said Ashley, opening the office door at the top of the stairs.
"I decided to try and help you, I was here yesterday, I came to see you. As I was just about to get out of my car, I saw a dark haired woman sneak up behind your friend, what's his name"?

“Hunter”
“Yes, well this dark haired woman whacked him on the back of the head with something. Then, another woman got out of the car, a young girl, and helped to bind up Hunter and put him in the boot of their car, a B.M.W, I think. The next thing I see, was a blonde haired woman coming out of your building and jumping into the car. They drove off. I decided to follow them. They drove to a little village called Dronfield. I stayed back, well back, in fact, I nearly lost them a couple of times. They ditched the man in a wooded area, tying him to a tree”.
“Where is he now Amanda”?
“He’s safe, he’s in my place”.
“Amanda, we are in deep trouble now, you know that, don’t you”.
“Oh yes, but I’m off tonight, I’m heading away from here, and from that sick bitch down stairs, I’ve had enough of her”.
“Ok Amanda, let me think, what can we do, we can’t all leave together”.
“I know that Ashley, listen, I’ve got enough money for me, I could go and bring your friend over, you and he, can make a break for it with your money, make a new start, that’s what I’m going to do. But I came here to kill that cunt down stairs Ashley, I wish you would let me finish the bastard off”.
“No Amanda, that’s the last thing we should do, now sit down there until I make us a cup of coffee, we’ll have to wait and see if there’s anyone else with her”.
Amanda threw herself down onto one of the chairs, like a sulking child.
As the kettle began to boil, Ashley turned to say something.
Amanda was gone, and the door was open.
“Shit!!” cursed Ashley.
“Amanda? Amanda!! Come back here. Now”!!
Three loud shots sounded out from Amanda’s’ gun.
“Oh fucking hell, great, just fucking great. Oh Amanda, now you’ve done it, shit, oh no”.
Ashley’s voice sounded like that of a young girl, trying their best to speak without bursting into tears.
“What the fuck are we going to do now”.
Blood was dripping from underneath the cover where Deborah Knowles’s body lay.

"You stupid fucking junkie bitch that you are, now you've really fucking done it. You've killed Britain's most respected policewoman, the Chief of Police if you don't mind. Fucking hell Amanda, you may as well have shot the fucking queen, now, I die, me, you, John, we all die now, that's for sure, ho, you've cooked the goose now. Why couldn't you just do what I fucking said, huh?
It was going to be alright Amanda. Do you think you were the only one who wanted her dead, you, you stupid fuck. Do you know what you've done Amanda? I'll tell you. Instead of just Deborah Knowles hunting our arses down, and maybe one or two of her faithful lick-arses, well now, we'll have the whole of the British police forces searching for us. There's not a city or a town on this whole fucking Island, or a village for that matter, where we can go. Everywhere, there'll be pictures and posters of us, there'll even be a reward for the public. Anyone who spots us, will be handsomely rewarded, fuck, we're done for".
Amanda stood with the gun, still in her hands, arms straight, and the gun pointing at Deborah Knowles.
"Amanda!
Get up those stairs, sit down, and wait for me, and don't touch anything".
Ashley lifted up the sheet, expecting to see Deborah Knowles's head blown apart. Instead, there was only one bullet hole, and that was in her side. There was still hope. Amanda had missed twice. She ran up the stairs.
"Come on Amanda, now"!
Ashley picked up the two bags from the bottom of the stairs.
"My car Amanda, we're going to your place.
Amanda drove Ashley's car across Sheffield, while Ashley phoned Angela Phorbes.
"Angela, please, it's Ashley, Steve Temple's house, as quick as you can. Please trust me, it's not a trap, I swear, I've got a big problem here, I need your help. I'll pay you whatever you ask, please just get to Steve Temple's house, I'll explain everything when we're there".
Ashley, if not before, was definitely regretting her actions now. The idea put forward to her by John Hunter had proved too tempting. A half a million pounds was a lot of money, but, to risk blackmailing the most ruthless woman ever to walk on God's earth to obtain that much money, was nothing less than ludicrous. If Angela didn't help her now, and why should she, then she was in deep trouble.

Ten minutes later, Ashley Amanda and John Hunter all sat in Amanda's living room, waiting. "She won't come Ashley" said Hunter. "She'll think it's a trap, and anyway, why should she do *us* any favours. You're a criminal Pathologist, she's a criminal, I work for the criminal forensic department, plus, we have just blackmailed someone for a million pounds, we are hardly candidates for the Samaritans of the year now are we"?
Ashley sat with a glass of brandy, trying to work out a plan if Angela did not show up.
Hunter interrupted her thoughts.
"Whilst we're on the subject of this, this Angela woman, did it ever occur to you Ashley, that this woman knows now, that we are in possession of a million pounds. What's to stop her coming over here and killing us, taking the lot, and just disappearing, have you thought about that?
And you" he pointed his finger at Amanda. How the fuck do *you* suddenly come in to the equation. How did you know where they'd tied me up? You must have been in it with them".
"No I wasn't in it with them, smart arse, and by the way, it's a good job I *did* find you, or you would have been dead by now, you ungrateful shit that you are"!
"Just shut up"! Hunter snapped, and then, looking to Ashley he said, "whatever we do Ashley, *she* is not a part of it, I can tell you that, fucking shooting Deborah Knowles, stupid bitch, fuck sakes, how stupid are you"?
"That will do" said Angela Phorbes, there's no need to snap at the young lady like that. And how stupid are you? I could have killed you, and you didn't even know I was here, you thick man".

"Angela, thank God you're here. She's shot Deborah Knowles" said Ashley, pointing to Amanda.
"Is she dead" said Angela.
"No, at least, she wasn't when we left there".
"Then what exactly do want from me Ashley? Come on in Sophie, it's alright".
Sophie stepped into the room and stood beside Angela.
"I eh, I was hoping you could help me out Angela".
"Help you out with what Ashley"?
"Well, this, this mess that I've landed myself in".

"You don't have a problem Ashley, she does" said Angela, pointing to Amanda. "You really don't".
Angela looked at Amanda.
"I'm leaving tonight" said Amanda. "I'm going away, I don't want anything more to do with this, or this house, or anything".
"Really"? Said Angela. "So, you just shoot Deborah Knowles, and leave her for dead, and leave Ashley here to deal with it, eh? Let *her* face the consequences of your actions, while you just ghost off into the sunset with Steve Temple's money, is that what you mean?
And you".
Hunter turned around to face Angela.
"What's your plans smart boy, what are you going to do, the same? Leave Ashley here in the soup"?
"I have no intentions of leaving Ashley to face anything alone, I'm in this as much as she is, and anyway, we have proof that Knowles is corrupt, we can prove it".
Angela smiled, "Mister Hunter, I'm not sure if you're quite aware of what you're dealing with here, I couldn't care less even if you had photographs of Deborah Knowles committing these crimes, there is no way you'll get a conviction against that woman".
Hunter cleared his throat, unnerved by what Angela had just said. "Well, in that case, why did she agree to pay the money, can you answer *that*"?
"She paid you the money Mister Hunter in order to give you a false sense of security. May I ask you, how far do you think she was going to let you get with her money. It wouldn't have mattered to her if you'd demanded two million pounds, three, you, weren't going anywhere, only to your grave, or worse. She may have had you in her new prison, Park Hill, and believe me Mister Hunter, your grave would have been the best option, either way, you were going nowhere with her money, and you're *still* not, if she survives, she's going to hound you".
"What should I do Angela, said Ashley, will you help me"?
Angela moved over to the drinks cabinet, and poured two vodka and cokes for herself and Sophie. Handing one of the glasses to Sophie, she said.
"Well, it depends on what you want to do".
"What do you mean Angela"?
"Well, if you are to stand any chance, you'll have to split up".
Hunter stood shaking his head and smiling sarcastically.

"How clever of you" he said, "I wish I could have thought of that"?
Angela ignored the sarcasm and continued talking to Ashley. She pointed to Hunter, and said, "you don't want to be anywhere near *this* idiot, when they come looking for you".
"Fine, suits me", said Hunter, "just give me my share of the money Ashley, and I'll be gone".
Ashley got up from her chair and walked over to the far side of the giant living room, she picked up one of the leather bags and said, "here, half a million in used notes, it's all there John, I've counted it".
"Have you really Ashley, well then, you won't mind if I take the other bag".
Ashley sighed "please yourself John".
Angela said to Amanda, "I hope you have *your* money ready to take with you".
"I have, it's up the stairs".
"Well go and get it, I would hurry if I were you.
Ashley? Phone for an ambulance for Knowles, it's an emergency, tell them where she is, tell them exactly where she is. Tell them it's for Deborah Knowles, and advise them to bring a surgeon with them, just in case.
Upstairs Amanda, on you go, quickly".
Ashley picked up her mobile and began to press the digits.
John Hunter was on his hunkers, and had opened one of the bags of money, picking up handfuls of notes, and counting them. Angela walked over to him.
"Have you ever trusted anyone in your entire life Mister Hunter"?
"Never"!
"Wise, "very wise" she said, as she continued screwing on the silencer onto her pistol ,and pointing it at the back of Hunter's head, and then pulling the trigger.
"Pour us another drink Sophie darling" Angela said to the stunned girl, "I'm just going up to see how Amanda's doing". Exactly one minute later, she came back down the stairs, alone, and carrying a large luggage bag.
"Right Ashley, you can either come with *us*, or you can go your own way, you're a millionaire now".
"Where's Amanda Angela"? Said Ashley, with a tremor in her voice.
"Amanda's not coming Ashley".

Ashley looked at Angela, who was lighting up a cigarette.
"Why? Angela, she was alright".
"No she wasn't Ashley, she was not alright. She was ready to leave you in the shit, read, traitor, if you and she had gone together she would have grassed you in, or you would have both been in a prison cell within three days, mark my words, and as for *that* piece of shit", She pointed to the corpse of John Hunter. "That was just a waste of a good skin, so, what's it to be Ashley? Are you coming with me and Sophie, or are you going it alone, you're welcome to do whichever you please, you'll have to make your mind up, because we're going to head off in a few minutes".
As Angela drew on her cigarette, she smiled. "Whatever you do, we've all got a few quid to spend, And as long as we keep away from Deborah Knowles, we'll be fine.
Ashley slumped down on her chair. "What a fucking mess Angela. How could I be so terribly stupid, I've fucked up my life now, there's no way Deborah will believe that I had nothing to do with shooting her. God, I blackmailed her for a million quid, and I have nowhere now to run or hide, my career lies in ruins".
"Yes you have Ashley, you could come with us, we're heading up to Scotland for a few weeks, way up in the hills somewhere. Peace and quiet, you're welcome to come along. Come on Ashley, what have you got to lose. As you say, Knowles will have you if you hang around here. She'll have you in that hell-hole they're calling Park Hill, for a good ten years, at least. She'll see to that, and as I'm sure you'll already know, it will not be an experience to relish, you can be assured of that.
So, come on, come to Scotland with us, away from all this shit down here. You'll be able to get some good Scottish beef into you, up there you know if you pardon the pun".
Ashley smiled. "Putting it like that Angela, how could I resist"?
"Ashley" smiled Angela, "I was referring to roast beef, you know, with potatoes, and vegetables and such".
Ashley smiled back at Angela. "I know" she said, "that's what I was meaning as well".
As Sophie drove out of Sheffield, and headed out onto the motorway, she said to the two women in the back seats, "I'm never coming back here, I swear".
"What about your little girl Sophie"? said Angela, "don't you want to try and get her back"?

“What would be the point Angela, she’s probably being looked after better than I ever could, and besides, if I *were* to win her back, I’d be monitored twenty four hours a day by the bastards, one slip up, one trip, anything, and they would take her back off me, no, fuck that Angela, she’s better off where she is, the little angel, God bless her, she’ll be fine”.

Angela said “what about *you* Ashley, are you ok with this”?

Ashley sighed heavily.

“Angela? I haven’t got a clue what the fuck I’m doing, honestly, I’m sitting here, heading up to Scotland with two people I don’t even know, and a million pounds in the boot of your car. All I know Angela, is, if I had stayed in Sheffield, I would have died, or I’d have been thrown into prison for a very long time. Knowles would have had me, I’d have been fucked. I may have stood a chance if that little junkie Amanda hadn’t came along and battered her senseless and then shot her, maybe”.

“Yes maybe” said Angela, “but believe me Ashley, it would have ended up worse than you could ever imagine, that’s to say, she survives, she might not”.

“She will” said Ashley, “she’s Satan’s sister, she’ll survive”.

“Yeah, you’re probably right Ashley.

“Yesterday, a very dear friend of mine topped herself, she’d been helping me try and get rid of Knowles. A few days ago, she lost her two little girls in a car crash, along with her lover, and her lover’s aunt, she couldn’t take it, she couldn’t take the loss, now she’s gone”. “I suppose, what I’m saying Sophie, is, you’re free to go any time, and that goes for you too Ashley”.

“Angela” said Sophie, “I only have you and now Ashley for friends, and I think I speak for both of us when I say, that all three of us, only have each other now, so I say, let’s make the best of it, what do you say ladies”?

SHEFFIELD CITY GENERAL HOSPITAL.

Deborah Knowles sat at the window of the recovery unit with her mobile phone. Where her window was situated, she could look right down onto the city. On her lap was a list of names she had kept when she and Karen Jones had been keeping in touch with Angela and Carla Paganni. She had sat here for almost an hour, wondering whether or not to try Angela's number. George Morton, the surgeon had confessed to Deborah that he had given Angela the phone whilst she was being kept in the military hospital. Knowles pressed the digits and waited.

"Hello"? Came the unmistakable voice of Angela Phorbes.

"Hello? Angela"?

"Oh hello Deborah, how are you keeping"?

"I'm fine, I'll survive Angela".

"That's a pity".

"Yes, I thought you'd say that".

"Did you".

"Yes, listen Angela, call it quits"?

Angela thought for a moment. "What's the catch Deborah"?

"There's no catch Angela, just don't come back here, ok? You, or Ashley, alright"?

"What are you talking about Deborah, I don't know where the hell Ashley is".

"Angela, oh my poor Angela, I've had people watching you, I know that Ashley is with you. You and that little girl, Sophie isn't it? I even know that you're all staying in the Regent hotel, up in Fife, but don't worry, I've ordered them to return here, you know, surveillance.

I've called to wish you all the best Angela, and your friends. Tell Ashley, I know that she had nothing to do with shooting me, simply because, if it had been her, she wouldn't have missed. I'm telling you now Miss Clark, that you are a free woman. Start again Angela, make a new start, and oh, tell Ashley to enjoy her money, it was drug money anyway, it wasn't mine. Look after yourself Angela, and like I say, stay away from Sheffield, and keep your nose clean".

"If you are genuine Deborah-".

"I am Angela".

“Well then, I wish you all the best too, although I will never forgive you, you know that”.
“Yes I do, and I can understand. I respect you Angela, and I would hate to have to hang you, I really would, I would have no-one to hate if you were dead”.
“Me too Deborah”.
“Ok then, we have a deal Angela? One last deal”.
“One last deal Deborah, only this time, keep your side of the deal, ok”?
“I will, oh, one last thing”.
“Yes”?
“My prison is nearly completed, and I am still one hundred per cent determined to keep Britain’s streets clean, if you don’t mind doing me a favour. If you *have* to kill, could you please make sure that they are scumbags, and not innocent people”.
“My killing days are over Deborah, unless I run into you”.
Deborah switched off her phone and laid it upon the small table by her bedside. She lit a cigarette and looked down onto the city below.
“God bless you Miss Clark” she said, smiling.
Angela switched off her phone, just as Sophie and Ashley came into the room.
“Everything ok”? Said Sophie, helping Ashley to carry two bottles of champagne and a basket of strawberries.
“Yeah, fine, everything’s just fine”.
“Come on Angela, grab a glass, let’s celebrate” said Ashley.
“Yeah, in a minute, I’m just going down stairs for something, I won’t be long”.
Angela walked down stairs and headed out into the gardens of the five star hotel.
As she walked around the gardens, taking in the fresh air, she began to reflect on her past, and the friends she once knew. She thought about Paul and Tools, Amy and Linda, and, of course, her dear cousin and friend, Tracy. If only she could have kept it together, for a little while longer, she would have been ok, but the loss of her two little girls was just too much for her to bear in the end. How strange, life. We plan things as if we were immortal. Days, weeks months, even years, we plan ahead…expecting to fulfill.
We take it all for granted.

One of Abba's songs was playing in her head now as she walked, she smiled at the words that came to her now from the song;... *The gods may throw a dice, their hearts as cold as ice, while someone way down here, loses someone dear".*

Tracy had moved up to Sheffield to get away from trouble, all the violence, but, of course, she would have no idea that she was about to marry a madman. Angela sighed, as she sat on a bench and lit up a cigarette.

"What now Miss Phorbes? What will you do with yourself now, God knows".

What road will my life take now I wonder? She sighed heavily, and rose to her feet. "There's only one way to find out I suppose". Angela walked around the car park and went back in to reception. She left a note for her friends, hoping they would understand. She then returned to the car park. She got into her car and sat crying for a few minutes. Ashley and Sophie would be fine, and she was quite sure they would both understand her leaving without saying goodbye. She then started the car and drove away, heading south. Still thinking about the life she once led with her old friends, particularly Tools, Amy and Linda, and what might have been with Carla Paganni. "You were the closest Carla, the closest I ever came to finding myself, and to finding complete happiness. Rest in peace my little angel". As she drove out of the town the song playing on her radio was Sinead O'Conners' "*Nothing compares to you".*

THE END,

William Hurst.

37487608R00431

Printed in Great Britain
by Amazon